OVER
THERE

Also by Thomas Fleming

Fiction
Time and Tide
The Spoils of War
The Officers' Wives
Promises to Keep
Rulers of the City
Liberty Tavern
The Good Shepherd
A Cry of Whiteness

Nonfiction
1776: Year of Illusions
The Man Who Dared the Lightning
The Man from Monticello
West Point: The Men and Times of the U.S. Military Academy
One Small Candle
Beat the Last Drum
Now We Are Enemies

TO LIEUTENANT THOMAS J. FLEMING
312th Infantry 78th Division
American Expeditionary Force

This war! It is the uprooting of all that has gone before. It is convulsion, madness, g   ress. Every element that human nature is capable of will   to the surface; unheard-of feats of courage will come out   ; despicable acts will be perpetrated; genius will triumf   raits unknown will be born. I want to be part of it, an in   simal speck to be sure, but still a speck in the great colossal   aval.

—Ge   Vanderbilt Whitney

CHRONOLOGY

1914

June 28: Francis Ferdinand, Crown Prince of Austria-Hungary, and his wife are assassinated at Sarajevo.

July 28: Austria declares war on Serbia and Russia declares war on Austria.

August 1: Germany declares war on Russia and her ally, France.

August 4: England declares war on Germany. President Woodrow Wilson declares America must be neutral "in thought and in action."

August 26–30: Germans crush Russian army at battle of Tannenberg but are stalemated at other points on the Eastern Front.

September 5–10: British and French armies stop the Germans along the River Marne. Later German attempts to break through in the north at Ypres fail, and trench warfare begins.

October 29: Turkey enters the war on the German side.

1915

April 25: British-Australian amphibious assault at Gallipoli fails to knock Turkey out of the war.

May 1: Germans and Austrians attack Russians on an 800-mile front from the Baltic Sea to Rumanian border, drive them back 300 miles.

May 7: German submarine torpedoes the British liner *Lusitania*, drowning almost 1,200 passengers, 128 of them Americans. Wilson says America is "too proud to fight" but protests the sinking, and Germany halts unrestricted submarine warfare.

May 23: Italy declares war on Germany and Austria-Hungary.

May 25: Another German offensive stopped at Ypres.

August 10: Proponents of preparedness led by Theodore Roosevelt open a military training camp for civilians at Plattsburg, N.Y.

September 26: French attack in Champagne and incur staggering losses. British and French attack in Artois with similiar results.

October 15: American bankers, organized by J. P. Morgan, lend Great Britain and France $500 million, largest loan in world history.

1916

February 21: German attack on Verdun attempts to "bleed French army white." Casualties on both sides exceed one million.

March 9: Woodrow Wilson orders General Pershing to cross the Mexican border with 11,000 men in pursuit of Pancho Villa.

May 31: Sea battle of Jutland between British and German fleets ends in draw. British blockade of Germany continues.

June 16: Immense Russian offensive hurls back Austrians but at a cost of one million men. Russian army veers toward collapse.

July 1: British and French attack on the Somme River fails. Casualties exceed one million.

November 7: Woodrow Wilson is narrowly reelected President on slogan "He kept us out of war."

1917

January 16: Woodrow Wilson calls for "peace without victory" and offers himself as a mediator. Both sides reject him.

January 28: Wilson orders General Pershing to end his pursuit of Pancho Villa in Mexico.

January 31: Germany announces resumption of unrestricted submarine warfare.

February 3: American freighter *Housatonic* is sunk by German submarine. Wilson breaks diplomatic relations with Germany.

March 1: U.S. State Department publishes intercepted telegram from German Secretary of State Zimmermann to Mexico proposing a military alliance.

March 16: Czar Nicholas of Russia abdicates.

April 2: Woodrow Wilson goes before Congress and asks for a declaration of war against Germany.

OVER THERE

OVERTURE

THE SMALL ERECT WOMAN IN A DARK GREEN BUSI-
ness suit paused on the steps of the Hotel Crillon
to admire the dramatic sweep of the Place de la Concorde—the
soaring obelisk from Luxor, the eight heroic statues saluting the
great cities of France, the twin fountains falling with hollow delicacy into the great frame of space, and beyond it the Seine and the
bright immensity of Paris. Beside the woman stood a stocky, cold-
eyed American general, his chest splashed with battle ribbons.

"I love this city," the woman said.

"I'll take Baltimore any time," the General said.

"You're a barbarian, just like your father," the woman said.

A gray Renault sedan was waiting at the curb. The plump red-
faced driver, a beret at a cocky angle on his big head, introduced
himself as Philippe and flung open the rear door.

"Please excuse my accent," the woman said in French as she settled onto the comfortable cushions. "I haven't spoken your beautiful
language for quite a while."

"Madame, your accent is superb," Philippe said. "You must have
spent a great deal of time in France."

"I lived here for eighteen months many years ago. I've only been
an occasional visitor since."

She gave Philippe a list of the places they wanted to visit. They
amounted to a tour of the entire Western Front of the First World
War, from Ypres in Belgium south to the Argonne and Verdun.
"We've reserved rooms at inns along the route," she said. "We want
to go slowly—and see everything."

Philippe headed up the Champs-Élysées toward the Arch of Triumph. "Madame is a historian?" he asked, casually cutting off a taxi and narrowly missing an elderly pedestrian, who saluted him with an obscene gesture that Philippe cheerfully returned.

"No," the woman said.

"So much has happened in fifty years. Revolutions. Other wars."

"Yes," the woman said.

"Now your country is embroiled in a third war begun by France. This thing in Vietnam."

"Let's not talk about that mess," the General growled. "First your army screwed it up, and now ours is doing a worse job."

"Maybe France is bad luck for the United States," Philippe said.

"Nonsense," the woman said. "We're like two old lovers who quarrel and always make up because the first memories are so strong."

"A beautiful thought," Philippe said. "But what do you hope to gain by recalling this old war?"

"She's writing a book about it for me and my sons," the General said. "I think a lot of other people will be interested. I'm going to try to get it published."

"Not while you're in the army," she said.

"Mother, you know I don't give a damn for what a lot of encrusted bureaucrats in Washington think," the General growled.

"Then give a damn for what I think—and what your wife thinks," the woman said.

"What excited your curiosity in this war?" Philippe said. "Did Madame have a husband or a brother who fought in France?"

"I was here. With many other American women."

"I thought American women were forbidden to do such things in those days."

"Women have always done a great many forbidden things."

"Madame, it's hard to believe you aren't French."

"For a while I almost was...."

Memories crowded against her heart and mind with almost suffocating intensity. Can it be recaptured? she wondered as the car rolled out of Paris into the green countryside. Can another generation grasp this old lost thing you have held and heard in imagination and in long night talks? Would anyone—even her grandsons—care?

A voice lectured her in blunt military style. She was wasting her time. Americans had no interest in their own history, which was why they would be condemned to repeat their mistakes in perpetuity until their luck finally ran out.

Other voices competed with this mordant military pessimist. One had an English accent. It told her firmly, almost ferociously, the book had to be written. It was important to tell the truth they had shared, from the inside—not as boring history but as the personal drama they had lived.

Another voice whispered in French, a voice that had once mocked and tormented her. Now it spoke gently, fondly, telling her not to worry about when, where, or if her book would be published. She was in France to speak with those she had loved, to summon from the depths of the past the improbable, inexplicable spirit of hope.

Yes, the woman thought. Yes. She settled back to enjoy her journey.

BOOK I

1. DAWN

COLONEL MALVERN HILL BLISS, COMMANDER OF the 10th U.S. Cavalry Regiment, drove his green Maxwell touring car down the darkening Texas highway between Fort Sam Houston and San Antonio as if he were being pursued by hostile Apaches. He weaved left and right and left again, whooping cheerfully above the screeches of the protesting tires.

Fortunately, he encountered only three cars on the road, and their drivers had the good sense to seek the safety of the sagebrush. When the Colonel reached the city, a semblance of sanity appeared: he shifted into first gear and drove carefully through the twilit back streets of San Antonio.

He was not doing badly, he was not doing badly at all, Bliss told himself. Not badly at all for a man who had downed five or six double bourbons for dinner.

The expression on the face of the man in the passenger's seat suggested another opinion. Sergeant Major John Henry Turner's frown was as black as his sun-dried skin. Turner did not approve of drunken colonels. He especially disapproved of a drunken colonel named Malvern Hill Bliss. Having devoted some twenty years of his life to keeping the son of a bitch alive in places as diverse as the deserts of Arizona, the heights overlooking Santiago, Cuba, and the jungles of Mindanao, Turner did not think Colonel Bliss had a right to kill himself on the highway between Fort Sam Houston and San Antonio.

Bliss disagreed: respectfully, earnestly, violently. The Sergeant knew that. He also knew why they never argued about it. There was always a reason why a man set out to drink himself to death.

Colonel Bliss's reason reduced him to an impotent black shadow who dragged Bliss from the bar of the officers' club at Fort Sam Houston to his silent empty quarters and followed him to San Antonio to preside over the sins he committed there, sins that Turner, a devout Baptist, could barely bring himself to contemplate.

Turner tried to take Bliss's mind—and his own conscience—off their destination. "We goin' to war, Colonel?"

"I hope not."

"You think them Germans as bad as they say?"

"No."

"Old Billy Sunday. I read in the paper he's tellin' people if you could turn hell upside down, you'd find Germany printed on it."

"Billy Sunday's full of shit. He always has been full of shit."

"He sure can preach up a storm, Colonel. Wish you'd heard him when he was here in San Antone."

Bite your tongue, Bliss told himself. Let Turner have his faith in Billy Sunday. You owe him that much. "Maybe you're right. I'm sorry I didn't go," he said.

It was the first hopeful sign Turner had seen in so long, he almost grew cheerful. He almost managed to forget Bliss's destination, Mama Juanita's House of Happiness, where the prettiest whores on either side of the Rio Grande were waiting for him. In fact, the Sergeant became almost grateful for the Colonel's decision to make Juanita's his destination tonight. It was infinitely preferable to a visit to the Church of the Blessed Sacrament.

There, in the hushed silence, with banks of candles glowing before the white altar, Colonel Bliss called God names that chilled Turner's soul, names he tried to banish from his mind the moment he heard them. As a soldier and a Christian, Turner simply could not comprehend the depths, the heights, of Bliss's insubordination. God was the Commander in Chief. His decrees were to be accepted and obeyed; a Christian had no other choice. But Colonel Bliss seemed to think he had the right to differ violently with God.

That line of thought nudged Turner uncomfortably close to the reason Bliss cursed God and made weekly visits to Mama Juanita's and got drunk every night with religious regularity. Turner saw it all again in the white-hot sunlight of that afternoon in Jolo, the ancient walled city on the island of the same name, overlooking the Sulu Sea. He saw it all for the thousandth time.

They had just returned from another punitive expedition into the interior. This trip had been messy. They had been forced to kill quite a few Moros. Usually, Colonel Bliss negotiated them into a peace treaty everyone knew would not last six months. But this time the datto, or chieftain, whose fort was inside the extinct volcano, Mount Bagsak, had shouted defiance and led a charge, whirling his gleaming campilan, a murderous two-handed sword, over his head.

They had to start shooting—which was exactly what the men in the ranks wanted to do in the first place. By the time they obeyed the Colonel's third order to cease fire, there were a hundred Moros on the ground with that uncanny smile of contentment on their faces. They really believed that a man who died in battle went to Paradise and spent eternity in the arms of beautiful women.

A day or two after that expedition, Sergeant Turner was strolling along the narrow twisting main street of Jolo. Half a block ahead of him he saw Mrs. Bliss come out of a store with the Colonel's thirteen-year-old son, Jack. She was like an angel of light there in the narrow rutted street, all in white, her blond hair gleaming in the tropic sun. Young Jack was in white too. He was blond like his mother. Behind them trotted the Malay houseboy, his arms loaded with groceries. Mrs. Bliss was celebrating the Colonel's return by giving a dinner.

Their bodyguard, a brawny wise guy from New Orleans named Price, sauntered out of the store after them. Turner felt the hair on the back of his neck bristle. Price should have casually preceded Mrs. Bliss into the street and looked the situation over before she came out. Worse, Price was not paying any attention to Mrs. Bliss and young Jack. He was talking to the daughter of the storekeeper, a lively little piece who kept half a dozen soldiers on the string.

What happened next was so fast—and so slow now, in memory, Turner almost believed the slow version. The Moro came out of the alley behind the grocery store and in three leaps was in front of Mrs. Bliss, his curved, gleaming Malay kris raised, his eyes closed, his mouth shouting his war cry, *La ilaha il-la'l-lahu*—"There is no God but Allah." He was small, as small as Mrs. Bliss. He was wearing only a sarong around his waist. His brown body seemed oiled, the way it gleamed in the blazing light.

The kris came down so fast—and so slow in the tropic sun of memory. Blood splashed across Mrs. Bliss's white dress. The kris went up into the sky and down again, and there was more blood on young Jack's white suit. Up and down again, and the houseboy's head was split in half like a melon. Price, the bodyguard, was trying to get his .45 out of his holster, but the kris went up and down again and he toppled, screaming, into the dark doorway of the grocery store, minus an arm.

Everyone started screaming. People scrambled down alleys and up the street past Turner. It was the only sensible thing to do in the presence of a *juramentado*, a Moro who had sworn a sacred oath to kill as many Christians as possible until someone killed him. Fortunately, Turner was there to perform that task. The Moro came at him with the kris raised but the Sergeant had his .45 out of the holster. The big pistol kicked in his hand as he pulled the trigger once, twice, three times and the bullets slammed the warrior on his back. He lay there smiling.

"Goddamn!" Colonel Bliss stamped on the brake as two boys and a dog skittered across the street in front of them. "Not bad for a drunken sot, wouldn't you say, Turner?"

"Not bad, Colonel," Turner said.

Maybe it really wasn't so bad, when you thought about the reason why the Colonel got drunk and cursed God and went to Mama Juanita's. Maybe—a shocking thought to Turner—he had a right to do these things. Maybe God had messed up.

Four or five hours later, Bliss was lying in bed with Grace.

No, Grace was his wife's name. Could he be that far gone, to go to bed with a whore named Grace?

Why not? Why not put it to God as bluntly as possible? Why not inform God that He was getting what He deserved from Malvern Hill Bliss, Colonel USA, who would soon write *Ret.* after his name and before whose name someone else would soon write *the late.*

"Oh, Colonel, it's so big," Grace murmured. "Come on. Do it again, Colonel. I want to be able to tell the other girls Colonel Bliss is better than Pancho Villa. My sister did it with him one night. Three times. You have done it twice, Colonel. Make it three so you can triumph over Villa again."

"You don't like Villa?"

"He's a pig."

"I just spent eleven months in Mexico trying to kill him."

"I hate him. He took my sister three times and paid nothing. He said it was her gift to the revolution. I'm not Mexican, I'm American. I have my papers."

"Land of opportunity."

"Come on, Colonel. I love you so. No one does it like you, so slow, so deep, so rich. You are the husband of my secret dreams."

Why not marry her? Bliss thought. Why not outrage the U.S. Army and the United States of America before retirement? Why not make a statement of absolute disillusion that might even shock Turner out of his incomprehensible devotion? A statement of fact, moreover, absolute moral fact. Why not marry a whore to demonstrate the moral bankruptcy of the United States Army, which blindly performed the orders of the commander in chief, President Whoever, to kill Moros, Mexicans, Indians, or striking American workmen with maximum efficiency.

You don't mean a word of that, Colonel, sighed Turner in the corner of Bliss's mind where he often stood, sorrowfully watching Bliss's disintegration.

Turner, Turner, why don't you go away and let me screw in peace? Screw whores, screw the army, screw the world.

This is what happens when you lose touch with Homer, intoned a third voice. *When you allow a woman to implant ridiculous ideas about a loving God in your soul. Why do you think I taught you to read Homer in the original Greek? Homer is the only world a soldier can inhabit, my dear Malvern. Homer and perhaps a touch of Dante. Io non piangeva, si dentro impietrai. I wailed not, so of stone grew I within.*

Father. Bliss could see him in his wheelchair, massaging the stump of the leg he lost to a Yankee shell in the slaughterous battle of Malvern Hill, ending his dreams of military glory. Dreams that his son, defiantly named for the battle, had been endlessly exhorted to fulfill.

Go away, he snarled to the hectoring ghost. I've stopped trying to satisfy your complicated dreams. I'm living my own stupid life; I'm going to hell on my own terms without the slightest reference to you or your crazy wife.

"Ohhh, Colonel. Three times. And each one better than Villa," Grace whispered, lowering herself on his numb but somehow erect member. Grace's body had a musky smell, almost Negro. Her thickly curled black hair fell over her sunken cheeks. Colonel Bliss placed his palms against her small snub breasts. Opposite, that was why he liked her. She was the opposite of his lost empress, his goddess of peace and purity, the soother of his soul. That Grace had exuded the odor of crushed flowers, of incensed holiness.

"*Ohhh, mi colonel, yo te amo, yo te amo,*" Grace murmured, moving up and down that throbbing rod of life. Why did it insist on rising, why did life refuse to stop beating in his blood? Why was the body so blind, so deaf to the soul's wishes?

"Jesus H. Christ!"

That voice was not in his head. That voice was in the room, just beyond the feeble glow of the candle on the night table. A hand came out of the darkness to seize Grace by the hair and fling her to the bottom of the bed.

Bliss stared up at the enraged face of a man wearing the uniform of a United States Army major general. The jutting jaw, the whipcord cheeks, the frowning brow were more than familiar. They had been part of Bliss's life since he toiled up the steep path from the West Shore Railroad on a broiling July day in 1882 to reach the parade ground of the U.S. Military Academy at West Point.

"Get out of that goddamn bed and into your uniform," John J. Pershing said. "We've got a train to catch."

"Why?" Bliss said.

"They want me in Washington the day after tomorrow. The President's going before Congress to declare war. He's giving me command of the expeditionary force to France."

"What the hell does that have to do with me?"

"You're coming with me. You're going to command a division.

You're going to do the best goddamn job of your life, or I will personally beat hell out of you."

Four hours later, the train rolled relentlessly across the vast Texas panhandle in the dawn. Colonel Bliss sat opposite Pershing in the otherwise empty car. How, why, does he endure? Bliss wondered. He has the same wound. Each day he faces the same emptiness.

On the night of August 26, 1915, while General Pershing was in El Paso patrolling the Mexican border against incursions from Pancho Villa, a fire broke out in his family's quarters in the Presidio, outside San Francisco. When it was over, Pershing's graceful darkhaired wife, Frances, was dead, along with their three daughters. Only his six-year-old son, Warren, survived, rescued by a courageous orderly.

Bliss had been on Jolo when it happened. He had written condolences, of course, and received a reply from Pershing, with the bitter comment, *All the promotions in the world would make no difference now.*

Bliss had sat there in his quarters overlooking Jolo City, smugly reading those mournful words. Oh, yes, grieving for his friend and classmate, of course, but pondering, Bliss style, the ironies of life. John J. Pershing had become a general by marrying Helen Frances Warren, daughter of Senator Francis E. Warren of Wyoming, chairman of the Military Affairs Committee. In 1906, Pershing had vaulted from captain to brigadier general over the outraged heads of 862 senior officers.

His friends and classmates insisted he deserved it. With a mere 700 men, Pershing had pacified the entire island of Mindanao in 1902, cajoling Moro dattus and sultans out of their forts when possible and storming them when necessary. His friend President Theodore Roosevelt had tried to make him a brigadier general then, but not even he could change the ossified army promotion system. It had taken Senator Warren's ability to smooth egos and threaten appropriations to make the army's mastodons swallow it.

So vaulted John J. Pershing: vaulted to heartbreak. The blaze had been caused by a hot coal, which had rolled out of the fireplace onto the highly polished wood floor in the middle of the night. The thick layer of wax on the floor had started a smoky fire that asphyxiated Frankie and her daughters while they slept. It was inevitable that Jack Pershing would insist on the highest possible polish on the floors of his house. Spit and polish, perfection in the smallest details, were the essence of his style.

Bliss sat on his veranda in Jolo, meditating on that irony. His family need never fear they would die in a fire started by too much wax on an army floor. Colonel Bliss was famous for his indifference to such trivia. From the day he got his commission, he had waged an underground war against the peacetime army's ridiculous insistence on polished floors, shoes, visors, belts. Against idiotic regulations of every sort, dreamed up by armchair generals in Washington to make life miserable for the men who did the fighting.

Four months later, the smug Colonel's wife and son lay dead on Jolo's main street. That was when Bliss began to wonder if there were graver lapses in his professional soldier's life, when he began examining the tasks he had performed in obedience to his oath to execute the orders of the blundering collection of politicians and uniformed bureaucrats that constituted the U.S. Army's chain of command.

The train groaned and rattled. Huge red streaks jutted across the slate-gray sky, the first glimpse of the rising sun. "This is always the worst time, isn't it," Pershing said, staring out the window. "You find yourself wishing it would stay this way forever. You don't want the goddamn sun to come up to start another day without them."

"Since we came back from Mexico, I've tried to get drunk enough every night to miss it," Bliss said.

Pershing's head turned like the barrel of a swiveling cannon. "You've done it for the last time, Mal. We can't let death break us."

John J. Pershing was thinking as a professional soldier about the fate that had gouged his soul. He was confronting the primal fear that the mystery and power of leadership had overcome on battlefields since men emerged from their caves with weapons in their hands. He was asking—no, ordering—Malvern Hill Bliss to become his ally in this private war within the public war.

He was also telling himself and Bliss not to lose faith in Pershing luck. This mysterious entity had kept him alive on bullet-swept battlefields and led him infallibly to the men and women who made his career, from the Commanding General of the Army, Nelson Miles, who chose him as his aide, to Theodore Roosevelt, whom Jack met on a chance visit to New York five years before Teddy became President, to Helen Frances Warren. Jack knew the murderous fire in the Presidio had sown dangerous doubts about Pershing luck in many soldiers' minds. But Malvern Hill Bliss was still a believer.

From the day Bliss walked into West Point, a strange inevitability had permeated his relationship with Pershing. Bliss's name—and his announced disdain for obeying rules and regulations—had instantly attracted Jack's attention. Four years older than the average plebe, Pershing had been the acknowledged leader of their class. When Jack found out Bliss was a distant relation of William S. "Perfect" Bliss, General Zachary Taylor's brilliant chief of staff in the Mexican War, he nicknamed him Imperfect Bliss—and made him his first test of his ability to command men. Under Pershing's glaring eye, Bliss ruefully surrendered his indifference to shining his shoes and cleaning his room, which had him at the top of the demerit list in plebe year, and stopped going over the wall to visit the saloons and cat houses of the Hudson River Valley.

But Bliss remained at the foot of their class, absorbing as little as possible of the awful doses of mathematics and civil engineering every cadet had to swallow. Southern pride—and a passionate preference for history and literature—saved him from unconditional surrender to Pershing's ferocity. After graduation, Pershing's friendship had kept Bliss in the army, that and a grudging loyalty to his father's dream of a reunited America, healed of the Civil War's awful wounds. In battle beside Pershing, Bliss had discovered the only kind of honor he respected. He had become a professional soldier.

Bliss had lost that soldier in the narrow streets of Jolo; he had disintegrated beneath that whirling Moro kris. But John J. Pershing was determined to resurrect him, because he needed him. No one else understood the invisible burden he carried on his ramrod back.

Maybe knowing Pershing needed him would make a difference.

Bliss was not sure. It might make a difference long enough for him to get to France. Then he could decide other things for himself. Such as whether death was an enemy or a friend.

Pershing began talking about how the American army was going to fight in France. "Open warfare is the key," he said. "We've got to get out of those stupid trenches into the open, where our superiority with the rifle and bayonet will count."

Bliss nodded. Open warfare was not a new idea. Fire and movement had been preached at West Point as the key to victory since the school's foundation.

Pershing stared into the emptiness around them for another moment. "Remember how we worried about what the goddamn reporters would say when we had a dozen men killed in an operation on Mindanao? We've got to forget that kind of thinking."

"Casualties don't matter, Jack?" Bliss said.

It was not an attitude Bliss associated with Pershing. He had always been parsimonious with his men's lives. They had pacified Mindanao in 1902 with a loss of only twenty men—six of whom had died of cholera. Bliss remembered talking with him after he returned from observing the Russo-Japanese war of 1904. Jack had been appalled at the reckless way both sides had wasted their infantry.

"Of course casualties matter. But you can't let them stop you. They didn't stop Grant and Lee."

Bliss started to say he thought Ulysses S. Grant and Robert E. Lee were a pair of military butchers. But it was not the time or place to vent his prejudices. Nodding noncommittally, he watched the rising sun flood sky and prairie. The whole world was drenched in red. It was the dawn of a new day.

2. PEACE THAT SURPASSETH UNDERSTANDING

DECLARE WAR! Red-haired Polly Warden rode up Fifth Avenue in a jouncing horse-drawn hansom cab glaring at the exhortation on top of the front page of the *New York Tribune*. Below it the stories reported the eagerness with which Congress and the nation were awaiting President Woodrow Wilson's speech calling for a declaration of war against Germany.

"It's so mindless," she said.

"They've got a lot of company," George Eagleton said. "The *Times*, the *World*, the *Sun*, and the *Herald* are all saying the same thing."

"And you agree with them?" Polly said.

"I'm beginning to think they have a point," George said.

"George. I'm disappointed in you."

George glowered at the mixture of high-roofed black motor taxis and open touring cars ahead of them. "I agree with Teddy Roosevelt. We can't let the Germans sink our ships, kill Americans on the high seas, and ignore our protests without turning into an international joke—a nation of cowards."

For a moment Polly was awed by the way George's size added intensity to his belligerent words. Six feet three, with massive shoulders, a thick neck, and a jaw that looked quarried from some primeval rock, he filled two thirds of the hansom's seat. Not for the first time, she reminded herself that brawn was not synonymous with brains. "George," she said, "that's simplistic thinking."

Polly knew George's detestation of Germany was not the real reason he was glowering at the traffic. Spring sunlight spangled the greening trees in Central Park and gleamed on the hansom cab's brass lamps. George had suggested the cab instead of a motor taxi because it was such a beautiful day. The old horse's sedate pace, the cab's small back seat, guaranteed him half an hour with his muscular arm around Polly's slim waist. She was spoiling this romantic interlude with her passion for peace at—in George's opinion—any price.

Polly regretted the quarrel too. She had no objection to George's arm around her waist, pressing her 110 pounds against his huge torso. Last summer at Bar Harbor they had done a lot of that sort of thing as they zoomed along the narrow roads in George's Pierce Arrow roadster. Occasionally they stopped at a certain bluff overlooking the sea and indulged in a little spooning—the exchange of a tender kiss or two. George's lips stirred remarkably pleasant sensations deep in Polly's body. It made her think that Viennese mind doctor, Sigmund Freud, might be right when he said women had sexual desires too.

But some spooning and an arm around her waist were all George got for the wear and tear on his tires. Finding out if Dr. Freud was right would have to wait a while. In Bar Harbor, Polly Warden liked to play. She stopped parties with her imitations of Marie Dressler and other Broadway musical comedy stars. She danced the smoothest, slinkiest Castle Gavotte on the Maine coast. Even George, a former Harvard fullback, said it was an athletic experience. In New York, Polly was a serious woman. Alone among her circle of fellow Wellesley graduates of the class of 1916, she had a job—teaching French to the young ladies of Miss Chapin's School. She devoted her afternoons and evenings to campaigning for the vote for women and fighting to keep America at peace.

Recently peace had become the more important cause. Was it simply because of the crisis atmosphere that had developed in the last two months? Or was the earnest young giant sitting beside her part of the anxiety that assailed her every time she saw a warmongering headline or editorial? Was she afraid the war would produce a crisis between her and George Eagleton?

"Eventually, Polly, the new woman's going to have to admit

the importance of manhood and courage," George said.

Polly's temper rose. It was that phrase new woman, the offhand, subtly contemptuous way George used it. The two words triggered complex emotions in Polly. Most of the time she thought of herself as a woman who had new ideas about her abilities and her future. But she hated anyone—especially George—to use the term as if she were a separate species, cut off from the rest of the world's women, some kind of freak.

"Why do you have to kill people to prove you're a man?" Polly said.

"No one wants to kill anybody. It's simple self-defense. No real man can sit back and let the Germans take over the world."

This was unquestionably a real man sitting beside her. But Polly remembered the skinny boy who had flung sand in her hair at Bar Harbor and heaped scorn on those feeble wailing creatures known as girls. She remembered her envy of George's teenage ability to throw a baseball and handle a sailboat—and his lack of interest in reading a book. She could still see the awkward Harvard freshman taking her to the spring dance at Wellesley with exactly two topics of conversation: last year's Yale-Harvard game and next year's Yale-Harvard game.

With no warning, in senior year George became interesting. He talked of hunting trips to Colorado and Alaska, of rambling around Inca ruins in South America with adventurous classmates. He teased Polly about being a suffragette, but there was nothing vicious in his sarcasm. He actually seemed interested in her opinions.

For a while Polly thought she was turning George Eagleton into a serious man. He seemed to accept her denunciation of the double standard in marriage. He even agreed that women should have the vote—risking the ire of his conservative father. Then George had displayed another kind of seriousness.

On a moonlit night at the end of last summer, George had driven the Pierce Arrow to that bluff overlooking the sea and kissed her gently, tenderly. Then he pressed her against his broad chest and talked about Life. He wanted to live it with her beside him. Was she interested in that idea?

Touched, even a little flustered, Polly told George she was very fond of him, but she was not ready for marriage. She wanted to wait a year or two, to work, to tackle the challenges of being an independent woman. She wanted to give her college education meaning and purpose.

All that was true. But Polly also knew there was something wrong with her feelings for George Eagleton. Part of it was her mother's fault. She was always talking about George. She seemed to keep a dossier on the other young women in New York who were supposedly pursuing him. Mother knew exactly how many times he danced with Suzy Astor at the fall cotillion and what he said to Caroline Russell at her cousin's wedding. She also knew exactly how much George was going to inherit when his father died: $20 million.

Having managed Polly's two older sisters into moneyed marriages, Mother seemed to think she was an expert on the subject. The anxiety—and occasional anger—this stirred in Polly was unfair to George. More than once, Polly had told her mother she would probably marry George Eagleton if she would let her alone. She liked him. He had a good sense of humor and no discernible bad habits. She simply could not see any reason to rush into his arms.

Even as Polly gave her mother this reassurance, a contrary voice within her was fiercely whispering *no!* She did not understand this voice. She sometimes thought of it as her counter-self, a shadowy opposite who lived in mirrors and midnight windows, an observer who both guarded and confused her. What was the meaning of that fierce *no?* Was it the voice of the new woman?

This personage, species, creature—her identity was as confusing as her origins—was unquestionably appearing in America and in other countries. For almost half a century, women had been graduating from colleges, entering professions, campaigning for the vote. They were still a small minority of the world's women, but they were growing steadily in numbers and self-confidence.

"It's that big gray house," George called to the cabman. "Eight eighty."

"Sure I know it well, sor," the Irishman said. "Kingswood's castle, we call it."

He edged them expertly to the curb in front of the four-story limestone château, a few doors from the corner of 69th Street. A plump Irish maid led them to the spacious front parlor, where some two dozen members of the League for International Peace were sipping tea from blue Sevres cups. Seven or eight were men. The rest were college women in their twenties or early thirties, dressed in colorful spring walking gowns or suits. Several, such as Polly's Wellesley classmate Martha Herzog, had bobbed their hair, a declaration of independence Polly knew her mother would never tolerate.

"Finally," Eleanor Kingswood said. "We wondered if you two had stopped to do a little spooning in the park."

"George doesn't look as if he enjoyed it," Arthur Hunthausen said. George grinned good-naturedly and pretended to sock his foxy-faced former Harvard roommate in the jaw.

Polly let the barbs pass unchallenged. She knew Eleanor Kingswood did not approve of George Eagleton. But Polly insisted a serious woman could change a man like George. Wasn't that what they were trying to do in the fight for peace, change them all from violent brutes into rational civilized beings?

The maid served Polly and George tea. "I've brought along the latest bad news," Polly said, throwing the *Tribune* on the couch.

Everyone groaned at the demand for war on top of the front page. "Now we know what Wall Street is thinking," Martha Herzog said.

"That presumes greed can think," snapped one of their Vassar friends, a dedicated socialist. The *Tribune* was the voice of the Republican Party and the voice of Wall Street—pretty much the same thing in New York.

Looking around her, Polly realized everyone was dazed by the sudden lurch toward war. It was less than a month since Woodrow Wilson had been sworn in for a second term. He had been elected on the slogan "He kept us out of war," with powerful support from pacifists and millions of other Americans who wanted nothing to do with the carnage that had been raging in Europe since the summer of 1914.

"It's the Zimmermann thing," Arthur Hunthausen said. In February the German foreign minister had sent a telegram to the government of Mexico, suggesting an alliance against the United

States. The British had intercepted it and given it to President Wilson, who gave it to the newspapers, creating instant national outrage.

Several men agreed the proposal to Mexico was an extremely unfriendly and stupid move by the Germans. But they did not think it explained why America was on the brink of war. "It's unrestricted submarine warfare," George Eagleton said.

The Germans had announced their decision to resume this policy, which meant they would torpedo all ships in the war zone. Most of the men agreed with George that this was far more serious than Zimmermann's telegram. Unrestricted submarine warfare killed American seamen. Several ships had already been sunk, with serious loss of lives.

"Why can't our ships stay out of the war zone?" Polly asked.

That stirred a chorus of male objections. Free trade was a basic American principle. Polly began to suspect every man in the room was like George Eagleton, eager to slug it out with the Germans. Polly had majored in French at Wellesley and sympathized with embattled France. But keeping America out of the war was more important than attachments—or antipathies—to either side. Only if America remained neutral could she be a true peacemaker. This had been Woodrow Wilson's creed until he was reelected.

"I've never been as disappointed with any man in my life as I am with Woodrow Wilson," Martha Herzog said. Small and dark, with a mannish nose and a strong severe mouth, Martha was their resident thinker. Her banker father was a major contributor to the Democratic Party.

"He's done nothing but bait the Germans since the day he got reelected," Eleanor Kingswood said.

Eleanor called the meeting to order. She stood as straight as a colonel, but there the resemblance ended. Eleanor's flawless face and superb figure drew envious stares from women and salacious ones from men. She wore her thick dark hair plaited in circular braids that formed a kind of crown. One night last summer Arthur Hunthausen had told her she looked like the incarnation of the goddess Athena. Eleanor had let him have an extra dance for that compliment.

Eleanor reviewed the drift toward war, with the *Tribune* as Exhibit A. Did anyone have a suggestion for a dramatic response? Polly suggested picketing all the bloodthirsty papers. "No," Eleanor said. "We need them for our other goal."

Everyone knew what Eleanor meant: the vote. Eighteen months ago, Eleanor had been one of the women behind what some people called the greatest parade in New York's history. Clad in white, carrying banners of brilliant yellow, she and other suffragists had led 23,450 women up Fifth Avenue, demanding the vote.

"I think the fight for peace is just as important, Eleanor," Martha Herzog said.

"But we seem to be losing it," Eleanor said. "We don't want to let them make fools of us."

Eleanor liked to win at everything, from tennis to politics. Polly sometimes wondered if that explained her initial attraction to the peace movement. The fight for peace was a relatively new idea that had won wide support among the younger generation. No less than forty-five different peace groups were now active in America.

Polly struggled to revive her best friend's enthusiasm. "Remember how we felt when the war in Europe began?" she said. It had been thrilling to believe they had an answer to the upheaval.

"These days the thrills are few and far between," Eleanor said.

Last year the war party, mostly Republicans led by former President Theodore Roosevelt, had opened a ferocious, sneering assault on the peace movement. Much of what George Eagleton said to Polly coming up Fifth Avenue was straight from their propaganda machine.

"The League's reserved forty cars on the Baltimore and Ohio for a last appeal to Congress," Arthur Hunthausen said. "They're leaving tomorrow at nine. Should we go?"

Eleanor hesitated. They had all made at least a dozen trips to Washington to urge peace on congressmen and senators. It was almost always a discouraging experience.

"No," Polly said. "We know talking to those idiots is a waste of time. Our fight is here. In our city. Let's all go down to Union Square tomorrow morning and tell the world, if we can't tell Congress, that New Yorkers hate war."

Eleanor looked testy. She did not like anyone, even Polly, to tell her what to do. "Isn't it obvious by now that you're wasting your time?" George Eagleton said.

"Why do you say that, George?" Eleanor said.

"I told Polly in the cab on the way up here. I think the President's finally making the right decision. We should have stopped those German swine long ago. They're raped Belgium and now they're raping France—"

"Really, George!" Eleanor said.

George turned scarlet. He had used a word no one ever uttered in polite New York society.

"I'm sorry," George said. "But that's what they're doing."

Eleanor gave Polly a mocking glance that said, Is this what you call changing the brute's mind? "Then you're not coming to Union Square?" she asked. George's opposition had made up her mind for her.

"I'm coming. To make sure some lug doesn't insult you or Polly—or the rest of you," George added with an embarrassed glance at the other women. Many of them were still glaring at him as if he had committed an unpardonable sin.

"We're used to being heckled," Martha Herzog said.

"I know," George said. "But I don't think any of you realize how unpopular pacifism has become."

"That's why we're going," Polly said. "To show the warmongers they can't intimidate us."

On Fifth Avenue, Polly briskly suggested George hail a motor taxi to return her to her home on Stuyvesant Square. In the roomy backseat she sat several feet away from him and struggled to keep her temper. "I saw absolutely no point in that argument. Were you trying to embarrass me with Eleanor?"

"I was just trying to talk a little common sense," George said. "But now that you mention it, there *are* times when I feel like I'm competing with Eleanor for your attention."

"Eleanor is my closest, dearest friend. I've known her almost as long as I've known you. She doesn't drive a Pierce Arrow and take me to dinner and the theater, but she has a very strong claim on my affections."

The muscles in George's freckled face bunched into ominous knots. For a moment Polly heard her mother warning her that no man would tolerate a woman who made impudent remarks. *Bridle your tongue if you want to be a bride.* It was one of Mother's favorite bits of woman's wisdom.

"Let's not argue about something that's practically irrelevant," George said. "The peace movement is a dead duck. I never thought you had a prayer of succeeding, but—"

George turned another shade of red, not quite as scarlet as the one he had displayed in the Kingswood parlor. He suddenly seemed overheated. He fussed with his high white collar and striped silk tie.

"But what?" Polly said. Was he reaching for some ultimate condescension?

"If Congress declares war I'm joining up. I might be over there a long time. Do you think—I mean, would you consider getting married before I go over?"

There it was. What her watcher voice, her guardian opposite, had feared. The war was giving George a chance to revoke his agreement to allow her two years of independence.

George swept her across the seat and crushed her against his broad chest. "I love you, Polly. I've loved you all my life," he said.

Polly struggled with clashing emotions. There was going to be a war. George was going to be in it. He wanted to be in it. Did he have the right to turn that into an obligation to marry him immediately?

There was this yearning, this warmth, his kisses aroused in her. Polly knew what else was involved, of course. Wellesley graduates had all heard earnest lectures from learned scientists on sex. But there was a gulf between knowing and doing; it was like imagining a trip to the moon and actually making one.

Unfortunately, on the trip to the marriage bed, there were no return tickets. If the moon was made of moldy sponge cake, a woman had to learn to like it. Only a handful of women in upper-class New York had dared to divorce their husbands, and they—not the husbands—had been ostracized. Most of them had fled to Italy or France.

The green mansard roof and splendid corner towers of the Plaza Hotel loomed against the blue sky on the right. The marble and limestone mansions of the very rich stared haughtily into Fifth Avenue on the left. She could live up here in a house almost as splendid with this man. She could, in the opinion of almost every other woman in New York, arrive.

Downtown on Stuyvesant Square the Wardens, like many other old New York families, struggled to maintain a façade of affluence. Polly's mother called it decency. They had one aging servant who doubled as cook. Her mother had not bought a new dress in a decade. Polly was lucky to buy one a year—and it was not from a Paris collection.

How could she decide whether she was marrying the man or the money? It was impossible in this crisis atmosphere, with newspapers and politicians—and George—shouting war. Polly wanted time, even a few days, to sort out these contradictory feelings and analyze them calmly, rationally, without this pendulum effect. "I've told you already, George. You're very special to me," she said. "But I'll have to think about marriage—so soon."

"I wish you would," George said. "I wish you'd give it some *very* serious thought." There was the hint of an ultimatum in his voice. Polly almost said something impudent in reply.

That night at dinner Polly waited until they had finished dessert and the coffee had been poured before mentioning George's proposal to her parents. "Everyone seems to think war is inevitable," she said, as her father, Alexander Hamilton Warden, gulped one of the half dozen pills he took at every meal. "Do you think so?"

"I not only think so, I hope so," her father said. As handsome as he was fastidious—in his youth his impeccable style had won him the nickname Beau Warden—this small compact man had been the source of Polly's interest in the peace movement. But he had abandoned it a year ago when Theodore Roosevelt announced it was imperative for America to join the Allies. If her father had a hero, it was the rambunctious ex-president. Their families had been friendly for generations. He had been a year behind Teddy at Harvard.

"George Eagleton says he's going to enlist. He wants me to marry him before he goes overseas."

"You don't sound enthusiastic," her father said. Although they had parted company on the peace movement, there was still a strong bond between them. He had supported Polly's passionate desire for a college education, in spite of her mother's fear that it would only make her more opinionated.

"I'm not enthusiastic about marrying a soldier," Polly said. "It might be better to wait until after this disgusting war is over. We'll beat the Germans to pieces in five or six months, don't you think?"

"That is hardly the point," her mother said, her blue eyes glinting ominously. "You're in no position to refuse him, Polly."

Alice Van Ness Warden had almost erupted last summer when Polly told her she had fended off George's moonlit overtures. They had come very close to having a serious quarrel—something no one in the family had with Mother if they could avoid it. When she got angry, her normally smooth, rounded cheeks sagged into sucking hollows and her sensitive mouth twisted into an ugly snarling loop.

"Polly. I've told you before. You'll never have another offer like this," her mother said.

"Mother, I've told *you* before that George's money is absolutely the last consideration. It always has been and always will be."

"Alice. I'm really quite—quite surprised," her father said. Money was never discussed so bluntly in old New York families. He had remained serenely aloof from the intricacies of Polly's sisters' marriages. Both had "settled," as her mother put it, for husbands from newly rich families who were eager to marry some of the bluest blood in New York.

"I don't care what you think!" her mother said. "Have you done *anything* since our wedding day to rescue this family from humiliation? When I think of the time I've spent flattering vulgarians from Chicago and nobodies from Philadelphia and Hartford, I almost explode!"

Polly winced as if her mother had struck the blow at her. She often winced when she thought about her parents' marriage. Polly was woman enough to understand, to sympathize with her mother. But she also sympathized with her father—no, she was proud of him. She was glad he had declined to plunge into the amoral world of Wall Street, where sharks like Jay Gould might have devoured him or turned him into a cold-eyed money worshiper like George Eagleton's father. She admired the way Alexander Warden served on charity boards and public committees to help the poor and gathered petitions calling on the state legislature to investigate New York City's corrupt politics. He was a good citizen, a kind, decent, loving man.

"I suspect you'll feel badly if you say no," her father said, ignoring his wife's outburst. He wanted to sympathize with Polly—he always wanted to sympathize with everyone—but he was on George's side on the question of war or peace. "Everyone's going to join up. There'll be a veritable tidal wave of patriotism. It'll be just like the Spanish-American War."

That was his war. He had been a captain in a New York regiment in 1898. He always made it sound like a lark. No one had gotten killed. The Spanish had surrendered before the regiment even landed in Puerto Rico. Wouldn't the Germans do the same thing when they saw a hundred million Americans marching toward them?

War, Polly thought, war was crowding into this modest dining room where she had sat as a chattering child, a stubborn adolescent. Both her parents were using war to intimidate her into surrendering her self, her life, to George Eagleton. It was invading her feelings for him too.

"I don't know what I should do," Polly said.

"I do!" her mother said.

Polly began to think war had already been declared.

3. THE CELTS ARE COMING

I DIDN'T RAISE MY BOY TO BE A SOLDIER,
I RAISED HIM UP TO BE MY PRIDE AND JOY.

Blaring from a phonograph positioned, with unconscious irony, at the foot of a statue of the Marquis de Lafayette, this favorite pacifist song drifted into Malvern Hill Bliss's ears as he strolled through the noontime crowds in New York's Union Square. He had just spent a somewhat disheartening twelve hours visiting his sister and her husband and two sons on East 20th Street. His brother-in-law, an unreconstructed Southerner—there were thousands of them making money in New York—found it hard to be civil to anyone in a U.S. Army uniform. His nephews barely remembered him.

The music stopped and a magnified woman's voice cried, "Fellow New Yorkers! Do you want peace or war? It's not too late to tell President Wilson to stop his reckless rush to slaughter! It's not too late to call him to account for his lies and equivocations."

Bliss was in no hurry. He had two hours to catch his train to Washington, D.C. As a soldier and a student of the American character, he was naturally interested in the pacifist crusade to keep America out of the war. He strolled toward Lafayette's statue and found a tall statuesque brunette talking through a megaphone. A six-footer in a well-tailored tan suit and vest stood beside her, a stern look on his angular face. The woman was telling everyone that Wilson was a liar and a warmonger.

"How much the Germans payin' you to say that?" yelled a man standing beside Bliss. He was a burly red-haired Irish American wearing a long-sleeved green athletic jersey.

"The Germans aren't paying me anything," the woman said.

"Yeah? What's your name?" the Irish American said.

"Eleanor Kingswood," the speaker said. "I'm chairman of the New York chapter of the League—"

"What's his name?" the Celt said.

"Arthur Hunthausen," the man said.

"Sounds like a Heinie to me," the Celt said.

"For your information, my ancestors arrived in New York a hundred years ago," Hunthausen said.

"So what? The Kaiser was just thinkin' ahead," the Irishman bellowed. "Ten bucks says you're a spy and your girlfriend's another one. We know what spies do, right? Who's she puttin' out for?"

"In the name of George Washington, who warned us against foreign entanglements, I ask you to ignore this vulgar interruption," Hunthausen said to the rest of the crowd. He pointed to a heroic statue of Washington on horseback in the middle of the intersection of Fourth Avenue and 14th Street. Bliss wondered how he could ignore Lafayette, who represented a foreign entanglement that had saved George and the infant United States from defeat and disgrace.

"Who's she puttin' out for?" the Irishman repeated. He grinned up at the brunette. "Who you puttin' out for, girlie? You got any generals on the string?"

He turned to Bliss and gave him a wink. "How about it, General. You know her?"

"I'm only a colonel," Bliss said. "I never saw her before in my life."

A hand seized the Irishman's shoulder. "You lowlife," Hunthausen said. "I won't permit you to spew such filth about the woman I love."

"What're you gonna do about it?" the Celt said.

"I'm going to thrash you," Hunthausen said, starting to take off his coat.

The Irishman hit him on the point of his jaw while his arms were behind his back, in the sleeves of his coat. It was a beautiful shot. Hunthausen flew at least twenty feet, almost knocking down a dozen office workers. There was a gasp of fright from the spectators. They seemed to sense instantly how dangerous the Irishman was.

No one tried to help Hunthausen as he struggled to his feet, tore off his coat, and advanced on the Irishman, his left fist extended for a jab, his right ready for a knockout punch—the classic amateur stance.

The Irishman stood there, hands on his hips, watching contemptuously. When Hunthausen was about six feet away, the Irishman dropped into a crouch and shuffled sideways, his left hand close to his chest, his right low, no more than waist high. It was a perfect imitation of lightweight champion Benny Leonard.

The Irishman feinted a rush with his right extended, and Hunthausen dropped his guard to protect himself from a body punch. The Irishman's left exploded against his jaw. An instant later the right, magically withdrawn and flung from less than six inches, caught Hunthausen in the belly. As he buckled, the Irishman hit him again with a one-two punch to the left eye and nose. Blood spurted, and the brunette started screaming for the police.

Hunthausen was on the sidewalk, groaning. The Irish slugger kicked him a couple of times to make sure he stayed there and hurtled through the crowd, roaring, "Let's take care of the rest of these traitors!"

Bliss followed him down the east side of Union Square Park, where a dozen other Irishmen in green jerseys were attacking pacifist women speakers and their male escorts. The gang was having no trouble disposing of the escorts—except for a big blond Harvard man in a crimson letter sweater who was mixing it up with one of their largest contenders, giving as good as he got.

The slugger who had flattened Hunthausen reached the scene just as a tiny redhead in a sky-blue dress banged Harvard's opponent on the head with a wooden placard on which PEACE was painted in red, white, and blue letters. The bozo's eyes glazed and he toppled to the ground. The slugger tore the placard out of the redhead's hands and smashed it against a tree, holding her at arm's length with his left hand.

"Get your paws off her!" shouted Harvard and clouted the slugger on the side of the jaw with a very good roundhouse right. He staggered away and Harvard rushed him. The slugger recovered in time to hit Harvard in the belt buckle with a right. Then he unleashed his left hook and Harvard was on the ground.

Spitting on his bruised knuckles, the slugger looked around. Who should be lurching toward him but his first victim, Hunthausen, blood oozing from his nose, one eye half shut, determined to go another round. The brunette was clinging to one arm, screaming, "No, Arthur, no! He's a hoodlum, an animal!"

She gave the slugger the perfect opportunity. Once more he clipped Arthur on the point of his unprotected jaw, and he and the brunette both went down in a tangle of high-priced tailoring.

"Scum!" screamed the brunette.

That word had a very unfortunate effect on the slugger. His face went blank with the kind of rage Bliss had seen only on a battle-field. He grabbed the groaning Hunthausen by his tie and lifted him two or three feet from the pavement for another left hook, obviously intending to pound his face into hamburger.

The tiny redhead seized his arm. She was afraid of nothing. "Stop it, you monster!" she cried. "Help, police! Help!"

There was no sign of a cop anywhere. Trying to shake the red-head loose, the slugger flung her back and forth like a toy. Bliss grabbed his other arm. "Don't waste another punch on him," he said. "Save it for the Germans."

The slugger laughed in a violent exultant way that, again, Bliss had only heard on a battlefield. "Maybe you're right, Colonel," he said.

The slugger let Hunthausen thud to the sidewalk. He shook off the redhead and surveyed the square. The pacifists were all out of action, the male protectors flattened, their placards smashed, their phonograph ditto. The slugger sucked in his lips and blew a short fierce whistle. "Let's go, guys. It's collection time," he shouted.

They assembled with the precision of trained soldiers and followed him east down 14th Street. Bliss watched until they disappeared into a large red-brick building several doors from the corner of Fourth Avenue.

The tiny redhead knelt beside her groggy Harvard stalwart. "Is this how you're going to fight the war?" she shouted at Bliss. "With brutes like that?"

"I hope so," Bliss said. "It's a relief to see not everyone listens to your pacifist nonsense."

"You'll regret saying that someday!" she cried. "The whole country will regret this stupid orgy of violence."

"This particular orgy didn't look stupid to me," Bliss said. "Those fellows seemed to know exactly what they were doing."

"All violence is stupid!" she cried.

Bliss shook his head. "Intelligent violence wins wars—and wars are the engine of history."

"Bunk!" the redhead shouted.

She was obviously a woman with a mind of her own. Quite a figure, too. He liked that sort of female: small enough to get your arms around. Goddess types like the tall brunette reminded him too much of his mother. They thought they were born to criticize the male sex.

Bliss strolled down 14th Street to the red-brick building. In a niche at the roofline stood the statue of an Indian. Engraved in bold letters above his head was an inscription: THE TAMMANY SOCIETY. It was the headquarters of Tammany Hall, the Democratic political machine that ran New York.

Inside, Bliss found himself in a room with the longest bar he had ever seen. There must have been five hundred bottles behind it. Three black-mustached bartenders, each a bruiser, looked him over. A beefy man in a derby was counting several hundred dollars onto the bar for the slugger and his friends.

"I knew you guys were good," the derby said.

"What can we do for you, Colonel?" one of the bartenders asked.

"Not a thing," Bliss said. "I just wanted to ask these fellows what's going on."

He introduced himself to the derby, who said his name was Alexander O'Sullivan. He introduced the slugger as Benny O'Connor. He had a handshake like Pershing's. Bliss could almost feel the bones crumbling from his wrist to his fingertips. The rest of them had equally Irish names and handshakes almost as murderous.

"Just a little political business, Colonel," O'Sullivan said. "We decided to make sure Wilson knows we're on his side in this war thing. There's gonna be a lot of jobs handed out, and we wanna make sure we got the okay on them."

O'Sullivan ordered steins of Ruppert's beer all around and continued his lecture. "We don't get along with Woodrow too well, as you may know. Last year we teamed up with the German Americans and tried to make him get as neutral with King George as he is with the Kaiser. We come within a dozen votes of passin' the thing in the Senate and scared the Preacher's socks off. He made that speech, sayin' we was pourin' poison into the veins of the American people."

As a White Anglo-Saxon Papist—his family had arrived in Maryland in 1668—Bliss had paid little attention to Wilson's speech. From the growls and glares of resentment on the Irish faces around him, it had obviously had an enormous impact on them.

"Ah, hell," said O'Connor. "I'm from New Jersey. Everyone over there knows Wilson's a liar and a bum. We elected him governor in 1910 and he broke every promise he made to us."

"Does that mean you won't fight the Germans?" Bliss said.

"He'll fight. They'll all fight," O'Sullivan said. "I just enlisted them in my national guard regiment, Ireland's Own. We're gonna make that Protestant pickle puss in the White House eat his words."

"You're the commander?"

O'Sullivan nodded cheerfully. "We're all gonna wind up as famous as Teddy Roosevelt on San Juan Hill. There ain't a German in New York who can stand up to an Irishman in a fight."

"The same goes for New Jersey," O'Connor said.

Bliss finished his beer, wished everyone luck in the U.S. Army, and said he had a train to catch. He headed for Penn Station feeling almost cheerful. The United States of America was a fascinating country.

That little redhead was fascinating too, not that Bliss ever expected to see her again. He was sure she and her snooty New York friends would snub a mere army officer from Baltimore, even if they agreed with his awful opinions about violence. Anyway, he had promised Pershing he was going to stay as celibate as St. Simeon Stylites on his pillar.

4. *GOD HELPING US*
WE CAN DO NO OTHER

ILLUMINATED BY SEARCHLIGHTS FROM BELOW, THE dome of the United States capitol loomed in the night like a great white symbol of sanctity, purity, and purpose. Malvern Hill Bliss stood near the bottom of the uneven marble steps beneath a big umbrella held by John J. Pershing. Rain drooled from the black sky above the dome. Bliss and Pershing were both in civilian clothes. The War Department did not want any premature publicity about Jack's appointment as commander of the American Expeditionary Force.

A block or so away on Constitution Avenue, several thousand pacifists stood before a line of troops and police, chanting, "Peace! Keep America at peace!" They had overrun the capitol and the congressional office buildings all day, shouting their slogans at lawmakers, most of whom ignored them.

The chants were abruptly drowned out by the thunder of hoofbeats. Up Pennsylvania Avenue came a squadron of cavalry. Behind them rode the President in a black touring car. The cavalry split into two columns and stopped just short of the capitol steps, forming twin walls of men and horses. The President's car cruised up to the steps between them. Cheers burst from the semidarkness on the left and right, where several thousand prowar partisans twirled small American flags. The President smiled and waved to them as he got out of the car.

"Waffling Woodrow's moment of truth," Bliss said. He was not an admirer of Woodrow Wilson. He thought the President's neutralist foreign policy and his whines about being too proud to fight had made Americans look ridiculous to the rest of the world. Even worse was Wilson's indifference to the pathetic weakness of the U.S. Army in a world maddened by all-out war. He knew Pershing felt the same way. But Jack did not respond in kind tonight.

"Let's go in," Pershing said.

An hour later, sitting beside Pershing in the gallery of the House of Representatives, Bliss listened to Woodrow Wilson reach the climax of his speech. Objectively, he had to admit it was a masterpiece, a classic example of how a gifted orator substituted rhetoric for the truth. Step by step, Wilson indicted the Germans for waging a war of aggression, for refusing to heed his calls for a negotiated peace.

But the President did not call on Americans to fight the German people. "We have no feeling towards them but one of sympathy and friendship," he insisted. It was the "government of the German empire" that was at fault. This idea was driven home with rhetorical drumfire. Phrases like "Prussian autocracy," "dynasties," "rulers," and "autocratic governments" exploded again and again.

Then the President was soaring into his peroration. Americans were going to war to fight "for the things which we have always carried nearest our hearts"—for democracy, for the rights and liberties of small nations, for "a concert of free peoples"—a world government that would guarantee "a universal dominion" of justice. "God helping her," Wilson declared, America "can do no other."

Magnificent, Bliss thought, especially that last phrase, cribbed from Martin Luther's declaration of faith, *Ich kann nicht anders*. But as the Frenchman said about the charge of the light brigade, it was not war. Wilson was calling for the impossible. He wanted a war without hate, without killing. He was telling the American people to smile through the apocalypse to achieve his parliamentary version of the Second Coming.

Beside him, Pershing's face was expressionless. What was he thinking? Bliss wondered. Maybe he did not give a damn what Wilson said. He was getting what he wanted, an army to command. He had been campaigning for the appointment ever since they came back from chasing Pancho Villa around Mexico four months ago.

Pershing had summoned the reporters covering the so-called Punitive Expedition to his quarters at Fort Sam Houston one night and
told them he wanted the big job. "Boys," he had said, "tell me how I
can help you so you can help me."

Outside on the capitol steps, General Tasker H. Bliss, Chief of
Staff of the U.S. Army, shook hands with Pershing. The Great Man
deigned to do likewise with Malvern Hill Bliss. "Hello, Little Rebel
Brother," he said, extending his big soft paw. He was in uniform; his
four stars gleamed on his massive shoulders.

A generation older than Pershing and Bliss, Tasker had long
found it amusing that there was a southern-born Bliss in the officer
corps to contrast—always unfavorably, of course—with the brilliant
northern-born Bliss.

"Greetings, BYB," Bliss said. That was supposed to be short for
Big Yankee Brother, but in Bliss's mind it stood for Bloated Yellow
Bastard. After serving under Tasker in pacified Cuba and the Philippines, he had concluded that this large slow-moving Pennsylvanian
personified the kind of soldier he despised.

General Bliss waved them to a waiting car, and they rode across
the Potomac toward his quarters in Fort Myer, Virginia.

"What did you think of the speech?" Pershing asked.

"It'll do the job, I think," Tasker said.

"What does that mean?" Bliss asked.

"It gives us the uplift we need to create an army. You can't beat
Wilson at that game. He learned a lot from his preacher father. We
need all the lift we can find. Last month one of my intelligence men
traveled as a civilian from Kansas City to San Francisco without
finding ten people in favor of the war."

"Do you really think we can make the world safe for democracy?" Bliss asked.

General Bliss sighed. "I see you're still a southern literalist, Little Brother."

Malvern Hill Bliss waited for Pershing to say something. In their
military travels had either of them seen any evidence that the world
was ready for democracy? Sioux ghost dancers? Cuban peasants?
Moro warriors? Did Wilson really think they wanted to settle things
with the ballot box when knives or guns were handy?

Pershing remained silent. "Maybe Teddy Roosevelt is right," Bliss said. "Whenever the situation calls for plain speaking and direct action, Wilson substitutes elocution."

Pershing kicked him hard in the right shin. Bliss shut up and listened while Tasker told them what else his intelligence men had found out about the supposedly United States. The German Americans, some ten million strong, had been intimidated by Wilson's tactic of impugning their patriotism. The same formula seemed to have worked for the seven million Irish Americans, though a lot of them still preferred to fight the British. In the South, the sons and grandsons of the ex-Confederates saw the war as a chance to rejoin the union. All of them could change their minds, of course, if the war went badly.

"What about the pacifists?" Pershing asked.

"I understand steps are being taken to shut them up," Tasker said.

"From what I saw in New York, most of them will be in the hospital by the end of the week," Bliss said.

In Tasker's comfortable living room, with numerous souvenirs of his years as an administrator in the Philippines and Cuba on the walls and tables, an orderly served them coffee and they got down to business.

"The President called for an army of half a million in his speech. Is that our goal?" Pershing asked.

"The British and the French are recommending two million," Tasker said.

"We better start picking out some generals," Pershing said.

"I've got a list of possibilities right here," Tasker said.

"So have I," Pershing said.

In spite of the matter-of-fact tone, the expressionless faces, the room's tension rose several notches. It occurred to Bliss that Pershing had not been General Bliss's choice to command the American Expeditionary Force. To Tasker's bureaucratic eyes, this was another Pershing vault over more deserving senior officers.

For the next two hours, Pershing and the Chief of Staff played my list against your list. Predictably, Tasker's list was composed of people like himself, men who had spent most of their careers in the engineers dredging harbors or building dams or shuffling papers in Cuba and the Philippines or bellying up to politicians in Washington. On Pershing's list were men who had impressed him with their brains and courage on a battlefield. Some were from West Point, others had risen from the ranks.

Pershing fought almost every man on Bliss's list.

"He was a tactical officer when I was at the academy. A windbag....

"A good staff man but no combat leader."

Tasker had not spent thirty years playing the Washington game without learning a few things. He had numerous objections to people on Pershing's list. They chased women. They lacked stature. They were "difficult." Tasker must have studied the fitness reports of every man whom Pershing might conceivably choose. Obviously Jack was not going to get his way more than half the time. A tight-lipped Pershing reluctantly accepted a dismaying number of over-age, overweight, underqualified generals.

Finally they reached Malvern Hill Bliss's name, strategically located at the bottom of Pershing's list. "I want this fellow," Pershing said. "He can fight a division."

Tasker contemplated his little rebel brother with his peering mastodon's eyes. "You're not serious?" he said.

"Why shouldn't I be?"

"I don't think a man who starts getting drunk every night at five o'clock can command a division."

"He's not going to do that anymore."

Bliss wanted to spring at Tasker's fat throat. His nasal drone, his condescending eyes, always clouded with his own self-satisfied thoughts, were pure Yankee.

"What about women? Can he keep his hands off them?"

"Of course," Pershing said.

Bliss saw what both these coldhearted Northerners were doing, each in his own way. They were forcing him to surrender his grief. They were tearing Grace and Jackie out of his heart, like a team of sadistic surgeons performing without benefit of anesthesia. They were forcing him to accept reenlistment in the khaki monolith, the uncaring juggernaut known as the U.S. Army.

Forty future generals had been selected, another forty marked as possibles, the rest of the colonels consigned to history's dustbin. The telephone rang. It was Senator Warren, Pershing's father-in-law, who had lobbied ferociously to get Jack the big job. The President wanted to see him for a midnight conference.

Pershing departed for the White House, remarking that he hoped the Chief of Staff would have some words of wisdom for his little rebel brother. Jack's look made it clear that he expected Bliss to summon some southern charm from his side of the new equation.

The two Blisses confronted each other across the living room. "I still don't think you can do it," Tasker said. "Though I understand, of course, why he wants you to try."

"You're so goddamn smart, Tasker, I sometimes think you understand more than God," Bliss said, defiantly spiking his coffee with bourbon from a nearby bar.

"We're going to organize the draftee divisions by states," Tasker continued in his unflappable bureaucrat's drone. "But we're taking some National Guard infantry regiments and other units from the thirteen original states to create one division that will be a sort of symbol of our unity, if you'll pardon that moderately laughable expression. We're going to call it the Lafayette Division. Are you interested?"

Bliss was no admirer of the National Guard. When Wilson had called them out to patrol the Mexican border last year, only one in four had shown up, and half of those were rejected by the army's doctors. But he could not afford to be choosy. "Very much," he said.

Tasker nodded, smiling in his supercilious way. "I thought you might be. I read that visionary letter your father wrote when you were admitted to the academy, portraying you as a vessel of reunion between North and South. It's still in your file. If you pull it off you might contribute to our elusive national identity. You'll have rebels and Yankees in the ranks—plus micks and yids and wops. It will take a man of experience, and you're that, at least. You've even commanded niggers. If you mess up, we can always say the job was impossible to start with."

"I won't mess up," Bliss said. He was dismayed by how defensive he sounded.

"What puzzles me is this," Tasker continued, unfazed and unassailable in his assumption of northern superiority. "Why isn't Pershing the drunk? He seemed reasonably happy with Frankie, while Grace drove you crazy most of the time."

You no-good Yankee bastard. The words crowded into Bliss's throat. But in that crucial corner of his mind, Sergeant John Henry Turner whispered, *Steady, Colonel. He wants you to lose your head.*

Tasker's sneer about Grace was true, of course. That was the terrible thing about the U.S. Army. It was all in a man's file—all the truths about himself he could not bear to face.

5. HIDDEN AGENDAS

"I HAVE SPENT MY LIFETIME GIVING SERMONS AND listening to them. Humility and admiration compel me to admit I never gave or heard a sermon as great as the one Woodrow Wilson offered to the nation last Monday night. It has made the war a crusade in which every Christian can and must gladly join. Out of the fiery crucible, my dear friends, I predict a new, spiritually refined America will arise to assume the burdens and privileges of world leadership."

Polly Warden sat in the front pew of St. George's Episcopal Church beside her parents, listening to the rector baptize the war. She had felt some of what he was saying when she read Woodrow Wilson's speech in the *New York World*. It was a totally unexpected reconciliation of the goals of pacifism with the brutality of war.

Did that mean Polly Warden should marry George Eagleton before he went overseas? Would that be her contribution to making the world safe for democracy, sending George to war as a satisfied husband, perhaps an expectant father? Had she spent four years studying literature and science and French at Wellesley to learn how to become a patriotic housewife?

Polly struggled to remain calm. It was not easy. War fever gripped New York. Almost every house on Stuyvesant Square displayed the American flag. Taxis and limousines flew little flags from their fenders. The fever quickly acquired a berserk quality. The city's twelve thousand policemen were put on twenty-four-hour alert. A flying squadron of 180 motor trucks full of machine-gunners and sharpshooters stood ready to crush potential uprisings of Germans and Irish. Groups of self-appointed Vigilance Squads dragged supposed spies and agitators to police stations, where they were thrown behind bars without even a hearing.

A block away on Third Avenue, the Wardens' butcher, Otto Eisenhauer, had his windows smashed, his store looted. Weeping, he came to Polly's mother, asking for help. "I luf America," he sobbed. "I haf boy at U.S. Naval Academy—Annapolis!" Other German merchants in the neighborhood were similarly abused.

Polly asked her father to denounce these senseless assaults on German Americans. The Wardens had lived on Stuyvesant Square for decades. Alexander Warden was an acknowledged community leader, chief vestryman of St. George's, head of the local Progressive Republican Club. He stonily declined. He said the Germans had bribed the Irish into joining their so-called neutrality campaign to starve the Allies and they were getting what they deserved.

At dinner, her father sat down with a most uncharacteristic frown on his handsome face. "Are you continuing your pacifist activities?" he said, in the sharpest tone of voice Polly had ever heard from him.

"I don't know. I rather doubt it," Polly said.

"I would very much appreciate it if you would transform your doubts into a decision as soon as possible."

"What happened at the vestry meeting last night?" Polly's mother asked.

"Charles Courter said he thought it was time someone told me that having a suffragette for a daughter was bad enough. But a pacifist rather strained the bounds of everyone's tolerance. It was a very unpleasant little speech. J. P. Morgan was there. He didn't say anything, but I could see he agreed completely."

"He's worried about the five hundred million dollars he's lent the English," Polly said.

"I've told you before, Polly, Mr. Morgan does not think that way," her father said. He valued his friendship with the great financier too much to tolerate criticism of his policies.

"George wants me to quit too, Father," Polly said. "But I refuse to do it to satisfy a bloated tub of Wall Street lard like Charles Courter. Some people are in favor of disbanding our chapter. We're meeting today to discuss it."

"You may quit any way you please, my dear. Just do it! Aside from the embarrassment it's caused me, I fear for your safety. Your creed has become violently unpopular with the American people. Isn't that obvious from your experience in Union Square the other day?"

An hour later, Polly rode uptown on a green Fifth Avenue omnibus to Eleanor Kingswood's house. Was her father simply intimidated by his wealthy friends, or was he joining her mother in remodeling her to George Eagleton's specifications? Could she resist everyone indefinitely? Already she found herself arguing in George's favor. She could imagine herself loving him quietly, steadily, for the rest of her life. She saw them proceeding serenely into middle age, busy with growing children, proud of George's war record, his success in business, his generosity to good causes she would select for him.

There was no passion in this portrait, but her mother maintained passion was not important in a marriage and might even cause problems later, when it inevitably cooled. There was nothing wrong—and a great deal right—about a husband who guaranteed you a comfortable life with no unpleasant surprises. Then there were those blushes every time George talked, however obliquely, about sex. Could he possibly be a virgin? Had he actually observed a single standard for her sake? That was a sobering thought.

But the inner voice who guarded Polly's future still whispered *no*. In her deepest heart was she still a pacifist? Or did she simply dislike the idea of publicly abandoning her commitment to peace and marrying George Eagleton in his uniform? She saw her mother and father watching with self-satisfied smiles, congratulating each other for persuading their headstrong daughter to be sensible. Worse, she saw a similar smirk on George's face.

In the Kingswoods' bay-windowed parlor looking out on Fifth Avenue, Polly found everyone talking about the President's speech. It had stunned them too. Only Eleanor, striding into the room with her usual brimming vitality, seemed undaunted. "Wilson's speech has changed everything," she said. "It's made the war nobler, more meaningful, than pacifism. More important, he's taken us a step closer to our primary goal: the vote, equality for women."

Polly was not impressed by this sweeping pronouncement. She suspected the ugly brawl in Union Square had lowered Eleanor's commitment to pacifism to the vanishing point.

Eleanor began to explain why an ennobled war was so important. "It permits women to support it, to make it spiritually meaningful. Women will demonstrate, by transforming the war, how they can transform American politics and society."

Martha Herzog wanted to know how supporting the war would work on a practical level. How were they going to prevent the carnage from arousing the warrior instincts their pacifism had hoped to extirpate? "We'll be over here, they'll be over there. Can you change a man's mind by writing him letters?" Martha said.

Eleanor's eyes sought Polly's for a moment. There was a glint of mockery in them. "Some of us—as many as possible—must go over there with them," Eleanor said. "We'll show them how a woman confronts the fever, the heat of battle, without allowing it to alter her soul."

"I like that," Martha said.

"What will we do when we get there?" Polly asked. "I don't think they'll let us join the infantry."

"I've already discussed that with some of Father's friends in Washington. There's going to be all sorts of jobs," Eleanor said. "The Red Cross, the YWCA, and ambulance and hospital work. The particular job is not as important as our *presence*."

"I like that too," Martha said.

Polly liked it even more. It was the answer to everything. She could marry George without humiliation, share his war with him, and ennoble it by her presence. All she had to do was make sure she did not get pregnant—not an insoluble problem for a modern woman. Her older sister had recently announced she was not having another baby for at least two years.

"There's only one barrier for women volunteers," Eleanor continued. "They can't be engaged or married to anyone in the army. Otherwise everyone would be demanding the right to go over and clutter up Paris, waiting to embrace their heroes."

Eleanor smiled at Polly. Or was it a leer? There were times when she almost disliked Eleanor. This was one of them. Everyone else in the room was staring at Polly. Martha Herzog and a few others seemed sympathetic; the rest were simply curious, coldly curious. Polly had told Eleanor about George's proposal. She had obviously spread the news all over the city. Her mother had predicted that a lot of women in New York would grind their teeth at the thought of Polly Warden walking off with George Eagleton.

Eleanor had urged her to refuse George, saying she wondered if he had ever had an idea that Polly or Arthur Hunthausen had not put in his head. When Polly defended George, Eleanor had revealed deeper, more alarming antipathies. She said she had begun to think marriage obliterated a woman's identity. She wondered how any women could submit to sexual intercourse.

Polly did not share these extreme feminist opinions. She did not think the New Woman had to regard men as irreconcilable enemies. Yet if she married George, or even became engaged to him, something very close to obliteration would be her fate. She would sit home and miss the Great Adventure, as Theodore Roosevelt was calling the war. She was the only one in the room who spoke fluent French. Here was a chance to put her years at Wellesley to work, and she was about to be debarred, disqualified, banned.

Polly concealed her dismay until the others had departed. "I can't stand the thought of your going to Paris without me," she cried. "Are you sure that regulation is unbreakable?"

"Absolutely sure. Father told me it was promulgated by General Pershing personally," Eleanor said.

As chairman of the board of U.S. Steel, Mr. Kingswood spent a lot of time in Washington making sure the government did nothing to interfere with his stupendous profits.

"There's a way out, darling," Eleanor said, "if you have the courage to take it."

"What? Talk the Kaiser into joining the League for International Peace?"

Eleanor nibbled a chocolate-filled cookie. "Pledge your eternal devotion but put the wedding off and come to France with us. When it's over, if you're still inclined, marry George at the American Cathedral in Paris. That's not only more romantic, it's more sensible. The thought that you'll be waiting for him the moment the Huns surrender will infuse the whole war with purpose for him. He'll come to you flushed with victory—and you can begin to deal with the fever in his blood before it infects his psyche."

Everything Polly had read in the papers since the President's speech convinced her the war would be brief and relatively blood-less. Many politicians and pundits predicted America's intervention would make the Germans sue for peace. The French and the British, from all accounts, were briskly driving the Kaiser's armies out of France. The Russians, having dumped their incompetent czar, were gathering their forces for a terrific blow from the east.

"Make it your first test of wifehood, darling," Eleanor said. "Find out if he really loves you."

Polly was already sure George loved her. That made her sure he would agree to wait. He would have his own great adventure to console him, plus the promise of her welcoming arms in Paris, within days of the beastly Germans' surrender.

"When do we sail?" Polly said.

6. ENTER LOUISE

As TWILIGHT SHROUDED THE MANICURED LAWNS and parade grounds of Fort Myer, Virginia, Malvern Hill Bliss sat in the parlor of his general's suite in the Bachelor Officers' Quarters, pondering a picture of Grace and Jackie, taken in Havana when his son was eight. Morro Castle loomed in the background like a shipwrecked galleon. Grace clutched the boy against her with a fierce, almost desperate intensity. Grace had hated Cuba. She had caught malaria there and worried constantly that Jackie would get it too.

Bliss pulled off the back of the frame, yanked out the photograph, and threw it into the blaze he had built in the fireplace. He watched the flames consume the two beautiful faces. On the coffee table was a scrapbook full of smaller photos. He began paging through it. His father had been right about going to war like a Greek. You had to sacrifice all your memories to the essential thing, the ability to command men to fight and die.

It had been the best of days and the worst of days. Precisely at noon, in his office at Fort Myer, Pershing had pinned on Bliss's shoulders the two stars of a major general. Ten minutes later they were having a violent argument. Congress had browbeaten the army into accepting two regiments of marines as part of the expeditionary force. Bliss had urged Pershing to put the Tenth Cavalry in the same division with the seagoing blowhards. He guaranteed the Tenth would show them up in combat.

Pershing stonily informed him that Negroes were going to fight in a separate segregated division. "These aren't Negroes," Bliss all but shouted. "These are the best regulars in the goddamn army. You know that as well as I do. We went up that hill with them in Cuba. Without them, Teddy Roosevelt and all those New York swells would be pushing up palm trees in a cemetery outside Santiago, and we might be lying next to them."

"I don't like it any more than you do," Pershing said. "But the goddamn Democrats are running the country. Wilson grew up in Augusta, Georgia. To him a Negro is a nigger. He thinks he's paying them a compliment by drafting them at all."

"But the Tenth Cavalry—"

"There isn't going to be a Tenth Cavalry the day after tomorrow. They're going to break them up and use them as noncoms in this Negro division and in the supply companies. Tell them you can't do a thing about it, any more than they can. Now let's get out there and take their salute."

They had walked into the hot Virginia sun together and mounted the wooden platform for the Tenth Cavalry's final review. Rank after rank they had swept past, not a foot or a hand out of line, the guidon flags snapping down, the black faces whipping to the right as Turner and other sergeants bellowed the command, while the band converted "St. Louis Blues," "My Gal Is a Highborn Lady," and similar tunes into marches.

Back in his quarters, Bliss found his orderly packing his uniforms and gear under Turner's supervision. Avoiding his eyes, Bliss told the Sergeant Major what was about to happen to his regiment. "Hell's bells," Turner said, the closest he ever came to profanity. "We thought when we come north with you we was on our way to Paree."

"You'll get there eventually—in a segregated division. The Democrats won't let you fight beside white men. They're afraid you might make us look bad."

Better to be brutal, à la Pershing, the owner of his soul. But Bliss could not offend John Henry Turner. "Maybe us and our nigger draftees'll get into the trenches next to the Lafayette Division, General," he said, smiling. "Be interestin' to see who chases them Germans the farthest."

"The Germans are good, Turner. Damn good."

Turner nodded, still smiling. "We'll both do our damnedest,

General," he said. "Like that guy in the cemetery in Arizona."

He was talking about one of their favorite jokes, an inscription on a tombstone near Tucson: HERE LIES JOE DOAKES: HE DONE HIS DAMNEDEST. Turner often said he wanted that to be his epitaph.

When the Sergeant Major handed Bliss a message from Tasker H. Bliss, any lingering euphoria he felt about becoming a general vanished. After cursory congratulations, Tasker informed him that he was appointing two of his favorite overweight, overage clones as the division's brigadier generals. For the Lafayette's chief of staff Bliss could look forward to dealing with Colonel Douglas Fairchild, widely known as the most ambitious glory hound in the U.S. Army. Tasker was reminding his little southern brother that he might be a general courtesy of John J. Pershing, but the Chief of Staff was still running the show.

With a sigh, Bliss pulled a picture from the album. It was Grace, standing alone on a desolate shore near Nome, Alaska, her glossy blond hair invisible, her beautiful face pinched inside a furry parka. This one was easy to consign to the flames. Grace had hated Alaska even more than Cuba. She called it hell in reverse, perpetual cold instead of heat. Jackie had gotten pneumonia twice, which per-suaded Bliss to hate it too.

The telephone rang. A woman's voice said, "Hello, General."

"Louise!" Bliss gasped. "Where the hell are you?"

"In Baltimore. I've retreated from Paris to straighten my front, as you generals would say. I'm now the proud owner of a bona fide divorce from your old pal Walter the-Wilted-Walrus Wolcott."

"What did he do wrong?"

"Let's put it this way. He didn't do anything right. According to the evening paper you got the big promotion today. May I drive over and congratulate you?"

"What a question. I'll have a man at the gate to show you the way."

"Not necessary. My chauffeur will ask directions."

Bliss could not believe it. Louise Wellington Wolcott, one of the few people in the world he gave a damn about. Ten years ago she had married his wealthy boyhood friend Walter Wolcott. Bliss had been stationed in Washington, attending the Army War College at the time. As a local celebrity, thanks to his charge up San Juan Hill and his exploits in the Philippines as Pershing's executive officer, Major Bliss and his wife became frequent guests at the Wolcotts' country house, Paradise Hill, outside Baltimore. They had fox-hunted and partied with them at the nearby Green Spring Valley Club.

By year's end Louise was visibly tiring of provincial Walter Wolcott. Born into New York's Four Hundred, she found the Maryland countryside much too tranquil for her temperament. She had headed for France, where she bought a château on the Loire, a town house in Paris, and a villa in Cannes and wowed the international set. Walter Wolcott had spun dazedly in her wake like an oversize pull toy.

An hour or so later, a white Lincoln limousine rumbled to a stop in front of the BOQ. Junior officers gawked from their windows as Louise emerged from the back seat in a slinky silver dress with a mocha Paris toque on her blond head. For a moment, Bliss had to clutch the back of a chair by his window. He had forgotten how much Louise looked like his dead wife. He had willed it out of his memory.

Everyone, including Louise, had been struck by the resemblance. During that golden year at Paradise Hill, Louise frequently bought two of everything and gave Grace the extras—dresses, suits, shoes, coats—so they could stroll around Baltimore and Washington making people look twice. Only on closer inspection did certain differences become apparent. Louise had seemingly blank dark-blue eyes, which could turn stormy or seductive at will, giving her an irresistible aura of command. Grace's eyes tended to be puzzled, as if she were perpetually trying to understand the rotten hand fate had dealt her.

Bliss opened the door, and Louise hurled herself into his arms. Her kiss went well beyond the comradely, the gin on her lips no doubt adding to the ardor. "Where's the party?" she said. "You mean they made you a general and they didn't give you a party?"

"They gave me a review instead."

"Good God."

Louise sauntered into the parlor and stretched her lanky body on the couch. Beneath the blond hair and Botticelli face she was constructed almost boyishly. In a flash her joie de vivre vanished. Her eyes had encountered the scrapbook on the coffee table. "Oh, Jesus," she said.

They had not seen each other since the catastrophe on Jolo. Louise had written him a sympathetic letter, of course: he had played stiff-lipped soldier and concealed his anguish.

"You're sitting here all by yourself, looking at them?" she said.

"I'm burning them," Bliss said.

"You son of a bitch! I won't let you. I'll take them." She grabbed the scrapbook and clutched it to her small breasts.

"It's yours," Bliss said. "One way or another, I've got to get rid of it so I can do this job—"

"Now I really need a drink. What have you got?"

"Nothing. I made a promise to Pershing. I won't touch the stuff until we march up the Unter den Linden."

"Is he nuts? Forbidding a soldier to drink? Is that the way he's going to run the army?"

Bliss shook his head. "It's a private program for yours truly." He gestured toward the scrapbook. "I've gotten drunk almost every night—since it happened."

"And Pershing still made you a general. That proves what I've always suspected. You're the best damn soldier in the army."

Bliss decided not to explain why Pershing made him a general. Louise spread the scrapbook on her lap and ran her fingers across the pictures. "I used to think about her in those godawful places you dragged her—Arizona, Alaska, the Philippines—while I was swilling champagne in Paris. She never complained. Not once in all the letters she wrote."

Would it help if she knew that Malvern Hill Bliss got all the complaints Grace had in her system? No. Speak no evil of the dead. Better to let her memory surround Grace with perfect love. His love, Bliss now admitted to himself, thanks to Tasker Bliss's ruthless reminder, had grown more and more imperfect. One of the reasons was sitting in front of him. Grace had brooded about her friend

Louise dancing at the Ritz and the Luxembourg Palace in Paris while she taught their Malay cook how to make french fried potatoes.

Tears were streaming down Louise's cheeks. The visit was turning into a mess. "Come on. We'll get a drink at the officers club," Bliss said.

The club's broad veranda was full of couples in wicker rocking chairs. All conversation ceased as they studied the white Lincoln and Louise. Inside, Louise ordered something called a French 75—champagne with a brandy base. Bliss chose Coca-Cola.

"What are you going to do with the rest of your life?" he asked.

Louise's smile was strange. Her eyes were not blank in the old romantic way he had enjoyed nine years ago. They were opaque and mocking. "Go back to Paris. It's the only place I can live."

"Why?"

"Do you know Gertrude Vanderbilt Whitney?"

"Not really. She's not the sort you meet in my line of work."

"She's the richest woman in the world, Mal. She was absolutely miserable with her louse of a husband—until she found Paris. Gertrude showed me how to live in Paris. That's why Walter divorced me. He gave me five million, but he kept our daughter. What do you think of that bargain?"

"It's your life."

"I wanted to be free, Mal. Free—in Paris. With five million dollars a woman can be freer there than in any other city in the world."

Bliss's soldierly disciplined side did not like what he was hearing. "You should marry again," he said.

"Why? I didn't find it very thrilling the first time."

"A man—the right man—will give you stability."

"Oh, my God. You're starting to sound like my stepfather. Is this what happens when you become a general?"

A figure loomed over them. "General Bliss," Major Harry Quickmeyer said. "I didn't get a chance to congratulate you at the review."

From the way he was looking at Louise, he had more than congratulations on his mind. Bliss introduced them. "I'm fond of this fellow," he said. "His father was one of the finest soldiers in the

American army. I was about ten feet away from him when he was killed on San Juan Hill."

"Sit down, Major," Louise said. "I just got divorced, and the General here is trying to take charge of my life. I need reinforcements."

"That's the way generals operate. They take charge of everything in sight," Quickmeyer said, a rakish grin on his shrewd angular face. Like most army brats, he was not intimidated by rank.

Quickmeyer decided to try a French 75, after Louise explained it to him. "Better get used to the wine of the country," he said.

"You're coming to Paris?" Louise said.

"I assume Pershing's going to make that his first stop. I'm on his staff."

"When you get there, give me a ring," Louise said.

She took a hefty swallow of her French 75 and leaned back in her red-cushioned chair. "I like soldiers, Major. I had a friend, an officer's wife, who sacrificed everything—beauty, money, finally her life itself—for a soldier she loved. I've never done anything remotely that noble. I'm not sure I even can. But I'd like to try. Do you know anyone who might be interested?"

"I'll give it some thought," Quickmeyer said, struggling to conceal his astonishment.

Bliss was awed by the uncanny way Louise penetrated Quickmeyer's defenses. How did she know that anyone who went to West Point and swallowed duty-honor-country for four years was an idealist somewhere, no matter how much the U.S. Army corrupted his soul?

"You'll love Paris, Major. It's like no other city in the world. It will change your ideas about so many things."

Louise's voice was like the rustle of silk on leather. For a moment Bliss was assailed by a desire to screw her until she begged for mercy. This was a new kind of American woman, wilder and freer than anything he had ever imagined. He did not like the way she was playing games with Harry Quickmeyer's soul.

"I think my ideas are changing already," Quickmeyer said.

They talked about life in Paris. Louise said if a man could not find the woman of his choice there, he was ready for interment. An estimated 75,000 beautiful demimondaines walked the boulevards, ready and eager to offer their devotion to a strong, tender protector. Love was Paris's secret weapon in the war. It was why the poilus and the Tommies fought so fiercely to defend the city.

A hand fell on Bliss's shoulder. He gazed up at a sight so unnerving he almost grabbed Louise's French 75 and belted down what was left of it. Mrs. Isadora Fairchild loomed above him in powdered and beribboned glory. Gray hair framed a face with two or three dumpling chins and cheeks dripping similar suet. The eyes were as cold and hard as musket balls, and the smile was so patently insincere it all but curdled Bliss's Coca-Cola.

"General Bliss," she cooed. "Malvern. What a delightful coincidence. Dougie and I just had dinner with the Chief of Staff and his darling wife. All he talked about was the contribution Dougie can make to this wonderful division you're going to command."

Bliss was familiar, if not friendly, with Mrs. Fairchild. Her husband, General Arthur Fairchild, had been his commander in chief for several seasons in the Philippines, and Bliss had made his required bows at more than one of her boring cocktail parties. Beside her stood the only child of their union, as handsome as a matinee idol and, Bliss suspected, as dumb: Colonel Douglas Fairchild. Although he should have been looking at his future leader, most of Dougie's attention was being diverted to Louise and Major Quickmeyer, who were gazing into each other's eyes, barely aware of the interruption.

Bliss introduced them, remarking that he assumed Quickmeyer and Fairchild knew each other. "We were in the same company for four years at that great institution of lower learning on the upper Hudson, weren't we, Dougie?" Quickmeyer said.

The expression on Fairchild's face suggested this was not one of his warmer memories of West Point.

"I've just been having the most fascinating tête-à-tête with Major Quickmeyer," Louise said. "We were wondering if idealism was still possible in our cynical world. If it could be the basis for something as mysterious and as complicated as love."

That last word seemed to take flight on Louise's dusky tones to circle Colonel Fairchild and his bulky hard-eyed mother, scattering incandescence like a Fourth of July rocket. "The heart and soul of the army, of this country, is idealism," Fairchild said.

"It's much too late in the evening for philosophy," Mrs. Fairchild said. "Come along, Dougie. It's hours past my bedtime."

Fairchild held out his hand to Bliss. "I look forward to serving with you, General." He seized Louise's hand and raised it to his lips. "What a privilege to encounter idealism and beauty in such an entrancing combination," he said.

"Come *along*, Dougie," said Mrs. Fairchild, who was halfway to the clubhouse door. Fairchild trudged obediently into the night in her wake.

"Whew!" Bliss said, collapsing into his seat.

"Quite a package, aren't they?" Quickmeyer said. "It's a good thing they're barring relatives from France, General. Otherwise you could look forward to sharing your command post with her."

"I can believe it," Bliss said.

"He's a lost boy," Louise said, gazing after Fairchild. "Walter was like that, before I took him to Paris. I have a weakness for lost boys. My father was one."

Bliss suggested it might be a good idea to get to bed before the sunrise gun went off. Quickmeyer looked at him as if he were speaking Urdu. Bliss saw he was a goner, his misery compounded by the possibility that Louise preferred Douglas Fairchild.

In the back seat of the Lincoln, Bliss played the censorious general. "Why are you trying to drive that fellow crazy?" he said.

Louise exhaled something between a sigh and a cry and hurled herself against him. "Oh, Mal, Mal, that was just persiflage. I came looking for a party and sort of hoping you'd introduce me to the great John J. Pershing, but now all I want to do is share your pain. Let me help you bear it for a night."

Desire thudded like a fist at the back of Bliss's skull. He was remembering how much he had wanted this woman nine years ago, how that desire had fouled his feelings for his wife until he could barely look at or listen to Grace without loathing. Night after night he had lain awake, undressing Louise in his mind, crowding his tongue into that mocking mouth. She was all the things earnest naïve Grace Semmes Bliss could never become.

Knowing Louise wanted him as much as he wanted her redoubled the agony. Bliss had dazzled her with his guerrilla exploits in the Philippines, his ability to bring to life the battles of the Civil War and other wars. They had walked the blood-soaked acres of Malvern Hill, Fredericksburg, and Antietam together. He had described the historic heroics of her distant ancestor Arthur Wellesley, Duke of Wellington, at Waterloo while her eyes whispered desire and her parted lips begged him to speak of love, not war.

"You're still the handsomest man I ever met, Mal," Louise whispered, her lips nuzzling his throat.

Now it was too late. Louise's wildness would destroy the soldier Pershing had resurrected. A part of Malvern Hill Bliss—the insubordinate naysayer who saw hypocrisy in every noble gesture—might still love her. He even saw why she instinctively reached out to him. A soldier's controlled wildness was the perfect match for the recklessness rampant in her soul. But he had to remain true to that obedient soldier, the one Jack Pershing had created and wide-eyed Grace Semmes had married. To take Louise now would be courting damnation, even if he no longer believed in a god of judgment. He would be his own judge, consigning his miserable wayward soul to a private hell.

"You deserved a woman like me, not a goody-goody like Gracie. How did you stand her all those years?" Louise said.

Bliss's whole body became rigid with a terrific vow not to touch this woman. A single caress, one kiss, and he was lost. "I loved the son she gave me. I loved Jackie so goddamn much," he said.

Louise hissed like a cobra. She coiled into a silvery ball in the opposite corner of the Lincoln's back seat. "American men are weird," she said. "You love sons, other men, fighting wars—more than you love a woman."

"There's some truth to that," Bliss said.

"Paris will change your mind," Louise said, the menacing hiss still in her voice. "Paris will change all your minds about so many things."

7. A NEW WOMAN

"YOU'RE MAKING THE GREATEST MISTAKE OF YOUR life!"

It was the fourth or fifth time Alice Warden had hurled this unnerving prophecy at her youngest daughter. Polly had expected an angry scene when she announced she was not going to marry George Eagleton before he went overseas, but the uproar had exceeded her worst expectations.

"Do you think Mrs. Eagleton will accept a daughter-in-law who's spent two years or even a year in Paris unchaperoned?" Alice Warden asked.

"Mother, I'm not fifteen!" Polly said. "I don't care what Mrs. Eagleton thinks—and neither does George."

"You'll care a great deal if Mrs. Eagleton refuses to receive you in her house. Many many people would follow her example."

They were in Polly's bedroom. She was dressing for dinner with George. If ever she needed to be calm and rational, now was the time. Her mother was making it impossible. She stood there, arms folded, watching Polly struggle to button her midnight-blue taffeta dress. It was last year's fashion but Polly liked it because the skirt fell just below the knee, giving her a feeling of freedom. Her mother still preferred the ankle-length skirts of 1914.

Polly made a last attempt to inspire a curl with a comb. Her auburn hair was hopelessly straight. "There's nothing to worry about, Mother. George is not going to object to this plan. How can he? It makes perfect sense."

"You may know more about a lot of things than I did when I was your age, but you don't know *anything* about men," her mother said.

* * *

George had reserved a table for eight o'clock at social New York's favorite restaurant, Delmonico's, on 25th Street off Madison Square Park. They paused to admire the flowers that filled the foyer and paused again in the dining room doorway while the diminutive French headwaiter greeted them. Polly's eyes drifted to the silver chandeliers, the frescoed ceiling, the flower-bordered fountain in the center of the room. Money bought so many things—comfort, pleasure, beauty.

Polly saw George slip the headwaiter a five-dollar bill as the man guided them to a secluded corner. The little Frenchman made George look more masculine than usual, if that was possible. His blond hair was damp from a shower at the University Club, where he had thrashed Arthur Hunthausen in squash.

Polly toasted the victory with Vichy water. "I sometimes think you're too impressed with Arthur," she said. "I'm tired of hearing you tell me what he thinks about this or that. You're just as intelligent as he is."

"I know that," George said. "But Art knows things I couldn't learn if I lived to be a hundred."

"For instance?"

George's smile was uncharacteristically rakish. "Mistresses. Arthur knows exactly who's got one—or in some cases two or three. Old J. P. Morgan, for instance. And Eleanor Kingswood's father."

"I don't think that's a particularly admirable form of knowledge."

Polly did not explain the real reason for her vehemence. Last year, on the eve of graduation, someone had sent Eleanor an anonymous letter about her father's long-running affair with an actress. Unable to believe it—she had worshiped her father—Eleanor had gone to see the woman and found out it was true. The revelation had filled her with icy rage, which often spilled over into her opinions about men in general.

George was surprised and a little irked by Polly's disapproval. "Maybe not, but it's interesting. Arthur's helped me grow up—get out from under my mother's thumb."

Polly preferred to think she was the one who had helped George escape his mother's heavy hand and his father's narrow mind. She decided not to point this out for the time being.

"Art's changing his name, incidentally—to Hunthouse. The English version. All sorts of German Americans are changing their names. Someone even suggested I ought to change mine. I guess it sounds German."

"Ridiculous," Polly said.

"I wouldn't change it without asking you first," George said with a playful grin. "It's going to be your name too."

"I hope so, George," Polly said, taking a nervous sip of her Vichy water. This was not going to be as easy as she had imagined. Sitting there in his well-tailored gray suit, his skin glowing from an hour of squash, George looked formidable. It was more than his size. His expression and his attitude seemed to have changed.

He summoned the headwaiter and ordered another Scotch and soda for himself. "And the menu," he said. "I've got to get this young lady home at a respectable hour."

The waiter brought the Scotch. George surveyed the menu. "We got our orders yesterday. We report to Plattsburg next week for six weeks of officers' training. Then we go to the Lafayette Division. They've been assigned to Camp Mills on Long Island. That's good news, isn't it? A lot of people are being shipped to the Deep South."

The headwaiter returned at George's wave and he placed their dinner order, adding a bottle of Chassagne-Montrachet. "I think you'll like that wine," he said. "Arthur and I drank a lot of it in Paris on our 1913 grand tour."

Polly had seldom seen George so self-assured. Did joining the army do this to a man?

"What a shame we can't go to Paris on our honeymoon. But we'll enjoy France twice as much after we kick the Germans back across the Rhine. Maybe we shouldn't even call the trip we take after the wedding a honeymoon. I'll be lucky to get a week's leave. It might be no more than a weekend. Lieutenants don't exactly run the army."

For a dazed moment Polly was engulfed by this torrent of wildly inappropriate words. "George," she said. "You're getting much too far ahead of things. I told you on the phone, I've made a decision I want to discuss with you."

George moved his drink to one side. "I'm listening."

"The other day I went to see Eleanor—"

George's blue eyes narrowed under his thick blond eyebrows as Polly described Eleanor's plan to go overseas and make a contribution to the war effort and how dismayed she was to learn there was a regulation barring women who were married or even engaged to soldiers. "It means I wouldn't be able to share this great adventure with them—or with you, George—if we got married before you go."

Deep furrows appeared on George's forehead. He gulped half his drink.

"I hope you'll understand this doesn't alter my feelings for you in the slightest," Polly went on. "I hope it won't alter yours for me."

George's jaw was clenched in a strange way Polly had never seen before. "I thought you loved me," he said.

"I do love you, George. I'm only talking about postponing the wedding until the war is over."

"Do you have any idea how long you're talking about?"

"There was a story in the *World* the other day. Some British diplomat said it would be over by the end of the year if we get enough men to France in a hurry."

"That's not what the army says. They're telling us to arrange to be gone two or possibly three years."

"Do you really think I want to sit home by myself that long, while my friends are all in Paris doing significant things?"

"You're joking," George said. "Either you're joking or you're crazy. What sort of significant things?"

"We don't know. We're going over there to find out."

"Polly, this is a *war*. They don't let women into wars. Women stay home. They've always stayed home."

"American women—modern American women—are going to change that idea."

"Bunk!"

"George. Do you realize you're coming very close to insulting me? Insulting women in general?"

"Polly, you're making a fool of me. I've told my friends we're getting married. I can hear Arthur saying I told you so. He's always thought you were wrong for me."

"Really? Why?"

"Because you have no money," George said. "Arthur thinks a man should marry a woman whose fortune matches or exceeds his. I didn't agree. I was dumb enough to think love was more important."

"George, I've told you I love you."

"This is a hell of a way to show it!"

At other tables, heads were turning in their direction. One particularly offensive older woman peered at them through her lorgnette. A jowled man who vaguely resembled George's father glared his disapproval. Polly's face, her whole body, burned with anger. "If you can't discuss this calmly, please take me home," she said.

"With pleasure," George said. He shoved some bills into the headwaiter's hand and escorted Polly into the warm spring night, striding ahead of her to his Pierce Arrow roadster parked in front of the restaurant.

"I simply don't understand you," Polly said, as he yanked open the car door. "I don't understand this—this outrage."

"You don't seem to understand a lot of things," George said.

"What am I supposed to think?" Polly said. "Is it simply a matter of—of bedding me? Is that what you want to brag about to your friends?"

George clutched the wheel with both hands. "Is that what you think love is all about? Is that what you think it means to me?"

"I didn't—now I'm not sure. You've aroused the worst sort of doubts."

With a terrific crash, George pounded both his fists on the Pierce Arrow's dashboard. "I told you I loved you!" he shouted. "To me that meant you were the most important person in the world! The thought of you giving yourself to me was so incredible, so amazing, I couldn't think about it when I was driving this car; I was afraid I'd run over somebody. I thought it was something I could take with me to France—something that would keep me going if things got tough. You don't understand any of that, do you?"

Rumbling omnibuses and honking cars and an occasional creaking hansom cab passed them on Fifth Avenue as George hurled this testament of love into the darkness. It was unreal. "Isn't the spiritual fact of my love just as important as the—the other thing?" Polly said.

"No!" George roared. "The other thing means we belong to each other for life. That's what I want. That's what I thought I needed. Now I'm going to do my goddamnedest to forget you."

"I'll make the same effort," Polly said. "I guarantee you I'll be completely successful."

The Pierce Arrow's motor rumbled. George ground the gears and swung across Fifth Avenue in a reckless U-turn. They hurtled downtown to Stuyvesant Square at forty miles an hour.

In front of the house, Polly made one more attempt to reason with this berserk male. "You didn't even give me a chance to tell you what I'm ready to do: marry you in Paris at the American Cathedral, as soon as the war ends."

"Isn't that wonderful," George said. "How do you know I'll be in any shape to walk down the aisle? I may be on crutches. Or in a wheelchair. Or in a coffin."

"Now you're trying to frighten me. You know that's ridiculous."

"I don't know what I know right now—except that I'm totally disgusted with you—and with your friend Eleanor. Good night!"

"Goodbye!" Polly said, flinging herself out of the car.

She slammed the door with all her strength and marched into the house. Her mother and father were sitting in the front parlor, playing their favorite card game, Hearts. "Well?" her mother said.

"I'm going to France," Polly said. "Unbeaten, unbowed, and unattached."

"I knew it, I knew it!" her mother cried.

Her father exhaled a mournful sigh. Was it because he disapproved, or because he knew his wife would be in a rage for the next six months?

Alice Warden flung back her chair and stalked toward Polly. "You were wrong. Will you admit it? Will you admit you were completely, idiotically wrong?"

"I admit I underestimated George Eagleton's capacity for insult, for—for cruelty. I'm glad I did. I'm glad I found out what he's really like."

"How can you stand there and say you're glad you turned your back on twenty million dollars? I won't let you do it. Tomorrow morning, you will pick up that telephone in the hall and call George. You will apologize and tell him you're ready to marry him as soon as it can be respectably arranged."

"No!"

The defiant cry made her mother stop short. She swayed there in the lamplight, her face growing more and more twisted until it was almost malevolent. "You know what I think? You want to go to Paris for the worst possible reason. You don't want to be a respectable woman. Since you've been thirteen, you've defied and disobeyed me in a thousand ways. You want to go to that immoral city to experiment with free love. That's what all this modern-woman talk comes down to."

Behind her mother, her father sat mute, his face contorted not with rage but with regret. Why didn't he say something to defend her? Alice Warden's sneer was triumphant, as if Polly had already confessed to immoral desires.

"Go upstairs and look at yourself in the mirror. Ask yourself if you want a lifetime of shame or a lifetime of happiness. Then come down here and agree to call George Eagleton in the morning."

Polly shook her head. "I'm sorry, Mother. The answer is still no, with or without mirrors."

She turned her back on her mother—and her father. She still loved them; but they were yesterday's people. She marched upstairs, stamping fiercely on each step. Unfortunately the stairs were carpeted, and instead of loud decisive noises she only produced dull thuds. At the bottom of the stairs her mother shrilled, "You won't be welcome back in this house, do you understand that? No Paris hoyden will be welcome in this house!"

In her bedroom, Polly stared at a photograph of her and George beside the Pierce Arrow on a bluff overlooking the ocean near Bar Harbor. Beside it was a picture of her and her two sisters at Bar Harbor when she was seven and they were nine and eleven. She tried to read the three innocent faces. Could her mother possibly be right?

Was she some sort of bad seed?

No. She was a pioneer, choosing unknown freedom to known submission, serfdom, bondage. Polly stuffed both pictures in the bottom drawer. Yesterday; it was all yesterday, she told herself.

She flung herself face down on the bed and wept. Why, why? she wondered as the tears soaked the pillow. She had no regrets. She had just escaped a horrible fate. She had just made a courageous choice. But for some reason Polly did not understand, the tears kept coming.

8. PLAYING THE OLD ARMY GAME

MAJOR GENERAL MALVERN HILL BLISS STOOD AT his office window in the two-story rectangular headquarters building of the Lafayette Division, grinding his teeth as a platoon of soldiers splashed past through Camp Mills's ubiquitous mud. It had rained every other day since they arrived in these godforsaken Long Island flatlands.

The soldiers were wearing broad-brimmed campaign hats; tan puttees covered their legs from ankle to knee. The hats were supposed to protect the wearers from a tropic sun; the puttees kept jungle insects from crawling up their legs. The uniforms made no sense whatsoever for fighting in Europe. But the mastodons in the army quartermaster department were incapable of rapid change. Their fellow slow-motion specialists in the bureau of ordnance were equally lousy at supplying the new American army with the weapons of war. On their shoulders, instead of Springfield rifles, the marching men carried broomsticks.

Around Bliss's headquarters, tents stretched out to the horizon, some four thousand of them. There were 28,397 men in the Lafayette Division: infantry regiments from New York and South Carolina in the first brigade, from Massachusetts and Pennsylvania in the second brigade; machine-gunners from New Hampshire and artillerymen from Maryland and Virginia and Connecticut. Most were so raw, so untrained, Bliss shuddered at the thought of them fighting German veterans.

Behind the mud-spattered platoon strode the division's chief of staff, Colonel Douglas Fairchild, and a dozen reporters completing a tour of Camp Mills. Colonel Fairchild knew a lot of reporters. He had been director of information on the General Staff in Washington. He seemed to spend half his time escorting these watchdogs around Camp Mills. Not once had he bothered to introduce them to Bliss. As far as the public was concerned, Colonel Fairchild, regularly described as the youngest chief of staff in the U.S. Army, was running the Lafayette Division.

Compounding Bliss's antipathy, Dougie's mother had taken a house in Centerville, only half an hour from camp. Bliss had already declined two invitations to dinner.

Bliss had seen more than one commanding officer overshadowed by his chief of staff. It was not going to happen in the Lafayette Division. He waited five minutes to give Fairchild time to get rid of the reporters and summoned him to his office. "Gentlemen of the press," he said, standing at the window watching the newsmen slosh across the muddy street. "That's the third or fourth contingent of those layabouts you've escorted around here this week."

"It's done wonders for our reputation, General. My mother tells me the Lafayette is the most talked about division in the army."

"Why?" Bliss said. "We're a shambles. We've been here a month, and they're still a bunch of civilians living in tents. Half of them don't even have rifles."

"Nevertheless, General, as I just told the reporters, we're making excellent progress at forging these men into soldiers. When we get over there and meet the test of battle, we'll garner the headlines."

Bliss almost groaned aloud. Fairchild talked like someone in a novel for adolescent boys. There had been a series set in West Point around the time he had been a cadet. It must have infected his vocabulary.

"I don't want press clippings from you, Fairchild," Bliss roared, "I want results! I want every man in this division to have a weapon by next Monday. I want enough ammunition to let them shoot until they can hit something. I want to train them in tactics more complicated than a bayonet charge. I want them to learn how to cooperate with our machine-gun battalions—when we finally get some machine guns. I want you to be a chief of staff, not a goddamn publicity man!"

Fairchild blinked with disbelief. It was probably the first time in his army career he had ever been criticized. "You will have those plans on your desk tomorrow afternoon, General."

"Make it the day after tomorrow. That will give you a day to transport your ass down to Washington and get us the equipment we need. Weren't you one of Tasker Bliss's favorite brownnoses on the general staff?"

"I never indulged in—brownnosing, General," Fairchild said, almost choking on the word. "I don't know any officer who would condone such a practice."

"Aren't you a graduate of the Command and General Staff School at Leavenworth?" Bliss said, pretending amazement. "I thought everyone who went there mastered the art and science of brownnosing. I've never seen a staff officer who wasn't good at it."

Bliss had not been invited to attend this elite new school, to which the army had sent many officers from Fairchild's generation. "Ask your mother to help us out. Tell her your reputation's at stake."

"If there's anything Mother can do, General, I assure you she'll do it," Fairchild said.

"Is it true what I've heard from one of your classmates, Fairchild," Bliss said. "Your mother lived at Craney's Hotel while you were at West Point to make sure no one mussed your hair?"

Craney's Hotel was on the military academy grounds. "Harry Quickmeyer probably told you that," Fairchild said, practically vibrating with antipathy. "I didn't ask for my mother's—solicitude—up there, General. I haven't asked her to follow me to every army post to which I've been sent. As one man to another, what the hell can I do about it? I'm her only son, almost her only living relative."

For a moment Bliss felt mildly ashamed of himself. He remembered his own problems with a formidable mother. "Find yourself a woman who can intimidate her, Fairchild," he said.

Dougie wobbled off, no doubt to tell Mother—and Tasker—the story of his atrocious abuse. Bliss hoped so. It was important for

Tasker to know Malvern Hill Bliss did not feel a shred of gratitude for making him a major general or for sending him Colonel Douglas Fairchild. Humming cheerfully, Bliss sat down to compose a letter to the one person who might actually get the weapons his men needed: John J. Pershing.

Seconds later his aide, chunky Captain Philip Sheridan Price, burst into his office, his eyes as round as a character in the funny papers. He was an eager beaver who got on Bliss's nerves. He had picked him off the army list for sentimental reasons; his father had served with Bliss in the Philippines.

"General," Price said, "there's a full-scale riot between the New York and South Carolina regiments in front of their mess hall."

There had been trouble between these two regiments from the day they saw each other. The New Yorkers—the 179th, Ireland's Own—were constantly ready to prove that one Irishman could beat four of anything else. The rebels—the 115th, Carolina's Pride— were out to prove their grandfathers had lost the Civil War only because the rest of the South quit on them.

"Call the Military Police and the headquarters companies from the second brigade," Bliss said, heading for the door.

"General, they're going wild. I don't think you'll be safe," Price said.

Bliss ignored him and squished through the mud to the first brigade's area. On the street in front of the flat-roofed mess hall at least two thousand men were punching, kicking, and cursing each other with marvelous enthusiasm. There was not an officer in sight. If there were any sergeants around, they were slugging it out in the goo. Two appalled MPs stood on the sidelines, waiting for reinforcements.

A captain came running from the Irish tents. He waded into the melee, dragging men apart, shouting, "Cut it out!" A flailing arm hit his campaign hat, knocking it into the mud. His blond hair glistened in the spring sunlight. Bliss was momentarily paralyzed. The resemblance to his dead son, Jackie, was uncanny.

The Captain waded back to the MPs and said, "Give me your whistle." He blew a long blast and shouted, "Attention! Attention!"

Not one of the battlers even glanced in his direction. Bliss charged around the edge of the brawl. "Give me your gun," he said to the MP.

He pointed the .45 toward the sky and pulled the trigger six times. That got everyone's attention. Moments later the entire company of military police, all army regulars, arrived, backed by the headquarters companies from the regiments in the second brigade, and surrounded the brawlers. Bliss gave a very short speech. "I don't give a damn who started it. You're all restricted to camp for the next two weeks. No passes, no leaves, nothing!"

Back at his office, Bliss resumed his letter to Pershing about the division's equipment shortages. He was interrupted by Father Francis Kelly, the chaplain of Ireland's Own, and Alexander O'Sullivan, their colonel. Kelly was a slim dark-haired man with the curving lips and high-cheeked good looks of an Irish tenor. Bliss had met him at a reception in the officers club when he arrived at Camp Mills and had been put off by his cheerfulness. O'Sullivan looked even fatter than the day Bliss had met him in Tammany Hall's headquarters.

"General, that sentence is extremely unfair," Kelly said, while O'Sullivan nervously nodded his assent. "Our boys haven't been picking fights with those Southerners. It's all the other way around."

"Come off it, Father," Bliss said. "Since when don't Irishmen pick fights?"

"That's the sort of prejudice we're in this war to overcome," Kelly said.

"Is that so?" Bliss said. "I've got news for you, Father. I'm in this war for only one reason: to beat the Germans. Any other reason is superfluous—and idiotic."

Kelly gave Bliss a condescending smile. "You don't know much about motivating Irish Americans, General. We're not only going to wipe out the prejudice against us with our deeds on the battlefield, we're going to free Ireland."

"That's quite an agenda, Father. I didn't know the Germans owned Ireland. I thought it was part of Great Britain—one of our allies."

This sarcasm produced a frown on the Celtic profile. "I think you're missing the spiritual dimension of this war, General. You're not communicating a vision of what we're fighting for. Maybe that's why the men are so restless."

"The men are restless because they haven't gotten laid lately. That's what makes soldiers restless."

"I consider that remark extremely inappropriate, General! Don't you agree, Colonel?"

O'Sullivan nodded unenthusiastically. Bliss suspected he was no paragon in the sexual purity department. "Don't try to pull spiritual rank on me, Father," Bliss roared. "I spent four years with the Jesuits in Baltimore before I went to West Point and figured out the Catholic Church was—and still is—the biggest farrago of nonsense since the Greeks stopped worshiping Zeus."

The dismay on both Celtic faces did such wonders for Bliss's morale, he decided to raise the ante. "If I had my way, Father, I'd ban chaplains from the army. They give men the absurd idea that God is going to protect them. Nothing keeps a man alive on a battlefield but brains, courage, and luck. Once a man realizes that, he's on his way to becoming a soldier."

Struggling to control his outrage, Kelly vowed the men in Ireland's Own would fight more fearlessly than anyone else in the division because they believed a loving God was waiting for them if a German bullet struck them down.

"Big ideas like God and country don't mean much on a battlefield," Bliss scoffed. "The real reason a man stands and fights is friendship. I've seen a lot of men lay down their lives for a friend in a firefight. I believe Jesus said that was the greatest love a man could manifest. The army is better at creating it than all the churches with their legions of pulpit blatherers."

"General, I reject your psychology as totally as I abhor your lack of faith!"

"Five dollars says by the time this war is over you'll admit I'm right."

"I'll take that bet!" Kelly cried. "Will you join me, Colonel?"

"I sure will!" said O'Sullivan, his evasive eyes admitting his knowledge of a battlefield came exclusively from the Hearst newspapers.

The Celts reeled out to spread the word that the Lafayette Division had a roaring atheist for a commander. That did not bother Bliss in the least. The tougher he could make himself sound, the harder his men would fight for him.

Bliss went back to work on his letter to Pershing. He had barely completed a paragraph when Captain Price's nasal voice was in his ear again. "General. Colonel Stuart of Carolina's Pride to see you."

Colonel Wade Hampton Stuart was almost as fat as Alexander O'Sullivan but he was somewhat taller. His suet had a sleeker, smoother look. A white-mustached lawyer from Charleston, he oozed a "fellow Southerner" cordiality from the moment he shook Bliss's hand. He did not seem to realize thirty years in the U.S. Army had purged this emotion from Bliss's system.

With Stuart was the first brigade's Tasker Bliss clone, Brigadier Wilson Cox. Out of earshot Bliss called him "Waffle ass," an old army term for an officer who spent too much time sitting on cane-bottom chairs in Washington.

"General," Stuart said. "I'm here to explain that little fracas down at the mess hall between our boys and those micks. They were teachin' them a lesson in southern courtesy. Last night, one of their officers made a derogatory remark about Robert E. Lee. Now you know any real Southerner can't let a thing like that pass unnoticed."

"I fully support Colonel Stuart in this matter, General," rumbled Brigadier Cox, who was from Georgia.

Bliss leaned back in his chair and tugged at his earlobe. "Have you ever been to Gettysburg, Colonel Stuart? I paid a visit the year I got out of West Point. When I stood at the foot of Cemetery Ridge and saw what Lee asked Pickett's men to do, I stopped believing he was the greatest man who ever lived. After I walked up Malvern Hill, where he threw away ten or fifteen thousand men charging massed Yankee artillery, I stopped believing he was a good general. His casualty rate was higher than Grant's. I'd shed this uniform before I'd imitate either one of those military butchers."

Colonel Stuart swayed, open-mouthed. Brigadier Cox looked as if he might collapse from shock or outrage or both. In that hidden corner of Bliss's mind, Sergeant Turner whispered, *Rein in, general, rein in. You're goin' too far.* Bliss ignored him. "If I hear another word about Robert E. Lee from either one of you, you'll be out of this division the next day," he thundered.

The cream of the South's chivalry reeled out, and Bliss resumed his letter to Pershing. A tentative knock on his open door interrupted him again. In the doorway stood the blond captain who had waded into the melee in front of the mess hall. Face-to-face, the resemblance to young Jack was not so acute, but it was still troubling. "General," the captain said, "I'd like to support Chaplain Kelly's complaint about the sentence you just handed down. At the very least you should conduct an investigation before you enforce it."

"Really, Captain. Are you also planning to take over this division and solve all its problems with a magic wand?"

The Captain's cheeks reddened. Jackie used to react the same way when Bliss teased him. "Of course not, General. But I thought you'd be interested in a report from someone who's in close touch with the situation."

"You're commanding a company in Ireland's Own?"

"Yes, sir."

"That hardly makes you an objective reporter."

"I assure you I am, General."

A captain who talked back to a general. Bliss told himself he should be outraged. But he had done it himself in his insubordinate youth. "What's your name and background, Captain?"

"Jonathan Alden, sir. I graduated from the military academy in 1915. I got stuck there teaching French until the war started, and I talked my way out."

"I'm interested in fighters, not talkers," Bliss said.

"I hope I can do both, General."

Bliss decided fileting Fairchild, shocking Chaplain Kelly and Colonel O'Sullivan, and deflating Colonel Stuart and Brigadier Cox was enough satisfaction for one day. "All right. I'll suspend the verdict, pending an investigation. You have forty-eight hours to prove your micks are innocent."

"Thank you, General. I was sure you'd say that. I told Chaplain Kelly you'd show him the army was fair."

The army fair? Bliss was so staggered by this naïveté, he let Captain Jonathan Alden stride triumphantly out the door, secure in his youthful faith.

The next day Bliss had Captain Alden's report on his desk. He must have stayed up all night writing it. There were half a dozen carefully described incidents, complete with names, dates, and epithets, which proved pretty conclusively that the South Carolinians, obsessed by ancestral defeat, were the ones who started the fights with Ireland's Own. Most of the Irish, Alden pointed out, were sons of immigrants who had not even been in the country when the Civil War was fought. They did not have the slightest interest in it.

The sun had actually come out, amazing everyone. Bliss strolled down to the tents of Ireland's Own, looking for Alden. The regiment's sergeant major told him the Captain and Company A were at bayonet practice. Bliss decided to take a look at how they were mastering this skill, on which Pershing placed great emphasis.

At the sawdust-strewn pit, the familiar straw dummy dangled from the iron overhead bar. On his chest in large letters was his name: FRITZ. A brawny red-haired sergeant was giving a demonstration. "Stick it in, twist it, and pull it up and out. Then stick it in again. Up! Out!"

The sergeant looked familiar. Bliss concentrated and made the connection. He was the slugger who had beaten up the pacifists in Union Square. What was his name? O'Connor. Over the years, Bliss had made a habit of remembering names. Nothing pleased an enlisted man more than an officer who recognized him after years of separation.

A rotund baby-faced soldier danced up to the dummy on tiptoes and poked it gingerly. "Jesus Christ, Fat," O'Connor roared. "Are you tryin' to tickle the son of a bitch to death? Slam it into his guts. He's tryin' to do the same thing to you."

This time Fat managed to penetrate the dummy, but the expression on his face resembled a small boy being forced to eat his spinach. "Get mad at him, Fat. Call him a name!" O'Connor said.

"You—dirty dog," said Fat, spearing the dummy again.

"Bastard, Fat. Fucking son-of-a-bitch bastard. Say that! Yell it and mean it!" O'Connor roared.

Fat retreated ten steps and took a deep breath. "You fucking son-of-a-bitch bastard!" he screamed. He hurled his bayonet into the hapless dummy so ferociously he ripped Fritz from his moorings and wound up in a tangled heap with him in the sawdust. The rest of the company doubled over laughing.

"Great!" O'Connor said. "The rest of you wise guys do it the same way."

"Attention!" Captain Alden had seen Bliss and was reacting in standard army fashion to the presence of a commanding officer.

"At ease, at ease," Bliss said. "I'm just a spectator. Your sergeant seems to be doing a fine job."

Alden called O'Connor over and introduced him. "He's caught on to the army very fast, General."

"Haven't I seen you someplace before, Sergeant? Union Square?" Bliss said.

O'Connor looked him in the eye. "I'm from New Jersey, General. I've never been in Union Square in my life."

Bliss liked a man with the nerve to lie that way. "How about the rest of the company? Are they catching on?" he said.

"They're comin' along, General," O'Connor said. "We're even makin' a soldier of Clymer, the guy you just saw in action. He's a poet."

"Get them in formation. I'll give them a little test," Bliss said.

Sergeant O'Connor bellowed an order. The company formed ranks. Bliss selected Fat Clymer for his test. He ordered him to step forward two paces and pointed to his rifle. "What's that?" he said.

"My gun, General," he said.

"The hell it is," Bliss said. "That's your weapon. This is your gun."

He grabbed Fat by the crotch. The man turned scarlet and everyone laughed. "I'm serious," Bliss said. "There aren't any guns in the army. Only weapons!"

He fastened Fat's hand around his crotch and ordered everyone else to do the same thing. "Now repeat after me.

"This is my weapon,
This is my gun;
This is for shooting,
This is for fun."

They thundered this old army refrain into the spring sunshine. Bliss glanced at Captain Alden and saw repugnance in his idealistic eyes. He controlled his temper and said, "I read your report, Captain. I'll withdraw my restrictions on the regiment for the time being."

He left Alden trying to figure out how a dirty-minded old curmudgeon could also be fair.

Two hours later, General Bliss was speaking to 269 amateur lieutenants from officers training camp. They looked so green he would not have been surprised to see twigs sprouting from their ears. Amateur enlisted men were bad enough. The thought of fighting a war with amateur officers appalled him. At OTC they had been taught to be gentlemen. Bliss tried to turn them into soldiers.

"The army has its own standard of excellence. It's not a woman's standard. It puts women out of the equation. The army says in its hard flat way, Obey me, be true to my code, and I'll call you a man. That's a far more exciting phrase than gentleman. You may be covered with mud and blood, you may stink like a slaughterhouse and be indifferent or even untrue to your wife, but if you do your job, you're still a person of value to the army, a man.

"At the heart of the army is a man's capacity for controlled violence. It's not easy for womanized Americans to accept the central importance of violence in our history—and in the world's history. It's even harder to grasp the concept of controlled violence—violence used as intelligently, as rationally as possible, under the tight rein of command. This combination makes a soldier a unique figure, a man who must master and contain in his soul opposite impulses.

"There's one more thing that goes to the heart of the word officer. You have the power to give orders that can cause men's deaths. That requires you to be as competent and professional as possible.

An incompetent officer, be he a lieutenant, a captain, a colonel, or a general, is nothing less than a murderer. Value your men, treasure them, serve them. Put them before your own comfort, your own health, your own safety. The men come first. That is the axiom on which I run this division. Any officer who doesn't live up to it will be in trouble with me."

As he spoke, Bliss's trick memory picked out two familiar faces in the first row: Hunthausen and his Harvard friend from Union Square. As the shavetails politely applauded his speech, Bliss turned to Captain Price, sitting behind him. "See those two guys at the end of the first row?" he said. "Put them in Company A of the first battalion of Ireland's Own."

How they got along with Sergeant O'Connor would make an interesting experiment in democracy, army style.

Rein in, General, rein in, Turner pleaded.

Go to hell, Bliss told him. A man who can't get drunk or get laid has to do something to amuse himself. Besides, I'm a general. What can they do to me now?

A week later, General Bliss sat at his desk, cursing under his breath at the latest nonresponse to his most recent letter to the Bureau of Ordnance, demanding the rifles, machine guns, hand grenades, and artillery the Lafayette Division needed to complete its training. Douglas Fairchild had come back from Washington empty-handed. Pershing had gloomily informed him that as the commander of the AEF he had no influence whatsoever with the mastodons in the bureaus. His authority began and ended in Europe.

In the doorway appeared Captain Philip Sheridan Price, who continued to grate on Bliss's nerves every time he opened his mouth. Lately he had gotten much too friendly with Fairchild. Twice in the last week, forced to go looking for him, Bliss had found him in Dougie's office.

"General, Chief of Staff General Tasker Bliss is on the telephone."

"I know his name," Bliss said. "What the hell does he want?"

"I have no idea, sir."

"That's part of your job, Price. Find out what people want before I answer the phone. That includes mucky-mucks like old Tasker."

Price's eyes widened with horror. Bliss had picked up the phone as he said this. The Chief of Staff had undoubtedly heard him.

"Have you read the newspapers today?" Tasker said.

"I never read the newspapers if I can help it."

"You better read today's *New York World*."

"Why?"

"In a story on page one, you're described as a prime example of the sort of general the army should discharge immediately. You're quoted as saying Washington is populated entirely by pinheads who are sabotaging the war effort. For good measure you've supposedly outraged the Southerners in your division by claiming that Robert E. Lee was a heartless butcher who never should have been permitted to put on a uniform. You've also insulted your Irish regiment by announcing you hate Catholics. Did you say any of these things?"

"Some of them. Don't you agree Lee was a butcher?"

"I'm serious, you idiot!" Tasker roared. "The *World* is our President's favorite paper. He's going to read that story. He was born in Virginia, and he's not inclined to laugh at insults to Robert E. Lee. I knew you'd turn into a walking, talking example of Pershing's bad judgment, but I never thought it would happen so soon!"

The telephone was suddenly sweaty in Bliss's hand. He had spent too much time in the field. He had forgotten, if he ever knew them, the games Washington insiders play.

Tasker was ranting about some of Bliss's previous imbroglios, obviously culled from a careful study of his file. He dwelt with particular relish on the time Bliss had gotten into a quarrel with the commander of the Seventh Cavalry about the generalship of the late George Armstrong Custer and had appeared for a review dressed as an Indian chief, complete to skin stained with berry juice, flaunting a sign that read: LITTLE BIG HORN, THIS WAY. "Pershing saved your neck that time, but he won't do it again!" Tasker thundered.

Pershing had been Commanding General Nelson Miles's aide and had spent days persuading the crusty old cavalryman to overrule Bliss's court-martial. It had helped that Miles also thought George Armstrong Custer was a birdbrained glory hound.

Tasker began dwelling on the word that every general dreaded to hear: "relieved." He talked about it as if it were already an accomplished fact. The only thing left to decide was what to do with Bliss. He would try to find some other job for him, in the Philippines or Panama, far away from reporters.

"There's only one man who can relieve me, Tasker," Bliss shouted. "I won't accept it until I hear it from him, not you."

"You will."

A half hour later, the telephone rang again. "Bliss?" Pershing growled. "I'm leaving for France in less than a week and I've got God knows how many things to worry about. Suddenly I'm getting phone calls from the White House asking me why I made you a general. What the hell's happening?"

Bliss told him the exact truth, not sparing his own excesses. He had learned long ago it was wiser to tell Pershing the truth because he eventually found it out anyway, in searing cross-examination. When Bliss got to Tasker's remarks about Pershing's judgment, Jack growled, "Say no more. I get the picture. The day after tomorrow, I'm coming out to review the division. Make sure the goddamn performance is perfect."

Bliss summoned Captain Alden to his office. "In two days, I want your men to perform the most ferocious bayonet assault in the history of warfare. Can they do it?"

"Yes, sir!" Alden said. "They could do it right now."

"No doubt you've heard all about this scandal that's erupted in the division. You believe it down to the last comma?"

"No, sir," Captain Alden said. "I know you wouldn't say anything like that about Robert E. Lee."

"Of course not. How would you like to be my aide, Captain? I've decided I need someone who speaks French."

"Sir, I was taught at the Academy the most satisfying thing an officer can do is lead men."

Bliss tugged at his earlobe. He felt a terrific need to disillusion this idealist. It was almost unbearable to confront this image of himself, the naïve true believer of 1886, who had graduated from the military monastery on the Hudson without a clue as to what the world or the army was really like.

"Leading men is the least satisfying thing a man can do if he's interested in promotion. Are you?"

"Of course, General. But—"

"I've led men all my life, in combat and out of it. I was about to expire into retirement when this war and Jack Pershing rescued me from oblivion—while my northern namesake, General Tasker Bliss, who never heard a bullet whistle in his life, soared to Chief of Staff. You could use someone like me, Captain, to complete your grossly inadequate military education. You have twenty-four hours to consider my offer. If you say no I'll mark you hopeless and ship you to an ammunition depot in Kansas not even Tasker Bliss has heard of. You'll decay there for the rest of the war, writing transfer letters no one in Washington will answer."

Bliss watched the slim figure trudge from his office, blond head drooping. For a moment he wanted to recall Captain Alden, affirm his idealism, and tell him to cling to it in spite of crazed cynics like Malvern Hill Bliss. But a father has a right to shape his son in his image, doesn't he?

Two days later, Pershing arrived in a big black Buick, trailed by a caravan of Fords and Hupmobiles and other cars containing more than fifty reporters. Word had gotten around that he was going to fire Bliss in front of the entire division.

The review was flawless. Bliss had spent the two previous days rehearsing it. Regiment after regiment went by the reviewing stand without a single stray foot in sight. Commands were executed with a precision that few regular army units displayed. They adjourned to the rifle range, where carefully selected companies from each regiment performed equally well. Finally they went to the field training area, where Pershing watched Alden's company execute a bayonet assault on a rival company of stuffed dummies with a ferocity worthy of the Sioux or the Iroquois in their heyday.

By this time the reporters were starting to look baffled. "What's your opinion of the Lafayette Division, General?" one of them asked Pershing.

"I haven't seen another division in the entire army in this state of battle readiness," Pershing said. "General Bliss is to be congratulated. His accomplishments are especially impressive when it's apparent from newspaper reports that he has to deal with some disloyal officers in his ranks."

As he said this, Pershing impaled Colonel Douglas Fairchild with a slitted glare. "I'm particularly amazed that this could happen when we have a man like Colonel Fairchild as chief of staff. He was first captain of his class at West Point, as I was. He knows the crucial value of teamwork and loyalty. That's what I hope to inculcate in the entire army: the spirit of the cadet corps, the sense that we're all a band of brothers."

Fairchild's eyes revolved in his handsome face like a pair of marbles in a spinning roulette wheel. "I guarantee you, General, we'll do our utmost to make sure the Lafayette Division achieves that ideal," he said.

"There isn't any truth to these reports of General Bliss's contempt for Robert E. Lee?" another reporter asked.

"Mal," Pershing said, "tell these fellows what you think of Robert E. Lee."

"I was brought up to believe he was the greatest soldier who ever lived," Bliss said. "When he was superintendent of West Point, he created that term band of brothers. I couldn't agree more heartily with General Pershing as to its importance."

"Do you agree with General Bliss's remarks on the way the Wilson administration is fighting the war?" another reporter asked.

Pershing shook his head, as if the mere idea of criticizing the commander in chief distressed him. "That has to be a misquotation. If General Bliss and I are in agreement on one thing, it's on Woodrow Wilson's wholehearted support of the war effort. We shared his reluctance to get into this war. Now we know that he shares our impatience to fight it to the finish as quickly and efficiently as possible. Is that a fair statement of your opinion, Mal?"

Oh, very fair, Jack. It omits one or two things, such as your opinion of Waffling Woodrow when he ordered you to retreat from

Mexico without Pancho Villa's scalp. That night you told me he was a white-livered son of a bitch without the guts of a mosquito. But this is a very fair statement of the public opinion we now have of our commander in chief. "I couldn't say it better, Jack," Bliss intoned.

"In fact," Pershing continued, "I'm so impressed with this division's readiness, I'm taking General Bliss and Colonel Fairchild to Europe with me for a special top-secret assignment while the men complete their training here."

Bliss was numb. Was Pershing relieving him covertly, after all? As soon as they were alone in his office, Bliss braced himself for the truth. "Are you taking the division away from me, Jack? I hope you're not going to give it to that glory hound, Fairchild."

"When and if I do take it away from you, it'll be in Europe, where I won't look like Tasker Bliss's errand boy," Pershing roared. "You can be goddamn sure I won't give it to Dougie. For the time being I'm taking you away from the division to cure your big mouth once and for all! One way or another you're going to learn to swallow the hot air that passes for thinking in your excuse for a brain! For the rest of this war, I don't want you even to say hello to a reporter without my permission!"

For another ten minutes Pershing belabored Bliss with undiminished fury. He exhumed the numerous other times he had rescued him from imminent official disgrace and made each one a scalding example of his inveterate stupidity. Bliss had absorbed this sort of battery from Pershing before, but somehow it was more humiliating with stars on his shoulders. When Pershing finally stamped out the door with a final order to pass on his punishment to Fairchild, Bliss slumped behind his desk like a man who had just gone ten rounds with heavyweight champion Jack Johnson.

What was the point of abusing Fairchild? Instead, Bliss began thinking about bourbon. He could feel its bite in the back of his throat, the smooth fire in his belly, the sweet comfort it would guarantee him for a few hours, immune from sons of bitches like Tasker H. Bliss and John J. Pershing.

"General?" said a voice in the doorway.

Captain Alden stood there, honesty and sincerity shining on his boyish face. "I've decided to accept your offer to be your aide—if you still want me."

Bliss's welts and bruises stopped aching. The sweet smell of bourbon vanished from his mind. "I was giving you one more hour," he said. "Then I was going to work on your transfer to that ammunition dump in Kansas."

Alden smiled, refusing to believe him. He looked so much like Jackie, Bliss's heart almost exploded. "Is there anything I can do for you, General?" he said.

"Tell Colonel Fairchild I want to see him. Advise him to put on a pair of asbestos pants. Because I'm going to roast his ass à la John J. Pershing."

BOOK II

9. ACROSS PERISCOPE POND

THE *BALTIC*, ERSTWHILE QUEEN OF THE WHITE Star Line, looked old and shabby in her ugly gray war paint. Through a drenching rain, Polly Warden had taxied to the pier with Eleanor Kingswood and Martha Herzog. They were the only members of their chapter of the League for International Peace who had been able to persuade—or defy—doubting parents and fiancés and arrange to go to Paris.

Eleanor and Martha were in high spirits; Polly struggled to share their elation. Her mother had made the final weeks at home an ordeal, endlessly reiterating that she had lost her last chance for happiness and listing the half-dozen women George Eagleton was now likely to marry. From Arthur Hunthouse via Eleanor had come news that George was having a wonderful time with a showgirl from the cast of *Stop! Look! Listen!*, a French revue with minimal costumes playing to packed houses on Broadway.

While stewards wrestled their trunks below to their cabin under Eleanor's supervision, Polly gazed at the silent empty dock, remembering a previous trip to Europe in 1912. The June sun had poured down and crowds of smiling friends had hurled streamers and whooped exuberant goodbyes. George Eagleton had been there, waving a straw hat.

"My mother's been having hysterics," Martha said, her usually solemn face full of incongruous cheer. "She's sure we're going to get torpedoed. I kept telling her the *Baltic* can outrun a submarine."

That's what they said about the *Lusitania*, Polly thought. She was awash in melancholy. Martha went below to unpack. Polly remained on deck while the *Baltic* shook off her tugs and began gliding down the river. The rain-drenched twilit city dwindled into the distance. They were on their way to the Great Adventure.

"What's this? Are you heading for France to stop the war in person?" said a masculine voice beside her.

"I beg your pardon?" Polly said, all the girlhood warnings about never speaking to strangers leaping into her head. The man was fairly short and quite handsome in a middle-aged way. He had a charming smile, a small well-trimmed brown mustache, and oddly somber blue eyes.

"We met in Union Square a few months ago. You told me my ideas about intelligent violence and war being the engine of history were bunk."

"You were in uniform!" Polly said, the memory of that awful day—and George Eagleton's courage—flooding her. This man was wearing a badly tailored gray tweed suit and a garish green tie that did not match anything.

"I'm still in the army. I'll only be wearing this civilian getup for a few more minutes."

"Then what happens?"

"General Pershing comes aboard and we can all put on our uniforms again."

"He's sailing with us?"

"He and his staff. About two hundred men. We're trying to keep it a secret from the Germans. Half of us came aboard in mufti."

Polly's heart skipped several beats. "Where is he now?"

"On board that ferry we're about to overtake."

He pointed ahead toward Gravesend Bay, where a small ferry was steaming in circles. "My name is Malvern Hill Bliss," he said. "Through some crazy mix-up in the files down in Washington, I'm not a colonel any more. They've made me a general."

Polly could only muster an awed "Oh!" After a moment she confessed her name, the supposedly fatal mistake when accosted by a stranger. But a general seemed to merit a measure of trust.

"Are you going to France to stop the war?" he asked.

"No. I'm going—to ennoble it. To—to contribute to an early victory. But I still don't believe war is the engine of history any more than, say, typhoid."

"Does that mean I'm a public menace? A sort of Typhoid Malvern?"

Suddenly Polly felt more like her old carefree self. "If women have their way, General, you'll have nothing to worry about. The whole world will be inoculated against typhoid—and war."

He smiled ruefully at her bravado. "Your big Harvard hero, the one who socked that mick who manhandled you—he's letting you go?"

Polly flushed. "We—we had a difference of opinion about that. A rather serious one."

"A *very* independent woman," General Bliss said. "That red hair probably explains it."

"I have an idea of myself—as a woman—that's more important than the color of my hair."

"Haven't you read that poem by the Irishman, Yeats, where he tells a woman, 'Only God, my dear, could love you for yourself alone and not your yellow hair'? Change it to red and I could recite it to you."

This man was incredibly forward by social New York's rigid standards. Polly found she liked it. She liked the thought of General Bliss—or anyone else—reciting poetry in praise of her hair.

"To be practical for a moment, what do you think you can do over there? You're not planning to sneak into the trenches, I hope."

"I speak fluent French. I can type, drive an ambulance—"

Bells rang and the *Baltic*'s whistle gave two tremendous hoots as they neared the circling ferry. A thirtyish woman with wide, strikingly beautiful blue eyes and shingled blond hair rushed up to them. She was wearing a pale blue suit with a split skirt in the latest tonneau silhouette style. She gave Bliss an enthusiastic kiss and ignored Polly.

"Will he mingle with the passengers?" she asked breathlessly.

"Of course. He's not a hermit," Bliss said. He introduced Polly to Louise Wolcott. "Miss Warden's going to Paris to help us win the war. Maybe even ennoble it. What do you think of that?"

Louise smiled but her eyes were not friendly. "My mother never let me go to Paris without a chaperone when I was her age."

"You're dating yourself, darling. This is a new woman, with new ideas about everything."

Louise retained her smile but her eyes grew even less friendly. "To be a new woman you have to experience what it means to be an old woman. That requires a certain *maturity*."

Polly knew exactly what Louise meant by maturity. So, she suspected, did General Bliss, who seemed to enjoy the antipathy he had generated. "I'm starting to change my mind about this trip. I thought it was going to be a prison sentence," he said.

After another round of hoots and bells, the ferry lashed itself to the lee side of the *Baltic* and about a hundred men in uniform came up the accommodation ladder. The first to arrive, greeted with a handshake by the *Baltic*'s portly captain, was General John J. Pershing. Polly instantly recognized his lean, erect figure, his jutting jaw and bristling mustache.

"Is he a good general?" Polly asked.

"He's never commanded more than sixteen thousand men. Now he's going to command a million. That makes him something of a question mark. But we don't have a better man, I can tell you that."

Something in the way Bliss said *man* made Polly shiver. She was on the edge of a world about which she knew nothing. The Great Adventure was beginning already.

The next morning, the *Baltic* plowed grandly through Atlantic swells as Polly, Eleanor, and Martha emerged for a stroll on the boat deck. Striding toward them in the dazzling June sunshine was none other than General Pershing. They had seen him from a distance last night in the first-class dining room, when he and his officers came in for dinner. The British captain of the *Baltic* had toasted them as "a promise of swift victory."

Eleanor introduced herself and Polly and Martha. She was used to hobnobbing with senators and congressmen and captains of industry. It seemed perfectly logical to her to enlist Pershing's help in France. That only doubled her astonishment when the General reacted with the cordiality of an offended grizzly.

"I'm sorry to inform you that I see absolutely no need for women—especially young women like you—to come to France," he growled. "If I have anything to say about it you'll take the next boat home!"

Eleanor began defending their mission. "General, we spent four years at Wellesley learning—"

"Wellesley?" Pershing said, his anger vanishing. "My wife—my wife, Frances—went to Wellesley."

"We were in our junior year when—when she died, General," Polly said. "We held a memorial service for her."

"I was invited but I couldn't—I couldn't come."

They could not believe their eyes. Pershing was close to tears. "Perhaps it might be better if we discussed our differences some other time, General," Martha said.

Pershing strode off, leaving them in a state of shock. Polly went in search of Malvern Hill Bliss. Last night, before they parted for dinner, he had talked about his long friendship with Pershing. She found him on the other side of the boat deck chatting with a young, remarkably handsome blond captain, whom he introduced as his aide, Captain Jonathan Alden. Bliss was intensely embarrassed by Polly's story. He began explaining that Pershing did not hate women, he just dreaded the possibility of scandal that would arouse critics in Congress and the newspapers.

"General, I can assure you my friends and I have no intention of getting pregnant in France!" Polly said.

Bliss glanced at the Captain, who was shocked by her bluntness. "Isn't she something?" he said. He tugged at his earlobe for a moment. "I can take care of Pershing. But wouldn't you rather do it yourself—by showing him you can make a contribution to the war effort here and now?"

"What do you mean?" Polly said, all her wariness of soldiers rising to the surface again.

"Give a crash course in French to a bunch of West Point ignoramuses, including me."

Three days later, Polly stood on a platform in the S.S. *Baltic*'s second-class salon. "We will now consider how to make comparisons in

French," she said. "When an adjective precedes a noun, as in '*La belle fille est assise*,' it is not necessary to repeat the definite article to form the superlative. You simply say, '*La plus belle fille est assise*.'"

Before her sat a dozen officers and two dozen enlisted men from General Pershing's staff. Other groups were being taught by Bliss's handsome young aide, Captain Alden, and two other officers with a working knowledge of the tongue of Lafayette.

Polly repeated the sentence: "*La ... plus ... belle ... fille ... est ... assise*."

"You can say that again," called a high-pitched voice in the back row.

"I beg your pardon, Lieutenant Patton," Polly said.

"Didn't you just tell us the prettiest girl has arrived?" Lieutenant George S. Patton, Jr., said. An intense snub-nosed young man with hair so blond his eyebrows were invisible, Patton was one of General Pershing's aides.

"The verb *asseoir* means to sit down, Lieutenant," Polly said.

"I got the most important part of it," Patton said. "You're definitely the prettiest girl on this boat. Give me a break and sit down for a second. If I flunk this course, General Pershing says he's going to put me in charge of the army's mules."

"It would help if you took the course seriously, Lieutenant."

"You make it awfully hard to concentrate, Miss Warden."

Every pair of military eyes in the salon seemed to confirm this compliment. Polly felt a flutter of pleasure similar to the one General Bliss (seated in the first row) had inspired with his praise of her hair. Three days at sea surrounded by these professional soldiers had banished her melancholy. They were all intensely, incredibly, masculine. Walking, sitting, standing, their shoulders were squared, their backs straight. They looked women in the eyes when they spoke to them—which they did as often as possible. There was an unquestionable erotic undertone to their attention, a hint of possible conquest, which Polly found exhilarating.

So did Eleanor and Martha, who were being showered with similar attention. They had already fallen half in love with two officers in Polly's class. Eleanor seemed violently attracted to tall broadchested Colonel Douglas Fairchild, who shared her fervent idealism about the war. Martha's favorite was lean wry Major Harry Quick-meyer. They had danced several times on previous nights in the salon and strolled the deck by day, discussing contemporary litera-ture and politics—subjects on which Martha was awesomely well informed.

Polly was amazed by how intelligent many of the officers were. Like most people, she had assumed professional soldiers were ignora-muses. Some of them, such as General Bliss, read William Dean Howells, Stephen Crane, and other advanced novelists. Even more of them were fond of poetry, although here their taste ran to Kipling and Robert Service.

Five tremendous blasts of the *Baltic's* whistle suddenly made French and masculine compliments superfluous. Everyone began struggling into their life jackets. For the last twenty-four hours, they had been sailing through the danger zone east of Iceland where Ger-man U-boats operated.

General Bliss helped Polly tie her life jacket, while Lieutenant Patton assured everyone it was just another drill. He had his jacket under his arm when they arrived on deck. Gun crews were manning the *Baltic's* two cannon, and lookouts were pointing to starboard. Someone had obviously spotted a periscope. The deck was jammed with frightened passengers. Patton led the way to Boat 14, which Polly was sharing with Eleanor, Martha, and a dozen officers.

"You better put on that life jacket, Patton," General Bliss said. "We're supposed to set a good example to the civilians."

"*Je suis le plus robuste nageur abord, mon général,*" Patton said.

Everyone burst out laughing. Patton's eyes bulged with mock outrage. "I stayed up half the night putting that sentence together. Tell my fellow scholars what it means, Miss Warden."

"I've heard army mules with better French accents," Major Quickmeyer said from the bow of the lifeboat. He specialized in needling everyone, especially Patton, who saw war as a kind of blood sport in which he was destined for greatness.

"Is that true?" Patton asked Polly.

"I don't know. I've never heard an army mule speak French," Polly said.

"Stick with George. You'll hear a lot of them," Quickmeyer said.

"What did he say?" another major asked.

"He's the strongest swimmer aboard," Polly translated.

"And the least intelligent," Quickmeyer said.

"*Je suis*—" Patton began, his brow furrowed. "Miss Warden. Give me a word."

"*Désespéré*," Quickmeyer said.

"That means hopeless, Patton," General Bliss said. "If you don't put that life jacket on, Quickmeyer will be right."

"*Je suis le plus robuste nageur abord*," Patton insisted, his life preserver still under his arm.

"Patton!" General Pershing said, materializing out of the crush of scurrying passengers. "Why aren't you in that boat? Why don't you have your life preserver on? Are you showing off?"

Eleanor Kingswood and Martha Herzog tried to edge by the General. Half a dozen officers reached down to help them into the boat. It swayed alarmingly, almost tipping Douglas Fairchild on top of Eleanor. "See what I mean?" Pershing said. "You've encouraged these headstrong young women to arrive late, on the assumption that George S. Patton, Jr., will save them."

"You're absolutely right, General," Patton said, frantically knotting his jacket.

"Tell the General what you just told us in French, George," Quickmeyer said.

"They're being unfair, General Pershing," Polly said. "Lieutenant Patton was just practicing his pronunciation. He's doing very well in his course."

There was a chorus of hoots from the lifeboat. "How do you say teacher's pet in French?" General Bliss said.

Pershing's eyes twinkled but he refused to smile. "I can't reprimand you, Miss Warden. You're not in the army. He is. That goes for the rest of you in Boat Fourteen! We're on display here. Who knows, there may be a reporter around. Have you spotted one, Bliss? You attract them like flies."

"I haven't seen a trace of one, Jack," Bliss said.

By now Polly knew the story of why General Bliss was aboard the ship. She thought it was cruel of Pershing to rub it in that way. But none of them, Bliss included, seemed to expect anything else.

They constantly hurled remarks at each other that would make most women burst into tears. They seemed to enjoy seeing cocky lieutenants like Patton terrorized. The one unforgivable sin in the U.S. Army seemed to be a swelled head.

After about five minutes of waiting in the lifeboats, one of the *Baltic*'s officers blew an all-clear call on a bugle. At lunch the waiters told them a ship just over the horizon had been torpedoed. By four o'clock, when Polly dismissed her French class, three more ships had been sunk within a twenty-five-mile radius. Three fourths of the *Baltic*'s civilian passengers were on deck, wearing their life jackets, their faces raw with terror. Polly strolled to the bow, wondering why she was not afraid. Was it from associating with soldiers? More than once their casual attitude toward death in the freezing Atlantic had helped her control her thumping heart.

"Hard to believe men are dying out there, isn't it?" General Bliss said, leaning on the rail beside her. "I'm glad I didn't join the navy. It's too impersonal. You never see who's shooting at you."

"Have you seen men die in battle, General?" Polly asked.

"Quite a few."

"It didn't change your mind about war?"

He shook his head. "People die all the time: in train wrecks, from pneumonia or cancer. It's part of life."

"I can't understand that attitude."

"You will, eventually. War is part of life too. It just speeds up the dying. It speeds up everything—even love."

Polly coolly ignored the reference to love, hoping it declared her disinterest in that subject. "We won't have many deaths over there, will we? Won't the whole thing be over in two or three months, when we get our millions of men into the fight?"

Bliss shook his head again. "Millions of men won't make a difference if they're not well trained and well led. Look at the Russians. They outnumbered the Germans five to one and have had the hell kicked out of them so far. Brainpower, not manpower, is what wins wars. I'm not sure how much we've got in our army. Pershing can't supply it all."

Polly shook her head with equal conviction. She still refused to believe that thinking had anything to do with war. To her it was all blind, senseless slaughter, which only proved men did not know the meaning of the word civilization. Even more upsetting was Bliss's pessimism. It was not the first time she had heard him express doubts about victory. "General," she said, "isn't it almost unpatriotic for you to talk that way?"

He threw back his head in mock horror. "That word doesn't scare me. A thinking soldier is almost de facto unpatriotic. But don't worry. I only tell the truth to people I trust. For the troops and reporters I'll obey orders and speak pure fustian."

"Why do you trust me?" Polly said.

"You're one of us," he said. "I don't care what's going on in your head at the moment. You're one of us at heart. I knew that from the moment I saw you grab that mick slugger's arm in Union Square."

One of the war lovers, the slaughterers? Polly wanted to be indignant. But her wrath was short-circuited by the oblique compliment, the offhand admiration. She found herself angry, flustered, and pleased—all at the same time.

That night, in the first-class salon, Polly, Eleanor, and Martha had a table reserved under a sign that proclaimed them LES PLUS BELLE FILLES—the prettiest girls aboard. Not even Eleanor could resist such flattery. Martha Herzog, who was no beauty, was embarrassed—until Major Quickmeyer asked her to dance.

Martha's elation was mild compared to Eleanor's when Colonel Fairchild invited her onto the floor. She glowed at the mere sight of this tall courtly soldier. General Bliss had given Polly a somewhat more jaundiced view of the romance when she told him that Eleanor was going to inherit forty or fifty million dollars in a few years. "That's the sort of wife Dougie is looking for," he said. He had also told her in his offhand way that Harry Quickmeyer "had a case" on Louise Wolcott.

Out on the dance floor, General Pershing was doing a stylish foxtrot with Louise, who looked exotic in a Chinese silk gown. Eleanor had filled Polly in on Mrs. Wolcott's New York past. Several Kingswood cousins had pursued her in her debutante days. Her father had died when she was a child and her mother had married a man Louise detested. She rebelled against both parents and soon had a reputation so bad she had been forced to seek a husband in Baltimore, whom she had shed a few months ago.

The dance ended, and Pershing led Louise over to their table. "I think this lady is unquestionably entitled to sit with you," he said, gesturing to the sign.

"I don't think they approve of me, General," Louise said. "They think I should be home knitting socks. Of course I think they should be home getting spanked regularly."

Pershing chuckled and sat her down without comment. "Miss Kingswood," he said, as Colonel Fairchild returned Eleanor to the table. "May I have the honor?"

Here was final, almost formal proof that the General had relented and would tolerate them in France. When General Bliss sat down at their table with Harry Quickmeyer, Polly thanked him for his help. Bliss nodded. "Jack's apologizing to your friend Eleanor at my suggestion. Telling her what a wonderful job you've done pounding French verbs into our skulls," he said.

He sipped some champagne. "But if you want the whole truth— if you weren't from Wellesley, you might still be in trouble."

"It awes me to think a woman can mean that much to a man like Pershing," Quickmeyer said. "I've carefully avoided falling in love that hard. Pershing did too until he was about my age. If the iron general can capitulate, what chance do I have?"

As he said this in his ironic style, his eyes, which were devoid of irony, drifted to Louise Wolcott's lovely face. General Bliss gave Louise a mocking smile and explained Quickmeyer's problem to him. "You don't have a chance because women defy rational analysis, Quick. They're mysteries to themselves and everyone else."

"I disagree," Polly said. "A woman can be as straightforward as a man. Every woman *should* be. But in our present state of subjection, too many women are afraid to be. They dissemble, flatter, and evade, because they're powerless."

Bliss chuckled. "I can see French isn't the only vocabulary you've mastered," he said.

Polly gave him a glare. She liked this man. He had been helpful to them. But his attitude toward women was almost intolerable.

"What if you new women find out you can't trust one another?" Quickmeyer said. "What if you abuse power just like men?" He stared gloomily at Louise Wolcott as he said this. She seemed to enjoy his distress.

For a moment Polly felt a premonition of pain, not for herself but for Martha, who was anxiously observing this exchange. Polly refused to include herself in the intuition. No man was going to invade her bruised heart.

Lieutenant Patton appeared beside them wearing his life jacket. "Orders from General Pershing. I have to wear this thing to make sure no—uh—undue contact with Miss Warden distracts me from my duties."

"Maybe that's the answer to our dilemma," Quickmeyer said.

The band began playing "A Hot Time in the Old Town Tonight." Patton launched Polly into a wild version of the Bunny Hug. It was probably the first time that risqué dance was ever performed in the *Baltic*'s main salon. Polly glimpsed disapproval on Eleanor's face, as she whirled past, and admiration in General Bliss's eyes. She hurled herself into the acrobatics, determined to show him she could be just as reckless as the wildest soldier aboard. Other dancers fled to the sidelines, and they soon had the floor to themselves. They got a round of applause when they ended with a dip that left Polly horizontal.

"Am I still *désespéré?*" Patton gasped, escorting her back to the table.

"*Non, tu es fou,*" she said.

"That means crazy," Patton said. "You're right. I'm crazy about you. If I wasn't a married man you'd need a hundred thousand gendarmes to protect you in Paris."

"There's no hope of competing with her," Louise Wolcott said, as Polly sat down. "She's going to be the sweetheart of the AEF."

"Really, Mrs. Wolcott," Polly said, "you're very good at what the French call *les mots piquants.*"

Patton asked for a translation. Polly told him to look it up in his dictionary. He would remember it better. Louise's sour smile made it clear she knew *les mots piquants* meant "cutting words" and now considered Polly an enemy. That was perfectly agreeable to Polly. It was amazing, the way women decided such things in a flash. Did men have similar intuitions?

"Me-ow," Bliss said. "And we thought the Germans were all we had to worry about in France."

"General," Polly said, "the most charitable thing I can say about your attitude toward women is—it's antediluvian."

He forced a smile but Polly saw she had hurt him. She realized the army's rough humor was all carefully calibrated by rank. Only General Pershing abused General Bliss. But it was not just the lèse-majesté of ignoring his rank. There was a personal dimension to his pain.

"I'd say that's a court-martial offense, General," Quickmeyer said. "I'll be glad to sit on the board. I guarantee a guilty verdict. What do you think her punishment should be?"

"The firing squad," Louise Wolcott said.

"It wouldn't work," Patton said. "There isn't a man in the army who'd pull the trigger."

"I think almost any lawyer could get the charges dismissed," Bliss said. "All he'd have to do is offer in evidence a lock of that red hair."

"General, I've already told you what I think of that opinion!" Polly said.

The soldiers decided maybe the firing squad was their only option—but they agreed to put off sentencing until after they defeated the Germans. They would hire a firing squad from them to perform the execution. By the time they finished this solemn foolery, Polly was pleased to see the pain was gone from Bliss's somber eyes. Why did she care about a man with such a closed mind? She found herself vowing with sudden intensity to prove to this stubborn, charming, confusing soldier what women could accomplish in his war.

10. THE DAY OF GLORY

SURROUNDED BY HOOTING TUGS AND SPOUTING fireboats, the S.S. *Baltic* edged into her berth in Liverpool. On the dock, a red-coated battalion of the Royal Welch Fusilers and their band greeted Pershing and his staff. The Lord Mayor of Liverpool in full medieval regalia, a squadron of British generals, and a regiment of newspapermen swarmed aboard.

The *plus belle filles* had said their goodbyes the night before. Polly had distributed at least a dozen copies of their Paris address. Friends such as Bliss, Quickmeyer, Patton, and Fairchild had assured her in atrocious French, their awful accents intact, that they would visit them as soon as possible.

The *belle filles* transferred to a small steamer that took them across the darkened English Channel. On deck after dinner they encountered two English lieutenants. They seemed incredibly young compared to most of the soldiers on the *Baltic*. One had classic English pink cheeks and blond hair, the other was dark and slim but no less boyish. Both had been wounded in Flanders and were returning to their regiments. They were delighted to meet some Americans and fascinated to learn they had crossed the Atlantic with General Pershing.

"How many troops did he bring with him?" the blond lieutenant asked.

"Only two hundred or so. His staff."

"When will your army come over?"

"One or two divisions will be arriving soon, but most of them aren't expected until October or November."

"October!" the dark-haired lieutenant said. "We'll both be dead by then."

No one knew what to say. Eleanor floundered into a discussion of the weather in Paris. The lieutenants said they were only familiar with the weather in Flanders. The last time the sun had been seen was the day of Jesus' resurrection. It had rained continuously ever since.

The *belle filles* soon said good night and retreated to their cabin. "Were they serious about getting killed?" Martha said.

"It must be some joke we don't understand," Polly said. "The English have an odd sense of humor."

The next morning they landed at Le Havre's Grand Quai. The huge docks nearby were jammed with British ships. The streets were full of British soldiers who eyed them curiously but kept a polite distance. In an hour they were on a train to Paris, and by nightfall they were in the City of Light, which no longer lived up to its name.

Everything seemed dim, even the street lamps. Most restaurants were shuttered and dark. The people on the sidewalks seemed subdued, depressed. Almost every second man was wearing a uniform. A surprising number of women wore black, not a color Polly remembered seeing on her previous visit in 1912.

They rode in a fiacre pulled by a half-starved horse to the Kingswood residence on the Rue de Verneuil, a short secluded block in the Faubourg-Saint-Germain, the most fashionable section of Paris. The house was a typical eighteenth-century Parisian mansion, which the French called an *hôtel*. Little was visible from the street. Tall brass gates opened on a walled courtyard, beyond which loomed the perfectly proportioned three-story house with its grayish-white shutters.

The staff greeted them in the marbled main hall. Madame Berrier, the *maîtresse d'hôtel*, tall and severe, with a crown of piled-up gray hair that gave her the look of a displaced aristocrat; Paulette, the cook, a smiling rotund Alsatian who looked as if she were her own best customer; and Madeleine, the pert *femme de chambre.* Madame Berrier explained in French, which Polly translated, that life was very difficult in Paris. Mondays and Tuesdays were meatless days. All except Saturday and Sunday were heatless days. For five days of the week there was no hot water. Coal was rationed. So were coffee, sugar, butter.

Eleanor assured her they had not come for pleasure. They were prepared to share the hardships with the people of France. She inquired for Madame Berrier's husband, who had been the butler: *"Mort sur la Marne."* Dead on the Marne. She asked for Madame Berrier's two sons: *"Mort à Verdun."* Dead at Verdun. She asked for the cook's husband, who had been the gardener. He was a prisoner of war. Polly understood why so many women were wearing black.

The *belle filles* of the *Baltic* helped carry their luggage upstairs and went to bed in a very sober mood. Polly dreamed she was dancing with George Eagleton instead of George Patton. They were both wearing life preservers. He kept trying to kiss her but their bulging fronts made contact impossible.

A hand shook her shoulder. It was Eleanor, candle in hand, looking like Lady Macbeth, her dark hair streaming down the back of her white nightgown. "I'm not sure I can stay in this house," she said. "Remember the letter I got a year ago about my father? It said he had assignations—with women here."

"Eleanor," Polly said. "I can only repeat what I told you when you got that awful letter. What your father does with his life is his business. We're women now, independent of all of them."

"I begin to wonder if we're ever independent of certain feelings, like loathing. I—I'm afraid I can never love a man."

Polly drew her down on the bed and embraced her. "Of course you can. There are good men in this world, men with ideals who live up to them. I thought you got on wonderfully with Colonel Fairchild."

"He told me he loves me spiritually. Our ideals are perfectly matched. But he's attracted to another woman, someone he met in Washington. He's hoping he can forget her on the battlefield."

The wail of a fire siren interrupted them. It was rapidly joined by a dozen more sirens. Was the whole city burning down? Madame

Berrier appeared in the doorway to announce they were having a visit from the *les Gothas*—German bombers. There was very little danger. Only a few dozen people were killed in each raid. But it might be best to spend some time in the cellar.

For an hour they sat in the dank dark basement by candlelight while bombs crunched in the distance and antiaircraft guns boomed ferociously nearby. There was a battery of guns across the Seine in the Tuileries Gardens, Madame Berrier explained. Finally a distant bugler blew the *berloque*—a signal that the raid was over—and they went back to bed.

The next morning three sleepy volunteers trudged to the head-quarters of the American Red Cross on the Boulevard Haussmann. It was an empty cavern, staffed by a handful of middle-aged American women who said the top people had not yet arrived. They talked to the woman in charge, a rawboned Maine schoolteacher named Givens, who told them what they could do in Paris to help win the war. There was the Red Cross, the YWCA, the various ambulance services, and nursing for the army or at one of the private estates that had been turned into hospitals by wealthy supporters of the Allied cause.

Eleanor said she thought a woman with a college degree ought to be an administrator. She had been trained to think, to organize things. Miss Givens's response was chilly. Administrators needed experience. They might be better off talking to the ambulance services, who might need women drivers—and possibly administrators—now that America was in the war and all the men would presumably want to get into the fighting with guns in their hands.

"We might as well have stayed home, for all the credit we're getting for being the first ones across Periscope Pond," Polly said.

Eleanor fired off a cable to her father, demanding he do something to get them jobs worthy of their abilities. Meanwhile they talked to people at the YWCA, who were eager to recruit them. They had plans to set up hundreds of rest homes and hotels for soldiers all over France. But for the moment there were no soldiers, so it was all on paper. The ambulance services said they were all fully staffed for the moment, thank you. The pompous overweight male in charge of the Norton-Harjes Unit assured them they would never let a woman drive an ambulance. It was much too dangerous. They went right into the front lines.

After a week of rebuffs, shrugs, and condescension, they were three rather discouraged adventurers. But Eleanor still insisted on sticking together and working as a group. "Maybe our friends on General Pershing's staff will help us when they arrive," Polly said, as they conferred over breakfast.

"They're coming tomorrow," Martha Herzog said, pointing to the headlines in the Paris edition of the *New York Herald.*

The next afternoon, the *belle filles* were part of an immense crowd on the Rue de Lafayette as Pershing and his men left the Gare de Nord railroad station in a motorcade. The sight of the General smiling and waving in the lead car beside Paul Painlevé, the French Minister of War, triggered an explosion of emotion unlike anything Polly had ever seen.

"*Vive l'Amérique,*" people screamed. "*Vive* Pair-shang! Heep heep hourrah!" They waved handkerchiefs and French and American flags, they blew kisses, they flung flowers by the thousands. Many wept hysterically and began bellowing the most electrifying national anthem in the world, "La Marseillaise":

> "*Allons, enfants de la Patrie!*
> *Le jour de gloire est arrivé!*"

Like an ocean in upheaval, the Parisians burst through the police lines and swept Polly and Eleanor and Martha into the middle of the avenue in a wild rush to get as close as possible to *les Américains*. The motorcade slowed to a crawl. Soon the open cars and their occupants were covered with flowers. Men pounded the Americans on the arms and backs. Women kissed and hugged every soldier they could reach.

To think of missing this excitement and sitting home as Mrs. George Eagleton knitting baby clothes! Once and for all Polly banished regret from her mind and heart. The Great Adventure was already reaching a magnificent crescendo.

A lurching, shouting man crashed into Polly, knocking her flat. Someone stepped on her hand; someone else kicked her in the ribs as she struggled to her feet. Maybe this was too adventurous! She found herself trapped in the screaming crowd swirling around the cars. There was no sign of Eleanor or Martha. They had been swept apart like shipwrecked sailors.

"Miss Warden! Polly! Hang on! *Nous sommes les plus robustes nageurs abord!*"

The American voice pierced the roar of the crowd. It was General Bliss, closely followed by Lieutenant Patton, battling through the surging, swaying bodies to her rescue. *"La belle fille est Américaine!"* Bliss shouted, flinging a muscular arm around her waist. He no longer looked middle-aged. His face was alive with a wild delight. Was it the joy of battle?

"*Bon! Bon! Vive l'Amérique,*" screamed the French around them. They pelted the three Americans with flowers. One plump middle-aged man tried to kiss Polly. "*Non, non!*" Patton yelled, shoving him away. "*C'est mon privilège exclusif!*"

"*Très bien!*" cried the man and kissed Patton instead.

"Let's find the cars before we get killed," Bliss said.

Polly had long since lost her hat. Somehow she clung to her purse as Bliss and Patton shouldered their way through the wild-eyed crowd. They finally reached a motorcar with smoke pouring ominously from beneath its hood. "Don't worry, it's just been running too long in low gear," Patton said. Bliss climbed in and sat Polly on his lap. Patton sprang onto the running board as the car lurched forward. In the front seat Martha was sitting on Major Harry Quickmeyer's lap.

"Colonel Fairchild rescued Eleanor. They're in the car behind us," Martha said, looking very satisfied with life minus Louise Wolcott.

Across the jammed Place de l'Opéra past the classic façade of the Church of the Madeleine, the sidewalks were packed with still more thousands of screaming, sobbing, singing Parisians. The Place de la Concorde was a solid mass of equally frantic welcomers. By the time they got there, Pershing had retreated into the Hotel Crillon, the former palace whose great windows and colonnaded façade dominated the north side of the square. The rest of the staff had orders to follow him. Bliss told Polly and Martha to wait for them in the front ranks of the crowd.

For an hour they watched while Pershing appeared and reappeared on the Crillon's balcony overlooking the huge *place*, where the guillotines of the French Revolution had once spread terror and Napoleon had celebrated his victories. Each time Pershing came out, the crowd's frenzy redoubled. It reached a crescendo when a breeze blew the French tricolor fluttering at one end of the balcony toward the General and he lifted the folds to his lips for a reverent kiss.

Gradually, the crowd grew exhausted—and so, probably, did Pershing. The numbers had dwindled and Polly's feet had begun to hurt by the time Bliss, Patton, and Quickmeyer slipped out a side door of the Crillon and proposed a drink at the Café de la Paix.

By a miracle they found an empty table at this world-famous watering place on the Place de l'Opéra. Patton was his usual outrageous self. "I'm worried. If the Germans hear about this reception, they may quit on the spot."

"If they do, it will only prove one thing, George. They've got people on their general staff who are dumber than you," Quickmeyer said.

"You're wondering how in the world we're going to satisfy the expectations we've raised, aren't you?" Martha said.

"If you weren't wearing skirts I'd tell Pershing to put you on our staff," Quickmeyer said.

Polly winced at the glow of pride—and affection—on Martha's face. Quickmeyer did not even notice it. "The young lady has it exactly right," Bliss said. "Pershing's a general without an army. At the rate the mastodons in Washington are moving, God knows how long it will take us to get one over here."

"That means fewer candidates to compete with for decorations, General," Patton said, his cockiness indestructible.

"I just escorted an old State Department friend of Pershing's to his room," Quickmeyer said. "He told the General not to pay any attention to this reception. It's all hysteria. The French are in terrible shape. There's a limit to what flesh and blood can stand, and they've reached it."

"He better be wrong," Bliss said. "Otherwise you young ladies should take the next boat home."

"*Vive l'Amérique!*" cried a fat Frenchman at the next table. He was several drinks ahead of them. They nodded and raised their glasses, as all the French in the café joined the cry. The fat Frenchman lurched over to them and began to sob out his story. He had lost his only son at Verdun. He had lost all hope for France. Today, hope had been reborn! At other tables, heads nodded and eyes glowed.

Was the whole celebration an illusion? Polly wondered. Were General Pershing and President Wilson—her country—playing a cruel trick on these desperate people? She told Bliss about their cool reception at the Red Cross and other places. "I'm going to do *something* as soon as possible," she said.

"Don't let that red hair do your thinking for you," Bliss said.

She gave him a glare, and he pretended to dodge a blow. "I know. Antediluvian thinking again. But I don't want you to do something dangerous."

He and Quickmeyer and Patton smiled at Polly and Martha in a superior male way, as if only they were qualified to deal with danger. Polly saw that Eleanor was wrong about their mere presence in France making a difference. The men intended to keep them as far as possible from the battle zone. Danger would be the only test of equality they would accept. Where and how could women find it?

11. LA GLOIRE

THE DAY AFTER GENERAL PERSHING ARRIVED, Polly announced she was going to the Red Cross and ask them if there was anything they could do for the French or British armies while waiting for the Americans to arrive. Eleanor opposed the idea. She was only interested in ennobling the American side of the war. Polly said it was all one war and they needed experience.

At the Red Cross offices on the Boulevard Haussmann, she broached the idea to Miss Givens. "Can you wrap your tongue around *française?*" Givens asked.

"Yes," Polly said, wincing at her pronunciation of *française*. It sounded more like franchise.

"Maybe you ought to speak to Captain de Rougemont. He left me his card. He's lookin' for volunteers who speak French to help out in their hospitals. They're havin' some sort of emergency up around Soissons." Her massacre of Soissons was even more mind-boggling.

Polly rode the Paris Metro to a street not far from the Gare de l'Est, the railroad station from which trains departed for the east— the fighting front. In a former drugstore she introduced herself to a small sad-eyed officer in the French army's Bureau de Santé, their medical corps. In rapid French, Captain de Rougemont told her the work would be close to the front lines and would be "*très difficile et très dangereux.*" A knowledge of French was essential because exact records had to be kept.

Polly assured the Captain danger and difficulty would not bother her in the least. The reference to exact records led her to

assume she would work as a medical secretary. The Captain congratulated her on her French accent and told her to meet him at the
Gare de l'Est at nine o'clock that very night.

Back at the Rue de Verneuil, Eleanor deplored the whole idea.
She was sure her father would cable the American embassy within
twenty-four hours and every door in Paris would be opened to them.
Martha wondered if she should go with Polly, but when Eleanor
complained she quickly dropped the idea. Polly suspected Martha
hoped to find some work that would give her frequent opportunities
to see Harry Quickmeyer.

"I'll just stay with the French while the emergency lasts," Polly
said. "That can't be more than a week or two."

That night at the silent empty Gare de l'Est, Polly found Captain de
Rougemont surrounded by ten American women who had volunteered for service in the French Red Cross before the United States
declared war. Most were like Miss Givens, middle-aged spinsters
who had volunteered because, Polly suspected, they were trying to
give more or less empty lives a sense of purpose.

No matter; they were cheerful and Polly liked them all. The
Captain escorted them to the station restaurant, ordered coffee for
them, and went off to arrange their transportation. Shirley Miller,
who was Polly's age, said her fiancé was in the newly formed 78th
Division. She displayed a gold watch he had given her just before
she sailed. She was hoping that in return for her work with wounded
Frenchmen, God would protect him on the battlefield.

"You don't have anyone special to worry about?"

"No," Polly said, pleased by how lighthearted the answer made
her feel. Maybe perpetually caring about men was what disabled so
many women, leaving them incapable of independence.

Captain de Rougemont returned with three women porters,
who carried their bags to a truck outside the station. It was a big
covered camion with no place to sit down. The driver apologized for
the rank odor. He had just finished carrying a load of mules to the
front.

"You must put on your uniforms in the truck," the Captain said.

"Mademoiselle Warden, you will be given a uniform at the hospital. Once more, I assure you of the gratitude of France!"

The last they saw of the Captain, he was standing at attention in the entrance of the Gare de l'Est, saluting them. In half an hour they were careening down bumpy roads outside Paris without head-lights, traveling at a suicidal speed. They bounced around inside the camion like dice in a box. Polly helped the other women get into their uniforms, which included white bibs, blue skirts, and veils of crisp white organdy, with a small red cross embroidered on the fore-head.

Shirley Miller had an extra uniform in her suitcase. She lent it to Polly, who protested that she knew nothing about nursing. "I don't know anything about it either," Shirley said. "Neither do most of the others. They didn't ask many questions, if you said you wanted to come. I guess they'll give us some on-the-job training at the hospital."

Ahead of them the horizon began to acquire a dull red glow. Over the hills came the rumble of guns. They really were going into the front lines! It was incredibly exciting, and a little scary. For a while they encouraged themselves with songs: "Keep the Home Fires Burning"; "Roses Are Blooming in Picardy."

The camion slowed to a crawl. They passed an endless column of marching men, guns on their shoulders, steel helmets on their heads. About 3 A.M. by Shirley Miller's watch, the camion lumbered into the courtyard of a château. A big central building loomed up in the darkness. Around it were at least a dozen flat-roofed wooden barracks. The ground near the barracks was covered with men, apparently asleep.

"They must be resting half their army here, before they attack," Shirley Miller said.

A cold rain began pelting down as they got out of the truck. Polly thought it was odd that none of the sleeping soldiers moved. They scampered into the château, where an elderly French major with a livid scar on his right cheek greeted them.

"Mademoiselles. Welcome to Château Givry, now known as Field Hospital Thirteen. It is in the Forbidden Zone, where only those who are actively serving the Army of France are permitted.

You must never leave these grounds without a pass signed by me. Anyone found on the road without a pass will be thrown into a military prison—not a pleasant experience."

He flung a sky-blue overcoat around his shoulders. "France is grateful for your presence here. You will go to work immediately." He pointed to Polly and Shirley Miller. "You two come with me. The others will be directed by Madame Leclerc, our head nurse."

He gestured to a sparrow of a woman who sat at a desk a few feet away, apparently indifferent to his lecture. She looked as if she might be asleep with her eyes open. Polly and Shirley Miller followed the Major into the rain. "You see our task," he said, as they scurried to keep up with him. "There are at least two thousand men out here. Some have been lying in the open for three days. We must speed up our system. Otherwise the men in the trenches will lose all confidence in France."

"What's he saying?" Shirley Miller asked. Her French could not deal with the Major's rapid speech.

"They're all wounded?" Polly asked in French.

"Yes. And a thousand more arrive each day."

By now they were stepping over and around the men on the ground. Cries and sobs rose out of the shadows. Orderlies stumbled among them, distributing water. "Don't drink too much," Polly heard one orderly growl. "We haven't any left in the tank and there's no wood to boil more."

In the sky above them, a rocket of red flame erupted out of the night and fell through the blackness into blackness beyond. "What's that?" Shirley Miller cried.

"*Avion*," the Major said, as if burning planes routinely crashed around them. "You must remember never to open a door or let light through a window. It will bring the bombers."

At the far end of the grounds, the Major opened the door of a barracks just wide enough to push Polly inside. She found herself in a long narrow room filled by perhaps a hundred men lying in beds jammed together so tightly that nurses and orderlies had to pass between them sideways. Dozens more men lay on stretchers in the aisles. The only light came from flickering candles. The air was thick with odors, none of them pleasant. The sounds were equally awful. Several men were screaming, many were sobbing. Others groaned like the motor of a car that refused to start.

A nurse with a blood-smeared skirt rushed up to Polly and thrust a huge hypodermic syringe into her hand. "All the men on this side"—she gestured to the right—"must have tetanus injections. Then you get them ready for surgery."

Polly stared at the syringe. She had never even seen an injection administered. The few times she had received one, she had closed her eyes. She watched the blood-smeared nurse snap on the glass tube containing the antitoxin, fill the upper part of the syringe, and jab the needle into the arm of an unconscious man. Polly took a deep breath, filled her syringe, and lifted the arm of the man in the first bed. She jammed the needle against his mud-caked flesh. The needle bent!

Her cry of dismay attracted a fat perspiring orderly. "He's an Arab," he said. "They have skin like leather. Try again."

She tried again, slanting the stroke; it worked. She pushed the plunger, and the antitoxin flowed into the Arab's arm. The next six French arms yielded without bending any needles. In half an hour she finished the row.

Now came getting them ready for surgery. What did that mean? Dazedly, Polly watched the blood-smeared nurse at work on the other side. Getting them ready meant undressing them: boots, leggings, belts, pants, shirts, underwear. Then you had to wash their wounds with a little tin basin of water and wrap them in clean sheets. Polly's hands trembled as she pulled at the boots of her first patient. He and all the others were covered with dried mud from head to foot. Their clothes were all but glued to them. It was impossible to undress them without hurting them.

In the next hour she was called *une espèce de con* (stupid fool), *une salope* (a bitch), *une vache* (a cow), and a dozen other uncomplimentary names. She barely noticed the succession of male organs as she dumped their filthy clothes in the aisle and tried to clean their appalling wounds. Some were punctures from bayonets or bullets; most were raw gaping gashes from shrapnel. One was a great cavity in the hip where a leg once was. When she unwrapped the bandages from another soldier's head, he had no eyes; she could see into the mucus back of his skull. Another one, only a boy, had bands of sopping gauze across his stomach. She pulled them away and recoiled from the horrible odor. "Gangrene," said the other nurse. "No hope for him."

Polly stumbled to the dim rear corner of the building and vomited into a bedpan. "Permit me, mademoiselle," the fat orderly said and took the slop from her clammy hands. "It happens to everyone the first night."

Time past and time future dissolve. There is only the present, this dim candle-lit nightmare, the cries of men in agony. German heavy guns thunder in the distance, nearby French batteries reply. The barracks vibrate. Eerie red flashes light up the cracks around the shuttered windows. For some insane reason, the words from "Roses Are Blooming in Picardy" begin crooning through Polly's mind.

For a moment she has an overwhelming desire to run screaming into the night. She goes on to the next man. Beneath his bandages, the lungs in his ripped chest are exposed. She stares at the reddish-gray flesh slowly rising and falling. A long shudder. They stop. She looks at the face. He is a young blond boy with a chilling resemblance to George Eagleton. His staring eyes are open. His mud-caked cheeks are streaked with tears.

The blood-soaked nurse pulls the blanket over his face and says, "*Au suivant!*" To the next one.

He is short and powerfully built. Beneath the bandages his right leg is a mass of putrefying flesh and shattered bone. He screams as she begins to undress him and raves in a patois she can barely understand. She realizes he is a Breton. She spent a summer in Brittany when she was twelve. Gradually she understands what he is saying. "I slit him open! Open, I tell you. Goddamn his soul!" He begins to shake with sobs.

His eyes bulge with sudden terror and revolve toward his leg. Blood is spurting from an artery in his thigh, a foot high fountain. "Help!" Polly cries. The fat orderly rushes to the bed and presses hard with both thumbs on the man's groin. "Hemorrhage!" he shouts. Another orderly arrives with a strip of rubber and ties a tourniquet on the man's upper thigh.

The guns continue to crash and rumble. As fast as a bed is emptied, it is filled with another mud-caked writhing man, and the tetanus injection and the struggle to undress him and clean his wounds begin all over again. Finally Polly asks the blood-soaked nurse how long a shift lasts. "I've been working for two days and nights," she says.

Her eyes glaze and she topples to the floor, as if the statement is a blow she has been trying to avoid. Two orderlies bring a stretcher and carry her away. Now both sides of the ward are the American mademoiselle's responsibility.

"Roses Are Blooming in Picardy." How could this be happening to pretty Polly Warden, favorite daughter of that do-gooding optimist, Alexander Hamilton Warden? Where did Eleanor Kingswood get the idea that their mere presence could ennoble this holocaust?

Mademoiselle needs fresh water and gauze? The orderly directs her to the operating room at the rear of the barracks. Polly rushes to the door and almost collides with a surgeon in a long white coat that is as blood-soaked as the recently collapsed nurse's skirt. He is young, slight, handsome, in spite of the exhaustion that deadens his face. His head is turned, speaking to someone inside the operating room. *"La gloire, la gloire! Bah. C'est de la merde!"* he says.

The words automatically translate in Polly's numbed brain. Glory, glory, it's nothing but shit!

He turns and finds Polly standing only a foot away from him. *"Pardon, mademoiselle."* He seems genuinely embarrassed. There is no time to do more than smile faintly and get the water and gauze.

Time continues to dissolve. A flood of men disabled by poison gas. Some are blind, others are retching blood from ruined lungs. Some scream in agony when Polly tries to undress them. The skin peels off with the clothing. The fat orderly explains: mustard gas. It causes awful burns, worse than flames.

More gunfire, occasional crashes that seem very close to the barracks. Once the wall sways and one of the shutters falls off its hinges onto a dying man beneath it. Polly wonders vaguely how long she has been working. A hand seizes her arm. It is the young surgeon, smoking a cigarette. "You must sleep sometime, mademoiselle," he says.

"What day is it?" she asks.

"Friday."

Friday! She arrived on Tuesday. She has been working three days and two nights.

"They've pushed them back a mile," the doctor says.

"What does that mean?"

"Never mind. Come with me."

He escorts her into blinding sunlight. The grounds of the château are no longer covered with wounded. Polly realizes her white bib and blue shirt are smeared with blood. She brushes at it. "This is the only uniform I have," she says.

"Never mind. For now you must sleep."

He escorts her into the château, where Madame Leclerc, the sparrowy head nurse, still sits behind the desk in the entrance hall. She does not look as if she has slept since Tuesday either. The doctor lectures her. They must become more *systématique*. Too many nurses are working until they collapse.

Madame Leclerc agrees with him automatically, as if only her ears are listening. "Is it true the counterattack was successful?"

"Yes. Paris is safe again. *Vive la France*."

He says this in such a bitter way, even Polly's exhausted mind grasps the depth of his disillusion. Madame Leclerc leads her through some of the château's main rooms, which are jammed with more wounded men. Nymphs and goddesses gaze down at them from panels on the walls and ceilings. From the uniforms on the floor, she gathers the wounded here are officers. She follows Leclerc up three flights of stairs and down a maze of corridors to a narrow room looking down on the row of barracks in which she has been working. On their roofs are painted huge red crosses.

Leclerc tells her to leave her uniform outside the door for washing. What about me? Polly wants to ask. Where do I wash? She feels filthy, inside and out. She wants to sink into a tub of hot water and scrub and scrub and scrub until she is pure, sweet-smelling Polly Warden of New York again. She dimly understands the futility of this wish.

The bed beckons. She strips off her uniform and flings it in a heap on the floor outside the door, just the way they dumped the clothes of the wounded in the ward. In the next room a woman is weeping. Shirley Miller? Is she horrified by what her fiancé will soon be facing?

Have you seen men die on a battlefield, General? La gloire, la gloire. C'est de la merde. The tears on the dead face of the blond boy who looked so much like George Eagleton. *We won't have many deaths over there, will we?* Hemorrhage! Blood spurting, a foot-high fountain. *War is part of life. It just speeds up the dying.* Polly's brain goes around and around these words and images like a cracked phonograph record. In the distance, the guns continue to boom.

12. MADEMOISELLES OF SAINT-NAZAIRE, PARLEZ-VOUS?

THE PORT OF SAINT-NAZAIRE SLOWLY EMERGED from the predawn murk as Malvern Hill Bliss stepped out on the main deck of the S.S. *George Washington*. Around him the 5,500 men of the Lafayette Division's first infantry brigade jammed the rails. The wharves of the two deep-water channels were cluttered with antiquated booms and shabby open sheds that looked a century old. Beyond them, small houses with slanted red and brown tiled roofs huddled along narrow cobblestone streets.

A few feet away, Bliss heard one soldier say, "It makes Hoboken look like Times Square."

"If they got some bars, some dames, it's Times Square as far as I'm concerned," the man beside him said.

"Cut the bullshit about dames," a sergeant standing next to them growled. "Any of you get the clap or the syph I'll personally beat the shit out of you before you go to the hospital. We're here to fight a war."

It was O'Connor, the slugger from Union Square.

"Listen to him," the first soldier said. "He thinks he's in the German army."

"You saw them films. How easy it is to get a dose," the Sergeant said.

"The Sergeant's right," said a huge blond lieutenant. It was Polly Warden's Harvard friend, Eagleton. "If those pictures don't make you careful, nothing will."

"I got news for you, Lieutenant, it's nothin'," said the Hoboken aficionado, who was as big as Eagleton.

"Okay, Killer," Eagleton said. "Just remember—after O'Connor works you over, I'll be next in line."

O'Connor and Eagleton were talking about a series of films on venereal disease the army had forced everyone to see at their embarkation depot. The cameras showed men and women blinded and insane, their bodies rotted from syphilis and gonorrhea. The brass was trying to scare the AEF into purity.

Bliss had rejoined the Lafayette Division when the *George Washington* and three other ships arrived in the roadstead off Saint-Nazaire a week ago. It had taken seven days for the French to find space for them at the port's ancient docks. That had given him time to reassert a semblance of authority over his brigadiers and colonels.

For the previous month, while Pershing and his staff got used to the pleasures of Paris, Bliss and Captain Alden had spent their days trudging through muddy villages and their nights in bedbug-ridden country inns, on a tour of the provinces to scout training sites for the AEF. It was Pershing's way of letting Bliss know he was still on the shit list. Along with working out a sensible plan to train the AEF in Lorraine, in the northeast corner of France, Bliss used the time to introduce Alden to the concept of the thinking soldier and begin his matriculation in the Bliss Command and General Staff School of Disillusion.

A pathetic-looking French band straggled onto the dock. It consisted of a tuba player and five or six broken-down buglers. They made a try at the "Star-Spangled Banner" while Bliss and his staff came down the gangplank. A short poker-faced French general and a cluster of officers in horizon-blue uniforms stood a few feet from the laboring musicians. Beyond them about fifty grayheaded stevedores and a scattering of women waved flags and shouted, "*Vive le Teddies!*"

"I guess they think Teddy Roosevelt sent us," Bliss said. "In a way, he did."

Bliss strode toward the General, his hand out. "Welcome to France," the Frenchman said with a heavy accent. "You are General Blaze?"

"Bliss."

"Viomenil."

The first battalion of Ireland's Own came down the gangplank to the "Marseillaise." The band did a slightly better job on the French anthem. The Teddies formed into two ranks and stood at attention while General Viomenil inspected them. He stopped in front of Sergeant O'Connor and said, "Are your men ready to fight?"

"You bet, General," O'Connor said.

Viomenil turned to Bliss. "Do all your sergeants express themselves in such casual terms to general officers?"

"Sergeant," Bliss snapped, "please give General Viomenil the correct response to his question."

"Yes, *sir!*" O'Connor said.

The inspection completed, Bliss struggled to make conversation as the rest of the brigade came down the gangplank and the band returned to massacring "The Star-Spangled Banner."

"Where did you learn to speak English, General Viomenil?"

"I am a descendant of the Viomenil who fought beside General Rochambeau and your Washington at Yorktown. I am a member of your Society of the Cincinnati. It has been a requirement in my family that we speak English."

"I was born within a few miles of Yorktown and grew up listening to my father tell me stories about it," Bliss said. "Do you know the one about your ancestor and Lafayette?"

"I'm afraid not," Viomenil said.

"Lafayette commanded the American light infantry in a night attack on two advanced British redoubts. Baron Viomenil commanded the French troops. The Baron assured Lafayette that if he needed help, his men would be standing by. Lafayette's men took their redoubt in ten minutes. Viomenil's boys had a much tougher time. When Lafayette saw they were still fighting, he sent a runner to ask him if *he* needed assistance."

Viomenil's smile was thin. "We have always considered Lafayette and his kind responsible for Baron Viomenil's murder. He died in 1789 defending his king against the scum of Paris. I can assure you, General, a majority of the ranking officers in the French army think your division should be named Rochambeau. Or Viomenil."

Bliss decided he was not going to be fond of General Viomenil.

"How long have you been in command at Saint-Nazaire, General?"

"I was relieved of my command of the Sixth Army almost exactly a year ago," Viomenil said. His bitterness was undisguised. "Lest you think this is unusual, I should explain that of the twenty-six officers in the highest commands of the French army in 1914, only three are still at the front. When a war goes badly, the politicians demand heads. Since they would never dream of offering one of their own, the sacrifice falls on a more suitable target, a soldier who cannot reply to their calumnies."

Bliss thought of Pershing and the list of incompetents Tasker Bliss had foisted on him. Would Jack's head be demanded by Wilson and his crowd if things went wrong? No doubt about it.

General Viomenil said members of his staff would conduct the brigade to their barracks on the outskirts of Saint-Nazaire. Rooms had been reserved for Bliss and his staff at the Grand Hôtel des Messagères, only a ten-minute walk from the docks. With a stiff bow, he withdrew.

A sagging French sedan careened out of a side street and skidded to a stop near the S.S. *George Washington*'s gangplank. Out climbed a short fat Frenchman with a red sash around his ample waist and black hair glued to his wide head by a quart of pomade. He introduced himself as the mayor of Saint-Nazaire. "You are General Bland?" he said.

"Bliss."

The Mayor exuded a stream of French courtesies, which Bliss let Captain Alden summarize in translation. Although his daily lessons with Polly Warden on the troopship had revived his West Point French, Bliss had decided to pretend not to understand the language. It was a trick he had picked up from Pershing in the Philippines. Often you could learn a great deal from the asides and mutters that translators ignored.

"His Honor the Mayor says he's here to hail the conquerors of the Germans and the saviors of France," Alden said, barely able to conceal his repugnance. "He's imported one hundred women of pleasure from Paris to console the troops after their long voyage."

"Ask him how much," Bliss said.

Looking even more appalled, Alden obeyed. "He says that

depends on the services required by the individual soldier. Such things are negotiated in France."

"How much for a simple lay?"

Alden had trouble putting this into French. "Ten francs," he said.

"Are the women clean? No venereal disease?"

This question inspired an oration, which Alden wearily condensed. "They're guaranteed by the government. They're examined every week by the finest doctors in Saint-Nazaire."

Another stream of French deepened the repugnance on Captain Alden's sensitive face. "He says one of the prettiest is ready to visit you tonight, General, free of charge."

"Tell him I'll pass on the offer."

The Grand Hôtel des Messagères had ceased to be grand around 1880. Everything had a faded, weary look. The same aura pervaded Bliss's suite; it was full of fake medieval chairs and dressers and a canopy bed. He let Captain Alden deal with the bellmen and the luggage. "I can see you don't approve of our arrangement with Monsieur le Mayor," Bliss said when they were alone.

"I'm afraid I don't, General. We're here for a noble purpose. I think you should shut those places down."

The sternness on the young face momentarily intimidated Bliss. "In the first place, this isn't our country. We can't shut them down," he said. "In the second place, it's an old army custom. Pershing set up a whole string of bordellos on the Mexican border last year and had army doctors inspect the ladies each week. It cut our usual VD rate by two thirds. In the third place, I've found a man fights a lot better if he's gotten laid recently. Don't ask me why. I'm just telling you my experience."

He might as well have been lecturing one of the fake medieval chairs or the canopy bed. Captain Alden still disagreed with General Bliss—and General Pershing, for that matter.

That night, Bliss strolled the streets of Saint-Nazaire with Captain Alden. Everywhere, Lafayette Division soldiers were being propositioned by Frenchwomen and disappearing down alleys and into bistros. Obviously the general staff's attempt to frighten the AEF into purity had not gotten very far. Bliss could hardly wait to write Tasker a letter, giving him the horse laugh. He was also enjoying the dismayed look on Captain Alden's face. He was seeing a side of the enlisted man they did not tell him about at West Point.

Dozens of men were streaming in and out of three houses with red lights in their windows. Ragtime music and raucous laughter echoed from their doorways. Bliss stepped into one of them and found himself in a narrow hall, decorated with wallpaper of shepherds and shepherdesses doing all sorts of naughty things to each other. At the end of the hall an American officer was talking to a large beaming Frenchwoman with frizzy, obviously dyed blond hair.

"Hello, Teddy," she said in a thick accent. "You want a juicy mademoiselle, eh?"

"No, I don't want a mademoiselle," Father Francis Kelly said. "I'm a priest. A chaplain."

"Ah, you wish directions to the cathedral? It is just down this street, one or two blocks."

"I want to inspect this place," he said. "I want to make sure none of the men from my regiment are in here."

"Impossible," the smiling madam said. "This is our property. We have a contract signed by the Mayor of Saint-Nazaire, who assured us he has the approval of your general. No one can come on these premises without our permission but the police and the doctor appointed to inspect the girls each Sunday."

"I don't believe you!" Kelly cried.

"I would be happy to show the agreement to you, but I don't have time," she said. She eased her bulk around Kelly to welcome two grinning members of Carolina's Pride. "Hello, Teddies. You want to have a good time, no?"

"We wanna have a good time, yes," the bigger of the two Carolinians said.

"This here's Man Mountain Jones. He wore out half the whores in Columbia, South Carolina, the night before we joined up," the smaller one said.

"Wear out?" the madam said. "Ah! You mean exhaust. You will find our mademoiselles don't tire so easily. Frenchwomen enjoy making love. Not like the English. You have learned bad habits from the English, you poor Americans. Welcome to French love!"

Kelly peered around the madam into the interior of the house. "Peter Foley!" he cried. "What are you doing in this place?"

"Father!" a blushing Foley gasped, coming to the door. "I—I'm lookin' for Bill Quinn. He come in here and I thought he might get sandbagged."

"The sooner you stop looking for him and get back to your barracks, the better it'll be for you the next time you go to confession!"

"Gee whiz, Father. I mean—"

"The poor boy has already paid his money. He's waiting for a *jeune fille*," the madam said. "Why don't you consult the bishop, Father? He will perhaps explain to you things about life in France."

"I'm going in there and make sure none of my boys are doing anything they'll regret," Kelly roared.

"Georges!" the madam cried.

From somewhere down the hall materialized a huge balding man with a steel hook where his right hand and lower arm had been. "Georges helps me keep order," the madam explained. "He was wounded on the Marne in 1914 but he has regained his strength, thank the good Lord. Please go now without more shouting."

Georges slipped his hook into Kelly's coat collar and escorted him rapidly into the street. On his way back he eyed Bliss and asked the madam if he should throw him out too. "I'm going," Bliss said and joined Kelly on the sidewalk.

"Is it true what that woman said?" Kelly asked. "You've agreed to these—these dens of iniquity?"

"Talk it over with the bishop of Saint-Nazaire before you blow your stack, Father," Bliss said.

Kelly vanished into the night. The disapproval on Captain Alden's face was too visible to ignore. "You seem to sympathize with the chaplain," Bliss said.

"I'm afraid I do, General. My father's a minister. He'd say and do the same things. So would I, if I had the authority."

"There's where you're wrong. Wearing this uniform doesn't give you any *moral* authority. Our authority is strictly *military*."

"That may be true in other armies, General. I'm not sure if it's true in the American army. We're a moral country, a moral people."

On the next block they encountered Sergeant O'Connor and three husky compatriots from Ireland's Own, all with Military Police brassards on their arms and clubs in their hands. Bliss had added a platoon of MPs to Saint-Nazaire's police force to keep order. "How do you like being a cop, Sergeant?" he said.

The Sergeant grew surprisingly thoughtful. "To tell you the truth, General, I never realized how hard they worked."

"How are you getting along with Lieutenants Eagleton and Hunthouse?" Bliss asked.

O'Connor looked him in the eye, as brazen as ever. "Lieutenant Eagleton's okay. I can't say the same for Captain Hunthouse. He's got some sort of grudge against me, General. I can't figure it out."

"Isn't Price your captain?" Bliss said.

"He got himself transferred to a nice safe staff job in Washington the day before we sailed. He recommended Hunthouse for captain, and Colonel Fairchild bought it."

The Sergeant and his squad continued their patrol. "Three months ago that fellow was on his way to becoming a gangster," Bliss said. "Now look at him. Enforcing the law—and criticizing the officer corps."

He gave Alden a quick summary of why he had put Hunthouse and Eagleton in O'Connor's company. "Don't you approve, Captain? Shouldn't the U.S. Army promote democracy along with other moral principles?"

"I suppose so, General. But aren't you also promoting dissension in the ranks?"

"Combat cures that sort of dissension overnight."

Confusion clouded Captain Alden's idealistic eyes. He still did not know he was matriculating at the Bliss Command and General Staff School of Disillusion.

Five hours later, in his bed in the Grand Hôtel des Messagères, Bliss stared into the predawn darkness. He had not slept more than five hours a night since Pershing had enlisted him in the American Expeditionary Force.

Bliss was thinking about Polly Warden's glowing auburn hair, her green eyes, her soft kissable mouth that blended innocence and anger and courage. He wondered where she was and what she was doing in her quest for adventure and nobility. He had no intention of seducing her. That would seal her low opinion of soldiers. But he could not stop imagining that small body in his arms, his lips on her white throat. There was a complete woman there, a creature who could be fire and ice, love in all its moods and tempos.

How long could he survive without a woman? Desire hammered at the base of his skull. It always seemed to swell there, a fist, pounding him. He was a celibate, like Chaplain Kelly, with his odd combination of innocence and arrogance. How did he and other priests manage it? Maybe virginity made it easier. You did not miss what you have never known. While you, Bliss, are like an amputee, trying to dance on a missing leg.

"General," Captain Alden said, rapping on Bliss's door. "General Pershing is calling from Paris."

Bliss grabbed for the phone. Pershing's voice went through his skull like a buzz saw. "We've just gotten a query cable direct from the Secretary of War asking if you've authorized three brothels in Saint-Nazaire for your division."

"It was the Mayor's idea, not mine, Jack."

"You're tolerating them. It amounts to the same thing. That's not going to be the policy of the AEF. I want those things shut down instantly."

"Last year on the Mexican border—"

"No one was watching us on the border except some drunken reporters. Over here we've got an army of do-gooders in the YMCA and the Red Cross and Christ knows how many preachers and politicians breathing down our necks. Plus a million mothers back in the States worrying about their darling boys' souls. Plus a President who thinks he's saving the world. If Wilson hears what you've done he'll try to stop the goddamn war!"

"We'll shut them down, Jack. But I think you're making a mistake."

"That's all the back talk I want to hear from you! We've got more important things to worry about."

There was something in Pershing's voice Bliss had never heard before, a strain of doubt and anxiety. "What's wrong, Jack?" he asked.

"The Russians are folding up. That's going to give the Germans a three-to-two advantage on the western front in a month or two. By this time next year, you may be fighting in Saint-Nazaire instead of screwing in it."

Bliss lay there for a long time, the silent telephone in his hand. It was not just the Russians folding up. Something else was wrong with Jack Pershing. For a moment all he could see was the Moro's kris swinging in the glare of the Jolo sun, the flames and suffocating smoke in the Pershing quarters at the Presidio.

"Bad news, General?" Captain Alden said.

Bliss looked into the unlined, unstained face. Young Jack's face. He felt a terrible wish to ask him to share his pain, his premonition of trouble. But it was impossible—and unwise. Generals had to remain armor-plated, no matter what they felt inside.

"The worst news imaginable. I've just been told I was wrong and you were right about those whorehouses. I hope this doesn't go to your head, Captain."

"I'll try not to let that happen, sir," Alden said, smiling.

"We'll close them tomorrow morning. Let the men have one more night."

"Isn't that—taking a chance, sir? General Pershing sounded pretty exercised."

There was no moral reproach in these words, only concern for Bliss's career. Bliss brusquely dismissed the idea. "In the purity department, Jack owes me a big one."

He told Captain Alden what he had done in 1907, after Teddy Roosevelt made Pershing a general. A lot of officers who had been passed over started a smear campaign about Jack's sex life in the Philippines. As his closest friend and executive officer, Bliss issued a statement denying the slurs. He said they spent their spare time growing orchids and teaching Sunday school to their little brown brothers, when in fact Pershing had enjoyed one of the great romances of his life with a beautiful Eurasian whose father ran a bar in Malabang.

"Was that honorable, Captain Alden? Should I have told the truth and destroyed my best friend's career?"

"I don't know, General," Alden said. He stared out the window at Saint-Nazaire, engulfed in predawn fog.

The uncertainty in his voice was another encouraging sign of his progress in the Bliss Command and General Staff School of Disillusion. By now he probably despised General Bliss. That was part of the plan. He must never suspect what was happening in the old fool's wayward heart.

13. LE CAFARD

"*SCHWESTER! WASSER!*"

Polly Warden tried to ignore the arrogance in the voice of the surly blond captain from the elite Prussian Guards division. He had been brought into the ward two nights ago, wounded in the legs. She did not want to dislike him, much less hate him. She wanted to regard all her patients as equally in need of care and kindness. But the German officers often tested her resolve. Many of the nurses and even some of the wounded poilus in nearby beds were intimidated by these overbearing creatures with their spiked helmets and gleaming black boots, their bulky coats crammed with pearl-handled Lügers and daggers and compasses.

"In a minute," Polly said. She was struggling to undress a French forward artillery observer who had been wounded by a shell. His body was riddled with shrapnel. He was delirious and probably dying.

"*Schwester! Verdammte Amerikanerin.*"

A slim figure in white hurtled from the operating room. It was Dr. Paul Lebrun, the surgeon who had rescued Polly from collapse last month, when she had worked three days and two nights without stopping. "Mademoiselle Warden, you will not give this Boche pig a drink until he apologizes in French. That is an order!" he said.

The German glared at Lebrun. "*Excusez-moi,*" he said.

Polly temporarily abandoned the babbling artillery observer and poured the captain a drink of water. "*Danke schön!*" he said sullenly.

"Headquarters, can you hear me? Barrage coming in," the artillery observer mumbled.

Engines growled overhead. "Boche," muttered a sergeant in the bed next to the artillery observer. German engines had an unmistakable dismal groan, several tones lower than French engines. The sergeant was wearing a cast on his broken left leg, which was elevated by a pulley to a frame above him. He could not hide under the bed, which some of the less badly wounded hastened to do.

Polly went back to grappling with the artillery observer. Outside, batteries of antiaircraft guns erupted with head-splitting crashes. The roar of the planes overhead seemed to pour down on them like a gigantic waterfall. Then the bombs: different, more menacing crashes. The walls swayed. Polly continued to undress the artillery observer.

Was it her tenth or eleventh air raid? She had thought hospitals were exempt from air attack. There were huge red crosses on the roofs of all the buildings. But the Germans bombed them relentlessly. Yesterday a 250-pound bomb had obliterated the barracks just a few hundred feet away from this one. Polly and the orderlies had rushed outside to find bits of sheets and bandages and parts of bodies dangling from a nearby tree. Two nurses and a doctor had been killed, along with more than forty patients.

Although the sense of nightmare persisted, Polly had acquired a semblance of order in her everyday life. She worked twelve-hour shifts, usually at night. She devoted much of her waking hours to becoming an educated nurse. She learned how to find the pressure points in the human body that controlled hemorrhages, how to turn and lift a wounded man in bed without hurting him, how to give injections and dress wounds.

Six of the ten Americans with whom she had ridden to the château in the camion had retreated to Paris. Madame Leclerc, the head nurse, told Polly this was an average dropout rate for both French and American nurses. There was a limit to what a woman could endure. "You'll find yours," she said in her spiteful way.

Never, Polly vowed. She would stay here until she died of exhaustion or a bomb killed her. She had simultaneously become an impassioned hater of war and a furious foe of the Germans. She had neither the time nor the inclination to resolve these contradictory emotions. Her visceral hatred of war was as tangible as the suffering men she nursed each day. It had nothing to do with the abstract rational pacifism of her college and New York protest days. Her rage at the Germans was equally visceral. It was rooted in her numerous collisions with their arrogance and condescension—and a growing fear that they were winning the war. Everywhere she looked, Polly saw defeat: in the listless silence of the wounded as they recovered from their surgery, in the haggard unshaven faces of the poilus (the word meant "hairy ones") as they trudged toward the front, in the wounded men's denunciations of their "butcher generals" who flung away lives by the thousands in futile attacks on German block-houses and trenches defended by hundreds of machine guns.

Polly often had breakfast with Shirley Miller when they came off the night shift. Shirley was still working, although she frequently cried herself to sleep. She had received a letter from her fiancé, full of martial valor. "How can I answer it?" she said. "How can I tell him the truth about this war?"

Polly thought of George Eagleton and shook her head. She was now glad they had quarreled, glad they were not writing to each other. She refused to think beyond this fact. She blanked out the memory of her dismay when she learned he had gone from her to a showgirl. She was not angry at George anymore. She was not angry at any soldier. One night she wrote Malvern Hill Bliss a long letter, warning him about the low morale, the atmosphere of imminent collapse all around her. It made her feel better for a day or two.

Some evenings before they went on duty she dined with Dr. Lebrun and the other surgeons. They were mostly young like him, but none had his lineage or good looks. Lebrun's great-grandfather had been a general in Napoleon's army. His grandfather had died fighting the Germans in 1870. An uncle on his mother's side was a general commanding a section of the front near Verdun. He described the present war as *un ancien démence,* an old madness that had raged between France and Germany since Roman times.

Dr. Lebrun talked almost exclusively to Polly. When he learned she was a college graduate, he wanted to know her philosophy of life. "I believe in the power and importance of ideals. I try to prac-tice them," she said.

"Ah. This then is the source of your marvelous innocence."

"I don't think of myself as innocent."

"Have you ever been in love?"

"No," Polly said, after a momentary hesitation.

"That too explains the radiance. Everyone in the ward talks of it. The poilus call you Mademoiselle Joyeuse."

Polly shook her head. "I'm as filled with sadness and horror as the rest of you."

Lebrun lit a cigarette. "Your soul is unspoiled by it. All of us have long since succumbed to *le cafard*. Do you know Verlaine?"

The guns rumbled. Cries from suffering men filtered into the château's dining room. Softly, slowly, Lebrun recited.

> *"C'est bien la pire peine*
> *De ne savoir pourquoi*
> *Sans amour et sans haine*
> *Mon coeur a tant de peine."*

Polly had read the poem. Verlaine was asking why his heart was full of pain even though he had transcended both love and hate.

"The poilus call that worst pain *le cafard*. I prefer it as a description of our state of soul. Those in the grip of *le cafard* both know and do not know why they suffer. *Le cafard* whispers of beloved things, gentleness and beauty that will never be known again. It also resonates with hunger, cold, the blood of brothers and foes, the dull reaction after killing. There is nothing vague about *le cafard*."

Polly trembled. She was being dragged across a border into a country where she knew neither the language nor the hearts and minds of the inhabitants. It was not the France of Molière and Victor Hugo and Flaubert. It was not even the France of Verlaine and Baudelaire, who redeemed their tormented decadence with the purity of their language. It was the France of the war, this daily unrelenting agony that had been uprooting all other realities for three years while Americans sat home and read lies in their newspapers.

"I too came here with a dream of the ideal in my heart," Lebrun said. "An ideal France in which brotherhood, equality, and liberty would be realities, not perpetual promises made by lying politicians. Now I only believe in *le cafard*."

For a moment Polly could feel nothing but grief and sympathy. She understood the power, the meaning, the hope of the ideal. She also knew, from her father's life, how indifferent the world was to it, how easily people ignored and even scorned it. The war multiplied and intensified this brutal process and made it happen faster. She heard General Bliss telling her the war speeded up everything: death, love. It was a kind of love Paul Lebrun had lost, she thought, as he talked forlornly of the stupidity and callousness of France's generals, the cowardice of the politicians who were supposed to control them. "*Cafard* gives the mind a peculiar clarity. It helps you see so many things," he said.

He took Polly's hand. She felt the strength of his long tapered surgeon's fingers. In the same low voice, he said, "Next Friday I have a weekend pass. Will you come to Paris with me?"

Stunned, Polly could only shake her head. She was still too American to see the connection between his cry of despair and this sudden plea. "We will do nothing, I will ask nothing, that you do not freely wish to give me," Lebrun said.

"*Absolument jamais!*" Polly said, freeing her hand. It was not good French but it was definitive. *Absolutely never.*

They walked through the deepening darkness to their surgical ward. Suddenly Lebrun's hand was on her shoulder. He spun her into his arms for a fierce desperate kiss. She smelled the sour sweat of his unwashed body, his matted hair. With a gasp she burst free.

She should slap him, denounce him. Instead she almost burst into tears. She understood in a dark inchoate way what he needed from her: ultimate sympathy, ultimate tenderness, a reward and a redemption from the daily brutality and death that surrounded them. But was it in her power?

"Forgive me," he said, stumbling back. "That won't happen again."

The next morning, Polly announced she was going to take a bath. She had asked Madame Leclerc for permission once before and had been scathingly informed that water was precious and she could bathe out of a bowl, like the rest of them. Now, with the number of patients reduced—there were actually vacant beds in several wards—Leclerc grudgingly relented.

A chill wind blew through a shattered window a few feet above the six inches of tepid water in the château's only bathtub. Nevertheless, Polly bathed. She half knew what she was doing; she was trying to regain her American self, to somehow splash her way back to that border Paul Lebrun had forced her to cross. It was necessary to become sweet-smelling Polly Warden again for a little while, desperately necessary. She had to escape the earthy anguished odors of France.

But it was impossible to escape this body that Lebrun imagined as a gift she might offer him. These rounded breasts, the clitoris and vagina beneath that mound of russet hair, the swelling thighs no man had ever touched—her womanness. Was it possible that this flesh, this hair, had a meaning that somehow transcended their mere existence?

That frightened her; she did not want to be a magical creature. She wanted to be simple and honest and direct like those epitomes of masculinity, the officers on the *Baltic*. But was there another side to these paragons? She remembered Pershing's tears for his dead wife, Major Quickmeyer's fascination with tantalizing Louise Wolcott, General Bliss saying, *You're one of us*. What did that mean? Did it explain why her heart went out to the poilus?

She tried to comb her hair before washing it. It was a greasy tangled mess, unlovely to touch, almost impossible to unsnarl. She decided to cut it off. For a moment she quailed at the thought of what her mother would say. But Mother was three thousand miles away. It was not a declaration of sexual liberation, it was an act of sanitation—and sanity. With no water to wash it regularly, it would be a mess again in a few days.

As her hair fell away in thick red strands, Polly was pleased to discover she had no sentimental attachment to it. She trimmed it carefully at the back and around her ears and decided she not only felt better, she looked better. More like a modern woman, less like Mademoiselle Joyeuse.

In her room as she finished dressing, a weasel-faced orderly delivered a message from Madame Leclerc. Dr. Lebrun had requested her as his nurse for the weekly inspection of the Maison Blanche. She was to report to the main gate immediately. The weasel struggled to suppress a leer, bowed mockingly, and vanished.

Lebrun was waiting for her in a staff car at the gate. Polly asked him what they were going to inspect at the Maison Blanche. "*Poules*," he said. That meant hens—but Polly suspected another meaning. She suspected even more as they drove through the shell-blasted landscape to a squat, ugly building on a hill about five miles from the Château Givry. A dozen camions were parked at the foot of the hill inside a high stone wall. Large signs announced the grounds were INTERDIT. Anyone inside the wall without a pass would be arrested.

A tall homely woman with misshapen yellow teeth and a sallow complexion greeted them at the door. She immediately began complaining about everything. The food they received from the army was abominable. Everyone wanted a week in Paris. One girl had tried to commit suicide. Lebrun nodded and promised to report the situation to the head of the hospital, who would speak to the commanding general. Polly had a feeling the exchange was a regular performance.

In what might have once been a sitting room, a table had been covered with a soiled white cloth. "Send them in," Lebrun said. One after another, women filed into the room, lifted dirty dresses over their heads, and lay down on the table. Most of them looked undernourished. None of them had taken a bath in months, to judge from the dirt on their skin. Lebrun used a speculum to examine their genital organs for venereal disease. After each examination he handed the instrument to Polly to be dipped in a sterilizing solution, while he used a fresh one.

The procedure was as impersonal, as matter-of-fact, as a task on a factory assembly line. Occasionally, Lebrun recognized one of the women by name and asked her if she was feeling better; apparently he had treated some of them for an illness. Most of the time he hummed to himself and muttered *bon*—unless he found something. Then he ordered Polly to take the woman's name.

They never gave a last name. It was always simply Annette or Marianne or Babette. If there were two with the same name, one was Big Annette or Fat Marianne or Blond Babette. The women's faces were mostly blank. They never met Polly's eyes. They pulled down their dresses and drifted out the door. A memory stirred in Polly's mind: reading she had done in college about slave auctions in the Old South. This was exactly the same. No last names, no recognition that these were human beings, women!

In an hour they had examined sixty *poules*. As they drove back to the Château Givry, Lebrun wrote a report on the visit. He was pleased. They had found only three cases of venereal disease. Usually the number was much higher. "Who—who goes to them?" Polly asked, almost gagging on the words.

"The poilus. Those trucks in the yard bring them in by the regiment. One woman will entertain thirty men a night. It's very important for morale."

Polly struggled to conceal her revulsion. "*Thirty* men?" she said. "Thirty men a *night?*"

"I asked for you as my assistant because I wanted you to see the difference between yourself and those creatures. I wanted you to understand why I need you."

That night the Germans launched a new attack. Another flood of wounded men poured into the hospital. By the end of her next shift, Mademoiselle Warden was as sweat-soaked and grimy as she had been before her ritual bath. She was back in the France of earthy, smelly pain.

Shortly after Polly fell into her bed, one of Dr. Lebrun's two operating-room nurses collapsed. Madame Leclerc dragged Polly out of an exhausted sleep and ordered her to replace her. She did not know the name of a single instrument. But she stood by, learning rapidly, meanwhile handing him simple objects, sutures and clamps to minimize the bleeding. She was amazed by how little bleeding there was.

As he worked, Lebrun whispered poetry. "*De la douceur, de la douceur, de la douceur!*"

Sweetness, oh, the sweetness! The sweetness! It was Verlaine again, his poem "*Lassitude,*" in which he tells his mistress to calm her feverish raptures. At the height of pleasure, he wants only a discreet abandonment, like the gentle love of a sister.

"*Sois langoureuse, fais ta caresse endormante,*" whispered Lebrun, as he searched a riddled stomach wall for bits of shrapnel. Be languorous, lull me with your caresses.

"*Mais oui, endormante,*" growled the anesthetist, Dolbier, a hulking older man with sagging pink cheeks and a bulbous nose. To him the word had its medical meaning, anesthetize.

The other nurse, a husky peasant girl named Marie Ribout, was giggling. Did she think Lebrun was talking to her?

"*Mais dans ton cher coeur d'or, me dis-tu, mon enfant, La fauve passion va sonnant l'oliphant.*" Child, in your dear golden heart you say savage passion sounds her clarion.

Polly replied with the poem's next line. "*Laisse-la trompeter a son aise, la geuse!*" The hussy, let her trumpet as she may!

"Ah, Dolbier, if I had such sophisticated nurses always at my table, I could operate indefinitely," Lebrun said.

Dolbier grunted. "A good thing most are stupid cows like Ribout."

Marie Ribout looked as if she might weep; she was in love with Dr. Lebrun. Shirley Miller, in spite of her fiancé's gifts and letters, said Lebrun was the handsomest man she had ever seen. Was everyone in love with him except Polly Warden?

With amazing swiftness, Lebrun began to sew up the ravaged stomach as he whispered the last three lines of the poem.

> "*Mets ton front sur mon front et ta main dans ma main*
> *Et fais-moi des serments que tu rompras demain,*
> *Et pleurons jusqu'au jour, O petite fougueuse!*"

The translation flowed through Polly's mind, into her blood and her flesh.

> Your cheek to mine and your hand in my hand,
> Make me those promises you'll break at dawn,
> And let us weep until then, my little firebrand.

Polly gazed into Lebrun's ashen face, his glazed eyes, and saw *le cafard*. He was insisting that she taste it, touch it, learn it. He was telling her she was his only hope of escaping it. He was warning her the hope might be only for a single night.

The door to the ward opened and shut. In the sterilizing room the boiler pounded and bubbled. Steam hissed sullenly. The cries and sobs of the wounded drifted around them. In the distance artillery thundered. On and on they worked, sleeping in fifteen-minute snatches on a cot in the corner of the operating room, Lebrun cutting into body after body, resectioning stomachs, removing kidneys, repairing ruptured lungs, whispering more Verlaine.

"*Mon rêve familier*," a poem about his yearning for a nameless woman who loves and understands him, a woman who knows how to wipe the sweat from his pale brow and cool it with her tears; "*Les Indolents*," in which two lovers debate whether it might be clever to die together; "*Colloque sentimental*," in which the ghosts of two lovers meet in a wintry park and discuss their old ecstasies.

> "*Ton coeur bat-il toujours à mon seul nom?*
> *Toujours vois-tu mon âme en rêve?—Non.*"

> When you hear my name does your heart always glow?
> Do you always see my soul in dreams? No.

Le cafard. Dr. Lebrun was operating on a poilu's shaven skull: sawing through bone to reveal the spongy pale-brown brain beneath it, draining off the blood that was crushing it, inserting a steel plate to hold the man's head together. With each word of the poet's amorous despair, each slice of the scalpel, was Polly Warden becoming a citizen of this new country, this landscape of named and nameless pain?

"Ah, Dolbier, do you think the war will enable modern women to triumph over us?" Lebrun asked the anesthetist.

"They've already triumphed over *un merdeux* (a twerp) like you." Dolbier grunted.

"I think it will have a precisely opposite effect. The war will evoke all the ancient virtues. They will surrender to pity, sympathy, admiration for men's valor. They'll become consolers, comforters, once more."

"*Je les emmerde,*" Dolbier growled. To hell with them.

"They're our only hope, Dolbier. Now even I, Lebrun the inde-fatigable, must sleep."

He handed Polly his bloody scalpel. She stood there with it in her hand for a full minute, paralyzed.

The following day was Friday. The whole middle of the week had vanished. The German attacks dwindled and the nightmare became more *systématique* again. At breakfast Lebrun told Polly he was leaving for Paris at noon. "Is the answer still *jamais?*" he said.

Polly saw her fingers on those pale cheeks, she felt her lips on that mournful mouth. A voice, the embryo of a wish, spoke in her soul. She almost knew why he was asking her now. But she willed not to know. She denied the radiance Paul Lebrun saw around her woman's body. She clung to her determination to be an independent woman with a self that transcended sex.

"I'll have to read more Verlaine, talk to more poilus about *le cafard.*"

It was a refusal—and a confession that never was no longer the inevitable word.

"Ah, *oui,*" he said. But there was no yes in his voice, his eyes. Did he think she was mocking him? He mocked himself so often. Half the poetry he recited was a mockery of Verlaine's mockery of love. She watched him mount a motorcycle with an empty sidecar and roar out the château's gate.

The next day Madame Leclerc assigned Polly to a new ward, populated only by German prisoners. Polly wondered if it was out of spite. It was hard to tell, because almost everything Madame Leclerc said to everyone was so full of loathing. The German officers were as obnoxious and demanding as the ones she had encountered in Lebrun's surgical ward. The ones who spoke English bragged incessantly about the genius of their commander in chief, General Erich von Ludendorff. Others boasted of the havoc wrought by his artillery commander, Colonel Georg Bruchmüller.

Some of the enlisted men were more docile and friendly. One private in particular tugged at Polly's heart. Otto was only sixteen and had lost his right leg above the knee. He had large gentle eyes and pale hair shaved close to his head. He called her "Kind *Schwester*," mixing English and German. He had visited an uncle in Milwaukee and knew quite a lot of English. He told her confidentially that he hated the war. At first it had seemed brave and glorious to fight for the Fatherland. Now he did not understand it at all.

A blast of curses from the next bed turned Otto deathly white. A major with his arm in a cast excoriated Otto for losing his faith in Germany. "*Gott mitt uns!*" he roared. "We will smash them all: Russians, French, English. Americans. *Gott mitt uns* against the whole world if need be!"

In one voice, the ward thundered, "*Gott mitt uns!*"

Polly's hand shook so badly for the next half hour, she could barely administer the scheduled injections of morphine.

On Sunday, they carried in a badly wounded German officer. Polly braced herself for the usual torrent of abuse as she began the struggle to undress him. Instead, the man whispered in flawless French, "Get the *Agent de Liaison*. Quickly!"

This was Major Mahone, the elderly French officer who had greeted Polly and the other Americans when they arrived at the hospital. Polly raced through the mud to the château, and Mahone rushed back to the barracks with her. He knelt beside the man's bed and listened for a moment, then summoned an orderly. They wheeled the man to a curtained-off section of the ward, where a doctor and his nurse soon joined them. An hour later, they wheeled the man out, his face covered. The nurse was weeping. So was the *Agent de Liaison*. "My God, my God, the sacrifices men make for France!" he said.

The man had been a French spy. He had been shot by French troops as he attempted to reach their lines. The doctor had kept him alive with saline solutions long enough for him to tell them precious information about German plans for a new offensive.

The night dwindled into the dawn with the usual cries and snarls. "*Schwester! Wasser!*" "Morphine! I'm bleeding!" Finally, a wan Shirley Miller relieved Polly. Madame Leclerc seemed to have made a policy of giving the Americans the job of nursing the Boche. Maybe it pleased her to remind the arrogant Teutons that the United States was now on France's side in the war.

"She wants to see you," Shirley said. "She's upset about something."

Madame Leclerc's sparrow's face looked more ghastly than usual, a feat in itself. "Come with me," she said with maximum bitterness.

Polly followed her into the east wing of the château, where the doctors lived. At the end of a long hall, Leclerc flung open a door and motioned Polly into the room. It stank of vomit. Paul Lebrun was lying on the bed, breathing in shallow gasps. An ugly blue black bruise disfigured one cheek.

"Absinthe," she said, rolling up the sleeve of his shirt. "One of these days he'll drink enough to destroy the central nervous system. He'll crawl in here and die—if he doesn't get killed first on that motorcycle."

She injected something into Lebrun's arm and glared at Polly, on the other side of the bed. "Why didn't you go to Paris with him? He's worth ten of you. A hundred of me, for that matter. I would have gone with him in an instant if he'd asked me. But we're used up. France is used up. We must depend on you Americans. God help us all."

Leclerc stalked to the door. "Clean him up," she said. "Treat him as you would any other wounded man."

Le cafard. Polly was across the border now. Tears streaming down her face, she pulled off Paul Lebrun's filthy clothes and bathed his fine-boned body. As her hands moved across his pale flesh, she knew it was only a matter of time before she joined him on his journey through this country of pain. Where else could she find a man who understood it so profoundly, who had explored the wounds of the mind and body and had somehow retained a memory of happiness?

14. WORDS TO LIVE BY

MAJOR GENERAL MALVERN HILL BLISS HATED ALL forms of paperwork. But a division commander could not avoid it. Feeding, disciplining, transporting 28,000 men involved a million details. At 7:30 A.M., after another night of broken sleep, he struggled to concentrate on a report from the Lafayette Division's quartermaster.

> The standard French military train is made up of thirty boxcars, seventeen flat cars, one coach for officers, and two cabooses for train crew. Forty men or eight horses can be transported in the boxcars. Sixty trains will be required to move the division to its training site. It will take two weeks, possibly longer, to assemble this much rolling stock.

Another report listed the animals and motor-driven vehicles they would soon be responsible for maintaining. There would be 3,900 horses, 2,617 mules, 238 bicycles, 319 motorcycles with sidecars, 122 motorcars, 41 ambulances, 64 tractors, and 638 trucks. He was going to be running a goddamn transportation system! At the moment, however, their system consisted of three decrepit Ford cars and one asthmatic motorcycle.

The telephone rang. Captain Alden answered it and practically came to attention. "Yes, General!... No, he's right here. We've been hard at work for the last hour."

He handed the phone to Bliss. "General Pershing."

"Glad to see you're not on banker's hours," Pershing said. "Can you come up to Paris tomorrow? I've got a meeting with Sir Douglas Haig, His Majesty's commander in chief, and his French opposite number, Henri Pétain. They're fighting over your division like coyotes over a piece of raw meat. I want you around to say the right things."

"I'll be there by car, train, or plane. Whatever I can find."

"The Brits are sending a car for you."

The next morning at 7 A.M. Bliss paced impatiently up and down the faded lobby of the Grand Hôtel des Messagères. Through the swinging door strode a tall slim young woman in a rumpled brown uniform. She had a wide sensual mouth, a strong, almost mannish nose, and bold gray eyes beneath thick dark eyebrows that gave her a sort of permanent frown. Clumps of carelessly combed dark hair were visible around her visored hat. "General Bliss?" she said in a soft, surprisingly feminine voice. "I'm Anita Sinclair, your driver."

She led him to a gleaming gray Rolls-Royce. "Do you mind if I sit up front?" he said. "I hate riding millionaire style."

"As you please, General," she said.

They headed for Paris on a good main road, giving Miss Sinclair a chance to demonstrate the top speed of the Rolls. The wheels did not seem to be touching the ground. She seldom slowed down to pass occasional trucks and wagons. Twice she just missed an oncoming truck. "It's four hundred thirty-three kilometers to Paris," she remarked after the second hairbreadth escape. "We have to dash a bit."

"I like fast driving," Bliss said. "How long have you been in France?"

"Two years. In 1915 I drove an ambulance at Artois and watched Douglas Haig and his fellow generals kill three hundred thousand men. Last year was even more fun. I watched him slaughter a half million on the Somme. If you hate Englishmen, war is a marvelous diversion."

She passed a horse and wagon hauling a load of wood. They missed another oncoming truck by inches. Bliss tried to assimilate the stunning assemblage of facts she had just dropped in his lap. In American newspapers, Artois and the Somme had been described as victories. He decided to start from the last and most interesting fact. "Why do you hate Englishmen?"

"Because they're so stupid," she said. "Will you tell me another species who'd allow themselves to be repeatedly slaughtered by generals who obviously don't know what they're doing? Even the Russians finally got the message and mutinied against their idiotic czar and his generals. Last spring the French tried to do the same thing. The English just go on brainlessly dying."

Bliss struggled to maintain his aplomb. He had heard nothing about a mutiny in the French army. "Why did the French mutiny?" he asked.

"They attacked in Champagne just after your president declared war. They lost two hundred thousand men in two days. The poilus shot their officers and started marching on Paris. The brass stopped them by executing a thousand or so of the most violent mutineers and firing half the generals."

"How did you learn all this?"

"By keeping my ears open as I drive Field Marshal Haig and his toadies around the countryside. You're on your way to see the F.M. in Paris, aren't you?"

Bliss nodded, wondering if he was dealing with a German spy or a crazy woman. "Would you like to know what he's going to tell you?" Anita Sinclair asked.

"It might help," Bliss said.

"If you give him a half million men immediately, he'll guarantee to win the war by Christmas. At his side will be Brigadier Charteris, his chief of intelligence. He'll fill your heads with evidence that the Germans are about to collapse. It's all lies. Johnny Charteris hasn't told the truth in so long he's forgotten it even exists. If you believe them and hand over your men, I'll add Americans to my list of champions of stupidity."

"I guarantee you Jack Pershing will do his damnedest to stay off that list. Why are you telling me all this?"

"I want to get rid of Douglas Haig and his whole bloody crew of mass murderers. The only way to topple them is to deny them men. As long as he's got men he'll attack-attack-attack and the slaughter will go on. My father's in the cabinet. He's persuaded the Prime Minister to refuse to send Haig another man. But he's planning another offensive at Ypres anyway, betting he can embarrass the

P.M. or you Americans into giving him the cannon fodder."

"They have men in England?"

"There's a good half million sitting around the training camps right now, doing absolutely nothing."

On they roared toward Paris, slowing down only for the winding main streets of the villages, where chickens, pigs, and children made headlong speed impossible. In the sunbaked fields, old men and women and boys toiled on the summer's crops. There were no young men anywhere. Bliss had learned from his travels around France that all the young men were either in uniform or in the cemetery.

"Is the war solely responsible for these violent opinions? Or have Englishmen given you other reasons to despise them?" he asked Anita Sinclair. He decided not to believe most of what she had told him. The woman must be having a nervous breakdown— though he could not figure out how anyone with ruined nerves could drive like Barney Oldfield.

"I used to adore them," she said. "I was a typical romantic ideal- ist. Men were all Lancelots. I was going to be their Lady of Shalott. Then I went to Oxford and learned the history of women's oppres- sion. I became a suffrage fighter."

"One of those charmers who maim policemen and try to blow up Parliament?"

She smiled briefly, pleased that he knew the violent tendencies of the English suffragists. "Particularly reprehensible on my part because my father happens to be a member."

"Why did you let anything so trivial as a war interrupt you?"

"It was a larger vortex. I see life as a series of vortices, General: some larger, some smaller, all drawing one into their whirling interi- ors. The war's vortex dwarfs everything else by far. You'll find that out very soon."

She said this with an intensity Bliss felt as heat. He wanted to loosen his tie and wipe sweat from his forehead. Could this war become a vortex for a professional soldier? He rejected the idea. A professional kept his equilibrium. War did not swallow him; he mas- tered it in his mind. Bliss heard himself telling Polly Warden, *Brain- power, not manpower, is what wins wars.* Unfortunately he also saw the skepticism in her green eyes.

"What about love?" he asked Anita Sinclair. "Has that ever become a vortex?"

"An extremely minor one, General. What else can you expect, when all the men I might love are on my stupidity list? Sex is another matter. I'm quite fond of one-night stands. How about you?"

She kept her eyes on the road, mockery twisting her mouth into a semblance of a smile. "I've been persuaded in my time," Bliss muttered, amazed to find himself embarrassed.

"I've shocked you, haven't I? If I were a randy sergeant major and said that to you with a wink and an ooo-la-la, you'd laugh and nudge me in the ribs, maybe even ask me where I was getting it. I think you'll find out this war is changing everyone's morals, women's as well as men's. It's changing the whole world."

"I hope you're wrong," Bliss said. "I haven't been too good at keeping some of the commandments, but I'm a believer in the moral law. It's what holds the world together."

"Bosh. Greed holds the world together, greed and power and lust. That's what this war is all about. Germany wants England's wealth and power. They've lusted after it for a half century. It's a contest between rival greeds. You're over here because American greed is part of the British system. You've learned to imitate us perfectly."

"Where do the French fit into it?"

"They're like the innocent bystander in the Charlie Chaplin comedy, the poor bloke who gets clobbered by both sides. We drubbed them a hundred years ago; now the Germans are getting in their licks."

"Is this what they're teaching at Oxford these days?"

"Of course not. If I survive this beastly war, I intend to become a historian and refute most of the drivel they're teaching at Oxford. I'm going to tell the truth about the wars, the empire, the whole rotten greed-driven system."

"Why did you quit driving ambulances?"

The dark eyebrows contracted into a genuine frown. "I broke down. I reached my limit. Everyone reaches it eventually, except for generals. They go on giving their orders well behind the lines and let the poor sods in the lower ranks do the crying and dying."

"That's not how generals operate in the American army," Bliss said. He told her about the way Brigadier Pershing attacked Mount Bagsak on Jolo in a 1911 clash with the Moros. When an American captain was killed and his company of Filipino scouts teetered on panic that could have infected the whole battle line, Pershing took charge and led them up the slope, pistol in hand, ignoring the lead whistling around him.

"Did the Moros have any machine guns?" Anita Sinclair asked.

"No."

"The Germans have a great many machine guns. I think if General Pershing or you try that sort of heroics on the western front you'll die very quickly."

Bliss felt a chill creep up his spine. There was something sybil-like about this young woman. He found her prophecies, her violent judgments, as unnerving as her reckless driving. But they were too bizarre to be true. He started telling her how the Americans would win by creating open warfare. She laughed and laughed. "Haig said the same thing when he took command," she said. "What does General Peshing think of the machine gun?"

"I don't know," Bliss said, uneasily recalling Jack's insistence on the rifle and bayonet as the crucial weapons.

"Field Marshal Haig considers the machine gun a much over-rated weapon," Anita Sinclair said. "Of course he never goes near the front, so how would he know it accounts for fifty percent of his casualties?"

An hour later, Paris loomed ahead of them. The Eiffel Tower poked its odd metallic majesty into the sky, proclaiming modernity in the midst of monuments and buildings from the centuries when France was at her zenith. They drove through surprisingly empty streets to American headquarters on the Rue de Constantine—two three-story private houses with symmetrical nineteenth-century façades and green mansard roofs.

"There's the tomb of Napoleon," Anita Sinclair said, pointing to the huge gilded dome of the Church of the Invalides a few blocks away. "Everyone finds it rather amusing that the French have parked you here in the Faubourg Saint-Germain, the most reactionary section of Paris. You won't find many of your neighbors even slightly interested in making the world safe for democracy. Most of them want either a resurrection of old Boney—or Louis the Sixteenth."

"Thanks for the ride," Bliss said. "And the conversation."

"Good luck with the F.M.," she said.

Inside the houses, Bliss found Pershing's two-hundred-man staff shoehorned into everything from cellars to attics. There were even desks in the halls. A sentry directed him to Harry Quickmeyer's office on the first floor. Around Quickmeyer's waist and over his chest gleamed a Sam Browne belt, created by the English officer of that name in India and now part of their army's regulation uniform. "What's this?" Bliss said uneasily. "Have we joined the limeys?"

"Pershing's orders," Quickmeyer said. "A good idea. You can't get into a restaurant in our regulation uniform. We don't look like officers."

Bliss asked Quickmeyer to buy him two Sam Brownes as soon as possible. "How are things going with my old friend Louise?" he asked.

Quickmeyer smiled wryly. "She's introducing me to Paris. Me and the rest of the staff."

"Don't let her forget that night in Fort Myer. She was at least fifty percent sincere."

If anyone could tame Louise, Bliss would bet on this man. He had a nice combination of toughness and disillusion. "I'll keep that in mind, General. If there's anything left of my mind after she's through with it," Quickmeyer said.

Quickmeyer gave Bliss directions to Pershing's residence on the Rue de Varenne, a few blocks away. A sentry came to attention, and the captain of the guard escorted him through two courtyards to the white and gold foyer of the house. Quickmeyer had called the place a palace and he was right. A marble staircase worthy of Versailles spiraled to the upper floors. The furniture had the sleek slim antiquity of the eighteenth century, with its inlaid woods and brilliant finishes. The American millionaire Ogden Mills had given it to Pershing for the duration.

Major James Collins, Pershing's diminutive senior aide, better known as "Little," parked Bliss in one of the ornate sitting rooms.

Five minutes later, Pershing stalked in, wearing a burnished Sam Browne belt. He looked thinner and grimmer. He had little interest in small talk. "Have you got things straightened out in Saint-Nazaire?" he growled.

"The town is as quiet as a Trappist monastery," Bliss said.

"General Viomenil was in Paris the other day. He was telling everyone he paid a surprise visit to your campgrounds. A sentry challenged him. When he identified himself, the guy bummed a cigarette and gave Viomenil his rifle while he lit up."

"That's absolute bunk!" Bliss roared.

"If I visit your outfit and a sentry does that, you'll be on your way home on the next boat."

All Bliss's resentments against Pershing's domineering, discipline-driven style danced around his head. He had walked in eager to tell him what he had heard from Anita Sinclair. Now he wondered why he should tell this son of a bitch anything.

With no warning, Pershing shifted from anger to an emotion Bliss could not quite identify. The hard edges of his face seemed to soften. His voice reached out to Bliss as a friend, not a commander. "Whether Viomenil is telling the truth or not is irrelevant. He's part of the dirty game they're playing, Mal. They want to make us look ridiculous, then take all the credit for turning our men into soldiers and grab them for their armies. We can't let them get away with it."

"The British are playing the same game?"

"More or less. But in a different way."

"What am I supposed to say to these characters?"

"I'll handle the hard stuff. Just sing along in the same key. Remember, we're stalling for time. We've only got two divisions over here. We need a minimum of ten before we can call ourselves an army."

"How long will it take to get them here?"

"At least six months. Maybe a year."

"Good Christ! One way or another Woodrow and Tasker are going to screw you yet, Jack."

A knock on the door; Field Marshal Sir Douglas Haig, commander in chief of the British army, and his chief of intelligence, Brigadier John Charteris, had arrived. Haig came toward them with a ponderous, authoritative stride. He had a big bulky body and a large head, which gave him a kind of accumulated force as he approached. His mouth was virtually covered by a wide brown mustache, focusing attention on his small hard eyes. Charteris was more elegantly constructed, slim and tall with a leading man's brush mustache and a mouth that seemed balanced between a smile and a sneer.

"France has not yet arrived?" Charteris said, as they sat down.

"Good," Haig said. "Perhaps we can have some intelligent conversation."

The conversation consisted of listening to Brigadier Charteris tell them the "exciting news" his intelligence staff had learned about the German army on the British front. There was dramatic evidence they were close to collapse. Division, regiment, and company size had been reduced to conceal manpower shortages. Recent captives were underfed morose conscripts as young as sixteen. Charteris's effortless flow of words, backed by numerous documents, was impressive—and might have convinced Bliss, if Anita Sinclair had not warned him he was dealing with one of the champion liars of the century.

Groping for a way to listen without really hearing anything, Bliss focused on the way the brigadier said "extraordinary." He simultaneously expelled and swallowed the word. "'Strawdnry." Maybe it was the key to telling lies with absolute aplomb.

"Little" Collins announced that General Henri Pétain, commander in chief of the French army, had arrived. He came equipped with a mustache even larger than Haig's, leaving Bliss with the feeling that he and Pershing were almost naked. He always wanted to see a man's mouth as well as his eyes when he talked with him. The Frenchman was short and seemed to wear a permanent scowl on his pouchy, weary face. He had an interpreter with him, a wizened colonel who looked equally weary.

Pétain asked Haig if he was going through with his plans for an offensive in the Ypres salient. "Absolutely," Haig said. "Our artillery has already wreaked havoc on the Hun's forward defenses. By this time next week, when our infantry goes forward, we expect to have him reeling."

Bliss had not heard such fustian since his last conversation with Douglas Fairchild. He thought he saw skepticism—and something else, perhaps contempt—in Pétain's veined eyes. "I hope you can attack without unacceptable losses," he said.

"We don't fight for *la gloire*. We fight to win," Haig said.

Bliss could hardly believe his ears. Pétain's eyes smoldered. That brought the Field Marshal to the purpose of this meeting as he saw it. He wanted to put Bliss's division—and the First Division, which had arrived two weeks ahead of the Lafayettes—into the trenches on the British front. They would be the vanguard of 500,000 Americans, who should be shipped to Flanders as fast as possible. He had persuaded the Admiralty to free up the transports to get them to Europe. The British would train them on the tactical level and integrate them into their companies. With this infusion of fresh men, he was confident he could smash through the Ypres salient, turn the German flank, and force them out of their trenches into open warfare, where they could be mauled by his cavalry reserve. "With your cooperation, General Pershing," Haig said, "I can end the war by Christmas."

Bliss sat transfixed, not by the prospect of ending the war but by the smug way he had dismissed Anita Sinclair's information. Everything she had predicted was coming true, including Haig's fondness for open warfare.

Pétain's translator murmured in his ear while Haig was speaking. The moment the Field Marshal paused, the French commander hurled a veritable hurricane of syntax at Pershing and Bliss. The translator struggled to keep up with him. "It seems inconceivable to General Pétain and to the people of France that the British—who occupy a front only a third the length of the French army's—can have the audacity to demand American men. To make the insult more atrocious, Britain has over a million men in the Middle East, in Africa, in Asia, defending her empire, while France sustains the brunt of the war. It is France whose country is being despoiled by the modern barbarians. We insist on the Americans serving in our sector of the front. But we agree with General Haig that it will not be necessary to organize the American forces as divisions or armies. Regiments will easily function as the unit of integration with the soldiers of France. We have a cadre of interpreters to serve as liaison officers to communicate orders in battle."

A vein in Pershing's forehead began to pulse. His hands balled into fists in his lap. Haig had just told him Americans above the rank of sergeant were superfluous. Pétain was telling him that Americans above the rank of colonel were superfluous. "General Bliss," Jack said. "How would your troops react if they were told that the division would be broken up and units integrated with the British or French army?"

Bliss solemnly declared they would have a mutiny in his Irish-American regiment if they were shoveled into the British army piecemeal. Given a choice, they would rather fight the English than the Germans. The rest of the division would be almost as unbalanced. The South Carolina regiment, for instance, found it difficult to take orders from someone born north of the Mason-Dixon line. He dreaded how they might react to foreigners.

Brigadier Charteris thought Bliss's assertions were "'Strawdnry." After all, the British army had integrated Canadians, Australians, New Zealanders, and South Africans into its ranks. Why not Americans?

"It may strike you as extraordinary, Brigadier, but Americans are different from Canadians, Australians, New Zealanders, and South Africans," Bliss said.

"General Pershing," Haig said, pretending Bliss had ceased to exist. "I wish to make it clear that this proposal is not simply my idea. It is supported at the highest levels of His Majesty's government. If my offensive falls short of its goals because we run out of reserves, a great many people in England may blame you. The consequences to your reputation, your career, could be grave."

"Isn't it possible, Field Marshal Haig, that other people may blame the politicians who are keeping half a million men in England because they've lost confidence in you?" Bliss said.

"I don't know where you got that information," Haig said. "I can only assure you it is completely erroneous."

"Completely!" Brigadier Charteris shrilled.

The earthquake in Britannia's aplomb made it clear that Anita Sinclair had again told the truth. Pershing was looking at Bliss with new warmth in his eyes. Maybe he had gotten off Jack's shit list. "I've had General Bliss scouring France for training sites," he said. "Tell us why you think it would be best for the American *army* to train in Lorraine, Mal."

Bliss discoursed on how difficult it would be to supply an American *army* through the channel ports used by the British, whereas, in Lorraine, the American *army* could be maintained by food and ammunition flowing through Saint-Nazaire and nearby ports, which were underused at present. He worked the word army into his presentation at least eight times. It was hard to tell whether that or his preference for Lorraine, where the French would be in charge of training the Americans, infuriated the Field Marshal more.

"How soon do you estimate your men will be ready to fight?" Pershing asked.

"Four months," Bliss said.

"In four months you'll be able to take over a sector of the front and confront the Germans with no support?" Haig sneered.

"I'll expect some support on my flanks," Bliss said.

"This of course you will have, on the honor of France," Pétain said.

"General Pershing," Haig said, "rather than reply to the aspersions General Pétain has cast on my nation's honor, may I ask you, as a commander with a sense of responsibility for the welfare and morale of your soldiers, how you can consider allowing them to be trained by an army that has on its escutcheon a mutiny so recent and so atrocious it threatened the entire conduct of the war? Let me add that this mutiny was brought on by a theory of generalship so inane and so ignorant it beggars description. I am speaking of the French army's so-called school of attack, which maintains a febrile reliance on élan, esprit, instead of the methodical preparations of artillery, the integration of tactics and strategy."

Pétain rose, a dour stump of authority. He admitted the French army had made horrendous mistakes. "Every army has its fools and madmen," he said. "I can assure General Pershing that they are no longer in control of the French army." He paused and studied Haig and Charteris with breathtaking contempt. "Field Marshal Haig cannot make such a statement."

Haig looked as if he might swallow his mustache. Bliss decided he liked Henri Pétain. "Gentlemen, gentlemen," Pershing said. "It distresses me to find myself the cause of so much antagonism between allies."

"Don't let it trouble your conscience, General Pershing," Haig said, glaring at Pétain. "The antagonism has always been there, and it will continue to roil our alliance as long as France considers herself the first power in Europe—with no basis whatsoever for that fact."

Bliss found himself wishing his chair had an arm so he could steady himself. *These are our* allies? The Germans could not hate them half as much as they hated each other.

Pétain directed another volley of French at Pershing. "The General wishes to know if he understands correctly that General Pershing rejects the idea of integrating regiments into French divisions. Will American troops fight only as divisions?" his interpreter gasped.

The General was still trying to acquire the Americans. He could give orders to divisions as easily as to regiments.

"Only as an American *army*," Pershing said.

Pétain fired another volley. The sweating interpreter informed them that the General would try to find a part of the French front suitable for the Lafayette Division the moment it completed its training. With that, France departed. Haig and Charteris contemplated Bliss with grave disappointment. "Do you speak French, General?" Charteris asked.

"No," Bliss lied.

"That's probably just as well. You'll miss the more atrocious insults."

Haig turned to Pershing. "As one soldier to another, I fear you're making a serious mistake. I also fear this won't be the last time we have this conversation."

"Are you going ahead with your offensive, Field Marshal?" Bliss asked.

"Absolutely. Though our frog-eating friend would never admit it, if we don't, the Germans will shift their reserves south and annihilate what's left of the French army. Do you realize, at the height of the mutiny, there was only one division willing to fight?"

Bliss and Pershing could only shudder.

"Even now, in order to keep them in the ranks, Pétain has agreed to grant the poilus so much leave time, no less than thirty percent of his army is hors de combat on any given day, either on trains going to or from the front or at home diddling their wives and girlfriends," Charteris fumed.

"And he has the gall—I choose the word advisedly—to accuse us of doing only a third of the fighting!" Haig rumbled.

Britannia departed. "Where the hell did you get that information about the half million men in England?" Jack asked.

Bliss told him about Anita Sinclair. "Maybe you ought to keep in touch with that girl," Pershing said.

Jack stared down at his clenched fists. Was he wishing he'd used them on Haig and Pétain? "We're going to win this thing, Mal," he said. "We're going to win it."

"Of course we're going to win it," Bliss said, concealing his alarm. Jack did not look or sound like a winner. "I didn't come to Europe to take orders from the limeys or the frogs. I came to take them from John J. Pershing."

Pershing's head rose. The fists unclenched. His jaw reacquired its iron jut. " 'Strawdnry," Bliss said.

"What?" Pershing said.

"It's the key to dealing with the Brits, Jack: learning how to say 'strawdnry the way they do. It'll stop them cold. I'm going to practice it and teach it to you. Then we'll figure out what to say to the frogs."

"Crazy bastard," Pershing said, almost smiling.

The smile faded before it reached Jack's lips. The crisis was too serious for humor, especially Imperfect Bliss's maniacal brand. Pershing reverted to his First Captain personality. "Remember what I said about discipline in that goddamn division!"

"I'll brand the word on my undershorts. In the meantime, let me give you some serious advice. Get the hell out of this part of town. Maybe even get out of Paris. Parking you here with the millionaires and what's left of the ancien régime is part of their plan to make you look silly."

"I've been having similar thoughts," Pershing said.

Little Collins stood at the door, a cable in his hand. "General. I thought you ought to see this immediately."

Pershing read it and handed it to Bliss.

GENERAL TASKER H. BLISS IS RETIRING AS CHIEF OF STAFF ON OCTOBER 1. I AM SENDING HIM TO FRANCE AS MY PERSONAL REPRESENTATIVE. HE WILL HELP YOU DEAL WITH POLITICAL ASPECTS OF THE DIFFICULT SITUATION YOU CONFRONT. I AM SURE YOU WILL WORK TOGETHER WITH THE UTMOST FRATERNITY AND CORDIALITY. WOODROW WILSON.

"Got any ideas on a word that will help us deal with Tasker?"

"Bullshit," Bliss said.

15. *PARIS MON AMOUR*

THEY RACED TOWARD PARIS LIKE FUGITIVES. THE motorcycle's thunder made conversation impossible. With goggles on his somber face, Paul Lebrun had a vaguely satanic look. In the swaying sidecar Polly Warden felt like baggage. Was it really happening? Had she abandoned her never?

It was the camion. She might have kept resisting the *cafard* of the surgical ward. But no one could survive the *cafard* of the camion.

A truck fitted out as an operating room, the camion was driven into the front-line trenches and the most badly wounded poilus, men who would not survive a trip to the Château Givry or even to an aid station a mile or two behind the lines, were dealt with by its surgical team. Moaning men mutilated by high explosives, without legs, arms, faces, genitals, were flung on the camion's table. The camion itself was armor-plated against shrapnel, but it could not withstand a direct hit by the heavier German guns. Three doctors and their nurses had already been killed working this way. The French army thought it was worth the price and sent a new camion to the sector each time the old one was destroyed.

Paul had volunteered for the camion and asked Polly with elaborate courtesy if she wished to transfer to another surgeon. Of course she had furiously insisted on going with him. It had been one of the camion's worst weeks. They broke the previous record for amputations. The truck was repeatedly bracketed by German artillery. Once a midnight German raid was beaten back by machine guns and hand grenades only yards away. The water-filled trenches full of rats as big as cats, the blasted treeless moonscape of no-man's-land, surrounded them with *cafard* as suffocating as poison gas. At the end of the week, Paul only had to whisper *Paris?* and Polly bowed her head in silent acquiescence.

As the city loomed in the distance, she told herself there was still time to say no. Eleanor Kingswood was in Paris. Eleanor and Martha Herzog. She could pick up a telephone and call them. She could hail a taxi and ride to the house on the Rue de Verneuil and recover her New York self any time she chose.

Polly knew she would do none of these things. She had crossed the border into Paul Lebrun's country, the desolated, defeat-racked France she could no longer deny. Her mother would denounce her; even Eleanor and Martha, raised in proper New York, would be dismayed. But proper New York and the United States of America were childish places and her mother was an infantile foreigner compared to the men and women of the country where *cafard* was king.

In Paris they drove swiftly down the empty boulevards and climbed the narrow streets of Montmartre. The white dome of Sacre Coeur cathedral loomed over them, dwarfing everything with its pretentious sanctity. Before a café called Les Trois Magots, Lebrun parked the motorcycle and helped Polly out of the sidecar. Magot meant many things in French: a baboon, an ugly or deformed person, a hidden treasure.

In the dim interior a harsh French voice called, "The mad doctor is back! Is this one of your patients?"

The voice belonged to the proprietor, behind the bar: a man who wore clown's makeup on his face. It was dead white, except for blue patches beneath his eyes, a yellow nose, wide red lips. Lebrun introduced Polly to Richelieu, also known as the Cardinal. "He's a poet who lost both legs on the Marne in 1914. Show her your croix de guerre, your eminence."

With a gasp Polly realized Richelieu was only half a man. He was strapped to a stool from which his long arms could reach every bottle in the small bar. He pulled a decanter of liquid off a shelf behind him. The croix de guerre, with its crossed swords and red and blue ribbons, floated in the middle of it. On the label was scrawled: *Do not drink: piss.*

There were half a dozen other customers at the bar. All were mutilated: one lacked a hand, another a leg, another a jaw. One man, whom everyone called Jean Valjean after the hero of Victor Hugo's novel *Les Misérables*, was blind. He asked Lebrun to describe their American visitor.

"She has the eyes of an angel before the world was created and God's clumsiness became apparent. Her russet hair would tempt Satan to bargain away his kingdom. Her mouth wears the inquiring innocence of Eve before she met the serpent. For the rest, only one word is necessary: Venus."

"Be glad you don't have eyes, Valjean. You'd circle her like a tormented moon forever," Richelieu said.

Cafard. All these men were believers in this strange new faith. They mocked the old faiths in its name. Beneath the mockery Polly sensed something dark and ominous. It crouched in the shadowy corners of Les Trois Magots, lurked in the painted smile on Richelieu's clown face.

"Sometimes I dream of harnessing the powers this war has unleashed: the hatred, the envy, the regret," Paul Lebrun said. "Converted into energy, it could annihilate all the kings and presidents and prime ministers of this world."

"It will happen soon in Russia," Richelieu said. "The bourgeoisie is tottering. The men of action, the Bolsheviks, are coming to the fore."

They drank a toast to "the Communards." To them the Bolsheviks were the descendants of the men and women who had been slaughtered by the French army when they seized Paris for a few months after the Germans defeated France in 1870. Richelieu gave Polly a copy of a newspaper, the *Bonnet Rouge*, which predicted the coming revolution in Russia would soon spread to France. He said the *Rouge* was the poilus' favorite paper.

Customers began arriving for dinner. The women wore the latest Paris dresses, which boldly advertised the female body with an absolute minimum of puffs and tucks. The men had the comfortable well-fed look of financiers and politicians, the two classes who were profiting most from the war. There was a scattering of American officers, some with women in Red Cross and YWCA uniforms. Paul Lebrun explained that Les Trois Magots had become popular for the entertainment it served with the food. Richelieu had set many of his poems to music. He called them *chansons de guerre*, war songs. But they were not ordinary war songs. "He didn't choose the name Richelieu by accident," Paul said. "He wants to rule France."

At a table in the darkest, most private corner, they dined on sweetbreads. Lebrun insisted they had to abandon Apollinaris water for a bottle of Bordeaux. Polly's head was swimming when the blind man, Jean Valjean, tapped his way into a cleared space in the center of the restaurant and introduced himself. His assumed name got a laugh. His shrill voice and bewildered timidity made him the total opposite of the indomitable Hugo hero of *Les Misérables*.

"We are here to celebrate the war, my friends, the famous war that extinguished my sight and altered the bodies of so many of my friends and relations. For your entertainment I present France's newest troubadour, Richelieu!"

Two of the mutilated drinkers carried Richelieu to the center of the room, strapped to his bar stool. Above him they unfurled the banner of Les Trois Magots: three baboons who saw no evil, heard no evil, and spoke no evil. Richelieu had a small accordion in his hands.

As Richelieu riffled some introductory notes, Eleanor Kingswood and Colonel Douglas Fairchild were escorted to a table a few feet away from them. Eleanor was wearing a blue and white YWCA uniform. They held hands on the tabletop and gazed into each other's eyes with desperate intensity.

Richelieu riffled his accordion again and sang in a husky atonal voice:

"Yesterday we invented a new weapon.
We expect it to devastate our enemies.
It is a woman with the body of a lion
And the voice of a hyena.

Her breath is as fatal as mustard gas.
Her eyes are death rays.
She has fangs that can tear out a heart,
Claws that can lacerate a soul.

Call her Saint Joan, call her Antoinette,
Call her mother, sister, wife.
She is our patron saint,
The queen of life and death.

She is also a bitch, a cow, a slut,
A vampire who sucks our blood
And screws the Pope and calls it paradise.
With her beside us in the trenches

This war becomes impossible to lose."

The audience applauded wildly. Eleanor, whose French was minimal, asked Fairchild what it was about. "He's making fun of the war," Fairchild said, "and sneering at women. This place should be shut down. It's subversive! I'll be damned if they get any of my money."

He seized Eleanor's arm and they worked their way through the jammed tables while Richelieu sang about his friend, the poilu named Perfect, who is hated by all the men in his regiment because he obeys every order and they are forced to imitate him. Eventually they are all dead except Richelieu and Perfect. Richelieu shoots Perfect. The ghosts of his dead comrades rise up to condemn the murder.

Colonel Fairchild was right, Polly thought. Richelieu and his fellow *magots* were subversive. They undermined everything that sustains a nation at war—heroism and obedience, love and duty. She only half understood why Paul had taken her here. It had something to do with *cafard*, but she sensed another purpose.

Paul's hand seized her arm. "There's my father," he said. A large middle-aged man with a haughty nose and an enormously self-assured smile was being seated at the table Eleanor and Colonel Fairchild had just abandoned. With him was a stunningly beautiful dark-haired young woman in a green silk dress. "That's his mistress, Annette," Paul said. The waiters added chairs and an extra table and two young French officers joined them, with two women almost as beautiful as Annette. "My brothers, Charles and Louis," Paul said.

"I told them we'd meet them here. But we're not going to speak to them. I just wanted you to see them."

Paul told Polly his father was one of the richest men in France, the King of the Bourse. He was the secret backer of the Trois Magots. He and certain friends in the government were working to promote peace with the Germans, a peace Paul feared would leave France defeated and disgraced. His brothers were what the poilus call *embusqués*—soldiers who never went near the trenches. "Study their faces," Paul said. "See the corruption, the egotism, the selfishness. They've become creatures of the abyss."

Waiters poured champagne and the maître d' hovered while Paul's father pointed imperiously to items on the menu. Richelieu was singing "Sacrament," in which he pretended to confess his sins to Jean Valjean. Each sin was a different form of cowardice. He was afraid of German planes, artillery, machine guns, and bayonets. He was even more afraid of French planes, artillery, machine guns, and bayonets.

The Lebruns and their women laughed delightedly. They seemed to have crossed the country of *cafard* to another even more mysterious land, where everything was mockery and cynicism. How had Paul escaped them?

"Shall we go upstairs?" Paul said. "Sometimes he sings until dawn."

Now was the moment, perhaps the final moment, to resurrect her never. Polly told herself if Eleanor had stayed she would have called out to her. She would have flung herself into the arms of friendship, the fiery circle of Douglas Fairchild's righteous American indignation.

They mounted a stairs behind the bar. Richelieu's droning songs, his wry accordion, receded. They were in a garret with a sloping roof and a double bed. "I promised I'd take nothing that you would not freely give me," Lebrun said. "But if you say no I must ask your permission to find another woman."

"Who is she?" Polly said dazedly.

"Anyone I meet on the street. I'll close my eyes and imagine she's you. I did it the last two times I came to Paris."

"No!" Polly said, thinking of the blank-eyed automatons at the Maison Blanche. "But you should understand—I'm not a magical creature—"

"I only understand how much I need you."

Polly pressed her lips against that tormented mouth. "Take me," she whispered. "Take me for whatever you can find in my soul."

"We must get beyond thought, beyond lies and truths," Paul whispered. "Fill me with your purity, your tenderness, your pity."

A series of thunderous crashes shook the building. A siren wailed. Searchlights probed the midnight sky. "Gothas," Paul said.

Crashes of a different kind: French antiaircraft guns. Yellow and orange flames flickered in the city below them. If there had been any possibility of resurrecting her never, this air raid ended it. They were back in the Château Givry, waging their nightly struggle against death while the bombs fell around them. Madame Leclerc's bitter mouth hissed, *He's worth ten of you, a hundred of me*. Verlaine whispered across the operating table, *De la douceur, de la douceur, de la douceur*. Sweetness, oh, the sweetness! The sweetness!

"Will you weep if I break my promises in the dawn?" Paul said.

"Yes. But it doesn't matter," Polly said. "I love you."

Trembling, she let him undress her and lead her to the double bed beneath the eaves. The only light came from the searchlights probing the sky for the Gotha bombers, the occasional flash of an explosion.

Paul's hands caressed her breasts, her thighs. She saw the long menacing fingers in her memory; she remembered what they explored in the bodies of the wounded. They seemed to have a separate existence on death's borderland. Polly shuddered and kissed him again. The fingers found the soft flesh between her thighs and sent waves of sweetness singing through her body.

He was naked now, beside her in the cold bed. He placed her hand on his penis. It was soft, as flaccid as those she saw when she stripped the wounded poilus. Slowly, irrevocably, it swelled and stiffened in her warm palm.

The searchlights flooded the window with vanilla light. The Gothas droned overhead, the bombs crunched, the antiaircraft guns thundered. Polly found herself desperately explaining it to someone, everyone: her mother, Eleanor, Martha. It was the war, engulfing her. The war and *cafard*. Was there a face at that flickering window? A watcher who deplored this irreversible act? George Eagleton?

The voice of the new woman who had defied George's sneers and threats awoke in Polly's throat. This was not deplorable. This was an act of courage, a woman's courage, a woman's war against *cafard*. There was only one man who might understand it: the strange general with the somber eyes, Malvern Hill Bliss, who said she was one of them, one of the fraternity of the brave, the soldiers.

The mystic medical fingers were inside her body now, probing the web of tissue, the last vestige of her *never*. "*N'es-tu pas l'oasis où je rêve?*" Lebrun whispered.

Baudelaire: Aren't you the oasis where I dream?

No, no, Polly thought. It was too extravagant. He was translating her into poetry when she wanted to be meaningful prose. But it was too late for *never*, too late to whisper regretful words to anyone. Paul's manhood was a thrusting presence.

Polly wanted it to be painful; she disdained the very idea of pleasure. But there was only a momentary twinge, like a cut finger or scraped knee in childhood, and he entered that place she strove to see as ordinary, natural, words that demythologized women, denied the male mysticism that simultaneously exalted and entrapped them.

But Polly could not deny what happened next, the surging tides of sweetness, oceans of it, filling her with exaltation and surrender as Lebrun's manhood began to move slowly, possessively within her.

"*Élan insensé et infini aux splendeurs invisibles, aux délices insensibles,*" he whispered.

Rimbaud: Insensate and infinite flight toward invisible splendors, toward immaterial delights.

The exotic words and those surges of sweetness were abolishing everything, her resolve to remain rational Polly Warden, to stay in touch with her prose self, her real feelings. She was being transformed into a creature of ecstasy and mystery by France, Paris, bombs, *cafard*.

"Les brasiers et le écumes. La musique, virement des gouffres, et chocs des glaçons aux astres."

Embers and foam. Music, veerings of chasms, and shock of icicles against the stars.

Rimbaud again. Perhaps only a madman who thought poetry had the power to transcend existence could speak for them.

The surges mounted in intensity, becoming a huge wave rolling toward a great cliff face fronting a landscape of unbearable beauty, an Edenic opposite of the seared world of no-man's-land. *"Douceurs!"* Paul cried as the wave exploded into a million drops of golden foam. They shimmered around Polly and within her, they filled the sky with ten thousand new stars, they emanated music beyond sound and poetry beyond words, they coalesced into an aureole that protected them from evil and pain forever.

Slowly, inexorably, the golden globules ebbed. Polly saw them flowing into a dark abyss: the sea, the night, the uncaring earth. Soon they were back in the real world of a garret above Les Trois Magots. Searchlights probed the sky beyond the window. An antiaircraft gun crashed one last time and fell silent. Below them the audience applauded another Richelieu war song.

"You must douche," Lebrun said. "We don't want a child. Not yet."

The voice was so calm, so clinical, it struck Polly like a blow. She had to remind herself he was a doctor. Behind drawn curtains on the opposite side of the room was a bathtub and a toilet. He ran water in the tub and helped her into it. From the wall he plucked a pink bag, resembling a hot water bottle, and a long tube. He filled the bag with water and some powder, then inserted the tube calmly, efficiently, into her vagina. He held the bag over her head and the irrigation began. He smiled down at her and toyed with her left nipple. *"Douceur,"* he murmured. But it was only an echo of his passionate cry.

Still dazed, shimmering, glowing, Polly realized she did not like this anticlimax. It was hard to deny its necessity. She certainly did not want to become a pregnant proof of her mother's—and General Pershing's—worst expectations. But she still did not like it.

Paul sensed her emotion. "Science is the enemy of love," he said.

The bag was empty, the irrigation complete. He turned on the water again. "Now bathe without my intrusion," he said. "A second irrigation does no harm. From now on, you can do both without me, don't you think?"

Polly lay in the steaming water for a long time, looking up at the douche bag on the wall. She was probably not the first woman to use it. What did she expect? This was France. She still did not like it. But what did her likes and dislikes have to do with it—with anything? she wondered, remembering that explosion of gold, that glimpse of Eden.

Paul drew back the curtains. Polly stepped from the tub to be wrapped in an oversize towel. He dried her as if she were a five-year-old, tied a woolen robe around her, and poured them glasses of cognac. "Now we must discuss the future," he said. "Where you will live between my visits. My mother owns a comfortable house near Auvers in the Île-de-France, south of Paris. It's closed at the moment, but it can easily be reopened and servants hired from the village. It's a place of beauty and peace. From the second-floor window you can see the steeple of the village church, rising above the trees like the voice of hope."

Paul had turned on only a single small lamp above the bathtub. Polly was grateful for the semidarkness; it concealed her amazement. "I don't understand," she said.

"You can't go back to the hospital," Paul said. "It was already coarsening your sensibility. A woman can't expose her soul to that kind of horror without becoming like Leclerc, an empty shell of embitterment."

"But a man can?" Polly said.

"A man must," Paul said. "But even he can't face it without the kind of redemption you offered me tonight."

"But—I want to go back," Polly said. "I want to share it with you. I want to face it as long as you face it."

"There are a thousand peasant girls like Marie Ribout who can replace you—and probably work harder with less risk of a breakdown. If patriotism is your motive, we'll find an American."

Polly struggled to grasp what he was saying. It was as if he had lapsed into some incomprehensible foreign language, like Hungarian. She felt entangled by what she was hearing, dragged toward some dark cavern or woods full of nameless dread. Everything in her body sang Yes, yes, take me into the darkness with you. But her mind reached out, groping for something to stop the abduction.

"I insist on going back!" she said. "I didn't come to France to be parked in some country house like a courtesan from the ancien régime."

"The anciens understood women!" Paul said. "They let them rule behind the scenes, where their delicacy, their wonder, their mystery remained undefiled."

"How will I rule you when I'm in Auvers and you're sixty miles away suturing stomachs?"

"You rule me already. If you turn your face away from me I won't go back. I'll stay here until I drown in absinthe. It's a good death compared to the ones we see at the hospital."

"I'll never turn my face away from you," Polly said. "But I have to go back."

Beyond the glow of the lamp, Paul seemed to condense into a knife blade of darkness. "I can't believe it. Behind that innocence, that radiance, lurks a modern woman."

Polly was staggered—and bewildered. How could a man of compassion with a heart full of poetry say such a thing? "A woman. Simply a woman," she said, flinging herself against him. "A woman who loves you. A woman who's sworn to defeat *le cafard* in your name."

"Go to bed," he said, thrusting her arms away from him. He hurled his empty cognac glass into the fireplace and left her standing forlornly in the center of the room. As his footsteps thudded on the stairs, Polly heard the screech of Richelieu's accordion, the beginning of another war song. *"Laissez-moi décrire ma saison en enfer."* Let me tell you about my season in hell.

16. DREAMS OF
LOVE AND GLORY

GENERAL JOHN J. PERSHING REQUESTS THE PLEA-sure of your company for dinner at his residence at 73 rue de Varenne at 6 p.m. on Wednesday, August 15, 1917.

The invitation had been radiating excitement on Louise Wellington Wolcott's bureau for a week. She dressed with excruciating care, trying on and discarding two dozen gowns to the exhaustion and irritation of her maid, Nanette. Finally Nanette made up her mind for her. "*Voilà!*" she said, as Louise pirouetted slowly before her full-length mirror in a clinging white lamé dinner dress by Madeleine Vionnet, the current queen of Paris fashion.

Nanette was right. The color gave her a virginal aura. Something told her from the fuss Pershing had made over that snip Polly Warden and her friends on the *Baltic* that he liked girlish women. She chose a white cloche, white gloves, shoes, stockings, purse. She was going to emanate purity, innocence.

Great shafts of fading August sunlight filled the streets of the Faubourg-Saint-Germain as Louise rode from her house on the Rue du Bac to Pershing's residence. Church bells boomed six o'clock as her chauffeur turned down the Rue de Varenne.

"Wait, Michel!" Louise decided it was a mistake to be on time. That suggested a certain eagerness, the very thing that would disenchant a man who was being pursued—literally or in imagination—by every woman in Paris.

She told Michel to drive around the Faubourg for a while. She wondered if Harry Quickmeyer would be at the dinner. Last night she had taken him to a bedroom in the Gare du Nord. It was a perfect way to remind him of the temporary nature of their love. Stupendous statues, symbols of continents and cities, guarded the immense windows. They had made love between the ankles of a masculine Africa and a feminine Marseilles while below them trains departed for Amiens and Audenarde and Ypres, where British soldiers were dying by the tens of thousands.

For a moment Louise let *made love* flutter in her mind like a toy plane. The phrase was unquestionably invented by a man. They thought they could create love in women's souls as inevitably as they manufactured babies in their bodies. But Harry Quickmeyer was finding out this was no longer the case. He was unquestionably intriguing, this soldier with the saturnine hawkish face. She liked the way his mouth melted from a harsh slit to a crafty, skeptical smile. It seemed to strike a musical note somewhere within her.

Still circling the Rue de Varenne, Michel cruised across the Place Vauban. Louise gazed idly up at the Church of the Dome of the Invalides, built for the kings of France in the seventeenth century, now the tomb of Napoleon. The great bands of gold on the dome gleamed magically in the fading light. "Stop!" Louise said. It was the perfect place to prepare for dinner with the commander of the American Expeditionary Force.

Beneath the three-hundred-foot-high dome, in a crypt of exactly the same circular dimensions, lay the man who was synonymous with military power and glory. The red porphyry sarcophagus rested on a base of green granite. Around it stood statues of twelve blank-eyed goddesses of victory with swords on their shoulders. Louise imagined herself as one of these angelic presences, presiding over the triumphs of John J. Pershing.

The church was practically deserted. Behind her Louise heard a man's heavy footsteps. A tall American officer, a colonel, spread his hands on the marble railing and gazed intensely at the sarcophagus. It was Douglas Fairchild, the self-proclaimed idealist with the stuffed dragon of a mother she had met at Fort Myer and danced with several times aboard the *Baltic*. He was young for a colonel and handsome in a classic American way: a firm, slightly cleft chin, a powerful nose, a broad furrowed brow beneath his visored cap.

"Are you here in search of inspiration, Colonel?" Louise said.

"Mrs. Wolcott!" he said. He seemed unnecessarily wary, defensive. "You might call it inspiration. But I hope you won't mention it to your friend Quickmeyer."

"Why not?"

"He'd never let me forget it."

Louise shrugged. "What's wrong with it?"

Wariness remained paramount. "Are you still looking for your soldier of the ideal?"

"In a way," she said, wary herself now. There was an unpleasant streak of sarcasm in his tone.

"I can't believe you've found him in Quickmeyer. There isn't an ideal drop of blood in his body."

The intensity of his antagonism fascinated her. He was pouring scorn on the man who had held her in his arms last night and volunteered to become the soldier she claimed to be seeking.

"Let me make up my own mind about Major Quickmeyer. Did you find anything here before I interrupted your meditation?"

His manner softened from wariness to embarrassment. She sensed he found it difficult to speak personally to a woman—perhaps to anyone. "I suppose you could draw a moral from his career. A man who was too ambitious. A soldier who never knew when to say enough."

"That's a history lesson. I mean the whole thing. The church. Those guardians. The tomb."

"I'd like to know what you found," he said, unexpectedly disarming her.

For a moment she floundered, then plunged. "It's a kind of defiance of defeat and death...."

She hesitated, groping for the rest of her thought. He finished it for her. "A statement of the way a soldier can become the nation. Can sum it up in his life, his soul."

"Yes," she said. "Maybe that's the essence of *la gloire*. Is that what you came here to find?"

"I've found it—thanks to you."

She asked him if he had been in battle. "A few skirmishes in the Philippines and Mexico. Nothing like the war they're fighting beyond the Marne."

"You haven't felt *la gloire?*"

"I've felt it in my mind. At West Point I lived in Robert E. Lee's old room. I felt it—felt him—all around me. Not many Americans understand the feeling any more. The ones who felt it in our Civil War—the Confederates—lost."

They both pondered the gleaming sarcophagus for a moment. The conversation was having a weird effect on Louise. Her voice sounded strange in her ears, blurred and throaty. Was it the setting or the intensity of the Colonel's gaze?

"May I buy you a coffee or an apéritif?" he said.

"A splendid idea. I could use some inner reinforcement. I have a dinner date with the new Napoleon, General Pershing."

"What a coincidence. So do I."

They found a sidewalk café on the Rue Cambon, on the other side of the Seine. He asked her why she was in Paris. "It's my home," she said. "I just bought a house on my favorite street, the Rue du Bac. Madame de Staël lived there. Do you know anything about her?"

"Wasn't she the mistress of one of the kings?"

"She was more a writer than anyone's mistress, though she had lovers. She attacked Napoleon in one of her books, and he sent her into exile. It was torment for her because she adored Paris. She had plenty of money, a comfortable house in Switzerland, beautiful views. She said she'd exchange it all for the gutter of the Rue du Bac."

Colonel Fairchild could only shake his head in bewilderment. Louise sensed behind his heroic façade a naïveté, even an ignorance, not only about France but about history, art, life. A waiter hovered. Louise ordered Pernod. Fairchild followed suit and found the yellow liquid almost undrinkable. Louise enjoyed watching him gamely sip it while she asked him questions about Pershing.

"Why do they call him Black Jack?"

"Because he commanded Negro troops, the Tenth Cavalry. It's not a compliment."

"Is he a good general?"

"Some people don't think so."

"Why do you dislike Harry Quickmeyer so much?"

Affability vanished from Colonel Fairchild's face. "My father was a general. Harry's father never got beyond captain. From the day we met at West Point, he went to work on me. He still does it, every time he sees me."

He gulped his Pernod and hunched over the glass as if he had just consumed an evil potion. More than dislike was on his face now. "In 1914, when we occupied Vera Cruz and were on the brink of war with Mexico, I went on reconnaissance to find railroad engines and boxcars to transport our army inland if necessary. It was rather dangerous. I had to shoot seven or eight Mexicans on the way back to our lines. Several people recommended me for the Medal of Honor. Quickmeyer was secretary of the board that heard the case. Pershing was the chairman. I was rejected."

How fascinating to learn the way men come to hate each other, Louise thought. For a marvelous moment she saw herself through Fairchild's eyes. She was an enigma in the fading summer sunshine, fondling her Pernod with delicate fingers, a hint of a smile on her red lips—a smile that dwindled into bewitching sympathy as he revealed his loathing of Harry Quickmeyer.

He leaned toward her, all reserve abandoned. "I want to be that soldier of the ideal," he said. "I need you to help me transcend the hate and envy that surrounds me."

His intensity ignited a rush of feeling in Louise. "My friend Gertrude Whitney says this war is going to change us all forever. I want to be part of the change—if she's right. It would be marvelous if I changed—that way, Colonel."

"Let me offer you something, by way of proof of my feelings."

He pulled a letter out of his pocket and handed it to her. An old-fashioned scent rose from the paper.

Dearest Dougie:

What you tell me about Eleanor Kingswood is most interesting. She's exactly the sort of woman I've always hoped you'd find. Someone who's young enough to be molded into an army wife—with a fortune that will enable you to live graciously and entertain lavishly, the keys to advancement in the U.S. Army. According to my informants, she's going to inherit at least forty million when her father dies.

Now for some good if explosive news from my side of the ocean. Tasker Bliss has been seconded to France to replace Jack Pershing. The complaints about Pershing's undiplomatic, intransigent handling of the French and British have convinced the President and the Secretary of War that he is the wrong choice to lead the expeditionary force. The prime ministers of England and France have personally written to Wilson urging his dismissal. The President is reluctant to do anything so severe because of the potential political repercussions. Pershing is a great favorite of the Republicans, because Teddy Roosevelt appointed him. (That monstrous creature, by the way, is rampaging up and down the country, denouncing Wilson's conduct of the war.) The President expects Tasker to make his presence felt as a superior in rank and political experience; then he will be elevated to command of the AEF and Pershing relegated to his deputy, with minimal duties. For Tasker to succeed in this job he will require a young vigorous chief of staff. Even his friends admit he is beginning to show his age. I trust I do not have to advise you about your next step—getting out of your dead-end indenture to that mountebank Malvern Hill Bliss and into a position to become that indispensable man. To arms, my darling! Mount your steed Ambition and do battle with the despicable Blisses and Quickmeyers of this world in my name.

Mother

Louise instantly saw the meaning of the first paragraph. He was abandoning his flirtation with Eleanor Kingswood's millions for her. The meaning of the second part was more obscure. Was he asking her help to unseat Pershing?

Fairchild tore the letter into small pieces, dumped them in the ashtray, and set them on fire. "I'm not taking Mother's advice. I'm going back to the Lafayette Division and stay a fighting soldier—for your sake."

That was not what Louise wanted to hear. She wanted the thrill, the suspense, the fascination of high intrigue with history reverberating around her like the beat of a kettledrum. "Don't," she said. "I'd be miserable—if you were killed."

"I won't be killed. I'm lucky," he said.

In a low fervid voice, Fairchild told her about a moment in the Philippines when he was leading a patrol down a jungle trail. An *insurrecto* had leaped from behind a tree and fired at him at point-blank range. He felt the muzzle blast against his face, the searing track of the bullet across his skull. He had been sure he was a dead man. A second later, an Irish sergeant behind him dispatched the gunman. The sergeant picked up Fairchild's campaign hat and poked his finger into the bullet hole in the crown. "Lieutenant," he said. "From now on life will be pure velvet."

Louise was awed. She had never thought of luck presiding over her life. For Fairchild it was part of his soldier's faith, as meaningful as the Virgin Mother of God to the women in mourning black who knelt in Notre Dame. Now he believed in Louise in the same charismatic way. He no longer wanted to be Tasker Bliss's devious right-hand man in his struggle to unseat Pershing. She had rescued him from his mother's intrigues, from duplicity unworthy of a soldier.

It was bizarre, romantic—and utterly appealing to some need or desire in Louise's soul. "Why are you going to dinner at Pershing's?" she asked.

"I have a friend on Pershing's staff. I was going to share the letter with him and see where he stood. He's not a Pershing man."

Perhaps she could have this reckless soldier of the ideal and intrigue. Louise struggled to conceal her excitement. What other woman in Paris had this glimpse of the turmoil in the American Expeditionary Force?

Fairchild glanced at his watch and gasped with dismay. It was almost seven o'clock. They were an hour late for dinner. Louise was unbothered by the news. She retired to the ladies' room to improve her makeup, a task that consumed a full ten minutes. She emerged to find a jittery Fairchild pacing beside her limousine. At 73 Rue de Varenne, an orderly led them to a salon from which the sound of voices drifted.

There were about two dozen people in the gilded room. Pershing's genial chief of staff, Colonel James Harbord, stood just inside the door, chatting with Harry Quickmeyer. Harbord gave them a warm smile of welcome that had no hint of reproof in it. From Quickmeyer came a very different response. Alarm—and pain—

coruscated his lean face at the sight of Louise with Douglas Fairchild.

It was one of the most pleasurable moments of Louise's life. She felt a similar vibration from Fairchild. He was discovering he could rattle his old enemy merely by walking through a door with Louise at his side.

"Mrs. Wolcott. What a pleasure to see you again," Harbord said.

"Without a life preserver on," Louise said. "That should double the pleasure."

"What have you and Dougie been up to?" Quickmeyer said. His tone implied it could not be anything important and might even be ludicrous.

"I encountered him seeking inspiration at the tomb of Napoleon," Louise said. "Something I doubt if many Americans have had the wit to do."

"Only a few of us have Dougie's vaulting ambition," Quick-meyer said. "Don't mention it to Pershing. He might get nervous."

Louise was sure by this time Fairchild would have been flustered and fuming under this onslaught. But her staring smile—akin to the blank-eyed gaze of those angels at Napoleon's tomb—steadied him. "Where is the General?" Fairchild said. "I'd better apologize for bringing Mrs. Wolcott an hour late."

"Relax," Harbord said. "He hasn't even come downstairs. He hasn't been on time for dinner or anything else since we've gotten here. He has absolutely no time sense."

The room's purring conversation abruptly ceased. Several officers who had sat down on couches along the wall leaped up. Pershing had just walked through a door at the opposite end of the salon. The straight back, the stern face, emanated a gloomy force that stirred warmth, excitement in Louise's flesh. With him was Malvern Hill Bliss, looking almost as gloomy. What sort of bad news had they just heard?

A smile transformed Pershing's melancholy as his eyes discovered Louise. He strode over to her and took both her hands. They began joking about their days on Periscope Pond. Harry Quick-meyer stood to one side, frowning. A similar frown creased Douglas Fairchild's brow. No doubt they were wondering if the rumors about

Pershing's prowess in the bedroom were true.

Louise decided not to discourage any of them. It was part of being a Parisian woman, this freedom to tantalize many men. For some reason she did not understand, she herself was tantalized by Douglas Fairchild. He had vowed to change her mind in a way Quickmeyer and even Pershing could not match—with deeds on a battlefield, a soldier's pursuit of *la gloire*.

17. INTRODUCING GENERAL DARLING

THE MUSIC OF A TEN-PIECE ORCHESTRA CHIRPED IN the background. An aging English tenor clutched a microphone and boozily croaked:

"At seventeen he falls in love quite madly
With eyes of tender blue;
At twenty-four he gets it rather badly
With eyes of a different hue."

"He's singing the story of my life," Malvern Hill Bliss said to the chubby blond woman in his arms.

"Mine too," the Countess Szechny said.

She had already told Bliss twice to call her Maisie. Before she changed her last name at the request of a Polish nobleman, she had been Margaret Anne Waters of Cleveland, daughter of one of the original partners of John D. Rockefeller. "I hope we'll see a lot of each other in Paris, General," Maisie cooed.

Bliss was tempted to tell her he had already seen more of Maisie than he had thought possible, without getting arrested. Maisie's gown revealed virtually everything above the waist but the nipples of her breasts. The cleavage plunged lower than any gentleman was supposed to look; the back was nonexistent. His left hand roamed an expanse of warm flesh that made him feel like a sultan in a seraglio.

Around him danced about a dozen members of John J. Pershing's staff and the General himself, all with their arms around similarly semidressed young or youngish women. The Paris styles for 1917 seemed determined to conceal nothing. Harry Quickmeyer, who was dancing nearby with Louise Wolcott, claimed it was a reaction to the need for secrecy in wartime. Pershing had already danced three times with Louise, who was wearing a diaphanous white silk outfit, revealing almost all of her lanky torso.

The French had coined a nasty term for the kind of war they were fighting: *la guerre de luxe*. The necessity of moving out of Paris was never more apparent. But Pershing seemed in no hurry. While the Lafayette Division sat outside Saint-Nazaire, waiting for the French to tell them they had figured out how to billet 28,000 men in the towns and villages around their training site in Lorraine, Pershing had kept Bliss in the city for the better part of a month discussing what the AEF should wear, shoot, fly, and drive. Bliss argued it was madness to wait for Woodrow Wilson's muddled war effort to send them what they needed. They had decided to buy French artillery and machine guns, British helmets and rifles, French planes and tanks. Without so much as a flicker of hesitation, Pershing had signed contracts committing several hundred million dollars on this equipment.

The Countess Szechny was explaining to Bliss that she had gotten rid of the Count years ago. He wanted to live on his Polish estates. She gave him four million and kissed him goodbye at the Gare de l'Est. "We're still good friends. But it leaves me with oceans of time to fill."

The Countess was the hostess for this little dinner dance for a mere fifty friends, including the English and American ambassadors and the French Minister of War. They were in her château a few miles beyond Versailles. "A real man would fill it nicely," Maisie murmured, nestling against Bliss's chest.

Did Pershing expect him to keep his promise of celibacy with this kind of temptation in his primrose path, Bliss wondered? Maisie might be a little used but her figure was still firm and inviting. She clearly wanted to be part of his great adventure.

How long you think it'd take for all that money to demote you from general to buck private? It was Sergeant Turner's voice in his head, warning him not to make a fool of himself.

At eleven o'clock Bliss and Pershing returned to Paris in his limousine. "The hell with the Lafayette Division, Jack," Bliss said. "I want to stay in Paree. How about making me your orderly? I'd outrank every other orderly in sight. You'd be sure of getting your hat first no matter where you had dinner."

Pershing chuckled. "It's pretty amazing, isn't it? All that pulchritude practically begging to be enjoyed?"

"I'm not sure how much longer I can resist it," Bliss said. "I bet half your staff is saying the same thing."

"I can't imagine a real soldier going for one of those overage social butterflies," Pershing said.

"They're not all overage," Bliss said, thinking of Louise Wolcott.

"I'm not talking about one-night stands," Pershing said.

Tonight Bliss was out with the other Pershing, the genial man of the world who lived inside the general's iron mask. The big car purred through the Versailles gate and rolled down dark empty streets. Bliss remarked that the natives kept later hours in Malabang.

"Can you stay awake a little longer?" Pershing said. "There's someone I'd like you to meet."

Without much geography of Paris in his head, Bliss had no idea where they were going. He noticed the two windshield signs that identified the car—the U.S. flag and the four stars—were lying flat on the dashboard. They were traveling incognito.

They nosed down a narrow street off the Boulevard Haussmann: the Rue Descombes. The driver stopped before Number 4—he had obviously been here before—and they mounted to the fifth floor of a small compact building. A slim young woman stood on the dim landing in yellow lamplight spilling from the open door. Her winsome face wore a delighted smile. "*Mon général*," she said, and eagerly embraced him in the French style, kissing him on both cheeks.

"Michette," Pershing said, "I want you to meet one of my oldest friends, Mal Bliss. Mal, this is Micheline Resco."

"*Enchanté*," Micheline said.

She was blond and not really pretty—the nose was a bit too long, the mobile mouth too wide—but these became trivial details in the glow of her smile, which practically illuminated the building. Everything about her was soft, sinuous, feminine, the opposite of the angular metallic military world in which they lived and worked. She was also young, not more than twenty-five, Bliss guessed. Her skin had the satiny sheen of youth.

Inside, Micheline had *Lohengrin* playing on a small phonograph—somewhat incongruous music for two men who were preparing to do battle with Imperial Germany. They sat down on an Empire couch a few feet from a grand piano draped with a brilliant red and black shawl and accepted cognac, served in warmed glasses. On the walls were half a dozen paintings, all religious, featuring the Blessed Virgin. Micheline raised her glass in a toast. "'Ow—are—you—Gen-ral?" she said.

Even that much English was a struggle. She blushed and glanced apologetically at Bliss. He realized she was dismayed at the prospect of trying to converse with two Americans in their own language.

"I—am—fine," Pershing said.

They sipped the cognac and smiled at each other. Bliss began to feel superfluous. Had he been brought along as a chaperone?

"Miss Resco is a very gifted artist," Pershing said. He smiled and added in an atrocious French accent, *"un artiste extraordinaire."* Micheline blushed again and bowed her head modestly. "She's done paintings of General Pétain and a number of other French leaders. Would you like to see the sketch she's made for my portrait?"

Lohengrin's music—it was the warrior's entrance into Valhalla—followed them down a hall to a studio in the rear. Tall windows and a skylight gleamed blackly against the night sky. The sketch stood on an easel. Bliss saw at a glance it was the other Pershing. The face looked inward. Dignity and pride were there but not the fierce outward glare that could impale a man.

Bliss summoned his wayward French to tell Micheline how much he liked it. "It's the face of my friend. His human face, the one he only shows to a few people."

"Ah, yes, yes," Micheline said in French. "He is not a man of iron, however much he yearns to be."

"What's all that about?" Pershing growled.

Bliss gave him a quick summary. Pershing smiled frostily. "I see I'm going to have to play censor around here. You both know too much about me."

Back in the parlor, they settled on the couch once more. "Mal," Pershing said. "I want you to tell Miss Resco that I love her. Every time I try to do it, my French makes her laugh."

"She looks as if she's gotten the idea, Jack."

"I want her to get more than the idea. Pour it on, Mal. Tell her I think she's the loveliest woman I've ever seen, except for Frankie. Tell her how much I need a woman's love if I'm going to handle this impossible job."

"*Chère mademoiselle*," Bliss began. He did not waste any time getting to the main point. When Micheline heard the verb "love," she trembled and her vivacity vanished. A solemn tenderness filled her eyes, suffused her face. She reached out and took Jack's hand.

"Perhaps you know the General's wife is dead," Bliss continued.

Micheline nodded. It was the one fact every woman in Paris knew. He and Pershing were displaying their ignorance of the feminine mind. Bliss paused to regroup his French. Should he tell Micheline Resco how Frankie and her daughters had died? He decided against it. Jack Pershing was the last man in the world who wanted a woman to pity him.

"Please tell the General he has had my love from the day I met him," Micheline said. "I have tried to conceal it, to deny it—because I saw no place for someone as insignificant as myself in the terrible drama that engulfs him."

Bliss communicated this word for word to Pershing, who raised Micheline's right hand to his lips. "Now tell her why circumstances make it impossible for me to marry her for the time being," Pershing said.

Bliss had barely begun this delicate topic when Micheline raised her hand. "I understand completely. But I am a believing Catholic. He must know in my eyes it will be a marriage—the only one I will ever make."

The moralist in Bliss almost got loose to warn her against such a heroic commitment. Jack Pershing had loved many women and would undoubtedly love many more. Could he, should he collaborate in this immolation of innocence?

Bliss decided it was none of his business. He was here as Jack's friend, his French voice, not his American conscience. He translated Micheline's answer and let Jack decide what to say about it.

"Tell her I understand—and pledge myself here and now to honor that marriage to the best of my ability for the rest of my life."

If that was a lie, it was a magnificent one. Bliss translated word for word again. Micheline pressed Pershing's hand to her heart and held it there, her head bowed.

"Now comes the hardest part," Pershing said, withdrawing his hand and perceptibly relaxing. "We have to teach Michette how to pronounce my name."

After ten minutes, in spite of Bliss's heroic efforts, "Pair-shang" was the best she could do. By that time all three were laughing so hard they had to abandon the attempt.

Micheline became solemn again. "There's only one solution," she said in French. "I'll call him *chéri*. How do you say that? General Chéri?"

"General Darling," Bliss translated, with some trepidation. "How do you like that, Jack?"

The other Pershing was still in charge. "I like it just fine— within these walls."

Bliss did not bother to translate that. Micheline seemed to understand. Twenty minutes later they were riding back to Pershing's residence. "How did you find her?" Bliss said.

"The frogs commissioned some character with a two-foot-long beard to paint my portrait the day after we arrived. Little Collins found out every general he'd painted had been relieved within six months. We got rid of him and found Micheline through Pétain."

Bliss saw the synergy of luck and defiance Micheline Resco represented to Pershing. She was his response to the way death had stripped and humiliated him. He was reaching back to a woman as young as Frankie on her wedding day, telling death his faith in his luck, in his soldier's destiny, was unbroken.

"I love her. It's amazing. When we haven't exchanged more than two dozen words," Pershing said. "Do you think I've gone nuts?"

"No," Bliss said.

Bliss wondered what Louise Wolcott, the Countess Szechny, and their friends would say when and if they found out this twenty-five-year-old painter had annihilated their hopes of snagging John J. Pershing. They would show Jack no mercy with their powerful friends in the embassies and parliaments. Micheline was a risk as well as a promise of luck and victory. But risk was basic to their business.

Inevitably, Bliss found himself wondering if he could find a similar woman. Polly Warden? She was hardly inclined to fall into a general's arms. Anyway, she seemed to have disappeared. According to Quickmeyer she had volunteered for duty at some French hospital near Soissons and vanished into the haze of secrecy around *La Zone Interdite*.

They crossed the Seine on the Pont Neuf bridge and cruised down the deserted streets of the Faubourg-Saint-Germain. The sentry at the gate of Number 73 Rue de Varenne snapped to attention as they slowed to a stop.

"Meanwhile," Pershing said, the growl back in his voice, "we've got a war to win. Haig's bombarding me with stuff about how well his offensive is going in Ypres. Maybe you ought to spend some more time with that talkative English driver. We'll arrange for her to take you up there for a visit. See what you can find out from her—and anyone else with loose lips. Pétain tells me the best bet is the commander of the Fifth Army, Hubert Gough. He seems to be on Haig's shit list for some reason."

General Pershing had replaced General Darling.

18. LOVE AMONG THE RUINS

THE CAR WAS THE SAME GRAY ROLLS-ROYCE THAT had brought Bliss from Saint-Nazaire. Anita Sinclair was at the wheel in her baggy brown uniform, greeting him with the same bold speculative eyes and ironic smile. They headed northwest on a good main road at her usual suicidal speed. Soon they were in Picardy, where, according to the song, roses bloomed in soldiers' hearts. It reminded Bliss of Maryland's Eastern Shore, lovely rolling country abounding with patches of green woodland. On nearby hills sat stately châteaus and an occasional ruined castle. The white road ran between double rows of tall trees, which added a processional quality to their passage.

"The high command suspects we're lovers, General," Anita Sinclair said, mockery again curving the sensuous mouth.

"I'm flattered. How do you know?"

"General Charteris paid me a visit yesterday in my lowly barracks. He turned himself into knots trying to tell me how to manipulate you without quite saying the obvious. He seems to think you're the key to changing General Pershing's mind about giving them your men. He all but promised me the Victoria Cross if I managed it."

"How's the Ypres offensive going?"

"According to Charteris, it's making wonderful progress. That makes me suspect the worst. He gave me this packet for your perusal, urging me to tell you I put it together with my own patriotic hands."

In an oversize oilskin envelope were copies of the London *Times* and other papers for the previous day. YPRES ATTACK RENEWED, the

Times proclaimed. TWO MILE ADVANCE. The reporter was jubilant. "Everywhere our objectives were attained ... we have broken the German line on the whole front attacked. Our casualties seem remarkably light." The Fourth Division of the Prussian Guard was "slaughtered." The end of Germany's resources was "within sight."

"If half of this is true, we ought to go home and save Uncle Sam a lot of money," Bliss said.

Miss Sinclair's ironic smile reappeared. She kept her eyes on the white road. They were now in the British zone. Trucks rumbled past, hurling clouds of chalky dust down Bliss's throat. Signs in English began to appear, directing ambulances to hospitals, warning drivers that certain side roads were under shell fire.

"What do you know about General Gough?" Bliss asked.

"He's the only senior general who's had the courage to cancel an attack when he decided it wasn't war, it was murder. That's put him in serious disfavor at headquarters."

Ten minutes later, Bliss noticed gray clouds building up to the northeast. "Bloody rain," Anita Sinclair said. "It never stops in Flanders."

The cloudburst broke as they cruised up a curving drive to a ramshackle hunting château that served as the headquarters of Lieutenant General Sir Hubert Gough, commander of the British Fifth Army. His aide-de-camp, a young captain named Blake whose blond hair and fair complexion reminded Bliss of Jonathan Alden, welcomed Anita Sinclair with more than ordinary warmth. He told her where to park and led Bliss to his general.

Gough was a ruddy, genial man of about fifty with a thick reddish-brown brush mustache and red-rimmed eyes that suggested sleepless nights. He greeted Bliss with a hearty hello and introduced his chief of staff, a colonel named Neil Malcolm. He was a hard-eyed Scot like Haig, with a grim uncompromising mouth.

They ate lunch in a dining room overlooking a broad lawn. The downpour formed huge puddles on the soggy grass. In the next room a trio of bagpipers played "The Harp That Once Through Tara's Halls" and other Irish songs. "I should have brought along the colonel of my Irish-American regiment," Bliss said. "He'd be trying to talk himself into your army by now."

"I'm Tipperary born and proud of it," Gough said. "The Irish Guards are one of my best regiments."

"The Colonel was born in the Bronx," Bliss said. "He just thinks he's Irish."

"Is it true, what I heard from a friend on Haig's staff?" Malcolm said. "You declined to serve with us because your Irish Americans objected?"

"I objected," Bliss said. "I didn't come to France to hand my men over to the British army—or to the French army."

"I would have done exactly the same thing," Gough said. "It's a damn fool idea. It only shows how desperate for men they are at GHQ."

"From the papers, I gather the offensive's going well," Bliss said.

Gough looked out at the sluicing rain. "What do you see out there, Bliss?"

"A lot of water."

"If you were a correspondent for the *Times*, you'd report it was bright clear summer weather. Those fellows are the worst liars in the world. Either that, or they actually believe the stuff that Charteris feeds them at GHQ. We never see them around here. I suspect they're afraid they might find out what's really happening, and then what would they do?"

Colonel Malcolm cleared his throat and asked Gough if he would like some more wine. The Irishman bristled at the suggestion that he drink more and say less. "We're talking to a fellow soldier, Malcolm. I see no point in telling him anything but the truth."

With anguish in his voice, Gough told Bliss he had driven to Haig's headquarters last night and urged him to abandon the offensive. The rain had turned the battlefield into a swamp. Horses were sinking up to their bellies in mud. He had withdrawn three divisions already, reduced to hollow shells. Just before they sat down to lunch, Haig had called with orders to continue the attack. "What can I do? He put these stars on my shoulders."

The pipers were playing "It's a Long Way to Tipperary." Bliss was touched by Gough's frankness—and shaken. He saw the similarity between Gough and Haig and Bliss and Pershing. What would he do if Pershing told him to spend his men's lives in a battle that made no sense?

"Is there any chance of giving me a look at the front this afternoon?"

"One of those, eh?" Gough said with a grin. "I've always been a front-line man myself. It's the only way to find out what's really going on. But getting close at Ypres can be a bit hairy. The Germans have the high ground on three sides." He looked inquiringly at Malcolm, who said it would be out of the question unless it stopped raining.

Malcolm clearly had no enthusiasm for letting Bliss anywhere near the front. Gough had to prod his chief of staff into admitting there was a local attack scheduled for 4 P.M. to seize two German strong points, Glencorse Wood and Winnipeg Farm.

By the time they finished a gooey English dessert called trifle, the rain had declined to a drizzle. Malcolm stamped out to prepare orders and a map that would get Bliss to the front. Gough began telling Bliss what he had learned from three years of war. It came down to trying to save the infantry's strength and morale whenever possible. Divisions should be rotated from front-line duty often. For an offensive, elaborate planning was crucial. Artillery, machine guns, planes, infantry—and the newest weapon, tanks—had to be meshed. "It's like leading an orchestra," Gough said.

Malcolm returned to report he had sent the map, orders, and passes to Bliss's driver. "You've only got an hour," he said, in his graceless way. "You'd better get moving."

In the entrance hall, General Gough's aide, Captain Blake, was arguing with Miss Sinclair. "I know the road better than any of your bloody motor-pool muckers," she said.

The Captain explained that the trip was going to be dangerous. He was afraid Miss Sinclair would be killed. "We'll let General Bliss decide," she said, transfixing him with her mocking gray eyes.

"I'm inclined to trust Miss Sinclair," Bliss said. "At the speed she usually drives, she must have someone watching over her."

They rolled into the damp gray afternoon. "They keep trying to protect us from the bloody war," Anita Sinclair said. They sloshed along for about five miles, then swung east. "Colonel Malcolm's sent you to the headquarters of the Seventeenth Corps," she said, gesturing to the map between them. "It's three miles behind the front. You won't see a bloody thing. You'll be a hundred feet underground watching them move pins on a map. Do you want a look at what's really happening?"

"That's the only reason I've made the trip—aside from the charm of your company," Bliss said.

"I've got an uncle who's commanding the forward artillery. We'll go there."

Ahead, the sky suddenly turned orange and lemon. The earth vibrated beneath their wheels. An accumulated boom rolled down on them. "There go the opening guns," she said.

In half an hour they were close enough to hear the guns more realistically. Earsplitting crashes flung shock waves against the car. Incoming shells exploded with gushes of flame several hundred yards to the left and right of the road. Was he out of his mind? Bliss wondered. He was exposing this young woman to mutilation or death.

"Don't worry, General. This is nothing compared to the Somme," Anita Sinclair said.

The shelling mounted in ferocity. Anita Sinclair recognized the rounds as if they were old friends. "That's a two-ten," she said, as a geyser of mud rose to the right. The 210 millimeter was the Germans' biggest gun. "That's a one-fifty," she said, as a smaller, darker geyser rose on the left. "We call them Jack Johnsons, after your black heavyweight champion."

A hiss, followed almost instantly by an explosion, sent shrapnel pattering against the car. "That's a seventy-seven," Anita Sinclair said. "Whizbangs. The men hate them the most. No time to duck."

Another *hiss-bang*. A chunk of shrapnel went through the rear side window, showering the back of Bliss's neck with glass. Anita Sinclair laughed. "That was a close one," she said.

At several points they were stopped by military policemen who were standing in the road, apparently as unconcerned about the shrapnel as she was. They studied Colonel Malcolm's pass and confirmed they were going in the right direction.

"I hate those bloody provosts," Anita Sinclair said.

"Why?"

"They arrest people. Most of them get shot."

"Deserters?"

"Frightened men. Poor sods who've gone batty."

They finally reached their destination, a sandbagged dugout in which the artillery commander for the sector sat talking on a telephone. All around them guns boomed incessantly. "I don't give a bloody goddamn what the road's like!" he shouted. "I want another ten thousand rounds up here by dark. We may be firing all night. Call GHQ. Call the bloody Parliament. Just get them here!"

He was a big man with massive shoulders and a thick neck. His small nose seemed lost on his broad face. "Hello, Anita," he said, with an amused squint. "I thought we got you out of this muck once and for all."

Anita Sinclair introduced her uncle, Colonel Harold Sinclair. She fluttered Colonel Malcolm's pass and said General Bliss was here with General Gough's approval. Colonel Sinclair shook hands and shouted, "Afraid we can't offer you much in the way of comforts, General."

"I'm here to learn a few things," Bliss bellowed.

"Afraid all you'll find is how not to fight a bloody war," Sinclair roared.

Anita watched, her ironic smile intact. At three forty-five the guns around them redoubled their tempo. Crash after crash blended until it was one continuous sound that threatened to turn Bliss's brain to jelly. Colonel Sinclair led Bliss outside, and with borrowed field glasses he watched the shells bursting on the German lines, hurling up red and yellow flame.

Colonel Sinclair glanced at his watch. "Zero hour!" he shouted. "Now we start the creeping barrage. We move it ahead a hundred yards every six minutes."

Out of the ruins of a village came a line of tiny figures, officers in front, the men burdened by bulging packs. There were about a thousand of them—a battalion. The barrage flung up mud a few hundred yards ahead of them. Their objective was a trench line on Winnipeg Farm, half a mile away.

The men were literally wading through mud that came up to their knees. Bliss could almost feel their growing exhaustion as they struggled to keep up with the barrage, which methodically advanced every six minutes no matter where the men were. When the barrage lifted, the men were supposed to be close enough to charge the German trenches. Instead, they were barely halfway across the swamp.

All along the German line, machine guns opened up on the floundering infantry. Three fourths of the first line melted away. Behind them a second line met the same fate. The exhausted survivors were trapped in mud that made it impossible to retreat or advance. Some dug holes in the ooze and fired back. But the operation was essentially a slaughter.

"Bloody hell!" Sinclair groaned. "What sort of general sends men to fight in that kind of muck?"

"Can't you give them more artillery cover?" Bliss asked.

Sinclair shook his head. "Against orders. They're on their own now."

German shells started falling among the soldiers in the mud. Several times men vanished in a burst that either buried them alive or blew them to pieces. "We can do something about that," Sinclair said. He turned to his guns. "Major McLeod," he shouted to his executive officer. "Shift to counterbattery fire. Call corps headquarters and see if aviation has sent in any new targets."

For another hour Bliss watched more waves of men join the survivors of the first two waves and inch toward Winnipeg Farm while machine-gun bullets churned the mud all around them. It was madness. He wanted to drive to Field Marshal Haig's headquarters and bang Brigadier Charteris's lying face into a wall map until it was pulp. As for the Field Marshal himself, he should be cashiered and shot before nightfall.

The longer Bliss watched, the harder he cursed. He used every obscenity in his vocabulary at least a hundred times. Suddenly Anita was standing beside him. "You see what I mean?" she said. "You see what I *mean*?" Through the drifting gunsmoke, Bliss saw tears on her face.

The battery's guns awoke, splitting Bliss's head apart. This time, firing on the German guns who were shelling the infantry, they started getting answers from their adversaries. Shells plowed up the fields all around them. Colonel Sinclair suggested a return to the dugout. "Can't have you killed on my hands, General," he said.

Bliss decided he had seen more than enough. As 210s and 150s whined over his head, he walked to the Rolls-Royce with all the nonchalance he could muster. Anita started the motor and clutched the wheel for a moment, struggling for self-control. "Could we take some wounded back with us, General?" she asked.

"Why not?"

To his astonishment, they turned left on the road and drove toward the German lines. All the British guns were dueling German batteries now. The air was livid with flame, vibrating with explosions of outgoing and incoming rounds. Above them, the sky remained the color of lead. "They'll be some walking wounded in a mile or two," Anita said.

The Rolls slithered and slewed on the slimy road. Up ahead, in about ten minutes, they saw stretcher-bearers wallowing toward them through the mud, up to their knees like the infantry in no-man's-land. On the right was a field dressing station with doctors and orderlies outside working in their shirt sleeves; nearby was a cluster of ambulances waiting for passengers.

It began to rain but no one paid any attention. Shells shrieked overhead or exploded nearby in a continuous bedlam. No one paid any attention to them either. Around them was nothing but mud, mud and a few shattered trees and bodies of dead horses and smashed wagons and gun carriages. Nature had been obliterated. War had created its own landscape.

Near the ambulances, Anita had a brief reunion with half a dozen people in unpressed grayish blue uniforms. Their visored hats covered half their faces. Bliss could not tell whether they were men or women. Anita pointed to the Rolls and they waved cheerily at Bliss, as if they were all at some summer resort. In a few minutes she came out of the dressing station with three limping young soldiers, their legs swathed in bandages. They were covered with mud from head to foot. It had dried on their faces, giving them weird whitish masks.

She introduced them to Bliss as if they were general officers.

Privates Leffingwell and Wilson and Corporal Tompkins, all of the Queen's Westminster Rifles. Bliss asked them if they were in the attack on Winnipeg Farm. They nodded numbly. "If you want to call it an attack, sir," said Private Wilson.

"We would have done them if it weren't for the mud," Corporal Tompkins said.

"Mud or not, there was still all them bloody machine guns," Wilson said.

"There's always machine guns," the Corporal said.

"Have it your way," Wilson said. "We've all got a ticket to blighty. There ain't no bloody machine guns there, thank God."

"What's blighty?" Bliss asked.

"It means home, sir," the Corporal said. "England."

"It's originally a Hindu word, meaning foreign country," Anita said.

"Jesus!" She slammed on the brakes, and the Rolls almost skidded off the road. Ahead of them a soldier was weaving along like a drunk, singing to himself. She pulled up beside him. "Chummy," she said, "what regiment are you with?"

"Yorkshires, Mum," he said with a dazed smile. "Nothing left of us now, though. Not enough to make a pudding."

"What's he doing over here?" the Corporal said. "They were in line a good mile away, going for Glencorse Wood. He's a bolter."

"Squeeze over," Anita said. "I know it'll hurt, but we've got to take him. The provosts are just up the road. They'll shoot him. They don't believe in shell shock."

"Why should they?" the Corporal said. "It's just an excuse for bloody funk."

"Squeeze over, you damn fool," Private Leffingwell said.

"What's this American general going to think?" the Corporal said. "First all this cheering for blighty and now we're ferrying bolters."

"It's all right," Bliss said. "Miss Sinclair's in command here. I'm just a passenger."

The Corporal gave him a look that clearly said he gave up on him. A general who let a woman order him around? He probably gave up on the whole American army. Anita shoved the Yorkshire private into the back seat beside the Corporal. "Careful, you sod, I've got a piece of bloody shrapnel in there," the Corporal said, clutching his bandaged thigh.

The Yorkshire man was still singing in a peculiar high-pitched voice, almost a whisper. His mud-caked lips barely moved as the words came out.

> "When the fighting is over and the war is won
> And the flags are waving free,
> When the bells are ringing
> And the boys are singing
> Songs of victory."

"Shut up," Corporal Tompkins said.

"Let him sing," Private Leffingwell said.

"I wish I was bonkers like him," Private Wilson said. "I wouldn't have to think how many mates we left in that bloody mud."

"That's war," the Corporal said. "You leave mates behind wet or dry, mud or dust."

Five miles down the road they found a field hospital. They left the wounded men and the shell-shock case in the hands of a young doctor Anita seemed to know well. He promised to protect the Yorkshireman—if Anita agreed to have dinner with him in Rouen next week.

She got back in the Rolls and sat behind the wheel, staring at bulky brown ambulances streaming down the road from the front. "I'm afraid we've ruined this beautiful car," Bliss said, looking over his shoulder at the smashed window and mud-covered backseat.

"Bugger it," Anita said, shoving the Rolls into first gear. "I feel like a human being for the first time in twelve months."

"I can see why. But it makes me wonder why you lied to me."

"About what?" she said, instantly furious.

"You said you hated Englishmen when you obviously love them. If anything, I'd say you love them too much."

The Rolls slewed crazily on the muddy road as Anita Sinclair slammed on the brakes. They wound up with two wheels in a watery ditch. "You bastard," she said. "You bloody American bastard."

She began sobbing and shaking. "I've never—actually seen it—before. Seen them dying—that way. I only heard the men talk about it."

Artillery thundered distantly, hurling ocher and scarlet against the darkening gray sky. Bliss put his arms around the tormented young woman. It was an instinctive gesture, a desire to soothe her rage and heal her pain—although he knew he lacked the power to do either. "They're brave men. There's nothing wrong with loving them," he said.

"But they're stupid! They die like sheep!"

"They die like soldiers. With their faces to the enemy."

She flung herself against him and sobbed uncontrollably for a full five minutes. "We have a lot in common," Bliss said, breathing a hint of perfume in her hair. "I hate stupidity too. I've gotten in trouble all my life for denouncing it wherever I saw it. But people learn from other people's mistakes. I'm going back to Paris and make sure the Americans fight this war differently—intelligently—thanks to your help."

With no warning she pressed her mouth on his. "You can take me to dinner in Rouen tonight," she said. "You've given me hope. I want to give you something in return."

"I think that would be a mistake," Bliss said. "I want to love you that way as much as I've wanted to love any woman. But I didn't say any of those things with seduction in mind."

Bliss thought of Pershing in Micheline Resco's arms. Was he crazy, refusing this woman? No. He was traveling down a current of feeling that formed his words with an inevitability that seemed outside his mind.

"I'm not talking about love," Anita said. "I have no love to give you—or anyone else. It died a year ago."

Her ferocity reminded him of Louise Wolcott in the back seat of another limousine. All these new women seemed riven, driven by rage. Was it the war, or had the war torn away some ancient restraint, permitting this primary lava to erupt? "It may sound strange, coming from a soldier, but I want—maybe I even need—your love."

"You don't understand the war," she raged. "There isn't any

place in it for love! Love only makes it worse when people die."

"I don't agree with you," Bliss said. "I've had people I love die in a war. It's better in the long run if you admit you loved them."

Or admit you didn't love them, whispered a mocking voice.

Was this his tormented way of expiating the failure of his love for Grace? Or a pathetic attempt to deny the agony of Jackie's loss? Bliss did not know. He could only cling to the current of feeling and a conviction that telling this woman the exact truth was better than accepting her terms for a one-night stand.

Anita shoved herself back behind the wheel, and the Rolls proved it was part tank by clawing its way out of the ditch. A half hour later, on the main road to Paris, she finally spoke. "You're the strangest bloody soldier I've ever met. Maybe you *will* fight this war differently."

Bliss wondered if he was risking his future in the U.S. Army with that heroic boast. Watching grief settle like a mask on Anita's fragile-boned face, he realized he had made the promise to himself as much as to her. He would defy the mud and blunders and death he had just seen beyond Ypres—or shuck his uniform.

19. LOVE AT WAR

"SCALPEL."

Polly Warden handed Paul Lebrun the gleaming steel instrument. He began cutting an incision in the poilu's stomach.

"Clamps."

She handed him the blunt-edged scissorlike devices that prevented the wounded man from losing more blood.

"Scalpel."

The gloved hand was extended again. Beneath the tan rubber were the fingers that caressed her breasts and thighs. Behind the mask on the hollow-cheeked face were the lips that pressed her lips, the tongue that explored her mouth.

Polly barely saw the swift savagery of the scalpel as it opened the soldier's stomach to explore the wound. Dr. Lebrun worked in silence. There was no poetry at his operating table these days. There was no mocking seduction in his voice when he spoke to his chief operating-room nurse. Most of the time his requests were a cold snarl.

"Forceps," he said.

She handed him the oversized tweezers, and he began picking out ugly pieces of black metal. The soldier had been wounded by an artillery shell. It had broken most of his ribs and shattered his left arm.

"His pulse is getting weaker," the anesthetist, Dolbier, said.

"Give him serum, five hundred cc's."

"I have. He's dying."

"Strychnine!"

"We're out of it."

Paul did not seem to hear him. He continued to explore the stomach. Polly watched the man's chest rise and fall, rise and fall, slower, slower, each time with more of a struggle. It was a broad muscular expanse, an athlete's chest. Surely he was strong enough to survive.

Dolbier's finger rested on the carotid artery in the soldier's neck. "I'm losing his pulse," he said.

The burly chest sank and did not rise. "He's dead," Dolbier said.

"*Putain!*" The word was the equivalent of goddamn it in French. It also meant whore. Lebrun flung the forceps against the operating-room wall. His bloodshot eyes glared at Polly. "A nitwit," he snarled, tearing off his mask. "That's what the Americans have sent us. Instead of soldiers they've sent female imbeciles to kill our best men."

"I think the Germans are somewhat more responsible," Dolbier said.

Paul paid no attention to him. "How many times must I tell you to make sure the worst cases are moved to the head of the list?" he shouted at Polly. "Are you incapable of learning the simplest lessons? Must you always get it all wrong?"

In French, the last question arrived as *foutre dans la merde* which literally translated as "put yourself in shit." Next came snarling variations on the basic idea that she was *une tête de linotte*, an idiot.

"If I was Mademoiselle Warden I'd use a scalpel on your gizzard," Dolbier said, as Polly picked up the forceps from the floor to return it to the sterilizing room.

"*Ça lui pend au nez,*" said the second nurse, sturdy Marie Ribout, gazing sympathetically at Polly. That meant, He's got it coming to him.

Antiaircraft guns erupted all around them. The growl of German airplane motors penetrated the thunder on the ground. Polly found herself wishing for a direct hit. A bomb would simplify everything. It would permit her to die a heroine's death, proving once and for all how much she loved this impossible man. Would Paul Lebrun weep beside her coffin, regret the names he called her? Of course. She had to believe that. There was not much else to believe now.

In the weeks that had passed since their trip to the Trois

Magots, Polly struggled and wavered and always came to the same conclusion. She wanted to stay in the hospital, working beside Paul, even though she now saw far more acutely what was tormenting him. It was not simply *cafard*. His defiance of his father and brothers was at least as fundamental. He had gone to war in the name of an ideal, a vision of a purified France that they mocked. The war—and their smiling scorn—had undermined that ideal. But she still refused to believe she could help him sustain it by becoming the keeper of a mystic shrine of love.

From the moment Paul heard this new never, he began sabotaging their love. The word, the idea, was uniquely French. It came from *sabot*, the wooden shoe peasants wore. The saboteur was invented by French workers in 1897 as part of their war with the capitalists. They worked as slowly, as clumsily, as maliciously as possible. Paul was applying the principle to love with cruel success.

He had begun the morning after Polly's surrender at the Trois Magots. She watched Richelieu pour an emerald green liquid into a glass. It turned cloudy white as the poet splashed water on it, and an odor of bitter herbs assailed her nostrils. "The green hour," Paul had said. "Will you join me?"

She had drunk the foul-tasting absinthe to prove to him that she was ready to follow him anywhere, even into madness. Her memory of the rest of the day was fragmentary. She remembered making love, hearing scraps of poetry whispered—or was it shouted?—flinching at the mocking laughter of Richelieu and his friends. Somewhere in the anarchy George Eagleton and her mother seemed to gaze reproachfully at her. *Cafard*, she had pleaded.

Where was she now? Polly found herself standing in the sterilizing room, the forceps in her hand. She dropped it into boiling water, fished out a replacement, and returned to the operating room. Another poilu had been wheeled in, a lung this time. They never had any names attached to them in the operating room. They were a stomach, a head, a lung, a leg. Had she too become part of the anatomy, as far as Dr. Lebrun was concerned?

Four hours later they sat side by side in the dining room. Paul seized Polly's hand and studied her palm. "I can read the future, you know," he said. He ran his finger along the line that angled across the center of her hand. "You will live a long time," he said. "Always regretting that you have refused to listen to your passionate nature. You will have several great loves but none as memorable as your first one."

"I'm beginning to think it's so memorable I'll spend the rest of my life trying to forget it."

Shirley Miller, the only other survivor of their original band of American volunteers, watched hungrily, disapproval in her tired eyes. She knew—everyone on the staff knew—about Polly and Dr. Lebrun. To the French it meant little, a liaison not much different from a million others in wartime. But Shirley combined envy and moral fervor to remind Polly she was American. At times she made Polly feel her capitulation was a national disgrace.

"All surgeons have tantrums," Paul said. "It goes with the profession. Especially when the surgeon is trapped in a nightmare like this one."

He raised Polly's hand to his lips and let the tip of his tongue wander around her palm. Shirley Miller gasped and looked away. "May I come to you tonight?" he murmured.

Polly let the touch of his tongue travel through her body, amazed by the electric way it stirred desire. "No," she said.

"You know I meant none of those appalling things. It was all spleen," he said.

"The answer is still no," she said.

It was the first time she had refused him. "Why?" he said.

Polly drank her bitter coffee and said nothing. "I think you know why," Paul said.

He was right. She knew. He had come to her small room at the top of the château night after night for a month. At first there had been poetry, even though it was spoken half in mockery. The poetry dwindled to their human voices, exchanging crucial words. *I love you. Always. Forever.* Those too had dwindled. Soon *cafard* crouched beside them in the darkness, a Caliban hurling accusations. Who were they, enjoying pleasure while around them thousands of men knew only pain and death?

Behind her closed eyes Polly searched for another glimpse of Eden, the crash of surf on a golden beach. Instead she heard the splash of her douche bag, the mocking laughter of Richelieu. Paul was right. In the Château Givry *cafard* was stronger than love.

That in turn opened her mind and heart to another voice. Last weekend in Paris, they had dined with Paul's father, Charles Louis Lebrun, and his brothers. Instead of the monster of selfishness and egotism Paul described, Polly found a man who drew her into a private corner during cocktails and pleaded with her to persuade Paul to accept a transfer to a hospital in Paris. She would come with him, of course.

His argument made sense in many ways. Paul had spent more time under fire than most poilus. He was close to a breakdown. But Paul's idealism—and her own—made this rational choice impossible. She could not use her love to persuade him to betray that visionary self who had welcomed the war, any more than she could retreat from this challenge and become the woman he wanted, a creature who lived in and through her passions, obliterating the war for him by annihilating her mind, her self.

"Will you come to Paris with me again next week?"

"Yes. But I won't drink absinthe. I won't let you drink it."

"How do you propose to stop me?"

"With the word I just spoke. No. I also propose to stop the tantrums the same way."

"The modern woman has declared herself," Lebrun said. "The creature who plans to rule the century."

"Not rule it. Just improve it, civilize it."

"You mean feminize it. Like your wonderful leader, Wilson, who was too proud to fight until he realized a defeated France and England would never repay their loans."

"Shut up," said the *Agent de Liaison*, Major Mahone.

Paul ignored him. "You should hear what my father says about the American army. They arrive with nothing: no artillery, no machine guns, no planes."

"We're going to have twenty thousand planes over here in a month or two," Shirley Miller said. "A hundred thousand cannon. My mother sent me a clipping from our hometown paper."

"Then why are you taking guns from us? My father says his cannon factories have been ordered to ship all their production to the

Americans for the next three months, leaving our own men with guns that are wearing out."

Polly stared into her coffee cup. She had no faith in Shirley Miller's hometown newspaper. She had seen how little truth the French newspapers printed. The poilus passed them from bed to bed and laughed at their reports of imaginary victories. The only paper they read with interest was the *Bonnet Rouge,* which told them to imitate the Russians and overthrow the government.

"I'm beginning to think my father is right: we're lurching toward catastrophe," Paul said. "The stupid British will butt their bulldog heads against a wall of steel in Ypres until they run out of men. The Russians have collapsed. The Italians will be next. Then France will be alone against the Boche. Maybe we should make peace while there's still time to negotiate."

Polly could almost see hope draining from Paul's exhausted mind and body. It was part of the reason she tried to forgive him for sabotaging their love. She had begun to think she deserved to be punished for her pacifism. Malvern Hill Bliss's worries aboard the *Baltic* were coming dolorously true. She and her friends had helped to disarm America, exposing everyone to the savagery of the German war machine.

Major Mahone tried to help. "How can you condemn the Americans when the young woman beside you is demonstrating, day after day, how much she cares for France?"

"You don't understand modern women, Grandfather," Paul said. "They care for nothing in their sterile souls. They act to prove a point, to demonstrate their program."

It was the same cruel argument. As Polly fled the dining room in a haze of tears, Madame Leclerc barked, "Mademoiselle Warden. You have received a letter. It's on my desk."

The letter was from General Bliss. He had gotten her address from a French liaison officer. He thanked her for telling him what she had seen and heard at the Château Givry. He had passed her letter along to General Pershing. It was the most realistic account of the condition of the French army they had received. In his candid way, he admitted it "did not encourage him" about their chances of winning the war. Men were still arriving from the United States in a trickle. The rest of his letter was a wry recounting of *la guerre de luxe* in Paris and his hope that Pershing would get his staff out of its enticing tentacles as soon as possible. He expected to leave for Lorraine soon to start training his division to fight on the western front. He signed himself *Your antediluvian friend.*

An American voice. She had been so engulfed by France and the war it seemed strange, almost foreign. She had traveled so far in the last two months, morally, spiritually, mentally. Was she even the same person who had knelt beside George Eagleton in Union Square and shouted "Bunk!" at Colonel Bliss for telling her war was the engine of history? For a while the memory filled Polly with sadness. She had been so naïve. All of them had been so naïve.

Polly's head drooped. It was time for bed. Quickly she washed herself in the single basin of water allowed her, turned out the light, and slipped under the covers of her narrow cot.

A knock resounded in the darkness. "It's the Knave of Hearts," Paul Lebrun said, "in search of the Queen of Spades."

"Some other time," she said. "I'm going to sleep."

"Don't you recognize the line? It's from Baudelaire's poem 'Spleen.'"

"Go to bed," Polly said. "We both have to work twelve hours tomorrow."

With a snarl Paul smashed the door's cheap lock and burst into the room. "Is that the voice of love?" he said. "The voice you promised to preserve here?"

"No," Polly said, sitting up in her bed. "You've sabotaged that voice. It's only a whisper now."

"Will you admit I was right? Will you come with me now, tonight? We'll go to that house in Auvers—"

"There'll be wounded men tomorrow, waiting for both of us."

"In six months the ones we save will be back at the front for the final German offensive, the one that will annihilate us. Don't you see how meaningless all this is compared to what we have in our hearts? Isn't love real to you? Is it only a word?"

"It's real. But wounded men are real too. The war is real."

He loomed over her in the narrow room. Outside, rain drummed on the roof and sluiced in the gutters. Distant artillery growled. Even in this weather, the killing continued.

"*Putain*," Paul Lebrun said. "*Putain moderne*." She was a modern whore, he said. She did not betray a man's love with other men. She betrayed it with ideas, with dreams of power and revenge for imaginary wrongs. "Would you like to see how a man makes love to a whore?"

She realized he was stripping off his clothes as he talked. He flung the covers back and thrust his finger deep into her vagina. She cried out with horror. He put his hand over her mouth and slid the finger back and forth with a relentless rhythm. Polly began to feel a desire that was not desire, a wanting her mind rejected.

"*Ton coeur bat-il toujours a mon seul nom?*"

When you hear my name does your heart always glow?

He was desecrating their memories. She grew more and more helpless. Her heart pounded, her breath was coming in gasps. "Please don't," she cried behind his suffocating hand.

She could not stop him. Perhaps in some anguished corner of her heart she did not want to stop him. He rolled on top of her and she opened herself to his cold swift thrusts while *le cafard* laughed drunkenly beside the bed. He was telling her she was getting what she deserved for thinking she could invade his country with her American pride, her naïve ideas about ennobling his war.

Paul came and Polly responded with a shudder, a cry. It was love's opposite, an eruption of shame and loathing. He gave her a brutal farewell kiss. "I'll see you in the operating room at six A.M.," he said.

Polly stumbled down the hall to the bathroom and douched, remembering other nights when it seemed to be a desecration of love. Now it was closer to a medicinal act, an attempt to prevent infection. She crept back to bed and lay there sobbing.

The door creaked. "Who's that?" she cried.

"Marie. I heard what happened. I've come to comfort you."

Marie Ribout slipped beneath the covers and took Polly in her strong arms. "Weep as much as you want," she said. "That will do the most good. I've been praying to the Virgin for you. She'll send you some consolation."

"I don't believe in your Virgin," Polly sobbed.

"She loves you anyway. You can't escape her love. No woman can. Especially someone who loves France as you do. She's our patron before the throne of God."

Polly wept and wept and wept. Marie held her in her warm embrace, murmuring consolation. Gradually Polly's tears ebbed. She began to realize this awkward homely girl was offering her something primary and important. It was more than sympathy, it was a quiet unassuming sense of herself as another woman, a bond that was deeper than nationality, stronger than desire, a fundamental kind of love.

Still in Marie's arms, Polly drifted into a shallow sleep. She was jolted awake by a rap on her door. An orderly's heavy voice told her she was to report to her operating room as soon as possible. The Germans had raided the front. There were many casualties.

It was 5 A.M. Marie Ribout was gone. Polly flung on her uniform and rushed downstairs for coffee and a brioche. Paul sat at another table, his eyes hooded, his face ashen. Once or twice he glanced in her direction. Polly was amazed to find she could meet his gaze without flinching. A cold clear anger seemed to rinse her mind of hesitation.

Outside, the rain continued to fall in a persistent drizzle. Paul walked beside her to their ward in morose silence. Inside, he drew her into the small room where the night nurse rested. "Can you forgive me?" he said.

"If you come into my room again, I'll report you to Major Mahone."

"Report me to General Pétain," he said. "Despise me. But don't stop loving me."

The Germans raided repeatedly along the front for the next two days. The wounded poured into the hospital, and they began working eighteen hours a day. Marie Ribout watched Polly with anxious eyes. Major Mahone seemed almost as concerned. Had Marie spoken to him?

At one point the he met Polly in the hall and seized her hand. "Mademoiselle, would you prefer another assignment? I've been led to believe you're unhappy working with Dr. Lebrun. I'll speak to Madame Leclerc if you wish."

Madame Leclerc would send her back to the German ward. No, it was better to stay where she was, to face the failure of love. Exhaustion inexorably drained Polly's anger until it was a muddle of guilt and personal defeat. The accusing voice, the one that berated her pacifism, extended its range. Her arrogance was responsible for George Eagleton's unhappiness too. If she had abandoned her pretentious feminism and married him, she would be home in New York, contented, pregnant, proud of her American hero husband.

The attacks continued into the third day. The wounds were awful, inflicted by hand grenades and flamethrowers. The poilus had to be so heavily sedated, many of them died on the operating table. But Paul did not throw a single temper tantrum. He was the voice of resignation, of grief, of weary philosophy. Above his mask, his penitent eyes asked Polly again and again for forgiveness.

She clung to her refusal, sensing that to abandon it would be a crucial step, possibly a fatal one. She would be confessing he had the right to abuse her. But exhaustion was like a spider, spinning a web of hopelessness around her. Marie Ribout sensed what was happening. She watched with anxious eyes that seemed to expect the inevitable.

"Tonight? I never needed you more," Paul murmured, after eighteen hours in the operating room. Polly wavered, then nodded wearily. It was easier to say yes.

They were like the lovers in a Verlaine poem, knowing in their hearts they would betray each other in the morning, yet too engulfed, too overwhelmed by their desire for each other to resist embracing.

Slowly, sadly, Paul began to recite "*Mon rêve familier*," a line with each deliberate stroke. Polly felt ideas and feelings separating in her mind and body, swirling down like doomed planes into a cloud of unknowing in which her sense of self vanished. She became the primary woman in the poem, whose hair was blond or red or brunette, who understood everything and nothing, whose transparent heart, purged of thought, cooled love's pale sweat-drenched brow with her tears.

Abandonment. That was what Paul Lebrun was demanding and she was giving him. She was surrendering to him and to *cafard*. She had surrendered her anger, and now she was surrendering her self. Tomorrow or the next day she would go anywhere with him, be anything he wished. She was too tired, too broken to resist him. She wanted the punishment she deserved for being an American, a modern woman in this warring world.

"*Les amants bizarres*," Polly whispered as the sweetness surged in her body. The bizarre lovers.

"*D'ajourner une exquise mort*," he said as she lost the last fragment of her self in his arms: postponing an exquisite death. "I wonder if that's what we've been doing all along."

The next day passed like a dream—or a nightmare. Whether Paul spoke in a voice with a silken caress or with the metallic snarl of a high-velocity shell did not matter. Polly belonged to him now in some deep incomprehensible way that created happiness and sadness in her heart, an alternating current over which she had no control.

The Germans were still raiding and shelling the front. The casualties flowed in, stomachs, chests, heads; the boiler huffed in the sterilizing room; the wounded cried and cursed in the ward. Shortly after nightfall, the antiaircraft guns erupted. Flares drifted down from the sky, their glaring light filtering around the edges of the burlap on the windows. The Germans seemed determined to punish the hospital tonight.

"What number raid is this, Dolbier?" Paul asked.

"The hundred and seventh," the anesthetist said.

"Isn't he remarkable?" Paul said to Polly. "Every country needs a Dolbier. He keeps track of things. He doesn't have the imagination of a railroad spike, but he devours facts. Which type of man do you prefer, Mademoiselle Warden, the factual or the imaginative?"

"I admire both," Polly said.

"Do you hear that, Dolbier? You may see the New World yet."

Is that what he called her when he was with his fellow doctors? Polly wondered. Did he brag about his visits to the New World? The Promised Land?

The antiaircraft guns thundered with unusual frenzy. The German motors seemed directly overhead. A bomb exploded not far away. The overhead light swayed. The ground shook beneath their feet. Paul bent over a stomach, the scalpel in his hand.

The next bomb's descending whine was the loudest yet. Marie Ribout was praying to the Virgin: "Holy Mary Mother of God—"

The bomb exploded just outside the rear wall. It blew in the window and most of the wall, turning the operating room into an instant shambles. The concussion flung Polly against the opposite wall, which buckled under the force of the explosion and the hurricane of shrapnel that came with it. A wave of intense heat engulfed her; for a moment she was sure she was going to suffocate. The anti-aircraft guns crashed and crashed. Two more bombs exploded nearby. Then there was silence.

Polly lay in the ruins wondering if she had gotten her wish. Was she dead? Was the enormous echoing in her ears the sound of eternity? The room, the whole building, was dark. The bomb had knocked out the generator.

From the ward came whimpering sounds. Someone was still alive in there. But in the operating room the silence remained profound. Footsteps crunched on broken glass. Major Mahone stood in the huge hole where the window had been, flashing a pencil of light around the wreckage. "Is anyone alive?"

Still wondering if she was dead, Polly did not speak. "I think I am," Dolbier said in his husky baritone.

The Major and several orderlies climbed through the hole and crunched over to the anesthetist. Another orderly with a flashlight played the beam toward Polly's side of the room. "The American mademoiselle," he said.

The Major joined him and helped Polly to her feet. Their beams played across her face and uniform. "My God, look at those shrapnel holes. She must be wounded," the Major said. Wisps of smoke curled from Polly's skirt and blouse. They were shredded by flying metal. She was going to die after all. Why didn't she feel any pain?

"Oh, look, Major, look," one of the other orderlies said.

Their united flashlights revealed Marie Ribout stretched across the patient on the operating table. Had she flung herself there to protect the wounded man, or was it a trick of the explosion? It did not matter, she was dead. Blood oozed from a wound in her head, creating dark red rivulets on her round cheeks.

"Lebrun. Where is Dr. Lebrun?" Dolbier asked.

"He's here," said the orderly who helped Polly to her feet.

Paul was lying face down less than a foot from where Polly had fallen. His left arm was flung out in her direction. Dolbier knelt and rolled him on his back. "Not a sign of a wound," he said, "but he's dead."

"I've seen it happen at the front when a large shell hits near a man," Major Mahone said. "The concussion crushes the skull."

In the flashlight beams, Paul's pale lips seemed curled in an ironic smile. As if they were about to whisper, *When you hear my name, does your heart always glow?*

BOOK III

20. IN DARKEST FRANCE

BENEATH GRAY SCUDDING CLOUDS, POLLY watched as Paul Lebrun and Marie Ribout were buried in the Château Givry's graveyard. The whole thing was incomprehensible. She should be lying beside Paul in Marie's coffin. She was the sinner, not innocent Marie, who had prayed to the Virgin for her. Paul's father, Charles Louis Lebrun, was there, his fleshy face haggard with grief, and his two brothers, their *guerre de luxe* gaiety banished by death's gravity. The father pressed her hand as he walked to his limousine, but he was too overwhelmed to speak.

As Polly returned to the château, Major Mahone fell in step beside her. "No one can believe your good fortune, mademoiselle. We counted thirty-eight shrapnel holes in your uniform. Not one piece of metal touched your flesh. We're changing your name, from Joyeuse to Heureuse."

The idea of calling her Mademoiselle Lucky almost made her weep. "I'll never be Joyeuse again," she said.

"You're young. Your heart will recover."

"Never," Polly said. "I should have died with him."

"Don't be absurd. You made him happy for a few months. So you quarreled? All lovers do."

Dr. Dolbier joined them, his heavy cheeks sagging with sadness. "I've been packing Paul's things. I thought you'd like to have this," he said.

He gave her a copy of Verlaine's poems, the pages smudged and worn by much turning. Polly could not bear to look at it. She thrust it into her suitcase and reported to Madame Leclerc for a new assignment. "Do you wish to continue to work in an operating room?" she asked, her usual loathing immensely reinforced by her rage at Paul's death.

"I'd like to work in the camion," Polly said.

"Why not?" Leclerc said, obviously delighted at the prospect of an early demise for *la putain moderne*.

An hour later she summoned Polly to her desk again, her sparrow face a grimace of disappointment. "The *Agent de Liasion* refuses to approve your transfer to the camion. I'm giving you the Germans instead."

Polly nodded numbly and walked away. "Everyone thinks you killed him, you know," Leclerc said. "You Americans have brought us nothing but bad luck."

The Germans were more arrogant and obnoxious than the last time Polly had nursed them. They chortled over the way they were slaughtering the British in the Ypres salient. They dismissed the French as already defeated, a cardboard enemy who could be knocked over with one more punch. Then they would deal with the Americans.

Sleep eluded Polly. She stared into the darkness, listening to the throb of distant artillery. She lay on her back, legs wide, waiting, almost wishing for someone to violate her. What was wrong with the rest of the doctors? Didn't they too want to visit the New World? When she slept her dreams were awful. Again and again, she found herself in Marie Ribout's coffin, gasping for air, clawing at the sealed top. A gray fog seemed to seep from her mind and turn her flesh to mud. She ate nothing but a little bread and fruit.

One day the *Agent de Liaison* seized her arm as she left the dining room, food untouched as usual. "We have a visiting doctor who would like to speak with you."

What now, a medical examination to get rid of her? Following the Major's directions, Polly trudged to the far end of the château, where the administrative offices were located in a set of rooms that had once been side parlors.

At a gilt-trimmed eighteenth-century desk sat a woman of about forty, wearing a horizon-blue army uniform covered by a dark blue cape. Her thick brown hair was cut short but retained a shimmering wave. Her mouth was full and strong but drawn severely at the corners. Her dark eyes emanated sternness, willpower. She gestured to a seat beside the desk. "I'm Dr. Marie Giroux-Langin, Director of Nurses in the Bureau de Santé," she said. "Charles Louis Lebrun asked me to see you. He's concerned for your state of mind since his son's death."

Polly began to weep. "Does he think I killed him?"

"Of course not. Who's been telling you such a thing?"

"Madame Leclerc. She says everyone thinks so. I don't blame them. I can see why you hate Americans. We've made you think we were going to win the war, and it isn't true. We're a bunch of fakes—poseurs."

"Mademoiselle. I've met your General Pershing. I didn't see a trace of the poseur in the man. I think—if I may speak one woman to another—you're somewhat hysterical. Tell me what transpired between you and Dr. Lebrun."

Dr. Giroux-Langin listened calmly, carefully, without a trace of disapproval, until Polly described Paul's plan to send her to his mother's summer house. The Doctor threw back her head and laughed. "That's so familiar! When I was in medical school, his father tried to do the same thing with me."

"What did you do?"

Her eyes flashed with dark fire. "He broke my heart. But I got my diploma, heart or no heart."

She stood up and strode to the window, her shoulders squared, struggling with some private emotion. "You must understand something about Frenchmen. They adore women. They like to treat them well. As well as they treat a valuable thoroughbred horse—or a pedigreed dog."

She looked over her shoulder at Polly. Her expression was the total opposite of those bitter words: compassionate, searching. "Does that wound you too much?"

Polly shook her head.

"When a woman tries to become a being in her own right, with an independent heart, most Frenchmen react with rage and fear. I think they fear us more than they fear the Germans. I can't explain it. Ultimately it's a spiritual question."

She paced up and down, more than a little agitated by her own remarks. "For the time being perhaps we should simply accept it as a mystery. That's better than letting it turn us into man-haters. No woman can hate men who die with the bravery of our poilus."

She paced again, deeply moved now, almost talking to herself. "There was a general at Verdun who said something wonderful to me. Wonderful and terrible. He said that when a brave man dies, the war creates two brave men to take his place. He said war diminishes the number of men but not the quantity of courage in the world. I believe that! Do you?"

"I hope I can, someday."

"Tell me the rest of the story."

Polly held nothing back, from the brutality of the uninvited visit to her room to the surrender of her deepest self a few days later. Dr. Giroux-Langin listened almost pensively, as if she knew it all in advance. Had she been tempted to such a surrender? Polly found it hard to believe.

Again there was a flash of icy fire in those commanding eyes. "You shouldn't spend another day in this hospital. There are too many unhappy thoughts and feelings here. Why don't you come back to Paris with me? I need someone with your experience on my staff. We're getting quite a lot of American volunteers, and my English is atrocious."

Polly said goodbye only to Dr. Dolbier and Major Mahone. Dolbier kissed her on both cheeks and said, "You've warmed all our hearts, even my humdrum factual one." Mahone insisted on a ceremony. He summoned Madame Leclerc and the head surgeon to his office and pinned the croix de guerre on Polly's blouse. "Mademoiselle has been wounded in the line of duty," he said.

"I have no record of a wound!" Leclerc said.

"Not every wound ruptures the skin, madame," the old man said.

In her room, Polly gazed at her uniform with the thirty-eight shrapnel holes in it. Leave it behind? No, said an inner voice that startled her, take it to show your grandchildren. Amazing. It was her obstreperous American self. Why should a talk with a French woman doctor revive that ghost?

At the château's front door, Dr. Giroux-Langin awaited her in a roomy tan staff car driven by a black Senegalese. She talked to Polly as a medical equal, asking her numerous questions about the procedures in the operating rooms at Château Givry. What did Polly think about sending wounded Americans to French hospitals? Would they adapt to the food, the treatment? Would American soldiers treat French nurses with respect? She had heard reports of a division that had landed at Saint-Nazaire and run wild.

"The Lafayette Division?" Polly asked.

"I think that was its name. Hardly surprising, if they take after their French namesake. I'm distantly related to him on his wife's side. Sainte Adrienne! That's what my mother used to call her. She was a model wife. No matter how many skirts the Marquis lifted, she continued to adore him."

"Was she sincere?"

"Perhaps not. But she suffered in silence."

Polly sensed this was not a virtue Dr. Giroux-Langin admired. "Did you volunteer for the army when the war began?"

The Doctor shook her head. "I was drafted. When I reported for duty in 1914, the battle of the Marne was raging. The army was appalled to discover Dr. M. Giroux-Langin was a woman. With a thousand casualties for every doctor, they decided to let me stay for the time being. Later, when they tried to discharge me, I went to General Pétain himself at Verdun. He inspected my hospital and told Paris to go to hell."

"Everyone at the Château Givry thinks France is beaten," Polly said.

"I thought that myself last year at Verdun," Dr. Giroux-Langin said. "I saw whole regiments flee, routed, reduced to blind panic by the German bombardment. But Pétain rallied them. Last spring, when a mutiny seemed about to destroy the army, he rallied them again. There are mysteries in war. One of the strangest is the mystery of leadership: why men respond to one man and not to another. It's something we women don't quite understand yet. But we'll learn."

By the time they reached Paris, Polly felt a precarious hope—for herself and for France. They drove swiftly across the city to Dr. Giroux-Langin's hospital, a rectangular yellow-brick building on the Rue Desnouettes, not far from the Versailles gate. Beside the main building, Polly saw two flat-roofed barracks that might have been transported intact from the grounds of the Château Givry. They had the same tarpaper roofs, burlapped windows, and jutting steam pipes in the rear. "That's where we train our nurses," the Doctor said. "I wanted to make the atmosphere as realistic as possible."

Would they have wounded men calling them bitches and cows and idiots? Polly wondered. And Paul Lebrun whispering Verlaine, inviting them to join him in Paris for absinthe's green hours? In a flash her sense of well-being vanished. She trembled and almost wept. *Cafard* was back.

Dr. Giroux-Langin did not seem in the least surprised. "You will not come to work for two weeks," she said, as they got out of the car. "What you see as the inexorable pull of lost love, the downward spiral of despair, I see as a depleted body and exhausted nerves. I have a regime I want you to follow."

In her office on the hospital's third floor, Dr. Giroux-Langin ordered Polly to devote fifteen minutes to deep breathing every morning, followed by a half hour of calisthenics and an ice-cold bath. "The breathing will diminish your anxiety, the exercise will tone your body, the bath will strengthen your self-confidence."

She walked Polly to the door, arm in arm. "Try not to think about the war for two weeks," she said. "Explore the Bois de Boulogne, the Louvre. Go to the theater, have dinner with friends. Become an American again for a little while."

Polly was amazed by how violently she resisted this last idea. "I'm not sure I want to be an American. I'm—almost ashamed of my country."

"There are many times each day when I'm ashamed of France," Dr. Giroux-Langin said, seizing her by the shoulders. "It's not the real country, but the ideal one we serve. Paul Lebrun saw that, in spite of his father and the war. Keep that faith alive in your heart for his sake, even if it makes no sense now."

At the Kingswood house on the Rue de Verneuil, the joy with

which Eleanor and Martha greeted her made Polly wince. General
Bliss had told them where she was working. "Everywhere we go we
talk about our friend in the Forbidden Zone," Eleanor said.

Polly forced cheer onto her face and listened to Eleanor and
Martha describe their adventures in Paris. Eleanor had taken a job
with the YWCA, setting up canteens in the training areas. Eventually some would be in the Forbidden Zone, when the Americans
took over a sector of the front. Martha was working as a secretary to
Brigadier General Charles Dawes, who was in charge of purchasing
equipment for the AEF. Harry Quickmeyer was often in the office,
consulting him on Pershing's behalf. The expression on Martha's
face made it clear that this was no small part of the job's attraction.

Polly asked Eleanor if she was still seeing Colonel Fairchild. The
answer was a pained, angry no. She had received a letter from him,
reporting that his heart had been surrendered elsewhere. It was the
first time Eleanor had ever been rejected by a man, and she did not
like it.

"Do you know the lucky woman?" Polly asked. From General
Bliss's comments, she did not see Colonel Fairchild as an ideal suitor
for Eleanor or anyone else.

"We suspect a certain femme fatale who apparently won't be satisfied until she's reduced the whole AEF to slavering adoration,"
Martha said.

"Louise Wolcott?"

"The uncrowned queen of *la guerre de luxe*," Martha said.

"I *hate* that woman," Eleanor said.

Upstairs in her bedroom Polly found two long letters from her
mother, crammed with news about all the things American women
were doing on the home front. She and Polly's sisters were serving
on committees to sell war bonds, wrap bandages, and knit warm
sweaters and socks for the "doughboys," a Civil War nickname that
reporters had fastened on the AEF. Mother added her usual diet of
gossip. Suzy Astor was writing a letter a day to George Eagleton, and
several other women were competing with her. But the replies were
sparse to nonexistent—prompting Mother to wonder if he was still
in love with Polly.

Beneath these letters was a note from George on army stationery. He had come up from Saint-Nazaire to see his friend Harry Quickmeyer. They had met at a national pistol competition two years ago, before Polly persuaded George to abandon such a warlike sport. Her name had "popped up" and Quickmeyer had directed him to the Kingswood house, where he discovered Polly was "already fighting the war." He hoped the Lafayette Division would soon imitate her example.

For a moment Polly was overwhelmed by a flood of melancholy. She knew exactly how George would react to her surrender to Paul Lebrun. The details would be irrelevant to him. A single standard— for women—was enshrined in George's mind. Ruefully, Polly understood its meaning and its value to George. Paul Lebrun had forced her to think realistically about the way men regarded women.

The maid reported a telephone call for Mademoiselle Warden. A masculine voice introduced himself as Charles Lebrun, Paul's brother. "My father wonders if you could join us at our hunting lodge in the Île-de-France this weekend. He would like to hear all you know about Paul's last hours."

How could she refuse such an invitation? It was a chance to expiate some of the guilt she felt for Paul's death. Promptly at three that Saturday, Charles Lebrun arrived in a gleaming gray Dion-Bouton, a luxury car often used by French presidents and premiers. They drove swiftly through the lush historic countryside of the Île-de-France with its sunny meadows and picturesque villages, favored subjects of Monet and other impressionist painters.

Polly asked Charles if he enjoyed his work as a liaison officer to the Belgian army. He made a wry face. "We have a saying, 'We'll fight till the last Belgian is expelled from French soil.' They're utterly useless soldiers. Which makes liaison work with them more or less superfluous."

They talked about the Lebruns. Paul had told her his parents were divorced. Was it recent? Charles Lebrun shook his head. "It happened years and years ago." He hesitated, then added, "You've met the principal reason: Dr. Giroux-Langin. I sometimes think my father's still in love with her."

The hunting lodge was a chaletlike two-story wooden house overlooking a placid brook that vanished into nearby sun-spangled woods. "We spent our boyhood summers here in a house my mother still owns," Charles said, as they got out of the car. "The whole neighborhood is full of sentimental memories. Father has come here every weekend since Paul's death."

In the lodge, Charles Louis Lebrun greeted Polly with an affectionate embrace that crushed the breath out of her body. He was looking bearlike in a rough hunter's shirt and leather knickers. As soon as she unpacked, he invited her to join him for a stroll in the woods. He strode along a path beside the swift clear brook at a pace that had Polly almost running to keep up with him.

The woods were open, the ground beneath the trees cleared of brush, although just enough shrubs were permitted to flourish to give an illusion of wildness. "The boys used to play here by the hour," Lebrun said. "We called it our forest primeval. Perhaps that's where Paul acquired his interest in America. He read dozens of books about your country. He organized games of cowboys against Indians with the local children. We called him our savage."

Polly was almost ashamed to confess Paul had never mentioned his interest in America to her. "You had other things to discuss," Lebrun said. "Tell me about his last days, hours."

"There was nothing unusual about them," Polly lied. She could not tell this man the truth.

"Did you quarrel about his refusal to transfer to Paris? The thought has troubled me—that I've added to your grief."

"We did quarrel," Polly admitted, "but we kept working. That's the important thing. We both remained committed to the war, to France."

Lebrun clutched Polly's hand, and his voice thickened with grief that was close to tears. "The family will never forget his nobility— or yours."

Ahead, the woods ended abruptly on a steep ridge. They looked across the brook as it wound through rolling pastures. About a quarter of a mile away stood a slope-roofed gray stone mansion with half a dozen chimneys. "That's Mon Repos, our old summer house," Lebrun said.

He seemed swept by melancholy. Polly was drowning in it. The landscape exuded peace, serenity, beauty. Behind the house was a garden full of topiary, shrubs sculpted in the French classical tradi-tion. In the distance she could see the church steeple Paul had com-pared to a voice of hope. He had wanted to share all this—the deep-est, richest part of his past—with her.

"Paul is dead," his father said. "What can we, the living, do to honor his memory?"

"I don't know," Polly said, still mesmerized by the lost happiness she might have known here.

"It seems to me the best thing we can do is bring peace to France—to the world."

Lebrun drew her back into the woods as if he wanted to make his next words as confidential as possible. Tonight at dinner Polly would hear a serious discussion of the possibility of peace with Ger-many. Not a red peace, a blood-soaked victorious peace, but a white peace, in which there were no victors except the soldiers on both sides who survived. To make it a reality would require a terrific political campaign, in which she could play an important part.

"We want you to organize the American women in Paris to join us, as you rallied pacifists in your own country before Wilson declared war. We want you to issue a statement, to parade before the American embassy and the British embassy and our foreign office on the Quai d'Orsay. We want you, in particular, to tell the world you've seen the futility of the war, to tell the story of your love for Paul and his tragic death. Will you do it?"

"Yes!" Polly said.

She was completely converted by Charles Louis Lebrun's melan-choly fervor for peace, by his readiness to forgive her for Paul's death, by his proposal of this act of expiation. It did not matter that her confession would ruin her reputation among respectable people, confirming her mother's worst predictions. Nothing mattered but this gift, this sacrifice he was asking her to make in Paul's memory.

"I was sure that would be your answer," Lebrun said.

He drew her to him for a fatherly embrace. At least it began as a fatherly embrace. But he did not let her go. Suddenly his lips were on Polly's throat. "My beautiful American child," he whispered. "Can you offer another gift to an old man? The same gift you offered Paul, a gift that will fill an empty heart with joy for a little while?"

No, whispered a voice in Polly's head. *This is wrong. No.* But she allowed him to keep his arm around her waist as they walked back into the woods. "There's a little cabin nearby where we rest during a hunt," he said.

It was hardly a hunter's cabin. There was a bed with clean sheets and a cabinet stocked with wine and liquor and a fire laid in the fireplace. One match produced a roaring blaze that quickly banished the late-afternoon chill. Polly stood there, paralyzed, while Lebrun took off her coat and began unbuttoning the back of her dress. The feeling, the word *wrong*, permeated her body. Not only wrong in the way others would use the word in prudish America but in some deeper more fundamental sense. She began to weep. Within seconds her tears became shuddering sobs.

"I want to love you—I want you to love me for Paul's sake—but not this way," she said. "I tried to love Paul this way, and we failed. He wanted to own me, and in the end I let him, but it was horrible. It wasn't love any more."

Polly told him about Paul's anguish, his rage, his despair, her forlorn attempts to defeat *cafard*. As she finished, thick teardrops oozed down Lebrun's cheeks. "You mustn't believe love ends this way. I hope—I'll even pray to whatever blind god presides over this berserk world—that you'll find another lover who brings you the happiness you deserve. In the meantime, what you've told me only makes me even more resolved to end this vile war. Do you still want to help us?"

"Yes, yes!" Polly said. She was engulfed by this new forgiveness, his love for Paul, her instinctive detestation of the war.

"You must understand it will be difficult, even dangerous. Many people in France and in your own country will disagree violently with the idea. They may call us traitors, betrayers."

Polly sensed he had not intended to tell her this. She also heard—or thought she heard, as Lebrun spoke out of emotions he had not anticipated—a division in his mind about this white peace. For a moment Polly heard Dr. Giroux-Langin, who had resisted this man for her own reasons, telling her the ideal country—whether it was France or America—deserved her loyalty.

"I'm not afraid of dangers or difficulties," Polly said. "Only one thing matters to me: Is this what Paul would want us to do in his memory?"

"I believe that with all my heart," Charles Louis Lebrun said.

Polly studied the fleshy, wordly face, trying to find sincerity, honesty, nobility there. But the financier had recovered his self-control. She saw only the implacable mask of masculine determination, the will to prevail.

Gwendolyn Victoria Warden, known to her American friends as Polly, was lost in the middle of darkest France.

21. THE VOICE OF HOPE

"WE HAVE RECEIVED INCONTROVERTIBLE WORD from our friends in Berlin that unless we propose an acceptable peace before January first, the German army will begin making plans for a final offensive that will end the war on their terms."

The speaker was black-mustached bald-headed Senator Joseph Caillaux, former premier, spokesman of the Radical Republicans, one of the largest parties in France's Chamber of Deputies, and the real leader of the plan to sign a white peace with Germany. He sat at the head of Charles Louis Lebrun's dinner table, flanked by the men who were working with him. One was a short dapper Marseilles playboy named Bolo Pasha, who had picked up his title doing some shadowy favors for the Khedive of Egypt. He was the owner of the *Bonnet Rouge*, the radical paper Polly had seen at the Trois Magots and the Château Givry. Another was bulky, garrulous Senator Charles Humbert, owner of one of the largest papers in Paris, *Le Journal*, and chairman of the Senate Committee on the Army. Next came pudgy, phlegmatic Louis Malvy, the Minister of the Interior, the man in charge of France's internal security. Finally there was a sullen hatchet-faced younger man named Almeyreda, whom Charles Louis Lebrun described as "king of the apaches"—one of the rulers of the Paris underworld.

Polly, Lebrun, and the others listened while Caillaux told them the government of the current premier, Paul Painlevé, was tottering. If President Raymond Poincaré, who was empowered under the constitution to choose a premier to organize a new government, balked at naming Caillaux, Humbert was to open fire on him in *Le Journal* and urge certain friends among the generals to threaten a coup d'état. Simultaneously, Almeyreda and his apaches would take to the streets shouting for peace and Polly Warden would lead her demonstrators in their wake.

"Paris might become dangerous for a few days," Caillaux said. "But I'm quite certain Poincaré will soon capitulate and offer me the premiership. I will immediately announce my intention to open negotiations for peace with Germany, without consulting our so-called allies in London."

"What about the Americans?" Lebrun asked.

"They can be informed in due course that the war is over," Caillaux said, with a smile that was close to a sneer. "Their millions of pacifists will rejoice, and Wilson, already with them in spirit, will soon join them. Don't you agree, Miss Warden?"

Polly nodded, but it was closer to a gesture of astonishment than agreement. "What sort of peace terms do you envision?" she asked.

Caillaux shrugged. "They won't be advantageous. For almost three years the Germans have possessed a quarter of France. The only way we can persuade them to retreat to the Rhine will be to offer large concessions. We'll have to give them Belgium and whatever they choose to occupy in the east—probably all of Poland and possibly the Ukraine."

"The Russians deserve nothing from us, the Belgians less," Senator Humbert said. "One is a country of blunderers, the other of cowards."

War is the engine of history, Malvern Hill Bliss had insisted. History was never a subject that had particularly interested Polly. She found herself wishing she had spent the previous eight years of her life studying it day and night. Were they rescuing the ideal France that Paul and Dr. Giroux-Langin treasured, or were they destroying it?

"When you say Paris might be dangerous, what do you mean?" she asked.

"There may be street fighting. The grudges of the Commune have never been settled," Caillaux said. "But Almeyreda here will protect our friends—and chastise our enemies."

A faint smile flitted across Almeyreda's sullen face. "There are many who need serious chastisement."

"I'm opposed to political murder!" Humbert cried.

"Almeyreda has promised to control his apaches," Louis Malvy said soothingly. "He's kept them quiet for the past two years."

The dinner broke up with Humbert vowing to assign one of his best reporters to write Polly's story for *Le Journal*. He looked forward to welcoming her in his office at the paper as soon as possible. Something in the way he said this, with a greedy smile in his eyes, made Polly uneasy. "She's not available for your delectation, Senator," Charles Louis Lebrun said.

Polly retreated to her bedroom while the guests departed in their cars and limousines. She sat at her open window watching them, still too astonished to think about what she had just heard. Lebrun's deep voice wished them a safe journey as they pulled away. The last to go was Joseph Caillaux. With a nervous cough, he told Lebrun they needed more money to keep Almeyreda and his followers happy until the plan was set in motion. "Cocaine is expensive," Caillaux said. "He's taken another mistress."

"You're sure about Malvy?" Lebrun said. "He could put us all in jail tomorrow."

"He's in too deep with Almeyreda and Bolo to back out now. Did things go as planned with Little Miss Liberty? She seemed a bit difficult, with her questions."

"She fell into my arms and agreed to everything," Lebrun said. "Her questions were perfectly natural. This business is new to her."

"I still don't see why you've insisted on bringing her into our plan," Caillaux said. "It's a sentimental idea."

"You can call it what you please. It makes me feel Paul's death is not completely meaningless."

"That's an illusion. All the deaths have been meaningless. A million Frenchman have died—not for France but for England."

"In their hearts they died for France. That counts for something."

"The heart doesn't think."

"True. But I still believe an outcry from American women will be useful. It will help to disarm their troops. They could be a complication you haven't foreseen, if they supported the government. The poilus wouldn't fight them as they would the English."

"You may be right. When can you have the money for Almeyreda? He wants a million francs."

"Monday at noon."

If a bomb had exploded outside the window and blown her across the bedroom, Polly could not have been more stunned. Why did Charles Louis Lebrun feel compelled to tell Joseph Caillaux he had seduced her? Because it made Caillaux feel she could now be trusted? Was Lebrun simply trying to maintain his reputation as an irresistible lover? Was he involved in a shadowy struggle with Caillaux for some kind of male superiority? Polly stumbled back from the window as Lebrun returned to the hunting lodge. It was the abyss Paul had warned her against. These men lived by a code that had nothing to do with ideals. There were only priorities: power, wealth, pleasure.

What did that imply for the peace they were proposing to negotiate? Wasn't anything that stopped the killing and maiming a good peace? Was she being the naïve American again, expecting the fervor of moral reformers from men who had no such tradition, whose history was a tangle of war and intrigue and hatred?

On Sunday morning, Polly came downstairs to find Charles Louis Lebrun at a huge desk in his study, surrounded by stock market reports from London, New York, and Geneva. He was briskly telephoning orders for the sale or purchase of various securities to a secretary in Paris. A half hour later, he emerged in a buoyant mood, predicting he had just made ten million francs.

He kissed Polly and asked if she had slept well. She lied and said yes. Charles Lebrun returned from a walk in the woods and they enjoyed a leisurely breakfast, during which the two men reminisced at length about Paul. "He was always the most adventurous one," the father said. "Always the most difficult to control."

The Lebruns and Polly departed for Paris around noon. She soon sensed tension between father and son. They stared out opposite windows. As the skyline of Paris appeared in the distance, the father uttered a bearlike growl. "Where the devil did you get these ideas?" he said.

"Last night I walked over to Mon Repos. I sat in my old room for a long time, thinking about what's happened to us," Charles said.

"Sentimentality."

Charles Lebrun began perspiring. "Perhaps, Father. But sentiment—sentiment is normal. Isn't it another word—for love?"

"Sometimes. More often it connotes feelings as a substitute for thought."

They resumed looking out opposite windows. "He's decided to ask for duty at the front. Doesn't that strike you as absolute idiocy?" Lebrun said. "Especially in the light of what you heard last night."

"I think this is a family quarrel," Polly said. "Outside opinions are worth nothing in such matters."

"I won't lecture you, Father. I don't have Paul's convictions. But those people sicken me: Almeyreda, Bolo."

"They sicken me too. But for the time being we need them. France needs them."

Charles Louis Lebrun picked up Polly's left hand. "Not a single ring on those pretty fingers. What would you like, a diamond? An emerald? What's the American taste in jewelry?"

"I've never been very interested in it," Polly said.

"We'll change that with a visit to the Rue Cambon."

That was where Paris's jewelers had their shops. "I'd rather see you give the money to war orphans and widows," Polly said.

"I gave them five million francs last month," Lebrun said. "That entitles me to spend a million on you."

The man was imperial. There was no way to stop him from doing what he pleased. It was easy to see why his son Charles perspired and stammered when they disagreed.

Polly wondered if Lebrun had abandoned his pursuit of the gift he had asked for in the Auvers woods. Was this breathtaking generosity another kind of seduction? Perhaps power was as erotic to this man as sex. Still in the grip of *cafard*, she felt too feeble, too confused, to escape him. His personal forgiveness for Paul's death was almost as important as this white peace he was using her to promote.

She parted at the house on the Rue de Verneuil with a promise to have lunch with him the following day. In the front hall, Eleanor

Kingswood greeted her with a somewhat distant hello. "That French woman doctor you told us about—Dr. Giroux-something?—called last night looking for you."

Eleanor wanted to hear all about the house party to which Polly had been transported in the Dion-Bouton. Polly put her off with vague generalities about French friends from her hospital and called Dr. Giroux-Langin. "Mademoiselle Warden," she said. "I think it's time you paid me a visit. I like to keep a close watch on cases like yours."

It was easier to say yes than make an excuse. Polly taxied to the yellow hospital on the Rue Desnouettes. In a crisp white coat, Dr. Giroux-Langin sat behind a desk piled with folders of patient records. "I try to read them all each week," she said. "I'm always behind."

She studied Polly for a moment. "I don't like your color. Have you followed my regime?"

"No. I've been—distracted."

"Perhaps your condition is more serious than I thought. Tell me what you've been thinking—feeling."

"I spent the weekend with Charles Louis Lebrun and several friends in Auvers."

The Doctor was suddenly as alert as a sentinel who hears a gunshot. She took off her glasses and placed them carefully on top of the pile of reports. "Why did he want to see you?"

Polly poured out the whole story, half defiant, half ashamed. "And at some point Lebrun seduced you—to guarantee your loyalty, your subservience," Dr. Giroux-Langin said.

"He—he tried," Polly said.

With an oath she must have learned at Verdun, Dr. Giroux-Langin flung her glasses across the room. She retrieved them and paced up and down the small office, unable to contain her fury. "This is a personal as well as a political affront! He could have had friends in the army transfer you from that hospital. He's deliberately involved me in this business to let me know how little he regards my opinions."

The war seemed in danger of disappearing in this firestorm of rage. "The awful thing is, I still agree with him," Polly said. "Isn't peace, some kind of peace, the only realistic alternative?"

Dr. Giroux-Langin pressed a buzzer on her desk. An orderly appeared. "Tell Jacques Marie Clemenceau I wish to see her immediately."

There was something vaguely oriental about the wide heavy face of the stocky, dark-haired nurse who soon joined them. Dr. Giroux-Langin introduced Polly. "Jacques Marie's father is the terrible old man we call the Tiger, the worst-tempered politician in France. Although I disagree with almost all his opinions—he's an unrepentant atheist, among other things—he's also the most honest man I've ever met. If you want to know the truth about the war, I think you should talk to him. He also publishes a newspaper. For that reason alone I think he'll be quite interested in Senator Caillaux's peace plans."

Jacques Marie Clemenceau's wide brow furrowed. "How ever did you meet that snake-oil specialist?" she said, in unaccented American.

In her direct way, Dr. Giroux-Langin explained how Polly had met Joseph Caillaux. Jacques Marie Clemenceau did not even blink. "May I use the telephone? I'll see if I can arrange a meeting," she said.

"Explain that it must be clandestine. A certain apache named Almeyreda might be inclined to cut Mademoiselle Warden's throat if he found out about it."

"We'll meet in Papa's apartment on the Rue Franklin. There's a secret entrance through the garden that few people know about."

They taxied across the Seine to the Rue Franklin, in the Passy quarter, with its splendid view of the Eiffel Tower and the green swath of the Champ de Mars. Was the street name an omen? Polly hoped so. On the Avenue Paul Doumer, one block below the Rue Franklin, a gray-haired concierge was waiting at the door of a large apartment. She bowed them inside and led them down into the cellar. In a dank corner, an invisible door swung open. Using a flashlight, she led them along a tunnel that reeked of the sewers of Paris. Another door opened on stairs that led to a small garden containing a few shrubs and a white gravel walk around an oval of faded grass.

In the center of the grass, playing with a white Aberdeen terrier, stood an old man dressed in a shabby unpressed dark suit. He had a fantastic fringe of white hair, bristling, fanglike white mustaches, swarthy, almost Mongolian features—and the most electrifying eyes Polly had ever encountered. They seemed to penetrate her mind and body in one concentrated glare.

"What's this?" he said. "I'm offered a rendezvous with one of the prettiest Americans in Paris, and she arrives with two chaperones: one of them my daughter, the other a woman who thinks she can order generals around as she pleases. This is an ambush, a plot to ruin me."

"It's very serious business, Papa," Jacques Marie said.

"I know that," he growled. "But you also know my weakness for American women." He put his arm around Polly's waist. "If this were twenty years ago, I'd send these two Amazons packing. I've only been in love twice in my life, both times with Americans. The first one was her mother." He gestured to his daughter. "She wisely gave up on me and fled back to America to save her own and her children's sanity."

"That's what Americans call 'the awful truth,'" Jacques Marie said with a tinge of sadness.

Georges Clemenceau led them into a study piled with books and papers and sat Polly down in a battered leather armchair. He fell into a swivel chair behind a big U-shaped desk. "Okay," he said. "Shoot the works."

He listened intently, scribbling an occasional note, while Polly told him everything she had seen and heard over the weekend at Auvers. "Dr. Giroux-Langin thought you could advise me. Is there a chance for peace?"

"It depends on what kind of peace you want, Caillaux's or mine," Clemenceau said.

"Yours?"

"I've been asked to form a government. I'm in the process of doing it now."

"How can you possibly do it, Papa?" his daughter said. "You don't have a party. You've insulted every major politician in France."

"It's an act of desperation on the part of our esteemed president. He hates me slightly less than he hates Caillaux, so he's throwing his influence behind me."

"Can France survive a German offensive?" Polly asked.

"I don't know. I only know this: France signed a peace of conciliation and surrender with Germany when I was a young man, forty-six years ago. We paid them a billion francs in reparations and surrendered two provinces rich in natural resources, Alsace and Lorraine. It only made the Germans more arrogant, more ambitious, more militaristic. Caillaux wants to repeat that performance. Do you think that makes sense? My peace envisions a Germany totally defeated, stripped of her grandiose ambition to rule the world, taught a lesson that will last a century."

"But that means another year—perhaps two years—of war, and you may not win," Polly said.

"I know that. But I'd rather die in the wreckage of a defeated France than live as a citizen in a humiliated France."

"Amen," Dr. Giroux-Langin said.

"Countries, like individuals, can become enslaved," Clemenceau said. "Ireland. Poland. Bulgaria. India. China. The world is full of them. It's an unspeakable fate, a living death."

The old man sprang out of his chair and strode up and down the narrow room. There was a catlike grace to his stumpy body, a kind of coiled determination. "In my long political life I've been everything, mademoiselle: a Catholic, a socialist, a republican. Now I believe in only one thing: force. Force triumphs over everything. Without force, freedom is meaningless."

Polly flinched from this total repudiation of her pacifism. Clemenceau paced the floor, gesticulating, his breath coming in rasps. "I'm talking about the extinction of liberty in Europe. If it's crushed in France, it will vanish in Italy, never arise in Spain, evaporate in Russia, and become a parody of the real thing in Germany and Austria."

He stopped pacing and glared at the three women. "Ah! I can see it on your faces, even hers," he said, gesturing to his daughter. "You're repelled by this nihilist who belches about force and then shouts apostrophes to liberty. But I'm not quite as cynical as I sound.

I'm convinced France and America have a special mission in this world. We were the first two nations to proclaim liberty, brother-hood, and equality as a cause. No matter how often we've failed to live up to those ideals, history—which just might be the voice of God—hauls us back to them. We come reluctantly, like all sinners. We whine and shudder at the sacrifices demanded. But we come, we come!"

Dr. Giroux-Langin's jaw was stiff with disagreement. Polly sensed she had a different vision of an ideal France. Clemenceau's daughter seemed equally unresponsive. For a moment the old man looked discouraged. His shoulders drooped as he shuffled around his desk and dropped into his chair.

"Get out of here, you two," he growled to the Doctor and his daughter. "Go back to your hospital. There are things I want to say to Mademoiselle Warden in private. When we're through I'll have her driven home."

The two women left through the front door. "Now we can get to some straight talk," Clemenceau said in his American English. "I have things to tell you that can't be said before other people."

He pulled a set of folders from the drawer of his desk. "Each of these is a dossier on the gentlemen you've gotten to know through the Lebruns. Our secret service has been watching them since the war began. They were all on what was called Carnet B—a list of people with questionable loyalty to France. But Malvy, our Minister of the Interior, is a trimmer by instinct. He's always been half inclined to agree with Caillaux. So nothing was done."

Clemenceau sprang up from his desk again. "When I become premier I'm going to jail them all, including Malvy and Caillaux. As a senator he's got immunity from arrest, but I'm going to ask the Chamber of Deputies to suspend that rule. I'm going to prove he and Bolo Pasha and Almeyreda are traitors. Every centime Bolo has put into the *Bonnet Rouge*—and the five million francs he lent Sen-ator Humbert to modernize *Le Journal*—came from Berlin."

History, Polly thought. It was twisting and coiling around her like a thousand hissing snakes in this small study. Though she flinched from its slimy entanglements, she was learning to face it. She was learning to judge men. She trusted this fierce old man more than she could ever trust shrill, arrogant Joseph Caillaux or suave, world-weary Charles Louis Lebrun. Clemenceau had Theodore Roosevelt's absolute uncompromising honesty and courage. For the first time she understood her father's worship of TR.

"The Lebruns are another matter. They're not politicians. They're rich and afraid of losing their privileges and comforts. Caillaux specializes in playing on the fears of such people, probably because he shares them. Maybe that's why I've never gotten rich. I was afraid it would interfere with my patriotism."

His eyes twinkled for a moment. "Of course, those who know how badly I run my newspaper assure me I never had anything to worry about."

The eyes abruptly regained their primal glare. "Are you with me—or with Caillaux?"

"With you," Polly said.

It made no sense. How could this stooped old man in his shabby suit save France? This penniless political outcast, a man without a party, growling defiance of imperial Germany in his run-down apartment? How could he defeat Caillaux and Lebrun and Bolo Pasha with their millions, their town houses and châteaus and hunting lodges, their Dion-Boutons? Polly had no idea. She was beyond thought, beyond grief, beyond *cafard* in a moment of pure feeling, pure faith.

"I want you to became my agent-in-place with Lebrun and Caillaux. Continue to cooperate with them. Go to Humbert. Tell him your story. I guarantee you it won't be used. The censor will never pass it while I'm premier."

He paused to light a cigarette. The acrid smoke of a Gauloise swirled around them. "Of course, if the deputies refuse to grant me the special powers I'm going to demand, I'll resign. Caillaux will succeed me. You'll be exposed to Humbert, to all of them."

Polly nodded, trying not to think too specifically about what the word exposed might imply.

"Naturally I want you to tell me everything you see and hear. I also want you to sow doubts about Caillaux and his peace plan in Lebrun's mind. Do you know any American soldiers?"

"I came over on the *Baltic* with General Pershing and his staff."

"Good. You can introduce them to Lebrun as a gesture of frater-nity. I'll do some orchestration in the background to make sure they say the right things. At a crucial moment I'll send you a signal to warn Lebrun he's in danger of arrest—which will, I think, scare him into switching sides. A good twenty or thirty deputies, who depend on him for their care and feeding, will follow him."

"Why should he believe me?"

"You can say Dr. Giroux-Langin told you. She could hear it from my daughter. The Doctor and Lebrun were lovers once, and I gather the parting was not friendly. He'd assume she mentioned it to you with the greatest glee."

Clemenceau drew on his Gauloise. Smoke swirled from his nos-trils, giving him a vaguely satanic look. "Madame le Docteur won't like what I'm asking you to do. She'll worry about your immortal soul."

More smoke swirled from the hard old mouth. "So will I. I'm not quite as much of an atheist as I pretend to be. No one is, in my opinion. But the Jesuits tell me no one ever went to hell for the sins of love."

He assumed she had already given herself to Charles Louis Lebrun or would have to do so in the near future, to guarantee her influence. Polly decided not to tell him about the scene in the hunter's cabin. There are secrets that transcend politics.

"Will you do it?"

Polly nodded. She would do it for Paul's sake, and her own sake, and for Charles Louis Lebrun's sake. No matter what he pretended to be to Joseph Caillaux, there was a core of decency in the man.

Clemenceau's lined face darkened. "Men will die. My soldiers—and yours."

With uncanny shrewdness the old man sensed this was where she was most vulnerable. Polly heard Major Mahone sighing, *The sacrifices men make for France!* Would she be able to bear someone saying the same thing about Americans? "I—I know that," she said.

The voice of hope, Paul whispered. She could only pray she was listening to it.

22. THE LOST WAR

AFTER SPENDING ALMOST A WEEK IN THE SERPENtine coils of the French railway system, the Lafayette Division finally arrived in Lorraine to begin training for the Western Front. Bliss set up headquarters in Neufchâteau, a hilly town of about five thousand on the meandering Meuse River. He took over the mayor's narrow stone house, which had been built in the seventeenth century and looked it. Water oozed from the taps in a trickle. The toilet was an outhouse in the back yard. Heating consisted of a few fireplaces.

In the nearby walled city of Toul, Bliss lunched with General Leon Castineau, the commander of the French 18th Division, which was in charge of training the Lafayettes. A portly man with deep pouches beneath his eyes and the jowls of a well-fed banker, the General spoke no English. A pale captain named Mercy with two wound stripes on his sleeve translated.

They consumed a delicious lunch, served by orderlies who must have trained at the Ritz in Paris. But neither the excellent wine nor the superb food cheered anyone up. Castineau's brow furrowed as Bliss explained what the Lafayette Division did not know. "We must play the game with the cards we are dealt," the Frenchman said with a sigh.

Unlike General Viomenil, with a year's vacation in Saint-Nazaire, Castineau was a very tired man. His division had been decimated in the disastrous spring offensive. He hurled aphorisms at Bliss, none of them even slightly encouraging.

"The machine gun is a flame that devours men.

"Artillery is the new queen of battles. The infantry merely occupies the ruins.

"The Germans have taught us that the spirit of attack is the spirit of folly."

The Lafayette Division was spread across twenty-five square miles of Lorraine countryside, the men living in houses and barns, inhaling the fragrant odors of French country life. To assemble even a regiment for a review or exercise required hours of driving to deliver the necessary orders. The transportation system promised by the War Department had yet to appear. The division's motor pool still consisted of three decrepit Fords and a single asthmatic motorcycle.

The weeks of boredom in Saint-Nazaire and the interminable railroad trip left Bliss with all sorts of disciplinary problems to resolve. Court-martial boards were busy handing down sentences for insubordination and something Bliss christened AWAP: Absent Without a Pass. The mademoiselles of Saint-Nazaire had transferred their operations to the local hotels after Pershing shut down their brothels, and numerous soldiers found their charms irresistible. Bliss waived most of the sentences, adding stern lectures against trying to obtain similar favors from the presumably virtuous farm girls of Lorraine.

Captain Alden persuaded Bliss to take a special interest in an uproar in his old company. Captain Hunthouse was demanding a court-martial for Sergeant O'Connor because he had transported a petite brunette named Solange from Saint-Nazaire on the troop train. O'Connor swore she was not a prostitute, she was a war widow he was bringing to Lorraine to set up a restaurant with money he had won playing craps.

Bliss announced he would be the restaurant's first customer. If Solange was a lousy cook, O'Connor would be a private for the rest of the war. A week later, with the Sergeant and a dozen of his fellow Celts watching anxiously, Bliss devoured escargots sizzling in garlic and coq au vin in a dark fragrant gravy. He dismissed the charges against O'Connor and became a regular customer, along with most of his staff. Even Captain Alden seemed to approve this departure from army discipline, although it was obvious that

O'Connor was enjoying a lot more of Solange than her table d'hôte.

During the last week of August, the men spent most of their time digging the trenches in which they would train, with French veterans showing them how to do it—without lifting a spade of the thick moist soil themselves. This did not raise the Americans' opinion of their allies. When Bliss suggested the 18th Division join in the digging, General Castineau nervously informed him the poilus were in a rest area, after a long tour in the trenches. Asking them to do manual labor might have "unfortunate consequences."

Back at his headquarters, a fuming Bliss was greeted by a beaming Captain Alden. "Good news, General," he said. "GHQ just called to tell us they're moving out of Paris. Going to a town called Chaumont, only about fifty kilometers from here."

Pershing had finally taken his advice. But Bliss quickly wiped the cheer off Captain Alden's face. "It's been my experience in the army, Captain, that the farther a man is from headquarters, the happier he is. GHQ is where eager beavers cluster and, for want of something better to do, jump in their cars to gnaw on the nearest targets."

"Maybe they'll concentrate on the First Division," Alden said.

This regular army outfit was training in another part of Lorraine. "I doubt it. Everyone, the Germans included, expects the regulars to perform. We're the big question mark—the amateurs."

The next day the weather went from summer to winter. The temperature plunged thirty degrees and a cold rain deluged the region, turning roads into gumbo. Bliss's headquarters became an enlarged icebox, in spite of blazes in every available fireplace. General Castineau called Chief of Staff Fairchild to tell him the day's exercise was canceled. "Tell him to uncancel it," Bliss said. "Ask him if the Germans will cancel a battle because it rains."

Bliss called for one of his three cars to go to Goussaincourt, where Ireland's Own was supposed to repel a simulated attack on their training trenches by the French. Captain Alden informed him none of the cars was running. Bliss said he would take the motorcycle.

Squashed in the sidecar, for twenty miles Bliss listened to an apparently endless supply of curses from his driver, a former racing-car daredevil named Mile-a-Minute Murphy. Icy rain drooled down his neck. Mud splattered in his face and on his uniform. Murphy had to use both arms to extricate his general when they finally reached the training site. Bliss found Colonel Alexander O'Sullivan and his 3,800 men standing around in huddled clumps. Only random squads were in the trenches.

"Haven't the French showed up?" Bliss asked.

"They're over in the woods. But we can't go into those trenches, General. There's a foot of water in them."

"Colonel. You have five minutes to get those men into the trenches, wet feet or no wet feet. You can't baby soldiers and expect them to follow orders under fire."

"I have friends in Congress who can have you hanged, drawn, and quartered for treating my men this way," O'Sullivan growled.

"I have a friend at GHQ who can have you shot. His name is Pershing."

As if the mere mention of his name caused him to materialize, over the hill came the big tan staff car with the four stars tilted against the windshield and small American flags fluttering on the front fenders. Bliss concealed it well but he was as shaken as O'Sullivan, who lumbered through the mud shouting orders to his untrenched battalions.

His helmet at a cocky angle, Major Joe Perry strutted over to Bliss and gave him a snappy salute. Joe would probably win a contest with Little Collins for the shortest officer in the American army. "Twenty-two imaginary machine guns are in position, General," he said.

Machine-Gun Joe, as he was known among the regulars, was a West Point classmate. He had ruined his career trying to persuade the mastodons in Washington to reorganize the army around this new weapon, which he worshiped with an ardor most men reserve for women. Bliss had found him in Saint-Nazaire working as a quartermaster and wangled his transfer to the Lafayette Division.

Pershing squished toward them through the mud. With him was a young colonel who had wise guy all over his florid face. "We were inspecting the First Division," Pershing growled. "Drum here called your aide and found out about this little show."

He introduced Hugh Drum, his assistant chief of staff. Bliss immediately put him on his Leavenworth geniuses hate list. He was the sort of crumb who believed in springing surprise inspections on people. Pershing's acquiescence was a bad sign. The pressure was giving him the jitters.

They watched the exercise from Colonel O'Sullivan's command post, a dugout several hundred yards behind the trenches. The French exploded a few small mines to simulate artillery and came out of the woods in squads, each man equipped with a dozen dummy hand grenades. They had their rifles strapped on their backs. They fell flat in front of imaginary machine-gun fire and squirmed through the mud until they were close enough to throw their fake grenades into the trenches. The two companies in the first trench line threw fake grenades of their own at the attackers and called O'Sullivan for artillery support. Eventually they retreated down a communication trench to the second trench line.

Another wave of French attacked that position. The Americans fell back to the third trench line. From there, under French instruction, they launched a counterattack. Mortars dropped dud shells into the first two trenches. Most of them missed by several hundred feet. The imaginary machine guns used what Joe Perry called indirect fire to harass the enemy. He nervously explained to Pershing how it looped over the heads of the counterattackers, like artillery. The infantry came forward in squads and grenaded the first two trenches until they were back where they started.

In the counterattack not a single American had fired his rifle or wielded his bayonet, the two things they had been trained to do in the United States. Bliss stood shivering in the rain, trying to absorb this astonishing fact. He had a feeling Pershing was not going to like it.

Pershing told O'Sullivan to summon the regiment's majors and lieutenant colonel to the command post. He glared at them and at O'Sullivan and Perry and Bliss. "I gather all you gentlemen are satisfied with this exercise?" he said.

"I think it showed continuing progress, Jack," Bliss said.

"I think it showed absolutely nothing!" Pershing roared. "We're not going to win this war by retreating from the first two trenches and fighting our way back to them. What about the bayonet? Where's the concept of a massed attack, delivered with overwhelming strength, an attack that drives the enemy out of his trenches into the open?"

"I didn't feel we were in a position to tell the French how to train us," Bliss said.

"But you *are* in a position to train your own men in American tactics! From now on I want part of each day devoted to attacks on fortified positions with fixed bayonets, by companies, battalions, full regiments. I want field maneuvers in which the rifle is used as a weapon. I want the art and science of patrols mastered. I want open warfare!"

"We'll get to work on it," Bliss said.

"The next time I visit this division," Pershing raged, his eyes on Bliss's mud-spattered uniform, "I also expect to see men looking like soldiers, not like a rabble in arms. Any officer who settles for less than perfection will be on his way back to the United States within twenty-four hours after his attitude comes to my attention. Is that clear to everyone?"

There was a veritable chorus of affirmatives. Pershing stamped off to his car, Hugh Drum smirking beside him. "Bayonet charges?" Joe Perry muttered. "Doesn't he know a machine gun fires five hundred bullets a minute?"

"Shut up," Bliss growled. "Until he's at least a mile away."

Led by a morose O'Sullivan, the regiment trudged past Bliss in the drizzle, the captains and lieutenants saluting in halfhearted fashion. A staff car edged past the column and pulled into the field beside Bliss. Captain Alden leaped out. "I've got dry clothes and whiskey in here, General."

"I don't need either one," Bliss snapped. "I'm going home the way I came—in that sidecar. If my men get rained on, I get rained on."

Alden turned to Joe Perry. "Can you reason with him, Major? He's soaking wet. He's going to get sick."

"You're acting like a damn fool, Bliss," Perry said. "Those kids can get chilled to the bone and laugh it off. You can't."

Perry had always been an outspoken little SOB. No wonder he wrecked his career fighting for machine guns in an army that still believed in bayonet charges. "You can both go to hell," Bliss said.

He bellowed for Mile-a-Minute Murphy and waited until the entire regiment was on the road. He told Murphy to go slow and shouted "Well done!" to every company they passed. By the time he got back to Neufchâteau he was shivering violently and getting terrific pains in his legs and back. A worried Captain Alden, with I-told-you-so all over his solemn face, called the division's medical department. The senior doctors were off visiting French hospitals. A doctor with a face so cherubic he looked as if he should be in diapers finally appeared. He introduced himself as Isaac Pinkus. "Where are you from, Doctor?" Bliss growled.

"Baltimore," Pinkus said. He even pronounced it correctly: "Bal-mer."

Bliss relaxed. He did not know why, but Baltimoreans trust each other. They compared notes on their hometown while the doctor examined him. They agreed they would swap the entire supply of fois gras in France for two or three Maryland crab cakes and wondered if they could find a recipe and persuade Madame Solange to make some. Pinkus said Bliss had a fever of 101 and was having an attack of neuritis.

"What the hell causes neuritis, Doctor?" Bliss asked, pretending he had never heard of it before.

"In your case, exposure to cold. Too much southern blood, perhaps."

That was an improvement over the doctor in Texas, who had told him it came from drinking too much whiskey. He had been bothered by the disease whenever he soldiered in a cold climate.

"If you mention this to a soul, Doctor, especially to my know-it-all aide, I'll transfer you to Mindanao. As far as the rest of the world's concerned, I've got the grippe."

"My lips are sealed," Pinkus said. There was no cure for neuritis, he said, but Calvados might dull the pain.

After a night spent gulping this fiery brandy, Bliss hobbled downstairs to do some desk work. Ten seconds later, Pershing was on the line. Bliss was in no mood for another going over. This time he was going to talk back—about charging machine guns with bayonets, among other things—but Jack had something more important than the Lafayette Division's training on his mind. "There's a frog politician named Clemenceau coming your way. The diplomats tell me he's going to be the next premier, so be nice to him. It's secret service stuff. You'll be amazed to find out who's spying for us."

Around four o'clock Georges Clemenceau stumped into Bliss's office. Bliss was shocked by his age; his face was a complex of crevices and pouches, and he walked with an arthritic stoop. "Bliss?" he said, mashing his hand American style. "I've spent the day visiting the poilus. I need a drink. Have you got any Calvados?"

Bliss poured him a hefty shot from his bottle. Clemenceau gulped it down and shook his head. "They kept asking me, 'Where are the Americans?'"

Revived by the brandy, Clemenceau began pacing. His big head thrust forward like a battering ram, he told Bliss that Pershing was too cautious, too conservative. "I'm about to become premier. I wanted to announce that the Lafayette Division had taken over a sector of the front. The poilus would think, At last, we've got a politician who can get some action out of the Americans. But he turned me down. Why aren't your men ready? Don't they have guns, ammunition?"

Bliss began explaining that his men had yet to work with their artillery officers, who had just returned from the special school the French army had set up for them. They had no training in poison gas tactics. The old man's attention wandered. "All right, all right," he said and abruptly switched the subject to Polly Warden. Could she be trusted to support the war to the bitter end? The French secret service had discovered she had a history of pacifism.

Floundering, Bliss had to ask the truculent old man what he was talking about. Irritation flared. Clemenceau thought Pershing had explained things to him. He described what Miss Warden was doing for France—and America, presuming that the Americans really wanted to win this war, a question that was beginning to worry him and other Frenchmen. Bliss could only shake his head in amazement and tell Clemenceau everything he had seen and heard convinced him Miss Warden was absolutely trustworthy.

"I think she was when she came to me. But she's spending her days and nights with one of the most artful seducers in France."

Clemenceau poured himself some more Calvados and returned to pacing the floor. "I'm going to stick with her. She's sent us a lot of good information about Caillaux and his gang. What's one more gamble on the edge of the precipice? She'll bring Lebrun down here in a week or two. Here's what I want you to do...."

When Clemenceau left half an hour later, Bliss was aghast, his neuritis twinging like a berserk fire alarm. It was stunning to discover this stooped old man was the only barrier to France's signing a separate peace that would leave the British army and Pershing's handful of Americans at the mercy of two million Germans. The prospect induced him to finish off the Calvados in a single gulp.

Two weeks later, after a flurry of telegrams and a long-distance phone call, Polly Warden arrived with Charles Louis Lebrun. She stepped out of the gray French limousine in a dark-green traveling suit and matching coat and cloche. She had cut her red hair and shaped it into interesting whorls around her ears. On her wrist glittered a gold bracelet that probably cost more than Bliss had earned since he graduated from West Point. She looked like Louise Wolcott's younger sister, a creature born for *la guerre de luxe*.

Lebrun was a charming predator. Bliss had seen his type in Washington. Sometimes they were senators, more usually businessmen working for the President they had helped elect. They purchased beautiful women as part of the furniture of their lives, another advertisement of their power. Why did he particularly abhor the idea that Polly Warden had sold herself to such a man? He did not give a damn if it was the most patriotic thing anyone had ever done, he still detested it.

Lebrun shook Bliss's hand and talked wittily about Miss Warden's patriotism. She had introduced him to General Pershing and other American officers, who had told him astonishing things about the American war effort. When she learned he was going to Lorraine in search of sites for new machine-gun factories, she had suggested he stop for a look at a division of American fighting men. He made it sound like a game he was playing to keep the little creature happy by day in return for the happiness she gave him at night.

Bliss ground his back teeth so hard his jaw ached. But the front of his mouth formed a smile. Pershing had told him to lay it on with a trowel, and he was in no position to disobey a direct order. During lunch Bliss strained his French vocabulary to the limit, talking with spread-eagle confidence about the way Americans were going to fight when they went into the lines. Lebrun sat there drinking champagne, muttering, "*Bon, bon.*"

After lunch they drove to the training sites and watched a simulated attack on an imaginary German-held trench by Ireland's Own. The Celts surged forward with furious enthusiasm, inspired by Bliss's promise that they would be rewarded with steak dinners and weekend passes to Toul. Joe Perry fired sheets of real machine-gun bullets inches above their heads. They ignored them as if they were raindrops.

After the exercise, Bliss asked Miss Warden if she wanted to say a few words to her former Harvard hero, Lieutenant Eagleton. He was only a few dozen yards away, covered with mud from head to foot, staring curiously at them. Color leaped in Miss Warden's cheeks. "No, thank you, General!" she said.

For some reason he did not understand, her agitation pleased Bliss. He wanted to believe this stunning creature from *la guerre de luxe* was still linked to the idealist he had met in Union Square.

Lebrun, with his limited English, missed this interesting exchange. Bliss led the financier and Miss Warden to the bayonet pits to watch some of the division's more ferocious bruisers spear the dummies. He had barred anyone under six feet two, which gave Lebrun the impression that the Lafayette's ranks were crowded with giants. "I wish the Kaiser could see your men in action, General," Lebrun said. "He might become more reasonable about peace."

"Do you know him well enough to invite him over? We'd be glad to give another performance," Bliss said.

"It would be a waste of time with the man France has just installed as premier," Lebrun said. "Clemenceau. A fanatic who only knows the language of hate. I predict he won't last a month."

Lebrun thanked Bliss for his hospitality. Polly Warden held out her hand. "You remember what you told me about war being the engine of history, General?" she asked.

Bliss nodded mechanically. "I believe it now—with all my heart," she said.

Trudging back to his icy office, his neuritis twinging, Bliss wondered if Polly Warden had just told him he was partly responsible for her fall from grace. Or was she trying to say she wanted him to understand—and forgive—what she was doing?

The sound of grinding gears outside the house interrupted Bliss's doleful puzzlement. Captain Alden threw open the door. "General Castineau to see you, General."

They shook hands. The Frenchman was grave. So was his interpreter, Captain Mercy. "We've come to say our farewells," the Captain said.

"You're going back into the lines?" Bliss said.

"We're going to Italy," General Castineau said. "There has been a catastrophe. Whether we shall become victims or saviors, God alone knows."

"What's happened?"

"The Germans reinforced the Austrians with six divisions and have broken through on a front of sixty miles. They've captured two hundred thousand prisoners and over a thousand guns," Captain Mercy said, getting ahead of his chief.

"Six German divisions have routed the whole Italian army? Over a million men?" Bliss said.

"Execrable but true," General Castineau said.

So much for Field Marshal Haig's strategy of keeping the enemy busy around Ypres. "I fear this will have a disastrous effect on French politics," Castineau said. "The defeatists in the Chamber of Deputies may soon be a majority."

Bliss could see how deeply shaken the man was. He felt his own confidence slide another notch. But he played the optimistic American. He pumped Castineau's hand and wished him the very best of luck. He was sure his men, thoroughly rested and their morale restored, would behave well.

Castineau glowered. "They'll behave well because there will be machine guns at their backs to shoot down the first man who runs."

* * *

That night, after an early supper, Bliss called for a car and rode to Grand, a tiny town near Neufchâteau with the ruins of an imitation of the Roman Colosseum on its outskirts. Almost two thousand years ago, Grand had been the headquarters of the Roman army in Gaul. Bliss told the driver to wait by the road and walked down the hill to the huge amphitheater. A full moon was breaking through scattered clouds, casting swaths of golden light through the wrecked walls.

It was a good place for a soldier to think about soldiering. He could almost hear them moving around, their armor chinking, their dice rattling: the old Roman regulars.

"*Bonjour, mon ami,*" said a man standing in the shadows near one of the exit ramps.

"Who goes there?" Bliss said good-naturedly.

"Corporal Chardin, Thirty-third Regiment, stretcher-bearer."

"Bliss, Lafayette Division historical section," he said.

"I'm honored," the Frenchman said, shaking hands. "I didn't know Americans had any interest in history."

"A few of us do. What brings you here, Corporal?"

"I'm an archaeologist by profession. I was estimating how much it might cost to excavate this place. I'm sure there are uncounted treasures under our feet: pottery, weapons, perhaps graves."

"Why are you doing it in the dark?"

"It was not dark when I arrived. I stayed to commune a little with the spirits of the old Romans. I'm interested in the history of the soul. I think it evolves, just as matter evolves."

"A mystic archaeologist?"

"I'm also a Jesuit priest."

"Why aren't you a chaplain?" Bliss asked.

"The French government is secular. It drafts priests into the army like other men. Priests are serving as machine-gunners, artillerymen."

"What do you think of the war, Corporal? You must have seen a lot of it. Has carting men off battlefields for three years shaken your faith?"

"On the contrary. It's strengthened my confidence in the indestructibility of the divine in the human heart. War reveals our savagery, our brutality—but it also evokes our extraordinary capacity for love."

"You think God willed the slaughter at Verdun last year and the one that's going on now at Ypres?"

"Monsieur, that is a complicated question. If it is possible for you to see the world as God, mankind as God, evolving toward a destiny utterly mysterious—"

"It isn't possible for me to see that!" Bliss said, refusing to abandon his grudge against the indifferent God who let Jackie and Grace die beneath that Moro kris on Jolo.

The Corporal sighed. "It will take a long time, perhaps centuries, for this new idea to grow in the human soul."

"Let me get a better look at you," Bliss said.

The Corporal stepped into a patch of moonlight. Bliss liked what he saw: intelligence and charm blended on the man's gaunt face. He felt momentarily ashamed of the contemptuous way he had dismissed his theology. "Let me ask you another question, Corporal," Bliss said. "Do you think we can win this war?"

"I don't know. Everything depends on you Americans."

23. WHEN LOVELY WOMAN STOOPS TO FOLLY

THE GERMANS WERE BOMBING PARIS AGAIN. Along the streets the fire trucks wailed the alarm. Searchlights probed the night sky, reflecting eerily on the low-hanging clouds. The antiaircraft guns flung up shells that exploded in ugly reddish-yellow flashes. Across the Seine bombs burst around the Gare de l'Est, one of the Germans' favorite targets. Flames flickered along the side streets. Louise Wolcott stood at the bedroom window of her house on the Rue du Bac, weeping.

"The bastards," she said. "Are they going to win the war after all?"

"It's starting to look that way," Harry Quickmeyer said.

Like everyone else he was appalled by the slow-motion American war effort. From their zenith of popularity in the summer, Americans were sinking lower than the British in Parisian opinion. Was that why she did not love this man? Louise wondered. Because he was failing to defend the city she loved? By becoming her lover, he had assumed enormous responsibility in her wandering heart.

Louise knew this did not make any sense. She had come back to Paris to find out how the heart of an independent woman worked, a woman who possessed five million dollars and a house on the Rue du Bac. So far she had discovered little but the free heart's unpredictability. There were moments when it palpitated at the thought of Harry Quickmeyer's lips on hers. There were other moments when she almost loathed his touch.

She was discovering how many different things the heart loved: Paris, for instance. Absurd, to love a city, a collection of streets and houses and restaurants and hotels and churches. But her heart defiantly loved Paris, no matter how absurd she thought it was.

Other women. Above all Gertrude Vanderbilt Whitney, her dark goddess, whose daring path she was trying to follow. Tormented Gertrude, who had opened her bitter heart to Louise and revealed the same ruined hopes of ideal love, the same blind wish to be chosen, lifted up on a great wave of absolute gift, absolute adoration. Louise would never forget the thunderous impact of Gertrude's revelation. If the richest woman in the world was unhappy, something was fatally wrong with American men.

Freedom. Was that what the heart loved above everything? Was that why Gertrude urged her to be imperious, to say yes and then no and then yes? For Louise, that was the hardest part. At one time she had nurtured a secret vision of herself as a woman of compassion—the opposite of her mother, who had scarcely shed a tear for Louise's father as he died a premature death from cancer. How many times as she wept in her room had twelve-year-old Louise imagined herself gathering him in her arms and kissing away his pain? In a totally unexpected way, Harry Quickmeyer had evoked that almost forgotten self.

He had told her everything: his boyhood in isolated forts on the plains, with no one but Indians for playmates. The father who waited five, ten, fifteen years for promotion to captain while alcohol destroyed a once-noble character and his wife's love; a brief moment of tragic glory in Cuba; a letter calling on his son to seek the fame that had eluded him. His mother had wept and told him to burn it, but he had hardened his heart against her—against every woman—in his father's name.

All the secrets so craftily concealed from the world by his mask of wry disillusion. The disguise, the single-minded pursuit of rank and fame, was brilliant and tormented and ultimately sad. Louise saw why her offhand challenge at Fort Myer had penetrated his guarded heart. She had the money and the beauty to right the wrong, banish bitterness from his future. With a wife like her, his path to a general's stars was assured.

Yet here she was, using the bitter truths he had confessed, the ambition he had concealed from everyone else, as another reason to evade compassion, elude love. "What's happening? What are we doing?" Louise said as more bombs gouged Paris, this time around the Gare du Nord. "Where's the armada of the air we were supposed to send by the end of the year? Where's our army? I'm almost ashamed to go to dinner with French friends."

"A lot of us are beginning to suspect Wilson thinks he can win without fighting," Quickmeyer said.

"How can you still love our oafish country?"

"Who said I loved it?" Quickmeyer said. "I made a commitment to it, knowing exactly how indifferent it could be to its soldiers. We're servants, not rulers, and servants are often treated badly."

"Everyone's starting to wonder if General Pershing is timid."

Quickmeyer laughed harshly. "You're jealous. Having him snatched away by a twenty-three-year-old French-Rumanian painter has been a shock to a lot of women in Paris."

She did not like the way he said *in Paris*. Since Pershing had moved his headquarters to distant Chaumont, too many of his officers talked about Paris that way. It was infuriating. No one was bombing Chaumont. The Americans sat out there and stuck pins in maps and fought fantasy battles with their imaginary army of a million men while Paris burned and France crumbled into defeat.

"Do you seriously think I wanted him for a lover along with you?"

"Am I your lover?" Quickmeyer said. "I've begun to think the term is irrelevant."

"Are you encouraging me to pursue Pershing, thinking I'd be in a position to make you a general?"

Quickmeyer lit a cigarette and offered her one. He held the match for her. "I almost blurted out something absurdly romantic," he said.

"What?"

"Becoming a general won't mean a thing without your love."

The bombs continued to fall on Paris. The aircraft guns continued to boom. But Louise's heart was no longer involved with the city's pain. It leaped with unaccustomed pleasure at those words. "You didn't say it because it isn't true, of course."

"Not entirely true. But there's some truth to it. I'm ready to

prove it by marrying you. Even though Pershing may ship me back
to the States dismembered."

So Pershing *was* interested in her. "I can't let you do such a
thing. Can you conceive of the possibility that I might love you too
much to let you do it?"

He turned away from the bombs and the antiaircraft bursts.
Were they a reproach to him? She hoped so. She was suddenly angry
at him for wanting her more than he wanted to defend Paris, more
than he wanted victory.

He inhaled his cigarette. "I don't understand you."

"I'm not sure I understand myself," Louise said. "That's why
Paris is so important. You can experiment with yourself here. You
can find out new rules, new hopes."

She sat down on the tousled bed where they had made love and
dozed in each other's arms until the air raid began. The bed
reminded her that their love was real on one level: subterranean
love, metro love, surging beneath Paris love with a strange roaring
anger in its ardor.

"I'm going to be spending quite a lot of time in Paris from now
on. Pershing's transferred me to the Services of Supply. It's an
incredible mess. There are thousands of tons of weapons, food, and
ammunition piling up on the docks at Saint-Nazaire and Brest."

How boring, Louise thought.

"It doesn't sound heroic, I know. But it's crucial to winning this
war if and when we ever start to fight it."

"Welcome back to *la guerre de luxe*," she said.

The antiaircraft guns sputtered and fell silent. The sullen drone
of the Gothas' motors dwindled into the distance. Louise sent Quickmeyer on his way with a final tantalizing kiss. Five minutes later the
telephone rang. She picked it up and a male voice whispered:

> "Louise, thy beauty is to me
> Like those Nicaean barks of yore
> That gently, o'er a perfumed sea,
> The weary, wayworn wanderer bore
> To his own native shore."

She felt an absolute, genuine thrill. Poe was her favorite poet. "Who is this?" she said.

"A survivor of the bombardment of the Gare de l'Est," he said.

"Do you need medical attention?"

"My wound is in the heart. I received it long before this trifling adventure."

"Poor man. Where and when did this awful thing happen?"

"At Napoleon's tomb. A woman in white said things to me that I can't forget."

"Colonel Fairchild?"

"Yes."

"Are you really at the Gare de l'Est?"

"I arrived just in time for the bombardment. It was very entertaining. I stood in the street and watched the whole thing."

He was telling her how indifferent he was to death—for her sake. Again she felt warmth rush through her body. "That was foolish. Dangerous. Why have you come to Paris?"

"To see you."

"No other reason?"

"None."

"Where are you staying?"

"I have no idea. If necessary I'll pitch a tent in the Tuileries. Can I see you for lunch tomorrow?"

They met at noon at the Pré Catalan, a restaurant in the Bois de Boulogne. She chose a table beside one of the curved floor-to-ceiling windows that looked out on Paris's favorite woods, subdued in the chill of oncoming winter. It was a clear sunny day, the first in weeks. The city was capped by a dome of transcendent blue.

Louise arrived early, wanting to see him from a distance as well as at close quarters. The headwaiter hovered. Parisian friends bowed and smiled: Caillaux, the former premier, and his buxom second wife; Humbert, the bloated senator from the Meuse, with his latest mistress. The women glared at her blond hair, knowing what raptures it incited in Frenchmen. Louise measured herself against the perfection of their dresses, the makeup that annihilated every blemish, the instinct for style that Frenchwomen acquired at birth and American women had to labor incessantly to achieve.

Suddenly Douglas Fairchild was stepping from a taxi, his Sam Browne belt gleaming on his broad chest, the hat's visor shadowing his face, making him look momentarily saturnine. But when he gazed at the Pré Catalan and the sunlight spilled across his features, he was an overgrown boy again. If it were simply a matter of faces, Quickmeyer had already won. His was a Shakespearean visage out of *Henry IV* or *Lear*, one of those truculent, knowing lesser nobles glowering around the king. Fairchild's face was out of Meyerbeer or Victor Herbert, a chocolate soldier profile that might burst into embarrassing song at any moment. What possible interest could her wandering heart have in him?

The headwaiter led him to her like an obedient horse to his stall. He kissed her hand and sat down slowly, gazing at her. "Now I know I'm in Paris."

Again, for a moment, she felt mirrored. She saw herself, her mauve cloche, her low-cut yellow chiffon dress. She liked it. "Last night you thought the train had taken a detour to the front?"

"I was hoping it had."

"Why?"

"I want to get there as soon as possible to show you the kind of man I am."

"I've told you that isn't necessary."

"For some reason, I think it is."

He ordered champagne. She sipped it and asked him why he thought he had to take risks for her.

"Otherwise you'll go on thinking I'm a fool."

"I don't think anything of the sort," she lied.

"Yes, you do. You don't like men who love you extravagantly. You prefer people like Quickmeyer, the Raffles type who comes in through the window and steals your heart. That's the modern style. You don't want to be swept away."

He was wrong, but it was interesting. "My husband swept me away. But he didn't, or couldn't—or wouldn't—follow through. He seemed to lose interest the moment he captured me," Louise said.

"Why?"

"When you get to Vienna at the head of your victorious troops, you might ask Dr. Sigmund Freud."

"He's a charlatan."

"You don't secretly love your mother?"

The question spilled half his champagne glass into his lap. Waiters rushed to dry him off. He was crimson. "I don't hate my father either," he said, trying to joke away his embarrassment.

She asked him if his mother and father were happily married. "Not really. My father was a sick man for most of his life. He was very badly wounded at the battle of Franklin in the Civil War."

"I used to wish my father had died in one of those battles."

"Why?"

"My mother might have respected him more."

The maître d' hovered. Fairchild let Louise make the choices. He began explaining why he had tried to win the Medal of Honor in the Philippines and in Mexico. He had decided it was the only way to overcome the envy a general's son aroused in the army. Louise sensed he was passing through a previous vision of himself into a persona he was creating for her. But she still sensed an enormous gap between them. It was more than personality, it was chronological. Like most Americans, he was still living in the nineteenth century, but his insulated army life left him even farther back—in the 1870s, perhaps. "Tell me about Paris. I'm an ignoramus about everything but war," he said.

"Do you see those two men dining with two women in front of the pillar?"

She was talking about Caillaux and Humbert.

"They're two of the most powerful men in Paris. The fat one, Humbert, owns *Le Journal,* one of the most important newspapers in the city. He's also a senator. The thin one, Caillaux, is a former premier. The woman with Humbert is known as Le Grand Horizontal. The other woman is Mrs. Caillaux. In 1914 she shot a newspaper editor to death for calling her an adulteress. They're discussing how to bring down the government of the current premier, Clemenceau, and put Caillaux in power so he can negotiate peace with the Germans."

He struggled to conceal his dismay. "I feel as if I just went from the third grade to senior year in college."

"Can you reconcile them and *la gloire?*" she said.

"That will only exist—only matter—between us," he said, taking her hand.

They barely spoke for the next hour. They drank and ate and communed with each other and with Paris beyond the Bois. It was the perfect place for two Americans to fall in love, in this wood within the most civilized city in the world. They needed the illusion of wildness to justify the excitement vibrating in the air between them. He was finding the courage to live a life of danger for her sake, the courage to overcome the hidden fear that he would end up like his father, half a man, a hollow soldier. She was letting her willful heart explore the possibility of loving a nineteenth-century hero, even though her twentieth-century head rejected the notion as absurd.

The check made him gasp with dismay but he paid it manfully. Outside, a taxi was waiting. Louise let Colonel Fairchild give the driver their destination: the Crillon, the Ritz—love in the gilded splendor of the ancien régime. She was ready to offer herself to him as a gift, a promise. But he said, "*Le Gare de l'Est.*"

"You're going back?"

"I have to be there in time to review the training schedules and plans for tomorrow. We're having another inspection. Pershing's bringing the president of France, Poincaré."

She was too stunned to speak as they raced out of the Bois toward the railroad station. He had ridden three hundred kilometers yesterday and would ride three hundred today for the privilege of having lunch with her. Incredible.

He began talking about another visit, next week or the week after. But there was not the slightest hint of an assignation. Gradually she realized that he was not going to ask her to become a *grand horizontal* until he had risked death on the battlefield. Even then, she suspected the proposal would come with a wedding ring attached to it.

Absurd, absurd, she told her pirouetting heart as he kissed her goodbye. Absurd to think you are falling in love with this American boy-man, this pursuer of *la gloire* out of a novel by Dumas, a musketeer *sans peur* but not *sans reproche*. She watched him stride across the station toward the train that would carry him back to Lorraine and his soldiers.

He was totally American. Was that why you love him? she asked her heart, which was now doing glissades and pas de deux. Or is it because he was ready to defend to the death your beloved Paris?

24. AGENT IN PLACE

"I WORRY ABOUT YOU DAY AND NIGHT," DR. Giroux-Langin said. "Especially at night."

"Doctor. How many times do I have to tell you nothing, absolutely nothing, has happened to merit your concern."

Ambivalence roiled Dr. Giroux-Langin's normally strong self-possession. She was talking to a younger woman who was spending nights and weekends with a man she had once loved. For two months now, Polly had been living *la guerre de luxe* with Charles Louis Lebrun. She had introduced him to Pershing and every officer above the rank of major on his staff. She had sat beside him while they told outrageous lies about the American war effort. All the time, she sensed their eyes were on her, imagining what she was doing after midnight to persuade Charles Louis Lebrun to believe this balderdash. They might consider her a patriot, but in another part of their minds she was a slut. Worst of all was her visit to Malvern Hill Bliss. She could still see his sad, puzzled eyes trying to solve the mystery of Miss Warden's fall.

Dr. Giroux-Langin flung her glasses on the desk and glared out the window at the gray wintry Seine only a few blocks away. "He's simply waiting for the right moment. Meanwhile he humors you by listening to your American propaganda. If Clemenceau's government falls, you'll see a very different man."

Polly struggled to conceal a panicky fear that the Doctor might also see a different woman. She was no longer sure what she thought and felt about Charles Louis Lebrun, peace, and Georges Clemenceau, who had become premier on Friday, November 13,

1917, six weeks after she saw him in his apartment on the Rue Franklin. She had heard nothing from the Tiger since that meeting. He had yet to make a major speech in the Chamber of Deputies. He seemed to be feeling his way while rumors of his imminent political collapse swirled through Paris following the rout of the Italian army.

No one in the blasé world of *la guerre de luxe* worried about her apparent affair with Charles Louis Lebrun. When she went to dinner and the theater with him, everyone assumed she also went back to his *hôtel* in the Faubourg-Saint-Germain and slept with him. It was impossible to explain to Dr. Giroux-Langin or anyone else that she and Charles Louis Lebrun were exploring a different kind of love, a precarious blend of the erotic and the paternal.

Freed of the need to play the seducer, Lebrun talked to her about his youth, his secret hopes, his even more secret disappointments. He was not a cynic by nature. He mourned the idealistic young man who had accepted his father's *réalisme* and become the heir to his fortune. Like most Frenchmen he made a fierce distinction between the dictates of the heart and the head. The heart was a woman's province. Modern men—especially modern Frenchmen—lived by the intellect. After all, it was a Frenchman, Descartes, who launched the modern world when he declared, "I think, therefore I am."

Yet the tears Charles Louis Lebrun wept for Paul, the nostalgia with which he talked about his student days, when he was an equally fierce advocate of an ideal France, made Lebrun's heart all too visible to Polly. It stirred sympathy for him—sympathy that often threatened to spill over into love. That in turn complicated her task of sowing doubt in his mind about Joseph Caillaux and his white peace.

"I will say no more to you on the subject," Dr. Giroux-Langin said. "From now on we'll discuss only professional topics. Which of the girls in the current class do you think suitable for work at the front?"

Polly was the supervisor of training new nurses. She suggested five names, and they parted coldly. Polly returned to the hospital's courtyard, where young Frenchwomen and a few Americans were learning how to care for wounded poilus.

* * *

At the Kingswood house that evening, Madame Berrier knocked on Polly's door. "A telephone call, mademoiselle."

"Polly?" said a male voice that was both familiar and strange. "I got a surprise overnight pass. Thought I'd run up to Paris and see a few friends."

It was George Eagleton. Was there a note of sullen suspicion in his voice? "How about dinner tonight?" George said.

"I'm afraid that's impossible."

"How about lunch tomorrow?"

"I'm on duty at the hospital," Polly said.

"A busy woman," George said. "Busy morning, noon, and night, I hear, with a certain French big shot. Did you enjoy watching us perform for his benefit?"

George had learned about Charles Louis Lebrun from Arthur Hunthouse via Eleanor Kingswood. It took Polly a moment to control the instinctive irrational shame that flooded her. She simply refused to yield to it. Somehow it was easier with George than it had been with General Bliss.

"How about a drink tonight?" George said.

"We could have an apéritif at the Ritz. I'm meeting Mr. Lebrun there at seven. We could meet earlier."

She would use George—instead of letting him abuse her.

At six-thirty, George waited at a table in the Ritz's long lofty lobby, watching gorgeously gowned women and mostly middle-aged men stream past the potted trees and other luxurious foliage. Polly had no trouble imagining what he thought of her in a dark green dinner dress and chinchilla wrap, her red hair cut short, her lips and cheeks made up like the women he had been watching. Disapproval blossomed on his wide earnest face.

"George," she said, sitting down opposite him, "I know you and other people think the worst about Charles Louis Lebrun and me. Someday I'll tell you about the whole thing, if you're interested. For the time being I need your help."

"Help! What kind of a fool do you think—"

A waiter hovered. They ordered vermouth. "I can't explain it now, George," Polly continued. "I'm going to introduce you as an old friend from New York. I want you to talk about how eager you are to fight the Germans. How much it means to you."

George's outrage left him speechless.

"I'm not doing this to defy you or humiliate you. We—we don't count in this situation, George. There are larger things at stake then your feelings—or my feelings. Before you explode, may I remind you of a certain actress you escorted around New York while you were at Camp Mills?"

George subsided, fuming. He only partially admitted the parallel between his showgirl and Charles Louis Lebrun. The double standard was alive and well in his head.

"How's Arthur?" Polly said.

George looked as if someone had poisoned his drink. "We're not friends anymore. He disgusts me. He keeps trying to get himself transferred to some staff job where he won't get shot at."

"Have you finished your training?"

"Almost. Yesterday we attacked live machine-gun nests with our gas masks on. General Bliss wants us to get used to the damn things. The guns fired a foot above our heads. It was terrific."

She asked him what he thought of General Bliss. "He's got a temper like a sick grizzly, but he cares about the men. He ate dinner with our company the other night, checking up on our chow. Our crazy Greek cook, Dukakis, has been feeding us a lot better ever since."

Charles Louis Lebrun loomed over them. "What a piquant picture: young America in Paris," he said in French.

Polly responded in French. "This is a very old and dear friend from New York. He's in the Lafayette Division. I hope you won't mind spending a few moments with him."

"Of course not," he said, kissing her on the cheek. Polly introduced them and George mashed Lebrun's hand. "Polly tells me you can't wait to get at the Germans," Lebrun said.

"We're going to wipe up the Western Front with them," George said.

"On what do you base your confidence?"

"I know my men. I know how they feel about it. They're a bunch of fighting Irishmen, and they're mad as hell."

"Mad—as—hell?" Lebrun said.

Polly supplied a translation in French. "Ah. Angry. Why?"

"They don't like the way the Germans are trying to push every-body else around. That goes against the American grain."

It was too good for George to make up on the spur of the moment. He was telling the truth. He was mad at the Germans—and he was even madder at Charles Louis Lebrun. He hunched his shoulders and glared at him.

"*Un vrai homme*," Lebrun said to Polly.

Polly nodded. "Monsieur Lebrun says you're a real man."

"We must go, *chérie*," Lebrun said in French. "We have almost an hour's journey."

"We're going to a private party, George. You'll have to excuse us," Polly said. She kissed him on the cheek. "I hope I see you again soon." Lebrun shook hands and said he was honored to meet an American fighting man.

They left George there in the gilded glitter of the Ritz, glower-ing into his empty glass. Polly felt triumphant and guilty in the same swirling moment. "He talks and looks so much like the men of 1914," Lebrun said as they waited for his car.

In the dark backseat of the Dion-Bouton, Lebrun fell unchA-acteristically silent as they rolled down the gloomy boulevards. "I had a narrow escape in the air raid last night," he said, as they went through the Versailles gate. "A Gotha must have been flying straight toward my house. He dropped his bombs one by one. You could feel the blasts moving closer. The last one exploded only a half block away. I lay in bed thinking I didn't really care whether the next one landed on my roof."

They rode in silence again for ten minutes. "That lieutenant. Is he the one you told me about, the one you declined to marry?"

"Yes."

"He's still in love with you."

"I'm not in love with him," Polly said.

"I could see that too," Lebrun said. "But that never stops a man his age from tormenting himself."

"I can't believe a mere woman can trouble a man that much," Polly said.

He laughed harshly. "Mere women have troubled me all my life. First my mother, then my wife. And others." Was he thinking about Dr. Giroux-Langin? "You're violently opinionated creatures. And you refuse to listen to reason."

"Perhaps men don't listen enough to their hearts."

He brooded again for a while. "I wasn't thinking of women when the bombs came toward me. It's this disgusting process of cutting a deal with the Germans. As Clemenceau grows weaker, the moment draws closer."

"Then why do it?"

"Grown men act on what their heads tell them, not their hearts."

"Perhaps your head should digest some new facts. What you've heard from General Pershing and his staff. What you saw when we visited General Bliss. What you heard tonight. The Americans are ready to fight."

"But there are so few of you. I have no faith in the million men you talk about. I think Wilson will never send so many. Meanwhile the Germans are shipping half a million, perhaps a million, from the Russian front."

In the country beyond Versailles, Joseph Caillaux had built a splendid imitation château of white sandstone and marble. Servants with blazing torches stood on the steps, illuminating the huge quadruple entrance doors. Inside, the first rooms were simple and severe, the dominant color a pale green. But the Salon d'Honneur was more sumptuous than anything in Versailles, with coupled columns and richly wrought gilded entablature and crimson upholstery.

"The architecture is perfect and logical," Caillaux explained to Polly in his self-satisfied way. "The outer rooms are simple because one merely passes through them. Have you succeeded in persuading any of your fellow Americans to join our crusade?"

"Not one," Polly said. "But I gave my story to Charles Humbert—and escaped without surrendering anything else to him."

"That must have taken some ingenuity," Caillaux said.

"Her story alone will have the appeal of a cry from thousands," Lebrun said. "A woman who's won the croix de guerre, calling for peace."

"I fear that's a somewhat prejudiced view, Charles."

By now Polly knew Caillaux never changed an opinion. He had opposed involving her in their plans, and he now opposed her even more since he suspected she might become a rival influence on Lebrun.

The dinner included a dozen members of the Chamber of Deputies and their wives or mistresses. The main topic of conversation was the Russian decision to drop out of the war. The Bolsheviks, who had seized power in October, were about to sign a treaty of peace with the Germans. Everyone seemed to think this development finished Georges Clemenceau as premier. He had been one of the architects of the policy of embracing Russia to humble Germany from the east. The French had lent the Czar's government hundreds of millions of francs that would now never be repaid.

Abruptly, Caillaux's harsh voice rang out. "The time has come for a vote of no confidence." A murmur of assent swept the table. Wineglasses were raised in salute. Polly kept her eyes on Lebrun, who was seated on the opposite side of the table beside Caillaux. He drank to the proposition without enthusiasm.

Beside Polly, Caillaux's plump wife, Henriette, was watching Lebrun too. "Your poor friend is upset and one can't blame him. I suppose you know his other son, Louis, has also decided to volunteer for the front."

"Yes, it's very distressing," Polly said, concealing her surprise.

The women retired for coffee to the Salon Blanc, a marvel of delicate eighteenth-century furniture and paneling. Polly found herself sitting on a couch with a shapely honey blonde who admired her diamond bracelet. "How wonderful it must be to charm a man as rich as Lebrun," she said.

Polly smiled politely. Her companion's eyes roamed the room. "It's time to tell him he's about to be arrested. Get him to the Chamber of Deputies tomorrow. Monsieur Clemenceau is making a speech."

An hour later, Polly and Lebrun rode back to Paris. "Madame Caillaux tells me your son Louis has also volunteered for the front," Polly said.

"I prefer not to talk about it," said the deep voice from the darkness on the other side of the back seat.

"I know someone who has an interesting theory that might explain it," Polly said. "She maintains that the amount of bravery in a nation remains constant. When a brave man dies, one and sometimes two spring up to take his place."

"Who is this sibyl?"

"Dr. Giroux-Langin."

"She'd believe that sort of thing."

"She told me something else she learned from Clemenceau's daughter, who works at the hospital. You're in danger."

"Why?"

"Clemenceau is going to arrest Monsieur Caillaux and everyone associated with him."

"Impossible. Caillaux's a senator. If that old madman touches Almeyreda, Paris will burn."

"He intends to force the Chamber of Deputies to revoke Monsieur Caillaux's immunity. I don't know what he plans to do about Almeyreda."

There was no response. "Dr. Giroux-Langin urges you to go to the Chamber of Deputies tomorrow. Monsieur Clemenceau is making an important speech that will clarify a good many things."

Lebrun was silent for a full five minutes. Ahead, the Germans were bombing Paris again. Searchlights crisscrossed the sky. They could hear the distant crack of antiaircraft guns, the *crump* of bombs. As they drew closer they saw flames gushing into the darkness from half a dozen buildings. The tinkling wail of fire sirens drifted toward them.

"The Tiger is trying to frighten me," Lebrun said.

"I'm only a messenger," Polly said. "But Dr. Giroux-Langin seemed concerned. Intensely concerned."

There was another long pause. "Hard to believe, after all these years," Lebrun said.

Clemenceau had advised her to portray Giroux-Langin as gloating over the prospect of Lebrun's fall. Polly was following her intuition that he was far more likely to believe the message she was pretending to deliver.

"I'd like to hear what Monsieur Clemenceau has to say tomorrow. Will you take me?"

There was a brief pause. "Meet me there half an hour before the session starts."

In the morning Polly telephoned Dr. Giroux-Langin to tell her she would not come to the hospital that day. She walked down the Rue de la Université to the home of France's National Assembly, the Palais Bourbon, one of the most magnificent eighteenth-century buildings in Paris. In the ornate pavilion to the right of the grand staircase, she found Lebrun talking to a stocky, cherubic young Englishman.

"This is Winston Churchill, the British Minister of Munitions," he said. "We see a good deal of each other, being in the same business."

"He means blowing up Germans," Churchill said. "He does it better than us, though our generals hate to admit it. His seventy-five-caliber gun is the best in the world."

A few feet away, the honey blonde who had passed Clemenceau's message last night was chatting with Louise Wolcott. The messenger's eyes met Polly's for a moment before she turned away to greet one of Caillaux's followers, Deputy Anatole Drouart, a swarthy, lupine man who looked as if he had nothing to recommend him but his power. Louise smiled at Lebrun, who greeted her warmly. Winston Churchill was even more effusive. "How does this woman keep getting more beautiful? It's the only secret I want to smuggle out of Paris," he said.

"It's the one France will do its best to keep," Lebrun said.

There were at least a dozen women like Louise and the blond messenger in the crowd, each exquisitely coiffed and dressed in the latest style. Polly felt an uneasy divided kinship with them, a camaraderie she half rejected. How little things had changed since the days of Madame Pompadour. Women still participated in politics by giving themselves to powerful men. Yet Polly could not deny the excitement it stirred in her blood.

A bell rang, summoning everyone to the Salle de Séances, the marvelously named chamber where the deputies met. Mr. Churchill sat beside Polly and Lebrun in the gallery. Below them on the floor, Polly easily identified Joseph Caillaux's bald head and bristling black mustache. He was sitting rigidly at his desk, glaring at the rostrum, as if he could already see Clemenceau there.

A hush fell over the gallery and the chamber floor as the Premier appeared on the rostrum. He waited for the quiet to deepen, his large head high, his eyes bright and hard, his mouth grim. He began with a single word: "Messieurs!"

He was calling the deputies gentlemen, but the word was edged with contempt. Everyone knew he did not regard many of them as worthy of the name. Briefly, almost curtly, he outlined the situation France faced. The army's morale remained low. The French people were discouraged and weary. Their ally Russia had abandoned the war. Italy was in disarray. American help was not arriving as quickly as they had hoped.

What should France do? What should he do, as Premier and President of the Council of Ministers? Some people urged peace negotiations. But he could think of only one answer that made sense to him: "Je fais la guerre!"

The ferocious words tore through the chamber like a high-explosive shell. Somehow they sounded more deadly, more awful, in French. Literally, je fais meant I make. I make war! Pacing up and down the rostrum, Clemenceau used the phrase like a whip to lash the reluctant politicians facing him.

"In domestic policies, I wage war!

"In foreign policies, I wage war!

"Always, everywhere, I wage war!

"Russia has betrayed us, but I still wage war. Unhappy Rumania has been forced to surrender, but I still wage war. Italy totters, but I still wage war.

"Before Paris, I wage war. Behind Paris, I wage war. If we retreat to the Pyrenees, I will still wage war!

"I will wage war until the last quarter hour because the last quarter hour will be ours!"

Two thirds of the sullen deputies no longer looked like the same men. They were on their feet, screaming "Long live France!" Some were weeping. They pounded their desks and waved clenched fists. Only the Socialists, sitting in a bloc, remained silent. The Socialists—and Joseph Caillaux, who sat with arms crossed on his chest, his head down, his bald head purpling with rage.

For fifteen minutes the cheering continued. As it ebbed, Winston Churchill said to Polly, "I thought we English had a monopoly on oratory. That's the greatest speech I've ever heard. I wonder if Clemenceau can back it up with action."

"I fear he will," Lebrun said.

Churchill departed. Lebrun stared down at the excited deputies on the floor of the chamber. It was the first time Polly had seen him lose his aplomb.

"Will you ask Dr. Giroux-Langin to send a message to Monsieur Clemenceau? I would like to meet him soon, in private. I think we can come to an understanding."

The voice of hope, Paul whispered.

Was it, Polly wondered? Or would she, along with this violent old man, be guilty of the deaths of thousands, perhaps millions? Polly thought of George Eagleton, hunched at the table at the Ritz, the personification of the American fighting man, truculently predicting victory. Was she consigning him and his men to the brutality and slaughter of no-man's-land?

She did not know. She was as blind as a child to the ultimate meaning of what was happening. She gazed into Charles Louis Lebrun's anguished eyes and pressed herself against him. "I'm sorry," she whispered.

25. PERFECTIONISTS AT WORK

FORTY FEET BELOW THE SURFACE OF THE LUNÉVILLE sector, in a foul-smelling dugout illuminated by a dozen flickering candles, Malvern Hill Bliss and the officers of Company A went over the map of the German position for the three hundred and thirty-third time. At Lieutenant Eagleton's suggestion, they called the sergeants down into the dugout to go over it with them once more.

"Are you ready?" Bliss asked.

"Just say the word, General," growled First Sergeant O'Connor. He and Eagleton had already volunteered for a dozen midnight patrols in no-man's-land. They knew the tricks of the trade out there: what to do if an enemy flare came down, the preferred weapons, the art and science of cutting barbed wire.

Nearby, as grim-eyed spectators, stood General John J. Pershing and Bliss's old acquaintance from Saint-Nazaire, General Yves St. Pierre Viomenil. He had replaced the ailing commander of the sector a week ago. Ordinarily a trench raid of this size would be handled by a captain and his battalion commander, a major. Bliss and the Commander-in-Chief of the AEF were on hand because the Americans could not afford to make any mistakes if they hoped to win the dirty game they were playing. A flubbed raid would be one more nail in the coffin of an independent American army in France.

Next to the generals were half a dozen nervous reporters and the regiment's chaplain, Father Kelly. At Pershing's suggestion he had given the men a special blessing before they moved to the forward trench. Nearby, a captain from the so-called Blue Devils, an elite French regiment, lectured his twenty men in their own language.

"What's he saying?" Bliss asked Captain Alden.

"He's telling them what to do if the Teddies panic," Alden said.

The Blue Devils were on hand at General Viomenil's insistence. It was a nice combination of French condescension and concern for their neophyte allies, impossible to refuse. Bliss noticed Lieutenant Eagleton was giving them surly glances.

"General, we don't need those guys," Eagleton said.

"Maybe not, but we're stuck with them," Bliss muttered, hoping he was out of Viomenil's earshot.

Viomenil and Pershing had already tangled over the choice of weapons. Jack had exploded when he found out the Lafayettes had been patrolling no-man's-land without their rifles and bayonets. "We can't change methods in midstream," he said. "The rifle and the bayonet are essential American weapons."

The Americans had discarded their sacks of grenades and entrenching shovels and pistols, the weapons the French considered best for patrolling and trench fighting. Bliss thought the French were right but he was not going to contradict Jack in front of Viomenil, who now looked as if he were digesting a live grenade.

A half hour later, miles behind the American trench, the sky flared with the brightness of a premature sunrise. Seconds later, shells shrieked overhead. "Now that's what I call pretty," Sergeant O'Connor said, as livid red and yellow flashes erupted on three sides of the selected two hundred yards of forward German trench line. It was a box barrage, which theoretically trapped the Germans in that slice of trench.

In the darkness O'Connor had discarded his rifle and bayonet and regained his sack of grenades and entrenching shovel. Bliss decided to say nothing and hope Pershing did not notice the contrary mick.

One of the French sergeants who had taken the Lafayettes on their first patrols, a chunky man they called Lucky Pierre, appeared out of the night and spoke in his usual rapid-fire style, gesturing toward the Blue Devils. Something about "*les chaud-lapins*" and "*tantes.*" Jonathan Alden translated. "He says they shouldn't let these sex maniacs worry them. They're really a bunch of aunties."

Pierre was demonstrating the typical infantryman's contempt for elite troops. He finally stopped abusing the Blue Devils and repeated his favorite piece of advice. *"La terre maternelle! La terre maternelle!"* Mother Earth. If an infantryman wanted to survive on the Western Front he had to bury his face in it early and often.

Out of the darkness loomed Colonel Douglas Fairchild. "General," he said to Pershing, "I'd like to go with them. A senior officer can steady the men if anything goes wrong. I know my way around out there. I've been going on patrols regularly."

"Is it all right with you, Bliss?" Pershing asked. "Can you get along without a chief of staff?"

"We'll manage."

Jack did not like Fairchild's grandstanding any more than Bliss did. But in the U.S. Army it was hard to refuse a man who offered to risk his neck. A colonel might help if things went wrong. Bliss did not have much confidence in Company A's commander, Captain Hunthouse, who had shown a marked disinterest in joining his men on patrols.

A detachment of engineers lugging long bangalore torpedoes led the way into the inky darkness of no-man's-land. Behind them they trailed white strips of cloth for the infantry to follow. The torpedoes would blast a hole in the German barbed wire through which Company A and the Blue Devils would attack. Soon everyone had vanished into the thunderous night. There was nothing for the generals to do but wait and hope.

It was hard to detect any sounds except the crash of the .75 shells around the German trench. Bliss thought he heard the sharper explosion of the bangalores and the popping of a German machine gun. Another ten minutes of suspense. A figure loomed out of the night, calling the password. It was Lieutenant Eagleton. "The trench is empty! Not a single German anywhere!" he gasped.

Old pros, the Germans had fled to their reserve trench the moment the barrage began, except for some machine gunners, who had also vanished when the Blue Devils grenaded them. "We want to attack the reserve trench," Eagleton said. "The Blue Devils captain says no. It's only another quarter of a mile. We'll surprise hell of out of them, General."

Bliss turned to Pershing. "Let's do it, Jack. I'll go with them."

"Okay," Pershing said. Bliss thought he saw a smirk of contempt on Viomenil's haughty face. He could almost hear him telling half of Paris the Americans needed a general and a colonel in command to execute a trench raid. But that was better than the stiff-necked aristocrat reporting to Pétain that an entire company had been massacred or captured by the Germans.

Bliss got on the telephone to his artillery commander and told him to lift the box barrage in exactly ten minutes. He followed Eagleton along the strips of white cloth to the forward German trench, where he found Colonel Fairchild arguing strenuously with the captain of the Blue Devils, who wanted to return to the French lines.

"We're going for the next trench in exactly three minutes," Bliss said, checking his watch. "Pass the word to the men."

In three minutes the box barrage ceased thundering. The night became eerily quiet. Bliss ordered O'Connor, Eagleton, and his platoon to join him and the Blue Devils in the first echelon. He put Hunthouse and Fairchild in charge of the second and third platoons following them. Within five minutes they were stopped by a mass of barbed wire. The Blue Devils crept forward with clippers and began chopping a hole in it. "If they are challenged, my men will throw themselves on the wire. You will attack over them," the French captain whispered. "The signal will be a grenade."

Each click sounded like an explosion in the silent darkness. Finally there was a nervous cry: "*Wer da?*" The grenade boomed ten seconds later.

"Kill the bastards!" Eagleton roared and stormed over the Blue Devils lying on the wire. Bliss was only a step behind him, his pistol in his hand, Sergeant O'Connor and the platoon beside him. It was a weird sensation, stamping on a man's legs, back, head. There was no time to think about how they were jamming barbed wire into his flesh.

Into the trench they hurtled to find it full of Germans, at least two hundred of them. "Surrender!" O'Connor roared and drove his trench shovel into the chest of the nearest man. He went down without a sound.

"*Kamerad!*" howled the man behind him, throwing up his hands.

"Der Feind!" (The enemy!) yelled a half dozen others and came at O'Connor with knives and clubs. The *kamerader* decided all bets were off and joined them.

Bliss soon saw the French were right about the uselessness of the rifle in a trench fight. It could only be fired from the hip, making it extremely likely that you would kill one of your friends. Compared to a knife or an entrenching shovel, a bayonet was also a lousy weapon in such close quarters. The Blue Devils swung small clubs studded with nails. The Americans used their fists and their rifles as clubs. The thing was closer to the cave than to the twentieth century.

O'Connor and Eagleton cut a swath through the Germans at their end of the trench, the sergeant wielding the shovel, the Lieutenant the butt of his .45. Ahead of them, a dugout door burst open, flinging light into the trench. Eagleton shot the first man out, an officer with a pistol in his hand. Several others retreated inside. Dozens of other Germans climbed out of the trench and fled into the darkness. In five minutes, those who were still on their feet were yelling *"Kamerad!"* and meaning it this time.

Fairchild rushed up to Bliss to report at least forty prisoners in his end of the trench. Bliss pointed to the dugout's open door. "Let's see if we can pick up an officer or two down there." He ordered Eagleton and O'Connor to follow him down the stairs, pistols ready.

Click. Someone below them threw a switch, and both stairs and dugout blazed with light. The Germans had electricity in the damn thing. The steps descended at least forty feet and they were concrete, not wood, like the French dugouts. "It looks like the entrance to the goddamn subway in Union Square," O'Connor said.

"Gives you the feeling they plan to stay for a while, doesn't it," Bliss said.

Peering cautiously around the corner at the bottom of the stairs, Bliss was so astonished he almost forgot where they were. The walls were lined with steel bunks. A gleaming potbellied stove squatted in one corner. Compared to the crumbling French dugouts, infested by lice and rats, it was a college dormitory.

The crack of a rifle restored Bliss's attention. The bullet chipped concrete an inch from his head. Four or five Germans were crouched behind a table in the corner near the stove. "Surrender!" he called. *"Kamerad!"*

"Gott mit uns!" one of them roared, and two more bullets bounced off the wall at the foot of the stairs.

"Let me get a shot at them, General," Eagleton said, easing past Bliss. He peered around the corner and got the same lead shave-and-a-haircut, accompanied by more shouts of *"Gott mitt uns!"* He banged four or five rounds at them to let them know you could not do that sort of thing to a Harvard man, but he was shooting wild.

"Does anyone in the company speak German?" Bliss asked.

Eagleton sent O'Connor to get Captain Hunthouse. He came down the stairs as if he were being invited to his own funeral. Bliss told him to persuade the holdouts to surrender. *"Gott mitt uns!"* was the reply, with gunfire for punctuation. Hunthouse almost recoiled to the top of the stairs.

The Blue Devils captain came down the stairs screaming curses in French. At any moment the Germans might counterattack with an entire battalion. When he discovered Bliss was trying to negotiate with the Germans, he became even more exercised. Bliss did not catch all the verbs, but he was sure General Viomenil would get them in triplicate and pass them on to the rest of the French army.

Bliss grabbed three grenades out of O'Connor's sack. Handing one to Eagleton and one to O'Connor, he waved them to the bottom of the stairs. He pulled the pin and flipped his grenade into the room. With a gesture he ordered them to do likewise. He could see from the expressions on their faces they hated the idea.

In the confined space the explosions were stupendous. *"Bon!"* said the Blue Devils captain and started up the stairs to the trench. As the Americans followed him, one of the Germans started screaming, *"Ach mein Gott ach mein Gott ach mein Gott!"* The captain took a fourth grenade from O'Connor's sack and flipped it into the dormitory. The screaming stopped.

"Is that how we're going to fight this war, General?" Lieutenant Eagleton said, as they emerged into the trench.

"Yes," Bliss said.

274 / THOMAS FLEMING

"They would've done the same thing to us if they had a chance, wouldn't they, General?" O'Connor asked, trying to apply the code of the slums to no-man's-land.

"Yes," Bliss said.

Suddenly he heard Polly Warden asking him if he had ever seen men die on a battlefield. He saw the dismay on her beautiful face at his tough offhand reply. A spear of regret, almost of shame, shot through his body. *He wailed not so of stone grew he within.* It was his job to impart stoniness to these amateurs, even though he knew it was nothing but an extravagant metaphor from a poetic exploration of hell.

An hour later, back in his headquarters in Lunéville, Bliss basked in that rarest of experiences, John J. Pershing's approval. They had captured fifty-eight German prisoners, left at least twenty Germans dead, and had only two Americans slightly wounded. His Celts had demonstrated all the qualities Pershing valued in soldiers: aggressiveness, ingenuity, toughness.

From the French side of the equation came only sour notes. After interrogating the prisoners, General Viomenil had announced they were from the 6th Bavarian Home Guard, a fourth-class German division. That had been more or less obvious. Half the captives had gray mustaches and snow-white hair. The Lunéville sector had been as quiet as a sanatorium for two years. Neither side saw much need for first-class troops to man its trenches.

"You must now prepare for a response, possibly from a first-class division," Viomenil said.

"I think they can handle it, General," Pershing said.

Bliss found himself standing uneasily between the two men, morally and emotionally confused. He agreed with Jack's need to establish his equality with General Viomenil. But Pershing was on the wrong side of the argument when it came to the choice of weapons.

"I hope you're right. I fear the entire process is premature," Viomenil said. "Your men never should have attacked that reserve trench. First-class troops would have cut them to pieces."

He left Pershing and Bliss with that happy thought. Bliss poured Pershing a bourbon and water and fixed one for himself. "Good show," Jack said, clinking glasses.

"I only wish you hadn't asked that sanctimonious chaplain, Kelly, to give them his blessing. He'll take credit for the whole damn thing," Bliss said.

"I figured we needed all the luck we could get," Pershing said. "Besides, he's good copy. The reporters are out to create some heroes, and your micks are naturals. You can't write about the Irish without working in a priest."

Bliss often forgot how well Pershing had mastered the art of manipulating the press. When they began their pursuit of Pancho Villa, Jack had obligingly posed in the middle of the Rio Grande on horseback. Actually, he had ridden across the inhospitable desert of northern Mexico in a Dodge touring car.

"How are we doing on the amalgamation front?"

"Next week I'm getting a visit from Field Marshal Haig, Prime Minister Lloyd George, Winston Churchill, and at least four other big shots. They're going all-out."

"Where the hell are our diplomats, Jack? Why do you have to deal with this on your own?"

"If we pull it off, Mal, we can claim all the credit."

This was the Pershing that Bliss would follow anywhere, the cool calculator who knew life was a series of gambles. They were both feeling high. Their men had performed. No one except General Viomenil knew they had been fighting fourth-rate soldiers.

Behind the flash of recklessness Bliss saw the tired harassed man who had arrived from Chaumont five hours ago. It was now 4 A.M. Bliss had hoped to talk to him about weapons and tactics, but he could not bring himself to add another burden at this hour. He would put it in writing, although he feared it would be pigeonholed by the Chaumont bureacracy. Already the AEF staff had swelled to five hundred Command and General Staff School eager beavers like Hugh Drum, who would never dream of letting Pershing take advice from a mere division commander.

"Have you settled things with Tasker?"

Within a day of his arrival in Paris, Tasker Bliss had begun spreading rumors about Wilson's dissatisfaction with Pershing and hinting that he was virtually deputized to replace him.

"Not yet. I've got to do it before I meet the British. Woodrow's appointed him to the Supreme War Council."

Bliss had not heard of this entity. Pershing explained they were a group of French and British politicians and generals who met in Versailles once a week to coordinate the war effort. "They don't have any power, but if Tasker starts talking amalgamation there it could be embarrassing."

"Make sliced salami out of him. I'm betting on you, Jack."

Pershing finished his drink and headed for the door. "Watch out for that first-class division. We can't afford any unpleasant surprises," he said as he got into his car.

The dirty game continued. Bliss hoped the Germans were not on to it.

26. *LA GUERRE DE LUXE*

"MY GOD, LOOK AT THIS!" MARTHA HERZOG gasped, seizing her January 14, 1918, copy of *Le Figaro* with both hands. "Premier Clemenceau's arrested Senator Joseph Caillaux and thrown him into the Prison de la Santé. He's also arrested Louis Malvy, the Minister of the Interior, and a lot of other people. He's going to try them for treason."

Wearing sweaters and winter coats, Polly, Martha, and Eleanor were having breakfast in the dining room of their heatless house on the Rue de Verneuil. With the temperature outside hovering around zero, the big stone building was a giant refrigerator. This morning, the water in Polly's bedroom jug had frozen and burst its container with an explosion like a small cannon. The savage cold was an almost visible image of the war's continuing grip on everyone's life.

"It's tantamount to Wilson's arresting Senator Henry Cabot Lodge and the Attorney General of the United States," Martha said.

Polly had been expecting the news for a week. A bitter Charles Louis Lebrun had kept her well informed of his negotiations with Georges Clemenceau. The Tiger had accepted Lebrun's surrender with the worst possible grace. He despised men like Lebrun, who had inherited wealth and added immeasurably to it with seemingly effortless ease. The Premier had demanded more from Lebrun than the delivery of the twenty-five deputies who were dependent on him. He had to agree to stop funding Almeyreda and his apaches, stop backing the *Bonnet Rouge*, the Trois Magots, and other critics of the war, and become a public supporter of Georges Clemenceau.

He wanted—and obtained—not merely Lebrun's surrender but his humiliation.

"May I see the paper?" Polly said. Among the names of the jailed were Bolo Pasha and Almeyreda, but there was no mention of Charles Louis Lebrun. At one point, the Tiger had threatened to include his name in the list of suspects who would be prosecuted later.

Polly had been dismayed by Clemenceau's savagery. He waged war on his political enemies as ferociously as he hurled defiance at the Germans. In her divided mind, she was torn between sympathy for Lebrun and her commitment to an Allied victory. Her struggle was immensely confused by a speech Woodrow Wilson made before Congress early in January, in which he offered Germany fourteen points, or principles, on which he was ready to negotiate peace. It was a paradigm of how Americans back home seemed totally ignorant of the situation in Europe. Not even the President of the United States seemed to be aware of the desperate struggle between surrender and victory racking France.

The day after Caillaux's arrest, Lebrun invited Polly to join him for the last night of the Trois Magots; tomorrow it was to be shuttered by order of the new Minister of the Interior. Never had Richelieu's satire of the war been more corrosive. He mocked generals, politicians (in particular, Clemenceau), patriotic writers, the Archbishop of Paris, the Pope—and Woodrow Wilson. He conducted an imaginary interview with Wilson, telling him if he really wanted a peace without victory, the French army was more than ready to give it to him. The audience, all followers of Caillaux, stamped and whistled and cheered. Polly felt like a traitor, sitting among them as Clemenceau's secret agent.

For his farewell song, Richelieu saluted the brave King Croesus, the man with the golden touch, who had made it possible for him to sing of bravery and patriotism and honor. What a pity that Croesus had learned nothing from his songs, that he had sold his kingdom to the enemy to preserve his hoard. As the words rang out, almost every head turned to stare contemptuously at Charles Louis Lebrun.

Much later, as they descended the steep streets of Montmartre in Lebrun's limousine, the financier said, "And you still believe in Clemenceau's victory?" His voice was slurred. It was the first time Polly had ever seen him drink too much.

"Yes," Polly said. The word left a bitter taste on her lips. Was it a lie?

Lebrun was silent until they passed the Palais Bourbon, home of the Chamber of Deputies. A streetlight cast random rays on the twelve heroic columns of the façade. Above them loomed the figure of France, surrounded by statues representing Liberty, Order, Commerce, and Peace—towering symbols of the ideal nation in which Paul believed. "I think you love victory more than you love me," he said.

"Why can't I love you both?"

"No woman loves a coward."

"I'll never think of you as a coward."

"Everyone else does. Why don't you?"

"I'm one of the few who know how much courage it took for you to listen to your heart. To your love for Paul—and for France."

"Nonsense. The truth is, I couldn't face a prison cell in January."

The chauffeur nosed down the narrow Rue de Verneuil and stopped before the Kingswood house. "I've lost you and my place in the world," Lebrun said. "Couldn't you see what you were doing, changing my mind little by little with your American optimism? There were times when I thought it was deliberate—that you were working for Clemenceau."

She kissed him violently on the mouth, even though the heavy cologne he used and the underlying odors of tobacco and brandy repelled her. "You'll never lose me," she said. She almost meant it. But she was also trying to stifle that surge of suspicion.

He held her for a moment. "If you could give me that gift I once asked for too rashly, too arrogantly—?"

Was this *cafard* again, a different, no less authentic kind? Polly felt the pull of pity, affection, guilt. But the voice, perhaps Paul's voice, still said no. "Let me listen to my heart, your heart, a little longer," she said.

* * *

At the hospital a few days later, Dr. Giroux-Langin summoned Polly to her office. "I met Charles Louis Lebrun at a dinner party last night," she said. "He told me you've broken off your affair. It was just as well you didn't mention it to me."

In a voice charged with compassion, the Doctor said she understood the brief liaison. It was *une feuille volante*, an endpaper in the history of their mutual love for Paul. "I'm glad you didn't succumb to him," she said.

The Doctor could accept a brief liaison as long as Polly did not become one of Lebrun's possessions. He had a history of degrading women and then tossing them aside like old clothing. Polly could only nod in bewilderment. It was exquisitely clever. If she denied there had been an affair, Dr. Giroux-Langin would think she was lying. By accepting it, the Doctor was admitting for the first time she had expected Polly to succumb. So how could she possibly object, when she found out she had succumbed?

Polly tried to fight back, using Lebrun's weapons. "I think he still loves you," she said.

Dr. Giroux-Langin almost lost her professional composure. "I find him essentially unchanged," she said. "I made that very clear to him. Clemenceau forced him to abandon Caillaux. But his heart is not with France."

There was color in the Doctor's cheeks. She looked almost girlish. "We're far beyond the bounds of our profession," she said, regaining her composure. "I hope you can now concentrate wholeheartedly on your work."

That exhortation soon acquired a hollow sound. Almost as if he wanted to savor his humiliation and simultaneously escape it, Lebrun changed his milieu from the followers of Caillaux to the aristocrats and ultra-Catholics of the right wing of French society. He took Polly to dinners at which she listened to paunchy marquises and scowling bankers hail Clemenceau's defiance of Germany and then harangue against the Jews and democracy while their wives complained about how difficult it was to find decent servants since the war started.

On the way home, the chauffeur would take them along the

Boulevard Clichy to the streets around the Place Pigalle in Mont-martre. Against the shuttered shops and oozing walls stood dozens of prostitutes, their blank white faces revealed by the occasional gas lamp, like souls of the dead. Lebrun would inquire for Popette or Angelique and invite the girl into the car to certify his stories about a certain count or marquis. Several times the teller of the tale was a man, wearing rouge and lipstick, even a skirt. A great many of these backers of Clemenceau seemed to prefer men to women. Always, Polly sensed Lebrun was asking her, Is this the ideal France you want me to defend to the death?

All this left Polly totally unprepared for Lebrun's announcement that he wanted to give a victory party for her and her American friends. "But there is no victory yet," Polly said.

"Ah, for those who fight the battles of *la guerre de luxe*, there are many kinds of victories. The mere thought of meeting the valiant Americans who are here to engineer our rescue will be a triumph for most of our guests."

He told her to invite everyone he had met from Pershing's staff—including the great man himself and his friend, General Bliss. The Americans would come in their uniforms, of course. The French would wear costumes that paid tribute to France's *gloire*.

She heard the sarcasm in his voice, but how could she object? Invitations went out to dozens of people for the Salute to Victory party at Lebrun's château in the Île-de-France. Eleanor and Martha were included, as was Louise Wolcott, who was among the first to accept. General Pershing claimed another engagement but Bliss, Quickmeyer, and a dozen members of the general staff accepted. When Martha reported George Patton was in Paris celebrating his promotion to captain, he too was put on the list.

Eleanor asked if she could bring a YMCA executive from Dubuque named Harold Holloway who seemed to fascinate her, though no one knew why. He was about six feet six, with the physique of an asthmatic whooping crane. Why not? Lebrun said. The YMCA too was part of America's program for the coming vic-tory. Their canteens would supply the doughnuts, the muffins, the coffee that would make the doughboys irresistible in battle!

On the appointed night, Lebrun's great château blazed with

light. In room after room there were enough hors d'oeuvres and fruit and sweetmeats to feed the poor of Paris for a week. Batteries of servants armed with champagne bottles stood ready to pour. Polly had told Lebrun she was coming in her French army nurse's uniform. He did not tell her what his costume would be. He came downstairs dressed as the traditional sad-faced French clown, Pierrot. His face was painted a dead white, his nose yellow, his lips blue. His suit was a rainbow of shreds and patches. "Why not admit to the world what I've become?" he said.

Captain Patton and Colonel Quickmeyer were among the first to arrive, along with Martha, Eleanor, and Harold Holloway. "*La plus belle fille de Paree!*" Patton shouted, in the same atrocious accent he had displayed aboard the S.S. *Baltic*, and gave Polly an enthusiastic kiss. A few minutes later General Bliss arrived. He was considerably more decorous than Captain Patton—and more disapproving. He clearly disliked the sight of Polly Warden receiving guests as if she were Charles Louis Lebrun's official hostess.

Champagne was poured in an immense room whose walls were crowded with portraits of French aristocrats from the reign of Louis XIV. Lebrun followed Polly to her circle of American friends from the *Baltic*. "What are you doing these days?" Polly asked Patton. "Have they put you in charge of the army's mules?"

"Not yet. I'm commander of Pershing's headquarters company."

"That means he's the world's greatest expert on how to shine shoes, boots, belts, and visors to the point where unwary visitors are temporarily blinded," General Bliss said.

"Is that all General Pershing cares about?" Polly asked.

"It impresses senators and congressmen and assorted Washington bureaucrats," Bliss said. "They're the ones we worry about most these days. They're swarming all over France."

"When are we going to start *fighting*?" Polly said, unable to conceal her anxiety.

"When Wavering Woodrow sends us an army," Bliss said.

"I think we're boring Miss Warden," Patton said. "She's a frontline veteran listening to a lot of *embusqués*."

"I'm an *embusqué* myself these days," Polly said.

"I like that word," Bliss said. "I looked it up. Literally it means a soldier not at the front, waiting to ambush the enemy. The French have a nice nasty sense of humor, don't they?"

"Irony, General. We love irony," Lebrun said. "We think it's the essence of life."

"Irony is just another word for history," Bliss said. "But we Americans believe in changing history. Don't you agree, Miss Warden?"

"What? Oh, yes," Polly said. Was he asking her—even telling her—to regain her lost idealism?

Swooping down on them was the Countess de Pougy and her diminutive French husband, whom Polly had met at several dinner parties. The Count was fourth or fifth in line for the throne, if the French ever decided to bring back the monarchy. The Countess supplied him with money; she was a Philadelphia Drexel. The tiny Count greeted them in the uniform of an officer of the French Foreign Legion, complete with a chestful of decorations. "Ah!" he said, kissing Polly's hand. "The heroine of the Forbidden Zone. I too have become a traveler to that infernal place."

"Doing what, buying up other guys' medals?" Patton asked, as Polly struggled with introductions.

"You'll find out later tonight, Captain," the Count said loftily, as if he were protecting a state secret.

Almost all the French guests were the aristocrats and royalists of the French right wing Lebrun had been cultivating in his Richelieuesque spirit of mockery. Most of the men wore martial uniforms like the Count de Pougy. The women's costumes were all faithful copies of the elaborate styles of the ancien régime. They gorged themselves on the hor d'oeuvres and strolled into the château's interior, eyeing everything like auctioneer's assistants, murmuring at Lebrun's extravagance. Each room was decorated in the style of a different period. It was like going from set to set in a play or movie.

"How do you like my costume?" Louise Wolcott said, cruising up on their right. She was wearing a black velvet dinner gown with cloth-of-gold panels and gold-beaded shoulder straps. A diamond-studded gold tiara sparkled on her glossy blond head. "I'm Queen of the May."

"Does that mean you may do anything you please?" Bliss said.

"That's Paris's motto. Some people have learned it much faster than I thought they would," Louise said. "Wouldn't you agree, Miss Warden?"

"Are you impugning the virtue of my *plus belle fille?*" George Patton asked.

"The word virtue isn't in any dictionary in Paris, George," Harry Quickmeyer said, handing Louise a bubbling glass of champagne.

"It's still in American dictionaries," Bliss said, his somber eyes drifting toward Polly.

A flash of sullen anger engulfed Polly. Why did those stars on his shoulders give this man the presumption to judge her? She had done more to help him win his stupid war than any other American in France.

A bell announced dinner. Polly found herself seated next to General Bliss, with the Count de Pougy on the other side. At the head of the table, Pierrot-Lebrun offered a toast to the "heroic Americans" who were going to rescue France. If Bliss caught the mockery, he did not give a sign. He asked Polly if her "business" with Lebrun was over—or would it continue as long as the war lasted?

"I—I hope not," she said.

"Maybe you ought to collect your Legion of Honor and go home," Bliss said.

That stirred new anger. He was treating her like a naughty child. "You still don't think we can win the war, General?" she said, loud enough for several people to look curiously at Bliss.

"I thought we had an understanding about what we could say to each other," he said.

"I'm sorry," Polly murmured, stunned that he would remember their conversation on the *Baltic*.

"Now comes the moment of excitement," cried Lebrun in his clown's face at the head of the table. "We're going to draw lots to see who accompanies Count de Pougy into the Forbidden Zone."

"Why?" Polly asked.

"To bring back some wounded poilus. It's the latest rage," Louise Wolcott said from the other side of the table.

"Madame! You've given away the secret," said the Count.

"There's a doctor in the vicinity who takes care of them," Louise said.

There were gasps and squeals of anticipation up and down the table as Lebrun passed out slips of paper with numbers on them. Duplicates were dropped into a huge brandy snifter. Lebrun tied a napkin around the Countess de Pougy's eyes, and she withdrew two slips.

"Seven and eleven," the Count said.

"I have eleven," Polly said.

"I have seven," Louise Wolcott said.

Groans and grumbles from the aristocrats. One woman said it was definitely unfair for two Americans to win. The butler brought them a stretcher and a flask of brandy. The whole party crowded to the door to see them depart in an official-looking Dion-Bouton.

They roared along pitch-black roads at top speed, the Count supplying directions from a map. In the back seat Louise abandoned her gibes and spoke to Polly in a far more intimate voice. "Why are you so cruel to poor Lebrun? He's turned to me for help. He can't understand your perpetual refusals. Everyone assumes you're sleeping with him. Why hesitate—especially when he needs you?"

The chauffeur cursed and swerved violently to the right to avoid an oncoming truck, thundering down the middle of the road. Louise told Polly she had been Lebrun's mistress for a year. In that time he gave her a million dollars' worth of jewelry. "I sold half of it and moved to a separate apartment, defying my husband for the first time. You orate about independence for women, but you're never going to experience it on a nurse's salary."

On Louise talked, urging Polly to learn from her example. Only when a woman had financial independence could she begin to explore her heart. Polly listened numbly, wearily, becoming more and more convinced it was impossible to escape Charles Louis Lebrun.

Up ahead the big guns rumbled; the night sky glowed with their muzzle flashes.

In about a half hour the Count de Pougy said, "There it is, on the right." The chauffeur hurtled through an arched gateway and up a long curving drive. Polly had no idea where they were. The guns were closer now. Their flashes glowed like ugly blotches of blood on the dark horizon.

Louise gripped Polly's arm. "My God, how I envy you. To go through this, night after night."

The big car squished through mud and puddles for another quarter of a mile. The chauffeur flashed his headlights for a moment. Several dozen bodies were lying in the open. A few feet away were the silhouettes of some narrow flat-roofed barracks. It was all so similar to the Château Givry, for a moment Polly could hear nothing but her thudding heart.

The chauffeur and the Count seized the stretcher and carried a wounded man back to the car. He cried out in agony when they bumped him against the door as they lifted him onto the back seat. A limousine was not designed to receive stretcher cases. Propping him up in one corner, they rushed back and picked up another man, who was equally difficult to get into the car. Polly and Louise sat on two smaller folding seats, facing the groaning poilus. They stank of mud and sweat and blood.

"Incredible. You can smell the war. You can breathe it," Louise said.

Polly was appalled. She had expected the Count de Pougy to have an arrangement with the directors of the hospital to pick up one or two of the less seriously wounded. She had no idea the expedition was clandestine, that they were going to scoop up new casualties before they were examined or treated.

As the chauffeur backed the car down the muddy side road to the highway, Polly took the first man's pulse. It was fluttering spasmodically. "Where are you wounded, *mon ami?*" she asked.

"In the chest." The man groaned. "It hurts."

"This man is dying," Polly said.

"He'd die out there on the ground," the Count said. "This way at least he'll die in comfort. It's a wonderful experience, watching a poilu die. It brings you close to the sacred meaning of France."

The second man had an almost normal pulse. He said he was wounded in the leg. "Give them some of this brandy," the Count said, thrusting the flask into Polly's hand.

The first man gagged and could not get the liquor down. The second man grabbed the flask and gulped it greedily. "Good stuff," he said.

"You're damn right it's good," the Count said. "It's fifty years old."

The poilu with the chest wound struggled for life, gasping and groaning all the way back to the Château Lebrun. The guests crowded around them as menservants carried the two wounded soldiers into the entrance hall. Towering over them was Charles Louis Lebrun's clown face. "Where's the doctor?" Polly said. "One of these men needs immediate surgery."

That sent a shiver of excitement through the onlookers. Gazing at the vacuous faces, the fat jeweled necks, the greedy eyes, Polly could have become a revolutionary on the spot. If there were a machine gun handy, she would have mowed down all of them.

The Count de Pougy gave orders to the servants in a voice that might have belonged to Napoleon at Austerlitz. They carried the two poilus upstairs. Led by Lebrun with his clown's smile, the crowd trooped after them. The servants carried the poilus into a bedroom with two canopied beds and left them on the floor beside them.

There was no sign of a doctor. The Countess de Pougy explained that there was only one doctor who cared for poilus brought to half a dozen nearby châteaus, including theirs. He was scheduled to arrive here in about an hour.

"Undress him," Polly said to Eleanor Kingswood, pointing to the poilu with the wounded leg. "I'll handle this man."

Polly knelt beside the man with the chest wound and began pulling off his boots. Eleanor stood in the doorway, frozen with disbelief, gazing at the mud-encrusted soldier she was supposed to strip.

"My dear girl, the maids will see to that sort of thing," the Countess de Pougy said.

"This man is dying!" Polly shouted. "He needs a doctor immediately!"

"They often die," the Countess de Pougy said. "The Count writes a beautiful letter to their families. He sends them a thousand francs."

George Patton shoved his way through the crowd at the door. "Tell me what to do," he said.

"They have to be undressed and bathed," Polly said. "Help me with this man."

The poilu with the chest wound was semiconscious, his eyes closed. His pulse was now barely discernible beneath Polly's fingers. Patton lifted him to a sitting position, getting mud and blood all over his immaculate uniform. Polly began cutting away the soldier's shirt.

The man's eyes opened. He looked past Patton at the soldier on the other stretcher. "*Salaud!*" he hissed. Bastard! He grabbed Patton's Sam Browne belt. "He ran away," he said in French, pointing to the other soldier. "That bastard ran away instead of sounding the alarm! The Boche—"

He slumped in Patton's arms, dead. The spectators in the doorway expelled a chorus of sympathetic cries. This was a truly wonderful show: courage, cowardice, betrayal, death.

"What the hell was he saying?" Patton asked.

Polly translated the dead man's last words. "It's not true," the leg wound said. He had a long lean cadaverous face. "I sounded the alarm. The Germans were on top of us before anyone could move! The bastards can see in the dark. I swear I sounded the alarm!"

"Let me see his wound," Patton said.

They cut off the bloody trouser on the man's left leg. The wound was a small red blotch in his calf, surrounded by a blackened border. "Powder burns," Patton said, pointing to the rim of scorched flesh. "A sure sign of a self-inflicted wound. No German got close enough to this guy to put the muzzle of a gun against his leg. He was running too fast."

"Messieurs, mesdames!" the leg wound cried. "I swear I sounded the alarm. I've been in the trenches four years!"

"Let's shoot the bastard," Patton said. "Ask them for a gun."

"Take me home," Polly said.

"You don't have to watch it. I'll handle it." Turning to the spectators in the doorway, Patton roared, "*Avez-vous un pistol?*"

"Take me home!" Polly said, tears trickling down her cheeks. It was the worst nightmare yet. There stood the man she had destroyed, the once imperial Charles Louis Lebrun, reduced by her treachery to a clown, waiting for her to give herself to his sad mocking mouth. Beside her was a poilu who had died to defend these abominable aristocrats who gawked at his death as if it were a sideshow for their delectation. A foot away was the soldier who had betrayed him. She was responsible for it all.

General Bliss shouldered his way into the room. "George, it's none of our business," he said. "It's not our army."

"It's our war!" Patton said.

"Please—take—me—home!" Polly said, beginning to sob. If they left her here she would belong to Charles Louis Lebrun before morning. She would belong to him until he discarded her with a million dollars' worth of jewelry and a worthless soul.

"Captain Patton, take Miss Warden out to my car. That's an order!" Bliss said.

"Yes, sir," Patton said.

He put his arm around Polly and shoved through the gaping crowd of millionaires and aristocrats at the bedroom door. Past Charles Louis Lebrun, who raised his hand in halfhearted protest and then allowed it to drop to his side in a gesture worthy of a forlorn Pierrot. Downstairs, Patton flung Polly's cloak around her and walked her out to the car.

In the cold dark backseat, a different George Patton started talking. "I'm sorry as hell. I lost my head in there. I can't stand the sight of blood. It almost makes me sick. I wonder if I'm a coward. Maybe that guy I was ready to shoot was really George S. Patton, Jr."

"You're not a coward," Polly said. "I am."

"You? You're the bravest woman I've ever met. I wish I wasn't married. I'd never let you out of my sight until you said yes. You were born to be a soldier's wife."

"I hate war!" Polly sobbed.

"You hate what it does to people. We all hate that," General Bliss said, opening the car door.

Bliss's chauffeur got behind the wheel, and they drove toward Paris. "La guerre de luxe," Bliss said. "It's not exactly inspiring, is it?"

"I'm going to see Pershing tomorrow and tell him I'm through being an embusqué," Patton said. "I don't care if I wind up courtmartialed."

"I have to go back to it," Polly said.

She did not recognize her own voice. It was as if an alien presence had taken control of her body. "Back to what?" Bliss said.

"The war."

"This time I hope you'll join the American army. I think you've done more than enough for *la belle France.*"

It was amazing, the way that tough American voice steadied her nerves. Polly found herself puzzling over why he had changed his mind about sending her home. Did those somber eyes, which seemed to intimate a *cafard* deeper than any she had seen, understand that only the front, the Forbidden Zone, the slashed gouged landscape of no-man's-land—only that domain of danger and death could purify her courage again?

27. *BAPTISM*

In the Maison Solange, Lunéville's most popular restaurant, Malvern Hill Bliss was entertaining Congressmen Finnerty, Mason, Bland, and Brewster. It was the fifth or sixth congressional delegation Solange had fed since they moved into the lines. The Lafayette Division, with men from thirteen different states, attracted them like flies to a picnic. They all had to be gorged at the army's expense, have pictures taken with some of their constituents, and pay a visit to the front lines.

The main topic of conversation was Woodrow Wilson's Fourteen Points. He had issued this blast of diplomatic gas in a speech to Congress a few weeks ago, calling on the Germans to surrender and accept eternal peace. All they had to do was give up Belgium, Russia, Poland, Rumania, and the huge slice of France they currently occupied. The congressmen seemed baffled to discover that the Germans had responded with a large horse laugh. They were even more puzzled to learn that the French and the British, who had not been consulted before Woodrow exhaled this peace proposal, were extremely upset and regarded Wilson as a combination menace and dimwit. The congressmen were all Democrats, and this naturally struck them as treason.

Captain Alden rushed into the restaurant. "General," he said, "we've just gotten a rather disturbing report from Major Perry. The Germans have been shelling our lines. He thinks it's registering fire. It could mean an attack."

Bliss began making apologies for an immediate departure to the front. Yesterday the forward trenches had reported an odd ceremony at sundown. From somewhere within the German lines, a band had played "Die Wacht am Rhein," one of their favorite war songs. The fourth-class division they had raided so successfully never played music at sundown. They probably did not rate a band. First-class divisions, on the other hand, no doubt came equipped with music to boost their already substantial pride.

The congressmen all insisted on coming to the front with Bliss. The army's policy, probably initiated under George Washington, was never to say no to a congressman. So they drafted another car from their motor pool and headed for the danger zone. They found Joe Perry in Ireland's Own regimental headquarters, a dugout about a mile behind the trench system, outside the tiny village of Bompère. There was no sign of Colonel Alexander O'Sullivan. Perry said he was having lunch in Lunéville with another congressman.

Bliss watched a salvo of German artillery fall about a hundred yards behind the forward trench. Ten seconds later, a salvo fell fifty yards in front of it. Similar salvos were falling all along the Lafayette trench line. The division was now manning almost four miles of the front. Their French instructors were gone; Bliss had decided they were no longer needed.

The salvos stopped when American artillery started firing back. A major artillery duel was soon in progress. The congressmen loved it, especially since none of the shells were falling anywhere near them. Bliss went down a communication trench to the forward trench, taking Perry with him. He was pleased to find Company A of the 1st Battalion, the men who had pulled off the raid, manning the trench.

Summoning Captain Hunthouse and Lieutenant Eagleton, Bliss pointed to Semperey, a wrecked village in no-man's-land. "I want a sergeant and twenty men to move into those houses as soon as it's dark. Major Perry is sending four machine-gun squads with them."

"Sir. May I go with them? I can guarantee twenty good men from my platoon," Eagleton said.

"All right," Bliss said, liking this Harvard man more and more.

The shrieks of incoming heavy shells gouged their eardrums. "Better get your men into the dugouts," Perry said. "These guys mean business. There's your proof."

He pointed toward the German lines. About a mile away a large sausage-shaped balloon was rising into the sky. In its gondola Bliss could make out two men with field glasses. A telephone wire ran from the gondola to the ground. Not by accident were they called barrage balloons. They were there to tell the artillery how to correct their ranges.

In a dugout christened the Waldorf, Bliss found Father Francis Kelly trying to cheer the men up. With him was a war correspondent named Charlie Murtagh from the Hearst papers. Since the raid, correspondents had been all over the Lafayette Division's sector. "This only proves how mad the Kaiser is," Kelly said. "We chewed up one of his best divisions the other night. Right, General?"

"If they attack, I want you all up there on the firing steps, giving them hell," Bliss said, ignoring Kelly's vainglory.

Heavy shells were landing all around the dugout. Sand drooled from the timbered roof. Bliss suddenly remembered that one of the officers in Ireland's Own had sent him a warning that some of these three-year-old French-built shelters were in danger of collapse.

"O'Brien, get up here!" a sergeant roared from the top of the dugout steps.

O'Brien, a chunky freckle-faced kid, reluctantly mounted the steps to the trench. He was replacing a lookout who had just become a casualty. The wooden stairs trembled as some of the biggest German shells exploded above them. O'Brien looked as if he were on his way to a firing squad. "Gimme ya blessin', Fadda," he whispered.

Father Kelly raised his hand in a rapid sign of the cross.

"That's really beautiful, Father," Charlie Murtagh said, scribbling notes.

"How about givin' us all ya blessin', Fadda?" said someone in the dim rear of the dugout.

"Sure," Father Kelly said. As he raised his hand to make another sign of the cross, a big shell landed very close to the dugout. A cascade of dirt showered from the ceiling. Two more big ones landed in rapid succession. A cracking, crumbling groan resounded through the gloom and part of the ceiling collapsed.

"Get out of here!" Joe Perry yelled, grabbing Bliss by the arm and hauling him up twenty or thirty feet of stairs into the muddy trench. Correspondent Murtagh and half a dozen soldiers, one of them dragging Father Kelly, landed on top of them. From the dugout drifted screams of terror and anguish and a dull roar as the entire ceiling, with its half ton of sandbags, buried the rest of the Waldorf's tenants.

The German barrage continued to rain down, filling the twilight with explosions. Bliss stumbled to his feet and summoned soldiers from other dugouts to try to rescue the trapped men. Sergeant O'Connor pulled six dazed, choking survivors from the wreckage near the foot of the steps. Diggers tunneled into the dugout from the opposite side and rescued two men who had crawled under bunks when they saw the collapse begin. But a head count, completed by the company clerk as darkness fell, concluded twenty-eight men had been buried alive.

"You've done all you can," Bliss shouted above the bombardment. "Get back in your dugouts. We can't waste any more men. I expect an attack before dawn."

"I reported that dugout as unsafe, General. Why wasn't something done about it?" Lieutenant Eagleton asked.

"Because the French are in charge here," Bliss shouted. "We don't have the right to rebuild dugouts or trenches. We're still fighting for the right to do those things, to run our own show."

He seized Eagleton's arm. "Instead of twenty men, take forty out to that village. Double the number of machine guns, too."

Father Kelly stared numbly at the dugout. "We can't just leave them down there!" he cried. "I knew most of them. They were from my first parish, Holy Innocents."

There was no sleep for Bliss that night. The German artillery relentlessly pounded the forward trench line. Without consulting Bliss, Colonel O'Sullivan evacuated a dozen other dugouts that looked unsafe. That dangerously thinned the numbers in this trench, which Bliss was determined to defend. He was sure Pershing would have a conniption if they surrendered a foot of ground.

A half hour before dawn, German infantry surged from their trenches behind an intensified barrage to keep Bliss's front-line troops in their dugouts until the last possible moment. It might have been a rout if Bliss had not stationed Lieutenant Eagleton and his infantrymen and Joe Perry's machine-gunners in Semperey. They disrupted the attack with devastating flanking fire from the middle of no-man's-land.

The infuriated Germans wheeled at least five hundred men to assault Semperey. Bliss reinforced Eagleton with the rest of Company A. Soon the battle enveloped the entire front line. The Germans were throwing at least five thousand men at them. Bliss had less than two thousand in his forward trenches. German artillery was furiously bombarding his reserve trenches to prevent reinforcements. What were they trying to do, smash the whole division? Seize the forward trench line and force them to pay a murderous price to regain it?

A worried Jonathan Alden told him General Viomenil was on the telephone. "I am informed you are under heavy attack, General," the Frenchman said. "I'm sending a brigade of experienced troops to your assistance immediately. They should be there by noon. Do you think you can hold on?"

"My men are contesting every inch of the line," Bliss said, well aware that Viomenil was hoping to make him eat the words Lafayette had said to his ancestor at Yorktown.

He had barely put down the phone when Captain Alden rushed in. "Colonel O'Sullivan says he's abandoning Remières Wood! His men are falling back to the trench line."

The Bois de Remières jutted into no-man's-land a thousand yards west of Semperey. The French had never dug trenches through it, deciding it was a natural barrier that could be defended with a few well-sited machine guns. Unfortunately, the wood flanked the forward trench line, and anyone who wanted to capture that line would try to seize control of Remières. Bliss had put two companies of the second battalion of Ireland's Own in the trees, reinforced by a machine gun company.

"Get up there and tell me what the hell's happening," Bliss said to Alden. "I'll be at Colonel O'Sullivan's command post in Bompère."

On the way to his car, he almost collided with Joe Perry, who had just leaped off a sputtering motorcycle. "Mal!" he said. "The

front line's under a lot of pressure. The Krauts are using flamethrowers, mortars, the works."

"Tell me about it in the car."

As they roared toward Bompère, Perry rapidly described what he
had seen and heard at the front. He recommended retreating to the
reserve trench, where he had sited most of his machine guns. He
thought they could tempt the Germans into an attack and massacre
them.

"What about the men in Semperey?" Bliss said. "I can't abandon
them."

"Pull them back too. I'll cover them. I'll shoot the living hell
out of the place."

"Let's see what O'Sullivan's got to say first. He's just abandoned
Remières Wood."

Bliss charged into O'Sullivan's headquarters to find him in an
easy chair, a glass of whiskey in his hand, entertaining a fat florid-
faced congressman. They might have been chatting in a corner of
the long bar at Tammany's headquarters. "What the hell are you
doing having a snort when your men just abandoned Remières
Wood, leaving our whole left flank exposed?" Bliss roared.

"They've dug in on the edge of the woods. The situation is contained, General," O'Sullivan said.

"Have you been up there to see how contained it really is?" Bliss
said.

"General," O'Sullivan said loftily, "my place is here, directing
my share of the battle. I've had reports from runners. I talked on the
field telephone with the captains of both companies—"

"Any regimental commander who thinks he can rely on runners
and reports from captains who are trying to cover their asses is a
fucking idiot!" Bliss roared.

The regimental sergeant major appeared in the doorway. "Captain Alden on the field telephone, General."

Alden's voice was charged with alarm. "It's a mess up here, General. Half of those two companies that fell back from the woods are
jammed into the forward trench. A lot of them are wounded. The
ones who are trying to dig in along the edge of the woods are getting
chewed up by grenade and rifle fire. There's panic in the air."

"We're going to fall back to the reserve trench. Get them organized for an orderly withdrawal. We'll start shelling the wood in a half hour."

Bliss slammed down the telephone. "Major Perry," he said, "I'm putting you in command of Ireland's Own as of this instant. Colonel O'Sullivan, you're relieved. I want you out of here by sundown. Report to headquarters at Chaumont for reassignment."

"I'll have your head on a platter for this!" O'Sullivan screamed.

"John J. Pershing has a prior claim on that item," Bliss said. "If this situation gets any worse, he'll exercise it."

O'Sullivan whirled to the gaping congressman. "Tell him, Neil. Tell him what you'll do to him when you get back to Washington."

"With you in command he won't get out of this dugout alive!" Bliss snarled. "There's five thousand Germans only a mile away. I suggest you head for the rear, Congressman."

In perfect punctuation, a large-caliber German shell landed only a few feet from the dugout. The walls bulged and the ceiling vibrated. The Congressman was out the door in a flash. Colonel O'Sullivan followed him at the same pace.

Leaving Perry in charge, Bliss rushed up a communication trench to the reserve trench as hundreds of men poured into it. Roaring orders, slapping backs, he organized them for defense. He sent two runners across no-man's-land to order Company A to pull out of Semperey. By telephone he coordinated the movement with Joe Perry at regimental headquarters.

The moment Company A started across no-man's-land, Perry poured a blizzard of indirect machine-gun fire into the ruined village. Through his field glasses Bliss saw dozens of Germans go down as they charged forward to annihilate the retreating Americans. The fugitives arrived in the reserve trench dragging their wounded and lugging their machine guns. "I'm proud of every one of you," Bliss shouted. "You broke up their attack."

"Tell us where you want us, General," Lieutenant Eagleton said. "We've got plenty of fight left in us. Right, Sergeant?"

"Sure!" O'Connor said. Somewhere he had gotten his hands on a French light machine gun, a Chauchat. He carried half-moon clips of extra ammunition on a bandolier across his chest.

"Where the hell did you get that thing?" Bliss asked.

"I slipped Lucky Pierre ten bucks for it," O'Connor said. "It fires fifteen rounds a clip, General. That's ten more than our lousy rifles."

Harvard and the school of hard knocks made a pretty good team, Bliss thought. Maybe they could make an army out of these amateurs. He would gladly surrender his standing as a world-class pessimist if they managed it.

A moment later, Jonathan Alden arrived with bad news. The men who had abandoned Remières Wood were trapped. The Germans had attacked in overwhelming strength and scattered the fragment of a company that was trying to hold at the edge of the trees. The Boche had severed the communication trench, and the men were too demoralized by the shell fire to fall back across open ground. They were fighting off attacks from both sides.

As he spoke, the German artillery shifted to a box barrage around the two trapped companies. Almost too late, Bliss grasped the German plan. They had no intention of trying to roll back the entire Lafayette Division. Their goal was to inflict a major humiliation on the Americans—to parade five or six hundred prisoners through the streets of Berlin.

Ten seconds later, General Viomenil was on the telephone. "Air reconnaissance tells me you have abandoned your forward trench line. Are you sure you don't require assistance?"

"It's a temporary withdrawal, General. I guarantee we'll reoccupy those trenches before nightfall."

"I hope you understand such promises become a matter of record."

Bliss had two battalions in the reserve trench—about two thousand men. He summoned their commanders. "There are two companies trapped on the other side of that barrage. We've got to reach them before they surrender."

Both majors looked out at the shells chewing up the muddy earth. Bliss could see the order did not make any sense to them. He had no time to explain the dirty game they were playing, even if an explanation was possible. "They'll fight to the last man, General," one of the majors said.

"We can't let them fight to the last man," Bliss shouted. "In an army it isn't every man or every company for himself. Those are our brothers, our friends, out there. When I give the signal, follow me."

"I presume I'm coming with you, General," Jonathan Alden said.

"No. I want you to stay here and keep in touch with Perry and the artillery. Tell them I want all the metal they can muster to seal off no-man's-land and Remières Wood against any and all German reinforcements."

It was an order he could have given himself. A flicker of resentment on Alden's face suggested he sensed he was being deliberately left behind. But he did not understand the General's motive. The General had made sure of that.

Within five minutes the machine guns and artillery opened fire. "Now!" Bliss yelled and mounted an attack ladder and ran toward the box barrage. Like everyone else, he found the first two hundred yards were easy. Then they were into the barrage and the world changed forever. Tremendous explosions knocked men off their feet. Others whirled and fell, writhing in agony as shrapnel tore into their bodies. The noise, the shock waves of the blasts, annihilated thought. It was like being in the ring with a hundred heavyweights, all of them screaming curses and throwing punches at your head.

Nothing in Bliss's experience in Cuba or the Philippines or Mexico had prepared him for this inferno. The lieutenant in command of the nearest platoon was flung high in the air by a shell that hit almost at his feet. The platoon sergeant just behind him went down in the same blast. A half dozen men stopped to help them. All six were hit by another blast. Similar things were happening all along the line.

A captain in front of another company was blowing his whistle in staccato bursts, a rhythm that rapidly grew hysterical. He broke into a run and dove headfirst into a shell hole. A lieutenant—it was Harvard's Own, Eagleton—ran over and shouted something at him. The Captain—it was Hunthouse—crawled out of the hole and lurched forward again through the smoky haze, some approximation of courage restored.

Whole companies seemed to have vanished. Bliss realized they were all face down in the mud with the shells crashing around them.

A figure rose from the ground and dragged Bliss down beside him. "Mother Earth!" Sergeant O'Connor roared. "Get acquainted with it, General. Those stars on your shoulders won't stop shrapnel."

Bliss pulled his arm free. "Get up!" he shouted. "There's no point in lying here until we're pulverized. Get up and do your job. Lead them out of this mess."

A figure loomed over them. It was Alden. "Are you hit, General?" he said. "I saw you go down."

"I told you to stay on that telephone. Don't you know an order when you hear it?" Bliss roared.

A private crawled over to the Sergeant and cried, "Slattery's got it. They just blew his goddamn head off."

"That's what'll happen to everybody. We've got to go forward," Bliss shouted at O'Connor. "Mother Earth isn't the answer here."

Mother Earth confirmed this analysis by shuddering and exploding all around them. Waves of heat from nearer hits made Bliss feel as if he was lying in an oven. A terrific rage convulsed O'Connor's face, worse than the one Bliss had seen in Union Square. Bliss suspected he wanted to kill him instead of the Germans.

Another figure loomed over them. "Let's get going, Sergeant. Get your men on their feet," said a calm, almost serene voice.

It was Colonel Douglas Fairchild. He was not wearing a helmet. He had a scarf slung around his neck as if he were out for a casual stroll. It was an amazing display of courage—or craziness. Bliss did not know and did not care. It was working.

Sergeant O'Connor leaped to his feet and roared, "Come on! If West Point can do it so can we!"

Men rose from the mud and lunged after him. Bliss joined Fairchild in getting others on their feet. The whole line surged forward, yelling, screaming, firing their rifles. More men went down in the shell fire, but the rest burst through the barrage and charged toward the forward trench. Sheets of machine-gun and artillery fire were falling in no-man's-land. The Germans attacking from that side were pinned down and taking terrific punishment. The gray uniforms attacking from behind the forward trench took one look at the howling mob running toward them and bolted for Remières Wood.

Two hours later, Bliss stared down at the bodies of the dead in the reserve trench. The battle of Semperey or Remières Wood—take your pick—was over. The division had lost about 100 dead and 250 wounded. The Germans had lost two or three times as many. There was no bag of prisoners to march through Berlin. But the dead were no longer interested in these reassuring facts.

For a moment Bliss was filled with self-loathing. He struggled to convince himself his order to rescue the two trapped companies had been necessary. The American army could not afford to lose the dirty game they were playing.

Or was it simply Jack Pershing who could not afford it? Were the two things one and the same? Bliss could only hope so.

They were still bringing back men lying in the mud between the forward and reserve trenches, where the box barrage had fallen. Dr. Pinkus was out there, applying tourniquets, bandaging wounds. Father Kelly was there too, raising his hand in another feckless blessing. His face had a haunted look. Bliss was not going to lose his bet—but did he really want to win it?

Three days later, Bliss sat in his office reading the story of the battle of Semperey on the front page of the Paris edition of the *New York Herald*. It described the clash as an American triumph on a scale comparable to the French victory at Verdun.

"General? Lieutenant General Viomenil is here to see you."

His old acquaintance from Saint-Nazaire strode into the room, as straight-backed and severe as ever. "I am here to congratulate your men and distribute croix de guerres."

"That's very kind of you."

"Kindness has nothing to do with it, my dear General. I trust by now you realize sending men through a box barrage is idiotic. One of the chief functions of the croix de guerre is to compensate men for a general's stupidity. You should recommend a similar decoration for your army."

Steady, General, steady, Sergeant Turner whispered. *It's only the baptism.*

BOOK IV

BOOK IV

28. THE STORMTROOPERS
ARE COMING

"DEAR GOD, GIRLS, WAIT'LL YOU HEAR THIS ONE! The American savior, Woodrow Wilson, known to his admirers as Jesus Christ Junior, has just announced he's absolutely confident the heroic Allies will handle the coming German offensive without the least difficulty! Have you ever heard more revolting hypocrisy? What do you think, Dandy?"

"I hope he's right," Polly Warden said.

"Of course he's right. We've got nothing to worry about with you in reserve. One year after your bloody declaration of war, the British Expeditionary Force can depend on the courage and ferocity of one female ambulance driver. It's enough to make a bloke stand up and sing the Star-Spangled Baloney."

The mocker was a big blowsy blonde named Letitia Gore-Blatchley, whom everyone called Bunky. In return she handed out nicknames to everyone else. Polly was Dandy, short for Yankee Doodle Dandy. Bunky's uncle was an earl, which apparently entitled her to unlimited amounts of regal scorn. She had been needling Polly from the moment she arrived at British Ambulance Group Three and became a member of the Voluntary Aid Detachment, better known as the VADs.

"Shut up, Bunky," Anita Sinclair said. "Polly's no more to blame for her politicians than we are for our bloody generals."

"There are times when I think I should report you!" Bunky said.

Anita was Bunky's physical opposite, slim and muscular, with a corresponding flintiness of temperament. Anger shimmered beneath her chiseled features, even in repose. Her father was a sub-some-thing in the British war cabinet. She seemed to have a much more positive attitude toward Americans, perhaps because they were not British. She was merciless in her criticism of the way the British generals were fighting the war. She and Bunky frequently tangled over her lack of patriotism.

The other ten drivers in the group were a cross section of the British upper middle class. They ranged from Thingy, a curvaceous empty-headed brunette who reminded Polly of a dozen New York debutantes, to the Bomber, a tiny bitter intellectual who wanted to end the war by a mass uprising of the working class. Day and night they drove their bulky ambulances along the atrocious roads of Picardy to aid stations in the lines around Saint-Quentin, at the southern end of the British trench line. On the other side of no-man's-land lurked the German army like a crouching monster in an ancient saga.

Polly had gone back to the war. It had not been easy. Dr. Giroux-Langin had opposed the idea. She told Polly she was not ready to return to the front, psychologically or physically. She refused to arrange for a transfer to a French field hospital and announced she would block any attempt Polly made to do it on her own.

Polly had been infuriated. She knew the Doctor's concern for her health was sincere. But her affection was mingled with her dom-ineering personality and her worries about Polly's spiritual welfare. After a week of sparring, Polly exploded. "I have one mother in America who keeps trying to run my life. I don't need another one in France!"

Barred from the French front, Polly turned to the Americans—and discovered her impromptu training left her trapped in a bureau-cratic maze. Although she had more field experience than any American nurse in France, she had no nursing certificate. A pompous colonel informed her there was no room for amateurs in the U.S. Army Nurse Corps. The most she could do was work as a ward maid at base hospitals far behind the lines.

In desperation Polly wrote to Malvern Hill Bliss, who ruefully informed her not even John J. Pershing could do anything about the encrusted red tape of the U.S. Army's medical department—or the quartermaster department or the ordnance department, for that matter. It was one of several reasons why they still did not have an American army in France. Bliss suggested Polly try the British army and gave her Anita Sinclair's address in Paris. He wrote to Anita and told her Polly was trying to escape *la guerre de luxe*.

Polly found Anita hurling shoes, underwear, and dresses into a foot locker in her barracks at the British motor pool on the outskirts of Paris. "Your timing is perfect," she said. "I'm on my way to Saint-Quentin to join Ambulance Group Three to find out if I can survive another nervous breakdown. Why don't you come along? Getting shelled in an ambulance is infinitely preferable to working for those monstrous bitches who pass for nurses in British hospitals. You also don't have to worry about doctors and recuperating officers trying to lift your skirt."

Polly became an instant convert to ambulance work. She wanted to get as close to the front as possible—and she did not want anyone lifting her skirt.

"Are you sleeping with General Bliss?" Anita asked, slamming down the lid of her bulging foot locker.

"No."

"He *is* an odd one. I offered my beautiful body to him, and he declined the honor. Does he prefer boys? Quite a few British generals do."

Polly vehemently doubted this suggestion. Anita shrugged and told Polly to ask Bliss to write a letter to his friend General Hubert Gough, who was in command at Saint-Quentin, telling him she was brave, dependable, and virtuous. "Gough's aide is slavishly devoted to me. I'll manage the rest," Anita said.

A week later Polly and Anita took a train to Saint-Quentin, where Polly discovered she was enrolled in Ambulance Group Three. Captain Rodney Blake, General Gough's blond affable young aide, met them at the station and assured them the matter had not caused the slightest trouble. Anita explained that in the British army, a general's authority was close to absolute in his zone of command. "If Goughie wanted to enroll his mother-in-law in Group Three as a convenient way of getting rid of the old bag, not a soul would object. Am I exaggerating, Captain Blake?"

"As a matter of fact the General's mother-in-law is expected to arrive next week," Captain Blake said. "You're going to be her training instructor. But I can get your orders changed, if you let me take you to dinner every night for the rest of the month."

"I prefer the mother-in-law," Anita said.

The General's mother-in-law failed to show up, which gave Anita time to help Polly pass the ambulance driver's test. A VAD had to learn enough about the inside of a combustion engine to fix obvious things like a broken fan belt; she also had to know how to change a tire in sixty seconds: a handy talent, Anita remarked, if the road was being shelled.

Polly found some aspects of the British medical service hard to bear. There was far more order and cleanliness in their hospitals than there had been at the Château Givry. The floors and the walls were scrubbed with Lysol twice a day, leaving the air drenched with fumes. The nurses, called sisters, ran the hospital like a prison. Everything—meals, scrubdowns, exercise—had precisely appointed hours. No one was allowed to do anything without official permission from the ward nurse or the head nurse or the doctor. Social life was even more stringently supervised. Volunteer aides and ambulance drivers slept in compounds guarded by armed sentries. They had to sign in and out and be in bed precisely at ten o'clock every night, except during an emergency.

The blast of a whistle interrupted Bunky Gore-Blatchley's argument with Anita about her lack of patriotism. The whistle shrilled not once or twice but four, five, six times, creating a whirlwind of anxiety. "Oh, kiss my knickers," Bunky bellowed, as everyone flew around the narrow barracks looking for gloves, caps, overcoats, boots.

They hurtled into the mud of the yard and struggled to shape themselves into the semblance of a military formation. Waiting for them was their nemesis, the Commandant. Beneath her stringently pressed gray uniform, she had a body that seemed as rectangular as a crate. Her face was also rectangular. The eyes, nose, and mouth were superfluous; you saw only the harsh lines, compounded by short black hair that fell in two rectangular flaps over her ears.

The roll was called by the Commandant's assistant, a tall birdlike woman named Stokes, whom everyone called the Stovepipe. The Commandant proceeded to inspect the thirteen drivers as if they were about to appear in a dress parade in front of Buckingham Palace. Thingy had a loose button on her overcoat; the Bomber's stockings were crooked: both received extra duty. Polly, last in line, got the hardest scrutiny.

"Warden. Your gloves are dirty."

"They're my only pair. I haven't had time to wash them."

"An American can't afford a second pair of gloves? I'm afraid that excuse won't do."

The Commandant seemed to think all American women in France were as rich as Gertrude Vanderbilt Whitney or Eleanor Kingswood. Further examination revealed Warden's shoes were not sufficiently shined, there was a grease spot on her cuff, and her neck was dirty. Polly was sure everyone had dirty necks. They received only half a pail of water a day to wash themselves. Writing down her dirty neck was pure discrimination.

Polly's deficiencies added up to six hours of extra duty. That meant fixing the Commandant's tea, cleaning her office, and serving as her orderly, carrying little messages or gifts to friends at hospitals in the area. The Commandant liked having a presumably rich American performing these menial tasks.

Another blast of the Commandant's whistle, and they piled into their ambulances and headed for the darkened front. The Commandant led the way, driving fast as usual. They did not use their headlights; that might attract enemy artillery. Hurtling past them on the other side of the narrow road were British army trucks on the way back to ammunition dumps and food depots. They too drove without headlights. A week ago one of them had collided head on with an ambulance in another group, killing the VAD instantly.

Up ahead the big guns rumbled and the night sky glared with their flashes. In an hour they were at a crossroads where a major in the British military police distributed orders. Polly and Anita Sinclair, bringing up the rear of the column, drew Field Dressing Station Three, one of the closest to the front. During the first two weeks of March, the sector had been quiet. Now a rising tempo of violence was visible to the ambulance drivers. Night after night for a week the casualties had mounted, as both sides raided across no-man's-land. Everyone wondered if this was the prelude to the expected German offensive. From what Captain Rodney Blake told Anita, the British generals thought it was a feint.

The aid station was on the reverse slope of a long low mountain the Tommies had named Dead Man's Ridge, because it had cost so many lives to capture it last year. The ridge was a frequent target of German artillery. As they came up the winding road, two big shells exploded in a field a hundred yards away. Polly struggled with a surge of nausea and fear.

Dr. Giroux-Langin was right. Her nerves were not ready for the battlefield. She willed herself under control and kept going. Anita, in the lead, was driving much too fast around the hairpin curves, several of which ran along the edge of the ridge with a drop of a thousand feet into a ravine.

By the time Polly reached the station, Anita was backing her ambulance to the door. Shells continued to hurtle over the ridge or land on the forward slope. The sergeant major in charge of the station greeted them cheerfully, as usual. "We've got a full load for you both tonight. Jerry did a nasty job on a forward trench. A lot of grenade cases. The docs are sewing them up as best they can."

Stretcher-bearers carried the wounded out to the ambulances. Each of the squarish shrapnel-proof vehicles carried four stretchers and a "sitter"—a walking wounded case—up front beside the driver. Polly knelt beside each man and introduced herself. "My name's Polly Warden. I'm driving the ambulance. I'm sorry you're hurt. You'll be in a nice clean bed in an hour or two, and you'll feel lots better."

They nodded and smiled vaguely. They had all been given maximum doses of morphine. Nevertheless, Anita Sinclair believed this routine often kept a badly wounded man alive. "Hope is as important as morphine," she insisted.

Beside her ambulance, Anita did the same thing. As the stretcher-bearers lifted them onto the racks, Anita took Polly's arm. "I'm going to fly," she said. "I've got a chest wound. They don't give him much of a chance. Don't try to keep up with me."

"Why not? If you have an accident it'd be better to have me around."

"I don't want to feel responsible if you muck up."

That was Anita, blunt to the brink of insult. She constantly took extra risks. A week ago, Polly had glimpsed why. On their weekly half day off, Anita had abruptly invited Polly to join her for a drive to Corbie, twenty miles or so north. Captain Blake, who continued to worship her no matter how badly she treated him, had supplied them with a staff car.

Outside Corbie they stopped at a small cemetery. Anita picked some wild flowers and put them on one of the graves. The white cross read CAPTAIN WILLIAM CONGREVE, DURHAM LIGHT INFANTRY. "We got engaged the night war was declared," Anita said. "We never did more than kiss. What bloody fools we were. Bloody idealistic fools."

Polly thought of Paul Lebrun. They had done more than kiss. Was that better, or worse? Maybe the war obliterated such moral discrimination the way it seemed to annihilate idealism. On the way back Anita talked brilliantly, compulsively, about the war as a vortex that consumed everyone's personal life. The next day, she handed Polly a letter addressed to Major General Malvern Hill Bliss. "I want you to give this to him if I get killed," she said. "I wish I'd slept with him. I hate the idea of dying owing anything to a man, even one I secretly admire."

The war had given Anita a ferocious contempt for conventional morality. It blended with her anger at women's oppression and her rage at her ultra-proper mother and her friends, who all blindly supported king and country and believed the propaganda the newspapers printed as a substitute for the truth. Polly wondered if she would feel the same way if the war lasted another three years.

The two ambulances started down the ridge, Anita careening around the curves with more than her usual recklessness. A big shell exploded close to the road, just behind her ambulance. "Oh my God," Polly gasped, fighting for control of the wheel.

"It's okay, miss. We're still on the road," said her sitter. His name was Billy Boggs. He was a private with two wound stripes on his sleeve. This time he had grenade fragments in his arm. Billy was frankly delighted to get such an easy trip to blighty. He said it saved him from going the ha'penny route.

"What's that?" Polly said, groping around the next hairpin curve.

"You cut a cross on the back of yer wrist and get some gummy and tape a ha'penny to it. In a day or two you've got a ripe old infection that could take your hand off if it ain't treated straight off. So off you go to blighty—or the rear, at least—for a week or two."

A lot of his friends had gotten out that way, Billy said. People were ready to do almost everything except desert to escape the Fifth Army. "Why?" Polly asked, as two more big shells exploded in the fields behind her.

Billy said the Fifth had run out of luck. Last year at Ypres (he called it "Wipers") they got all the rotten jobs, ridges and blockhouses crammed with more German machine guns than they had rifles. "You stay in the lines for a while and you soon see how much luck counts in this business. Any man who comes back from leave and goes over the top within a week's time is dead and he knows it. Never seen it to fail. Luck works like that. It gives you good times and then bad. The Fifth Army's got nothin' but bad waitin' for it."

They finally reached the bottom of the winding road down Dead Man's Ridge and discovered a new problem. From the fields on both sides of the road ground fog swirled, thicker than Polly had ever seen it. In sixty seconds she did not know whether they were on the left, the right, or in the middle of the road. If an ammunition lorry came along they would all be smithereens. She crawled along at ten miles an hour, her heart pounding. Not even Anita Sinclair could drive fast in this soup.

At the crossroads, Polly had to get out and walk around the intersection to find the road to the hospital. She had gone less than a mile when shapes loomed up. It was an ambulance. She heard Anita Sinclair's voice asking if she was from Group Three. Thingy had collided with a lorry. She was alive, but her beautiful face was a mess from flying glass. The Commandant was rushing her to the hospital.

It took an hour for them to clear the road. By this time it was almost dawn. Anita was in a fury. Her chest case had died. The fog remained impenetrable. She crawled along, Polly a dozen feet behind her.

Polly's rearview mirror suddenly glared so brightly it almost blinded her. A second later, a dull boom rolled toward them from the front. Seconds later came the eerie whistle of hundreds of descending shells. They exploded in the fields all around them. "Holy bloody Christmas!" yelled her sitter, Billy Boggs.

Again the sky glared, and again the shells rained down to fill the dawn with thunder. Amid the crashes Polly heard some that seemed to go *plop* rather than explode. Billy Boggs heard them too. "Gas!" he shouted and pulled on his mask.

Polly slammed on the brakes and groped frantically under the seat for her mask. They were supposed to wear the bulky things on their chests at all times, but it made the wheel hard to handle. She located the mask and pulled it on as the first sickeningly sweet odor of mustard gas mingled with the dewy smell of the fog.

"Come on!" she shouted to Billy Boggs and leaped out to get masks on the faces of her stretcher cases. Billy held her flashlight in his good hand while Polly struggled with the sticky rubber suction cups. One man had a thick bandage on his head. She ripped it off, ignoring his screams of pain. "I'm sorry. Gas!" she yelled, before she realized she was talking through her own mask and he could barely hear her.

Anita Sinclair rushed up as Polly climbed out of the back of the ambulance. "Two of mine don't have masks!" she cried. "The bloody fools at the aid station must have misplaced them. I'm going ahead full speed. Wish me luck."

She vanished into the fog. Polly continued to crawl toward safety. Again and again the sky glared and the shells hurtled down. It was like riding through a hurricane without the wind. There was only the noise, raised to the level of absolute chaos. On both sides of the road, British batteries began replying, but their fire was sporadic and often ended in an explosion as German shells landed on them.

A far bigger explosion leaped above the fog. "There goes an ammo dump for sure," Billy Boggs said. Mustard gas was all around them now. Polly could feel it burning her hands on the wheel. She pulled on her gloves. Lorries and command cars roared past them toward the front. Once a man ran beside them screaming, "Help me! My mask don't work!" Polly kept going, and he vanished with a choking cry.

Several times she was sure she too was choking inside the foul rubbery mask. Her lips, her tongue burned from sucking at the mouthpiece, while saliva bubbled in the tube. She had to fight an impulse to tear it off and gulp down air. Beside her Billy Boggs was hunched into a ball, grotesque in his rubber face and breathing tube.

It was seven o'clock by the time Polly reached Hospital Three and stripped off her gas mask. Orderlies unloaded her stretcher cases and led Billy Boggs to a bed. "I wish we had a few like you in the front line," Billy said, shaking Polly's hand. "You've got what it takes."

At Group Three's compound, Polly found the ambulances in their usual precise row and the Commandant raging up and down, berating everyone. Polly got the worst abuse for being the last arrival. "Four hours overdue!" the Commandant fumed.

"It's a miracle I'm here at all," Polly said.

"Your nationality does not give you the slightest license to be insubordinate! There's a major attack under way. Casualties are already heavy. We must leave for the front immediately."

By the time they reached the crossroads, about ten miles behind the forward trenches, it was apparent that this was not going to be a routine trip. All around them fires burned in smashed batteries and supply dumps. Mustard gas was still so thick, they had to put on their masks. At the crossroads the major in charge of the traffic was wild-eyed, almost incoherent. "Who sent you out here?" he yelled. "We've got to clear the roads. There's no room for bloody ambulances!"

"We were told the aid stations are full," the Commandant said.

"There aren't any bloody aid stations left, as far as I know. The Germans have overrun everything: Dead Man's Ridge, every strongpoint in line. They're only a mile or two up that road, and there's nothing between them and us but the wreck of the Ninety-fourth Division."

"You mean we're being beaten?" the Commandant gasped.

"They're coming on like bloody giants in seven-league boots!" the officer said. "Now turn around and get the blazes out of here."

"We will not go back without wounded men!" the Commandant said. "I think you're in a state of shock, Major. Sinclair, Warden—go up that road to Aid Station Three. Skelton, Boscawen—go down that road to Station Two."

Polly followed Anita Sinclair up the road. Within a mile she heard the chatter of machine guns and the crash of rifles. Over a rise came about five hundred British soldiers, running as fast as possible, many without guns, packs, or helmets. Anita Sinclair slammed on her brakes and leaped out of her cab. "What's happening? Where are you going?" she screamed.

"To hell or blighty!" one of them yelled. "There's ten thousand Jerries just over that hill!"

"British soldiers don't run away!"

"Take a good look and change yer mind about that one!" howled another man, not even bothering to break his stride.

Anita stood there, immobilized. Polly jumped out of her cab and ran up to her. "Turn around. They must be telling the truth," she cried.

Anita did not seem to hear her. She stared at the rise, as if she was waiting for the Germans to appear. "Anita!" Polly said, grabbing her arm.

"Get your bloody American hands off me!" Anita said, jerking her arm away.

Polly was too stunned to even try to answer her. While they watched, over the rise came a thin line of British soldiers—no more than a hundred, with six or seven officers. They turned on the crest and fired at an unseen enemy. A blast of gunfire sent a dozen of them tumbling down the hill. The rest, officers included, started running toward them, some dragging wounded friends.

The officer at the head of the pack, a captain, came gasping up to them. "What the devil are you women doing in the middle of a battlefield?" he said.

"What does it look like we're doing?" Anita said, pointing to the ambulances with the huge red crosses on their sides.

"It's a rout," he said. "They outnumbered us ten to one. They grenaded us to pieces." He started to sob. "I can't believe it."

"There's nothing to do now but die," Anita said.

"I suppose you're right," the Captain said, miraculously regaining his composure. He was about the same age as the two lieutenants Polly had met on the channel steamer, the ones who said *Oh, we'll be dead by then.*

The men dragging or carrying wounded caught up to them. They surrounded the ambulances, calling out, "Can you take these lads? They'll never make it on foot and neither will we, carryin' them."

"Load them in," Polly said.

They packed at least eighteen men into the vans. British artillery started shrieking overhead to fall on the crest of the rise. "Now will you stop standing there like a goddamned would-be martyr?" Polly shouted to Anita.

She nodded and got behind the wheel. Polly led the way back down the road, a sergeant with a head wound slumped beside her. At the crossroads, the major in charge of traffic was lying on his back in the center of the intersection, a ribbon of blood running from his riddled chest.

"Stormtroopers," the sergeant muttered. "The buggers slide all around us. Keep going. They'll shoot up anything they see."

The ground fog had lifted. The road ahead seemed clear. Polly slammed down the accelerator and careened through the intersection, Anita Sinclair behind her. They roared down the long straight road past wrecked batteries and smoldering supply dumps and houses. Several times they had to slow down to edge around shell holes. Once they had to pull aside for a division rushing forward to reinforce the collapsing front. "What's it like up there, mate?" one of the marchers called to Polly's sergeant.

"Bloody hell!" he said.

They reached the hospital about ten o'clock and helped the orderlies carry the wounded into the receiving room. The beds, the floor, the hall leading out of it were covered with more wounded men. A sister rushed up to Anita. "Who authorized you to bring these men in here?" she cried. "We can't handle another case."

"Nobody authorized us. We picked them up on the battlefield," Anita said and turned her back on the woman.

Outside, she stared sullenly at Polly. Was she breaking down again? Polly wondered. Maybe they were both breaking down. "I would like to tell you something," Polly said. "You're not the only one who's come here because someone she loved has been killed and she's ashamed of still being alive. Maybe ashamed of a lot of things. Even if you've seen or felt worse pain than I have—which I doubt—that doesn't justify what you said to me up there. I thought you saw me as a person, not some living example of national folly."

"You're right," Anita said. "I apologize."

Her voice was empty. The words were meaningless. The sight of those fleeing Tommies had crushed or broken something vital inside her. Below them in the valley the battle crackled and thundered. "Do you still have that letter to General Bliss?" Anita said.

"Yes."

"Tear it up."

She climbed into her cab and began backing away from the receiving platform.

"Where are you going?" Polly said.

"Back to the bloody front, wherever it is."

"I'm right behind you."

29. THE PARIS GUN

AS USUAL LOUISE WOLCOTT FOUND SLEEP ELUDING her in the dawn. She seldom slept more than four or five hours a night. Last night's slumber had been even skimpier. She had lost two hours to the sirens announcing an air raid and the bells and bugles declaring the danger was over—without a bomb being dropped, as far as she could tell. In the hours between, she had been troubled by a distant rumble of guns from the north, where the Germans were attacking the British army with reportedly alarming success.

She lay in her canopied bed wondering what Harry Quickmeyer was doing in Saint-Nazaire. Was he making love to his dark-eyed Jewish volunteer who gazed so adoringly at him? Not likely. Colonel Quickmeyer was Louise Wolcott's anxious, submissive warrior. In a certain sense she was almost as submissive to him. In spite of her heart's glissades over Douglas Fairchild, she was still seeing Quick-meyer. The mere thought of him sent shivers of desire through her flesh. But she denied him the triumph of arousing the ideal in her soul. That was impossible, as long as he was an *embusqué*, fighting *la guerre de luxe*.

Colonel Quickmeyer's toils in the Services of Supply, overcoming the million and one obstructions of stubborn French railroad officials, dealing with the problems of quartering and entertaining twenty thousand Negro stevedores in Saint-Nazaire and other ports, could not match Colonel Fairchild's exploits. He had come to Paris a week ago to take her to dinner, wearing the croix de guerre he had received for his daring in no-man's-land. Louise had clipped and pasted in a scrapbook the newspaper stories describing these duels with death. He had written her a breathtaking letter after each expedition, telling her how her name, uttered like a prayer in his heart, gave him the courage to stride through shell fire while everyone else burrowed into the muddy earth.

Drama, Louise thought. Drama was the key to happiness. Where else but Paris could a woman find herself at or near the center of so many dramas? There was General Pershing himself, who continued to pay remarkable attention to her whenever they met at a dinner or a reception. His affair with this French-Rumanian painter could not last. She was too young, too naïve, too devout. A victorious general wanted—needed—a woman of the world.

Then there was Malvern Hill Bliss. She still wanted him in her arms, even if it was only for a single night. She wanted to make him admit how much he had desired her in Maryland ten years ago. She wanted him to confess he regretted his marriage to his simpering, worshipful wife.

A liberated woman did not merely count her blessings. She listed the ones she wanted and pursued them. Louise Wolcott was going to set all sorts of records in the pursuit of happiness. A new world was being born in the battlefields a few dozen miles away, a world in which the old morality was irrelevant and God was a bad joke. Louise was determined to enjoy the great upheaval.

By 7 A.M. Paris sparkled in bright spring sunshine. The rumble of guns from the British front seemed closer. But it would be impossible to lose the war on such a beautiful day. The British would stop them. They were clumsy lovers, but they had bulldog courage. The headlines in the Paris edition of the *New York Herald* exuded optimism.

Today she would launch a new drama. Louise had persuaded Eleanor Kingswood to join her for lunch in Natalie Barney's garden on the Rue Jacob. Known to some as the Amazon, dark-haired Natalie, born to wealth in San Francisco, saw herself as a modern Sappho. Louise's affair with her had terrified Walter Wolcott into agreeing to an immediate divorce and that glorious five-million-dollar settlement. Even Gertrude Vanderbilt Whitney had been shocked—and, Louise suspected, secretly fascinated. Natalie represented a horizon of freedom that many women hesitated to explore.

She was a forbidden zone, in which Louise risked her reputation in the world from which John J. Pershing would choose a mistress—or a wife.

Most women would hesitate to approach someone from whom they had stolen a man as handsome as Douglas Fairchild. But Louise had adapted the language of military tactics to personal relationships. The key to success was boldness, a faith in the spirit of the attack. At Charles Louis Lebrun's victory party, she had drawn Eleanor Kingswood into a corner and apologized for taking Fairchild away from her. She swore she had done nothing to encourage him. Eleanor had gestured feebly to Harold Holloway, her elongated YMCA man, and said she was content for the moment. Louise told her no one in Paris should ever be content with her current love. She proposed to introduce her to a woman who knew more about love than anyone else in Paris, male or female.

Always on the prowl, Natalie had seen Eleanor on the street (the Rue Jacob was less than a block from the Rue de Verneuil) and pronounced her interesting. Behind Eleanor's self-confident manner, Natalie saw an American innocent. After twenty years in Paris, Natalie found innocence especially tempting. She had asked Louise to arrange an introduction.

Louise chose a clinging mauve frock with a deep V-neck. Although Natalie no longer professed any interest, Louise could not resist flirting with her. Michel, her aging Alsatian chauffeur, drove her to the Kingswood house on the Rue de Verneuil. "Who's winning the battle around Saint-Quentin?" Louise asked. Michel always seemed to know what was happening at the front.

"The Germans. The French are sending reinforcements to the British. Slowly."

The guns rumbled in the distance. Michel hated the British. He blamed them for the loss of Alsace-Lorraine in 1870. They should have come to France's aid against the Germans then. Europeans never forgot or forgave anything.

At the Kingswood house, Eleanor was wearing a dark-blue suit and a white silk blouse with a ruffled collar. She was on her way to becoming a YWCA woman, an interchangeable part of colorless

Protestant America. Louise took charge. "You can't go to Natalie Barney's in an outfit like that."

They examined Eleanor's wardrobe. It was all in the same conservative mode. "I'm glad I came early," Louise said. "There's still time to get something at Bon Marché."

The crossed the Seine and headed down the wide Boulevard de Strasbourg. Eleanor remarked that her friend Martha Herzog had warned her Natalie Barney had a bad reputation. "Most poets have bad reputations," Louise said. "She's different. You'll never meet anyone like her in the YWCA."

They were passing the dark-brown soot-stained façade of the Gare de l'Est. Crowds were pouring out of the train station and out of three Metro stations that formed a junction at this point. Fifty feet in front of the car something exploded with a tremendous crash. Louise saw bodies flying through the air. With a tinkling, tearing sound the windshield in front of Michel evaporated. He cried out in pain or terror and the Rolls-Royce careened left, sideswiped a taxi, and hurtled across the boulevard straight at one of the Metro stations. Ten feet short of the open mouth, Michel regained control and screeched to a stop.

Eleanor and Louise climbed out of the car. Smoke rose from a huge hole in the center of the boulevard. At least twenty people were lying on the ground, some writhing in agony, others very still. Those who had escaped injury were scanning the sky, looking for the plane that must have dropped the bomb. How could a Hun pilot commit this bestiality without an alarm being sounded? Were there traitors in the French Air Service?

Police and ambulances came clanging out of side streets. A black-mustached gendarme examined the car and began asking questions. Had they seen a bomb fall? Heard a plane? Seen anyone throw an explosive device from a passing car? A wild-eyed older man rushed up to the policeman and shouted, "We're being shelled by our own army because we haven't subscribed to the government's latest bond issue. It's part of the capitalist plot to turn us all into serfs of the millionaires." The gendarme told him to shut up or he would arrest him.

Michel was sweeping glass out of the front seat of the Rolls. He had several slivers in his arms and neck. Leaving him with orders to get the car to a garage and himself to the nearest hospital, Louise hailed a taxi and continued their journey to Bon Marché. In this grandmother of all department stores, she selected a luncheon costume for Eleanor: a pale blue frock with a white sailor color, a wide-brimmed blue hat with artificial white roses on one side. A seamstress did a few tucks and they started back to Natalie Barney's house in their taxi.

As the driver took a short cut down a narrow side street, the Rue de Givry, a tremendous blast blew out all the windows a block ahead of them. Whatever or whoever was bombing Paris seemed to be following them. For a moment Louise felt panic claw at her flesh. Was this God's way of warning her there was a limit to her pursuit of happiness? She thought she had mastered that childish fear.

Once more ambulances, police cars, and fire trucks rushed to the scene. Their driver backed out of the Rue de Givry and got them to Natalie Barney's house only fifteen minutes late. She met them at the courtyard gate in one of her clinging Greek costumes, her dark hair in the usual disarray over her shoulders. Although Natalie was no longer young, there was not a hint of a wrinkle on her sensual face. Her figure seemed equally immune to age, except for a certain fleshiness—which somehow suited her.

"Have you heard the news?" she said. "The Germans are bombing Paris with an invisible airplane. A secret weapon."

"We've not only heard it, we've seen the bombs exploding," Louise said.

"How thrilling," Natalie said. "To think you've risked death to visit me."

Natalie led them into her dim incense-scented parlor, with brocaded hangings on the wall, embroidered with lilies, her favorite flower. On the backs of the chairs were faded chasubles, echoes of old cathedrals. Beyond another door was the garden, magically insulated from the rest of Paris, an oasis of green shaded by four ancient trees.

At a round table sat Natalie's favorite male guest, André Germain. He was a social and literary butterfly, so frail he looked as if a puff of wind would knock him over. In his cups he pretended to be Natalie's lover, a laughable idea on the face of it. Louise was quite certain his inclination was in the other direction. "This is my elf," Natalie said. "He tells me everything that's happening in Paris."

The crash of another shell or bomb rolled over the tops of the trees. "You say it's an invisible plane?" Louise asked.

"One of my friends in the Chamber of Deputies told me at breakfast. The first bomb landed on the Quai de Seine this morning," Germain said.

"How does a plane become invisible?" Louise said.

"It's done with mirrors. Refraction of light. The Germans are enormously ingenious," Germain said.

"What does your friend tell you about the attack on the British?" Eleanor asked.

"It's an utter rout."

"Enough!" Natalie said. "We're not here to discuss the war. I don't believe in it. The thing is a vile fiction, a nightmare."

"My darling!" In strode the Baroness Deslandes, Natalie's current love. Compact and formidable as a tank, she was half German. Natalie embraced her with merely ordinary warmth. Her kiss was on the cheek, almost perfunctory.

Dumpling-shaped Gertrude Stein and her worshipful friend, Alice B. Toklas, arrived. They too had seen one of the explosions. "I forbid you to talk about it," Natalie said. "It's part of the war. In this garden there is no such thing as war."

Another explosion—thankfully some distance away—contradicted her words. Gertrude Stein said she had written a poem about the war. It imagined the upheaval as a metronome, beating time to a danse macabre. She saw the soldiers, the pilots, and the generals all performing on a vast stage. In the last stanza their strings become visible. They are all puppets.

Natalie applauded the idea. But she wanted to discuss that outmoded form of heroism, love. In her low sultry voice, she began discoursing on the importance of embracing your desires, no matter what it cost in terms of social ostracism.

"I agree with all my heart!" Baroness Deslandes declared. Natalie barely noticed her.

Another explosion, this one much closer. They were occurring every fifteen minutes. The invisible airplane never seemed to run out of gas. "My father is the one I've followed," Natalie said. "He never hesitated to embrace his desires. Night after night after night."

"My father—is the same way," Eleanor said.

"Why should they have the privilege and not us?"

The Baroness Deslandes was frowning. She obviously had no idea Natalie was pursuing a new love. To see it taking place in front of her eyes was disconcerting.

A maid served vermouth. They sipped their drinks and Natalie talked about the importance of the great Roman maxim *carpe diem*, seize the day. The war had made everyone realize the lover who hesitates is lost. It was the only good thing to be said for the war.

"How true!" the Baroness said, seizing Natalie's hand. She coolly withdrew it.

Another explosion. This time it seemed part of the orchestra, a drum beat emphasizing Natalie's point. André Germain watched, a quizzical smile on his gamin face. He had written a book about the suicide of Renée Vivien, a novelist Natalie had loved and abandoned. He knew how dangerous Natalie could be; that was part of her fascination. "Have you read Goethe's poem 'Die Lorelei'?" André asked Eleanor.

"No."

"I recommend it. The Lorelei is more than a myth, in my opinion. She's a type of woman. The Enchantress."

Gertrude Stein weighed in with a skeptical snort. She did not believe in enchantment. The modern artist was an analyst of reality. The modern writer was an analyst of emotion. Enchantment was a romantic idea and romance was dead. It had been dying for thirty years, and the war had unquestionably killed it.

The Baroness Deslandes stormed to the defense of Goethe. "Die Lorelei" was an immortal poem that would never die. Neither would Goethe's ideas. They were part of the world soul.

Drama. Louise watched it unfold, while another bomb exploded in the middle distance. The maid served lunch: oysters on the half shell, cold shrimp in dill sauce, a Sancerre white wine. Eleanor

Kingswood talked about creating leave sites for American soldiers. The YWCA was taking over hotels and spas in the south of France. The idea was to keep the men out of Paris.

"What about women? Will you bring them south from the boulevards?" André Germain said.

"We certainly will not!" Eleanor said. "The Y is committed to the idea that men don't need sex for a happy, enjoyable leave."

The Baroness Deslandes made an exclamation in German that Louise did not understand, but it did not need translation. "It will be an interesting experiment," Gertrude Stein said.

"A very interesting experiment," Alice Toklas said. She had a habit of echoing Gertrude.

"Surely you must have an opinion on this great question, Natalie darling," Louise said.

Natalie showed her white teeth. In her wilder moments she had been known to use them to express her love. "I think Miss Kingswood will discover the truth or falsity of her position from a voice within her own heart."

Another explosion. This time, Louise suspected it coincided with an upheaval within Eleanor Kingswood. She suddenly seemed timid, virginal. "We may be wrong," she said. "I hope not."

"Hope not?" Natalie cooed, Lorelei again. "Never say hope not. Paris is where all of us have come to fulfill our hopes."

"Amen," Louise said. "Or should it be Awoman?"

Everyone except the Baroness approved that line. André Germain even jotted it in his notebook. It would appear in one of his articles within the year. The Baroness was growing more and more agitated. She glared from Natalie to Eleanor to Natalie again, while another explosion boomed into the azure sky, so close it could have been in the next block.

This bomb—and the caress in Natalie's voice as she lectured Eleanor on the theology of Parisian hope—was too much for the Baroness Deslandes. She leaped to her feet, clutching her purse. "Isn't it enough that I risk my life to see you? I could be comfortable and safe in my cellar. Why should I endure this imbecility?"

She lapsed into German, calling Natalie a number of presumably nasty names. Natalie smiled up at her. "That won't do, Ilse," she said. "Either you say goodbye nicely or it's goodbye forever."

The Baroness drew herself into a compact mass. "In two or three weeks, when German troops are marching down the Champs Élysées, we will see who says goodbye forever."

"*Putain!*" shrilled André Germain in an outburst of patriotism.

As the Baroness stormed out, all the air raid sirens in Paris wailed. Finally, the authorities were admitting these mysterious explosions constituted an emergency. Ignoring the clamor, Gertrude Stein startled Louise by expressing furious resentment at the Baroness's prediction of a German victory. "The Americans haven't begun to fight. Wait till they go into action!" she said.

Natalie rushed after the Baroness. Gertrude, still vibrating with patriotism, turned to Eleanor Kingswood. "Alice and I would like to visit your leave camps and entertain the boys. Alice has a lovely voice."

"Gertrude plays the piano beautifully," Alice said.

Eleanor murmured something about arranging a visit. Louise suspected the troops would be more interested in hearing and seeing Elsie Janis, a shapely star of stage and screen who had recently arrived in France. Still, who was she to decide what would best inoculate American soldiers against temptation? Gertrude and Alice might well do the trick.

Another explosion; this one was at least a mile away. Natalie returned, looking gloomy. "Do you think she's right?" she asked Louise. "You consort with military men. Are the Germans about to win the war?"

"My resident expert is in Saint-Nazaire unloading ammunition," she said. "But anyone can see it doesn't look promising."

"When the madness began, I shipped all my furniture, my paintings, back to San Francisco. But I couldn't bring myself to leave Paris," Natalie said, her dark eyes on Eleanor Kingswood. "I think you would have done exactly the same thing. I've passed you frequently on the street, when the personality is least guarded. I sensed behind your formality a heart full of courage—a heart that cried out for a great love—but full of doubt about where and how to achieve it."

"That's true!" Eleanor said.

The all-clear sounded. Natalie's instinct for the dramatic found it irresistible. She announced the luncheon too was over. She had poems to write and letters to send by her elf, André, who was looking more and more dismayed. "Do you think Deslandes knows something?" he said.

"She knows I no longer love her," Natalie said.

Louise and Eleanor walked down streets clotted with fear. In cafés, at shop doors, Parisians scanned the sky for the invisible German bomber. For almost three years, they had endured air raids by night and rationing by day. They had frozen through awful winters. How much more could they take? Louise wondered.

"She's an extraordinary person," Eleanor said.

"Natalie? Of course," Louise said. Natalie no longer seemed important.

"I think she's right—about my longing for a splendid love."

"We all long for that," Louise said, as they turned into the Rue de Verneuil.

"I can't decide between Harold Holloway and a man you haven't met, an infantry captain in the Lafayette Division. He writes me stunning letters, describing his feats of courage."

"I know exactly what you mean," Louise said. "It's difficult— almost impossible—to love an *embusqué*."

"Yes," Eleanor said with a sigh. "I never thought the other man—his name is Arthur Hunthouse—had any grasp of the ideal. Now I wonder if a man can discover it on the battlefield."

"Maybe the answer is neither one, now that you've aroused Natalie's hopes."

"Hopes? What do you mean?"

Louise sighed. Eleanor's naïveté did not matter for the time being. The drama was only beginning. Eleanor would soon discover how ferocious Natalie became when her hopes were aroused. The answer Louise wanted to find at the moment was the source of those explosions. If they came from an invisible plane, the war might be almost over. Getting out of Paris could be a very good idea, loathsome as it was in other ways. She left Eleanor at her courtyard gate and hurried to her house on the Rue du Bac.

Her maid Nanette greeted her with a troubled bonjour. She had feared Louise had been killed by the bombs. The newspapers said seventeen were dead and many more wounded. As Louise mounted the stairs, Nanette added, "Colonel Quickmeyer is here, madame."

He was standing by the window in the upstairs sitting room smoking a cigarette. "You survived," he said, with a wintry smile.

She kissed him on the cheek. "Tell me what's happening. All I've heard is rumors, each one more ridiculous than the next. Do the Germans have an invisible airplane?"

"They've got something worse, a gun that can hit Paris from seventy-five miles away."

"A cannon?"

"A very big cannon. The French are going to try to blow it up, from the air or from the ground. I don't rate their chances as very good."

"What's happening to the British army?"

"It's a disaster. It took the British all last year and a half million casualties to gain six miles against the Germans. Yesterday and today the Germans gained twenty. They've captured at least thirty thousand men. They're driving a huge wedge between the British and French armies. If they pull it off, the war's over."

"My God. What are we doing?"

"Nothing. What can we do? We've got a hundred thousand half-trained troops in France. I'm not sure the British or the French even want them."

"What's wrong with our supposedly marvelous country?" Louise cried.

"We could discuss that for hours. I'd rather talk about what's wrong with you," Quickmeyer said.

"Oh?"

"It isn't very subtle, is it—to leave these things in full view?"

He pointed to a table where she had spread the scrapbook with Douglas Fairchild's newspaper clippings. She had not yet pasted in the letters. They were in a neat pile beside it.

"Are you in the habit of reading other people's mail?"

"When it's left out for obvious reasons, yes."

"I didn't expect you back from Saint-Nazaire for days. A week."

"Are you serious about him?"

"I'm serious about any man who risks his life in my name."

"Jesus Christ! When are you going to grow up? Dougie Fairchild isn't waltzing around no-man's-land to prove he loves you. He's doing it to get to be a general as fast as possible."

"I don't think you're an objective judge."

"The hell I'm not. I've studied that monster from close range. He's a terrifying phenomenon: the type of soldier who gets a lot of other people killed while he collects the glory."

"He risks getting killed himself. Can you say that, on your shuttle train to Saint-Nazaire?"

"I thought we were both intelligent enough to realize there's more than one way to win this war. I thought what we had between us made the war more or less irrelevant."

"A war that's about to drive me out of Paris can never be irrelevant," Louise said.

He stubbed out his cigarette and walked up and down the blue-and-gold sitting room. "Do you love him?" he said.

"No."

"Do you love me?"

A mirror filled one panel on the wall where he was standing. She was able to see his face, even though he was turning away from her as he spoke. She saw the haunted pain on it and remembered the fear that had surged in her when the shell exploded on the Boulevard de Strasbourg. Somehow the fear connected now to her power to heal this pain. That suddenly became the most important thing she would ever do. The words surged in her throat: Of course I love you.

But that would end all the dramas: with Fairchild, with Pershing, with Malvern Hill Bliss, with Natalie Barney, even—she faced it for the first time—with Eleanor Kingswood. It was too much to sacrifice for the power to heal this man's pain. After all, he was an *embusqué*.

"Not yet," Louise said.

Now all the dramas would continue. Including this one.

30. MY COUNTRY
SHAME ON THEE

HER BRAIN NUMB FROM LACK OF SLEEP, POLLY Warden drove her ambulance along a winding road between the towns of Bapaume and Péronne, in the valley of the Somme River. Anita Sinclair and four other drivers, including the Commandant, were just ahead of her. On both sides of the road trudged thousands of British soldiers, weary, dirty, dejected men, retreating south toward the river.

It was the most demoralizing sight Polly had ever seen. Defeat oozed from every face. Again and again, she saw men throw away rifles, packs, even their gas masks. Many sat on the side of the road, too sick or exhausted to keep going. Others staggered along, swigging from liquor bottles they had looted from abandoned officers' messes.

Often she saw men filling canteens from gas-contaminated water in the shell holes. No one stopped them. Officers seemed to have vanished. There was no sense of an army, organized into companies and regiments. This was a beaten mob. Their numbers continued to grow as men abandoned positions on the ridge above the road to join the column.

"Do you know where you're going?" Polly called as the ambulances slowed down to work their way around a shell hole in the road.

"Haven't a clue," one soldier yelled. "Ask the bloody general you're sleeping with." It was an article of faith among the soldiers that the generals and their staff officers enjoyed the VADs whenever they felt like it.

Down the hill streamed about two hundred men shouting, "German cavalry. They're surrounding us!"

Panic rippled through the column like a breaking wave. The retreat became a wild flight. Men too tired or too sick or wounded to join it were shoved into the shallow trench that paralleled the road. A few officers stood on the edge of the trench shouting orders and recriminations. One captain managed to persuade about thirty men to fix their bayonets and crouch in the trench, facing the ridge line.

The Commandant slammed on her brakes, stopping their little column. She ran over to the Captain and asked him if he thought they should turn around. "Might not be a bad idea, mum," he said, pulling off his helmet to wipe his mud-streaked forehead. Beneath the mud was a schoolboy's anxious face.

"I'm not going back. I'm going to find those men," Anita Sinclair said.

They had been told there was a battalion with heavy gas casualties somewhere along this road. For the past two days they had been responding to such emergencies, as the British Fifth Army collapsed around them. Half their ambulances had been commandeered to help evacuate Hospital Three as the Germans approached it. The rest raced up and down the chaotic battlefield, offering help wherever it was needed.

Polly had picked up wounded men with German machine-gun fire pattering against the trees all around them. Once, a stormtrooper had risen from behind a bush and thrown a hand grenade at her ambulance. Their infiltration tactics made the idea of a front line meaningless. Anita Sinclair began carrying a pistol she had taken from a dead British officer. She insisted Polly carry one too.

Anita was now the real leader of Ambulance Group Three. The Commandant was too demoralized to exercise any authority. The system into which they had once been so tightly woven had disintegrated. There were no longer any military police to guard their compound. Gone too were General Gough's amiable staff officers. They had all fled to Villers-Bretonneux, twenty miles closer to the Channel ports. Everyone wondered if that decision was an ominous indication of what Gough and his fellow generals were thinking.

"I think we should turn around and follow the army. I'm sure the General has a plan," the Commandant said.

"Anyone who wants to come along is welcome," Anita said, striding toward her ambulance.

Polly trudged grimly after her, vowing to prove she was as committed to the war as this English amazon. Bunky Gore-Blatchley lurched after them. "I'm coming too, though I don't know why," she said. "I think you've gone quite loony, Anita."

"So has the whole world," Anita said, studying a map. They drove another ten miles, stopping to ask soldiers if they knew anything about a badly gassed battalion in a wood. One sergeant said it might be up the next road to the northeast. That was toward the advancing Germans, but Anita took the turn without even slowing down. Over the ridge they saw a stand of trees in a small valley, with several dead horses lying on the edge of the wood. "That may be it," Anita said.

They bumped across an open field to the dead horses. Overhead the sky reverberated with the snarl of engines as British and German planes tangled in a huge dogfight. Anita got out of her ambulance and called, "Hello! Anyone here who needs help?"

Not a sound. To the north, artillery rumbled. A German plane swooped low, hotly pursued by an English ship. The Englishman's machine guns chattered. They walked into the woods, which were open, cleared like the woods near Auvers. They could see a shallow trench a hundred feet away. Men were crouched in it, facing northeast, toward the front. "Hello!" Anita called again.

Not a man moved. "Oh my God," Polly said. They were all dead. Riflemen peered down their barrels. Machine-gunners squatted behind their guns. All dead. Behind them slumped officers, clutching pistols.

The dogfight raged above them. Anita Sinclair walked along the entire trench line. Polly and Bunky followed her, mesmerized by the sight of mass death. Most of the faces were resolutely blank. Some wore a grimace. A few had twisted in a final agony. There were at least a thousand men. A whole battalion, annihilated by German gas.

"Why didn't they use their masks?" Bunky said.

"Maybe gas concentrates quickly in a valley like this," Polly said.

"Is anyone alive?" Anita Sinclair shouted. Her voice echoed through the dim woods. She was close to hysteria.

A stumpy soldier without a helmet emerged from a dugout about a hundred feet behind the trench. "I am!" he cried in a high trembling voice. He reeled toward them and shuddered at the sight of the dead men in the trench. "Oh, Jesus, are they still there?" he wailed. He threw himself behind a tree, his back to the silent ranks.

They climbed over the dead men and confronted Private Tommy Prince of the Third Cornwall Fusiliers. They were all Cornwall Fusiliers. He wept as he told his story. "The Colonel was in his dugout. He was hard man, very set in his ways. Fought in India, Burma. Knew his business. He didn't believe in fightin' with masks on, you see? He said it was better to lose a man or two to gas at first. Later, if the gas got really bad, then masks was all right. But the fog was so thick this mornin' you couldn't see the stuff. The officers sent the Colonel word that gas was bad and they needed masks. But he wouldn't give the order. Then it was too late. They was all dead. It was phosgene. You could barely smell it in the fog."

"How did you survive, you miserable little worm?" Anita snarled.

"The Colonel sent me to run a message up to the battalion on the ridge. I had me mask on when I come back. They was all masked up there. I come back and these was all dead. I didn't know what to do."

"You're a liar. You ran away. I'm going to shoot you," Anita said. "Bunky, go get my gun."

"I swear it's the truth!" the soldier screamed. He began to weep hysterically. "I was ready to die here with the rest of'm. The Colonel said we was all gonna die here. But I couldn't fight the whole German army. They come by here. I could hear'm laughin' while I hid in the dugout."

"You're not going to shoot him," Polly said. "Not while I'm around. What's happening to you?"

"This is none of your business!" Anita raged. "Why don't you go back to Paris now and start spreading the story of our disgrace? Isn't that what you're going to do? You've had a smirk on your face ever since this mess began."

There it was again, this mindless hatred of her because she was an American. It burst out of Anita, out of all of them, with uncontrollable fury. Polly tried to excuse it, to blame it on the catastrophe that was engulfing them, but it was not easy. "You can insult me as much as you please. You're not going to shoot him," she said.

Bunky put her arm around the shaking soldier. "Come on, lad. You can ride with me."

As they rejoined the retreating column a major waved them down. "They're evacuating Péronne. The clearing stations are desperate for ambulances." They headed for this walled city on the north bank of the Somme. As they neared it they were slowed to a crawl by a tidal wave of civilian refugees pouring down the road. Old men and women of all ages dragged carts with their household goods piled on them. Herds of cows and pigs were in the procession.

Anita pounded on her horn and they finally edged their way into Péronne. The streets were full of lorries and staff cars, lugging away papers and men from various army offices. An excited sergeant major directed them to a high school that had been converted into a casualty clearing station. Inside, in what must have been the school gymnasium, two young doctors were working on about fifty wounded men on stretchers. They looked at the three VADs with amazement. "How on earth did you get here?" the taller of the two asked.

"Sheer accident," Anita said. "We can only take twelve stretcher cases and three sitters."

Anyone lightly wounded enough to be a sitter had long since joined the retreat. That meant they were limited to the twelve stretcher cases. The doctors looked at each other as if neither wanted to make the choice. "They're all rather badly hurt," said the taller doctor, who had a delicate, intellectual mouth.

The other doctor, shorter, burly, took a deep breath. "We'll pick twelve. It's no different from the sort of thing we do in the field all the time."

Polly had done the same thing at the Château Givry. But it was one thing to exercise such judgments in the turmoil of a front-line hospital, where the individual soldier does not know he is being judged, and another here, where every man knew that if he was left behind he was probably going to die.

Quickly, the burly doctor chose twelve men. Two stretcher-bearers began carrying them out to the ambulances. "So long and good luck, you bloody apostles," someone called.

"If we find Jesus, we'll tell him to come back for you," one of the outgoing stretcher cases said.

Their casual courage brought tears to Polly's eyes. "I can see why you've fallen in love with them all," she said to Anita.

She barely nodded. At the door, Anita asked the doctor where they should take the men. "I don't have a clue," he said. "Try Gough's headquarters at Villers-Bretonneux. They should know where the hospitals are setting up."

"What are you going to do?"

"We're staying with the men," the tall doctor said.

Crossing the river, they ran into another mass of refugees and retreating soldiers. A military policeman suggested they take a side road along a ridge that looked down on the whole valley of the Somme. It was an astonishing, terrifying sight. The landscape for ten or fifteen miles was dotted with burning villages, supply dumps, field hospitals. They could see masses of German infantry advancing toward thin lines of waiting British. There was no artillery firing, but an immense clatter of machine guns and rifles drifted up to them.

War is the engine of history. If Polly had any lingering doubts that Malvern Hill Bliss was right, this view of the valley of the Somme erased them forever. She was watching a nation on the march, imbued with fanatical faith in its destiny to rule the world. It was hard to believe it was all being directed by a few men far behind the lines. How could anyone grasp such immensity, master such violent confusion?

They raced on to Villers-Bretonneux, arriving in the last light of afternoon. A military policeman directed them to General Gough's headquarters in the town hall. As they got out of their cabs to check the wounded, a big car hurtled into the town square and braked to a stop a few feet away. In her daze of exhaustion it took Polly a moment to realize there was a small American flag on the fender.

Out of the front seat stepped a short slim officer wearing a Sam Browne belt: Malvern Hill Bliss. "Anita!" he said. "I was hoping I might see you—and Miss Warden—but I didn't really think it was possible. I'm so glad you're safe."

"I wouldn't call this safe," Anita said. "The Germans are no more than five miles away. Doesn't that worry you?"

"It worries me a great deal. That's why I'm here."

"Are you hoping to evacuate your excuse for an army along with Gough's?"

Astonishment and pain mingled on General Bliss's face. He was one of those men who had always charmed women. He did not know how to deal with this berserk creature in front of him. "I'm here to find out what the situation is and report back to General Pershing," he said. "We want to know what we can do to help."

"The situation is hopeless. We've been beaten, humiliated, disgraced—and I hate myself for contributing to it. I hate you almost as much, with your smarmy talent for appealing to a woman's worst instincts. You've helped me betray my country, my army, my dead. Now get out of my way. I have to find out where to take these wounded men."

She stormed past him into Gough's headquarters. Bunky Gore-Blatchley retreated to her ambulance. Polly felt obligated to say something. "Anita's been under a tremendous strain, General," Polly said. "None of us have had more than an hour's sleep in the last three days."

He nodded mechanically. "Is it all over? Have the Germans won?" Polly asked.

"They're winning around here," Bliss said. "But there's a lot more soldiers in France they haven't beaten yet. The French are moving up on their left flank. If the British can hang on to Amiens, the Germans'll find themselves in a salient."

He pulled out a piece of paper and sketched a salient for her, showing how the bulge was vulnerable to attack from three sides. For the first time Polly glimpsed how generals thought. They stepped back from the chaos and terror of the battlefield and saw shapes and patterns and possibilities beyond the comprehension of civilians. It was momentarily reassuring. But a primary question remained. "What's happened to our army? Why are we letting the British and French do all the fighting? I hate to say it, but I'm almost ashamed to be an American."

"Can you keep a secret?" General Bliss said. "I'm ashamed too. So are Pershing and every other man in the AEF."

Anita came out of the town hall and strode over to them. "Hospital Three, what's left of it, is setting up shop in Albert, north of here. I've got directions."

"Can we talk, even for five minutes?" General Bliss said. "I still value your—your friendship."

Polly wondered if he had been going to say love. Had her presence stopped him? "I've said all I've got to say," Anita snarled, climbing into her cab.

"Miss Warden," Bliss said, turning to Polly. "If you want to come back to Paris with me—"

Polly saw the flash of disdain in Anita's eyes. Even if she had been tempted to say yes, that look made it impossible. "General," Polly said. "I told you once your ideas about women were antediluvian. This proves it! There are wounded men in this ambulance. They're my responsibility!"

They left Malvern Hill Bliss standing forlornly in front of Hubert Gough's headquarters. As the General dwindled in Polly's rearview mirror, she found herself wishing she had rejected his attempt to rescue her in a softer voice. It was already open season on Americans in the British zone. It did not seem right to humiliate a man who had admitted he was ashamed of his country.

31. *HUMBLE PIE*

MODERN WOMEN! BLISS THOUGHT AS HE WATCHED the three ambulances recede into the twilight shrouding the narrow main street of Villers-Bretonneux. He was learning about them the hard way. He still thought it was all wrong, letting them within range of German artillery, but he had to admit they had earned his respect. Unfortunately it did not seem to be working the other way around.

"General Gough will see you whenever you're ready, sir," Jonathan Alden said.

Bliss turned away, almost grateful for the epic upheaval engulfing them; it made personal emotions unimportant for the time being. To the north and to the south, guns thudded relentlessly. The Germans were pouring in division after division. One army was driving toward the key rail center of Amiens, on the Fifth Army's left flank; another one tore an ever widening gap between the French and British on the right flank.

Pershing had called him at dawn, as the Lafayette Division was emerging from a month in the Lunéville lines. He told him about the collapse of the British Fifth Army and the growing French fear that Haig might fall back to the channel ports. Pétain wanted to take the American divisions apart and brigade them with French divisions for the emergency. Pershing insisted on keeping them together and fighting as an army corps under a French or a British general. He told Bliss to get up to Picardy and find out what was really happening.

Bliss followed Jonathan Alden into Fifth Army headquarters. Everything had a seedy, temporary air. Gone were the immaculate servants, the kilted bagpipers. Papers and maps were spread on tables, boxes of documents were piled in corners. Gough slumped in his chair and shook hands without bothering to stand up. "I've barely been out of my car for the last forty-eight hours," he said. "Running from hole to hole like the little Dutch boy."

"I'm here to find out what we can do to help," Bliss said. "Pershing's ready to commit every man we've got."

"Men is what we need," Gough said. "If we'd had the men we wouldn't be in this mess. We'd have stopped them inside our battle zone."

With barely concealed bitterness, Gough said Haig had been convinced the German assault would hit the Ypres salient. He had given Gough only eight divisions to defend forty-two miles of front and not a single labor battalion to build a defense in depth.

"Why in God's name did he think the Germans would attack where you're strongest?" Bliss asked.

Gough sighed. "Haig is convinced he won a victory at Ypres last fall, believe it or not. He imagined the Germans wanted to remove the stain from their escutcheon."

"Have you committed your reserves?" Bliss asked.

"Yesterday. Two divisions. They've been thoroughly chewed up. We need a minimum of ten French divisions. We're fighting at least thirty German divisions."

"Four American divisions have the same number of men as ten French ones. If we commit our men under you, what would you do with them?"

"Put you in as a corps on my left flank to cover Amiens, and tell the French to go to hell."

"I like the sound of that. I think Pershing will too."

"You'll have to talk it over with Haig, of course. He's on his way to Doullens to confer with the French. My staff will map you a route."

Bliss held out his hand. "Good luck, old man. You've got some coming to you."

Did they both sense the words were meaningless? Somewhere, somehow, Gough had lost his luck and there was not much hope of getting it back.

In the corridor, Bliss found Alden talking to his virtual double,

Gough's aide. "Captain Blake tells me they're putting together a pickup force of about two thousand under a brigadier to fill the gap between the Fifth Army and the French," Alden said. "About five hundred of them are American engineers who were up here to help build defenses. They're short of officers. What do you say to letting me take charge of a company for a day or two?"

It was exactly the sort of thing Captain Malvern Hill Bliss would have wanted to do at the age of twenty-five. But General Bliss knew too much about the situation on the battlefield to see it as anything but a chance to commit suicide. "Absolutely out of the question," he said. "I've got to get to Doullens and see General Haig as soon as possible."

"You don't need me there, General. I'll join you in Lunéville as soon as we stabilize things. It shouldn't take more than a week."

"I'm going with them myself, sir," Captain Blake said. "It should be a very good show. We've got plenty of ammo and forty or fifty machine guns."

In his mind's eye Bliss saw what would happen when German stormtroopers hit this makeshift brigade with their infiltration tactics. "I said it was absolutely out of the question!" he roared. "Captain Alden can't be my aide and double as a free-lance infantry officer in another army!"

Anger and disbelief mingled so visibly on Alden's face, Bliss felt thoroughly ashamed of himself. The chastened young British captain seized a map and showed them how to reach Doullens without getting shot or captured by the advancing Germans. They drove through the night with the horizon lurid with the flames of burning villages and supply dumps. After a wordless hour on the road, Bliss said, "I'm sorry I lost my temper."

The blond head nodded, acknowledging the lapse. "Has it occurred to you that I was thinking of your safety? Every officer wants combat experience. But leading a bunch of men you've never seen before into a losing fight is not the best way to get it."

Still the blond head drooped, the mouth remained sullen. "You don't seem to have any confidence in me, General. You treat me like I was twelve or thirteen years old."

That inadvertent direct hit left Bliss temporarily speechless.

* * *

The sixty-mile trip to Doullens took most of the night. Again and again they had to pull off the road as columns of retreating British soldiers trudged past them. A colonel told Bliss they were part of the British Third Army, whose mission was the defense of Amiens, the key rail center connecting Picardy to the rest of France. If Amiens fell, there would be no way to get the Americans to the battle zone.

His jitters growing, Bliss reached Doullens as German artillery began crackling and booming a few miles away. The town square was full of limousines. He got out of his car in front of the city hall and found himself face-to-face with none other than Georges Clemenceau, who was striding up and down in the chilly morning air, beating his arms against his body to keep warm. "Aha!" said the old man in English. "The Americans to our rescue! What brings you here, my friend?"

Bliss said he was looking for Field Marshal Haig. "So are we," Clemenceau said. "We're hoping to persuade him to stay in the war. He's inside, conferring with his generals. The British secretary of war, Lord Milner, and their chief of staff, Wilson, will be joining us. Also my mutton-headed confrere, President Poincaré, and the only two generals in whom I have a shred of confidence, Pétain and Foch."

Concealing his astonishment at Clemenceau's frankness, Bliss asked him if the French were reinforcing the British Fifth Army. "Is there a Fifth Army? Pétain tells me it no longer exists," Clemenceau growled. He seized Bliss's arm as if he needed support. "Do you know what Pétain told me yesterday? The Germans will beat the British in the open country. Then they'll beat us too. Do you think a general should talk or even think like that?"

Bliss groped for a reply. "Sometimes it's useful to fear the worst. I'm sure he's taking steps to prevent it."

Clemenceau lit a cigarette and told Bliss he was afraid Pétain was going to fall back on Paris and "let the British go to hell." If that happened, Clemenceau would have to go "hat in hand to the Kaiser" and ask for peace terms. He had brought General Foch to Doullens to counteract Pétain, an act of desperation in itself.

Bliss knew General Ferdinand Foch only by name. Although he had the large-sounding title of Chief of Staff of the French army, he had been shunted off to the Supreme War Council since the disastrous spring offensive and the mutiny that followed.

Personally, Clemenceau continued, he despised "Ferdinand the Great" as much as Foch hated Clemenceau. The General was "devout to the point of imbecility," a daily mass goer, a prude about women. But he was a fighter. If he had only ten men left in his command, he would order an attack. Whether anyone would obey him was another matter. "The poilus loathe him. He's slaughtered too many of them."

They were interrupted by the arrival of General Pétain, General Foch, and President Poincaré. Clemenceau introduced Bliss. Pétain barely managed a grunt of recognition. Bliss began to appreciate his nickname, The Sphinx. Poincaré, whose office was mostly ceremonial, smiled wanly. He had met Bliss when he inspected the Lafayette Division with Pershing. The short dapper Foch shook Bliss's hand perfunctorily, with a stiff little bow. He was more interested in Clemenceau.

"The Kaiser is making his final lunge for glory," Foch said. "His recklessness is our opportunity. Provided, of course, that we can rescue the British from their deplorable panic."

"A rather large proviso," Pétain said.

Field Marshal Haig emerged from the city hall with his army commanders. Bliss was dismayed to note that Gough was not among them. It was an ominous sign. He excused himself from the French conclave and shook hands with Haig. "I had no idea a conference of this magnitude was taking place," he said, and quickly explained his visit to the battlefield, his talk with Gough, the proposal to commit the four American divisions as an army corps.

"That proposition can only be discussed after this meeting," Haig said, and strode past Bliss to greet the French.

A few minutes later, Lord Alfred Milner, Prime Minister Lloyd George's right-hand man in the British war cabinet, and General Henry Wilson, the British chief of staff, theoretically Haig's superior, arrived. Milner, shaggy-haired, with heavily lidded eyes, looked formidable. Wilson was an elongated giant with a shrewd bony face.

It dawned on Bliss that the commanders of the French and British armies were meeting, backed by their top politicians, and no one had bothered to invite John J. Pershing or any other American representative. It was one more humiliation to swallow, one more demonstration of the way Woodrow Wilson had shipped the AEF to Europe without an iota of political support.

Haig introduced Bliss to Milner and Wilson. "I see no harm in allowing him to join the conference, provided he understands he has no official role and his name will not be included in the minutes. In the long run it may facilitate our communication with General Pershing."

"A blessing for which we've prayed on bended knee for the last ten months," Milner said.

The French were equally agreeable to Bliss's invisible participation. They trooped into the ornate three-story city hall and sat down in a corner of the council chamber around an oval table. Overhead, a crystal chandelier lent a touch of the ancien régime. A high window overlooking the town square was flung open. Through it came the distant rumble of artillery and, closer, the clank and rattle and roar of some sort of machinery. Clemenceau asked what it was. "Tanks," Haig said. "To defend the town in case the Germans break through."

President Poincaré volunteered to be chairman. Clemenceau spoke first without bothering to ask permission. He wanted to know if Haig was abandoning Amiens. Haig said it was all a terrible misunderstanding. He intended to fight for Amiens, if the French helped him. He was sending reserves from his armies in the north. The British government was shipping him another 170,000 men from England as fast as possible. But French help was essential, especially on the Fifth Army front.

"There is no Fifth Army," Pétain snapped. "They've run like the Italians at Caporetto."

"They're still fighting hard," Haig insisted.

"The Germans report ninety thousand prisoners," Pétain said.

Poincaré pleaded for calm and asked Pétain to assess the situation from the French point of view. The Sphinx stressed his responsibility for the safety of Paris. But since Field Marshal Haig had agreed to defend Amiens, he too was prepared to take some risks. He was ready to send twenty-four divisions into the battle, but not all of them were first class, and it would take "a considerable time" to get these units ready to march. It might be necessary to retreat beyond Amiens temporarily.

Foch exploded. Pounding the table, his mustache bristling, he shouted, "We must not talk of giving up Amiens! We must fight in front of it and behind it! We must fight where we are now!"

Field Marshal Haig turned his large head toward the excited Frenchman. "If General Foch will consent to give me his advice, I will gladly follow it."

For a moment a wild mixture of incredulity and tension filled the room. Haig was agreeing to an idea the British had opposed violently and systematically for three years. He was going to put his troops under the command of a Frenchman. He was choosing Foch because he had no hope of getting any help from the pessimistic Pétain.

In a matter of minutes, they were drafting a note to be signed by Clemenceau and Lord Milner.

> General Foch is charged by the British and French governments to coordinate the action of the Allied armies on the Western Front. He will work to this end with the generals in chief, who are asked to furnish him with all necessary information.

A supreme commander had been appointed—and John J. Pershing had not even been consulted about the choice. The Americans were obviously regarded as superfluities, to be manipulated or ignored at will. Never had Bliss felt so humiliated, not only personally but as an American soldier.

"I believe, gentlemen," said a beaming President Poincaré, "we have worked well for victory."

The conference broke up in this atmosphere of mutual congratulation. Through the window, the growl and crackle of German artillery seemed closer. As the politicians hastened to their cars to escape the danger zone, Haig seized Foch's arm and led him over to Bliss. "Pershing says he wants to help, but only if he's permitted to fight his divisions as an army corps. What do you think of the proposition?"

"What do you think?" Foch said.

"I have grave doubts," Haig said, impaling Bliss with his hard eyes. Bliss had no trouble reading their message. The Field Marshal was asking if he remembered his smart answers when Haig and General Charteris came to Paris. Now Bliss—and Pershing—were to get their reward. Haig did not need any Americans. He had twenty-four French divisions and a French general who would deliver them in time to fight for Amiens.

"I concur completely," Foch said. "The Americans have no training or experience to coordinate something as large as an army corps. It would lead to bungling and slaughter. I will see Pershing as soon as possible and order him to break up his oversized divisions and send battalions to us and to you—if you want them."

Haig clapped Bliss on the shoulder in an outrageous imitation of cordiality. "So there you have it, old man. Generalissimo Foch's answer, by which we all must abide."

Bliss did not need a diagram to tell him what he was seeing: the creation of a new partnership, Haig-Foch Ltd., with the emphasis on the limited. Outsiders like Pétain and Pershing need not apply. From now on their job was to take orders.

Bliss stalked out of the Doullens city hall and drove south with Jonathan Alden, telling him about the bizarre conference. Alden could only shake his head in bewilderment. It was one more example of how little a real war resembled the ones fought in the textbooks at West Point.

As they approached Villers-Bretonneux, Bliss decided to pay General Gough another visit. He at least might be cheered by the news that twenty-four French divisions were coming to reinforce him. The Irishman also might tell Bliss whether Douglas Haig was really going to take orders from Ferdinand Foch. It might help Bliss advise Pershing on how to react to this new phenomenon.

Gough was just getting out of a staff car as they arrived. He looked a little more cheerful. "What's left of the army is showing a lot of fight," he said. "But my right flank continues a bit of a mess. The French are retreating faster than we are. We could certainly use some Americans. Did you find Haig? What did he say?"

Bliss told him what he had found at Doullens. Gough was too Irish to disguise his humiliation. "Seems a bit thick not to invite me, don't you think?" he said. "I'm the only fellow who knows what's happening down here."

Bliss followed him into his headquarters. A worried colonel was waiting in Gough's office. "We've just learned the Third Army has retreated without the slightest consultation," the Colonel said.

"What's their new line?"

The Colonel drew a ragged red curve on the wall map. Gough all but collapsed into his chair. "That leaves a good six miles of our left flank exposed. It won't take Jerry long to exploit that. My God, what else can go wrong?"

"Do you want to order a withdrawal, General?"

"I don't see that we have any choice."

"There will be no more withdrawals!"

Standing in the doorway, hands on his hips, was the new Allied commander in chief. The staff colonel hastily excused himself. Bliss was about to follow him when Foch waved him to a seat. "There's no need for you to go. You may learn something, General," he said.

His kepi at the cockiest possible angle, Foch strode over to a wall map and glared at it for a moment. Then he whirled and bellowed at Gough. "Why are you at your headquarters and not with your troops in the fighting line?"

Gough flushed. "As General Bliss can tell you, I returned from a tour of my lines less than twenty minutes ago."

Foch did not seem to hear this reply. "Your corps commanders will be on your heels, and everyone will stampede. Go forward! The whole line will stand fast, and so will your men."

"I can assure you, Generalissimo Foch, my corps commanders are not the sort of men who stampede."

Again, Foch ignored the reply. He was in a kind of frenzy of arrogance. "Why did your army retire? What were your orders to the army?" he shouted.

To Bliss's amazement, Gough continued to answer the Frenchman in a calm reasoned voice. He told him the Fifth Army's defense plans were based on General Pétain's ideas: to give ground in the forward zone and fight harder in the next two zones. "I believe he calls it *un defense élastique*," Gough said.

"Pétain is a cowardly old woman. Foch is in command now! There must be no more retreats. The line must be held at all costs!"

Like a bad actor in an operetta, Foch gave Gough one more glare of contempt and strutted out the door. He had not bothered to ask the Irishman anything about the whereabouts of the Fifth Army's battered divisions, or about their strength or morale. Nor had he given Gough a chance to tell him about the Third Army's retreat, or about the French divisions on his right flank that were falling back faster than his own exhausted men. In the light of these realities, Foch's prohibition of any retreat was murderous lunacy.

"Excuse me, General," Bliss said and followed Foch out the door.

He caught up to the Generalissimo of the Allied Armies as he was getting into his car. "I want to thank you for that very educational lecture," Bliss said in French. "May I make a small suggestion that I hope is equally educational?"

"I have no time to waste on trivialities," Foch said.

"Don't ever talk like that to me or any other American general. If you do, you'll get kicked in the balls."

Bliss spoke these words with grave deliberation, especially the last ones: *les couilles*. He left the Generalissimo standing beside his car. It took a full minute for the door to slam.

32. MESSAGE FROM ON HIGH

FOR THREE DAYS THE PARIS GUN HAD NOT FIRED A shell. German planes had raided Paris by night, but they were familiar terrors. It was the Paris gun, distributing random death by daylight, that had shaken everyone's nerves. In comparative tranquillity, Louise Wolcott had lunch with Harry Quickmeyer in the Ritz Hotel's garden restaurant. The upper half of the Place Vendôme's majestic column, spiraled with the bronze of 1,250 cannons captured at Austerlitz, with Napoleon's statue on top, loomed above the outer wall. Spring sunshine spangled the flowering trees and glistened on the red and white table umbrellas. In two days it would be Easter.

"Are the Germans still winning in Picardy?" Louise asked.

French newspaper headlines were thunderous with reports that the British were about to abandon Amiens and retreat to the English Channel. "They're running out of steam. Foch has reinforced the British with twenty-four French divisions," Quickmeyer said.

"Is Foch going to take Pershing's offer?"

Like all Americans in Paris, she had been thrilled to read that Pershing had made a dramatic visit to Foch's headquarters to tell him that all the doughboys in France were ready to fight under his command.

"No. The Generalissimo and Field Marshal Haig still think they can get American troops on their terms, not ours."

"Why did Pershing make the offer?"

"To see if he could embarrass Foch into agreeing to let us fight as a unified army. He was also trying to outmaneuver General Tasker

Bliss, who voted in favor of amalgamation on the Supreme War Council."

It was marvelous, having someone on Pershing's staff as a lover. Louise picked up all sorts of fascinating tidbits to float across the table at dinner parties. She was rapidly becoming the most sought-after guest in Paris. Most people had to depend for their rumors on windy French senators and pretentious subministers who knew next to nothing.

"Pershing's a genius at political infighting. But when I think of the gamble he's taking, I break into a cold sweat," Quickmeyer said. "If the British and French fold up, they're going to blame it on him. I don't know how he sleeps at night."

Louise saw he was wondering whether he was cut out to be a general. Was his failure to conquer her part of his self-doubt? Probably. All the dramas were continuing. Over their apéritifs, Louise had amused Quickmeyer with the story of Natalie Barney's pursuit of Eleanor Kingswood. Natalie was bombarding her quarry with bouquets, poems, letters. She paced the courtyard of the house on the Rue de Verneuil like a lioness in search of prey. She threatened to challenge an appalled Harold Holloway to a duel. Louise did not mention how often a tearful Eleanor sought her advice, or how frequently they exchanged consoling kisses.

There were limits to what Colonel Quickmeyer would tolerate. Louise had convinced him she had done little to encourage Douglas Fairchild and would do even less in the future. She almost meant it. Lately she was frightened by the intensity of Quickmeyer's love, his too visible pain at the prospect of losing her.

"That air raid last night was the worst yet," Quickmeyer said. "They dropped thousand-pound bombs. Ain't progress wonderful? They were dropping fifty-pounders only a year ago."

"I watched the whole thing from my balcony," Louise said.

"You shouldn't do that," Quickmeyer said. "Go down in the cellar and stay there!"

There it was again, the pain, combined this time with masculine arrogance. Louise chose to be sullen. "I'll hire a miner and dig a dugout forty feet deep underneath the cellar and cower there. Will that satisfy you?"

Behind her flippant mask, Louise was shaken by the thought of thousand-pound bombs. It was not dying but dying with so much of her life incomplete that she feared. She wanted to be so many things, to savor so many dramas.

"I'm sorry," Quickmeyer said.

"It's all right," she said, smiling gently.

She was defeating this lean, hitherto triumphant male. It would be delicious, except for his pain, which she could banish with a word. They parted in the Place Vendôme with a kiss and she rode through Paris, thoughtful, almost solemn. Finally she tapped Michel on the back. "Take me to Saint-Gervais."

Opposite city hall, a block from the Seine, Saint-Gervais was her favorite Paris church. It was large enough to give God some grandeur, but not so stupendous that a human being felt insignificant—Louise's reaction to Notre-Dame. As she arrived, the three-hour Good Friday service commemorating Christ's crucifixion and death had just ended. But the church remained full of kneeling worshipers. The incense-rich air seemed pervaded by a mournful spiritual light.

Louise sat in one of the rear pews, as befitted a Protestant and a sinner. She had often gone to Good Friday services during her first years in Paris. The aura of penitence the priests created with their sermons and chants had evoked memories of her dying father, his slow crucifixion by cancer. Was there a secret in the mystery of the suffering Savior that she had somehow missed? Was it her failure to offer even a shred of sacrifice or pain that had doomed her father in spite of her febrile prayers? Was that the source of her reckless offer to Harry Quickmeyer at Fort Myer?

On the right of the main altar was a smaller altar with a statue of Mary, Jesus's mother. To Frenchwomen she was more important than Jesus. They prayed to her with the same intensity Protestants prayed to the Savior. Louise, who never liked her own mother, had found it strange at first. But the more French she became, the more intrigued she was by the idea of a woman who had special access to God. If only she believed in God, what a difference it would make!

Louise glanced across the aisle and saw the Jewish poet Max Jacob, his head bowed in prayer. His lean Semitic features, his fringe of beard, made him seem Christlike, though he was much too short to be Jesus as Louise imagined him. Her Jesus was a tall striding figure with a voice of thunder. Jacob sensed her eyes on him. He smiled and nodded, his eyes full of curiosity. He was probably wondering what a rich American divorcée was doing in Saint-Gervais. They had met at Natalie Barney's house. Jacob knew her wild side. Was he, the Jewish convert, sent here by God to tell her even the most improbable hearts could be rescued by Jesus' sacrifice?

What if Quickmeyer's fears came true, the British collapsed, and the French army retreated inside Paris for a last stand? Louise saw herself in a besieged city, carrying water and ammunition to the men in the forts, bandaging their wounds, asking them with fear clutching her throat, Have you seen Colonel Quickmeyer? It would be the ultimate drama.

A tremendous explosion reverberated through the church. The Paris gun! It was still pursuing her! Terrified eyes, Louise's included, bulged up at the pall of smoke and dust descending on them. Halfway down the nave, a stone pillar crumpled. The arched vault supported by the pillar cracked. In a second tons of stone came crashing down on the kneelers in the center of Saint-Gervais. The spiritual air was filled with screams of pain and terror.

Louise did not remember running. She only realized where she was many minutes later, as she stood in the Place Saint-Gervais watching hundreds of would-be rescuers—soldiers, Red Cross workers, ambulance drivers—stumbling through the wreckage, wrestling with the stones. Nearby was the Archbishop of Paris, wringing his hands. Premier Clemenceau and President Poincaré showed up to imitate him, with the addition of curses and vows of revenge. But the one who best expressed Louise's feelings was Max Jacob. He raised his fist to the heavens and denounced God. "How could you be so careless?" he screamed. "These were your faithful servants!"

The survivors of Saint-Gervais were displeased by Jacob's shouts. Eventually several gendarmes threw him into a van and took him away. Louise rode home thinking: a narrow escape, in more ways than one.

On the Monday after Easter, Louise went to a dinner at the American embassy honoring supporters of the American Red Cross.

She had given them twenty-five thousand dollars. She found herself sitting next to a fleshy pink-cheeked French general, Denis Duchêne. Opposite her was none other than John J. Pershing.

The AEF's commander scarcely took his eyes off her. Not too surprising, of course. She was wearing another diaphanous gown that revealed enough to tantalize without quite sacrificing modesty—at least by French standards. General Duchêne complimented her on the dress. "You've made yourself at home here, madame. It is good to see Americans adopting French ways. Would that General Pershing were more inclined that way."

"We're eager to learn," Pershing said. "I've assured General Foch of that, as you probably know."

"I wish I could share that assurance, General. Today I proposed to my good friend Foch a daring plan: to place a platoon of your men in each of our French companies. Our poilus would take heart to see at first hand, at last, the long-awaited Americans. Your men would swiftly learn the French way of war. General Foch thoroughly approved this idea. But he told me, with a sigh, you would never agree to it."

"I don't think this is the time or place to discuss such delicate matters, General," Pershing said.

Duchêne shrugged. "When the war hangs in the balance, time is more important than punctilio."

"Now I know why your troops call you the Tiger, General," Louise said to Duchêne.

"I don't mince words, like Clemenceau. I mince Germans," Duchêne said.

"What would you prefer for a nickname, General?" Louise asked Pershing.

"The Tortoise?" General Duchêne said.

"Remember, he won the race," Louise said.

"But he wasn't fighting a war," Duchêne said. "I fear General Pershing resembles our Pétain. He's too deliberate. It's speed that wins the battle. Speed and valor."

Pershing's face remained an impassive mask. But Louise thought she saw something very close to rage in his eyes, which had narrowed to slits.

Ambassador William Sharp, a self-effacing man who seldom got his name in the papers, spoke from the head of the table. "There are a number of us on the political side, General Pershing, who think a proposition such as General Duchêne is making has some merit. It would get us through the present emergency—"

"I'm afraid it might get us through to a surrender in the field to a victorious German army," Pershing said.

The man was incredible. He was ready to fight the entire room. He seemed indifferent to the shocked looks on all the civilian faces.

"Absurd!" Duchêne said. "Even if the Boche succeeds in breaking the British front, he'll find my troops astride the Chemin des Dames, the outer rampart of Paris, refusing to yield an inch of soil."

The French were marvelous too, in their way. They had a gift for the vivid phrase, the heroic stance. When it came to drama, the British and the Americans could not touch them. Louise's smile emanated admiration. Across the table, she could almost feel John J. Pershing bristle—which was exactly what she wanted him to do.

After the usual boring speeches, including a labored one by Pershing about the importance of the Red Cross, the dinner wound down to coffee and departures. General Duchêne asked if he could escort Louise home. "I'm sure you want to get back to your troops, General," Pershing said. "Who knows, the Chemin des Dames may be where the next German offensive will begin."

"They'd never dare attack such a position. It would be a slaughter," General Duchêne said, refusing to take his eyes off Louise.

"Mrs. Wolcott lives only a few blocks from my residence. I insist," Pershing said.

"I think madame should decide—between the Tiger and the Tortoise," Duchêne said.

"General," Louise said, "you're forcing me to choose between my love for France and my love for my country. In such a contest, patriotism must always conquer."

Duchêne clicked his heels and kissed her hand. "The last thing I would ever do is wound a heart that is so obviously capable of tenderness. I can only hope that some other night you will find room in it for your adopted country."

"Hope is a noble virtue, General. Persist in it."

Pershing briskly bundled Louise into his car in the embassy courtyard. "Whew!" he said. "Have you ever seen anything like that fellow Duchêne? He makes Foch seem tongue-tied. I wish these frogs fought as well as they talk."

"Isn't he a good general?" Louise said.

"Let's not worry about him," Pershing said, as the big car swung down the Rue du Bac. "May I come in for a drink?"

"Of course," Louise said.

In ten minutes they were in her upstairs sitting room, sipping brandy. "I like that dress too," Pershing said. "I'd like it even more if it were hanging in the closet and you were in something more comfortable."

"That can be arranged," Louise said. "But what about Micheline Resco?"

"What about her? What do you know about her?" Pershing said.

"Only what almost every woman in Paris knows."

"I'm still very fond of her," Pershing said. "But we're not married. Why are you worried about her, if I'm not worried about General Duchêne?"

The pain on Harry Quickmeyer's face and her desire to heal it, Max Jacob's Christlike smile, the explosion, the crumbling pillar in Saint-Gervais—all these things suddenly seemed part of a triumphant procession that had carried Louise to this breathtaking moment. What was pulsing between her and Pershing?

Recklessness. That was what she meant to this man. Micheline Resco had personified the admiration of suffering France. Now, a year later, instead of admiration there were insults between him and General Duchêne—and no doubt between him and Generalissimo Foch and Premier Clemenceau. Pershing was defying them all, taking an enormous gamble on his embryo American army's ability to beat the Germans. When a man is taking a risk that huge, he wants a woman who can dance on the edge of an abyss.

"Give me five minutes," Louise said, strolling into her dressing room.

33. IN FLANDERS FIELDS

"MY GOD, ARE THEY SENDING THEM INTO THE lines?" Polly Warden asked.

She was watching companies of British replacements march past the tents of Ambulance Group Three. They were children, pink-cheeked, flushed under the weight of their unaccustomed packs, with their steel helmets on the backs of their heads, the straps hanging loosely on their rounded baby chins.

"They've lowered the draft age to eighteen," the Bomber said. "And raised it to fifty." She twisted her thin lips and glared at Polly. "And not a sign of your heroic Americans."

March had dwindled into April. They were still camped outside Amiens, waiting for orders to depart for Soissons, where they were going to be assigned to a French hospital. It was a gesture of mutual aid and British pride. The French were sending thousands of troops north to fight for Amiens. The British wanted to give something in return.

Meanwhile, where *were* the Americans? Polly could only read the newspapers and wonder. She had thrilled to Pershing's dramatic offer to Marshal Foch, but for weeks now there had been nothing but silence. From everything she heard around Amiens, only British and French troops were manning the shaky lines.

Anita Sinclair strode up to them, her face ashen. "Our orders have been changed. We're going north. To bloody Ypres, I bet. I don't know whether I can stand that. I'd rather stay here and risk Fritz's next offensive."

Everyone was sure the Germans would renew their drive on Amiens as soon as they brought up more ammunition and fresh troops. The British had moved all their field hospitals out of harm's way. Wounded were carried from aid stations to trains and shipped to Étaples on the French coast near Boulogne, where there was a complex of base hospitals.

Polly knew why Anita wanted to stay near Amiens. The headlong retreat of the Fifth Army had forced the British to abandon Corbie. Polly would never forget the pain in Anita's eyes when she realized her fiancé's grave was now in German territory. "It isn't just William," she said, trying to be stoic. "It's all the others who died on the Somme. For what?"

Anita's anti-American fury had subsided to a permanent melancholy, a hopelessness about the war that extended to all the armies. She no longer berated Polly or anyone else. Polly was grateful for the respite. The sleepless nights and days of the Fifth Army's debacle had pushed her close to the breaking point again. For days after the battle subsided, she had wrestled with nightmarish dreams.

Instead of Ypres, Ambulance Group Three was sent to Hazebrouck, another rail center from which wounded were shipped to Étaples. It sat in the middle of the flat Flanders plain, without so much as a hillock for miles. They were assigned a grimy barracks near the rail yards. The Commandant tried to reestablish some control: ambulances had to be polished every day, uniforms were inspected with baleful glares. But it did not last. The collapse of the Fifth Army had shaken something deep inside the woman. She spent most of the day in her room. Her assistant, the Smokestack, revealed she was drinking gin.

For the first week, the front was relatively quiet. Most of their stretcher cases were illnesses: dysentery, trench foot, and a strange fever that left a man so weak he could hardly walk. At first the doctors had accused the victims of faking, but now they accepted it as a new kind of flu.

Hazebrouck and the next town en route to the lines, Bailleul, had an international flavor. Australians, Canadians, and Portuguese mingled with the British in the cafés and bistros. The Portuguese were particularly numerous. There were about twenty thousand of them in two divisions, manning the front lines. With the Commandant hors de combat and no military police available to guard their barracks, the VADs were free to accept invitations to dinner from army friends. After three years of warfare, Anita Sinclair had an astonishing number of them. She often invited Polly to join her.

Polly sensed Anita was trying to lure her into her own agony of sympathy and guilt for these young men who were likely to be killed at any moment. But Polly found it hard to penetrate their indefatigable good cheer. They sat around the bistros and cafés singing endless verses, all of them indecent, to Mademoiselle from Armentières, a town a few miles away. If *cafard* was loose in the British army, it was layers deep, behind tight smiles and wry jokes. Only someone who was also English could sense it.

One night, they had dinner with General Gough's handsome former aide Rodney Blake, now a major in command of a machine-gun battalion in a division that was in reserve. Blake was worried about the Portuguese. "They're having some sort of bloody revolution back home à la Moscow," he said. "They don't want to shoot anybody but their officers. I don't know what Haig thinks he's doing, putting them in the lines."

He was still loyal to General Gough, who had been sent home in disgrace. His bitter remarks on Haig and other generals stirred Anita's sympathy. After several glasses of wine, she let him hold her hand and tell her how much he loved her. He called on Polly to authenticate his plea. "Have you ever seen a more desperate case, Miss Warden?" he said. "Either in Europe or America?"

"Never," Polly said.

As their ten o'clock curfew neared, Major Blake went off to the bar to buy a final round of drinks. "Sign me in," Anita said. "I'm going for a stroll with the boy major."

Polly forged a passable imitation of Anita's signature in their doomsday book. Bunky Gore-Blatchley wanted to know where she was. "Raising morale," Polly said.

"Incredible. She was the most awful prig at school. No one could even say bloody without turning her scarlet."

Much later, groping through the dark barracks to her cot, Anita stumbled over someone's boots and fell on top of Polly. She apologized and lay down without undressing. "Poor Rodney." She sighed. "He needed that terribly."

Polly said nothing.

"He's so bitter about Goughie."

Polly almost said something sarcastic. But who was she to cast stones? She was glad she had held her tongue when Anita continued. "It was William. I kept hearing him in Rodney's voice. They went to school together. They use the same slang."

She lit a cigarette. "That's stupid, isn't it. I'm just a slut. The war's given me an excuse to be a slut. Isn't that what you think?"

Bunky Gore-Blatchley's voice came out of the darkness. "If you don't shut up you'll be a dead slut."

"What time is it?" Polly asked.

"About five. Hardly worth going to sleep," Anita said.

A second later, the earth shook. Their windows glared with weird white and yellow light. The thunder of thousands of guns swept toward them. "Oh my God," Anita said.

It was another German offensive, aimed not at Amiens but at the British army's lifeline, the channel ports. The Commandant stumbled out of her room at the head of the barracks. "Get dressed. There's bound to be a call within the hour," she croaked.

The sky continued to glow, and the thunder of the guns was undiminished. Above them came the familiar growl of German planes. Bombs crashed between their barracks and the rail yards. They ran outside and crawled into some muddy ditches. The anti-aircraft guns barked at the planes. At dawn a runner arrived from local army headquarters. They were ordered to Bailleul, where additional directions would be supplied.

A military policeman stopped them on the edge of town. "You can't go in there!" he shouted. "The place is chaos. The whole front is chaos. The bloody Portuguese have run away like so many sheep. They've taken over the town. The Germans aren't far behind them."

The Commandant burst into tears. "Not another rout. I can't stand another rout," she said.

"We're going in," Anita said.

Thousands of Portuguese were milling around Bailleul, their faces streaked with mud and terror, their uniforms stained yellow by the gas bombardment. They paid no attention to Ambulance Group Three. They were too busy having political meetings. Orators stood on tables in the cafés, haranguing them on the virtues of socialism. Around them swirled excited French men and women, shouting they were all cowards.

Group Three headed up the road to Armentières. Anita, in the lead, saw a stream of Tommies coming toward them. "Where are you going?" she shouted.

"Any place but here!" one of them yelled.

She jumped out of her cab and pointed her gun at them. "Get in these ambulances, you rotten cowards. We'll take you back to the front."

"You pull that trigger, miss, and it'll be the last thing you ever do," the spokesman, a private, said.

"Bloody hell!" snarled a corporal. "Are we goin' to let a woman shame us? Let's get in, boys. It's easier than walkin' back. We'll have to do it anyway when the old man catches up to us."

They piled into the ambulances. Dozens of them were the young boys Polly had seen earlier in the day, moving up. They were in the King's Own Royal Fusiliers, the KOs for short. The boy in her front seat was blubbering. "My corporal was going to take care of me. A shell killed him. Who'll take care of me now?"

Anita finally found a short fierce-looking brigadier who said he would take charge of the hundred and fifty men they were carrying. "If the Germans catch you doing this, miss," he said to Anita, "they'll shoot you."

For two days, it was the Fifth Army all over again. Aid stations were overrun, Armentières fell, the Portuguese panic infected more and more British regiments. Again and again yawning gaps opened in the front as troops broke and fled. On April 11, a messenger posted an exhortation from Field Marshal Sir Douglas Haig on Group Three's bulletin board.

> There is no other course open to us but to fight it out! Every position must be held to the last man; there must be no retirement. With our backs to the wall, and believing in the justice of our cause, each one of us must fight to the end. The safety of our homes and the freedom of mankind alike depend on the conduct of each one of us at this critical moment.

Anita Sinclair doubled as their military expert. She pointed to their map of Flanders. "If they take Bailleul and Hazebrouck, it's goodbye Dunkirk," she said. "That leaves only Boulogne and Calais to get the army out. They won't be able to do it."

The war was on the brink of being lost again. Still there were no Americans in sight. By this time Polly was almost British enough to assail any American general she saw. She imagined herself screaming, *Where are your bloody men?*

Toward the end of the second day, Polly and Anita launched a free-lance search for wounded. Beyond Bailleul, the rumble and crash of battle were all too audible. A British battalion came toward them, led by a lieutenant colonel, his face a frozen mask of fear. Behind him his men were a swarming mob. Anita jumped out of her cab and asked him if he had read Field Marshal Haig's orders, forbidding retreat.

"The Field Marshal's forty miles behind the lines," the lieutenant colonel said.

"What the hell's going on?" It was Major Rodney Blake on a bicycle. He jumped off and also asked the lieutenant colonel why he was retreating.

"To save my life and the lives of my men," he answered.

"We're digging in on that ridge," Blake said, pointing to a long low hill south of Bailleul. "Take your men up there and join my machine-gun battalion. We could use some infantry."

"I don't take orders from a major," the lieutenant colonel said.

Blake knocked him flat with a right to the jaw. A grimy sergeant gazed disgustedly at his fallen leader. "I've been waitin' the whole war for someone to do that," he said. "Show us where to go, Major."

Blake gave them directions and told Anita to go with them to make sure they got there. He drew Polly aside and said in a low voice, "I want you to take me back to Hazebrouck like the wind. There's nothing up on that hill but a cycle patrol with two machine guns. I've got to bring up the rest of my battalion as fast as possible."

They raced back to Hazebrouck along a road that was now under fire from German long-range artillery. Huge explosions tore up the fields around them. Polly gasped for breath and struggled to stay in control. Blake patted her arm. "It's all right, it's all right, everyone shakes when those damn things hit close."

In Hazebrouck, Polly followed Blake into the office of a colonel in charge of transportation. Hundreds of trucks were parked in a motor pool outside his window. "I need thirty lorries to transport my battalion to Bailleul," Blake said.

"Thirty lorries!" the Colonel said. He was a pudgy man with drooping reddish brown mustaches. "I'll need orders for anything like that. Just fill out this requisition form and I'll pass it up the line. Come back about this time tomorrow."

Blake pulled out his pistol and whacked the Colonel on the forehead. He slid to the floor, unconscious. The boy major swiftly filled out the form and handed the pen to Polly. "Sign it where it says 'commanding general,'" he said.

Polly then scribbled her name, appalled by the magnitude of the crime they were committing. "Don't worry. They won't shoot you. The most you'll get is fifty years in Dartmoor," Blake said.

In ten minutes, thirty lorries rumbled out of the motor pool behind Polly's ambulance. In another half hour, Blake had loaded them with his men and machine guns, and they raced up the road to Bailleul.

As darkness fell, an ecstatic Anita Sinclair arrived in the compound. "They're making a smashing stand on that ridge," she said. "The Germans haven't gained a foot. I wanted to stay for the night but Rodney made me leave."

"You're both bloody insane," Bunky Gore-Blatchley said. "It's time we remembered we're noncombatants and aren't supposed to be driving soldiers up to the lines or wherever. The same goes for driving about picking up wounded. You're going to get killed, and what will that accomplish?"

Anita smiled conspiratorially at Polly. "We like it. Right, Yank?"

"Right," Polly said, although her stomach had done a loop while Bunky was warning them of sudden death. Her nerves were still shaky.

That night there was another German air raid on the rail yards. They scattered to their slit trenches again, lest one bomb wipe out the whole group. Polly crouched beside Anita in the dark as the bombs crashed sporadically a few hundred feet away. "It's time I apologized for the awful bloody way I acted when the Fifth Army went up," Anita said. "I mean *really* apologized."

"I might have felt the same way if the situation were reversed," Polly said. "I don't understand why the American army isn't fighting."

"There's a good reason, no doubt. It isn't lack of courage. You've shown me that."

A bomb hit only fifty yards away. Shrapnel hissed over their heads. Polly trembled violently. "But I'm afraid all the time," she said.

Anita put her arms around her and held her until she stopped shaking. "So is everybody else."

The next morning Polly awoke without a trace of the anxiety that often seized her at the beginning of the day. Something indefinable, a kind of healing force, had passed between her and Anita last night. She felt amazonian as they drove up the road to Bailleul again. Above them in the gray Flanders sky swarmed dozens of British planes on their way to bomb and strafe the Germans. Jouncing past them in trucks were reinforcements from the Amiens front, Australians who howled and whistled at them and yelled things like "Nothin' more to worry about, girls! The Outbackers are on the scene!" On the other side of the road streamed civilian refugees with their usual pitiful bundles of possessions on their backs.

On the outskirts of Bailleul they met a crowd of British stragglers, dirty, exhausted, demoralized men. "Don't go in there. Jerry's got half the town. They're shootin' from every bloody window," one private yelled.

"Get in," Anita said. "We'll give you a free ride to the picture show."

The Private declined, but a sergeant persuaded a dozen men to board Anita's ambulance. Another dozen crowded into Polly's rear compartment, with a corporal in the seat beside her. As they approached the town square the crash of rifles, the hammer of machine guns, grew intense. A hulking lieutenant with an unmistakably Irish face stood in a doorway waving to them. "Stop!" he yelled. "The square's in German hands. We've got a lot of wounded in here."

"We've got a lot of reinforcements in here," Anita said.

The men jumped out of the ambulances and ran for the building. A German machine gun flung bullets along the stone wall above the doorway. A rifle bullet smashed Polly's windshield, showering her with broken glass. Anita backed her ambulance to the doorway, and the soldiers inside the building loaded it with wounded men. Bullets continued to splat against the building. From windows above the doorway, British rifles barked and a machine gun clattered.

Polly backed her ambulance to the door. A sergeant tried to carry out a wounded man to sit beside her. The machine gun chattered. Both went down groaning. With bullets skittering off the paving stones, clunking against the armored sides of her ambulance, Polly tried to drag the Sergeant into her cab. Anita ran over and helped lift him in. "If you're not careful, you're going to wind up with a Victoria Cross, Yank," she shouted.

With Polly's help, she hoisted the other wounded man to his feet, slung his arm over her shoulder, and staggered through another hail of machine-gun bullets to her cab. She boosted the man into the seat and started around the front of her ambulance to the driver's side.

A rifle boomed from a window on the other side of the narrow street. The bullet struck Anita in the back, just below the shoulder. She cried out and crumpled against the front of the ambulance. The rifle boomed again. Another bullet struck her, lower in the back. "Bastard!" shouted the Irish lieutenant in the doorway. He emptied his pistol at the German.

Somehow, Anita pulled herself erect and reeled around the fender to her cab. She got behind the wheel and lurched into gear. Polly followed her down the winding streets to the road to Hazebrouck. That was as far as Anita could go. She veered off the highway and rolled to a stop.

Polly ran up to her. Overhead an air battle was raging. Artillery pounded the ridge where Rodney Blake's machine-gun battalion was fighting waves of Germans. "I'm afraid—I'll kill these poor fellows—" Anita said. The seat of the cab was drenched with blood, Anita's and the wounded man's beside her.

Polly seized the pistol under the seat and looked around her.

Half a dozen stragglers had just drifted out of Bailleul. She ran up to one of them, a scrawny little man who had thrown away his rifle, and thrust the pistol in his face. "Can you drive?" she said.

He nodded, terrified. "Get behind the wheel of that ambulance and follow me."

He helped her move Anita to Polly's cab. They put her wounded sitter in the back. Polly pulled off the straggler's shirt and packed it around Anita's wounds to try to slow the bleeding. They started down the road beneath the snarling planes. More long-range shells gouged the fields around them. The air vibrated with the bedlam of war.

"You're bad, but I've seen worse," Polly said. "Hang on."

"No—point in—trying to build up my hopes, Yank," Anita said.

More truckloads of whistling Australians whizzed past. The artillery dwindled to a grumble, the small arms to a faint crackle. "Did you—tear up that letter to—General Bliss?" Anita said.

"No."

"Good. Send it—to him. Tell him—I'm sorry."

She slumped in the corner, staring out at the road for a long time. Hazebrouck loomed in the distance, guarded by half a dozen balloons to fend off German bombers. "Polly!" Anita gasped. "I just saw William. He was standing by the road—hands on hips—smiling at me. Do you think it's possible—the ghosts of all the—"

She struggled for breath. "He looked—so young."

Her head lolled. She was dead.

"Anita!" Polly cried. The road became a haze of tears. She rubbed them away and drove on, clear-eyed, to the field hospital beyond the railroad yards. Orderlies rushed out to help as she backed to the loading dock. Polly cradled Anita in her arms. "She's dead," she said. "Take care of the others. I want to hold her for another minute."

34. LUCK, FATE, AND DANGEROUS ADVICE

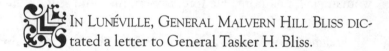 In Lunéville, General Malvern Hill Bliss dictated a letter to General Tasker H. Bliss.

Dear Tasker:

I just heard about your attempt to top Pershing by telling Generalissimo Foch, "We have come over here to get ourselves killed. If you want to use us, what are you waiting for?" Never have I seen a more sickening example of bureaucratic arrogance and ignorance. You, who have never had a shot fired at you in anger, are telling a man who has thrown away whole army groups in crazy offensives that he can slaughter American troops at will. It shows what ambition will do to an aging man's brain.

I used to at least concede you were intelligent in a certain academic way. Now I withdraw even that compliment. Don't you see that these German offensives require us to rethink our whole approach to warfare on the western front? If we attack like Foch our men will be massacred. We've got to attack like Ludendorff's stormtroopers, we've got to use our artillery like Bruchmüller. We've also got to figure out how to defend ourselves against these tactics. The Germans are demonstrating their mastery of the art of warfare. You have demonstrated nothing but a mastery of the art of bullshit.

The secretary's eyes bulged but he said nothing. "Type that up immediately," Bliss growled.

The secretary, whom Bliss had privately nicknamed the office ballet dancer, rushed back to his desk and began typing at record speed. Bliss glowered at a map on which he had shaded the latest German gains in Flanders. The British had gotten mauled again, but they had managed to stop another offensive. It had not been as bad as the collapse of the Fifth Army, but in Flanders Haig had less room to maneuver. The month of April had ended with the Germans in possession of more crucial territory.

Captain Alden strolled in looking glum. The whole division was glum. They were sitting around two dozen French villages waiting for marching orders that never came. "Some mail from Chaumont, General," Alden said.

The handwriting was distinctly feminine. A letter from a woman via Chaumont? He tore it open, his mind still on Tasker and the Germans in Flanders.

Fragments of Polly Warden's letter tore through his brain. *Heavy street fighting ... Bailleul ... machine-gun and rifle fire.* He stared at Anita's letter. The handwriting was bolder, more masculine than Polly's. *Major General Malvern Hill Bliss.* Nothing else on the enve-lope. He opened it. The secretary had stopped typing his letter to Tasker. There was not a sound in the building.

> *Dear General:*
>
> What a shame I still think of you by that awful title. No doubt you still think of me in the same impersonal way, as "the British VAD" or "the sexy chauffeur"—or possibly "the easy lay." Yet there was the begin-ning of something more personal between us, and that's what I want to commemorate in this letter. In spite of having 28,000 men ready to die at your command, you conveyed an amazing humanity. You made me think there may actually be something to the American obsession with equality. It may create better people.
>
> As I've arranged things, if you get this letter I'll be dead, a condi-tion I find incomprehensible. Isn't it fortunate that none of us can imag-ine our own deaths? If I survive, I may send the silly thing to you as a sort of comradely joke. I may even add a postscript telling you my offer still stands!
>
> *Fondly,*
> *Anita*

Bliss sat there, fingering the paper, suddenly hating war. Not merely this war but all wars. Was that what women's participation in wars would eventually accomplish? The idea that a man could fire a bullet into the body of a woman as fine as Anita was so revolting it made the whole idea of war intolerable. In the next moment he saw other bullets tearing into Polly Warden's body, shattering that lovely face. It was insanity, obscenity.

"General?" Captain Alden was standing in front of his desk, shifting from one foot to the other. "You can't send this letter to Tasker Bliss. He'll use it to discredit you. It's much too intemperate."

"Send it anyway."

"General, I just won't do it. You'll have to relieve me and send me back to the infantry."

"That's where you want to go, isn't it?"

The cheeks were flushed now, the blue eyes bright with anger. "General, you don't seem to understand. You seem to think you can worry about me but I'm forbidden to worry about you. It works both ways."

"All right," Bliss said. "Put it in the file marked Memoirs."

Alden grinned. "I can't wait to read those, General."

Ten seconds later, into Bliss's office strutted General Viomenil's chief of staff, Colonel Jacques de Coeur. Extremely tall, at least six feet four, with a nose that qualified him to play Cyrano de Bergerac, he was at least as arrogant as his boss. Bliss called him Colonel de Heartburn.

"General," de Coeur said, dropping a sheaf of papers on Bliss's desk, "I have here a plan by which your division will be split into three brigades, who will join the Eighteenth, Twenty-sixth, and Thirty-fourth divisions of General Viomenil's Ninth Army. General Viomenil hopes you will give it immediate consideration so the task of integration can begin as soon as possible."

Colonel, I have here a foot which I am about to plant a yard up your backside. He did not say it, of course. "A fascinating idea. Whose is it, General Viomenil's?" Bliss asked.

"The General has developed the concept in collaboration with his old friend Generalissimo Foch. These divisions will eventually be placed in the strategic reserve Generalissimo Foch is creating.

They will participate in the offensive that will smash the Germans back to the Rhine. General Viomenil will be the field commander. He would, of course, welcome your presence on his staff."

As his chief pencil sharpener. Bliss did not say this either. "I'm surprised to hear General Foch is thinking of an offensive. You don't expect the Germans to attack again?"

"They may make one more try at the British. But where can they attack us without unacceptable losses? We taught them their lesson at Verdun. The British are simply inept at war. But we can stabilize their front with a few divisions when they begin to buckle again. We'll keep them in the game."

"What a relief to know you have the situation so well in hand. Tell General Viomenil that as soon as I discuss these plans with General Pershing I'll get to work on them."

Colonel de Coeur smiled loftily. "As I understand it, General Pershing is no longer in a position to object to them. They have been approved by President Wilson."

De Coeur strutted out. Bliss thumbed through the plan to dismember his division. It was very thorough. Doctors, engineers, machine-gun battalions were all neatly dispersed. Even his staff officers were assigned to corresponding French staffers—in subordinate positions, of course.

"General," Captain Alden asked, "can you spare a few minutes for Colonel Quickmeyer, the new Chaumont G-Two?"

"I never needed an intelligence officer more in my life," Bliss said.

Harry Quickmeyer strolled into the office, his hand extended. His smile was perfunctory. He seemed as glum as his opposite number in the Lafayette Division, who recently complained to Bliss that he had nothing to do. "I've talked my way out of the Services of Supply and gotten a little closer to the front," Quickmeyer said.

"I can get you a lot closer if you want to work for me," Bliss said.

"I'll keep that in mind, General. I'm collecting information for Pershing from division intelligence officers to try to put together a picture of German intentions. There's something funny going on. The French have lost track of no less than forty-five German divisions, about half of them first class. That sounds like another offensive to me."

"What do you think they'll do?"

"I'm more interested in what you think, General," Quickmeyer said. "What would you do if you were Ludendorff?"

Bliss pondered the map of France, with the trench lines snaking from Switzerland to the North Sea, and tried to imagine himself with two million men at his disposal. "I wouldn't attack again in Flanders, tempting though the targets are. Haig and Foch have moved every available man up there. The same goes for Amiens. I'd do a number on the French to scare them into pulling their troops back to protect Paris. Then I'd hit the British with a knockout punch."

"Where would you attack the French, Verdun? Reims?"

"Too obvious," Bliss said, studying the map. "The French are dug in to their chins on those fronts. They've had years to do it. A better bet would be someplace they haven't had time to fortify."

His finger fell on a strip of road that ran along the map northeast of Paris. "Up here. The Chemin des Dames. The French captured it last spring. It's been quiet ever since."

"It's very rough country," Quickmeyer said.

"Stormtroopers don't worry about rough country. It suits their style. Haven't you armchair specialists worked up any reports on how the Germans tore apart the Italians and the British?"

Quickmeyer shook his head. "It just sounded like open warfare to us," Quickmeyer said.

"It's a new way to wage war, Quick. Light-years beyond our ideas about open warfare. No one's ever used infantry like Ludendorff's using his stormtroopers."

The blank look on Quickmeyer's usually intelligent face made Bliss's heart sink. If one of their brightest was not getting this message, what would it take to penetrate the craniums of run-of-the-staff types?

"Speaking of new ideas, what do you know about this?" He handed Quickmeyer the orders he had just gotten from Colonel de Heartburn. "Can he possibly be telling the truth about Waffling Woodrow approving this?"

Quickmeyer nodded mournfully. While Bliss stared in shock, Quickmeyer told him the British had frightened Wilson into agreeing to ship them 120,000 men a month—infantry and machine-gunners only. No division staff, no artillery, just raw manpower. "The French are getting in on the act with this idea."

"I can't believe it," Bliss said. "Pershing's accepted it?"

"What can he do? Tasker Bliss is telling the President it's the only way to stop the Germans."

Tasker was still playing the dirty game. But the real villain was the Haig-Foch partnership, which was getting each general what he wanted. Haig would have enough Americans to stop the next German lunge for the channel ports. Foch would have enough to try another fit of offensive grandeur.

"How's my old friend Louise Wolcott treating you? Worthy of your rank and prestige, I hope?"

Quickmeyer's glumness slipped into full-fledged gloom. "I'm afraid I've been outranked and outprestiged, General."

"Good God. I always suspected that woman had no judgment. Her ex-husband was one of my oldest friends, but I never respected him. In grade school he used to pay me to do his fighting for him. Who's the new hero?"

"John J. Pershing."

Bliss managed to absorb the shock without losing his composure. "Who else knows that?"

"Half of Paris, probably. But no one worries about that sort of thing in the City of Light."

"In Foggy Bottom, also known as Washington, D.C., they do."

Quickmeyer was in no mood to fret about John J. Pershing's reputation.

"I should have warned you about her," Bliss said. "But you looked like a fellow who could take care of himself. I hope she didn't do too much damage."

Quickmeyer shook his head. "I keep getting urges to strangle her and then tell everything I know to General von Ludendorff. But it passes. In the first place, strangling is too good for her. In the second place, I don't know enough to interest Ludendorff."

Quickmeyer went on his morose way. Half an hour later, Bliss headed for Paris. What he planned to do there was not at all clear in his mind. He was propelled by a blind instinct that Pershing needed him. He hurtled down the long straight roads, repeatedly asking Mile-a-Minute Murphy why they were going so slowly. Finally, the man asked in a strangled voice, "Do you think ninety miles an hour is slow, General?"

"Today I do," Bliss said.

He was amazed by how deserted Paris was. As he rolled down the Avenue de la Grande Armée, he learned why. A shell from the German long-range gun exploded a block away. "I'll be god-damned," he said. "Action at last."

He headed for Pershing's residence in the Faubourg Saint-Germain. The diminutive senior aide, Little Collins, wanted to know if he had an appointment. "Nope," Bliss said. "Just tell him Mal Bliss is here and it's urgent."

In a sitting room he found George Patton. He was now a lieutenant colonel wearing a uniform that had a red, yellow, and blue patch on the shoulder and a collar insignia with a silhouette of a tank set within a brass wreath. He informed Bliss he was second in command of the brand-new American tank brigade. The tricolor patch declared that tanks had the firepower of artillery, the mobility of cavalry, and the ability to hold ground like infantry.

Bliss was in no mood to listen to such nonsense. "Oh, bullshit, George," he said.

"Please don't say that to Pershing, General. I'm trying to talk him into buying another hundred and fifty French tanks. He doesn't see much point to them either. I think they can win the goddamn war for us."

"Are the Germans building any?"

"According to French intelligence, they're building trucks instead. I can't figure out why."

"With their new infantry tactics, they don't need tanks."

Collins told Bliss to go upstairs. Patton would have to wait. He found Pershing at a desk in a study off his bedroom. He looked haggard. Bliss dropped General Viomenil's plan to dismember his division on the desk and asked him what he should do about it. Pershing thumbed it listlessly. "Stall. That's the only move we've got left."

"Jack, what the hell's happening?"

"Wilson folded when Clemenceau and Lloyd George hit him with simultaneous cables demanding amalgamation on their terms and Tasker seconded the motion."

Pershing glared down at his clenched fists on the desk. "Why did I ever take this miserable job, knowing I'd be working for a lily-livered son of a bitch like Wilson? I'm a damn fool, Mal. A stupid, overambitious fool who thought he could outsmart everybody. I'm getting exactly what I deserve."

The resignation in Pershing's voice appalled Bliss. Jack was letting Haig-Foch Ltd. become the voice of fate. Every soldier played a lifelong game with the blind goddess, mocking her when the going was good, too often collapsing into numb acquiescence when the going turned bad. No one was more vulnerable to this temptation that Jack Pershing.

"Wait a minute, Jack. You've got six trained divisions under your command now. You haven't agreed to bust *them* up. All you did—and I admit it's awful—was agree to reinforce the English with men who haven't arrived yet. That makes sense. They've lost well over three hundred thousand men in the last two months. The French haven't lost a man. I wouldn't agree to this goddamn dismemberment plan no matter how loud old Georges Clemenceau screams. I'd tell Ferdinand Foch to go eat his kepi."

"Can I get away with it?" Pershing said, his fighter's jaw tightening.

"Sure you can," Bliss said. "What's Wilson going to do if you stand your ground? If he fires you, he'll have a hell of a time explaining why to Congress. Can you imagine what your pal Teddy Roosevelt would do with this plan if we sent it to him?"

"You've got a point," Pershing said. He walked over to the window. A distant boom rattled the glass as another German long-range shell landed. He punched his fist into his left hand. "You've got a point."

"There's another point—I mean matter—I'd like to discuss with you, Jack."

Pershing stayed at the window, his back to Bliss. Did he know what was coming? Bliss's pulses pounded. His mouth went dry. He was back in plebe year, with John J. Pershing glaring at his unshined shoes. "I understand you've been seeing Louise Wolcott."

Pershing whirled, his eyes wild. "I know it's none of my business, Jack. But I'm sort of—involved for several reasons. One is that night you took me along as interpreter for Micheline Resco. The other is, I know Louise. You're making a hell of a mistake. You made a promise to Michie; you gave her your word you'd do your best to honor that promise. Fooling around with Louise isn't—doing your best, Jack."

"I don't need this kind of advice from you—from anyone!" Pershing roared.

"Maybe not. It's from the gut, Jack. I don't think a man can walk out on a woman like Micheline Resco without ruining his luck—maybe forever."

Luck was not the same as fate. Luck was a goddess a man could cajole, propitiate—and alienate. Pershing had brought Bliss to Europe as a witness, a defiant witness, to the indestructibility of his luck. It added weight to what Bliss was telling him. It almost made it a threat.

"I've always believed a man should take advice from his friends. But you're pushing the principle to the limit!" Pershing roared. "Now get the hell out of here. I'll handle this thing with the French. Don't worry about it. I'll handle the other matter too. Just forget it. Worry about your own goddamn personal life."

"Jack, there's something else I wanted to discuss. These German offensives—"

"I said get the hell out of here! I've had enough advice from you to last me for the rest of the century."

Bliss found himself out in the hall, almost suffocating with dismay. He had blown it. He should have saved Louise until last. Someone needed to tell Pershing what these offensives meant, the importance of the new tactics the Germans had developed. Jack was too harassed by Haig, Foch, Pétain, Clemenceau, and Lloyd George to think about them. Someone had to persuade him to change their tactics to deal with massed artillery, gas, machine guns by the thousand. They had to be ready to try anything and everything to save lives, even tanks.

Downstairs, Patton rushed into the hall to say goodbye. "Did you get a chance to mention tanks?" he said.

"Sorry, George. We didn't get to it. We didn't get to a hell of a lot of things."

Outside in the May sunshine, Bliss decided there was one more thing he was going to get to, even if it cost him his stars. "Take me to 27 Rue du Bac," he told Mile-a-Minute Murphy.

In five minutes he was knocking at Louise Wolcott's door. She was dressing for dinner but she told him to come upstairs anyway. He found her in a lacy peignoir, putting on makeup at her dressing table. "What an unexpected pleasure!" she cried, jumping up to kiss him on the mouth just hard enough to suggest desire.

"I'm not here for pleasure," he said. "I'm here to do something very unpleasant."

"What in the world could that be?" she said, resuming the makeup job.

"To tell you to quit seeing Jack Pershing."

Everything stopped. The makeup, the glow in the blue eyes, the brightness on the beautiful face. "Who told you?" she said.

"Never mind. I'm telling you to cut it out."

"Since when are you in charge of my life?"

"I'm not. But I'm still telling you to cut it out."

"You're jealous," she said.

"I stopped being jealous about you a long time ago," he said.

"You're jealous because you never touched me. You didn't have the nerve."

"I screwed you in my mind. Just like you screwed me. Neither of us had the nerve to do anything more than that, ten years ago. The difference between us was, you enjoyed it. You enjoyed wrecking my marriage, while you pretended to be Grace's best friend. That's why I don't want you anywhere near Jack Pershing. You betrayed Grace. You'll betray him."

She leaped up, the sensuous mouth twisted, the beautiful face contorted with rage. "I love him. He needs a woman like me."

"A woman like you is the last thing he needs. He's got the kind of woman he needs."

"That simp of a portrait painter? Don't be ridiculous."

"I'm not being ridiculous. I know Jack. That's the kind of woman he needs, not someone who'll start playing games with his feelings when he needs her most."

"I told you I love him!"

"You don't love anyone or anything. The way you've treated Harry Quickmeyer proves it. I was there the night you put the moves on him. You've reduced him to an embittered wreck. You'll do the same thing to Pershing."

Quickmeyer's name had a strange effect on Louise. Her anger faltered. Her mouth went bitter. "You have no idea what goes on in a woman's heart. Can you conceive of the possibility I might love Harry Quickmeyer—and Jack Pershing?"

"No. I'm also not interested in how many angels can dance on the head of a pin. That was a favorite topic around Paris in the Middle Ages. I'm an American. I believe in a woman loving one man at a time."

A hairbrush whizzed by his head and smashed a vase on the fireplace. "Get out!" Louise screamed. "I'm going to tell Jack about this! I'm going to have you transferred to Pago Pago!"

"I don't think we have an army installation there."

"You can start one. Get out before I kill you." She pulled a pistol out of the drawer of her dressing table.

"Go ahead, shoot me," Bliss said. "It'll make my reputation in Paris."

He strolled out. The pistol sailed by his head and hit the wall in the corridor. He picked it up and broke open the chamber. It had six bullets in it.

He was flung back in memory to a night in Jolo: Grace, reeling around their quarters drunk, his .45 in her hand, swearing she was going to shoot him because he did not love her. She knew, she had known for years he really loved Louise Wolcott. He, just as drunk, inviting her to do the job: *Grace, Grace, I couldn't help it. I tried to stop it again and again. But it's over now.*

Half an hour later, Mile-a-Minute Murphy roared out of darkened Paris toward Lunéville at his usual speed. *A good day's work, General*, Sergeant Turner whispered.

The hell with the compliments, Bliss replied. If you've got any pull with God, tell him to make Ludendorff attack the French as soon as possible.

35. THE JEALOUS LOVER

ARTILLERY RUMBLED IN THE DISTANCE. THE LARGE Englishwoman behind the makeshift table glared at Polly Warden. "Do you or don't you admit that you frequently drove your ambulance into the battle zone without orders—often in defiance of orders?" she said.

"I don't remember defying any orders," Polly said. "The situation was so chaotic no one was giving any orders."

"The record contradicts this assertion. The Commandant claims you and Miss Sinclair were constantly insubordinate."

"How would she know? She was drunk most of the time."

"A lie!" cried the Commandant.

"Strike Miss Warden's remark from the record."

"Yes, Miss Bassett." The Stovepipe, acting as clerk of the court, scribbled furiously.

In their gritty barracks in Hazebrouck, Polly Warden was being court-martialed. Anita Sinclair's death had triggered what the British call a flap. A larger and more formidable version of the Commandant arrived from London to find out what VADs and their ambulances were doing in the middle of the street fight for Bailleul.

A lull had fallen over the battlefield. No one had any illusion that it was more than temporary. Gloom and anxiety pervaded all ranks of the British army. The casualties for the month of April had been as horrendous as those for March. There were no replacements except half-trained eighteen-year-olds.

None of this mattered to the Investigator, as everyone in Ambulance Group Three called their London visitor. She conducted her hearing with the aplomb of a governor general in a long-pacified colony. Polly swiftly became her explanation for the scandal. As an American, she was naturally undisciplined and disrespectful. She had infected Anita Sinclair with her insubordinate spirit.

"Miss Warden," said the Investigator, sucking in the corners of her mouth in a way she seemed to think was authoritative, "it is becoming more and more evident to me that you have failed to absorb the proper attitude toward the Voluntary Aid Detachment idea. Volunteers are expected to display a constant subordination toward the professional women who have been given responsibility for their direction. Under the circumstances, I think it would be best if you resigned immediately."

The Investigator glared at the rest of Group Three, who were sitting on their cots watching the proceedings. "Anyone else who fails to show a proper spirit of subordination will be dismissed in the same way."

After the Commandant and the Investigator departed, meekly followed by the Stovepipe, Bunky Gore-Blatchley and the others assured Polly they did not agree with a word of her condemnation. "I wish I had the guts to resign in protest," Bunky said. "I'd do it if it wouldn't look like I was running away because we're losing the war."

"It's one more piece of evidence that women are their own worst enemies," the Bomber said. "Only a workers' revolution can rescue us."

"The hell with that. Let's give the Yank a good send-off," Bunky said.

They pooled their resources and raised enough for a bottle of wine. After dark, they boosted the Bomber over the fence (the Commandant had reestablished the prison system for their compound) to buy some vin rouge in Hazebrouck. It took her two hours to return with the wine and a breathless tale of two Australians who wanted to spend the night with her. Bunky said that proved how desperate the Allies were; they were putting uniforms on the blind. The Bomber vowed the Gore-Blatchleys would be first on the firing squad list when the workers rose.

Divided by twelve, there was barely a mouthful of wine for each of them, but it was enough to raise their spirits above the general gloom and defeatism. "Let's say this for the Yank," Bunky said. "She's enabled us to believe there are such things as Americans. They're not a figment of the P.M.'s imagination. I only hope the rest of them, if they ever arrive, have as much pluck."

Polly felt tears on her cheeks. They had been through a lot together. "I wish I could stay with you until the war is won. You've helped me understand a little of what it means to be English. Your pride, which can be a bit obnoxious at times—"

"And why not, when you get a good look at the rest of the bloody world?" Bunky cheerfully demanded.

"—but above all, your courage. I think I've absorbed a little of it from you. I hope we'll meet on some road under shell fire before too long. Cheers!"

The next morning eleven subdued VADs each gave Polly an embrace and headed for the front. She trudged to the railroad station, where she waited for hours while troop trains full of French and Australian soldiers rolled into Hazebrouck. The Allies were betting that the Germans would make another lunge for the channel ports. Finally her Paris train was cleared for departure. She rode south with refugees from Bailleul and other towns, disconsolate people who had defeat stamped on their faces.

At the Gare du Nord, she hailed a taxi and headed for the Rue de Verneuil. She wondered about the sparseness of pedestrians on the streets and asked the cabdriver why. "The Paris gun," he replied, "the cannon our magnificent generals and fliers can't silence."

Polly had heard about the gun. As they drove along the Rue de Rivoli, a shell landed half a block ahead of them, only a few hundred yards from the Louvre. At least six people were killed. One was an old woman in black, another a blond young girl in a blue-and-gray school uniform. Polly stared at their blood-spattered bodies and thought, We can't lose this war. We can't let people who do things like this rule the world!

She had seen enough in Picardy and Flanders to know that the war was being lost. Beastliness did not seem to have much to do with winning or losing wars. God seemed indifferent on the subject.

The Americans were the only hope. Why were they doing nothing while the Germans smashed up the British and humiliated the French this way?

At the Kingswood house on the Rue de Verneuil, Martha and Eleanor were just sitting down to supper. Polly was greeted with acclaim and kisses. "Have they given you leave?" Eleanor asked.

"More like a permanent reassignment," Polly said. "I've been kicked out of another Allied medical department. There's nothing left for me now but the Italians."

They set a place for her at the table and began telling her what life was like in Paris under bombardment by the long-range gun. "People are leaving the city by the thousands," Martha said.

"I've been thinking of getting out of the city for several reasons," Eleanor said. "The long-range gun is just one of them."

She glanced uneasily at Martha as she said this. Polly sensed she was not being told the whole story. Eleanor said she was tired of working for the YWCA. Running canteens, figuring out how many doughnuts you can make from a thousand pounds of flour, was not her line.

"I told my father it would be good politics for him to create an ambulance group. He sent me the money, and we've bought the ambulances and signed a contract with the French Red Cross. I need someone to train drivers and run things in the field."

"I accept unconditionally!" Polly said. "Where will we operate?"

"I've talked to a French general named Duchêne. He's in command on the Chemin des Dames front," Eleanor said. "He says he can arrange things with the hospitals up there, above Soissons."

Soissons evoked memories of the Château Givry, Paul Lebrun, *le cafard*. "I'd rather work with Americans," Polly said. "Haven't they taken over a sector of the front yet?"

Eleanor rolled her eyes and waited until the maid had served coffee and dessert. "Instead of fighting, most of our troops are sitting around Lorraine, playing craps and poker. Everyone says General Pershing's a complete incompetent and should be sent home."

Polly remembered Malvern Hill Bliss telling her he was ashamed of his country. Did he really mean ashamed of General Pershing? The man who had kissed the French flag on the balcony of the Hôtel Crillon was refusing to fight? It did not make sense. "Who are these critics?"

Eleanor toyed uneasily with her hair. "One of them is Louise Wolcott. You'll probably be surprised to hear she and I have become friends. She and Pershing had a violent affair, until she found General Duchêne more attractive—and much more intelligent. She says she's thinking of putting a plaque on her house that says, 'Site of Pershing's first defeat.'"

Eleven months in France had made them women of the world, Polly thought. Last June they would have been shocked speechless to hear that General Pershing had succumbed to Louise Wolcott.

That night, as she was getting ready for bed, Martha Herzog knocked on her door. "Can I sign up as your first volunteer for the Kingswood Ambulance Group?" she asked.

"I'd love to have you. But I thought you were one of the essential cogs in the Services of Supply. I don't want to be court-martialed twice in the same week."

"I'm inclined to think I'd be happier elsewhere."

Polly decided to be blunt. "What's happened to Colonel Quickmeyer?"

"He transferred to intelligence and spends most of his time at Chaumont. He's also taken a dislike to American women."

"Louise Wolcott at work again?"

"Who else? She decided she preferred generals to colonels."

Martha launched a searing assault on Louise. She worried about her influence on Eleanor. Polly listened with disbelief as Martha told her about Natalie Barney's pursuit of Eleanor, which had sent her fleeing to Louise for protection. Natalie was the real reason Eleanor wanted to get out of Paris.

Polly fell back on her pillows. "Louise makes you wonder if you want to become a liberated woman."

"I'm not sure what I want to become at this point," Martha said. She flung herself into Polly's arms and wept fiercely, bitterly. "It's so awful to want someone, to know how much you could mean to him—and have him ignore you," she sobbed.

"Let him go, once and for all, Martha," Polly said. "You can't keep hurting yourself this way."

"How did you do it—with George?"

"He's the one who had to let me go. I hope he's done a good job of it. I'm sure he's found at least six mademoiselles by now."

Polly found George Eagleton a troubling name. She thought she would sleep like a child; it was the first time she had encountered anything that resembled a real bed in three months. Instead, she found herself tossing from one side of the down-filled mattress to the other, wondering if everything that had happened to her in France was a punishment for the way she had treated George, then angrily rejecting the accusation in a private court-martial that raged until 3 A.M.

The next week was full of frenzied activity. Recruiting drivers for the Kingswood Ambulance Corps was no problem. The difficulty was selecting the twenty best from six hundred and fifty volunteers. Many women were bored with the trivial jobs they had been able to find in Paris. Others wanted to get out of the city, not to avoid the bombardment but to escape the omnipresence of sex for sale on every boulevard and avenue. It made many American women profoundly uneasy.

For another week, under the supervision of expert French mechanics, the volunteers learned how to change tires and make simple repairs to the ambulance's Ford motors. They also acquired red-trimmed gray uniforms and temporary quarters in a former French barracks outside Missy, a French town six or seven miles east of Soissons. That city was a wreck from three years of artillery and aerial bombardment. Most of its twenty thousand civilians had long since fled, but it was full of French soldiers, some on generals' staffs, others in the medical and transportation departments. Soissons was another vital rail center connecting the northern and central fronts.

Polly and Eleanor had lunch at General Duchêne's headquarters, an elegant château a few miles outside Soissons. The General was almost too charming—and so were his staff officers. They were bored with their quiet sector and looked forward to the prospect of entertaining twenty American mademoiselles. Polly began wonder-

ing if she would have to establish curfews and bed checks to safe-
guard her drivers. Would she turn into the Commandant? An
appalling thought.

Back in Soissons, Eleanor produced an address and told Polly to
drop her off at the local headquarters of the YMCA. Harold Holloway was stationed there, working on plans for American canteens
in Champagne. Teasing, Polly asked if he was the real reason why
Eleanor wanted to leave Paris for Soissons.

"Harold is still very dear to me," she said, "but I find it difficult
to love someone who's never going to see action. Arthur Hunthouse's letters have made me see how combat matures a man."

There was an aura of unreality in this transfer of Eleanor's affection; it was a mental exercise, not an emotional commitment. There
were times when Polly found it hard to imagine Eleanor loving any
man, she was so relentlessly determined to seize the moral high
ground.

Just up the street was an imposing cathedral that had somehow
survived German shells and bombs. In the dim stillness, Polly knelt
and remembered Anita, Paul Lebrun, Marie Ribout, the poilus of
Château Givry, and the Tommies who had ridden with Ambulance
Group Three. She no longer had enough faith to pray for them in
the old-fashioned way. She simply tried to surround them with rev-
erence.

A voice whispered in her ear. "Mademoiselle Joyeuse." It was
Dr. Dolbier, the anesthetist from Château Givry. She leaped up and
embraced him. "At the hospital, things are so slow we're reduced
to becoming tourists," he said. "When are you coming back to work
for us?"

"Soon," Polly said, "but not in the operating room." She told
him about the ambulance group.

"We'll have a reception for you at the château as soon as possible. I'll have Madame Leclerc bake a cake, which I will personally
test to make sure it's free of strychnine. She never ceases denouncing
Americans these days. Your poor friend Shirley Miller broke down
under the lash of her sarcasm and went home. I must confess that
even I, who am still in love with you and therefore can't criticize

your country, don't understand why your soldiers aren't fighting."

"I can't understand it either," Polly said, again feeling a flush of shame that was almost as demoralizing as her old fear.

Back at the car, Polly found Eleanor pacing up and down. "I told Harold the way I felt," she said. "He didn't take it well, I'm afraid."

"Personally, Eleanor, I'd be delighted to be in love with someone who wasn't at the front."

"That's easy for you to say. You don't have anyone," Eleanor said. "I had to make a choice."

You don't have anyone. The words reminded Polly of the brutal way the war had deprived her of those she loved. The war seemed to insist that anyone who entered its vortex had to be prepared to face a strange loneliness. Though massed millions surrounded everyone, grief remained private, personal, creating a painful distance between individuals. The war was a jealous lover.

36. A TIGER IN THE BEDROOM

"AN AMERICAN INTELLIGENCE OFFICER CAME TO see me yesterday," General Denis Duchêne said as he pulled off his boots.

"Oh?" Louise Wolcott said. "What was his name?"

"Quickman or something like that. Sounded German."

"Quickmeyer?"

"Yes. He proceeded to tell me that he had become convinced the Germans were going to attack me on the Chemin des Dames. Have you ever heard anything more ridiculous? The staff and I had a good laugh over it at lunch."

Louise was lying in bed, awaiting the General. Most of the time she found him a satisfactory lover. Then there was the thought that every kiss, every caress, every thrust from General Duchêne was more revenge on John J. Pershing and Malvern Hill Bliss. Usually, that was enough to inflame her.

But Harry Quickmeyer's name extinguished all desire in her flesh. She felt cold, dry, almost dead. It was uncanny. It made her wonder if there were some things a liberated woman could not control. That was a demoralizing thought.

The General padded into the bathroom, continuing his derision through the half-open door. *Splash splash.* "The fellow claimed to have identified no less than fifteen German divisions in Laon, opposite the center of my lines. As if that could happen without our intelligence service finding out about it."

The General had a bad habit of talking too much before they made love. The subject was always military. Louise tried to excuse it. War was his business; he had spent his whole life in the army. But her interest in troop movements and tactics was minimal. She found it hard to follow the dispute with Pétain over *la defense élastique* versus the school of *attaque* to which Duchêne and Foch belonged.

Occasionally it was interesting—when Duchêne talked about his plan to win the war, which involved getting rid of Pétain. Together he and Foch would launch an offensive that would hurtle irresistibly across the Rhine. The Americans would lead the way. "Young fresh troops, unblooded," the General said. "They will consume the Germans' first lines of defense. After them will come the poilus to reap the fruits of victory. While the stupid British sit up to their necks in the mud in Flanders!"

Splash splash from the bathroom. The General had a bladder the size of an elephant. A pity the rest of him was not so generously endowed. "I thanked Colonel Quickman," Duchêne said, "and told him French intelligence would file his warning under 'idle speculations.'"

Hearty laughter. *Splash splash.* "Idle speculations!"

The General also had a bad habit of laughing too hard at his own jokes. It reminded Louise of what else she did not like about Frenchmen as lovers. They were always too pleased with their performances. They expected praise from a woman. If they did not get it, their passion swiftly cooled.

From that viewpoint, Americans were much more satisfactory. They were always so grateful for the privilege, so eager to please, so anxious not to disappoint. Even Pershing. In the bedroom he was a totally different man from the iron-jawed general seen by the public.

For a moment Louise was seized by the rage she had felt when Pershing stopped seeing her. Just stopped, without a note or a call of explanation. After a week of mounting fury, she had written a letter to Harry Quickmeyer. She could still remember every line.

> *Dear Colonel Quickmeyer:*
>
> Some men, when they are defeated in love, behave like men nevertheless. They do not whine, they do not tell tales, they do not slink around behind the scenes attempting to ruin the happiness of the woman they supposedly loved and the reputation of their successful rival. You differ from such men on all points. You have bored me with

your whines from the start. Now you have angered me with your tale-bearing, your skulking, your attempts to interfere with the love I feel for a man who is immeasurably superior to you in every way. I don't mean John J. Pershing; he was no more than an interlude, which unfortunately evoked all that is contemptible in your character. I mean General Denis Duchêne, commander of France's Sixth Army, a man who does not know how to slink, much less retreat. I suppose I should have foreseen all this from the positions you sought since you arrived in France—jobs that kept you as far behind the lines as possible. Surely you should have known a woman like me could never love an embusqué. But I suppose a consuming cowardice warps everything in a man, even his judgment.

Louise

General Duchêne emerged from the bathroom in his underwear, a smile on his wide handsome face. Here he comes, God's gift to women, whispered an aberrant voice in Louise's head. She banished it and opened her arms. "*Chéri*," she cooed. "I've been on fire all day, just thinking about you."

He slipped beneath the covers and cupped a big hand over her left breast. "Someday you must tell me of your indiscretions. Especially with a certain woman poet, also American."

"How do you know so much?"

"I've read your file in the Sûreté. It would have been indiscreet on my part to fall in love with someone who might be a German spy. Instead, I found only an explorer of love."

"Who's found a master of the art at last."

"Practice makes perfect," Duchêne said, his hand roaming her belly, her thighs.

When it was over, twenty minutes later, Louise breathed an ecstasy she did not feel. "My D'Artagnan," she murmured. "My Bayard."

"*Magnifique*," the General murmured. Whether he was congratulating her or himself was not clear. A moment later he began to snore. He usually slept for an hour or two and departed around 3 A.M., in time to be back with his troops in the dawn. He was famous for his fierce discipline. During the mutinies last year, he had executed several hundred rebels at drumhead court-martials.

Sleep eluded Louise. She sought satisfaction in imagining Harry Quickmeyer's humiliation at General Duchêne's headquarters. A double humiliation, really, since Quickmeyer knew Duchêne was her lover. There were always some compensations for disappointments. Life had a way of balancing things out. The account she had yet to balance was revenge against Malvern Hill Bliss. That would have to be profound—and exquisite.

To think she had once wanted to sleep with the loathsome toady. How did a man like that exercise such influence over Pershing? It had to be something peculiar they did to each other at West Point. Band of brothers! More likely a band of pederasts.

Snort, snuffle. General Duchêne was a world-class snorer.

The downstairs clock struck midnight. It was May 27, her birthday. Louise had no intention of celebrating it. She would be thirty-six, a terrifying age. Only four years from forty. But her life—at least her Paris life—had been full. She discounted the years in New York under the oppressive eyes of her mother and stepfather. But she had finally escaped to Paris and a lifetime of dramas.

The double window in her bedroom facing east suddenly glowed as if someone had cast a searchlight on it. A few seconds later a deep rumble rattled the glass. Louise got up and peered across darkened Paris. On the eastern horizon, the sky glowed again and again, and the rumble became continuous like the thunder of an angry surf. What was it?

Artillery! What else could it be? Were the Germans attacking? Of course not. All the newspapers said they were exhausted by their losses against the British. Was it the French? The Americans? Why hadn't the General told her about it? Perhaps he wanted it to be a surprise. Louise rushed back to the bed. "General," she said, "has your offensive begun?"

"*Uh? Offensive?*" It was a French as well as an English word.

General Duchêne struggled up on one elbow. The glow in the eastern window was almost continuous now, like the rumble. It flickered and glimmered like the flames of a gigantic conflagration.

"*La barbe! Putain!*" the General cried, springing out of bed. That meant Damn! Goddamn it!, not the sort of language Louise was used to hearing in her bedroom.

"Is there a mixup? Has your offensive begun at the wrong time?"

"My offensive, my ass!" the General roared. "It's the Germans!"

"Really, General."

"Shut up. Where the hell are my boots, my pants? Put on a goddamn light!"

With a trembling hand Louise lit a candle. Her Bayard was on his hands and knees, his large posterior high in the air, looking under the bed for his boots. It was not a very heroic pose.

The eastern window seemed to glow brighter. The rumble deepened. The General pulled on his pants and boots, snarling obscenities Louise had never heard before. Somehow she felt they were being aimed at her.

"What have I done to deserve such abuse?" Louise cried.

"*Putain Américaine!*" the General roared, grabbing Louise by the nightgown in a gesture that was totally lacking in love. "Listen to me," he said. "I wasn't here tonight. Understand? If you ever tell anyone I was here tonight, you'll disappear. I have men who take care of such matters for me. Do you understand?"

"You're hurting me!" Louise cried.

"*La barbe! Putain!*"

The General flung her aside and dashed for the stairs. Louise crashed into her dressing table and slid to the floor, makeup and perfume and toilet water spilling all around her. The eastern window continued to glow. The rumble of the guns had become part of Paris, like the daytime roar of traffic. But Louise was no longer part of Paris. Louise had become a terrified, humiliated American.

37. RETURN OF THE SUPERMEN

AT MIDNIGHT IN THE KINGSWOOD AMBULANCE Group's barracks outside Missy, sleep eluded Polly Warden. The hot humid darkness reminded her of New York in June. Last evening she and Martha had driven to the Château Givry for dinner with Dolbier and several other doctors. Now she found herself wishing she had visited Paul's grave. Here she was, posing as a battlefield veteran with her green drivers, and she was afraid to face the truth about her grief. It was still a raw wound. She was a coward, a fake!

The French had plenty of ambulances. Dolbier had assigned the Kingswood group to the sector of the front that had just been taken over by three British divisions. In the morning Polly and Martha Herzog had driven up there to meet the doctors and medical orderlies at the casualty clearing stations. The road ran through a countryside that seemed drenched in peace. Every little valley was lush with cornfields and grapevines. Picture-postcard villages nestled against the hills. North of the Aisne River, the woods were green on the slopes of the fifteen-mile ridge known as the Chemin des Dames, the Road of the Ladies. It seemed a particularly suitable name for a sector to be served by the first all-female American ambulance group.

There was no business at the casualty clearing stations. The orderlies sat around drinking tea and smoking pipes and cigarettes. Polly and Martha had to hunt down the doctors at their billets in the nearby villages. They were served tea and sandwiches, the British version of hospitality, and teased about the nonappearance of the American army, a topic the tactful French had avoided at Château Givry.

As they walked toward their ambulances in one village, a voice called "Miss Warden!" It was Anita's friend Major Rodney Blake, as handsome but more subdued than the last time she saw him. With him was a husky red-faced colonel. Blake had heard about Anita's death. They discussed it briefly, in stoical British style. "She told me not to cry for her if it happened. I've obeyed orders," he said.

He explained what the British were doing in the sector, serving under a French general. "Haig's trying to embarrass Pershing into putting his men under Foch's command. Naturally he expects to get his share of them if it works," he said with a wry grin.

"We're glad it's a quiet sector. The men need rest and recuperation badly," he added. The three divisions were refugees from the Fifth Army. They had been mauled in the fighting around Saint-Quentin and then shifted north, where they had taken another beating in the second German offensive.

"Let's hope it stays a quiet sector," growled the red-faced colonel. "Our local Napoleon, General Duchêne, has got us packed into a front only three miles deep with the Aisne River at our backs. I can't imagine a more perfect recipe for disaster."

"Let's hope we meet soon at a dance," Major Blake said as they parted. "*Not* in one of your ambulances."

Outside several villages, sergeants were drilling formations of the eighteen-year-olds Polly had seen marching into the lines in Flanders. Martha was shocked by how young they looked. Polly nodded ruefully. "All three divisions are probably full of green kids like these. The veterans are dead in Picardy."

She drove back to their quarters at Missy in a thoughtful mood. "I don't like the feel of things up there," she said.

That night after supper Polly called a meeting of the drivers in their barracks. For the first hour they rehearsed putting on their gas masks and breathing through them. Next they studied maps of the sector, pinpointing the British casualty clearing stations. She told them what it felt like to be in a poison gas attack and how frightened they would be under shell fire at first.

Now she lay awake, her body tense, almost braced, as if she expected someone to strike a blow at any moment. Woman's intuition or bad nerves? Only Dr. Giroux-Langin would know for sure, she thought wryly. As the field director, Polly had a private room at the head of the barracks. She lit a candle and began reading Paul Lebrun's smudged book of Verlaine's poems. She could hear his voice reciting them. She thought of Auvers and was swept by regret so engulfing it seemed moon-driven, tidal, sucking her down into a cold underworld of melancholy.

Suddenly the earth rumbled, the walls swayed. Polly flung on her uniform and rushed outside. For the entire length of the Chemin des Dames the night sky was alive with evil yellow light. She shuddered at the thought of how many guns were flinging poison gas and exploding steel into the French and British divisions jammed into forward trenches on the crest of the ridge.

She ordered Martha and the other drivers to make coffee and sandwiches. For three hours they sat in anxious silence while the bombardment continued. No calls came from the hospitals or casualty clearing stations. Were they being ignored because they were new and untried?

At 4 A.M. Polly telephoned Château Givry and asked for Dr. Dolbier. "There's nothing left beyond the Aisne," he said. "Casualty stations, command post—they've all been blown away. The French Twenty-first Division has surrendered en masse!"

"Should we move up?" Polly asked.

"I'm not sure it's safe," Dolbier said.

"We're not here to play it safe," Polly said.

Polly decided to take ten ambulances to Givry and leave Martha and the other nine drivers at Missy to respond to calls from other hospitals. As they drove through the predawn darkness Polly realized the German artillery had stopped firing. Instead, over the hills and valleys rolled the crackle and crash of machine guns and rifles. The stormtroopers were attacking.

On the main road, as they neared the gates of the château, a group of figures reeled past them. "*La guerre est fini!*" one of them yelled. They were poilus running away. Had they galloped the full nine miles from the front lines already? "Don't be too alarmed by those stragglers," she told the others as they got out of their ambulances. "In every battle some men panic."

In the main building, a distraught Dr. Dolbier was talking with Major Mahone, the *Agent de liaison*. "You shouldn't have come," Dolbier said to Polly. "Unless reserves arrive within the next two or three hours, we may be overrun by the German infantry."

"Surely the reserves will come up," Polly said.

"I fear our resident idiot, General Duchêne, had all his reserves in the front lines," Mahone said.

"Have you heard from the British?"

"They've called for ambulances—"

Dolbier and Mahone wanted Polly to head for Soissons or Paris. Instead she led her column toward the British sector. About 7 A.M. they reached Braine, a tiny town several miles south of the Aisne, dominated by a thirteenth-century Gothic church. As they drove up the main street, an English sergeant on a big black horse rode toward them. He had a wounded man in front of him and another wounded man behind him. "There's a lot more up the road," he said. "I've been runnin' them back here on this German colonel's horse for an hour now. I shot the bastard off him. Was he surprised!"

"Where are the doctors?" Polly said. Both men had severe body wounds. Their uniforms were soaked with blood.

"Who the hell knows? Take my lads. They're in the church," he said. "I figured even the Boche wouldn't shoot a man in a church."

They put the two wounded men in the ambulance in back of Polly and drove to the church. The crackle of small-arms fire seemed to be growing closer. Lying in the nave were another dozen Tommies, all badly wounded in the head or body. They quickly loaded three ambulances and sent them back to the Château Givry.

"Now take us up the road to the others," Polly said.

They followed their guide on the horse for about a mile, while the roar of battle grew closer. It was abruptly joined by another roar, as four bright red German Fokkers swooped down. Machine guns sparkled on the cowlings of their motors. They were strafing soldiers on the crest of a hill less than half a mile away.

The lead plane banked and hurtled toward the ambulances on the road. He came at them like a giant insect, barely fifty feet off the ground. Polly was sure he was going to strafe them. Was there any difference between strafing ambulances and firing high-explosive shells into Paris?

The Fokker's machine guns twinkled. A hail of bullets struck the sergeant and his horse, flinging both into a roadside gully. Polly leaped out and ran over to help. The horse was screaming and thrashing, blood spurting from a dozen wounds. The sergeant was almost as riddled. "Get a gun. Kill the poor—beast," he said, as his eyes glazed in death.

The six new drivers clustered on the edge of the gully, staring in horror at the dead man and the dying animal. "You'll see lots worse before this is over. Let's go," Polly said.

The plane roared toward them again. "Get down!" Polly cried.

They flung themselves into the grass by the side of the road. Instead of strafing them, the pilot dropped something that landed with a clunk a few feet from Polly's ambulance. It was a wrench, to which he had tied a note.

Captain Udet presents his compliments to the ladies of the American Ambulance Corps. He looks forward to taking them to dinner in Paris.

"Nuts to you!" Polly shouted as Udet banked above them, climbed straight into the sky, and dove exuberantly to strafe the British on the ridge again. His acrobatics seemed to sum up the arrogance of these apparently unbeatable supermen.

They climbed back into the ambulances and Polly led them up the road in search of the other British wounded. As they reached a grove of trees on a hill a few hundred yards away from the one the Germans were strafing, a soldier ran out to them. "Jesus, are we glad to see you!" he yelled. "We've got a hundred wounded men in here."

They piled them on top of one another in the ambulances like cordwood. There was no time to separate any but the most obviously dying. As Polly struggled with the last choices, the defenders of the other hill broke and ran down the reverse slope toward them. They raced across a valley full of yellow wild flowers. The German planes swooped down to strafe them. Scores went down in the murderous hail of bullets. On the crest of the hill appeared a line of

Germans, who quickly set up machine guns and added more vic-tims. Of the five hundred who made the dash, at least two hundred lay crumpled in the wild flowers.

An officer shouted orders to the fleeing soldiers. "Get into the woods and start digging!" He pulled out a map and studied it, then grabbed a runner and scribbled a message. "Take this to brigade headquarters and tell them where we are. The Bois de Santenay."

The man saluted and raced off. The officer took off his helmet to wipe his sweaty forehead and Polly recognized Anita's friend, Major Rodney Blake. He strode into the trees and saw Polly. "Miss Warden!" he said. "This isn't much of a dance, is it."

"I've heard better music," Polly said.

"You better clear out immediately," he said. "I'm the only officer in my battalion still alive. Possibly the only one in the division. Unless a miracle occurs, they'll overrun this hill in the next fifteen minutes."

"Major!" yelled one of the men. "Look what's bloody comin'."

He pointed into the sky beyond the hill they had just aban-doned. Moving toward them was a line of gray German observation balloons with huge white-edged black crosses on their sides. Trailing ropes ran down to the trucks that were towing them. "They mean artillery," Major Blake said to Polly. "Get going."

With seventy wounded jammed into the six ambulances, they headed for the Château Givry. As they went down the hill, shells started crashing into the trees where Major Blake and his men were hoping to make a stand. The ugly black explosions drifted into the blue sky. The balloons with the artillery spotters in the dangling gondolas came on inexorably, like the eyes of a gigantic monster with a million legs. Polly realized Major Blake was probably going to die in the Bois de Santenay.

The sitter in Polly's cab was a disconsolate sergeant with a shat-tered leg. "My poor kiddies," he muttered. "They never had a chance, miss. They was on top of us before we could aim our rifles. What's wrong with our bloody generals?"

The convoy reached Château Givry about 11 A.M. The day was even hotter than the night. A summer sun beat down on the parched grass. On the road outside, camions rushed past carrying reinforcements to the front. Maybe General Duchêne was not an idiot after all. The poilus would hold. The British would rush reinforcements to the Bois de Santenay and other strongpoints along the line. They could not let the Germans beat them again.

"They'll stop them. Don't worry," Polly told her anxious drivers. For a while she seemed to be a prophet. In the afternoon the front stabilized. Polly led her group on quick trips that brought in another two hundred wounded. She telephoned Martha Herzog at Missy and told her to bring the other ten ambulances to Givry at nightfall so the tired drivers with Polly could get some rest.

Telling herself she did not need sleep during a battle, Polly promptly led the fresh drivers into the darkness to collect more men along the British front. In Bouvancourt, a village several miles west of Braine, there were wounded men propped against the sides of houses, lying in doorways and in the street. Stretcher-bearers carried in more every second. Judging from the vicious crash of the rifles, the clatter of the machine guns, the battle was raging only a few hundred yards away.

The ambulances were soon as jammed as they had been at the Bois de Santenay. As they headed back to Givry, another convoy of ambulances came toward them. The leader slowed down and a British male voice shouted, "Is the town still in our possession?"

"Just barely," Polly said.

The British ambulances vanished down the road. Five minutes later, Polly saw two men ahead of her swinging flashlights. She stopped and found herself staring up at a lieutenant in a dusty gray serge uniform and steel helmet that curved down to his eyebrows. Behind him were a half dozen men in similar outfits.

"You are in German territory now, miss," the lieutenant said in excellent English. He turned his flashlight on the flag painted on the ambulance's fender. "You are American?"

"Yes."

"According to the articles of war, you are captives. But stormtroopers don't have time to worry about women and wounded soldiers. Go on your way. Don't come back to Bouvancourt again. We'll keep the ambulances that just went in. Look for us. We'll drive them down the Champs-Élysées in our victory parade."

Several of the Lieutenant's men laughed and fired their guns in the air as Polly pulled away. Her sitter, a private with a head wound, moaned in terror. He was probably dying. Hope began dying with him. The Germans were invincible.

Numb from mounting despair and lack of sleep, Polly kept going throughout the night and into the next day, making another six trips to the French and English fronts. Everywhere she saw signs of demoralization: more and more stragglers on the roads, frantic officers rounding them up, majors and colonels who could not tell her where the front was or what had happened to a certain casualty clearing station.

Around noon, they returned to Givry with more English wounded and began unloading them. The *Agent de Liaison* burst out of the château and ran toward them. "No, no!" he cried. "The hospital is being abandoned. The Germans are only a mile away."

The old man's usually impeccable blue uniform was a blood-smeared mess. "Forgive my appearance. I helped load the wounded. I sent your other ambulances to Missy." He began to weep. "Oh, mademoiselle, it's all over. They've beaten us. The poilus simply won't fight. There's no heart left in them."

Through Polly's exhausted mind filtered the realization that Paul's grave would be in German-held territory now. If she had not been responsible for her drivers and their cargoes of wounded men, she would have imitated Anita Sinclair that day. She would have driven across the chaotic battlefield, collecting stragglers, ferrying them up to places like the Bois de Santenay, daring the Germans to kill her.

Instead, she rearranged the wounded in the ambulances to make them as comfortable as possible and gave them drinks of water and shots of morphine. She told them where they were going and assured them they would find doctors soon. Meanwhile, they would pick up more ambulances at Missy and relieve the overcrowding.

Polly knew something was wrong the moment they entered Missy's winding main street. The town was full of poilus, many of them drunk. They were looting the houses—smashing windows, kicking in doors, beating up the terrified inhabitants who tried to resist them. They leered at Polly and her drivers and shouted insults. *"Putains américaines!"* was among the milder epithets.

Polly found Martha and the other nine drivers cowering in their barracks, defended by their three elderly French mechanics, armed with tire irons. "They took our ambulances and drove off yelling 'To Paris!' Martha said. "I thought they were going to rape all of us. They don't seem to like Americans."

"Mademoiselle! They're coming!" yelled one of the mechanics, pointing out a window.

A swarm of drunken poilus was pouring out of Missy, heading for the ambulances full of wounded men. Polly ran to the nearest ambulance and asked a sergeant for his gun. Groggy with morphine, he gave it to her. She hefted the big automatic. "How do you fire it?" she said.

He slipped the safety catch on the handle, and she strode around the ambulance to confront the oncoming mob. There were at least fifty of them. When they were about twenty yards away, she pointed the gun at them, holding it with both hands. "Stop!" she said in French. "I'll shoot the first man who takes another step."

"And I'll shoot the next one," said a voice behind her. Another sergeant, with a ghastly shrapnel wound in his leg, had managed to drag himself out of the front seat of his ambulance. He was too weak to hold his gun at arm's length. He leveled it on the hood of the ambulance.

"And I'll shoot the one after that," said a woman's voice. One of the drivers, a tall blonde from Minnesota named Alice Hedberg, aimed another gun.

For a moment the poilus swayed there, wondering if they were serious. They could have overwhelmed them in a rush, but the guns gave them second thoughts. Having run from the Germans, they were not feeling very brave. Polly sensed their mood and shouted, "These ambulances are full of English soldiers who've been wounded fighting for France! We're not going to let a bunch of drunken cowards throw them in the ditch."

"The English are fighting for gold, not for France," a tall thin poilu shouted.

"Spoken like a true friend of Germany!" Polly shouted back. "Anyway, at least they fight. They don't run away like sheep. Get out of here. Find your guns and go back to the front."

"*Putain!* We're going to Paris!" shouted the man who spouted German propaganda.

They milled around until they achieved some sort of formation and headed down the road to Soissons. Polly told the mechanics to gas up the ambulances and set the rest of the fuel on fire. They gave the wounded men more water and found three of them had died. They left the bodies in the barracks and headed for Soissons, with the extra drivers jammed into the front seats with the wounded sitters.

The road was crowded with fleeing civilians and clumps of poilus, the standard flotsam of defeat. About a mile outside Soissons, they saw their stolen ambulances, parked helter-skelter in a field. Nearby was a company of French cavalry, manning a roadblock; their horses were tethered in a grove of trees. The roadblock was reinforced by five or six machine-gunners on both sides of the highway. A grim-faced French major waved Polly to a stop and asked for her papers. She quickly proved she was the director of the group. "May we take our ambulances?" she said.

The Major nodded. "Perhaps you would also like to see how we deal with the swine who stole them?"

The Major led Polly and Martha and the extra drivers over to the ambulances. Farther into the field, another company of cavalrymen was guarding several dozen dirty haggard poilus. The Major shouted an order. They dragged six men out of the group at random and shoved them into the center of the field. Two more cavalrymen crouched behind a machine gun. The six men went down in a blast of bullets. One of them tried to rise. The machine gun chattered again. He lay still.

Two of Polly's drivers burst into tears. Martha Herzog turned her head away. Polly was too stunned to speak. Were those men—boys, really—any different from the poilus she had nursed at Givry, the men who called her Mademoiselle Joyeuse?

Concealing her revulsion, Polly asked where she could find a hospital for her wounded Englishmen. The Major shrugged. Hospitals were not his department. He was absorbed in shooting French-men to make them fight.

Polly decided it was madness to wander around the countryside with dying men. She left her column outside Soissons and drove to General Duchêne's headquarters. Surely his staff would know where she could find a hospital. Inside the mansion, once so crisply mar-tial, so polished and serene, officers scurried from room to room, shouting orders. Papers were being flung into boxes. They were get-ting ready to retreat!

Time and again Polly would find an officer who looked familiar and ask for help. Each time she was brushed aside. She finally stormed down a corridor into the office of General Duchêne him-self. He and two other officers had their backs to the door, ponder-ing a huge map on the wall.

"My reserves are gone!" Duchêne cried. "I committed four divi-sions. The Germans went through them as if they were cheese-cloth."

"General," Polly said. "Please excuse this interruption. I have sixty wounded men in my ambulances. No one will give me direc-tions to a hospital."

Duchêne glared wildly over his shoulder at her. "Who let this female in here? Arrest her!"

One of the officers in front of the map turned to look at Polly with an amused smile. "I'll take care of her, General. She's an old friend," he said.

It was Malvern Hill Bliss. He took Polly by the arm and led her into the corridor. "One of us always seems to be in trouble when we meet," he said.

Polly was too exhausted to make jokes. "What are you doing here? We don't need a general. We need soldiers who'll fight. Where's your men?"

"They're on their way," Bliss said. "Thanks to General von Ludendorff and his pals, the Yanks are finally coming."

38. DIE WACHT AM MARNE

MALVERN HILL BLISS'S DAY HAD BEGUN AT 4 A.M. with a phone call from Pershing. "I think it's time for you to go see Foch," he said. "The Germans gained thirteen or fourteen miles yesterday on the Chemin des Dames front."

"I'll be on the road in ten minutes," Bliss said, concealing his weariness. He had spent the previous ten days in the field with his division, experimenting with new assault tactics designed to deal with machine guns. "How are things going in our First Division show at Cantigny?" he asked.

"Beautifully. They took the town with only fifty casualties, and they're holding it against heavy counterattacks."

Cantigny was a village on high ground in Picardy, captured by the Germans in their attack on the Fifth Army. Foch had put the American First Division into the lines opposite it so he could send some French divisions to the British in Flanders. Yesterday, a regiment of the First Division had attacked the town and captured it. The news had flashed through the American Expeditionary Force at telegraphic speed.

Bliss's relations with Pershing were still strained. That did not stop Jack from using him as his son of a bitch in his negotiations with Foch. Bliss explained it to Captain Alden as they raced through the predawn murk toward Foch's headquarters. "The mere fact that he's sending me to Foch instead of going himself is a statement. But when he meets him face to face he can still be charming."

In Foch's headquarters at Clermont, staff officers spoke in hushed tones, as if they were visitors to a sickroom or attendants in a funeral home. There was no delay in ushering Bliss and Alden into the Generalissimo's office. He was bent over a map, conferring with General Pétain. That sphinxlike character did not even bother to say hello. "Where is General Pershing? He's the man we must see," Foch said.

"He sends his compliments," Bliss said, "as well as his deep concern about the situation on the Chemin des Dames. He wants you to know we're ready to commit all six of our trained *divisions* wherever you want them."

Foch's mustache quivered at Bliss's emphasis on divisions. He was being told that his plan to break the Lafayette and other divisions into brigades for distribution to the French army was hors de combat. "These *divisions* will take orders from you or any other general you designate, and we'll do our best to execute them without question. I think we demonstrated what Americans can do yesterday at Cantigny."

"A pinprick," Foch snapped. "You think a successful attack by one regiment on a two-mile front can counterbalance what we're facing on the Chemin des Dames? The Germans are on the high road to Paris! They'll throw in every soldier within reach to exploit this breakthrough. Have you proven you can stand against their best attack divisions?"

"Generalissimo," Bliss said, carefully curling mockery around the word, "you don't have much choice. I'm afraid you'll have to take it our way—or leave it and try to explain to Premier Clemenceau and the French people why you refused this offer. Six American divisions are a hundred and eighty thousand men. That's almost twice as many soldiers as Napoleon commanded at Waterloo."

Hatred glittered in Foch's tired eyes. The raison d'être of his supreme command, his deal with the British to insist on American amalgamation, was unraveling. General Pétain, who despised Foch for a dozen reasons, not the least of which was the conviction that he himself was a far better general, yanked on the final threads. "I see no reason why we should reject this offer," he said. "An American division can occupy the front of three French divisions. Put them in line while I build up reserves for a defense in depth. If we fight this battle prudently, we may teach Ludendorff a lesson from which he'll never recover."

"Prudence, prudence!" Foch raged. "Wars aren't won by prudence. They're won by attacks. We must build up a reserve, not to be chewed up in the next German offensive but to strike a blow at this salient Ludendorff is creating. It's a gigantic trap if we have the courage to spring it!"

Foch pounded the map with his fist. Much as he disliked the man, Bliss had to admit there was something to what he was saying. The German advance was a huge bulge reaching toward Paris. If the French could hold the corners of the bulge, in the north at Reims, in the south at Soissons, they might bag a half million Germans.

The Sphinx stonily pointed out the flaw in Foch's strategy. "The poilus won't attack. It will be a miracle if we can persuade them to hold the line. That's why the American divisions are needed immediately."

Foch sank into a chair and eyed Bliss. "Is this another offer like the one I received from Pershing two months ago? One that comes with hidden terms?"

"I think you're the one who produced the hidden terms, Generalissimo."

"Divisions," Foch muttered, as if the word was an obscenity. "The commanders, including yourself, will obey every order without question?"

"It's a pledge of honor, Generalissimo," Bliss said.

He was assailed by a horrendous fear that he was risking his division, his men, with that promise. But there was no time to organize an independent American army and grandly take over a sector of the front. He found himself wishing he had not worsened this bitter feud with his big mouth.

"I'm on my way to General Duchêne's headquarters," Pétain said to Bliss. "Come along. It might help to see firsthand how the battle is developing."

At Soissons they found a frantic Duchêne pacing the floor of his headquarters like a man about to blow out his brains. Pétain was merciless. Briefly introducing Bliss, he proceeded to flay Duchêne alive for refusing to take his advice about an elastic defense. "The Germans demonstrated its worth last year on this very front," Pétain said. "You and your hero Foch are too proud to learn from the enemy. You sit like stupid puffed-up frogs in your little pond, croaking *Attack*, while the Boches' nets are coming down on your heads. Now he's dining on your flesh!"

As they turned to the situation map to get a grasp of the battle, Polly Warden burst in on them. Bliss escorted her beyond the range of Duchêne's wrath, took her to Captain Alden, who was waiting in an anteroom and told him to find directions to a hospital for her—at gunpoint, if necessary.

She thanked him in the surliest possible manner. Either she was still angry at him for his attempt to rescue her from danger in Picardy or she was too tired to be charming. Her eyes were glazed with exhaustion.

"When's the last time you had some sleep?" he said.

"Two days ago," she said. "I don't need a lecture about it. Everywhere I've been in this miserable war men have been telling me to run and hide. I'm sick of it! I've had more bullets and shells shot at me than your whole damn division!"

Bliss leaned into the blast this time. "Sleep may be as antediluvian as my other ideas. But I think you need some."

She rubbed her eyes like an exhausted child. "I'm sorry," she said. "It's so awful up there, a total rout. Ten times worse than Picardy or Flanders. Why have you waited so long to *fight*? I'm so ashamed I want to die!"

He realized she meant every word of that. "Someday I hope I can explain why we've waited," he said. "In the meantime, give us a chance to perform before you kill yourself."

Bliss went back to Duchêne and Pétain. The Sphinx was flaying him again. Duchêne had failed to blow up the bridges over the Vesle River, five miles south of the Aisne. He thought Pétain was going to send reinforcements over them. "Idiot!" Pétain said. "We might have held on that river for a few days. Now we've got nothing left but the Marne."

"The Marne?" Duchêne said. The Germans had gotten to the Marne in 1914. It was a symbol of the last ditch to everyone in France. To let the Germans get there again struck him as madness. "It will demoralize the country!" he cried.

Bliss was inclined to agree with him. Beyond the Marne there were no natural barriers between the Germans and Paris. If they crossed in strength the war was over. "Demoralize—or galvanize," Pétain said. "Either way, we have no choice."

Back in Paris, Bliss found an exultant Pershing at his residence on the Rue de Varenne. "Foch called. He's taking all six divisions."

Jack listened impassively to Bliss's account of his confrontation with the Generalissimo. Beyond a skeptical grunt, he made no comment on the pledge of obedience. That was going to be Bliss's problem. He seemed almost as uninterested in his report on Pétain's meeting with the panicky Duchêne.

"They're coming on like a brigade of steamrollers," Bliss said. "Tomorrow they'll be on the Marne."

Pershing nodded, as if Bliss had just told him it might rain tomorrow.

If their green troops, still dependent on French artillery and air support, could not stop the Germans on that mystic river, John J. Pershing would go down as one of the blunderers of the millennium. A footnote in the international best seller, *How Germany Won the Great War* by General Erich von Ludendorff, might mention that according to General Foch, who signed the surrender for the Allies, Pershing was advised by a certain Malvern Hill Bliss, an even more *incroyable* dunderhead.

"If we don't stop them, Jack, it's all over," Bliss said.

"We'll do it," Pershing said. His jaw looked like the Rock of Gibraltar. Bliss struggled to absorb some of this granitic faith in Pershing luck into his own less stable nervous system.

I'm so ashamed I want to die, Polly Warden had sobbed. To his amazement, those words did more to steady Bliss than his shaken faith in Pershing luck. Repealing that cry, deflecting its potential tragedy, became as serious as defying death's dark challenge beside Pershing, as important as winning their awesome gamble for the future of the world.

BOOK V

39. WITH THE HELP OF GOD—AND A LOT OF DEAD MARINES

BACK IN LUNÉVILLE, MALVERN HILL BLISS DISCOV-
ered the prospect of Germans on the Marne had
produced hysterical paralysis in France's already creaky transportation system. Frantic telegrams to Foch and Pétain produced
promises but nothing with wheels. Finally, into Lunéville's central
square rolled proof of their desperation: some sixty green-and-white-
trimmed Paris buses.

Bliss crammed the first battalion of Ireland's Own and half the
regiment's machine-gun battalion aboard the stubby sputtering
vehicles, whose top speed was twenty-five miles an hour. He told
Chief of Staff Fairchild and his brigadiers to start marching the rest
of the division behind them and headed for Château-Thierry, the
enemy's probable objective on the Marne. He knew a thousand men
could not stop the German army. He could only hope other divisions were having better luck with their railroad connections or
knew how to conjure trucks out of the bureaucratic fog.

They reached the sprawling red-roofed rail center overlooking
the Marne in time to see thousands of beaten poilus streaming
across the last remaining bridge shouting, "la guerre est fini!" Bliss
deployed his machine-gunners and most of his infantry along the
south bank below the bridge and sent a strong patrol commanded by
Lieutenant Eagleton and Sergeant O'Connor into the city. Gunfire
soon broke out. Bliss found Eagleton and his men occupying a stone

house a few blocks from the bridge, exchanging fire with two or three hundred Germans. The firefight continued for the better part of an hour, with the stormtroopers showing no inclination to attack. Bliss ordered Eagleton to withdraw to the south side of the river. The Germans did not make the slightest effort to pursue them, nor did they show any interest in seizing the bridge, which Bliss permitted French engineers to dynamite.

For the next two days, the fifteen hundred Lafayettes remained the only military obstacle between the Germans and Paris. They did nothing more exciting than exchange shots with two or three more German patrols. There was no sign of the main enemy army, with its massed battalions and awesome artillery. Bliss gradually realized the stormtroopers had run out of steam, not too surprising after lunging forty miles in seven days. General von Ludendorff was not going to try to cross the Marne until he rested his elite troops and consolidated the enormous salient he had carved in the last week. Meanwhile, trucks, trains, Paris buses, and old-fashioned shoe leather gradually delivered the rest of the Lafayette Division and three other divisions to the front.

The Paris newspapers, desperate for good news, crowed nonsensically about the way the Americans had stopped the enemy offensive. While the Germans regrouped, the French attempted to do likewise. Bliss was summoned to the headquarters of General Jean Degoutte, who had replaced General Duchêne as the commander of the French Sixth Army. People said Degoutte had the temperament of a Chinese cook, although his carefully waxed mustaches made him look more like a mandarin. His opening gambit was a rehash of the old amalgamation recipe. *La critique*—the emergency—made it vital to slice the American divisions into wedges, he said, and sandwich them into what was left of the Sixth Army.

"I'm sorry, General," Bliss said. "The Lafayette Division will be happy to take over any part of the front you suggest, as a unit. But I will not allow it to be carved into little pieces and fed into your divisions. That exceeds the agreement we made with Generalissimo Foch."

"The same thing goes for us," said Colonel Wiley Parker, chief of staff of the Second Division. The burly, gimlet-eyed Parker had begun the war as a captain and leapfrogged from Chaumont to his current job, acquiring a Napoleonic brusqueness along the way.

Degoutte shrugged and turned to a wall map. With crisp authority he assigned the Second Division nine kilometers of the front west of Château-Thierry and the Lafayettes another nine on their left, with the French 125th Division between them. "Understand, gentlemen, the line must be held at all costs. Our reserves are gone."

"We want to do more than hold the line," Parker said. "We want to attack."

A brief smile played across Degoutte's haughty face. "We'll try to give you an opportunity as soon as possible."

Bliss felt uneasy. Degoutte was another member of the Foch School of Attack. Mentioning the word to one of these characters was like giving a drunk a bottle of bourbon for his birthday.

The Second Division and the Lafayette Division dug in west of Château-Thierry under the guidance of General Degoutte's staff officers. During the next two days, the Germans launched a half dozen probing attacks along the Lafayette's front. The three regiments Bliss put in the line fought well, beating the stormtroopers back with accurate rifle and machine-gun fire. Ireland's Own even extended its front, not an easy thing to do under fire, when the 125th French Division on their right flank melted away.

Instead of taking advantage of the disappearance of the 125th Division, the Germans pulled back. For the next four days, there were no attacks, only mortar and artillery fire, which took their usual toll. The German shells were mostly .77 millimeter whizbangs, the kind used as harassing fire. The barrages did not have the concentrated fury of the prelude to an attack. The German infantry remained out of sight in the towns and woods they had captured, a mile or so away.

Bliss decided they needed information and ordered a raid to bring back some prisoners. A party led by Douglas Fairchild captured a German lieutenant, who told them the offensive that had begun on the Chemin des Dames was over. They had been ordered to go on the defensive. Fairchild confirmed the statement from what he had seen in the woods where they captured the *leutnant:* the Germans were digging fortifications and siting machine guns by the dozen.

The following day, General Degoutte ordered the Lafayette Division to feint an attack while the Second Division's marine brigade assaulted the woods known as the Bois de Belleau and the nearby town of Bouresches. Bliss jumped in his car and drove to Sixth Army headquarters, where he gave General Degoutte a summary of the German lieutenant's statement. The Chinese cook asked why Bliss had driven twenty miles to tell him what he already knew.

Pointing to the wall map, Bliss argued that attacking Belleau Wood and Bouresches made no sense. They were not on the road to Paris. The prime route to the capital was east of Château-Thierry— a good twenty kilometers from Belleau Wood. Degoutte fingered his mustaches and admitted Bliss had a point. But Colonel Wiley Parker had repeatedly asked him for permission to attack. Everyone in the French army was eager to see the American concept of open warfare displayed for their "education."

The Chinese cook produced an oriental smile. The interview was over. Bliss rode to the headquarters of the Second Division, in a farmhouse about two miles behind the front. He found Wiley Parker and James Harbord, until a week ago Pershing's chief of staff, poring over maps, while the division commander, Major General Omar Bundy, stood to one side, more like a sentry than a participant.

One of Tasker Bliss's selections, Bundy was a fussy little man with a Pétain-sized mustache and a haughty manner. Harbord had a brand new star on his shoulders. Pershing had appointed him commander of the Second Division's marine brigade. No one in the army had been enthused about letting the marines into the AEF. Bliss wondered if Pershing had appointed Harbord their commander to make sure they did not try to pull their usual grandstanding act and claim they won the war singlehanded.

"I thought you fellows might want to take a look at this report of a raid we pulled off last night," Bliss said. "Have you sent any patrols into Belleau Wood?"

"Haven't had time," Wiley Parker said. "We got the order to

attack this morning. The French tell us the Germans have only occupied the northeast corner of the wood."

"They don't know where half their own army is," Bliss said. "You're going to take their word for what the Germans are doing?"

Parker shrugged. "Marines are trained to fight in the woods."

"Against guys with machine guns and hand grenades, backed by artillery?" Bliss said.

Parker grew testy. "General. Have we missed something? Has General Pershing made you commander of both divisions?"

"I believe I'm the senior officer in this sector, Bliss," Bundy said in his piffling way. If Tasker Bliss was the personification of the military bureaucrat, Bundy was the quintessential peacetime post commander, someone whose mind could not transcend polished boots and precedence based on seniority.

Fuming, Bliss drove back to his headquarters, issued orders for the fake attack, and told Captain Alden to find a hill on their right flank from which he could watch the marine assault. Around 4 P.M., while the Lafayette's artillery thundered and two battalions of South Carolinians pretended to assail a hill two miles to the west, they drove to the site Alden had selected, a small grove of old trees on the crest of a ridge with a good view of the southern edge of Belleau Wood, the village of Bouresches just to the west, and the fields around them, which were planted in corn and wheat. Their French liaison officer and Machine-Gun Joe Perry, the new commander of Ireland's Own, joined them.

At four-thirty the Second Division's artillery opened up with a tremendous crash. But most of the shells hurtled over the mile-square forest to fall far behind it. The French and American gunners took twenty minutes to adjust their ranges. For another ten minutes they actually landed some shells in Bouresches and Belleau Wood. Then it was five o'clock and the timetable silenced the artillery. Out of their foxholes came the marines, two battalions of them, two thousand men, advancing in four waves, five yards apart, twenty yards between each wave, through the waist-high young corn and wheat.

Bliss was shocked by how young the marines were. These were not the swaggering lifers who demolished bars brawling with soldiers

414 / THOMAS FLEMING

and sailors. They were nineteen- and twenty-year-olds who had signed up for the Great Adventure a year ago. He could see the tension and determination on their boyish faces. Occasionally, across the distance drifted the shrill blast of an officer's whistle, the fainter echo of a shouted command.

For a hundred yards they advanced without a bullet or a shell fired at them. "*Mon Dieu*," gasped the French liaison officer, lapsing into his native tongue. "No one has attacked like this on the Western Front since 1914."

Ten seconds later, Bliss saw why. Across the fields of green corn and brown wheat came a sound like a thousand snapping sticks as German machine-gunners pressed their triggers. The whole first wave of marines melted into the ground. Still they kept coming, and the snapping popping sounds continued to pour from Bouresches and the otherwise silent green woods. Huge swaths were cut through the next wave, and still the third wave kept coming for another hundred yards, to meet the same brutal fate.

"It's fucking insanity!" Joe Perry said. "Haven't these stupid bastards even heard of the machine gun?"

Bliss was jamming the cups of his field glasses so hard against his eyes they were practically boring into his skull. It was Malvern Hill and Gettysburg all over again. How could any American commander commit this bestiality?

By now the marines in the fourth wave were thinking for themselves, discarding the idiot orders that had sent 80 percent of their friends to death and disfigurement. On the left flank they were flat on their faces in the wheat, no longer even trying to advance. On the right flank, where the American line bent closer to the woods, they had a shorter distance to go and they covered the last yards in a wild rush that cost them more casualties but at least got them into the cover of the trees.

Until darkness fell, Bliss stayed on the hill watching small groups of marines try to get into Bouresches. Every time they were cut down. Machine-gun and rifle fire and the crash of hand grenades drifted from Belleau Wood, where the Germans were undoubtedly taking advantage of superior numbers to annihilate the handful who had gotten into the trees.

Bliss went back to his headquarters and summoned the Office Ballet Dancer to take a letter to John J. Pershing. He described the attack on Belleau Wood as the most appalling piece of military stupidity since the charge of the British Light Brigade in the Crimean War in 1854. He urged Pershing to relieve Bundy, Harbord, and Wiley Parker and order the division to abandon the attack. The miserable square mile of trees was not worth the life of a single American. They needed to husband every man to meet the next German offensive.

Ten minutes later, Captain Alden appeared with the letter in his hand. "General," he said, "I'm afraid this is another one you shouldn't send."

"Why not?" Bliss roared.

"I've been talking to some newspapermen. They're calling the attack on Belleau Wood the bravest thing Americans have ever done. It *was* tremendously brave, General."

"And incredibly stupid!"

"The bravery is what people will remember. It's what I'll remember. I just finished writing a letter to my father about it. We're showing the whole world what Americans are ready to do to win this war."

"If you believe that, my attempt to educate you as an army officer is a failure! Bravery is assumed in this business. Brainpower is what's lacking most of the time. Haven't you heard me say an officer who throws away the lives of his men is no better than a common murderer?"

Alden gazed forlornly at him, like a loving father regarding a son having a tantrum. It was a bizarre reversal of roles. "General, please don't send this letter. Hold it for a day or two. Let's see what happens in Belleau Wood. If the place isn't worth anything, maybe the Germans will retreat. Even if they don't, by then you might have some idea of what General Pershing thinks about the situation."

"I want to influence what he thinks. It's part of my job!"

"Is it, General?"

The words were spoken so softly, so sadly. There was nothing but concern and anxiety on the young face, redoubling the force of the question. Slowly, bitterly, Bliss admitted Captain Alden was right. He was presuming his friendship entitled him to tell John J. Pershing how to run the American Expeditionary Force. Pershing—and a lot of other people—might have some reservations about that idea. "All right. We'll save it for two days," he said.

40. SLAUGHTERHOUSE SIX

"ALERT! ALERT! ALL AVAILABLE AMBULANCES will proceed immediately to the Evacuation Depot on the Lucy–Torcy road nine kilometers west of Château-Thierry. An emergency situation exists there. Gas casualties are numerous."

Polly Warden roused her exhausted drivers from fitful sleep in the big dormitory they shared with some fifty French nurses. For two weeks they had been working sixteen hours a day, ferrying American wounded from the Second Division and the Lafayette Division to this base hospital south of the Marne.

They joined a long line of ambulances heading for the front. MPs routed all of them to the field hospital that was servicing the marine brigade, fighting in Belleau Wood. Polly had never seen so many ambulances. There must have been at least a hundred of them, in a winding brown procession along the road to the huddle of tents with red crosses on them.

When her ambulances got to the muddy field behind the tents, Polly breathed the sickening odor of mustard gas. She had seen occasional victims in the hospital at Givry. But here were almost a thousand of them: lying in the dirt; stumbling aimlessly, pursued by orderlies; raving deliriously, strapped to stretchers. They had strips of cloth over their seared eyes, making them look like players in some nightmare version of blind-man's buff.

A grim-faced medical corpsman told her what had happened. "The Germans caught the second battalion of the Sixth Marines as they were withdrawing from the woods. They covered them with a blanket of the stuff."

A young doctor rushed up to them, his eyes streaming. "Put on your gas masks," he said. "We just had an orderly collapse and die after he spent half an hour in a tent with some of the worst cases. Their uniforms are soaked with gas."

"You ought to put your own mask on, Doctor," Martha Herzog said.

"You're absolutely right," he said. "But it's out of the—the—question."

He coughed violently, gulped down air, and rushed back into the tent. Polly and her drivers pulled on the hated masks and helped load their ambulances. They tried to limit the delirious cases to one per ambulance. The orderly told her a number of earlier drivers had refused to take sitters; they were afraid of the gas. "We'll take them," Polly said.

The young doctor came back, coughing violently. "I—I've been told to hitch a ride with you. I—I'm afraid I've got a dose of this stuff."

"You can be my sitter," Martha Herzog said, leading him to her ambulance.

Polly's sitter was a young marine lieutenant. He sat rigidly, staring ahead as if he could see through the strip of cloth over his eyes. His breath came in rasping gulps. "Where are we going?" he asked.

"To a French hospital. They've had plenty of experience with mustard gas. I used to be a nurse in one. They'll take good care of you."

"Then they give you—dark glasses and a white cane—and send you home?"

"No. In about a week you should be seeing normally."

"My God. Why didn't they tell us that? All of us—think we're blind for life. One of my sergeants blew his brains out."

They joined the procession along the narrow road. Trucks carrying food and ammunition rumbled past them toward the front, almost crowding the ambulances into the ditch. "Are we winning this battle?" Polly asked.

The Lieutenant shook his head. "It's rifles—against machine guns," he croaked. "We got slaughtered—the first day—and we're still getting slaughtered."

At the crossroads where Polly expected to turn east toward the Marne, a French military policeman was stopping each ambulance. When she told him her group was going to the French hospital at Lizy, he shook his head. "They're full. Stay on this road to American Evacuation Hospital Six at Juilly."

The Americans had finally set up a hospital. It was in a three-story sandstone central building that had been some sort of school. Around it the medical corps had built a series of wooden wings. Polly helped her sitter out of the cab. "Take me around—to the other ambulances. I want to tell—the boys we're not—blind for life," he said, still gasping for every breath.

Polly led the Lieutenant to each ambulance, where he croaked the good news to the occupants. It produced cries of relief from many men. Putting their gas masks on again, Polly and her drivers helped to unload their gasping passengers and carry them into an admitting ward, where several hundred earlier cases were lying on the floor. The Lieutenant stumbled around, croaking Polly's good news to all of them. "Just put up—with it—fellows. In a week you'll be able—to shoot a German—at a thousand yards."

The young doctor, still coughing violently, seized Polly's arm. "Who told him that?" he said. "It may not be true for him. He got a double dose of the stuff. Hero type. Wouldn't put on his mask till all his men were accounted for."

Not for the first time, Polly felt the pain of ignorance. She was still only an amateur in the world of medicine. "I'm sorry," she said. "I was trying to help."

The doctor relented and smiled cheerfully. "On the other hand, you may be right. We doctors don't know everything. We just pretend we do. For instance, I didn't know there was such a thing—as a woman's ambulance group. Miss Herzog here has enlightened me—marvelously."

He doubled over in another spasm of coughing. "You'd better sit down and stop talking, Doctor," Martha said. His name was Isaac Pinkus. He was with the Lafayette Division. They had taken over the fighting in Belleau Wood.

Polly excused herself and asked a nurse where she could find the hospital's chief medical officer. She followed directions to a small cubicle in one of the wooden wings, where a bulky gray-haired man sat behind a desk. His name was Hoar, and he was both a doctor and an army colonel. He almost levitated when he heard Polly had twenty ambulances to offer him. "We could certainly use you," he said. "We're relying on the division ambulances, and they don't have nearly enough."

By the end of the day, after two more trips to the field hospital to pick up gassed marines, it was all arranged. The Kingswood Ambulance Group was part of U.S. Army Evacuation Hospital Six. They cleared some orderlies out of a nearby barracks and handed it over to Polly and her drivers. Everyone was delighted, especially Martha Herzog, who looked forward to seeing more of Dr. Pinkus. "I never realized a yid could be so intelligent," she said.

It took Polly a moment to remember that German Jews such as the Herzogs took a dim view of more recent Jewish immigrants from Russia and Poland, who spoke Yiddish and lacked *Kultur*. "I never realized you were such a snob," Polly said.

"Only about brains," Martha said. "That's the essential component in my ideal man."

Polly was tempted to remind Martha that her last intelligent man, Harry Quickmeyer, had broken her heart. But she refrained from pontificating. Who was she to advise people on their love lives?

The next morning, before they could respond to any calls, Colonel Hoar summoned Polly to his office and informed her that henceforth the Kingswood Ambulance Group would stay at least ten miles from the front. Chaumont did not want any women drivers killed by German shells. It would look terrible in the newspapers.

Infuriated, Polly pointed out that most field hospitals were within five miles of the front. Hoar said they could meet division ambulances on the road and transfer men, saving miles of driving. Polly vowed to protest the order to General Pershing himself. Hoar told her to go right ahead—but in the meantime she and her drivers would observe the ten-mile rule. "You're part of the U.S. Army now," he said with a condescending smile.

There was only one solution: find someone who outranked Colonel Hoar and the faceless bureaucrats at Chaumont. Polly asked Dr. Pinkus for directions to General Bliss's headquarters. She found him operating from the basement of a bombed-out château about a mile behind the front. A covey of cars, motorcycles, and trucks surrounded the house. Inside, Captain Alden greeted her warmly, but he looked dubious when she explained why she was there.

"He's in a terrible mood," he said. "I'm not sure this is a good time to bother him."

Polly sat down in his office. "I'll wait until the General has a free moment. I've got all day."

Ten minutes later she was face-to-face with Malvern Hill Bliss. "Well, well, well, if it isn't the terrible-tempered angel of mercy. Or angle of death. Which do you prefer?" he said.

"The first, naturally, General. How are you?"

"I'm absolutely miserable. What can I do for you?"

"I know you're fighting a war and what I'm about to ask isn't truly vital. But it's important to me—and the women of my group."

She told him about the regulation from Chaumont. He did not look very interested. "Are you still ashamed of your country?" he said. "Do you still want to die of sheer embarrassment?"

"No," she said. "I'm tremendously proud of the way we've stopped the Germans."

He laughed violently, as if she had said something that amused him in a bitter way. "Do you like to fuss over men who've been shot to pieces, gassed, demoralized by rotten leadership? Do you get some sort of kick out of it?"

"Of course not," Polly said.

"Do you talk to your wounded? Do you try to find out what's really going on?"

"I try to give them a little hope. I don't pretend to know enough about tactics or strategy to understand what's happening."

"Why don't you try to find out? Somebody ought to know, someone who can tell the story someday. Or are you just looking for excitement? Do you like to risk getting killed for the hell of it?"

Polly found that question extremely disturbing. "I don't want to get killed any more than you do, General. But I do want to risk getting killed. I could give you an abstract explanation for that: all about the importance of women showing they can share danger and death with men because otherwise we'll never be truly equal. But it might be simpler to say I want to help fight this war and win it in memory of someone we both loved—Anita Sinclair."

The name had a terrific impact. He lowered his head, and for a moment Polly thought he was going to weep. "I don't want to be reminded of her," he said. "I don't want to be reminded of the way I sneered at English generals. Now I'm watching American generals do the same moronic things. You should change the name of that evacuation hospital to Slaughterhouse Six!"

Polly finally grasped what was tormenting him. The realization left her numb. "Is it really that bad?"

He looked past her, out the window. "If I were you I'd get out of this war right now. A woman can't handle the stupidity, the madness of it. Get out while you're still sane. Otherwise you'll end up like Anita."

"I can't get out of it any more than you can," Polly said. "People I loved have died in it. Including Anita. If you'd only stop thinking of me as some fragile creature that has to be protected, I think we could resolve this very minor matter and get on with the war."

She braced herself for an explosion. But General Bliss seemed to regard her impudence as a logical part of the conversation. "You're right," he said.

He sat there, still looking away from her, drumming his fingers on the desk for a full minute. In the lines on his face, his tight soldier's mouth, his proud deep-socketed eyes, she sensed a profound sorrow that went beyond the personal. It was a philosophical sadness, a combination of bitter knowledge and harsh disappointment in life itself.

Polly felt a vibration of sympathy in the root meaning of the word, a similar blend of grief and memory. *Cafard,* whispered a voice in her head. She found herself wishing she could comfort this man—and ask him for wisdom and knowledge about the war in return.

Bliss's fingers stopped drumming on his desk. A different man was looking at her: smiling, genial, full of southern charm. "Okay," he said. "I'll beard the lions of Chaumont for you."

He summoned a stenographer and dictated a letter to Colonel Hoar, informing him that he was countermanding the ten-mile regulation. The Lafayette Division's medical department had advised him wounded soldiers could not possibly benefit from an extra transfer en route to the hospital. As for the danger of the Kingswood drivers getting killed, so what? If it happened, it would only "add heroines to the heroes that are being created on the battlefield every day."

"How do you like that?" Bliss asked. "I can write bushwah as good as any of these damned reporters."

Polly was amazed by the transformation. There seemed to be two people warring for possession of General Bliss's soul. One was the anguished soldier she had met when she entered his office. The other was this smiling cynic. Which was the real man?

Bliss signed the letter as soon as it was typed and gave it to her. They stood up and shook hands. "I'll see you at the field hospital, perhaps," Bliss said. "I'll be visiting it quite a lot now that we've taken over this mess in Belleau Wood." For a fleeting second the sorrowful man was talking to her again.

"I wish I understood more of what's troubling you," Polly said.

"That might take the rest of your life—which I have no hope of claiming."

Had he felt it too, that vibration of sympathy? Polly found herself in the outer office talking dazedly to Captain Alden. He was surprised and pleased that the General had granted her request. She drove back to Evacuation Hospital Six through the green glowing June countryside, trying to make sense of Malvern Hill Bliss. The war rumbled over the hills after her.

41. RESCUE: A LOVE STORY

"GENTLEMEN," SAID GENERAL DEGOUTTE, IN HIS best mandarin style, "I think it's time we ended this business in Belleau Wood with a new approach. Perhaps by now you are prepared to admit you have learned something from your experience."

"Yeah," Wiley Parker said. "Never call on the Lafayette Division for help. In six days they've gained a grand total of twenty feet."

Bliss and Parker regarded each other with absolute detestation. The same could unquestionably be said for Major General Omar Bundy. Normally genial Brigadier James Harbord, sitting beside Parker, was not much friendlier. When they had asked Bliss for two regiments to relieve the exhausted marines in Belleau, he had excoriated them for turning the struggle for the woods into a publicity contest. He was still in an excoriating mood.

"I sent my men into that woods with very specific orders," Bliss said. "They were not to give up any ground. They were also not to waste men charging machine guns to make a few headlines. That goddamn collection of ruined trees isn't worth the five hundred casualties I've taken. It sure as hell isn't worth the five thousand you've taken."

"You don't seem to understand, Mal," Harbord said. "This has become a test of strength between us and the enemy. A question of who's going to have moral ascendancy."

"Jim, that's balderdash," Bliss said. "Are you claiming that if we take this stupid little forest, the whole German army is going to roll over on its back and surrender? Bunk!"

For the hundredth time Bliss cursed himself for not sending his letter to Pershing the day the marines attacked. Now it was too late. The whole world had begun watching the meaningless struggle as a test of American prowess. The marines' brainless bravery had triumphed over prudence, intelligence, military professionalism.

"This bickering among soldiers of the same army is most unbecoming," General Degoutte said, as if the French army had never known so much as a murmur of dissension. "The wonderful sacrifices of the marine brigade must be preserved for posterity. But there are alarming indications that the Germans are about to launch another offensive to the east of Château-Thierry. We can no longer afford your little sideshow. Here is how we will end the battle of Belleau Wood."

A smirking aide pinned a map to the wall. Degoutte picked up a pointer and began lecturing them as if they were plebes at West Point. "By tomorrow we will have assembled seven hundred guns. When General Bliss's regiments withdraw from Belleau tonight, we will begin a fourteen-hour bombardment. Tomorrow, the marines will reenter the wood. They will advance behind the rolling barrage to the northern edge of the forest. They will, I assure you, find only dead Germans—and a few dazed survivors who will be happy to surrender."

The condescension made Bliss writhe. It was insufferable, but they had brought it on themselves. They had displayed their colossal ignorance of how to fight on the Western Front. He could hear Pétain and Foch and Haig saying "I told you so" to everyone they met. After nineteen days and six thousand casualties, the French came to the Americans' rescue in Belleau Wood so they could get on with the war.

Outside Degoutte's headquarters, Bliss turned to Harbord. "How do you like feeling militarily inferior?"

Harbord walked away without answering him. Wiley Parker raised a clenched fist. "Pershing's going to hear about this!" he snarled.

Back at his own headquarters, when Captain Alden asked him how the meeting had gone, Bliss exploded like a Jack Johnson. He described Degoutte's condescension and the smirks of his staff officers. "I hope you're pleased with what you've accomplished with your cowardly advice to tear up my letter to Pershing," he raged. "You've arranged for the American army to be treated like nincompoops for the rest of the war."

A white-lipped Alden stood his ground. "General, I think you're letting personal pique interfere with your judgment. You don't seem to grasp that this is a war for the soul of the world—and Belleau Wood will go down in history as an example of a kind of courage, a nobility, that's uniquely American. People will never forget what those men did to make the world safe for democracy."

"Get out of my sight before I transfer you back to the States to drill draftees!" Bliss shouted. He could not deal with this sacrificial idealism as a substitute for professionalism.

The Captain stalked out, his head down. *That was a pretty bad performance, General,* Sergeant Turner whispered.

Shut the hell up! Bliss snarled.

Five days later, Bliss received an invitation to a dinner in Paris, celebrating the Fourth of July. On the engraved card was scribbled a note from Pershing: *Drop in to see me before this shindig.*

Bliss told his orderly to brush his best uniform and drove to the City of Light, wishing he had thought of some clever excuse to skip the party. He did not want to see Pershing. He was afraid of what he might say to his old friend. He was even more uneasy about what Jim Harbord and Wiley Parker's friends at Chaumont may have already said to him.

The French had rushed to make as much as possible out of the marines' so-called victory in Belleau Wood. General Degoutte had renamed it the Bois de la Brigade de Marine. Foch had distributed croix de guerres. The marines had cooperated in their usual vainglorious style. When they mopped up the handful of Germans who had survived the French artillery, their commander had sent back a message: ENTIRE WOOD NOW PROPERTY OF U.S. MARINE CORPS.

Pershing's residence on the Rue de Varenne was full of civilian and military flunkies. He was still entertaining all sorts of visiting firemen from the United States. Eventually, his senior aide, Little Collins, led Bliss to an ornate bedroom where Jack was dressing for dinner. "I've been hearing some bad things about you from the Second Division," he said, adjusting his tie in the mirror. "They say your men didn't show much drive when they went into Belleau Wood."

"There was no way you could drive through the second German defense line. It had over fifty interlocking machine guns in it."

"The marines got through it."

"After a fourteen-hour artillery barrage that smashed everything in the woods as flat as this rug."

There was a pause. No one had told Pershing about the barrage. Jack tried to regain his authority. "They won the thing, that's the main point."

"With fifty percent casualties. I don't call that winning. That's about what the Americans inflicted on the British at Bunker Hill. We've been calling that a victory for almost a hundred and fifty years, even though the thing ended with the Yankees running for their lives. The Germans didn't run. They just fell back to another fortified woods."

Pershing spun around to give him his most ferocious glare. "Don't you remember what I said to you in Texas? We had to expect heavy casualties?"

"I can accept heavy casualties when they accomplish something significant. This Belleau thing accomplished zero, strategically and tactically. Can anybody justify it? Can you?"

"We won the goddamn thing. That's how I justify it!" Pershing roared. "I don't want you to sound off to another living soul about those casualties. Do you get me?"

He went back to adjusting his tie. "I'm relieving Bundy. I'm giving Harbord the job."

Harbord! The co-perpetrator of the massacre, along with Wiley Parker. Harbord was being rewarded with the command of the Second Division? Didn't Pershing realize the message he was sending to the rest of the AEF? If you wanted to prove you were doing your job, you had better produce a big casualty list. For some dunderheads, the bigger the list, the better the job would become an axiom. How could Jack not know this?

"I've asked Pétain to transfer you out of the Sixth Army. Get you away from the Second Division. Harbord and Parker don't want to have anything to do with you. I can't blame them, if some of the things they claim you said to them are true."

Bliss said nothing. It was his only hope of survival. He wanted to survive. That was the shameful part of it. He wanted to remain in command of the Lafayette Division.

"I thought you understood the dirty game we're playing. Did you really think we could walk away from Belleau Wood and let the Germans say they'd beaten us?"

"I guess not, Jack," he said.

Pershing was buying the publicity approach to the war. He was so desperate to create an American army he could not pass up any opportunity to promote it, no matter how drenched in blood it was. The beating he had taken from Foch, Pétain, Haig, and Tasker Bliss had taken a terrible toll. It was going to take an even worse toll on the American Expeditionary Force.

"Keep your head, for Christ's sake. I still need you around," Pershing said. "Have a good time at this dinner. It's the last rest you're likely to get for a while. The Germans are cooking up the biggest push yet. I want to see the Lafayette Division stop them dead on its front. Do you hear? Dead!"

Bliss spent the next hour wandering around Paris. Again and again beautiful streetwalkers offered to make him happy. All he could think about were the marines going down in rows before the German machine guns. Was this what Pershing meant by open warfare?

The Independence Day dinner was at the American embassy, an eighteenth-century palace with dozens of white and gold rooms full of the usual paintings of cupids and shepherdesses and horny Greek gods. There were plenty of women and at least forty French and American generals. He saw Louise Wolcott in the middle distance, wearing one of her anatomy-lesson gowns. She gave him a cold stare.

From another angle a familiar voice said, "Hello, General."

It was Polly Warden. She was looking more American than Parisian in a gauzy blue dress that buttoned to her neck—definitely not the sort of thing that would excite Charles Louis Lebrun. Did she have several personalities, depending on the company she kept?

"I just saw Harry Quickmeyer," she said. "He says Jim Harbord's been promoted to major general. He's going to command the Second Division."

"The heroes of Belleau Wood," Bliss said.

She studied him for a moment. "You don't think that's right, do you?"

"I think it's wonderful. He's a fine soldier. An old friend." Bliss grabbed a glass of champagne from a passing tray and downed it in a single swallow. "That's what I've been told to say, and I'm saying it. I'm a good soldier."

"Anita told me you were too honest to be a general."

"That's damned nonsense," Bliss said, polishing off another glass of champagne. "Dangerous nonsense, in fact. A reputation for honesty could ruin a man in this army."

"Please. You don't have to talk that way to me."

Suddenly they were alone in this crowded glittering room. A dazed Bliss was trying to understand the enormous echoing need this auburn-haired young woman was evoking in his soul. Without Pershing he did not have a single human being he could trust, much less love. He had lost Jonathan Alden with his vicious tongue. Did Polly Warden somehow understand all this?

Of course not. She was not a mind reader. When she visited his headquarters, she had been baffled by his bizarre behavior. But she saw something in him he did not see very often and when he saw it he did not trust it. What was it?

You don't have to talk that way to me. She was making him face what he was on the way to becoming, a drunken cynic who would let arrogant Frenchmen like Foch and Degoutte throw his men away in doomed assaults while he consumed a quart a day and waited for Pershing to find out about it.

"What's happened to Charles Louis Lebrun?"

She colored slightly, the flush reaching the edge of the coils of auburn hair above her ears. Bliss could almost feel its silky beauty beneath his fingers. "He's become a patriot—thanks in part to you."

"I can't imagine how my influence could compare to yours. Would you get as interested in me if I confessed to a total loss of patriotism?"

She seemed to sense he was not entirely joking. "I'd still be your friend," she said. "You've been a good friend to me."

He wanted to tell her a beautiful woman could not alter a man's soul without making him her lover. But he did not want to embarrass her—or be told he was being antediluvian again. Besides, he had no room for love in his life. He had to get himself and his men ready for this new German offensive.

A waiter thrust another tray full of champagne glasses under Bliss's chin. He waved it away. "You've already been more of a friend than you realize," he said. "Someday I hope I can explain it to you."

"I'd like that." She hesitated and the next words came in a rush. "That little talk we had in front of Fifth Army headquarters in March was tremendously helpful. I wish I understood more about the war. So much of what I see is so awful, it wipes out thought. That makes it much harder to bear."

Briefly, bitterly, Bliss described everything that had happened along the Marne so far, including Belleau Wood, as a newspaper sideshow. "In a week—two at the most—the Germans will launch their final offensive."

"Can we stop them?" Polly Warden asked, her eyes full of pain. She was seeing field hospitals, ambulances crammed with bleeding men.

"It all depends on Pershing's luck. Does that sound crazy to you?"

"Yes," she said.

"Welcome to the American Expeditionary Force."

42. THE SPAWN OF WAR

Louise Wolcott could not believe it. Suddenly, appallingly, Paris trembled on the ultimate brink. The newspaper headlines about the Americans stopping the Germans on the Marne, defeating them in Belleau Wood, had vanished like sea spray. It became chillingly apparent that the Germans had stopped themselves and were now marshaling their gray-clad hosts for an awesome coup de grace.

In the past week, a million people had fled Paris. The boulevards were deserts. The department stores, the shops, were empty caverns and abandoned caves. The whores of Montmartre were starving, the cafés and bistros were empty or shuttered. Louise's omniscient chauffeur, Michel, warned her that the city's embittered underclass, the seamstresses who toiled in the salons for a pitiful twenty francs a week, the munitions workers who inhaled poisonous chemicals twelve hours a day, the descendants of the victims of the Commune, were waiting to rise—and their first target would be the Faubourg-Saint-Germain.

Still Louise stood her ground. She saw herself as American, preempting a Paris the decadent French could no longer defend. She was sustained by love. She reread her latest letter from Douglas Fairchild, telling her about his six days of hell in Belleau Wood. He added a commentary on the mediocre generalship of Malvern Hill Bliss. Knowing nothing of their descent into eternal enmity, Fairchild was reluctant to be critical. But he was clearly disappointed in Bliss's performance. He had refused to order an all-out attack. As a result, the Lafayette Division scarcely gained a yard.

The marines had returned to finish the job, mortifying Fairchild and many other officers in the division.

Juicy material to spread around Paris; it would inevitably reach a jittery Pershing's ears. She knew why he had brought Bliss to Europe. She also knew he yearned to escape the awful memory that haunted him. Louise—not Bliss or worshipful Micheline Resco—was his only hope. Pershing knew that, but he still let Bliss poison his mind against her. The thought filled Louise with a dark rage at the entire male sex.

At the Fourth of July dinner at the American embassy, Harry Quickmeyer had gazed at her with cold bitter desire. She had almost invited him to the Rue du Bac. She had imagined him tying her to the bed and lashing her with a cane or whip until she bled, then raping her on the bloody sheet while she moaned and writhed in a crucifixion of desire.

Was it the Americans in the war that filled her daydreams and night dreams with violence? The images carried her back to her childhood fantasies, when her father told her she was descended from the Iron Duke, the flinty, ferocious Englishman who had defeated Napoleon. She was the spawn of war. Why should she be surprised by her spiritual participation in this one?

Louise put Fairchild's letter in an envelope addressed to General Tasker H. Bliss. She had met him at the Fourth of July dinner and unquestionably made a conquest when she expressed her profound detestation of Malvern Hill Bliss. The older (and obviously wiser) Bliss seemed fascinated by her assertion that he was an evil influence on John J. Pershing. She added a note to the General accepting his invitation to dinner. Then she wrote to Fairchild, telling him how much his letter had thrilled her and urging him to tell her more "about the timidity of a certain general."

Dressing with her usual meticulous care, Louise strolled to the Rue de Verneuil. It was a hot July day. The sun glared down on Paris. In Louise's mind's eye it reflected nothing, no glamour, no glitter. The City of Light had lost its glow for her.

Each day for a week now she had made this journey to Eleanor Kingswood's house to calm her panic about the imminent arrival of the stormtroopers. Her turmoil had been ignited by the Baroness

Delandes, who had offered Eleanor her Teutonic protection—in return for a pledge of eternal devotion. Instead, Eleanor had sent a frantic telegram to Polly Warden, suggesting the entire ambulance group should flee to the Pyrenees. That redhaired would-be Amazon had rejected the proposal with curtness bordering on contempt.

The unexpected drama had evoked an idea in Louise's mind revolving around that marvelous phrase no-man's-land. It would be her answer to the looming threat north of the Marne, her bravery, her defiance of Pershing, Bliss, and all the other moralists and order givers who were about to be engulfed by this tidal wave of steel and blood.

It would also be delicious revenge on Natalie Barney. Occasionally Louise admitted that had been in the back of her mind from the start. Now that she was no longer in love with Paris, Louise could remember the anguish she had felt when Lorelei conquered her— and then abandoned her.

Louise found Eleanor in her bedroom, reading a letter from Arthur Hunthouse. Louise had met this fortune hunter on one of his several trips to Paris and saw cowardice beneath his foxy-faced posturing. She was sure every sentence in his grandiloquent letters was a lie.

Eleanor listened anxiously as Louise recounted the political and military news of the day. Clemenceau's government had come within a whisker of falling in the Chamber of Deputies, as the frantic politicians demanded to know how the Germans had advanced forty miles in six days, in the very heart of France, against the presumed flower of the French army. Many people were calling for the release of Senator Joseph Caillaux as the best way to forestall the next German offensive. But Clemenceau had survived a vote of confidence and Caillaux was not likely to get out of jail. Which meant the German offensive would begin—possibly tomorrow. Some people thought the French army would not fight. Everything depended on the Americans, but were there enough of them?

By the time Louise finished, Eleanor was wide-eyed with terror. "Aren't they perfectly detestable?" Louise said.

"Who?" Eleanor asked.

"Men," Louise said. "Natalie Barney is right about the impossibility of loving them. Men and love are contradictory terms. They exclude each other. You came to France thinking you could ennoble them by your presence. What have you found? Doughnut eaters. *Embusqués* like your YMCA hero, Holloway. You're reduced to believing the nonsense this fellow Hunthouse writes to you about his heroism."

"How do you know it's nonsense?"

"I asked Colonel Fairchild to investigate him. He says he's the most cowardly captain in the division."

Louise sat down on the chaise longue and kissed Eleanor firmly on the mouth. "Forget him. Forget all of them. Let's create our own no-man's-land, our own bravery. Come with me tonight to the Gare du Nord. On the second floor there are immense bedrooms filled with gigantic statues that symbolize the great cities and continents of the world. Once I loved a man there—a man I've come to detest. He tried to break my heart. Instead, I broke his. Tonight we'll celebrate that victory. We'll fight our own woman's war for happiness and win."

"How wonderful you are," Eleanor said as *no-man's-land* gathered force in her mind. Lorelei had sown the seeds, but Louise was about to reap the harvest.

"Let me tell you the real secret of everything: the war, love, hate," Louise said. "No one is watching. Father, mother, God: none of them are watching. We're free to do whatever we want to do. Whatever fills us with joy and happiness."

Louise kissed her again, more passionately this time. Eleanor clung to her, weeping. They sat together, kissing and whispering words of love until twilight.

Dramas, Louise thought. Would life ever be so full of them again? She saw Douglas Fairchild rallying his men against the German onslaught for her sake; Harry Quickmeyer hunched over his scraps of intelligence at Chaumont; John J. Pershing awake in his sweaty bed, fearing the worst; Malvern Hill Bliss cowering in a dugout, wondering who or what would save him now.

No one was watching. That was the most marvelous part of it. No one was watching except Louise, the spawn of war, doing exactly what she pleased in no-man's-land.

43. ROCKS OF THE MARNE

ON THE AFTERNOON OF JULY 13, 1918, MALVERN Hill Bliss and Colonel Joe Perry watched the men of Company A of the First Battalion of Ireland's Own move warily along the trench they had dug on the south bank of the Marne. There was no sign of any Germans on the wooded bluffs on the north bank of the river. Five miles to the west, the red roofs of Château-Thierry were toy size. The Marne was eighteen feet deep and eighty yards wide in front of the Lafayette Division: a formidable obstacle. But the Germans were planning to cross it. Beyond those bluffs an immense host was gathering.

Screened by some trees, Bliss and Perry listened to Company A grouse about their assignment in standard infantry fashion. The ten-foot-deep trench had been a backbreaker to dig. Today, when they thought they could catch a little rest, they got a new assignment: to dig another trench, facing the French division on their right flank. "What's the story, Lieutenant?" a stumpy private asked George Eagleton. "We gonna stand off the frogs as well as the fritzies?"

"Orders from General Bliss," Eagleton said.

"Hey, Lieutenant. Look who's here," Sergeant O'Connor said.

He had his arm around a fat smiling French sergeant. It was their old freind from Lorraine, Lucky Pierre, the proponent of Mother Earth. He had a bottle of wine in his hand, which he passed around to the trench diggers. Pierre was already celebrating Bastille Day, the French Fourth of July, which the rest of France would cele-brate the next day.

Pierre spoke rapidly in French. Ex-poet Fat Clymer, the lion of the bayonet pits, translated. "He says he's going across the Marne tonight to take some prisoners. He wants you and Sergeant O'Connor to go with him, Lieutenant. He says the guys in his division are *nullissime*. I think that means useless."

"*Oui, nullissime. Merde,*" Pierre said.

"We can't turn down an invitation like that, can we, Sergeant?" Eagleton said.

"Hell, no," O'Connor said. "But don't it worry you a little that we got *nullissimes* on our right flank?"

"Now you know why we're digging these trenches," Eagleton said.

Five hours later, at the headquarters of the French Ninth Army, Malvern Hill Bliss, Charles H. Muir, the commander of the AEF's 28th Division, and an Italian general named Fabrizio Zorgniotti confronted Bliss's old nemesis, General Viomenil. "General Pétain was good enough to pay me a visit only yesterday," Bliss said. "I understand he urged you to prepare an elastic defense, with only a skeleton force on the river and most of our men out of range of German artillery. We agree wholeheartedly with him."

"General," the Italian general said in French. "We learned a harsh lesson at Caporetto—"

"This is neither the time nor the place for lectures on the history of Italian ineptitude," Viomenil said.

"General, I don't like the way you're splitting up my division. It's very bad for my men's morale," Charlie Muir said.

Viomenil had taken a battalion of the 28th Division and planted it on the Marne in the middle of his French divisions. The rest of the 28th was five miles back, in reserve. Viomenil coolly explained that he had no confidence in the 28th Division. He wanted them to learn by fighting beside veterans.

Bliss suppressed an impulse to help Muir by reminding Viomenil that Foch had agreed not to split up American divisions. He was through giving advice to other division commanders. It was every man—or at least every general—for himself in Pershing's AEF.

General Viomenil opened a jeweled snuff box and inhaled a pinch. "We must keep our forward defense lines fully manned. We cannot allow the enemy to occupy a foot of France's sacred soil on this side of the river."

Viomenil regarded Bliss as if he were a piece of fois gras ready for chewing. "It is my understanding that you assured Generalissimo Foch you would obey his orders—and the orders of his subordinates, of which I have the honor to be one."

Bliss cursed under his breath. There was no time left to drag Pétain or Pershing into the argument. East of Reims, a French patrol had captured some prisoners who said the Germans were going to attack at 12:10 A.M. on July 15.

Outside Viomenil's Ninth Army headquarters, an inn about ten miles south of the Marne, Bliss shook hands with Charlie Muir and General Zorgniotti and wished them luck. Zorgniotti's interpreter translated. "We'll need it," the General said in French.

The panicky French government had hornswoggled two divisions from Italy to bolster their collapsing army. On their right flank the Lafayette Division had the Italians and half a dozen glued-together fragments of the French divisions shattered on the Chemin des Dames. Bliss had suspected they were *nullissimes* before Lucky Pierre confirmed it.

Back at his headquarters, Bliss found a letter on his desk from Captain Jonathan Alden.

Dear General Bliss:

It has become more and more apparent to me that I am unable to meet your standards as an aide-de-camp. I have tried to do the job honestly and diligently, but I have obviously failed to satisfy you. Under the circumstances, I think it would be best if I returned to the infantry as a company commander.

I have talked with the captain of my old company, Arthur Hunthouse, who says he is quite amenable to changing jobs with me. He is intelligent, a Harvard graduate, and he speaks fluent French and German. I think he would be a good aide. I hope you will make this decision as soon as possible.

Sincerely,
Jonathan Alden
Captain, USA

Bliss sat there in the hot July twilight, cursing himself. He should have seen this coming. For the past two weeks Alden had been dragging himself around headquarters like a dying gladiator. Once or twice Bliss thought of apologizing for his explosion over Belleau Wood but he had resisted it. In his harried brain he had blended Alden's naïve idealism and Pershing's blood-soaked opportunism, both of which infuriated him.

"Captain Alden!" he roared.

He came to the door, pale, tight-lipped. "Yes, General?"

"I wish I had time to discuss this matter with you in more depth. For the moment I can only assure you I'm not dissatisfied with your work as my aide. If we survive this battle—and you still insist on a transfer—I'll take a look at this fellow Hunthouse."

"General, I'd like to transfer as soon as possible. I'm sick of being an *embusqué*."

The frowning young face confronted him, its boyishness undiminished by anger. Was he going to lose this accidentally adopted son to the idealism blazing in the souls of the Americans of his generation? A prayer, a plea for mercy crowded Bliss's lips for the first time in thirty years. But he could not say it. He could not be that hypocritical. He would take what came, knowing he deserved it. "It's always been part of my creed never to deny a man's request for action," he said. "I'll do my best to meet your timetable, Captain. But first I've got a battle to fight."

He summoned Chief of Staff Douglas Fairchild to his office. "I'm about to risk a court-martial," he said, studying the map. "I'm going to reduce our forces on the riverbank to the minimum. Tell each regiment to leave only one company there, with plenty of machine guns. Pull a battalion from each back to this railroad embankment, a half mile from the river. Put the rest on this plateau, two miles back, with orders to be ready to counterattack on a moment's notice."

"You're going to let the Germans land on this side?" Fairchild said incredulously.

For a moment Bliss wavered. Was it madness to let the stormtroopers across the Marne? Bliss clung to his memory of Pétain's grim-jawed insistence on an elastic defense, even here. The

Sphinx, that gloomy, unlovable son of a bitch, had become his hero. He told Fairchild to get the orders out to the regiments. He wanted everyone moved by daylight.

Fairchild clumped out, shaking his head. Captain Alden came to the door looking almost cheerful. "General, a couple of men from Company A went across the river with a French patrol to grab some prisoners. They divided them up and want you to talk to their share. Captain Hunthouse has come along to interpret."

Two soaking-wet Germans were pushed into the room by an equally soggy Sergeant O'Connor. He had a Chauchat slung over his shoulder; the wicked-looking light machine gun seemed to have become part of his uniform. Lieutenant Eagleton followed them, then Captain Hunthouse, his future aide. Bliss liked him less every time he saw him. His eyes were shifty, his mouth uncertain. Combat had shaken his nerve.

"Ask them if they're planning to attack," Bliss said.

Hunthouse rattled off some Deutsch. The smaller of the two Germans replied, his pale lips curled with disdain. "He says if you hope to keep them prisoners, you'd better move them inland a few dozen miles. The German army will occupy this house within hours of their assault."

"Ja!" said the other German, a big-jawed bruiser without much brain.

"What are they calling this offensive?" Bliss said. All the other offensives had code names, which were important to identify. They could be picked up on German radio traffic by French and British eavesdroppers.

Hunthouse asked the question. "Friedensturm!" said the smaller soldier. "Ja, Friedensturm!" added the bruiser with an almost joyous arrogance. "Peace offensive," Hunthouse translated.

Bliss sat down at his desk and toyed with a corner of the map of Champagne. He pondered the crude red-crayoned edges of the forty-two-mile-wide bulge the Germans had punched into the French lines between Soissons and Reims. Peace offensive. For the first time in months he saw a glimmer of hope. Any general who had to tell his troops they were launching an offensive that was guaranteed to end the war was worried about his men's morale.

"When will they attack?"

Hunthouse asked the question in German. Both men shook their heads. That was a secret.

"Tell them if they don't give us the day, the hour, and the minute, we're going to turn them over to the French—as uncooperative prisoners," Bliss said.

The ultimatum wiped out most of the *Friedensturm* exaltation. The big bruiser cracked first. He babbled in German. "*Schwein!*" snarled the smaller trooper.

"Tomorrow night," Hunthouse said. "At ten minutes after midnight."

That confirmed the day—July 15—and hour the French had picked up yesterday. "They're betting the frogs will be plastered from celebrating Bastille Day. I hope to God they're wrong," Bliss said.

Twenty-six hours later, precisely on that fateful tenth minute after midnight, Bliss was standing outside his headquarters, a farmhouse five miles south of the Marne, when the German barrage began. From Reims on the east to Soissons on the west, Colonel Bruchmüller's murderous mixture of poison gas and high explosives descended on the French and American lines. It was the closest thing to Judgment Day that Bliss ever hoped to see. The night sky whitened and thickened to yellow and whitened again and again. The air swished and swirled like a hurricane, bringing a rain that burst with a red crash.

In his mind's eye Bliss saw four hundred thousand Frenchmen and Americans shuddering in their watery trenches and foul dugouts beneath this incessant bludgeoning. Not a few of the blows were falling on the four companies he had left along the Marne. The commander of one of those companies was Captain Jonathan Alden USA. He had embarrassed Bliss into making the switch with Hunthouse immediately after they finished interrogating the prisoners. Hunthouse was pathetically eager to change places. Maybe some German ancestor had warned him in a dream about what was coming.

Until 4 A.M. Colonel Bruchmüller's fiendish musicians played their doomsday concerto without a second's letup. They must have dropped in exhaustion beside their guns when the blaze of destruction ceased and the stormtroopers went forward. Almost instantly the German thunder was replaced by ferocious salvos from French and Americans guns, zeroed in on no-man's-land in anticipation of this opportunity for gruesome revenge. On Bliss's front the target was the dawn-gray Marne, soon aswarm with Germans in rubber boats, paddling grimly into the shell and machine-gun fire. Brave men, Bliss thought, watching them through his field glasses.

Eight hours later, Bliss strode up and down his headquarters in torment while the thunder of battle shook the windows. He felt like a man trapped in a pitch-black attic room while his family and best friends were fighting for their lives on the lower floors. Occasionally, one of them struggled to a telephone to tell him what was happening.

"Perry here," said Machine-Gun Joe's crisp voice. "Things aren't looking too good on our right. Those French divisions seem to have evaporated. Germans are pouring past us."

"I know. Keep calm and fight your battle."

He had watched the shattered remnants of the French divisions, all of whom had been crammed into trenches on the riverbank, heading for the rear the moment the Germans started across the river.

"Mal, I've lost all contact with my battalion on the river," Charlie Muir said. "It looks as if the French retreated without telling them. They're surrounded by Germans!"

"I think you better start saying some prayers for them, Charlie," Bliss said. "Throw in a few curses on Viomenil for me."

"General," quavered Colonel Wade Hampton Stuart, commander of Carolina's Pride, "my company on the river is under terrific pressure. Do I have permission to withdraw them?"

"In the words of Robert E. Lee, Colonel, no," Bliss said.

"Mal," Joe Perry said. "I just heard from Captain Alden. He thinks it's time to fall back to the railroad embankment. His men are running low on ammunition. They've taken a lot of casualties."

"I want them to hold for another half hour. I'll send them some ammunition."

Bliss got on the phone to Viomenil. "My compliments, General," he said. "Would you mind telling me where the rest of the

Ninth Army is? We're still fighting on the riverbank. So is the American Third Division on my left flank. Everyone else seems to be heading for Paris—or the Pyrenees."

"We've stabilized a line about two miles from the river, on the plateau," Viomenil said.

"Two miles. Is that about as far as a stormtrooper can advance before he gets out of breath?" Bliss said.

"Do you wish to withdraw? You have my permission," Viomenil snarled.

"My orders are from John J. Pershing, General. He told me he wanted me to stop the Germans dead. That's what I'm trying to do. If you order me to withdraw, I'll of course obey. But my preference is to fight it out here with my right flank refused. I've got a nice long trench dug along it. Do you have any objections to that?"

"None."

He was making Viomenil eat more of the American crow his ancestor had found so hard to digest at Yorktown. Bliss was forgetting the Frenchman had the power to return the compliment—in the raw.

A motorcycle roared up to the door. Douglas Fairchild, covered with dust and grime, burst into the office. "General, the situation is deteriorating along the river. You've got to withdraw those companies. They've fought magnificently. It would be criminal to leave them there to the last man."

Bliss nodded. "Pull them back to the railroad embankment and hold there at all costs until two o'clock. Then we're going to counterattack."

An hour later, Bliss stood on the railroad embankment, his second line of defense, watching Company A of Ireland's Own and companies from his other three regiments falling back before the German onslaught. It was a fighting retreat, a good performance for men who had been under fire since 12:10 A.M.

Sergeant O'Connor and Lieutenant Eagleton were among the last to arrive. They both had acquired Chauchats. In fact, half the company seemed to have them. Bliss reminded himself to ask Machine-Gun Joe Perry where the hell he had stolen them. As Harvard and the School of Hard Knocks labored up the embankment together with German bullets whizzing around them, the Sergeant said, "We're rollin' with the punch, Lieutenant. Calm down. Maybe the General knows what he's doin' for a change."

"Oh, yeah? Look at that," Eagleton said, pointing to their right. "We're about to be up to our ass in Germans."

A good third of the twenty thousand stormtroopers who had gotten across the Marne when the French evaporated were advancing on their right flank.

"Don't give up on the General too soon, Lieutenant," Bliss said. "Watch closely."

The flank attackers came forward without artillery and only a scattering of mortar fire. They expected a walkover and were stunned to encounter a trench line from which ferocious machine-gun and rifle fire swept through their ranks. The survivors hastily retreated out of range.

"That's good stuff, General," Lieutenant Eagleton conceded. "But what about those guys? They're the ones I want to even things with." He pointed to the gray-clad battalions briskly positioning machine guns and mortars as they prepared to storm the railroad embankment.

"You're going to chase them all the way back to the river."

Lieutenant Eagleton looked at his men. Exhaustion had drained almost every face of life. Even Sergeant O'Connor looked like a walking dead man.

"You'll have lots of help," Bliss said. "The whole division's going forward at two o'clock. Here they come."

He pointed toward the plateau. Their regiment's two reserve battalions were pouring down the slope in open ranks. To the west, toward Château-Thierry, battalions from the other regiments were moving forward too, in a series of brown waves. Twenty thousand fresh men were heading for the Germans in the half mile between the embankment and the river.

The sight had a miraculous effect on Company A, transforming faces, stiffening backs. Captain Alden strolled through their ranks, telling everyone to make sure they had all the ammunition and grenades they needed. The Captain was showing his SOB general how much happier he was as a company commander.

"Here comes our artillery!" Bliss shouted. Over their heads whined a salvo of .75 millimeter shells to crash in the fields and trees where the Germans were organizing their attack. For half an hour the artillery pounded the Germans with a hurricane of high explosives. At a signal from Bliss, Major Patrick Logan, the cocky First Battalion commander, blew his whistle and led Company A and the rest of the battalion down the embankment.

"Open up, operate by squads!" Alden roared. Other lieutenants and captains shouted similar orders. They split into the ten-man teams Bliss and Joe Perry had created as the best way to attack machine guns. Each squad had four men with sacks of grenades, four with rifles, and a ninth man with a Chauchat. The tenth man was the squad leader.

They headed for the Germans in low quick rushes, the Chauchat gunners covering their advance. Bliss kept his eyes on Captain Alden and Company A. "Take that gun!" the Captain shouted, sending a squad crawling toward a machine gun in a woods.

"Kilpatrick, take that one." Another gun was firing from a fox-hole to the right of the woods. Sergeant O'Connor and Lieutenant Eagleton were shouting similar orders. Grenades sailed through the hot smoky air. The Maxims fell silent. Through the crash of guns and grenades Bliss heard O'Connor roaring a battle cry: *To Hell or Hoboken!*"

About twenty Germans burst out of the woods and ran back toward the river. O'Connor crouched, and his Chauchat crackled. Most of the men in gray went down. The half dozen survivors turned, their hands in the air. Bliss did a dance and pounded Joe Perry on the back. "We've got some soldiers down there, Joe!"

The squads continued their rushing-crawling advances. One of Alden's men got a burst in the chest when he rose to throw a grenade. The squad fell back. The soldier lay there, writhing. O'Connor sprayed the German gun with his Chauchat while Alden ran out and hauled the wounded man back to the shelter of a knoll. Bliss's heart almost stopped beating.

Everywhere, Germans were falling back, carrying machine guns, mortars, trailing their rifles. The river was less than a quarter of a mile away. It was a rout! "To Hell or Hoboken!" howled Company A. It was starting to look easy. Like running downhill.

With no warning, the momentum of the battle changed. Gray figures flitted toward the Americans in the trees; mortar shells exploded all around them. Men went down screaming, clutching shattered arms and legs. Rifle and machine-gun bullets thudded into bodies. Bliss saw squads running back toward the embankment. It was a counterattack, one of the many surprises veteran troops have in their repertoire.

Forgetting he was a general, Bliss followed Perry down the embankment to take charge of the men within reach of his voice. "Get down in the gully. Under cover," he yelled to Eagleton and his rattled platoon.

Alden rushed up to him. "You have no business out here, General!" he shouted.

"You're absolutely right," Bliss said and sent a runner racing back for reinforcements.

The Germans came at them in the same little rushes, grenading, inching around the flanks. Bliss could see panic gnawing at Company A's exhausted men. They were wondering how they could lose and win and lose in the same day.

A company from another battalion arrived. The captain was a ruddy-faced Irishman well over six feet. From their clean uniforms they had been in reserve all day. "Let us at the bastards!" he said. "Why the hell are you hanging back like this?" He led them out of the gully in a headlong charge.

Obviously he and his battalion commander had paid no attention to Bliss's attempt to reform their tactics. "Jesus Christ," Bliss gasped as half the company went down in blasts of machine-gun fire. The captain lay among the dead. The survivors fled back to the gully, wild-eyed, shaking.

"Okay, dumbjohns," Alden roared. "We're going out there again. The smart way." He shoved them into Company A's depleted squads and told them to imitate their example.

"This time it's the Marne or bust!" Eagleton shouted.

"To Hell or Hoboken!" O'Connor roared.

"Or Baltimore!" Bliss howled.

They came out of the gully firing Chauchats, inching forward, flinging grenades, bellowing their battle cry. The German counterattack faltered, and the gray figures began drifting back toward the river again. "We're going to win this goddamn war!" Bliss yelled. If he had gotten killed by one of the hundred thousand bullets whizzing around him on July 15, 1918, he would have died a happy man.

By nine o'clock, the sounds of battle along the Marne had dwindled to random rifle shots. Malvern Hill Bliss telephoned General Viomenil. "I would like to report the situation on the Lafayette Division's front," he said in French when the General came to the phone. "There are no living Germans between my third line of defense and the river. They're all either dead or prisoners of war."

"*Bon,*" the General said and hung up.

Bliss telephoned him again. "What happened to the Twenty-eighth Division battalion that was left on the riverbank?"

"Unfortunately they were wiped out."

Bliss called Pershing at Chaumont and gave him the same report that he had given Viomenil. "I've still got at least twenty thousand Germans across the river on my right flank," he said. "If they go after Viomenil's sprinters again they may be behind me tomorrow."

"Maybe not. Finding out the exact date of the attack was the luckiest break of the war. The artillery chewed up a lot of stormtroopers. Foch wants to counterattack as soon as possible. I've given him the First and Second divisions."

As Bliss put down the phone, Arthur Hunthouse appeared in the doorway to ask if there was anything he needed done. Bliss felt the bravado, the exultance of victory drain out of his body. For some reason he had temporarily forgotten Jonathan Alden was no longer his aide. The Captain no longer cared that General Bliss had gotten himself back on General Pershing's approval list. He was in another drama now, a dance of death between the ideal and the real. Again, a prayer rose to Bliss's lips. Again, he stifled it.

44. INITIATIVES

SEARCHLIGHTS, THE WAIL OF SIRENS, THE ODD pulsing beat of German motors. Bombs rained down on Paris, the ghost city from which two million people had fled. In her house on the Rue du Bac, Louise Wolcott soothed a trembling Eleanor Kingswood. "It's their last gasp," she said. "Tasker Bliss told me last night the war was as good as won. The Germans have lost the initiative."

"What does that mean?" Eleanor said.

"We're in control of the game. The moves are up to us now. All they can do is respond. General Foch will launch offensives when and where he chooses. He has six American divisions ready to attack when he gives the word. There'll be ten more by the end of summer."

The windows rattled as a large bomb exploded only a few blocks away on the other side of the Seine. It was amazing how much she had learned from her dinner with Tasker Bliss. The old wheezer fancied himself succeeding where Pershing had failed. He literally gushed inside information.

"I might as well be at the front with my ambulance group," Eleanor said, as more bomb blasts shook the house. "It's no more dangerous than it is here."

"Your friend Polly would only order you around the way she bosses everyone else."

Louise and Eleanor had driven out to Evacuation Hospital Six to visit the Kingswood Ambulance Group last week. Louise had asked if she could go to the front in an ambulance. Polly Warden had said no. She would be taking up space they could use for a wounded man.

"Speaking of the initiative, you've lost it with her. You'd think it was the Warden Ambulance Group," Louise said.

"I can't bear the thought of being away from you even for a day," Eleanor said.

Another stupendous blast. Louise sighed. Her conquest of Eleanor Kingswood could not be more complete. She had the initiative now and forever. It was a delicious triumph. Natalie Barney had written her a virulent letter, telling her she was barred from her salon on the Rue Jacob for life.

The other dramas continued. Douglas Fairchild filled Louise's mailbox with letters describing his narrow escapes from German machine guns and shell fire and his continuing adoration. She had no fear of losing the initiative there. Tasker Bliss was awed by Fairchild's courage. He said he deserved to be a general and would see what he could do to make him one.

"I love you, I love you, I love you," Eleanor whispered. "Let me kiss you everywhere." Her lips and her tongue roved Louise's body. She felt it, of course. But no ardor stirred in her flesh. That seemed to be the one thing wrong with having the initiative. Love involved feelings more complicated than conquest. After the first few days of wild caresses and kisses, Eleanor ceased to arouse her. She was a possession, a drama, like Fairchild, like Tasker Bliss, like so many others.

With Natalie Barney it had been different. Natalie had wielded the initiative. She had been the ultimate exploration, the unimagined territory beyond ordinary freedom. Louise had been her adoring slave. At the time she had hated it, but now she remembered it with an aura of sweet longing.

There was another problem with Eleanor. She was boring. She was relentlessly high-minded. She wanted to justify, to ennoble everything with lofty slogans. She wanted to make the world safe for democracy—by giving women the vote. She wanted Louise to join her in a crusade against male arrogance and aggression. She wanted their love to have historic dimensions.

History bored Louise. It was full of cautionary lessons, reasons for not doing things. Lugubrious old men like George Washington and Robert E. Lee and William McKinley. So-called saints like Francis of Assisi, who lived in a frenzy of holiness. History was an enemy of freedom. After listening to Eleanor she had begun to suspect the woman's movement was another enemy. Who needed a vote to be free?

Oh! Eleanor's tongue was in a place that inspired extremely pleasant sensations. It was not quite ardor but it was in the family, a cousin. For some reason it reminded her of Harry Quickmeyer. Someone—was it Tasker Bliss or Douglas Fairchild?—had told her he had quit his safe job at Chaumont and joined the Lafayette Division as colonel of a regiment.

He had never replied to her scathing letter. Although strictly speaking she had not lost the initiative, Quickmeyer's silence made it tantamount to losing it. She was suddenly flailing at a shadow, a ghost of love. The thought filled her with bitter sadness.

Ohhh! Eleanor had an educated tongue. Was it something they taught at Wellesley? No, she had taught Eleanor the art and science of loving sensations. But had she taught her the art of love? Was that still eluding Louise among the bomb blasts?

What if Harry Quickmeyer was out there in these bomb blasts or even uglier explosions at the front? What if shrapnel shredded his bitter heart? What would she do? Louise's soul fled across the dark miles to the chalky fields of Champagne and knelt beside him, weeping, weeping, weeping.

"That's enough!" Louise cried. She flung Eleanor aside and sprang out of bed to clutch a peignoir.

"Did I hurt you?" Eleanor asked.

"No."

"When I kiss you I feel it in the same place." Eleanor sighed. "That must be the final proof of love. To feel exactly what the beloved is feeling."

Louise pondered Eleanor's magnificent body: the long slim legs, the full breasts, the curving belly. It did not stir an iota of desire. The affair was over. The drama was about to move to the third act. That was the best part of retaining the initiative. You decided when the drama began—and ended. "You're a darling creature," Louise said. "You've brought spring sunshine into my life. But now it's summer."

As dawn streaked the Paris sky, Eleanor stood sobbing in the vestibule of Louise's house on the Rue du Bac. "Please tell me what I did wrong!" she said.

"For the hundredth time, nothing. These amours are part of Paris, part of being a free woman, darling."

"I can't live without you! I'll kill myself!"

"You'll find other lovers. We'll meet from time to time and recall our happiness. It's better to end it now, before quarrels and boredom ruin it."

"Nothing could ruin it!"

"I'm much older than you. So many things ruin love: memories, accidental parts of our pasts that intrude on the tenderest moments."

Eleanor sobbed her way into the waiting taxi. Upstairs, Louise found a pen and paper.

> *Dear Colonel:*
>
> I heard through mutual friends of your decision to seek action at the front. It stirred the most peculiar emotions in my heart. A strange fear that I might be the reason for it. An even stranger fear that I might be responsible if the worst happened. A sudden longing to see you, to try to sort out the awful confusion in which our love became entangled. Part of the fault lies in your presumption of the right to command me. But I freely admit part of it lies in my wayward woman's heart, in complications past and present I might explain to you. There is probably no hope of my doing this, but I want you to know you are in my prayers. The French believe a sinner's prayers are especially welcome to God. I hope they're right.
>
> *Regretfully,*
> *Louise*

Did that regain the initiative? Louise wondered. Suddenly it did not matter. She paced the bedroom, tears streaming down her face. She loved him. She loved the woman who had proposed to share his soldier's pain and danger that night in Fort Myer. Why had she betrayed that woman? Was freedom a game she had been playing in a desperate attempt to amuse herself until love appeared? Was retaining the initiative a kind of cowardice, an avoidance of the surrender love demanded—and she had refused? Had Paris betrayed her again?

Across the hills and valleys east of Paris came the rumble of guns from the banks of the Marne. The next offensive was beginning. Generalissimo Foch, with two hundred thousand Americans in his ranks, was retaining the initiative. Louise wondered if it would be as ruinous in war as it was in love.

45. BRAVERY

"DEAD MEN," THE LAFAYETTE DIVISION PRIVATE beside Polly Warden muttered as she drove him toward the evacuation hospital. "Dead men floatin' in the river."

He was a shell-shock case, one of a growing number in the AEF. No one had shot him, but he was no longer a fighting man. If someone gave him an order or asked him if he wanted something to eat, the answer was the same. "Dead men. Dead men floatin' in the river."

Polly knew the story. She had heard it from the ashen lips of Dr. Isaac Pinkus at the field hospital. The Lafayette Division had been ordered to attack across the Marne. For a whole day the South Carolina regiment and the engineers had tried to get pontoon bridges in place with the help of artillery and covering machine-gun fire. German artillery and machine guns had devastated them. The next morning, when they braced themselves for another assault, the Germans were gone. During the night they had retreated a half dozen miles to the River Ourcq.

"If we'd waited twenty-four hours, five hundred men would still be alive," Pinkus said, shaking his head.

Polly was appalled. Why would Malvern Hill Bliss do such a thing after he had criticized other generals for wasting men's lives? She had met him at the evacuation hospital during the first American offensive, the attack on the Marne salient from Soissons by the First and Second divisions. The casualties had been horrendous. One regiment in the Second Division had been reduced from thirty-eight hundred men to three hundred. After two days of fighting the division had virtually collapsed and had to be withdrawn. Bliss had denounced General Harbord and Colonel Parker, the division's chief of staff, as executioners.

"Dead men. Dead men floatin' in the river," the private said.

General Bliss remained an enigma. When she asked him why he had exchanged Arthur Hunthouse for Jonathan Alden as his aide, he had snapped, "I grew unfond of Captain Alden and he reciprocated." When she still looked puzzled, he had added, "I'm not a nice man, Miss Warden." The scowl on his face and her low opinion of Arthur made her wonder if that was true.

The army had shifted the Kingswood Ambulance Group to a new evacuation hospital south of the Marne, east of Château-Thierry. Most of the four American divisions in line were fighting in this area. The field hospitals had crossed the Marne while the French and Americans moved up to assault the Germans on the Ourcq.

Several of Polly's drivers were showing signs of strain. Even Martha Herzog and Alice Hedberg, the most dependable of the group, were smoking cigarettes by the dozen and talking desperately about the week's vacation they were supposed to get after six months on duty. Polly recognized the symptoms. It was *cafard* American style.

The war had no discernible end. The Germans retreated from one river to another river, but who knew when they might attack again and regain the initiative? Meanwhile the torrent of wounded men flowed from the front in their ambulances. Each was a small defeat, a loss inflicted by German shrapnel or bullets. Each day *cafard* seeped into her drivers' minds and hearts. Especially when the shell-shock cases muttered things like "Dead men floatin' in the river."

The next day, heavy fighting began along the Ourcq. The casualties mounted to crisis proportions. The weather turned rainy, making the roads treacherous strips of gumbo. As usual, Polly pushed herself harder than anyone else. Sleep became something she snatched dozing at the wheel of her ambulance in the endless lines of trucks and cars waiting to cross the Marne.

At the field hospital toward the end of the last week in July, a harried Dr. Pinkus rushed up to her. "Can you take a gassed lieutenant? He's got a mild dose of mustard. His clothes stink of the stuff. Put on your mask."

Five minutes later, an orderly led George Eagleton out to her ambulance. He had a bandage around his streaming eyes. Naturally he did not recognize the gas-masked woman behind the wheel. The orderly was telling him his eyes would be all right in a few days. "The hell—with that," he choked. "Give me something for them now. Send me back to my men."

"You need some hospital time, Lieutenant."

They headed south toward the Marne in a hard rain. As Polly edged across the narrow pontoon bridge, with ammunition trucks lumbering at her from the opposite direction, George said, "Are they kidding me? Will I be blind for life?"

Polly pulled off her mask. She would risk the fumes to talk to him in a normal voice. "No," she said. "With luck you'll be fine in a week. You'll be back with your men."

"Polly," George said. "Is that you?"

Was it the fumes or emotion that filled her eyes with bitter tears? "Yes."

They rode in silence for a long time. "I stopped—thinking about you," George said, gasping out the words. "One of the consolations—of combat."

"Don't try to talk," Polly said.

He ignored her. "Are you still enjoying—your great—adventure?"

"No," she said. "Are you?"

"Believe it or—not, the answer—is yes. I'm—good at what I do up there. I like—the feeling."

"I never doubted for a moment you'd be a good soldier."

"But not good—enough for you?" he choked. "You were saving—yourself for French—aristocrats. Are you going—to marry that paunchy—old tycoon?"

"No."

"Are you still—his mistress?"

The road was a haze of tears. "I probably couldn't explain what happened to me, George. But I can see there's no point in even trying."

"A lot's happened to me too."

"I know that," Polly said.

"No, you don't. You don't—understand the good part of it—up there—the solidarity—between me and my men. We're forging something—that will last—for the rest of our lives. Something—no woman—will ever share."

"I may not share it but I admire it."

"Stuff," George said.

Somehow the bandage around his eyes made the words even more unbearable. He was blind to every and any protestation or apology. The war had given him nothing but the strength to hate her.

"That night I saw you at the Ritz—on the way back I met a streetwalker. She'd just started in the business. I was one of her first customers. I tried to talk her out of it. I offered to give her enough money to live as an honest woman. She laughed at me. But I admired her—for her honesty. She was a whore—and she admitted it. You won't admit—it."

He choked for breath until Polly thought he was in serious danger of strangling. "George, what I did that night at the Ritz was cruel, but it had a purpose. I thought I was helping to win the war. Now I don't know what it accomplished, except to kill and maim another million men."

He was not listening to her. It was as if she had ceased to exist. He spoke into the darkness around his eyes. "You know what you were? My charity case. You made me feel noble. I was marrying poverty-stricken Polly, even though she didn't have a dime. Now I realize there are a lot more important things a man can do with his money."

In the same enraged voice, George told her about his growing determination to make the sacrifices of the war mean something back in America. He was going to eradicate the slums in which most of his Irish enlisted men had been raised, fight for decent medical care for the poor. "Sergeant O'Connor grew up in a tenement with no running water. His mother died of heart disease from lugging pails of water up six flights of stairs. We can't let that sort of thing happen in America anymore."

"I agree with everything you say. Why do you have to hate me to say it?"

"Because your goddamn feminism is selfish. You're missing the real point: the way poverty divides Americans of both sexes, turns them against each other. You're nothing but a bunch of spoiled bitches who want to be superior to men."

He relapsed into a coughing fit. "You've got us all wrong, George," Polly said.

At the evacuation hospital they led George off to the gas ward. In terrific turmoil, Polly retreated to the ambulance group's office in the basement of the hospital. She found Eleanor Kingswood there, going over the records. She looked haggard, as if she was not sleeping well. Was she embarrassed over her panicky proposal to flee the German offensive? Polly gave her a wary greeting, hoping they could avoid a quarrel.

"Martha tells me you're letting some people have forty-eight-hour leaves in Paris," Eleanor said.

"They need it. The pressure's getting to them."

"Martha thinks you need a leave too. Why don't you come back with me tonight? Spend the weekend in Paris."

Polly shook her head. "I just brought George Eagleton to the hospital," she said.

"Is he badly hurt?"

"Gassed. Not seriously, as far as I could tell."

"Then there's no reason for you to stay."

"I'm afraid there is," Polly said. "We talked—quite a lot on the way from the front. I think we have some more to say."

"Darling. Martha is very concerned about you. So am I."

Paris. The house on the Rue de Verneuil. For a moment all Polly could see was the huge bathtub at the end of the second-floor hall. It had been a month since she had a real bath. Maybe she needed forty-eight hours away from shell-shock cases babbling about dead men in the Marne. Maybe there was nothing left to say to George Eagleton. "All right," she said.

On the way to Paris in her tiny English two-seater, Eleanor talked obsessively about Louise Wolcott. She no longer liked her. She had no education, no philosophy, no sense of the ideal. She was nothing more than a sensualist, an adventuress, more French than American, like her poet friend Natalie Barney. She was equally scathing about Arthur Hunthouse. He was a fake, a liar, a coward. She had found out his letters from the battlefield were fiction.

Polly struggled to stay awake and listen intelligently, but it was impossible. She dozed off at least three times, missing whole sections of Eleanor's monologue. She apologized for her exhaustion and vowed a bath and a night's sleep would restore her to full consciousness.

At the house on the Rue de Verneuil, Polly reeled upstairs and stripped off her smelly clothes for the first time in a week. Madame Berrier and the *femme de chambre* cheerfully lugged pots of boiling water to the bathtub. In twenty minutes Polly was in the tub, lapped by warm water, remembering her bath at the Château Givry. She had failed to recapture pure sweet-smelling Polly Warden of New York that night. Was this another, even more doomed attempt, inspired by George Eagleton? Or was it mere sensuality? She did not know, and she was so tired she did not care.

As she toweled herself, the bedroom door opened. Eleanor stood there, a strange tension on her face. There was nothing unusual about her assuming she had the freedom to stroll into Polly's bedroom. They had shared a room for four years at Wellesley. But Polly was not prepared for the way Eleanor put her arms around her and kissed her on the mouth.

"What in the world is that for?" Polly said, wrapping her nightrobe around her.

"For love," Eleanor said. "I want to show you I love you as much as you love me. You do still love me, don't you?"

"Of course I do," Polly said.

"I've been thinking about us. I see great flaws in our friendship, flaws that only love can repair."

"I don't know what you're talking about," Polly said. "I think our friendship is perfect as it is."

"No, it isn't. I've been the egotist, the rich woman, too full of pride, too absorbed in my own ideas. I've alienated you in a hundred small ways. I want to make up for it. I want to love you—the way you've loved me—selflessly, tenderly, nobly, for the rest of our lives."

"Darling," Polly said. "Are you sure you're all right? Your nerves have been horribly strained—"

"Listen to me!" Eleanor said. "Listen to what I'm offering you. A lifetime of love. An absolute equality of sharing everything I own now and in the future. I need you for my happiness—my sanity!"

Polly sank into a chair. "Tell me what happened between you and Louise Wolcott."

"Forget her. Forget that bitch. She pretended to love me. I'm offering you genuine love. Something a sensualist like her wouldn't understand in a million years."

Eleanor's dark hair streamed down the back of her Alice-blue robe, wild, Valkyriean. She sank to the floor and rested her head on Polly's knees. "Let me show you how much pleasure I can give you. Pleasure without humiliation, ugliness, domination," she whispered.

Polly knew what Eleanor was proposing. She knew women fell in love with each other. At Wellesley, most "cases," as they called them, were innocent outbursts of adolescent affection. A few women were anything but innocent. They played dangerous emotional games with their victims' feelings. Beyond these youthful uproars were serious commitments between older women, some of them on the faculty. People called them "Boston marriages." These women became a pair, apparently as meaningful to each other as husband and wife.

Polly thought of Eleanor's panicky proposal to flee the final German offensive. It was not only Louise Wolcott; the war had wounded Eleanor. It revealed her ideas about ennobling it were naïve, even ridiculous. It had shouldered her aside, leaving her a frightened spectator. Polly was flooded with sympathy and pity, with memories of Eleanor's generosity, her boldness and courage in the fight for equality.

Half dazed with exhaustion, hurt by her bitter conversation with George Eagleton, Polly veered toward surrender. Eleanor was offering to share her life, her wealth, with her. Was she the answer to her loneliness, her refuge from *cafard*, the endless meaningless pain of the war? The solution to the incomprehensible blank the future had become, when and if the war ever ended?

"Eleanor, I love you. I'll always love you."

"No, you won't. There'll be a man, some warrior like George

Eagleton, who'll convince you his heroism on the battlefield has entitled him to your lifelong devotion."

Polly laughed bitterly. "George isn't my candidate. He spent most of his time in the ambulance calling me a whore."

"You haven't found the right man yet. But he'll turn up. Young, handsome, wounded, possibly as rich as George. Probably twice as stupid. They're all stupid, lost in their fantasies of heroism. Risking their lives to convince us they're worthy of our love. Or lying about it, like Arthur Hunthouse."

Polly was back in the operating room at Château Givry. Paul Lebrun bent over a wounded poilu, murmuring, *Ah, Dolbier, do you think the war will enable modern women to triumph over us? I think it will have a precisely opposite effect. The war will evoke all the ancient virtues. They will surrender to pity, sympathy, admiration for men's valor. They will become consolers, comforters, once more.*

"Their bravery means something, Eleanor. It will always mean something," Polly said.

"It doesn't!" Eleanor said.

"In Picardy I had a friend you never met, a British woman named Anita Sinclair. She was a feminist of the most militant kind. One of Mrs. Pankhurst's shock troops. But she gave it up for the war. She said life was a series of vortices and the war was the greatest vortex of all. She died proving a woman could—and should—share men's bravery."

"Idiocy!" Eleanor said.

"No," Polly said. "Bravery. I could never turn my back on bravery, Eleanor. I could never call it stupid."

"Idiocy!" Eleanor insisted, flinging herself away from Polly to glare at her with remarkably unloving eyes. For all Eleanor's talk of love without domination, Polly suspected that bad habit would persist, no matter whom Eleanor embraced.

"I'm offering you a future of accomplishment and happiness! Think about it," Eleanor said, stalking out of the room.

Polly crawled into bed and fell asleep instantly. She dreamed she was in Maine with George Eagleton, sitting in his roadster on the cliffs in the moonlight. But he was in uniform, complete with his helmet. He kept trying to kiss her, but she was wearing her gas mask. She awoke in the dawn, her flesh vibrating with melancholy.

She dressed and tiptoed out of the house. The rumble of guns from the east seemed louder in the gray stillness. She took a taxi to the Gare de l'Est and a train from there to Neuilly, which was only a few miles from the evacuation hospital. At the railroad station, ambulances were loading wounded men onto a train going to base hospitals on the other side of Paris. She had no trouble hitching a ride in an empty, driven by a yawning Red Cross man.

The guns were much louder now. Their thunder drifted across the summery green pastures, as aged farmers led their plodding cows out to graze. "Heavy fighting?" she asked.

"Very heavy," the Red Cross man said.

At the hospital, Polly checked the admitting office and found George Eagleton's ward. She mounted the stairs with determined steps. This was not the sort of bravery Anita Sinclair would applaud. But it was still bravery. She was going to try to talk to George again. Even though it was clear he no longer loved her, she was not going to let him say goodbye in that atrocious fashion.

At the entrance to the ward, she asked a short brisk nurse how Lieutenant Eagleton was doing. "He must be feeling fine," she snapped. "He walked out of here sometime during the night. Put on his uniform in the toilet and just walked out. If he gets another dose of mustard gas he'll be a dead man."

Polly's eyes misted; she felt her throat fill. How could you not admire such men? She knew she had given Eleanor the right answer.

"You'd think they didn't have any other lieutenants in the army," scoffed Miss Brisk.

"Have you been over here long?"

"I got here a week ago on a six months' contract."

"When you've been here for a while, you'll call it bravery," Polly said.

46. DEATH VALLEY

CAPTAIN HUNTHOUSE ADVANCED ON GENERAL Bliss, a brown piece of paper in his hand. Bliss knew what it was before he spoke. "Another communication from Ninth Army headquarters, General."

Bliss tore open the envelope and read the message in one mordant glance.

> You will renew attacks by both your brigades at 5:30 A.M. tomorrow. You will be supported by the 62nd French Division on your left, the 28th American Division on your right. Your objective remains the same: the Vesle River. Viomenil.

Bliss stared out at the ruins of the village of Beauvardes. Rain sluiced from the gray sky. His lunch, a vile concoction of chili beans and ham, lay half eaten on his desk. He was in the cellar of Beauvardes' shattered city hall. The whitewashed walls oozed moisture. He slept on a cot in the corner. Was he living like an infantryman to guarantee he was as miserable as his men?

Bliss avoided Captain Hunthouse's eyes. He was beginning to detest this man, for no obvious reason. He was an adequate aide, alert, subservient, eager to please.

"Bad news, General?" Hunthouse asked. He was trying to be sympathetic, but it only made him more repugnant. In a desperate attempt to amuse himself Bliss had given Hunthouse a secret name: Arthur Asskisser.

"Not really. Just another order to send our men back into the German army's favorite shooting gallery."

Hunthouse stared ravenously. Not a word of reproach or correction for his intemperate general. On the contrary, Bliss suspected everything he said to Arthur Asskisser was circulated rapidly through headquarters and the division.

"Have you gotten yesterday's casualty list yet?"

"It'll be on your desk in a half hour."

The hastily typed sheaf of papers arrived within minutes. Bliss only looked at the fifty names of the dead and wounded from the 179th Regiment's A Company. Captain Jonathan Alden USA was not among them. Bliss stuffed the list in the drawer, cursing his weakness.

A half hour later, a big staff car with a four-star pennant hanging limply from the fender splashed to a stop in front of Bliss's headquarters. Into his dank dim dungeon strode John J. Pershing. His gleaming boots and Sam Browne belt made Bliss's soiled sweaty uniform feel twice as grubby. "I just saw Viomenil," Pershing said. "He can't understand why you're stalled on the Ourcq."

We're stalled on the Ourcq for the same reason Haig stalled on the Somme in 1916 and the Germans stalled on the Marne last month. Without surprise you can't get far against machine guns and artillery. These probably fatal words leaped to Bliss's lips, but he did not say them.

"If Viomenil gave us time to plan our attacks, to coordinate our artillery and indirect fire from our machine guns, we'd be across that miserable river and beyond it."

That got nothing but a grunt from the commander in chief. "How's Quickmeyer doing?"

"Great. The rebels love him."

Quickmeyer's call to Bliss had coincided nicely with the collapse of Colonel Wade Hampton Stuart. He had come unglued in the attempted crossing of the Marne. The division's one thousand casualties in that atrocity were mostly in his regiment. He had protested wildly that Bliss was persecuting him and his men. Instead of telling him that Pickett had not complained to Robert E. Lee, Bliss had sent him to the doctors, who diagnosed nervous prostration.

"I hated to lose Quick," Pershing said.

Bliss grimly dragged the subject back to his nemesis, Viomenil. "I think we're wasting men, Jack. All we have to do is keep the pressure on with patrols and artillery until the Germans do what they're going to do anyway, when they're ready: pull back to the Vesle."

"We can't afford to gamble on your goddamn predictions," Pershing snapped. "If we're going to get an army of our own, we've got to prove we can go all out."

Bliss saw there was no point in telling Pershing what it was like to serve under General Viomenil. The division's ordeal had begun with the order to launch an assault across the Marne. The day after their savage repulse, the Germans retreated without a shot being fired at them—as Bliss had predicted they would. Viomenil immediately flung the Lafayettes across the river and ordered a headlong pursuit by the entire Ninth Army. Assuming the Germans retreated like the French on the Chemin des Dames, he predicted he would trap the enemy against the Vesle River, twenty miles north of the Marne, and destroy them.

In the forest of Fère, the Lafayette Division ran into ferocious opposition, especially around Croix Rouge Farm, half a dozen stone buildings in a big clearing that dominated the main road north. It was taken only after a vicious struggle and another thousand casualties. Other divisions met equally stubborn rearguard resistance while the rest of the German army retreated north of the River Ourcq, a muddy little stream about half the distance to the Vesle.

Viomenil, still convinced the Germans were fleeing to the Vesle, immediately ordered an attack across the Ourcq. Once more there was no time to reconnoiter, to plan, to coordinate infantry and artillery. But Bliss had swallowed his doubts and complied. Both of the Lafayette's infantry brigades had stormed across the river, only to discover the Germans had lost interest in retreating.

The hills north of the Ourcq were two hundred feet high and gave the Germans irresistible fields of fire for machine guns. A deluge of gas and heavy artillery added to the carnage. Nevertheless, his New York Irishmen and South Carolina rebels fought their way into the town of Sergy, just north of the river. Ferocious counterattacks by the crack 4th Prussian Guards Division drove them out seven times in the course of the day, which ended with the Germans in control of Sergy at sunset.

"I want you to take Sergy today and keep it," Pershing said, running his finger along the map. "Show that picklepuss Viomenil your boys can do anything he asks."

"We'll do our damnedest, Jack."

Pershing loomed over him like a figure in a nightmare. "Say that again—and mean it."

Bliss tried to tell himself Pershing was trapped too. The French had maneuvered him into obeying every order, no matter how outrageous, as the price of an independent American army. They were all trapped. Didn't that somehow make the whole thing honorable? "We'll—do—our—damnedest," Bliss said.

Twenty-four hours later, the Lafayette Division had Sergy, after taking it and losing it four more times. The little town's sloping streets were finally conquered by a mixed bag of companies from the Celts and the rebels, led by an equally skewed group of officers ranging from Colonels Harry Quickmeyer and Joe Perry to Lieutenant George Eagleton, with Captain Jonathan Alden somewhere in the middle performing deeds of total recklessness. By the time it was over, both Quickmeyer and Perry had recommended him for the Distinguished Service Cross.

At twilight Bliss and Hunthouse walked through the ruins of Sergy, past bodies of dead Germans and Americans killed during the last two days. Father Kelly knelt beside one of them, writing his name on a pad. After the battle on the Marne, Bliss had put him in charge of the burial detail. Joe Perry had suggested forming one after seeing men break down in the middle of burying their friends. Kelly looked up at Bliss with eyes that seemed to plead for an explanation.

On the outskirts of Sergy, Bliss heard a worried voice asking a lieutenant if he was okay. The answer was a series of strangled coughs. He found Sergeant O'Connor standing over Lieutenant

Eagleton, who was doubled up in a foxhole. "What's wrong with you, Lieutenant?" Bliss asked.

More strangulation. "Nothing—sir," Eagleton said.

O'Connor said Eagleton had gotten a bad dose of gas four days ago. The division doctors had shipped him to the hospital. "He was back the next day, coughin' like hell. We were glad to have him around in this fight, but—"

"Shut up," Eagleton said. "I'm—fine, General."

Bliss found Captain Alden a few hundred yards away, siting machine guns. "Congratulations," he said. "You won a DSC today."

"I'd rather have a hot meal for my men, General."

"That's on its way. What about that lieutenant who's a walking gas casualty? Are you going to let him keep ruining his lungs?"

"He'll survive," Alden said. "I told him I wanted him back as soon as possible. I'm learning a lot from combat, General. How to motivate men. How to challenge them to be braver than they thought they were."

The words cut. The Captain intended them to cut. The son was telling his army father he could do things the pathetic old fogy could no longer manage. What was the General supposed to say? In the lexicon of their profession, there was only one phrase. "Well done," Bliss said and retreated into the night.

The next morning he drove to Viomenil's headquarters for breakfast. As they discussed how to attack the Germans beyond Sergy, Colonel Douglas Fairchild burst in on them. His uniform was mud-smeared, his eyes glazed with exhaustion. He told them he had spent the night patrolling the front with a small escort. He had irrefutable evidence that the Germans were retreating. Batteries of artillery had passed him in the darkness, heading north toward the Vesle. There was nothing left along the front but a thin line of machine-gunners.

"Such enterprise deserves another palm on your croix de guerre, Colonel," Viomenil said.

Fairchild glowed. Bliss was tempted to ask how many reporters he had taken with him. A chief of staff was not supposed to be patrolling no-man's-land. He was supposed to be planning the next battle. But with Viomenil in command, that was impossible. So why not let Dougie collect his medal?

"Our pursuit must be immediate and vigorous. We still have a chance to crush them against the Vesle," Viomenil said.

"My staff is already drafting orders," Fairchild said.

"The orders will specify there will be no advance without strong preliminary patrols," Bliss said. "I don't intend to lose another thousand men to the German rearguard."

"Nonsense!" Viomenil said. "Push both your brigades forward in force. Brush aside any resistance."

"Is that an order, General?" Bliss said.

"I am not here to give advice."

Three days later, Bliss stood on a denuded hilltop looking down on the valley of the Vesle River. On the south the land was bare and flat, with few trees or any other kind of natural cover. To the north, the hills came down close to the river and several towns clung to their slopes, as Sergy did above the Ourcq.

Not a single German had been trapped on the south bank of the Vesle. They trudged to safety over numerous pontoon bridges, which they promptly collected on the north shore and hauled away to be used another day. Now, instead of Germans, the Americans were the ones who were trapped on the south shore. As Bliss watched, one, two, three, four, five whizbangs exploded around foxholes that belonged to Ireland's Own. Medics ran forward lugging stretchers and went flat as more shells came in. They dragged a wounded man out of a hole and struggled rearward in ankle-deep mud.

In its present depleted state, the Lafayette Division could no more cross the Vesle than it could fly in a body to Berlin. Some battalions were down to the size of companies. A quarter of the officers were dead or wounded. Shell-shock cases were multiplying by the hour. The colonels of all four regiments had warned him the men had reached the limit of their endurance.

Cursing, Bliss walked back down the hill to a field hospital on the reverse slope, out of sight of German artillery observers. Ambulances were arriving to evacuate the day's wounded. Who should step out of the first one but Polly Warden. Her gray uniform was clean and crisp. Her red hair glistened in the sunlight. "Hello, General," she said. "Are you as unhappy as you look?"

"Unhappier, by far. I'm actually trying to look cheerful. It's my job."

"Death Valley," she said. "That's what the men call it down there."

"It's apt."

"Can't you do something about it?"

The words reached the Bliss who was raging behind the obedient servant of General Viomenil. "I'm going to try," he said.

He leaped into his car and Mile-a-Minute Murphy hurtled back to Sergy, where Viomenil had set up a temporary headquarters. As usual, his aides let Bliss wait for twenty or thirty minutes while the General said his prayers to God or Generalissimo Foch. Finally the audience was granted.

"General," Bliss said, "I'm requesting you to relieve my division. The men are dangerously exhausted. The shell and machine-gun fire to which they're exposed is demoralizing them. You've relieved half a dozen other divisions in your army since we crossed the Ourcq."

"They've been in line a long time, I admit," Viomenil said. "But they must remain a little longer. Surely they want to be able to say they are the men who drove the Germans not only from the hills of the Ourcq but from the Vesle."

"How do you propose to do that, General? Those hills are twice as high and far more heavily fortified. As I told you more than once, the Germans never planned to stand on the Ourcq. Here there's every evidence of determination."

"We can only find that out by putting them to the test," Viomenil said. "I wish to establish bridgeheads across the Vesle. We'll begin with the town of Fismette, which our intelligence tells us is lightly held. Put a reinforced company in there tonight. Let's see what the Germans do."

"See what they'll do? They'll wipe it out to the last man. If we're going to try to cross that river, let's attack with our whole army. Let's make a serious effort."

"General, you are the vocal critic of our faith in the spirit of the attack. Everything we hear from your headquarters reeks of sarcasm and hostility. That's why I'm bending to your inclinations, as it were, and risking only a company to explore the enemy's intentions. If they're serious about standing on the north bank, we've only lost a company to discover this important fact."

Bliss shook his head dazedly. "General, did you ever command a company?" he said.

"Of course. In my captaincy days."

"So did I. It was the most meaningful experience of my life. I grew to love every one of my men. Even the screw-ups and the bad apples and the cowards. I worked with them day and night to make them better soldiers. If some general ordered me to lose that company, I would have been tempted to do the unthinkable—kill him."

"I fear you lack aloofness, a requisite of the successful general officer. Perhaps you should have remained a captain. Such speculations aside, I want that company across the river in Fismette by tomorrow morning."

"Another order, General?"

"Another order—with the compliments of Generalissimo Foch, as well as my own."

47. *INTO THE FLAME*

BLISS SCRUPULOUSLY AVOIDED HAVING ANYTHING to do with selecting the company to go into Fismette. He made the order as impersonal as possible and sent it to Chief of Staff Fairchild via Hunthouse with no comment. In the morning, he issued orders to support them with machine guns and artillery if they were attacked. Only then did he ask Fairchild what company had been chosen. "Company A of the first battalion of Ireland's Own," Fairchild said. "I thought the assignment called for one of our most reliable officers. I saw Captain Alden in action at Sergy—"

"Of course," Bliss said.

Fairchild had brought Company A up to strength with drafts from two other companies who had fought well in Sergy. They had crossed the Vesle on the spanners of a wrecked bridge at midnight and occupied the town against light resistance. So far the Germans had not reacted.

Bliss called for his car and headed for the front with Hunthouse. As they descended the hills overlooking Death Valley, Bliss got a picture-postcard view of the dark swift Vesle rushing between sprawling Fismes and its satellite village, Fismette, on the north bank of the river. The summer sun beat down, making every detail in the landscape glow.

Behind Fismette's single main street stretched walled gardens that ran a good hundred yards up a steep hill to the right and angled down to the river on the left. You did not have to be a general to see Company A's position was lousy. The hill on the right was at least three hundred feet high and presumably owned by the Germans.

More hills loomed on the left, about a quarter of a mile inland.

The Germans began shelling Bliss's car as it hurtled across Death Valley. Shrapnel whanged against the fenders. Hunthouse all but curled into a ball in the seat beside him. In another time and place Bliss would have been amused. He strode into Joe Perry's command post in the cellar of a ruined house in Fismes. He was on the field telephone, talking to their artillery on the hills behind Death Valley.

Perry hung up and regarded Bliss with unfriendly eyes. "I don't get this, Mal," he said.

"A probe. Orders from General Viomenil."

"Why didn't you tell him to stuff it in his ragout?"

"That's against the rules, Joe. We're in the French army. You wouldn't expect me to say that to Pershing, would you?"

"If he gave you an order this dumb? Yes."

Was that why Perry was a temporary colonel and Bliss was a general? Before he could find an answer to that question, the world started to explode. From the hills on both sides of Fismette, mortars rained down, blowing apart whole houses, demolishing a barricade Jonathan Alden had built at the head of the street along with most of the soldiers manning it, tearing up chunks of the gardens. From three sides at least two thousand German infantry swarmed forward in their usual style, covered by at least fifty heavy machine guns firing from the hills. No American could move from behind a wall or come out of a house without getting killed.

"Jesus Christ, Joe, give them some help," Bliss said.

"It's coming," Perry said.

The division artillery began plastering the machine guns in the hills. Machine-gunners on the roofs of Fismes poured indirect fire over the roofs of Fismette into the oncoming German infantry. From a roof beside one of the machine guns, Bliss watched Sergeant O'Connor, identifiable by the Chauchat slung on his shoulder, jumping in and out of windows to get from house to house, organizing a pullback on the left. A big lieutenant, almost certainly Eagleton, was doing the same thing on the right.

Company A fought from house to house, firing out windows, flinging grenades down on Germans in the gardens and in the main street. About a hundred and fifty of them made it back to a huddle of small houses by the river. Captain Alden was one of the last to arrive, lugging a heavy machine gun on his shoulder, the ammunition belts wrapped around his body. Through his field glasses Bliss could see exaltation on the young face. He was showing his general what bravery could do.

A rocket soared into the blue sky. "What's that mean?" Bliss said.

"He wants reinforcements," Joe Perry said. "Should I send him another company?"

"No. Tell him to get the hell out of there."

A runner with the order to retire started across the ruined bridge. German shells blew him off. Two more runners died the same way. Their bodies drifted downstream in the dark current. Mortars and artillery rained down on the bridge. The Germans had no intention of letting Company A escape.

Numbly, Bliss watched Captain Alden attempt the impossible. Without reinforcements, Company A started north again. It was dirty work. There were still hundreds of Germans in the town, and they soon knew what was coming. Light machine guns blasted from windows. Some of the machine guns on the hills recovered from the shell fire and went to work again, shooting men in the back as they rushed the houses.

Bliss watched O'Connor slither along a wall, throw a grenade in a window, and fire his Chauchat ahead of him as he jumped after it. A moment later he bolted out the door, pursued by half a dozen Germans firing rifles. He dove over a wall and leveled his Chauchat at them. Nothing. The machine gun had jammed. It was a symbolic moment. O'Connor threw the gun at them and shot three of them with his pistol. The survivors ran back in the house but O'Connor did not follow them.

The counterattack sputtered out on both sides of the main street. In five minutes about fifty survivors were back where they started, in the houses by the river. Bliss watched Alden and Eagleton organize them for a last stand along the garden walls. "Send another runner. Get them out of there," Bliss said.

"It's no go, Mal. Alden will have to make up his own mind,"

Perry said, pointing to the twisted remnants of the bridge, still under relentless shell fire.

Alden ordered the machine gun set up in the north corner of the wall of the garden closest to the river, where it could cover a retreat to the riverbank. Engulfed by dread, Bliss knew what he was thinking: *The men come first.*

From the other side of the river, Perry's machine guns did their best. The artillery continued to blast the Germans in the hills. But there were too many Germans already inside Fismette and in the fields within grenade range. They crawled closer and closer, and grenades sailed over the stone walls to wound and kill. The single heavy machine gun could not stop them. Neither could half a dozen Chauchats firing from the upper windows of two of the houses.

Over the wall of the garden above the one with the machine gun leaped a great tongue of fire. The men crouched along the wall screamed in agony and tried to run away. A few of them managed to get to their feet but they were living torches. It was a *Flammenwerfer*, a weapon that added a new dimension of terror to infantry warfare.

What was left of Company A ran for the riverbank. Captain Alden took charge of the machine gun. Eagleton ran up to him and shouted something. Alden waved him away and the Lieutenant joined the sprint to the river. There was no hope of getting across the shell-smashed bridge. The fugitives had to swim or die.

Bullets from the German machine guns on the hill churned the water around the swimmers. Two of them rolled over in agony and went under. Perry was shouting orders. Bliss followed him down from the roof like a man walking through a nightmare. Men were lugging machine guns to the riverbank. Others were already there, shooting at Germans attacking the machine gun which was still firing staccato bursts from the angle of the garden wall.

A sodden Lieutenant Eagleton was on the riverbank, dragging exhausted swimmers to safety. Chaplain Kelly, Joe Perry, and a dozen others joined him. The machine gun in the garden continued to fire. From the riverbank, Bliss could no longer see it. At any moment it would stop and Captain Alden would run for the river. It was the sensible thing to do. He had killed enough Germans for one day.

Instead there was a tremendous *whoosh* of flame and a curling funnel of black smoke: the *Flammenwerfer* again. The machine gun was silent. Over the garden wall leaped two figures in khaki. One was Sergeant O'Connor; the other was Fat Clymer. O'Connor raced to the riverbank as Germans leaped over the wall in pursuit. Clymer turned, leveled his bayonet, and charged. "Fucking sons of bitches!" he screamed and bayoneted the first two before they could raise their rifles. But there were five, six, seven of them. They riddled him with bullets as he raised his bayonet for another thrust. "Oh, God, oh, God!" Father Kelly cried.

O'Connor ran up and down the bank while more and more Germans appeared on the wall to shoot at him. Lieutenant Eagleton was pointing at the river. "Jump in!" he shouted.

"I can't swim!" O'Connor roared.

Eagleton dove into the river and started swimming toward him. Harvard was risking his life to save the slum mug who had beaten him up in Union Square. It was a parable of American democracy. The Lieutenant was proving beyond debate Bliss's prophecy to Father Kelly about a soldier's readiness to risk his life for a friend. But Bliss watched it without emotion. He was a statue general made of lead.

Eagleton was treading water within ten feet of the north bank. The Vesle was not a wide river, no more than thirty yards. "Jump in. That's a goddamn order!" Eagleton bellowed.

O'Connor jumped and went down as if he were made of cement. Eagleton dove after him and surfaced with his arm around the Sergeant's chest, hauling him toward the other shore. Germans ran down to the riverbank and started shooting at them. Joe Perry's machine guns and riflemen on the south bank soon discouraged that activity. The German machine guns on the hills poured bullets at the swimmers, but it was long-range shooting. Bliss stood on the bank watching eager hands drag them to safety.

O'Connor lay on the grass beside Eagleton, gasping and choking. "Lieutenant," he said. "If we get through this thing, you got a friend for life."

"Sergeant," Bliss said, "is anyone left alive over there?"

Bullets whizzed around them. Captain Hunthouse ran up to

him. "General, you shouldn't expose yourself—"

"Shut up," Bliss said. He repeated his question.

The Sergeant shook his head. "We put up a hell of a fight, General," he said, "but there was just too damn many of them."

"Why were we there, General? What the hell were we trying to prove?" Eagleton asked.

"We were obeying orders from General Yves St. Pierre Viomenil, commander of the French Ninth Army," Bliss said. "I'm putting you in for a Distinguished Service Cross for what you just did in that river."

"General," the Sergeant said. "Captain Alden gave me a message for you. He said—to thank you for everything."

Bliss wanted one of the random German bullets whizzing around them to smash into his skull. It was the only possible antidote to his pain. As he walked numbly toward his car, Joe Perry grabbed him by the arm. "Mal," he said. "Don't blame yourself for this. You're still the best damn division commander in this army."

Shells exploded around the car as Mile-a-Minute Murphy raced across Death Valley, but Bliss barely noticed them. He was contemplating the absolute justice of Colonel Fairchild's choice of Company A of Ireland's Own, commanded by Captain Jonathan Alden USA. It was a peculiarly perfect punishment for Malvern Hill Bliss's gutless inability to stand up to Jack Pershing and Yves St. Pierre Viomenil and Ferdinand Foch and their readiness to waste American lives to win themselves more ink in the history books.

"Where are we going, General?" Arthur Hunthouse asked.

Ah. The perfect question from Arthur Asskisser, the aide he also deserved. What was he but an asskisser with stars on his shoulders? "Ninth Army headquarters," he said.

Big-nosed Colonel de Heartburn told him General Viomenil was busy. Bliss brushed him aside and strode into the great man's office. "Your experiment on the north bank of the Vesle is over, General," he said. "I want the Lafayette Division withdrawn to a rest area tonight."

"I've just been briefed on the unfortunate affair," Viomenil said. "We're issuing a communiqué, reporting that the Lafayette Division repelled a strong enemy attack this morning. I hope that will be some consolation."

Did this man think he could be comforted by an official lie? Was that all history amounted to, in the end? Was this what he was trying to tell him?

Viomenil inhaled some snuff. "At the battle of the Marne in 1914, I commanded the right flank. I sent whole divisions forward, only to see them annihilated in an hour. You cannot allow your feelings of sympathy and pity to be engaged in such matters. They must be reserved for your private life."

"Ah. Private life."

Bliss thought of Polly Warden and his desire to fill his hands with that silken red hair. That was forbidden now. All private pleasures, even the approximations of love, were forbidden. The unofficial man behind the official general—the man he thought women evoked—was equally detestable. As soon as possible, he would go before a psychological firing squad.

"We'll send your division to a rest area south of the Marne, around Épernay. Pleasant country—and not too far from Paris."

"Ah. Paris."

He would show this Frenchman who could be aloof. From now on he would be immune to every emotion, private and public. From this day forward Malvern Hill Bliss was a dead man disguised as a living general. Only his military brain would continue to function. His treacherous heart, his traitorous nervous system, would be impervious to love. He would live like a trapped beast, gnawing on his own flesh, waiting for the bullet or shell that would end his ordeal.

48. IN THE HEART OF THE HEART OF PARIS

Dear General Bliss:

    I heard from one of your wounded about Captain Alden's death in the fighting for Fismette. I know you grieve for all your losses, but I also know this loss must be particularly hard to bear. In spite of your quarrel, I am sure there was still a great deal of mutual affection between you. I want you to know how deeply I was saddened and extend to you my deepest sympathy.

                                    Gwendolyn (Polly) Warden

As she sealed this letter, Polly struggled against a wave of melancholy compounded by exhaustion. The day had begun with a tense meeting with Eleanor Kingswood. She still spent most of her time in Paris, but when she appeared at the hospital she was full of criticisms of the way Polly was running the ambulance group. Eleanor thought she was too lenient with emergency leaves and too careless about allowing the women to date officers from the hospital. What would they do if one of the drivers became pregnant? Did Polly want the Kingswood Ambulance Group to fulfill the nasty prophecies they had heard aboard the *Baltic*?

"Aboard the *Baltic* they thought we'd *all* go home pregnant," Polly said. "We can survive one or two accidents. I hope we don't have any, but you have to treat people like adults. You have to trust them."

Eleanor made it clear that one or two pregnancies might be enough to force her to find a new field director of the ambulance group.

"If you'd be happier with someone else, by all means hire her," Polly said. "I only hope you'll let me keep driving for you."

That temporarily shamed Eleanor into silence. She retreated to Paris and Polly headed for Death Valley. She drew four shell-shock cases for her ambulance. Strapped to their stretchers, they screamed and sobbed every time she hit a bump.

Back in the office, she found Martha Herzog waiting for her with a smile that was so cheerful, Polly almost said something nasty. Did anyone have the right to be cheerful? Martha had just come back from forty-eight hours in Paris. By now, everyone in the ambulance group had taken these emergency leaves except the field director.

In Paris, Martha had met Dr. Isaac Pinkus—not by accident. The glow in her eyes suggested her anguish over Harry Quickmeyer might be diminishing. She hoped to see more of Dr. Pinkus. The Lafayette Division was in a rest area only twenty miles away. Their morale, according to Pinkus, was poor. Their sojourn in Death Valley, the defeat at Fismette, had left everyone depressed and bitter.

The following day, after an especially grueling run to the front—the Germans had shelled the road during the night and almost destroyed it, making the return trip agony for the wounded— Polly was astonished to find Malvern Hill Bliss sitting in her office. He looked ghastly. There were dark circles under his bloodshot eyes. His skin was gray, his lips bloodless.

"Got your lovely letter. Wanted to thank you," he said. "You understand. I don't know why. But you—unnerstand."

She realized he had been drinking. In fact, he was drunk.

"Of course you don't completely unnerstand why Captain Alden died. That's what I want to tell you. It was my fault. I ordered him to cross that river and die. Because I'm a coward."

"I find that hard to believe, General."

"It's the truth," Bliss said. "I'm going through the hospital now. Going to visit each wounded man and apologize to him personally for my disgusting cowardice—that betrayed him and his friends. Going to explain this whole murderous farce and who's responsible for it."

Polly was back in the Château Givry, hearing herself say similar things to Dr. Giroux-Langin. "General Bliss," she said. "I don't think you should do any such thing. You're extremely distraught—and a bit drunk, I'm afraid. I think you should come with me to Paris. There's a doctor I want you to see, one who helped me last year when I was in a similar state of mind."

He shook his head. "I've got a division to run. Eight thousand replacements to train. Once I get this off my chest I'll be all right. Isn't confession good for the soul?"

"Perhaps. But I doubt if it's good for a general's reputation."

"Goddamn my reputation! Just another word for career. You don't know what I've done for my career, Miss Warden. I've betrayed everyone who ever loved me. Sacrificed them with cold-blooded cowardice to get these stars on my shoulders. Don't feel sorry for me. I'm not worth it."

A rumble of heavy guns from Death Valley redoubled Polly's determination. "You're suffering from a serious case of exhausted nerves, General. I insist on your coming with me to Paris now. I will not let you go into that hospital and make a fool of yourself!"

Bliss slumped in his chair. "Why do women think they can rescue hopeless cases?" he said.

Outside, Polly found Arthur Hunthouse leaning against Bliss's car, smoking a cigarette. She told him General Bliss had decided to go to Paris for a few days' rest. He would have to hitch a ride back to the division.

Hunthouse goggled at her. "You're going with him?"

"That's none of your business, Arthur."

Hunthouse's expression made it clear he intended to spread the story across France. Polly decided it was better to let him think the worst about her than tell him the truth about Bliss. Thanks to Charles Louis Lebrun, she no longer had a reputation to lose.

"I guess those rumors Eleanor told me about you are true," Arthur said. "The war has a way of bringing out hidden character traits in everybody."

Polly considered telling Arthur what the war had brought out in Eleanor, but she decided to let him find out for himself. She sent Hunthouse on his way and put Martha Herzog in charge of the ambulance group. Trusting Martha's discretion, she told her the whole story.

"We'll be fine. Don't worry about us," Martha said. "Those forty-eight-hour leaves have done wonders for everyone."

In two hours Polly was escorting General Bliss into Dr. Giroux-Langin's hospital on the Rue Desnouettes. He had said very little to her on the way except a few cryptic remarks about the danger of altering a man's soul. Not without some anxiety, she told him he was going to see a woman doctor. He did not seem bothered by this news.

Upstairs, to her immense relief, Polly found Dr. Giroux-Langin was on duty and delighted to see her. Polly swiftly explained the situation. The doctor nodded briskly. "There's nothing unusual about it. I saw half a dozen French generals break down at Verdun."

She studied Polly for a moment with pursed lips. "Ambulance drivers break down too," she said. "When is the last time you've had a leave?"

"Three or four months."

"Abominable! You've learned nothing from your previous experience. Bring in the General. You will stay and translate for us, I presume?"

The consultation began pleasantly, with the Doctor gravely thanking Bliss for stopping the Germans on the Marne. But Polly was soon flinching as she translated Giroux-Langin's blunt questions and the General's candid answers about his marriage, his sex life, his work habits, his lack of religious faith. She almost wept as she repeated in French the story of his wife and son's deaths in the Philippines. She trembled as he described his brutal clashes with Foch, Degoutte, Viomenil, and other French generals and the order that led to Captain Alden's death at Fismette. Would Giroux-Langin accuse him of slandering France?

"I too have small regard for Foch and his school of attack, General," the Doctor said. "I've seen the results in this and other hospitals. For me, France has only one real general, Pétain."

"Would that it were true, Doctor," Bliss said.

Giroux-Langin pondered her notes for a moment. "Miss Warden's diagnosis is essentially correct, General Bliss. You're suffering from exhausted nerves, worsened by severe emotional trauma. You cannot under any circumstances return to duty for at least a week. You must let go, turn your back on what seems unbearable for a while. Confess your limitations, even your helplessness, always a difficult thing for a man to do. Allow faith and hope and love to revive in your soul. These are not merely religious terms—they're natural drives, the basic components of the human spirit."

Polly translated as Giroux-Langin spoke. It was a curious experience, turning another woman's words into her own. She felt drawn beyond the neutral tone of the translator into a desire to make the words personal, to express not only their meaning but her sympathy.

The rest of Giroux-Langin's advice was similar to what she had given Polly last year. General Bliss was to drink nothing stronger than wine, ignore the newspapers, toughen his spirit with cold baths, and go for long walks in the Bois. She gave him a prescription for some pills that would help him sleep.

She presumed he would not want to stay in her hospital for his week of rest. That would require explanations to superiors. She suggested he check into a small quiet hotel. "For the first few days, at least, you'll require supervision. I suggest putting yourself in Miss Warden's care. She's an experienced nurse. Young as she is, I have great confidence in her judgment."

That did not exactly jibe with the "Abominable!" Giroux-Langin had flung at Miss Warden's judgment minutes before the consultation began. Polly suspected the Doctor was using the General's crisis to order both of them to spend a week in Paris. But she had gone too far to turn back now. In a half hour, she and her patient were checking into the Hôtel du Quai Voltaire overlooking the Seine. It had only thirty-three rooms, most of them empty.

Polly rented adjoining rooms on the third floor. General Bliss telephoned the Lafayette Division headquarters and told Arthur Hunthouse to dispatch a valise with enough clothes and money for a week in Paris as soon as possible. Polly telephoned the evacuation hospital and told Martha Herzog where she would be if an emergency developed.

The rooms were clean and decorated with bright prints of paintings by Degas and Monet. Across the Seine loomed the majestic buildings of the Louvre and the green trees and shrubs of the Tuileries. The General sat down on his bed. "Now what, Doctor?"

"I think it would be best if you went to sleep as soon as possible. I'll get this prescription filled—"

The hesitant smile on his face accentuated the sadness in his eyes. "Maybe I don't need any pills. Maybe I only need what you've already given me," he said. "Your love."

He said this so calmly, with such assurance, for a moment Polly was angry. Why did he assume such a thing? This was a purely professional arrangement. One of the best doctors in Paris had assigned her to care for him.

Somewhere in her body, the word love acquired enormous weight. She sat down on the bed beside him. Could he possibly be right? Did she already love this man? He took her hands. "I've loved you since that night at the American embassy when you stopped me from turning into a drunken cynic in front of your eyes. But without your love, I couldn't keep up the performance," he said.

George Eagleton and Paul Lebrun had told Polly they needed her love. But they had demanded she hide from the war, ignore its ugliness and pain and death. This man was asking her to share the war with him. He wanted her to love his anguished sense of responsibility for the lives of his men, his pain, his grief. "I thought about loving you, but it seemed—impossible," she said.

"I thought the same thing. But here we are."

Together in a hotel room in the middle of Paris. Was it all an immensely clever scheme on his part? No. He could not possibly have anticipated her reaction to his drunken visit to the hospital or known about Dr. Giroux-Langin. It was the war, bending their lives from parallel lines to a mysterious convergence.

The General was kissing her gently on her lips, her throat. "If Dr. Giroux-Langin hears about this—" Polly said.

"She's French. She won't be as shocked as she pretends to be," Bliss said.

"There are Americans to worry about too," Polly said, thinking of Eleanor Kingswood and Arthur Hunthouse.

"There's no one to worry about," Bliss said. "That includes John

J. Pershing and Woodrow Wilson and Ferdinand Foch. For one entire week we've been forbidden to worry about anyone but each other."

First they bathed—it was one of the two days a week when Paris had hot water—and then they made silken tender love in the double bed with Paris murmuring outside the open window. Love in the center of Paris. Love that somehow centered Polly's life for the first time. This man was where she wanted to be, at the center of the war.

She also sensed a spiritual centering. There was gravity as well as tenderness, sadness as well as joy in this love. It was an amazing blend of loneliness and discovery, pity and admiration. It momentarily abolished the war, the sobbing and the screaming wounded, the tumbled dead, yet refused to deny them. It challenged the carnage with a new kind of courage.

Polly never filled Dr. Giroux-Langin's prescription for sleeping pills. She and Bliss slept in each other's arms from 6 P.M. until 9 A.M. It was her first full night's sleep in months. She awoke to random traffic sounds and lay there slowly remembering yesterday. Her body and her mind felt new. Months of the war's grime had vanished. *Cafard* was only a memory. An enormous, formless gratitude flooded her heart.

She kissed him softly until he awoke. "I want to make sure you're real," she said.

"I haven't felt this real since I landed in Saint-Nazaire," he said. He drew her against him for a long deep kiss. "You know all about me," he said. "But I know almost nothing about you. I want to hear everything."

Wrapped in his arms, she told him about her college dreams of feminine glory and about George Eagleton. Then, in a rush, the hospital at Château Givry, Paul Lebrun, his father, Clemenceau, Anita. Trying to tell him exactly what she had felt about each of them, she revealed herself as both vulnerable and strong, reckless and afraid, proud and ashamed. It was another kind of giving, more profound than her physical gift last night—a blending of self with self that left her weeping when it was over.

"*Cafard*," Bliss said. "It's at the heart of it all, isn't it. For both of us."

He was talking to himself as much as to her. But the understanding was as shared, as real, as his hand on her breast. It was emanating from both their lives, flooding them with intensity, meaning, hope. They made love within this aura, their minds as well as their hearts alive with desire. Somewhere in her soul Polly felt barriers crumbling and crashing. Behind her closed eyes she surrendered every denial, every fear, every reservation, to this man. He had become her need as much as she was his. She reached out to him, groping for new strength, new understanding.

For the next three days they wandered Paris. They ate at obscure bistros and avoided the Champs-Élysées and the boulevards. In the late afternoon they drank coffee in little side-street cafés where the sun threw sparks the color of burnt topaz from a glass of brandy on the next table. In those hours they sampled one of Paris's most precious gifts, *langueur*—the exquisite pleasure of doing absolutely nothing.

They visited Notre-Dame, which was full of women in black, praying for their men at the front—or the souls of their dead. Bliss lit a candle before a side altar. "What's that for?" Polly said.

"To thank the Virgin for sending you to me."

"Do you believe in her?"

"Not exactly. She's like God. I don't understand why, but I suspect she has something to do with the way things work."

They went to the Church of the Dome of the Invalides and pondered the tomb of Napoleon. They breathed the incense of *la gloire*, and Bliss talked again about war as the engine of history, a science and an art a nation had to master if it hoped to survive. To her surprise, Polly found herself still resisting the idea. For the rest of the morning they were separate selves again. She poured out her woman's abomination of war, and he replied with his male insistence on its inevitability—and the necessity for men and women to think intelligently about it.

"I'm beginning to see there's a large residue of pacifism lurking in your psyche, Dr. Warden," he said. "You may be very good at repairing damaged nerves, but I think you need a long course of treatment to detoxify you from your bout of peace-at-any-price fever. Fortunately, you've met the perfect therapist."

"I thought I was cured by the war," Polly said ruefully.

He shook his head. "Pacifism requires mental as well as emotional treatment."

"You can say what you please, but I admire that pacifist agitator you saw in Union Square. She was a wholehearted idealist."

"Without a brain."

"I begin to see why you're a general."

"I was just as obnoxious when I was a lieutenant."

They were sitting in one of their favorite small cafés in the Place des Vosges. The ancient square with its rose-red fifteenth-century buildings, their first floors concealed by an arched arcade, was an island of peace in the late afternoon. The man at the next table opened up a newspaper. The huge headlines shouted in French: GREAT BRITISH VICTORY! 26,000 PRISONERS! GERMANS IN FULL RETREAT! Bliss immediately bought copies of every paper on the nearest newsstand and rushed back to the hotel to read them with Polly's help.

The day before, August 8, 1918, the British army had taken the offensive against the German salient around Amiens created by Ludendorff's rout of the Fifth Army in March. Striking into its left flank as the American First and Second divisions had hit the Marne salient near Soissons they had scored one of the most spectacular victories of the war. "Maybe Haig's finally figured out how to do it the right way," Bliss said. "Or the Germans are starting to crack. This could change a lot of things. I'd better get back to the division."

"No!" Polly said. "As your nurse—and as a woman who loves you—I absolutely forbid it. Your nerves have only started to heal. You should stay here another four days. It could make a tremendous difference."

The telephone rang. Bliss picked it up. Standing a foot away, Polly heard a voice like the rasp of a file on iron. "I'll be there in fifteen minutes, Jack," Bliss said.

He hung up and began putting on his tie. "Pershing's at his residence. He wants to see me."

He tried to kiss away Polly's frown. "I'm all right. I feel fine," he said.

Polly spent the next hour alone in the room, reading about the British victory. She thought about Anita Sinclair and Major Rodney Blake and so many others she had seen in torment over the irresistible German offensive of the spring. It seemed like a dream. The last three days seemed like another dream.

The key turned in the lock, and Bliss walked into the room. In the late-afternoon light, he looked tired, almost frail. He sighed and sat down in an armchair. "Pershing just had lunch with Foch. We're going to form an independent American army and launch an offensive in three weeks. I'm going to command a corps."

"What does that mean?"

"Three divisions. Almost a hundred thousand men."

"You're not ready to take on that much responsibility," she said.

For a moment anger flared in his somber eyes. He heard the word ready in another context, as a challenge to his ability. Then he realized she was talking about his nerves. "Wars don't run on schedule, Doctor," he said. "None of us are ready. We haven't solved those problems I told you about—such as what open warfare really means."

Dread swelled in Polly's heart. She heard Georges Clemenceau saying, Men will die. Mine and yours. She wept sudden bitter tears. "I hate the thought of you going back. I wish I didn't have to go back either. I hate it. I hate it!" she cried.

"I'm glad you hate it," Bliss said, kissing her gently. "But you'll go back too. I know you will. I need the thought of you there with me. Let me be there with you—in the same way."

BOOK VI

49. A BIRTHDAY PRESENT FROM LADY LUCK

IN THE CROWDED HEADQUARTERS OF THE U.S. First Army's V Corps in the little French village of Maricourt, on the banks of the River Meuse, Malvern Hill Bliss pondered a map of the Saint-Mihiel salient, the big bulge in the French lines south of Verdun that was the target of the coming American offensive.

V Corps was to strike the west face of the salient. There was every reason to expect it would be a bloody business. The French had not attacked here since 1915, when they had been beaten back with terrific losses. The Germans had spent three years fortifying the twenty-five-mile-wide swath of woods and fields that guarded the Woëvre Plain, a kind of back door to the heart of Germany.

Somehow, throughout two weeks of frantic preparation, a part of Bliss remained free to think about the transformation of his soul that had taken place in Paris. He who was totally unworthy of being blessed had received a gift he could only describe as sacred. He felt awed—and alarmed by the responsibility he had assumed. He was torn between the bargain he had made to share the war with Polly Warden and a desire to protect her from the worst of it, now that he understood the source of the pain in her green eyes.

At times those eyes acquired an accusatory glare, reminding him that he may have convinced her war was an inevitable part of history but she still regarded it with loathing. At times he wondered if he really wanted to protect himself from thinking about the way they were plunging ahead, massing almost half a million men for this attack—without reforming their tactics. Had he allowed Jack Pershing to silence him with this promotion to corps commander?

No, no, there was no time to retrain the entire American Expeditionary Force. All he could do was hope for the best and try to run his share of the battle his way.

"General, an update from First Army headquarters on the artillery," Arthur Hunthouse said, dropping a sheaf of papers as thick as a Russian novel on his desk. Bliss shoved it aside and began writing to Polly.

> Burn this letter the minute you finish reading it. Certain characters with "von" for middle names would be delighted to get their hands on it.
>
> When I'm not thinking about you I'm up to my eyeballs in intelligence reports on the depths of various rivers and creeks, the width of thirteen or fourteen fields of barbed wire, and what happens to a tank if it rains. (It sinks into the mud and disappears—a wonderful weapon! But your friend George Patton is still convinced it's going to change the course of military history.) I'm delighted with my fellow corps commanders, particularly Hunter Liggett, who's running I Corps. He's fatter than Tasker Bliss and almost as old, but he's got a brain twice as big as Tasker's—and mine, too, for that matter. Pershing thought he was too fat to stand the strain over here. Liggett stopped him cold with: "There's nothing wrong with fat as long as it isn't above the neck."
>
> In V Corps I've got three division commanders to deal with—all major generals, naturally. Two of them are former Academy classmates, which makes for fairly smooth going. The third, who happens to be my replacement in the Lafayette Division, is Wiley Parker, the insufferable ex-chief of staff of the Second Division and architect of the Belleau Wood slaughter. He and I have been at each other's throats a number of times already. My corps chief of staff, a skeletonic six-foot-three double-dome named George Jorgenson, is of the same generation and agrees with him on everything. I have some hopes of educating Jorgenson, but Parker is hopeless. I lie awake nights trying to figure out ways to stop him from wrecking the Lafayette Division.
>
> Lest you are tempted to urge your friend Clemenceau to open peace negotiations immediately, let me assure you there are just as many feuds raging in the British and French and German armies. You no doubt wonder why my friend Jack Pershing handed my division over to the likes of Wiley Parker. That's Jack's shy way of letting me know who's

boss. He's still my friend, of course—but he feels perfectly free to step on my face now and then.

Another bit of face stepping occurred the day I left the division to become corps commander. Old Waffleass Cox, my antiquated brigadier, collapsed with his third case of the grippe, which turned into pleurisy. I recommended Colonel Harry Quickmeyer to succeed him. Pershing gave the star to Douglas Fairchild instead. Why? Number one, Tasker Bliss was backing Fairchild, and Jack thought it was good politics to let Tasker win a trivial victory now and then. Two, Jack had just gotten a letter from Dougie's mother telling him how much she wanted her darling to become a general before she croaked. She also name-dropped half a dozen senators on the Military Affairs Committee, plus having tea regularly with the Secretary of War. So your pal Quickmeyer, who thoroughly deserves the promotion for the terrific job he's done with Carolina's Pride, the last surviving regiment of the Confederate Army, gets nothing for his sweat and tears but a pat on the back from yours truly.

Is that enough inside information on how the great and glorious U.S. Army works for this lecture period, Dr. Warden? To make sure it does not revive your latent pacifism, you need another session with your therapist as soon as possible. Perhaps we can meet in a certain town we hope to liberate in a week or so. Your lonely ex-patient,

Malvern Hill Bliss

The next day the French officially relinquished their control of the Saint-Mihiel lines, and American troops moved into the trench system. In the middle of fretting over this shuffling of almost two hundred thousand men in and out of his sector, Bliss received an abrupt summons to Pershing's headquarters at Ligny-en-Barrois, a good sixty miles from Maricourt. Mile-a-Minute Murphy got him there in sixty-two minutes, almost living up to his nickname.

Bliss wondered if he was being invited to a celebration. It was an auspicious moment in the checkered history of the American Expeditionary Force. Instead, Pershing was pacing up and down his office, looking as if he had swallowed a live porcupine for lunch. "The goddamn limeys have reneged on the heavy tanks," he said.

That meant they lost three hundred six-pound guns—the equivalent of seventy-five batteries—and six hundred machine guns. Pershing told him he would have to rely on artillery to break the barbed wire on V Corps' front. He was going to assign the American-manned tanks to the corps attacking from the east and south, where the terrain was less swampy.

"Did the bastards give you an explanation?" Bliss asked.

"No. But I've got one. Remember those hundred and twenty thousand men they browbeat me into giving Haig last spring during the German offensives? I asked for most of them for this operation. This is how Haig's getting even."

The tanks were one more example of the mess Woodrow Wilson had made of the American war effort. Eighteen months after his declaration of war, they finally had an independent American army—but every artillery piece supporting it was French made. Ditto for every plane in the air service and every tank in Patton's brigade: all French Renaults, too light to deal with those thirteen belts of German barbed wire.

"What's this I hear about you telling your division commanders not to advance until they've got artillery support every time they see a machine gun?" Pershing growled.

As Bliss feared, Wiley Parker had converted his advice into a slander and passed it on to friends on Pershing's staff. "I told them to use artillery as often as possible. It will save a lot of lives, Jack."

He started to tell Pershing about Hubert Gough's idea of the modern army as an orchestra. Pershing cut him off in mid-sentence. "I want you in Vigneulles on the fourteenth of September. I'm not interested in any excuses about lack of artillery support." Vigneulles was a key town in the center of the salient. Its capture would, they hoped, trap tens of thousands of German troops in the apex around Saint-Mihiel.

An aide appeared in the doorway. "General, Field Marshal Foch is outside."

In strutted the Generalissimo, his interpreter, and General Maxime Weygand, his close-mouthed chief of staff, who many said was his brains. Foch was looking very cocky in his gold-braided field marshal's kepi. Two weeks ago, Clemenceau had elevated him—and Pétain—to that ultimate rank. His high spirits ebbed noticeably at the sight of Bliss. "Excuse me," he said in French, which the interpreter smoothly translated. "I thought you were alone."

"General Bliss is commanding Five Corps," Pershing said with cool deliberation. Bliss wondered if he was finding out why he had been appointed to his lofty post. Was it Pershing's way of telling Foch he still liked the man who had threatened to kick the Generalissimo in the balls?

"Of course," Foch said. "I had momentarily forgotten." He paused, perhaps considering the possibility of congratulating Bliss. Instead, he spread a map on Pershing's desk and started talking so fast his interpreter grew frantic.

"Two days ago I met with Field Marshal Haig. He pointed out to me that the entire German line, from Verdun to the North Sea, is really one huge salient. An attack on it from the north, south, and center has a good chance of collapsing their entire front. The British are already attacking the northern flank. We French and Americans should thrust from the other directions. This makes your Saint-Mihiel operation superfluous."

Pershing had been sitting at his desk listening almost complacently. After all, he finally had his independent American army. He did not see what Foch and Haig could do about it now. The word superfluous made him sit up straight. His eyes narrowed to slits.

"I don't propose to cancel your attack outright," Foch continued. "But I think it should be foreshortened so we can resume operations as soon as possible in a drive to the north."

Gesturing at his map, Foch announced he wanted Pershing to attack only the southern face of the salient. Meanwhile, Foch would shift six American divisions to the French Second Army under General Viomenil, who would attack north through the valley of the Argonne—and transfer the rest of the army farther north to the valley of the Aisne, where they would fight under General Degoutte.

It was mind-boggling. On the very day that the AEF took over a major sector of the front, Foch was telling Pershing to split the army into three separate groups and give two of them to French generals—leaving Jack with the smallest piece!

"Marshal Foch," Pershing said, speaking so carefully every word came at the Frenchman like a bullet, "the American people and the American government expect the American army to act as a unit, a single force. They do not want it dispersed all over the Western Front. Nor—do—I."

Bliss began to breathe again. The last gasp of the Haig-Foch Ltd. plan to finance the war with American bodies was in sight. Methodically, grimly, like a heavy tank crunching through barbed war, Pershing continued. "General Bliss here has told me—and the casualty figures on my desk support his argument—that General Degoutte and General Viomenil have a regrettable tendency to waste American lives."

"Your men's lives are wasted because they attack like fools!" Foch shouted.

"They attack, that's the main thing. That's why you want them so badly. But you're not going to get them."

"*Voulez-vous aller à la battaille?*" Foch screamed.

"Do you wish—to participate—in the battle?" said the gulping French translator, who had all but dissolved in perspiration turning Pershing's blast into French. Foch's sneer was the ultimate insult one general could fling at another.

Pershing somehow kept his temper. "Yes, I wish to go to the battle," he said, letting Foch knew he understood the literal French as well as the English. "But as an American army. In no other way."

"I insist upon my arrangement!" Foch bellowed. He was the one who had lost his temper. A purplish shade was tingeing his neck and cheeks, his hands were trembling.

Pershing stuck out his pugnacious jaw. "Marshal Foch, you may insist all you please, but I absolutely decline to agree to your plan. Our army will fight wherever you may decide—but it will only fight as an independent American army."

Both men were on their feet now. For a moment, Bliss thought Pershing was going to hit Foch with a roundhouse right. What would the world say if the Generalissimo of the Armies was carted out of the headquarters of the commander of the AEF?

Instead, Pershing seized a map and pointed to the valley of the Argonne. "Give us that job. Why assign it to the French Second Army, if it's too weak to handle it?"

"The attack must begin on September twenty-fifth to mesh with the British offensive. Can you attack Saint-Mihiel on September twelfth and then shift your entire army sixty miles to the Argonne in two weeks?" Foch said.

Pershing glared at Bliss. Was he asking a question or telling him to keep his mouth shut? "Yes," he said.

"Very well," Foch said. "Your theater of operations will be the Argonne valley."

As Bliss stared at the map, he was assailed by foreboding. A fundamental military principle was being violated. Any time an army fought along the edge of a natural barrier like a forest or a river, it should be responsible for both sides of it. Otherwise, there was grave danger that the army on the other side might lag behind, exposing the attacker to murderous flank assaults and artillery fire. The Argonne valley was bounded by a forest on the west and a river on the east—with French armies responsible for one side in each case.

Foch gathered up his map, his face still purple. "In my opinion, General, what you are attempting requires veteran troops."

"We've got some veteran troops," Pershing said. "By the time we get to the Argonne, we'll have a lot more."

Two nights later, in a cold pelting rain, Bliss and Arthur Hunthouse trudged toward the woods where the Lafayette Division's Irish regiment was to jump off in a few hours. Bliss was not drawn to this part of his twenty-five-mile battle line for sentimental reasons. He was continuing his personal feud with Wiley Parker.

When Parker inspected Ireland's Own, he had become incensed over the number of Chauchats being carried in the ranks. He insisted they all be exchanged for rifles. Joe Perry tried to explain their squad tactics, but Parker only began shouting insults at him. Perry had complained to Bliss, who had rescinded Parker's order. He was here to make sure Parker did not take it out on Ireland's Own by demanding some impossible task.

Finally Bliss saw figures moving in the darkness ahead of them. "What outfit is this?" Hunthouse asked nervously.

"Company A," growled a familiar voice. "Who the hell are you?" It was Sergeant O'Connor. Bliss asked him if Solange planned to start a restaurant in Maricourt. She had opened her third bistro of the war in Épernay, where the division recuperated after their nightmare on the Vesle. The tables were packed with hungry Lafayettes from noon to midnight. O'Connor said Maricourt was too small. Solange was ready for Paris.

The Sergeant summoned the company's new commander, George Eagleton. "I'm not supposed to be here, Captain," Bliss said. "I just want to get an idea of the planning at company level. What's your objective?"

Eagleton got out his map and showed him a farmhouse on the far side of a woods, about half a mile away across the belts of barbed wire. Both woods and farmhouse were probably full of machine guns, but it was a reasonable job for a veteran company. "You think you can handle it?" Bliss said.

"Now that we got our Chauchats back, it shouldn't be too bad. Sergeant O'Connor here's done a hell of a job of breaking in the replacements. They were pretty green, General."

All the divisions were complaining about the poor quality of the replacements arriving from the States. Eagleton began telling Bliss some of them did not know how to load their rifles. The crash of the opening barrage ended the conversation. Two thousand guns set the horizon afire on three sides of the Saint-Mihiel salient. Bliss watched Eagleton move around the company, checking the platoons and his green lieutenants.

One shavetail seemed especially jittery. He feverishly ordered two men to dig him a foxhole. "Hurry up, goddamn it," he shrilled. "They're going to fire back any minute."

Eagleton seized him by the shoulder and drew him into the trees. "In this company, the officers dig their own foxholes, Lieutenant Korda," he shouted above the thundering guns.

How did a little weasel like Korda become an officer? Bliss wondered. Should he do something dramatic about it, like cashiering the cowardly son of a bitch on the spot? No, it would only throw his platoon into confusion. Maybe a few days under fire would make a soldier out of him.

For the next five hours the artillery poured destruction on the Germans. Bliss slogged back to Joe Perry's regimental command post through the thunder and discussed what they would do if the shells failed to destroy the thirteen belts of barbed wire. There was the dismaying possibility of a slaughter as the men tried to cross them. The Germans undoubtedly had them zeroed in.

At 5 A.M. the guns fell silent. Bliss and Perry climbed to the top of a nearby hill and listened to the officers' whistles shrilling, the distant shouts and curses, as the advance began. Behind them the regiment's machine-gun battalion began firing over the infantry's heads. In the gray half-light Bliss could see swarms of bullets vanishing into the woods half a mile away.

Company A and the rest of the first battalion were crossing a series of open fields. As far as Bliss could see in either direction, a line of steel-helmeted Americans was walking forward at a steady, well-rehearsed pace. A second line was already out of the trenches behind them. Bliss braced himself for the moment when German artillery opened up on them.

Shells began exploding erratically here and there. But the bombardment lacked the intensity they had expected. Ahead of the infantry, engineers were flinging their long bangalore torpedoes on the beds of barbed wire, blowing big holes in it. Scarcely a shell fell anywhere near them. Bliss was baffled—but immensely relieved.

In thirty minutes, the first wave was within machine-gun range of the woods. The companies broke into squads and began attacking in cautious rushes. Maxims popped here and there. Squads hugged the earth, squirmed forward, flung grenades. They plunged into the woods without a single casualty. Now, surely, all hell would break loose, Bliss thought.

The woods remained silent. The random machine-gunners had been the only defenders. One of them had survived the grenade attack and surrendered. In Perry's command post, Bliss ordered Hunthouse to ask him where the German army was. "*Gegangen*," said the German, waving to the east. "*Alles gegangen.*"

"Gone, all gone," Hunthouse translated.

"I'm beginning to think this thing could be a walkover," Perry said.

Back in corps headquarters, Bliss could not believe his eyes as the reports poured in from the front. By 11 A.M., his three divisions had reached their objectives for the day. By 3 P.M. they had reached their objectives for the second day! A mud-spattered motorcyclist delivered a message from Pershing, urging him to push on to

Vigneulles as fast as possible. ENEMY IN FULL RETREAT. VITAL TO CUT OFF HIS ESCAPE.

Bliss found Wiley Parker in a farmhouse five miles beyond the line from which they had jumped off that morning. He asked him if the Lafayettes had enough left to keep going to Vigneulles. "Pershing wants it ahead of schedule."

"I'll have the micks there by midnight," Parker said.

War had no logic. Here he was, giving a man he detested a chance to win a smile and probably a medal from Pershing. "Where the hell are the Germans?" Bliss said.

"According to the prisoners we've interrogated, they got orders to withdraw from the whole damn salient two days ago," Parker said. "They'd already moved out most of their artillery by the time we attacked."

Pershing luck, Bliss thought. How much longer would it hold? "It'll still look good in the newspapers," Parker said.

"Parker," Bliss snarled. "When are you going to get it through your head that Ludendorff and his friends don't read our newspapers?"

At half a dozen points in his other two divisions' sectors, their infantry had encountered machine-gun nests in woods and houses. In every case, there were thirty or forty dead Americans sprawled in a neat line, as if they were toy soldiers someone had knocked over with the swing of a hand. Bliss dragged the division commanders out of their headquarters and forced them to take a personal look at these small slaughters.

With the commander of the Fifth Division, Bliss pointed to a dozen men who had been killed two hundred yards from a machine gun. "Even when they start to retreat, they back up facing the gun, still standing up. Get them down on their stupid faces," he said.

The Fifth Division commander had been near the head of their class at West Point. He found it hard to take such blunt advice from Imperfect Bliss, the class goat. "Americans don't like to crawl. I think my men would rather die standing up," he said. Bliss purpled the air around his ears until he admitted the idiocy of that idea.

At 1 A.M. that night, a messenger arrived from Wiley Parker. IRELAND'S OWN ENTERED VIGNEULLES AT MIDNIGHT. THEY FOUND

TOWN DESERTED. REINFORCEMENTS HAVE JOINED THEM AND DUG IN AGAINST POSSIBLE COUNTERATTACK. Bliss sent it on to Pershing's headquarters and tried to get a few hours' sleep.

The next day, September 13, was Pershing's birthday. The advance continued against extremely light German resistance. Again and again, large numbers of their rearguard surrendered after putting up a fight that was little more than a formality.

Late that afternoon, Pershing's big car sloshed to a stop in front of Bliss's headquarters. He strode in, beaming. Seldom had Bliss seen him so cheerful. "What do you think of this thing?" he said. "We're beating their pants off. Sixteen thousand prisoners, four hundred and fifty guns."

Pershing paced excitedly up and down the room. "This proves the superiority of the American soldier, Mal. It's a genetic thing, in my opinion. The people who left Europe for America were better stock. They had more courage, more initiative. It makes for superior people, superior soldiers."

Bliss thought of the rows of Americans cut down by machine guns in the sectors of his green divisions. If this was initiative, he'd take a healthy dose of timidity.

He understood why Pershing was here. It was Jack's birthday, and he had just pulled off what looked like the biggest Allied victory so far. Could there be better proof that his luck had been restored, that fate was no longer his enemy? He wanted to share his sense of escape with the man who appreciated it better than anyone else.

Still, Bliss felt compelled to hint at the truth. "They were retreating before we attacked, Jack. I don't think they'll do that in the Argonne."

Pershing glowered at him. "I can always depend on you for the bright side of things."

"Well—it'll look good in the newspapers," Bliss said.

He realized with horror he was quoting Wiley Parker. Polly Warden's mournful green eyes accused him. What was he becoming?

50. THE BURDEN OF TRUTH

HUGE EXPLOSIONS WERE TEARING UP CHUNKS OF earth around the narrow rutted road running across the flat Woëvre Plain beyond Vigneulles, in the center of the Saint-Mihiel salient. A marine MP stuck his head over the edge of a ditch and shouted, "You can't go up there. They're shootin' at everything that moves."

"Is the field hospital still at Véry-sur-Lac?" Polly Warden said.

"Maybe. Maybe there's nothin' in Véry," the marine shouted. "Their long-range guns have been goin' full blast for the last twelve hours."

The astonishing American victory at Saint-Mihiel was entering a bloody aftermath. The Germans had retreated to their main defenses, the Hindenburg Line, and were ferociously bombarding the forward American divisions. After virtually no casualties in the first two days, wounded men were now piling up in the field hospitals.

"We'll drive fast," Polly said. She shoved the accelerator to the floorboard and careened up the road, Martha Herzog and Alice Hedberg behind her. Ambulances and all other vehicles had been warned to travel only in small groups. Any large procession would be suicidal. On the far side of a large lake near the town of Véry-sur-Lac, German barrage balloons swung in the gray September sky, watching hungrily for targets for their artillery.

About five miles beyond Vigneulles, Polly's left front wheel hit a deep rut in the road and she heard the ominous *pop* and hiss of a flat tire. Martha and Alice stopped to help her. "Keep going," Polly said. "I can fix it myself."

Four men emerged from some nearby shell holes as Polly slid a jack under the front bumper and began taking off the tire. "I can handle it," she said, as they came toward her in a crouch, their eyes darting into the sky in search of shells.

"Listen," said the first man, a tall lanky private with bad teeth. "We wanna get the hell outa here. Me and my buddies've been gassed. We wanna get back to a hospital."

"Report to the field hospital at Véry-sur-Lac," Polly said.

"Véry-sur-hell," one of the other men croaked. "You can get killed pretty easy around that crummy town."

"What's your outfit?" Polly said. "Where are your officers?"

"Ain't much left of our outfit," the tall private said. "We wanna get the hell outa here."

Their sullen eyes were the only thing alive in their dirt-smeared faces. These were stragglers, like the ones she had seen during the British retreat in Flanders and the rout at the Chemin des Dames. "I'm not taking you anywhere," Polly said. "You're a bunch of deserters."

The last word made the tall private take two steps backward, as if she had suddenly revealed fangs or claws. Polly finished working a new inner tube into the tire, put it back on the wheel, pumped it up, and climbed into the cab. "You," she said to the tall private. "Crank that motor."

He obeyed. As she pulled away, the private snarled, "Bitch!" The others gathered in the road behind him to echo his opinion. "Bitch!" they shouted.

A hissing roar seemed to all but crush the ambulance roof. In her rearview mirror Polly saw a shell explode at the tall private's feet. When the dirt settled he had vanished. His three friends were lying beside the road in a tangled writhing heap. She ran back and found two had gaping stomach wounds; they would be dead in a few minutes. The third had a nearly severed lower right arm. She half dragged, half carried him to the ambulance, thrust him inside, and put a tourniquet on the upper arm. "I'm sorry. I'm sorry!" she said.

She drove for Véry-sur-Lac, pursued by more shells. Should she have taken them back to the evacuation hospital? Was she guilty of their deaths? Of course not, Malvern Hill Bliss said. You're not thinking intelligently about this war.

It's easy for you, Polly told him. You've been doing it for thirty years. I'm trying to think. But I can't stop these feelings. Is it because I'm a woman?

In the shattered town, she handed the wounded man over to the orderlies at the Lafayette Division field hospital, which was in the basement of a smashed-up church. Dozens of wounded men were lying on the floor. Surgeons were operating by candlelight in dim curtained-off corners. Dr. Isaac Pinkus rushed up to her, blood all over his white surgical gown, to ask why she or someone else was not sending more ambulances.

"There aren't many left. Most of the army and Red Cross ambulances have been ordered north to some other battle. We're going tomorrow," Polly said.

Shells exploded in the ruins of Véry-sur-Lac while nervous orderlies loaded the ambulances. A terrific blast blew a chunk of concrete from the top of a nearby ruined wall. Alice Hedberg trembled. "Do you think the men are right? Eventually one of them has your number on it?" she asked.

"Yes. And you won't hear it when it hits you, so there's no point in worrying about it," Polly said.

Hard-boiled. That was the only style for a leader of men—or women. Inwardly Polly winced at Alice's admiring smile. She did not want to become as hard and tough as a man. Yet what was the alternative, whimpering and whining?

Polly led Martha and Alice back through the shell fire, praying no one got a flat. That would mean unloading the wounded to jack up the ambulance. Her sitter, a husky blond lieutenant with an ugly leg wound, reminded her of George Eagleton until he started talking. He had a Massachusetts accent so broad he sounded as if he were practicing for a career as a vaudeville comedian. But there was nothing amusing about his story. He had lost four fifths of his company when they attacked the Hindenburg Line. His captain was on a stretcher behind them, with a bullet in his brain.

"It doesn't make sense," he muttered, growing groggy from morphine. "We knew we couldn't break through the damn thing with the whole division. Why did we attack it with two companies?"

Polly could have told him why. They were helping Wiley Parker lengthen his casualty list and thereby prove to John J. Pershing that he was the most aggressive general in his army, even after the victory was won. Thanks to Malvern Hill Bliss, she knew what was happening inside the American army. Lately she was beginning to think she knew too much.

The ambulance jolted over a half-filled shell hole. The Lieutenant clutched his leg and almost cried out. "We're making the world safe for democracy," he said through gritted teeth. "I guess that's what counts."

So many Americans believed in Woodrow Wilson's crusade. It constantly surprised Polly, who had seen so much of the war from the French and British side. No one in their armies talked about changing the world. The only thing they wanted to change was the direction of the German army.

"Do you believe we're making a better world, miss?" the Lieutenant asked.

"Of course," Polly lied. She wished she believed it. Maybe she was too tired to believe it. Maybe she was too tired to believe anything.

For a while after returning from her three days in Paris, Polly had met the war with renewed energy and hope. But this upsurge had dwindled steadily over the next weeks. Gradually she realized what Bliss had told her about the war—and continued to tell her in his letters—made it even more unbearable. Before, the war had been merely abominable in its random cruelty. Now it often seemed deliberately murderous.

Martha and the other drivers were moving in the opposite direction. For them the war was becoming sacred. It was being consecrated in American blood. Martha sat in Polly's office at night, talking about what they would do with the rest of their lives if they survived the shell fire. She had lost her fervor for their crusade for woman's equality. Whatever they accomplished to make a better world, men and women had to do it together. Men capable of sacrificing so much for an ideal were more than worthy companions. They would be the leaders, the pacesetters.

Back at the hospital, Polly dispatched three more ambulances to

Véry-sur-Lac. In her office, she found another letter from Bliss, hand-delivered as usual by his speed-demon driver. Murphy. The General was exultant over the American victory.

> Believe it or not, it's happened so fast I've got all of 24 hours free before the next battle. Maybe it's time for that session with your therapist, to make sure your pacifism remains dormant. I've found a decent hotel in Saint-Mihiel, the Logis de la Reine. I hope you can meet me there at 1800 hours.

She did not like it. She wanted to make another trip to Véry-sur-Lac to bring out those wounded men. She brooded on the possibility of simply sending him a message, saying no. I have a war to fight too, General, a war that doesn't give me time for therapy sessions. Would that somehow balance out the mangled stragglers, the captain with the bullet in his brain?

No, no, no. Polly told herself to stop seeing everything through a glaze of guilt. She was only a very tiny speck in the war's vortex. She told herself to accept the reality of her love for Malvern Hill Bliss, to stop trying to undermine it. Love has happened to you. It was an event, like a victory—or a defeat.

At 1500 hours she turned her ambulance over to one of the other drivers and asked Martha to drive her to Saint-Mihiel to have dinner with General Bliss. The euphemism reminded her acutely of Anita Sinclair. Maybe she had already given too much of herself to this man. Maybe the whole thing had been nothing more significant than Anita's encounters with British soldiers who needed her for a night. Maybe the mistake was calling it love.

In Saint-Mihiel, French and American flags were fluttering on every lamppost. "They had a big celebration here this morning," Martha said. "The town's been in German hands for over three years. Marshal Pétain made a speech, thanking the Americans for liberating it."

There was nothing celebratory about the atmosphere in Saint-Mihiel now. From every side street French troops dragged screaming, sobbing young women, followed by crowds of older women and some men and boys. The poilus ordered the young women aboard a line of trucks in the town square, cursing them and threatening them with bayonets when they hesitated. Polly asked one of the officers what the women had done.

"They became whores. They lived with Germans," he said.

Soon there were at least a hundred women in the trucks. "Where are you taking them?" Polly asked.

"To the Fourth Army. They will offer their charms to French soldiers from now on," the officer replied.

Polly remembered the *poules* in the Maison Blanche. For a moment she was ashamed of France. She could not bring herself to tell Martha these deportees would soon entertain thirty poilus a night. Martha was outraged by the mere fact of their arrest. "I bet half the men in this rotten town collaborated with the Germans," she said. "No one's persecuting them."

At the Logis de la Reine, a dilapidated four-story hotel a block from the main square, Polly found General Bliss in Room 17, overlooking a pleasant rear garden. He had his tie off; a bottle of champagne tilted in a cooler on the dresser. He kissed her and said she looked tired.

"I am," she said. She did not return the kiss. She felt oddly passive, almost numb.

"What else is wrong?" he said.

"I didn't like your summons. It had a rather smug tone."

"Forgive me. I keep forgetting I'm dealing with a modern woman."

"Where is this battle you're rushing off to in twenty-four hours?"

"I can't tell you the geographical name. But it may fill your ambulances for the rest of the year."

"Am I supposed to laugh at that or groan?"

"Take your pick. It might be best to laugh. Gallows humor is an old army custom."

"I'm not in a laughing mood." She stared sullenly into the inoffensive garden. A small dog, a terrier like Clemenceau's, was scampering around it, chasing birds. That only seemed to intensify her anger. "I didn't spend the day in some comfortable château planning another battle. I was under shell fire, carting back the victims of the current victory."

In a furious, accusatory voice she told him about the stragglers, the dying captain and his decimated company, the women in the trucks in the town square. "Should any of these things put me in a laughing mood?"

German artillery thudded beyond distant Vigneulles. There was not a sound in the room. Polly turned to find Bliss sitting on the edge of the bed, a rueful smile on his face. "I had a feeling those letters were a mistake," he said. "But I let love overcome my judgment. In your job it's probably better not to know what's really going on. It only makes what you see in the field hospitals that much harder to take."

"I disagree completely!" Polly said, too angry now to even consider the possibility that he had just told her the truth. "The next thing I'm going to hear is some paternal advice about taking a month off in Paris, where you can visit me in more comfort and style."

"When I change my mind about something that important, you'll hear about it without any rigamarole," he said. "I told you I wanted—maybe even needed—the thought that you were sharing this miserable business with me. But there's more than one way to do that. You don't have to know the name, rank, and serial number of every foul ball in the American army."

"Can you do anything about those women in the trucks?"

He was already irritated, and the question took him by surprise. "We're not here to tell the French how to run their lives."

"You don't care about them, do you?"

"There's a limit to how many things a man can care about—or a woman, for that matter—without turning into a nag."

"I'm beginning to think less and less of your skills as a therapist, General."

For a moment she thought he was going to demolish her. Instead, with an odd explosive sigh, he strode over to a window overlooking the street. He stood there, jingling some change in his pocket. "I should have known Paris was too good to be true," he said. "Beautiful young women like you don't fall in love with men like me. Only guys like Jack Pershing have that kind of luck."

His glance fell away from her, as if he was hoping he would find something else on her face and was already disappointed. "Isn't that what you're trying to tell me? The whole thing in Paris was a mistake—you were carried away by pity?"

No! The word flashed in Polly's mind, but she was too angry to voice it. Whatever had happened in Paris, it was much more complicated than pity. She knew that emotion all too well. She lived with it every day.

He walked over to her, took both her hands, and raised them to his lips. "It's okay. What you gave me in Paris should last me for the rest of the war, at least."

He was giving her up. Why was this happening? Polly felt immensely confused. On the one hand he deserved everything she had said to him because in some bizarre sense he was responsible for her war. He had been a constant presence from that violent day in Union Square, to the deck of the *Baltic* as New York vanished in the mist, to that day of disaster and defeat in Picardy. He had always been there, with his somber eyes and murderous wisdom.

On the other hand there was Paris, that moment of transcendent surrender. Maybe that was what she begrudged him. Why had she surrendered to a man who told her what was wrong with the U.S. Army and the war and did almost nothing about it? A man who could not muster an iota of sympathy for those pathetic women in the trucks in the town square?

"I'm sorry," she said.

She started to say she still cared for him, but the memory of offering those same words to George Eagleton curdled them on her tongue. Perhaps there was something fatally, forlornly wrong with her after all. Maybe she was incapable of love for a man. Maybe this was the price she had to pay to be a new woman.

His arm around her shoulder, he led her to the door. "Murphy's downstairs in the bar. He'll take you back to the hospital," he said.

"I really am sorry," she said.

"So am I," he said.

Twelve hours later, somewhere west of Saint-Mihiel, Polly and her ambulance group sat in a tremendous traffic jam. Past them streamed a river of marching men. The ambulances were empty.

They were joining the massive movement of the American First Army to the new battle Bliss and his fellow generals had been planning while the men fought at Saint-Mihiel.

Martha Herzog got out of her ambulance and strolled down the column. She was in no danger of blocking traffic. Nothing had moved for two hours. Five minutes later, she returned with a thoughtful look on her face. "Those women from Saint-Mihiel are about three hundred yards up the road," she said.

Polly got out of her cab and walked up to the trucks with Martha. There was no sign of the obnoxious officer who had been in charge of rounding up the women yesterday. The trucks were being driven by Vietnamese. A single guard sat beside them, in every case fast asleep.

"We saw you arrested yesterday," Polly said to the women in the first truck. "Do you want to escape? You can hide in our ambulances, and we'll drive you back to Saint-Mihiel. Or Paris. Wherever you want to go."

They gazed at her in astonishment. Slowly, ruefully, they shook their heads. "We have no identity cards. We might be shot as spies—or starve," a plump brunette said.

"It won't be so bad," another woman said. She was a bleached blonde with a gaunt, heavily rouged face. "You get a lot of presents from soldiers. They know they're going to die soon. They have no use for their money."

In the gray afternoon light, it was painfully apparent that most of these women were professional prostitutes. Their faces wore the lost blankness of the *poules* at the Maison Blanche. Polly and Martha trudged back to their ambulances. "Maybe we're the ones who are crazy," Martha said.

"No, we're just Americans," Polly said. "We don't realize how hard it is for people to change."

Suddenly she was back in the hotel room raging at Malvern Hill Bliss. Was she blaming him for the world's intractable ways? For two thousand years of injustices against women, for the cowardice that produced stragglers in every war, for the perpetual barbarity of some generals, for the eternal possessiveness of men like Paul Lebrun and George Eagleton?

The column began to move. They crawled along in first gear until twilight. A hard rain began to fall. Polly's heart went out to the soldiers slogging past them, their shoulders hunched, their heads bowed in the downpour. Many of them were not wearing their rain-coats. Instead they had wrapped them around their rifles and light machine guns.

Veterans, she thought. Marching to another battle, knowing it meant kill or be killed. Behind her a horn began beeping angrily. Someone or something very important was coming through. Follow-ing the rules of the road, Polly edged the ambulances into the col-umn of marching men. A staff car came roaring past them. Just ahead of Polly, it hit a puddle, flinging a sheet of muddy water in the soldiers' faces. "You son of a bitch!" someone shouted.

The car skidded to a stop. A tall fat colonel got out. "Who said that?" he shouted. A dozen voices yelled "I did" from the safety of the inner ranks. In the rainy darkness there was no hope of identify-ing them.

"What outfit is this? Who's in command?" the Colonel bel-lowed.

"I am." A giant of a man stepped into the road, saluted, and identified himself and the company. It was George Eagleton.

"You call this discipline, Captain? Shouting that sort of epithet at a superior officer?"

"I call it justifiable anger, sir. You just threw about three gallons of muddy water all over us."

"I'm going to put you on report, Captain."

"Go ahead. When I get out of this lousy army I'm going to run for Congress. From the day I get to Washington I'll make your life miserable!" George roared.

The men in the ranks cheered. The Colonel vowed to see George court-martialed and drove on to a chorus from the ranks calling him names far worse than son of a bitch.

Men, Polly thought. American fighting men. If she could not love them individually, she could still love them collectively, the way Anita Sinclair had loved her Tommies.

51. A PRAYER FROM THE HEART

OH, MY DARLING, MY DARLING, MY DARLING. *I love you like that idiot Elizabeth Barrett Browning, to depths and heights, past moons and stars, over mountains and valleys, seas and oceans. The thought of your death is my purgatory, my crucifixion. Take me, take me, take me. Take me with love, take me with loathing. But take me.*

The words roared through Louise Wolcott's mind with the berserk violence of a North Atlantic squall. There was only one thing wrong. She was alone in her canopied bed on the Rue du Bac. Her imploring arms enclosed nothing but cold September air.

She stumbled into the darkness and finally found a candle on her dressing table. She sat there, staring at the ghost of herself in the mirror. Finally she picked up the letter and read it again.

Dear Mrs. Wolcott:

Thank you for the letter you sent me from the curious woman named Louise. She is surely the strangest creature I have ever encountered in my worldwide roaming. She seems to be a compound of oriental cruelty, Russian madness, German clumsiness, French passion, and American naïveté. Who could have spawned such a creature? I doubt if any country would want to take responsibility for her.

It seems a thousand years ago since I met her in America and heard her talk the most wonderful nonsense. I was entranced, I freely admit it. We went to France together, where we both encountered an equally fascinating creature, the War. I thought the War was pretty stupid, but

Louise fell in love with it. That caused all sorts of trouble.

Apparently now she is no longer in love with the War. But fate, with that pleasure it seems to take in the perverse, has meanwhile changed my mind. Now I'm in love with the War. The next time you see Louise, tell her that. Maybe it will give her something to think about.

Sincerely,
Colonel Harry S. Quickmeyer, USA

She roamed the house, the letter in her hand, weeping. Her maid Nanette emerged, saw it was nothing more unusual than madame having another crying fit, and went back to bed. Finally in the dawn Louise sat down and wrote a reply.

Dearest Bastard:

How strange it is to love someone who hates you. It's a new experience for me. I find it oddly refreshing, almost a restorative. It frees the mind to think and say the most daring things. Can you ever believe the sincerity of what I told you that night at Fort Myer? Apparently not. The male mind is like the gearshift of a car. It can only go forward or in reverse in the universal mud. The female mind partakes of flight and its risks. It exults in acrobatics, spins, and loops with recovery in doubt until the last moment.

The other night I dreamed I was in no-man's-land. I found you lying in a shell hole, covered with blood. I was wearing white. I flung myself on top of you and kissed and kissed your dead face until my clothes were covered with your blood. Then I picked up your rifle and charged the enemy with the bayonet fixed.

Louise

She awoke at 11 A.M. and called for coffee and the newspapers. The headlines trumpeted the usual nonsense about Germany's imminent defeat. Her telephone rang. "A general is calling, madame," Nanette announced. "A General Faire—chilled."

The ebullient voice swarmed over her sleep-starved nerves. "Darling. I've come to Paris to celebrate our victory at Saint-Mihiel—and my promotion to brigadier general. I waited until the battle was over before I told you, because I wanted to bring you something more than a mere promotion. Where would you like to go to dinner?"

She chose the Ritz, always a good place to dine when the feelings have to be concealed. Everything at the Ritz was as formal as a solemn high mass. She watched the waiters circle them, their faces grave as acolytes. There was no need to worry about a mocking eye, a reckless word.

Bursting with exultation and exaltation, Douglas Fairchild flung his promotion and the Saint-Mihiel victory at her feet. He declared them her trophies, the first of many holy grails he would seek on the battlefield to give her joy and pride. Now he was on his way to an even more violent show in the Argonne. It was a profound military secret. He was entrusting it to her as a token of his trust, his faith in her loyalty.

"I'm not worthy of you," she said. "I'll make you miserable."

He shook his head. "Impossible," he said. "You've become part of my luck. It's never failed me. It will never fail me now. It's part of a divine plan that's leading me to a great height, a great responsibility. Without you I won't be worthy of it."

Louise did not even know what she was eating. She paid no attention to the wine that passed her lips. She was not even sure what she was wearing. All she could think about was the letter she had written in the dawn. What if that dream came true?

General Fairchild told her about Malvern Hill Bliss's promotion to corps commander. He was baffled by it. The man was fundamentally unstable. He had quarreled with every French general under whom they had served. He was cautious to the point of timidity, always worrying about the enemy's strength and dispositions. Wiley Parker, the man who had replaced him as Lafayette Division commander, was a distinct improvement, a fighting general who believed in the spirit of the attack. The French had the right idea. Attack-attack-attack! That was how wars were won.

General Fairchild described their future life together as he rose through the army's ranks to Chief of Staff. She would preside at chaste dinners for presidents and senators. She would charm foreign politicians and diplomats. She was his guarantee of inexorable ascension. Again and again Louise had to stifle an impulse to scream, "I don't care!"

Finally the oratory ended. He escorted her to a taxi and ordered the driver to take them to the Church of the Dome of the Invalides. A ten-franc note persuaded the night watchman to let them in. Their footsteps echoed high up in the immense dark vaults. The only light came from banks of flickering candles. They walked to the tomb and gazed down at the gleaming sarcophagus of the emperor. "We'll come back here again and again," he said. "It's where we began our journey together."

With a stifled cry Louise stumbled away from him to light a candle before a shrouded statue. She dropped to her knees and prayed, *Oh, God, don't let the dream come true.*

The General's footsteps pursued her. They sounded like a whole army on the march. Fairchild lifted her to her feet and pressed her to his chest. She felt the cold leather of the Sam Browne belt against her cheek. "You don't have to pray for me. My luck will protect me."

Louise barely listened. She was thinking about the War. She was no longer in love with it. What if the War did not care? What if the War had its own plans for her? What if the War was God?

52. ARGONNE

WEARING A GOLD-BRAIDED FRENCH KEPI AND A horizon-blue overcoat at least a size too big for him, Malvern Hill Bliss peered through field glasses at the valley of the Argonne. He was standing on top of a hump of ground that had earned its name during the 1916 battle for Verdun: Mort-Homme—Dead Man's Hill. Beside him, his chief of staff, Brigadier General George Jorgenson, and the commanders of the three divisions in V Corps were also wearing French overcoats and high-crowned French hats. If a German observer was studying the activity on Mort-Homme, he would see nothing but Frenchmen.

Ten miles away, three enemy barrage balloons swung on their ropes beneath the leaden sky. Nothing else seemed to be moving in the valley of the Argonne. From the looming forest to the west, which stood on a ridge a thousand feet above sea level, to the steep slopes of a dominant hill named Montfaucon in the center, to the swampy lowlands along the unfordable Meuse River on the east, the fields and woods seemed devoid of Germans. But the French intelligence officer standing beside Bliss said there were five divisions out there, about 50,000 men, manning three "stellungs"—lines of concrete bunkers and machine-gun nests and trenches. They had named them after the witches in Richard Wagner's Ring cycle: Giselher, Kriemhilde, and Freya.

Pershing's plan was as bold as it was simple. He hoped to overwhelm these 50,000 Germans with a tidal wave of infantry. On September 26 he was going to hurl 250,000 Americans at them. On the first day he wanted to gain no less then ten miles. That would crack the Giselher and Kriemhilde Stellungs and carry them to the northern tip of the Argonne Forest, forcing the Germans inside it to abandon this natural fortress. Linking up there with the French Fourth Army, they would lunge another ten miles to smash through the Freya Stellung, the last and presumably toughest German line.

Pershing had not personally worked out this plan, of course. He had been busy attacking Saint-Mihiel while the Argonne assault was concocted by the Leavenworth geniuses on his staff. The more Bliss saw through his field glasses, the less he liked it. "How much German artillery is on those heights east of the Meuse?" he asked the French intelligence officer.

"That's hard to say. But there's room to conceal at least twenty batteries," he said.

"That means the Germans have hidden twenty-five," Bliss said. "How much have they got on those bluffs along the Argonne Forest?"

"I think we can assume at least as many," the Frenchman said. "Plus heavy machine guns."

The looming height of Montfaucon split the southern part of the valley in half. That meant the two corps attacking east and west of it would be forced into two smaller valleys, each about six miles wide. They would be exposed to artillery and machine-gun fire from both flanks. Bliss's V Corps was supposed to bull straight up the valley at Montfaucon, keeping the German defenders so busy they would neglect to fire on the Americans on both sides.

The plan had the finesse of a blackjack between the eyes. If your opponent ducked the first swing, you were in trouble. "I think we're attacking in the wrong place," Bliss said. "We should start by clearing those heights east of the Meuse. That would outflank the first two stellungs and rattle their whole setup. We'd have artillery on their flank instead of vice versa."

Brigadier General Jorgenson frowned furiously at the mere thought of criticizing his fellow geniuses from the Command and General Staff School. Tall and angular, with prissy lips and a professorial frown, he had already earned a Bliss private nickname: Grimjaw. "That would betray our intentions, General," he said. "The key to the success of this operation is surprise. The Germans expect us to continue to attack east from Saint-Mihiel. That's why we've left so many veteran divisions back there."

Bliss decided not to argue with his chief of staff in front of half a dozen French colonels. Grimjaw had just pointed out another flaw in the Leavenworth geniuses' plan. Instead of bringing the best divisions from Saint-Mihiel, they were trying to execute this ten-mile-in-a-day advance up the Argonne valley with a mostly green army. No one in the three divisions Bliss had been given for V Corps— the 91st, the 37th, and the 79th—had fired a shot in battle.

"I've seen enough to give me *beaucoup cafard*," Bliss said to the French intelligence officer, who actually looked intelligent, a rare thing in his business.

"It will be very difficult. We wish you luck," the officer said.

"What's this *cafard* stuff?" Grimjaw Jorgenson asked as they rode back to corps headquarters in the village of Cousances. He frequently talked to Bliss like a psychiatrist dealing with a mental case.

"Just an expression I picked up from the French," Bliss said. He felt a terrible need to share his foreboding with someone. But it would be bad form for the corps commander to sow doubts in the minds of his subordinates, and no one else in his life could tolerate his candor.

He told himself he was glad Polly Warden was gone. She had been an unreal presence, giving him the illusion that he was being honest, when he swallowed his doubts and fought his battles like everyone else. Their interlude in Paris had been as accidental, as meaningless as a million other encounters between horny soldiers and sympathetic women in this and other wars. It was time to strip his mind of everything but the brutal business at hand.

At headquarters, Arthur Hunthouse greeted Bliss with the air of a man who has just performed a heroic deed. "We've had quite an altercation, General. A nigger sergeant and two of his friends showed up, claiming they knew you. They got rather uppity when I told them they couldn't wait in here. I put them in the cellar under guard."

"Hunthouse," Bliss said. "I've got a new job for you. Front-line liaison officer. You're going forward with the Seventy-ninth Division when they attack this Thursday. In the meantime, send those niggers to my office immediately."

Bliss could not believe it. There stood Sergeant Major John

Henry Turner in the flesh beside two other sergeants from the old Tenth Cavalry. They were all in the 92nd Division, which had been assigned to I Corps. "What took you so long to get here?" Bliss asked.

"They didn't want to send us over as combat troops, General," Turner said.

"What sort of an outfit have you got?"

"Pretty bad, General. We got a lot of white officers who don't think much of niggers. And we got a lot of niggers who ain't much good."

The other two sergeants nodded in glum agreement. "Why aren't they any good?" Bliss asked.

"Draftees, General. Can't make a soldier out of a man who don't want to fight in the first place."

Turner said they also had a fair number of Negro officers and some were not bad, considering they were amateurs. But most of them spent too much time signing petitions to get into the officers' clubs. "Ain't many's concentrated on the main thing, General: how to fight Germans. You got any advice for some old sergeants?"

"I'll put you in touch with a first sergeant from the Lafayette Division. They're on the way up here to go into reserve. He can give you some real inside dope."

"Guess we're gettin' ready for a big fight, General. All that traffic on the roads."

"It's going to be the biggest battle in American history, Turner."

Turner nodded. "You ain't changed your opinion of the Germans, General?"

Bliss shook his head. "Especially when you combine the Germans with the place we're attacking: the Argonne."

"Argonne," Turner said. "It's got a kind of groan in it."

"I'm worried about who's going to do the groaning," Bliss said.

Three days later, Bliss drove to Mort-Homme before dawn to watch the infantry assault go forward. He got there in time to see the climax of the Argonne bombardment. Four thousand guns belched flame from the eastern to the western horizon. Huge jets of fire leaped from the giant howitzers, pinpricks from the smaller .75s, a fountain of fiery sparks from the biggest trench mortars. But he saw little else besides these fireworks. The entire valley was blanketed in a thick white fog.

An omen? Bliss wondered. Every reader of military history was familiar with the phrase the fog of war. It was what always descended on a battlefield once the shooting started and most men lost the ability to think coherently. Above the mist five miles away loomed Montfaucon, the Hill of the Falcon. That was also the name of a famous gibbet in fifteenth-century Paris. François Villon had written a poem about it, giving voices to the dead thieves swinging from the beams. The poem ended with two lines that Bliss had never forgotten. He thought they applied equally to soldiers.

> Be ye not then of our fraternity.
> But pray to God that we all be forgiven.

The fog refused to lift. Bliss finally gave up and drove back to his headquarters, where he paced the floor and waited for news. Around 11 A.M. the first reports trickled in. All three V Corps divisions were meeting only light resistance. For an hour or two it looked as if it might be a replay of Saint-Mihiel.

Around 1 P.M. the fog lifted and Grimjaw Jorgenson rushed in to report the 91st Division, a Pacific Coast outfit operating on V Corps's left flank, was taking a terrific pounding from German artillery. In the center, the Ohioans of the 37th Division had vanished into the four-mile-wide Forest of Montfaucon. On the right flank, the 79th Division, the Maryland-Pennsylvania outfit that was supposed to capture Montfaucon Hill, was entangled with itself, regiments stumbling into each other and into stiffening German resistance.

Bliss piled into his car and started toward the 79th Division's headquarters. The drive should have taken him twenty minutes. After an hour sitting in the worst traffic jam he had ever seen, Bliss returned to his headquarters and called for a horse. While he waited, Captain Hunthouse wobbled in from the 79th's front, looking as if he had spent a lot of time face down in the mud. "General, it's chaos up there!" he said. "People are lost in the fog. No one knows what's happening a hundred yards away."

"Get a horse and join me. We'll see if we can straighten things out."

Riding cross country, they got to the 79th's headquarters in half an hour. Joe Kuhn, the crusty commander, was another West Point classmate who took a dim view of Imperfect Bliss as his superior officer. He haughtily informed Bliss no one knew much about what was happening at the front. Telephone communications had broken down. Runners were not getting through. His green infantrymen had bypassed machine-gun nests and pillboxes where the enemy looked dead, but the Germans had since come to life and were shooting up everything that moved.

Bliss not too politely suggested Kuhn get the hell out of his command post and head for the front to find out a few things. He demanded a situation map and announced he was going to visit some regimental headquarters while Joe digested the advice.

Bliss and Hunthouse rode east toward the frowning face of Montfaucon. The battle chattered and rumbled ahead of them. Skirting a wood, they encountered about twenty-five infantrymen heading for the rear. They had the blank, scared look of men under fire for the first time. "Where the hell are you going?" Bliss asked.

"The captain and our lieutenant got themselves killed," a corporal drawled, his accent instantly identifying him to Bliss as a Marylander. "We're goin' back for orders."

"You're getting one right now," Bliss said. "Turn around and attach yourselves to the first officer you see."

They about-faced and trudged toward the front again. Bliss and Hunthouse paused to consult their map. Ahead of them, as the infantrymen crossed an open field toward another woods, a Jack Johnson came whooshing down from the east. Ninety-five pounds of death caught the infantrymen in the middle of the field, bunched up like school kids on their way to a picnic. Shrapnel hissed around Bliss and Hunthouse, who dove headfirst off his horse. In the field there were parts of bodies everywhere. The wounded were screaming and sobbing and crawling like crushed roaches. Four or five survivors lurched to their feet and ran toward the rear.

Bliss was consumed by bewilderment. Had God arranged for him to encounter those Eastern shore farmboys, turn them around, and send them across the field in time to meet that shell? Or was that French Jesuit right? Was God out there in that field, bleeding and dying? Nothing else made sense except the obvious alternative: no God at all, a world of blind murderous chance.

Another *whoosh*, another Jack Johnson. This one landed in the woods up ahead. They were coming from German batteries on the heights east of the Meuse. What idiocy, to let them have target practice on these green kids.

"Get up," Bliss said to Hunthouse, who was still nuzzling Mother Earth. They rode on through a landscape that grew more and more grisly. Again and again clumps of Marylanders and Pennsylvanians were mowed down by the traversing fire of a single machine gun. Often they saw a whole platoon, fifty-eight men in a neat row, the lieutenant and sergeant in front of them, all dead. "Murderers," Bliss muttered. "We're a bunch of goddamn murderers."

About a mile farther on, they found some 150 infantrymen lying down on the reverse slope of a hill while George Patton lectured them profanely. "I found these SOBs straggling to the rear," he said. "This thing is a hell of a mess, General. Have you ever seen so many dead men?"

"Where are your tanks?" Bliss asked. V Corps was supposed to have about a hundred of the metal monsters. Patton said there was a platoon of Renaults just ahead of them, badly in need of help from these recalcitrant infantrymen. Leaving his horse with Hunthouse, Bliss browbeat the infantrymen into crossing the bullet-swept crest of the hill with Patton and found twelve American-manned light tanks stuck behind a French-manned heavy tank, incongruously known as a Schneider. It was tilted on its side in a huge ditch the Germans had blown in the road. The American tankers were trying to dig out the Frenchmen.

Bliss ordered the infantrymen to join the excavation effort. It was dangerous work. At least forty men went down from bullets or shrapnel before they got the Schneider righted. With each casualty, Patton grew more frantic, cursing the diggers, the German artillery, the makers of the clumsy Schneider. As the French tank finally clawed up the opposite side of the trench, Patton spotted some enemy machine guns about a hundred yards away. "Let's go get them!" he roared and charged out of the ditch. Seven men followed him.

In seconds, six of them were dead and Patton was on the ground, blood gushing from a gaping wound in his thigh. The surviving soldier dragged him back to the ditch and tied a tourniquet on his leg. "That was the bravest dumbest thing I've seen anyone do in this war, George," Bliss said.

"Maybe I just figured it was time I died," Patton gasped.

He had succumbed to the worst temptation an officer faces on a battlefield, the desire to join the dead. It happened most often to the Pattons, the glory seekers.

Bliss tried to organize the infantrymen for an attack on the machine guns. "Who's got some hand grenades?" he said.

Everyone looked blank. No one in their regiment had been issued hand grenades. Bliss gave them up as hopeless and followed the tanks toward their objective, the town of Cuisy. He watched them swing out of column into line and come down the road toward the town, infantry bunched behind them. The tanks' 37-millimeter cannon blasted German pillboxes in the hills above the houses, and their machine guns cut down the German gunners when they ran for cover. They wreaked similar destruction in the town itself. In twenty minutes there was not a living German in Cuisy.

"Why don't we have two thousand of those things instead of two hundred and fifty?" Bliss said. Once more he damned Woodrow Wilson and the American war effort. The greatest steel manufacturer in the Western World had sent a million men to France and not a single tank.

The Germans reacted ferociously to this tank attack. Artillery fire pounded Cuisy. Tank after tank took a direct hit and turned into a flaming coffin for its crew. Six survivors fled to the cover of the nearest woods and refused to emerge until someone had silenced the German guns.

Bliss and Hunthouse rode toward Montfaucon again. In the cellar of a wrecked farmhouse, they finally found the command post of the 313th Regiment, which was leading the 79th Division's advance. The colonel, a big broad-chested Pennsylvanian named Swaney, said his forward battalions were still about a mile from Montfaucon, unable to cross a wide clearing, the Golfe de Malancourt.

Bliss asked Swaney if his men could take Montfaucon before dark. "Maybe. If we had some tanks," Swaney said.

Bliss told Hunthouse to go back to 79th Division headquarters and ask for more tanks. If he saw any along the way, he was to turn them around and head them in this direction. "If we don't take Montfaucon today, this whole offensive may be kaput," Bliss said. "Did they explain that to you, Colonel?"

The Colonel looked grave. He was a civilian soldier but he was an intelligent man.

"We can't advance a foot beyond it on either flank," Bliss said. "You don't leave fortresses in your rear. Even another day spent on it will give the Germans time to move an extra ten divisions into this fight."

Around 4 P.M. Hunthouse returned with eight French-crewed tanks. They led the way across the Golfe de Malancourt, two battalions of the 313th Regiment behind them. In the gloomy woods on the other side, machine guns chattered, rifles cracked, and the green Pennsylvanians charged brainlessly, heroically, wasting men by the dozen. Eventually the Germans, no more than a company strong, broke and ran for Montfaucon. Colonel Swaney collected what was left of his two battalions. They barely mustered nine hundred men. The only officers still on their feet were two captains and a lieutenant.

The Colonel looked pleadingly at Bliss. "Montfaucon," Bliss said. They followed the tanks into the dusk. As they neared the base of the hill, a hurricane of machine-gun fire and point-blank 77-millimeter shell fire descended on them. A whizbang hit a tank and it exploded into a fireball. The French tank commander rumbled back to the edge of the woods, where Bliss and Swaney were waiting with a reserve company. "It's madness," he said. "You don't have enough men to hold the hill even if you take it. They'll come back and kick you off during the night."

Bliss could have threatened him with a court-martial. But he agreed with his estimate of the situation. What was left of the attacking battalion crawled and crouched and stumbled back to the woods. From the shrouded bulk of Montfaucon, German machine guns spat fire into the gloom. Although the sun had long since gone down, the Hill of the Falcon seemed to cast a shadow on the entire valley of the Argonne.

At 4 A.M. the next morning, Hunthouse awakened Bliss from an uneasy sleep to tell him General Pershing had just arrived at V Corps headquarters. Bliss found Pershing talking to Chief of Staff Jorgenson. "I want you to call each division and tell the commanding officer in my name that I expect results today."

"Yes, General," Jorgenson said, barely able to conceal his delight with the assignment.

Jorgenson departed and Pershing went to work on Bliss. "The Fourth Division reached its objectives at two o'clock yesterday afternoon and sat there for three hours waiting for the Seventy-ninth Division to catch up with it. They say they could have taken Montfaucon."

The Fourth Division was part of III Corps. Bliss had no control over them and there was no way he could have known where they were or what they were doing. "Why the hell didn't they advance?" Bliss said. "Your Leavenworth geniuses are trying to make everyone move in lockstep. A battlefield doesn't work that way, Jack. You probe for weak spots and when you find one, you exploit the hell out of it."

"It was a good plan if everyone did his job."

"That's never happened on any battlefield since the Athenians tangled with the Spartans. Those kids in my divisions don't know what the hell they're doing, Jack."

"I heard you had a regiment at the base of Montfaucon. Why didn't you keep going?"

Bliss told him it was only one battalion of the 313th Regiment. He described the gathering darkness and the refusal of the French tank commander to advance.

"You should have sent the infantry in without him," Pershing said.

"It would have been a slaughter. They'd lost most of their officers."

Pershing stamped up and down the room. "I don't want any more excuses from anybody, Mal."

"I'm not giving you excuses. I'm telling you the goddamn truth! If you don't trust my judgment, throw me the hell out of here."

"I hope I don't have to do that," Pershing said, stalking out the door.

Bliss got on the telephone to the commanders of the 79th and 37th divisions and told them to coordinate their attacks and commit every available man to taking Montfaucon. He ordered a bleary-eyed Grimjaw Jorgenson to work out the details. "I want that hill by noon," he said.

At 4:30 A.M. the big guns spewed metal and fire into the sky again. From the forest of the Argonne to the banks of the Meuse, the infantry went forward at 5:30 A.M. behind a rolling barrage. Almost immediately things started to go wrong. The tired troops, who had gotten little or no sleep, fell behind the barrage. The Germans hunkered down in dugouts and when the barrage passed over them rushed to their machine guns and poured killing fire into the oncoming battalions. Artillery from the heights of the Meuse and the bluffs of the Argonne Forest added to the carnage.

The only good news came from the 79th and 37th divisions. Converging on Montfaucon, by sheer numbers they fought their way up its steep slopes to the ruined town on the crest. By noon the Germans had abandoned the Hill of the Falcon. Bliss leaped on his horse and rode to the scene to distribute congratulations. On the crest he found Generals Joe Kuhn of the 91st and Charlie Farnsworth of the 37th, studying the terrain through field glasses.

Bliss ordered an immediate advance on the next objective, the town of Nantillois, two miles beyond Montfaucon. Both commanders urged him to take a look through their field glasses. Machine guns jutted from every third window in Nantillois. Trench lines and barbed wire snaked through the fields around the town. Fresh troops, their gray uniforms unblemished, were busily setting up more machine guns. Bliss remembered Pershing's farewell warning and said, "I want it by six o'clock."

The generals slouched back to their divisions. Their attack on Nantillois got nowhere. Their men were spent. Montfaucon was still casting its deadly shadow on the battlefield. The picture grew darker that afternoon when Bliss got a telephone call from Hunter Liggett, the commander of I Corps, asking him if he knew anything about the whereabouts of the 35th Division. "They've disappeared!"

Twenty-eight thousand men disappeared? It soon became apparent that the 35th Division might as well have vanished. The Missourians had lost all semblance of cohesion. Colonels could not find their regiments, their artillery was firing blind. Bliss's 91st Division was getting plastered by flanking fire from Germans the Midwesterners were supposed to be fighting.

In the Argonne Forest, the 77th Division was getting nowhere. The French Fourth Army, in relatively open country on their left, had yet to advance a foot, giving the Germans out there all the leisure they needed to torment the New Yorkers' flanks. A regiment of the 92nd Division, inserted between the French and the 77th for liaison, had run away. Hunthouse reported this last bit of news with a note of triumph in his voice, as if it proved he was right about Sergeant Turner and his friends.

Bliss was too harried to excoriate him. As the afternoon lengthened, V Corps was flooded with complaints from its three divisions. The men were not getting any food. Ammunition was running low. Where was their artillery? German guns were pounding them with impunity. They were being forced to attack machine guns with their bare hands. No one was evacuating the wounded.

Bliss ordered Hunthouse to saddle up. He knew what was wrong but he wanted to see it for himself—and he could not do it by automobile. They cantered two miles west to the single road that was supposed to supply the 90,000 men in V Corps. From north to south, as far as Bliss could see, there was an apparently endless line of trucks, artillery with teams of horses sagging in their traces, cars, ambulances, even a few tanks, all as motionless as if they were engraved on the landscape.

Standing beside one of the stalled ambulances was Polly Warden and her friend Martha Herzog. He asked how long they had been there. "Since four o'clock yesterday afternoon, General," Martha replied. Polly said nothing. But Bliss read fresh accusations in her green eyes.

Over the next two days, Montfaucon's shadow grew darker and more ominous. By September 29, their fourth day in the Argonne, the situation report from First Army headquarters read, "Troops do not seem to be making an organized attack, or to be making any advance."

The weather turned cold and rainy. The men were still wearing summer uniforms. Many of them had left their blankets and packs behind when they attacked on the twenty-sixth, and the traffic jams made it impossible to regain them. Bliss's three division commanders begged him to relieve their half-starved men. They were living on sardines and drinking water from shell holes. Dysentery and flu were rampant.

Bliss summoned his horse again and rode across country to Pershing's forward headquarters, a railroad car on a siding in Souilly, a few miles behind their jump-off line. As he dismounted, Field Marshall Foch and General Weygand descended from Pershing's car. "Here we have an example of the pitiful state of the American army," Foch said to Weygand. "A corps commander can't telephone his chief or use a motorcar to reach him. He must ride through the woods on his horse. Napoleon had better communications."

"How are things going elsewhere on the Western Front, Field Marshal?" Bliss said.

"The British have broken through the main German line, and the French armies are making magnificent progress everywhere."

"Including the Second and Fourth armies?" Bliss asked. As far as he knew, the Fourth had yet to gain a foot in their so-called attacks west of the Argonne Forest. The Second Army, on the other side of the Meuse, was equally immobile.

"They're waiting for progress here in the Argonne before they advance," Foch replied.

"You should be Pope, Field Marshal," Bliss said. "Your infallibility is unshakable."

In the railroad car, Bliss found a wrathful Pershing. "What did you say to the little son of a bitch?" Jack growled.

"Nothing worth repeating. What did he say to you?"

Pershing slumped in a chair, his fists knotted. "He said we were going nowhere and the solution was to break up the army, give half to the French, half to the British. I told him to go to hell."

"So? What else is new?" Bliss said.

Pershing lowered his head; his voice dropped. "He called me a fool. He says Clemenceau is cabling Wilson, demanding my relief. He wants to replace me with Tasker."

"Jack," Bliss said. "There's nothing left of those green kids. It's time to send in the veterans: the First and Second Division, the Forty-second, the Twenty-sixth. Give me the Lafayette Division."

Pershing nodded bleakly. "You think they can do the job?"

If ever a soldier needed an injection of optimism, it was John J. Pershing. But Bliss could not lie to this man. "If they can't, nobody can," he said.

53. LA GUERRE DE FOLIE

"I'M SORRY, MISS WARDEN. I CAN'T TAKE ANY more," said the chunky blond driver sitting beside Polly's desk. Her name was Susan Griscom. She was from Indianapolis and normally exuded midwestern optimism and cheerfulness.

"You've had a bad trip. Why don't you take a day off and think it over?" Polly said.

Susan shook her head. "It's ten times worse than Belleau Wood or the Vesle."

She had brought a full ambulance out of the Argonne last night and gotten caught in the usual traffic jam. After eight hours on the road, three of her four stretcher cases had died. On her previous trip, two men had died.

"You're tired," Polly said. "We're all tired. I want you to think it over for twenty-four hours."

Three other drivers had collapsed in the last five days. They were operating on two or three hours' sleep a night. Every trip into the battle zone took anywhere from six to twelve hours to complete. They dozed behind the wheel as they sat in the traffic jams, but it was hardly genuine sleep. The sounds from the backs of their ambulances often turned it into a nightmare.

Polly's head throbbed. Was she getting the flu? Four drivers had come down with it. The cold weather was multiplying the number of cases at an epidemic pace.

A worse miasma emanated from the Argonne: the stench of defeat. It was infecting everyone, drivers, nurses, doctors, soldiers.

The sitters talked in numbed disbelieving voices about the machine guns, the shells, the poison gas, the dead. They told stories of German determination. Machine-gun squads fought to the last man. Often when they surrendered, they walked up to the Americans, hands in the air, and flung grenades in their faces. In the night they infiltrated the American lines and shouted orders to fall back, creating chaos.

Polly thought of Malvern Hill Bliss, commanding a third of the men in this murderous cauldron. What was he thinking, feeling? When she saw him on horseback the other day, she thought he looked at her with a mixture of pride and contempt. He was telling her he could survive without her love. One-night—or three-night—stands would do the trick very nicely, thank you.

Did she really believe that? Or was she letting the war's cruelty do her thinking for her? It did not really matter. She was fairly certain she was never going to talk to General Bliss again. No man could remain interested in a woman who showed up for an assignation and harangued him like a bad-tempered schoolteacher.

Five hours later, Polly drove her ambulance to the edge of an American field hospital behind Montfaucon. German shells crashed into the ruins of the town on the crest of the mountain, only a few hundred yards away. She was surprised to discover massive Sergeant Desmond Walsh of the Lafayette Division in charge of evacuation. An army regular, he had disapproved of women so close to the front at first. But lately he had changed his mind and become one of their friends.

"I thought you were in reserve," Polly said.

Walsh shook his head gloomily. "They needed us to finish the job up here," he said. "The doctors talked the General into lettin' them come first to set things up."

"Is Dr. Pinkus here?" Martha Herzog said.

"He's out collectin' wounded already," Walsh said. "Instead of gettin' some sleep. I never seen anything like the guy."

"Aren't the stretcher-bearers supposed to do that?" Martha asked.

"Our guys ain't arrived. We're usin' what's left of the Thirty-seventh Division, and there ain't many of them," Walsh said. He was unaware that Martha was in love with Dr. Pinkus.

Martha looked as if she might burst into tears at any moment.

"Here he comes now," Walsh said.

He pointed into the fields beyond the sheltering bulk of Montfaucon. Isaac Pinkus was rushing toward them carrying a wounded man on his back. Stretcher-bearers were carrying another man beside him. Pinkus was wearing his helmet at a cockeyed angle. On his round chubby face was an expression of stunning cheer. Polly was filled with admiration and bewilderment. It was a marvelous glimpse of a man doing a job he loved so much he was oblivious to imminent death.

"Ain't he somethin'?" Walsh said. "I useta think Hebes had no guts. But he's got enough for a whole damn division." The Sergeant had no idea Martha was also Jewish.

Shells spewed dirt and mud into the air only a dozen yards behind Pinkus and the stetcher-bearers. One of the bearers cried out and fell, hit by shrapnel. Pinkus tried to pick up the stretcher and balance the man on his back at the same time. Martha Herzog uttered a little cry and ran out of the hospital into the open field.

"Hey, she shouldn't do that," Sergeant Walsh said.

Shell fire was still gouging the field when Martha reached the stretcher. She picked it up and they resumed the trip to the hospital, Pinkus chatting cheerfully with her. In the admitting tent, he carefully lowered the man he was carrying to the ground. "He's got a bad chest wound," he said. "I sewed it up before we started. Let's see if the stitches held."

He pulled open the man's bloody shirt and nodded, pleased by what he saw. "Good old silk gut," he said.

"Dr. Pinkus," Sergeant Walsh said. "No-man's-land is a hell of a place to practice emergency surgery."

"I'm saving lives, Walshie," Pinkus said. He beamed at Polly and Martha. "How are things in the ambulance service?"

"You're the best cure for *cafard* I've found yet, Doctor," Polly said. "I wish we could put you on film."

"I wish we were winning this battle," Pinkus said.

* * *

Eight hours later, still without any real sleep, Polly reached the evacuation hospital with her wounded and found Eleanor Kingswood waiting for her with three new drivers. Eleanor was still briskly formal in letters and conversations. She remained in Paris most of the time, running the business side of the ambulance group.

Eleanor announced the imminent arrival of Suzy Astor and Caroline Russell, daughters of two of the Kingswood Group's most generous supporters. They had come over to do canteen work for the YWCA and were simply dying to see the front. Eleanor wanted Polly to escort them close enough to make a good story for the newspapers—but not too close. She did not want them to get frightened or hurt.

Suzy and Caroline arrived within the hour. Polly had partied with them in Bar Harbor and elsewhere. Both honey blondes, they were typical New York debutantes; neither had encountered an idea since they were born. Giddy with excitement, they stepped out of a tan Dion-Bouton touring car wearing Paris frocks. In the car's front seat was the Astors' butler, who was going to help them set up the canteen.

Polly gave the chauffeur directions to Souilly, where the two tourists were thrilled by a glimpse of General Pershing's railroad car headquarters. A mile or two up the road into the Argonne, the traffic jam began. The divisions that had begun the battle were trudging out of the combat zone. On the other side of the road, fresh divisions were streaming toward the front. Polly suggested it was a good place to set up their canteen. The chauffeur and the butler hauled a plank and two wooden horses from the trunk and unpacked boxes of candy and cookies. The two debutantes stood behind their impromptu counter and tossed the sweets to the surprised soldiers.

"Aren't they darling?" Suzy said.

"How many Germans have you killed?" Caroline asked a grimy exhausted corporal.

The man stopped and stared at these apparitions. Then he burst out laughing and resumed his shuffle to the rear. Most of his friends imitated him. A few held out their helmets for the candy and cookies. Polly watched, gagging. It was worse than *la guerre de luxe*. *It was la guerre de folie*—idiocy.

"There's George Eagleton!" Suzy said, pointing to the other side of the road.

It was George, with a burly sergeant striding beside him, a menacing-looking machine gun slung over his shoulder.

"George!" Suzy called.

Captain Eagleton crossed the road, smiling, a hint of a swagger in his walk. From the Army 45 on his hip to the grenades clipped to his belt, he emanated masculinity. "What's this? Did you girls take a wrong turn coming down Fifth Avenue?" he said.

He let Suzy and Caroline give him enthusiastic kisses. "And Polly Warden. What are you doing here? Have you quit ambulance driving?"

"She's giving us a look at the front," Suzy said.

"I hear she's even better at giving people a look around Paris," George said. "She knows all sorts of important people in Paris."

Caroline was drinking in this sarcasm. She was one of the nastiest gossips in New York. Suzy was too light-headed to pay attention. "How many Germans have you killed, George?" she asked.

"Oh, I don't know," George said. "How many Germans have we killed, O'Connor?"

"About twenty thousand," the Sergeant said.

"He tends to exaggerate," George said. "It's really closer to five thousand."

"Really?" Suzy gasped.

"Fill up my helmet," George said.

They crammed candy and cookies into the helmet, and George strolled through his company, giving them to the men. "Doesn't he look marvelous?" Suzy sighed. "I've been writing to him. You don't mind, do you, Polly dear?"

"Of course not," Polly said.

Back at the hospital, Polly watched while reporters interviewed the misses Astor and Russell. Suzy cooed about how *thrilling* it was to hear the guns in the distance and how *certain* everyone was of beating the Germans. She told how they filled the boys' "tin bonnets" with goodies and wished they could have kissed every one of them. They were all heroes.

An hour later, Polly drove her ambulance into the Argonne again. She told herself she did not care what George Eagleton thought of her. But the ghost of the New York Polly did not quite agree. In her fleshless heart there was still a quiver of affection, attraction, for him. He was so American. "Don't let him die," she murmured, even though she no longer believed in a God who paid attention to prayers.

54. OVER THE EDGE

MALVERN HILL BLISS PACED HIS HEADQUARTERS, waiting for news. With green divisions withdrawn and veteran divisions in line, the First Army had attacked again at 5 A.M. It had taken four days to move in the veterans. That gave the Germans time to insert at least five fresh first-class divisions, according to First Army intelligence.

There was nothing especially surprising about Ludendorff's determination to defend this chunk of France. Elsewhere on the western front, the German army could retreat sixty to one hundred miles before they had to fight for anything vital. In the Argonne, the crucial railroads supplying their armies in the north were only twenty-two miles from the line of the original American attack on September 26. The Germans were defending their jugular, and they had no intention of letting the AEF win without a ferocious fight.

Did Marshal Foch know this when he maneuvered Pershing into volunteering for the Argonne? Probably. But Pershing should have known it too. Bliss should have known it. He should have warned Pershing. He had stars on his shoulders. He was just as responsible for the growing mountain of corpses as his commander in chief.

Arthur Hunthouse rushed in with situation reports from their three divisions. The Germans had pulled every trick in their well-thumbed book of tactics. The American rolling barrage had concentrated on the tops of hills; the Germans had dug machine guns into the slopes and decimated a brigade of the Third Division when they went forward. The artillery bombarded the edge of the woods, where you might expect machine guns to be; the Germans pulled the guns back to the center of the woods and slaughtered a battalion of the 80th Division with indirect fire. Only the Lafayette Division's first brigade, led by Brigadier General Douglas Fairchild, reported some gains. They had captured a vital hill and were in the outskirts of Romagne.

On the left, in I Corps, the First Division had smashed through German defenses along the Aire River. Ignoring artillery raining death on them from the bluffs of the Argonne Forest, they drove ahead on a narrow front, pushing a long salient into the German lines. That was the only good news from that flank. Inside the forest the 77th Division had a thousand men cut off and surrounded. In III Corps, on the right, good news was nonexistent. Killing fire from enemy artillery on the heights east of the Meuse had stopped all three divisions and caused near rout and panic in the Fifth.

For the next three days it was more of the same. Even the Lafayette Division slowed to a crawl. The Germans fought house to house through Romagne and fell back to the huge forest of the same name beyond the town, where they had blockhouses and belts of interlocking machine guns that seemed impregnable. The heights beyond it, the Côte Dame Marie, the division's objective, were beyond reach.

After frantic pleas from Bliss and seven division commanders, the Leavenworth geniuses finally advised Pershing to attack east of the Meuse to silence that murderous artillery. On October 8, two French and two American divisions were given the job, under a French general. It was too late and probably too little. In twenty-four hours they were trapped in a pocket on the banks of the Meuse, pounded by artillery and deluged with poison gas.

Behind the lines, the horrendous traffic jams continued. Food still failed to reach the troops. The wounded lay unevacuated for two full days in some divisions. Only ammunition was getting through, thanks to special passes that forced other vehicles, including ambulances, into the muck on the side of the road.

Early on October 10, Wiley Parker stalked into Bliss's headquarters. "I'm relieving every regimental commander in the Lafayette Division!" he snarled. "They're insubordinate. They're refusing my direct orders to attack!"

"You can't decapitate four regiments in the middle of a battle," Bliss said.

He mounted his horse and took a terrified Hunthouse with him for amusement. They found Machine-Gun Joe Perry in the ruins of a house in the southern outskirts of Romagne. The Germans had counterattacked during the night and driven them out of the forest and most of the town. Perry vowed they would get it back by nightfall. Whizbangs crashed around them as they talked. Hunthouse skittered into the command post, leaving the horses to their fate.

Perry insisted they were attacking, but not Wiley Parker–style in suicidal charges. "A long casualty list is the only excuse he'll accept. I told him to go to hell," Perry said.

A mile away, Quickmeyer was in a former German dugout, complete with electric lights and running water. He looked exhausted. The South Carolinians around him were equally worn. Quickmeyer dismissed Parker's threat with a shrug. "The guy's a parody of a general. We gained four hundred yards yesterday and lost two hundred and fifty men. Parker said it should have been eight hundred yards and the casualties should have been a thousand."

Bliss heard similar stories from the other two colonels. He rode back to Parker's command post in a rage. "I'm countermanding those relief orders," he said.

"We'll let Pershing decide," Parker said.

He was betting on his friends among the Leavenworth geniuses at headquarters to eviscerate the corps commander. Bliss decided to go directly to Pershing. A division commander ordinarily had the authority to relieve anyone he chose, but Parker was overreaching himself with this mass removal.

For a full day Bliss could not reach Pershing. He was on the road, stuck in traffic jams, trying to brace division commanders. The situation continued to deteriorate. On the left, the First Division had been withdrawn from their salient. Their casualties were reported to be over nine thousand. The 33rd Division, in the pocket east of the Meuse, suffered two thousand casualties from poison gas alone and was close to collapse. The Germans crammed a full regiment into Romagne, and Ireland's Own was lucky to hang on to a single house on the outskirts of the miserable ruin.

For another day, while progress on the V Corps front was measured in yards and occasionally in inches, Pershing did not return Bliss's calls. Chief of Staff Jorgenson reported massive straggling from all three divisions in V Corps. As many as 20,000 men were wandering around the rear area, hiding in dugouts, faking gas injuries. The same situation prevailed in the two flank corps.

Bliss asked if they were doing anything about the stragglers. Jorgenson looked plaintive. "The MPs are swamped. Maybe this will help."

He handed Bliss a copy of a letter Pershing had sent to all the division commanders. He ordered them to tell junior officers they had the authority to shoot any man who ran away. Here was proof of the First Army's descent into desperation.

"Where's the Ninety-second Division?" Bliss asked.

"They're in reserve behind I Corps."

"Get me Sergeant John Henry Turner and the three best companies in his regiment. Let him pick them out. Find some trucks to bring them back here."

In three hours Jorgenson returned with the three companies. The ebony faces were a tonic to Bliss. He told them what he wanted them to do. "It's going to be a lousy job. They're going to call you every dirty name you ever heard. But I don't want you to shoot anybody unless they shoot first."

For the next four hours, Bliss watched Turner and his men round up stragglers in and around the towns of Montfaucon and Nantillois. Several times bullets were fired at them from dugouts, and the occupants emerged only when they were told a grenade was about to land in their laps. Bliss told them if they were found straggling again they would be shot. MPs marched them back to their divisions.

By nightfall they had returned about 5,000 runaways. Bliss hoped twice that many would go back voluntarily, now they saw there was no place to hide. He handed Turner and his men over to the colonel in command of the military police and ordered them to spend another day on the job. As they rode back to headquarters, Jorgenson shook his head in dismay. "I never dreamed we'd have to do that to American soldiers," he said.

"By the end of the Civil War, the Confederacy had more deserters than men in the ranks. Lincoln had twenty thousand men in Indiana and Ohio looking for Union skeedaddlers," Bliss said.

Jorgenson asked him why he had used black troops. "To deepen the humiliation for the whites. And let the blacks see Ole Massa and his boys can do some running too."

Jorgenson looked thoughtful. He was learning a few things they did not teach at the Command and General Staff School. Back at headquarters, Hunthouse reported Pershing's senior aide, Major Collins, had called to tell Bliss to come to the railroad car at Souilly that night at 11 P.M.

A cold rain began drooling from the wintry sky. Bliss decided going by horse would risk an attack of neuritis—not to mention a good chance of breaking his neck in a shell hole. He started the ten-mile trip at 8 P.M. in his automobile. Mile-a-Minute Murphy almost went crazy in the crawling traffic but they got there by 11 o'clock.

Little Collins met him on the steps of the railroad car. "I'm worried about the General," he said. "I don't know who to talk to about it except you."

"What's wrong?"

"I'm afraid he's pushing himself over the edge. He's on the road all day giving pep talks to everybody, from sergeants to generals. He stays up until three or four A.M. reading situation reports. Yesterday—"

Collins hesitated, not sure how far he should go, even with Bliss. "We were driving up to One Corps. He put his face in his hands and said, 'Frankie, Frankie, I don't know how I can go on.'"

Bliss squeezed Collins's shoulder, trying to say he knew they both shared Pershing's pain. "I'm glad you told me."

The night sky flickered with yellow flame. The guns rumbled across the miles. In his mind's eye Bliss saw the First Army's ordeal: on the outskirts of Romagne where the Lafayettes were fighting house to house, in the swamps along the Meuse where III Corps was butting its head against outcroppings known as the Cunel Heights, in the forest of the Argonne where the 77th Division was still trying to extricate its lost battalion from surrounding Germans. He saw the wounded dying in ambulances on the clogged roads, the stragglers in the woods and cellars trying to decide whether to fight again.

Bliss did not expect to see a happy general. Even so, he was shocked by Pershing's appearance. He looked as if he had aged five years in the last ten days. There were deep lines in his face, flecks of gray in his hair. "What's on your mind?" he asked in a leaden voice.

"I came here to squawk about the mess Wiley Parker is making of the Lafayette Division. But that's not important, compared to what I'm seeing in front of my eyes."

"What?"

"Jack Pershing in danger of acting like Malvern Hill Bliss. Letting death defeat him."

"Death," Pershing said, avoiding the accusation. He was pretending he thought Bliss was talking about the deaths by bullets or shells his men were dying a few miles away. Like all soldiers he was contemptuous of that death. It simplified things.

Bliss was not talking about anything that simple, although it was part of the many meanings in the serpentine word. "You know what I mean," he said.

"You think I'm licked?"

Bliss shook his head. "Never. But you're acting like you're licked."

"Is there anything else we can do? Anything we haven't tried?"

"Go on the defensive," Bliss said. "Step back and rethink this whole thing. Sort out that mess on the roads. Let everyone get some sleep, some food—and some new tactics."

Pershing shook his head. "Foch won't buy it. He'll be crawling down my throat again."

"Tell him to stuff it. Tell them all to stuff it. Tell them you're reorganizing the whole setup. You're trying to do too much anyway. One man can't be a field commander of the biggest army on the Western Front and a diplomat and a supply officer and Christ knows what else."

Bliss told Pershing to imitate Haig. Make himself the commander of an army group. Split the AEF up into two armies, one to operate in the Argonne, the other east of the Meuse, instead of leaving that mess for the French to fix. The arrangement would make him less vulnerable if either army fell on its face. The British did not relieve Haig when Gough's army collapsed; they relieved Gough.

Pershing shook his head. "This is my army. You know what I went through to get it. I can't let go of it."

Bliss wondered how close he could come to telling Jack Pershing he had failed as a field commander. It was not all his fault—and yet, in the savage game they were playing, the fault could be laid nowhere else. "You've got to do it, Jack. For your own sake—and for the sake of the men up there. They need a breathing spell."

Bliss could not tell if the stony silence was assent or refusal. He took a deep breath and made his next move. "When's the last time you saw Michie?"

A very long silence. "I don't know. Six weeks at least. Before Saint-Mihiel," Pershing said.

"Go see her. Announce this new setup, the two armies—and then go see her."

The guns rumbled in the distance. More flashes of yellow fire glared on the railroad car's black windows. Bliss took his longest chance yet. "It's what Frankie would want you to do," he said.

He thought Pershing nodded. It was barely perceptible, but Bliss thought he saw Jack's head move. Another part of his exhausted mind resisted Bliss. It was not hard to understand why. John J. Pershing, First Captain of the Corps, taking this much advice from Imperfect Bliss? It was almost unthinkable.

Pershing's hand picked up some papers on the desk in front of him. He stared numbly at them. Bliss took them away from him. "Forget this stuff. Have a drink and get some sleep," he said.

"What's Parker doing to the Lafayette Division?"

"It isn't important."

"Tell me."

He told him. Pershing's eyes narrowed to those familiar slits. The iron jaw came at Bliss. The fist crashed on the desk. "Parker is right! You can't win this goddamn war without attacking-attacking-attacking!"

It was the most terrible moment of Bliss's life. He had to face what he had tried to avoid again and again. "If you mean that, Jack, I quit," Bliss said. "I'm not going to serve another day under a man whose idea of good tactics is a ten-mile-long casualty list."

"I didn't say that!" Pershing roared.

"That's what it comes down to," Bliss shouted. "That's what you're tolerating if you let that son of a bitch stay in command of my division. It was the best goddamn division in this army until he got his hands on it!"

"I accept your fucking resignation! Now get the hell out of here!" Pershing bellowed.

Bliss found himself outside in a freezing drizzle. Inside the darkened railroad car, Pershing was kicking over furniture, flinging lamps and telephones at the walls, roaring curses into the night. An appalled Little Collins appeared on the steps. "Jesus, General, what the hell did you say to him?" he gasped.

"Everything," Bliss said.

55. FRIEND DEATH

As Bliss's car edged into the endless line of trucks and tractors and horse-drawn artillery inching toward the Argonne, an alien voice whispered, *Now is the time, Malvern. You've been putting it off in all sorts of clever ways. Young women, substitute sons, playing faithful friend. Now is the time to admit you have only one real friend. He's out there on the battlefield, waiting to end your ridiculous charade.*

Whose voice was it, his father's? Telling him what every thinking soldier finally knows? Or his real self, the cold intellect above, behind, beneath his unstable southern heart, the watcher who knew from boyhood it would probably end this way?

There were some consolations. On a battlefield, he could make it look honorable. Glory seekers like George Patton and Douglas Fairchild had made acts of suicidal recklessness almost commonplace. He had always recoiled from blowing out his own brains. It was too easy, and it left an aura of cowardice. It was a Yankee way to die. He would die like a Southerner, his face to the enemy.

"Get off this goddamn road," he said to Mile-a-Minute Murphy. "Get out there in the muck and push it as far as you can go."

"That won't be far, General," Murphy said.

"It's an order, Murph."

They got about a mile, with Murphy working the clutch like a man with St. Vitus' dance and the motor shrieking protests as they plowed through mud up to the axles. A final lunge landed them in a miniature lake that sent water lapping to the headlights. "I'll walk from here," Bliss said.

Murphy waded after him in the drizzle. "General, are you okay? Where are you going?"

"That's a military secret, Murph. You hitch a ride with one of these trucks and get yourself some sleep. I'll be perfectly okay. Tell the boys at Corps not to worry about me. I know exactly what I'm doing."

He mushed on through the mud and rain toward the rumbling, flickering front, puzzling over the catastrophic failure of his resignation in protest. Why was there not an atom, not a molecule of the soaring sense of triumph he had always expected to feel if he acted out of pure principle? Wasn't it a perfect example of doing his damnedest? Hadn't he told Pershing the brutal naked truth? Why was he the one who felt stripped of every spiritual and moral consolation?

In that secret corner of his brain Sergeant Turner declined to say a word. Maybe he had finally decided there was no point in wasting advice on a man who had ignored it so maliciously all his life. That was fair enough. The whole thing was eminently fair. A man who has never taken advice from anyone ruins his career, throws away thirty years of his life, because his best friend won't take advice from *him*. What could be more satisfactory? It was Greek drama, a perfect balancing of tragic ironies. Except in his case it was tragicomic, like everything else in his impromptu life.

The cold rain soon had neuritis twingeing from his toes to his fingertips. That was all right too. It would be very un-Greek if he did not suffer some pain before he met his friend Death. Only one thing still puzzled him—why he had been given a temporary reprieve from his fate by encountering Polly Warden. Perhaps it was a reward for his twisted fitful fidelity to the ideals of the thinking soldier. That was what she saw, what she loved with those sad green eyes. She was another idealist, pursued by private furies, the contradictions of being a modern woman.

Where the hell was he? Rosy-fingered dawn, as the Greeks called her, was beginning to toy with the night sky. Except in the Argonne, Rosie's finger painting was strictly gray. Up ahead were the ruins of a fair-sized town. Random crackles of rifle fire drifted toward him, punctuated by the popping and chatter of rival machine guns.

It was Romagne, where his Celts, Ireland's Own, his sentimental favorites, were still slugging it out with the Prussian Guards. A perfect place to shake hands with his friend Death.

He strolled into the regimental command post, still in a cellar at the southern end of the town. Joe Perry and Douglas Fairchild were drawing lines on a map for the benefit of Harvard's Own, Captain Eagleton, and four other captains. Sergeant O'Connor and the weasel-eyed lieutenant, Korda, were in the circle. They sprang to attention and Bliss quickly put them at ease. No one was surprised to see the corps commander. He had long since established his fondness for visiting the front.

Perry and Fairchild thought Bliss was here to chew them out for being in the same place. They started telling him they had kicked the Germans out of Romagne yesterday afternoon and last night another regiment of Prussian Guards had stormed back, shattering the Celts' second battalion. They were throwing the first battalion at them in exactly ten minutes.

"I'm here to emphasize the importance of this fight," Bliss said. "General Pershing wants this town today. He wants it taken—and held! I'm going to personally lead the assault."

Joe Perry looked suspicious. Corps commanders did not lead infantry assaults at the battalion level. But he could not think of anything to say besides, "We're expecting some artillery in five minutes."

The captains and lieutenants and sergeants departed to their companies. Bliss joined Eagleton and Company A, who were leading the assault up the east side of the street. They crouched behind a garden wall while the division's .75s pumped shells into the upper end of the town. Eagleton identified the houses the Germans were holding in strength and detailed squads to attack them. Bliss said he would take a squad up the street to keep them busy on that side.

In exactly ten minutes the .75s stopped shooting and whistles blew. Sergeant O'Connor and a dozen others bellowed the regiment's war cry "To Hell or Hoboken!" and the company went to work. Bliss led his squad into the street. The bodies of dead Irish

Americans sprawled in the gutters and slumped in windows. The squad hugged the walls and dove in and out doorways, as German machine-gun and rifle fire erupted. Bliss strolled down the middle of the street, pistol in hand, trading single bullets for every hundred fired at him.

Germans ran into the street to escape the squads attacking from the rear. Bliss shot at them and vice versa. One fired a light machine gun at him from no more than a hundred feet and missed. The Chauchat gunner in his squad took care of most of these fugitives. Bliss doubted if he hit one with his pistol, but he was having a wonderful time. His friend Death was letting him go out in style.

Squads from other companies were in the street now, bellowing "To Hell or Hoboken!" Grenades sailed through windows; more Germans headed out of town. O'Connor appeared in the second-floor window of a house at the far end of the street and shot quite a few of them. Joe Perry ran up to Bliss, babbling congratulations. "I didn't think these guys had anything left, Mal. You pulled it out of them."

Douglas Fairchild was equally breathless. "General, if ever I've seen a man earn a Distinguished Service Cross—"

Sergeant O'Connor appeared to report they had cleaned out all the houses on his side of the street. He added some choice comments about the utter uselessness of Lieutenant Korda. "The son of a bitch wet his pants. He really did," the Sergeant said.

An American airplane dove low over the town. Bliss saw dozens of wads of paper spilling from its cockpit. What the hell was going on? Five minutes later, Sergeant O'Connor reappeared with a copy of the Paris edition of the *New York Herald* in his hand. The headline was huge: CENTRAL EMPIRES ASK FOR PEACE. Underneath it in smaller type was: ENEMY APPEALS TO PRESIDENT WILSON ASKING END OF WAR.

"What the hell does it mean, General?" Eagleton asked.

"I haven't a clue," Bliss said.

A frantic scream came from the street, accompanied by staccato bursts of rifle fire and grenade explosions. Lieutenant Korda appeared in the doorway, shaking with terror. "They're counterattacking!" he wailed.

"Come on!" O'Connor roared. Company A swarmed into the street and the rear gardens to fight off a battalion of oncoming Germans. Bliss followed them, determined to give his incompetent friend Death another chance.

"These guys haven't gotten the news of the armistice, General!" O'Connor yelled as machine-gun fire blew all the glass out of a window above his head.

"Maybe this is what the Germans call an armistice!" Bliss yelled back, shooting the German major leading the assault.

They were barely holding their own when a strange sound echoed through the ruins of Romagne: the yi-yi-yi of the rebel yell. Up the street and over the garden walls came a battalion of Carolina's Pride with Harry Quickmeyer in the lead.

"What the hell are you Yankees waiting for?" Quickmeyer said. "Let's go get these guys!" Soon there were rebels on roofs, in windows, and running up the street firing Chauchats from the hip: typical southern craziness, but all beautifully coordinated. In ten minutes the Germans decided maybe they didn't want Romagne after all. They fled into the forest north of town, leaving Bliss and friend Death still at arm's length.

Bliss decided maybe he did not want to die for the moment. The war was still interesting, even if he was no longer a general. He began strolling back to his headquarters. The shell fire from the batteries east of the Meuse was horrendous. As he trudged through a veritable barrage, he saw another would-be suicide approaching from the opposite direction.

It was his old friend Chaplain Kelly. "What are you doing out here?" Bliss said.

"Looking for wounded," Kelly said. His bloodshot eyes suggested he had not slept for a week. His face and uniform were caked with mud.

A voice cried from a shell hole. "Medic. Help. Someone help!"

At the watery bottom of the hole lay a runner with a message clutched in his hand. Kelly knelt beside him in the slop. "Where are you hurt, Mickey?" he said.

"It don't matter, Fadda," Mickey said. "Get this to the artillery." He thrust the grimy piece of paper at Kelly.

"Let me give you absolution, Mickey," the Chaplain said.

"Wasta time, Fadda. Get movin'!"

The shells crashed down, spewing dirt and mud on top of them. Kelly muttered the words of absolution and started to raise his hand in a final blessing. He saw Mickey was dead. "He was the last of my Holy Innocents boys," Kelly said.

The Chaplain and Bliss resumed their journey across the churned earth. "That fellow died like a soldier," Bliss said. "I wish I could be that lucky."

Kelly ignored him. He probably thought Bliss was showing off. Up ahead, behind a shattered farmhouse, was an aid station. Two stretcher-bearers appeared on their right, carrying a wounded man. A Jack Johnson exploded with a blast that knocked Kelly and Bliss flat on their backs. Is this it? Bliss wondered, as the whining roar echoed inside his head. He peered through the smoke, expecting to see friend Death grinning there, his hand out.

The smoke cleared and no one was there but the stretcher-bearers and the wounded man and Kelly stumbling toward them. Both bearers had been killed. The wounded man was a little Italian, like many of the replacements for Ireland's Own. Kelly slung him over his shoulder and carried him to the aid station.

As two nurses relieved him of his burden, a voice cried, "Magnificent, Father."

It was Charlie Murtagh, the big toothy Hearst reporter who had already written several stories about Kelly and Ireland's Own. "I heard about what you're doing, Father. Everyone in the division's talking about it. They call you the Savior of No-man's-land. How many men have you brought back, counting this one?"

Kelly glared at Bliss. "Did you send this fellow up here?" he said.

"I had nothing to do with it, Father. Publicity is General Fairchild's specialty, not mine."

Murtagh grinned wolfishly. "It's almost over. The Germans are asking for an armistice. Now it's time to put Wilson's feet to the fire and free Ireland."

"Ireland?" Kelly said. "Screw Ireland. I'm an American. There are Americans dying out there. Get out of my way. I've got to get this message to the artillery."

The Chaplain had become a soldier. Bliss, the big-mouthed cynic, had become an ex-soldier, an *embusqué* slated for early deportation to Hoboken. He decided he did not give a damn whether peace was breaking out. He was going back to the front, and this time friend Death would not elude him. He would find him crouched behind a German machine gun, pressing the trigger at point-blank range. He would die like the young marines at Belleau Wood, proving generals too could be brainlessly brave.

A half hour later, Bliss reached the main road in V Corps's sector. Standing beside her ambulance in the usual stupendous traffic jam was Polly Warden. This time she was alone. She was putting a hypodermic needle back into a black bag, after giving morphine injections to her wounded men.

She looked sad, even funereal—and as beautiful as he remembered her in Paris. Why not cheer her up, tell her he had managed to self-destruct after all? She was the one person in France who would appreciate the humor of it.

She listened to the story of his brawl with Pershing without the slightest trace of amusement on her face. It made him wonder if these new women lacked a sense of irony. That might turn out to be their fatal flaw. It was hard to get through a war, let alone the rest of life, without it. "My only regret," he said, "is wasting Dr. Giroux-Langin's time—and yours. Maybe it will teach you to select your patients more carefully."

He turned his back on her, finally and forever. Dismissed the pursuit of happiness once and for all. He had never really believed in it anyway, coming from the South, where the bitter taste of defeat made the idea laughable for most people.

"General! Malvern!" Polly Warden was running after him. There were tears on her face. "I just saw Pershing at the field hospital, talking to the wounded. He didn't act like a man who wanted long casualty lists."

The flotsam of the battlefield drifted past them: walking wounded and messengers heading for the rear, engineers and signal troops lugging equipment forward on their backs. The distant crash of rifles and the chatter of machine guns echoed over the blasted trees on either side of the road. Several truck drivers stared from their cabs at this welcome break in the monotony. A team of mules pulling a rolling kitchen also looked interested.

What was she trying to tell him? That he had gone too far, said too much, as usual—his fatal flaw? "If—if you love someone the way you—love Pershing, you have to forgive him for what's happening," Polly said. "If a friend like you can't do it, the whole thing could become unbearable for him."

She took his muddy hands and raised them to her lips, replicating the gesture he had made in the hotel room at Saint-Mihiel. "I've been thinking and thinking and thinking about love while I sit in these traffic jams. How I found it in Paris and lost it in Saint-Mihiel. Are you—even slightly interested?"

Bliss suddenly wished he could sit down or at least lean against a tree or a truck. He had not slept for thirty-six hours. Exhaustion seemed a perfect condition in which to meet friend Death. But the possibility of life, love, happiness made his flesh feel papery, his bones so fragile a single harsh word might snap them like matchsticks.

"I saw that when you love someone, they become the center of your world and you attribute all your happiness to them. But you also start to blame them for your unhappiness. In marriage this takes ten or fifteen years, but in a war—as I was told by a fascinating philosophic militarist I met crossing the Atlantic—everything is speeded up. You can go from happiness to blame in a month. Especially if you love a general, who gives you the impression that he has all this power, when in fact he's as trapped by the whole business as you are."

She wiped at her tears, getting a big smudge of mud on her left cheek. "Am I making any sense?"

All Bliss could do was nod. She wiped at her tears again, making the smudge bigger. "I've also realized love has to include forgiveness. I hope you can put me on your list—after Pershing."

The traffic chose this worst of all moments to start unjamming. She kissed him unashamedly, with truck drivers, mules, and two or three hundred infantrymen watching, and ran back to her ambulance. Bliss stood there, as dazed as he had been half an hour ago when the Jack Johnson landed ten feet away from him. A modern woman, he thought. But a woman first, a woman who knew things that elude male rationalists, with their principles and pronouncements.

Bliss slogged to the field hospital and walked through the tents full of bandaged men until he found Pershing, leaning over a red-haired kid. "Where were you hit, son?" Jack asked.

"Just beyond that crossroads outside Romagne, General, about halfway up the hill."

The kid assumed his commander-in-chief knew every inch of the battlefield intimately. Pershing started to explain he had meant where the bullet or shrapnel had hit him. Then his eyes traveled to the lower half of the blanket, which lay flat where the kid's right leg should have been. He nodded mournfully, patted his shoulder, and walked on to the next cot.

"Jack," Bliss said.

"I've been looking for you," Pershing growled.

"I want to stay in this fight. I'll take any job you give me, from corps commander to latrine officer."

"I'll talk to you tonight," Pershing said and went back to consoling the wounded.

Hitching a ride on a motorcycle, the one vehicle that could get through the traffic, Bliss reached the rear of the battle zone in time to see the last of V Corps's stragglers marched to the front. The colonel in command of the military police could not say enough good things about Sergeant Turner and his men.

At corps headquarters Bliss called for paper and ink and wrote Hunter Liggett, commander of I Corps, urging him to give the 92nd Division or some part of it another chance in the front lines. He told him what a superb job Turner and his men had done as temporary military police. It seemed fitting, somehow, for his last act as a general.

For the rest of the day Bliss waited for the blow to fall. John J. Pershing valued loyalty above everything else. Malvern Hill Bliss had been disloyal. His retraction at the field hospital would be seen as a pathetic attempt to rescue himself from dismissal and disgrace. There was no possibility of explaining that it had been inspired by a red-haired ambulance driver who had untangled the nature of love for him in a voice ragged with exhaustion.

God knows there were ample reasons to dismiss him. The Lafayette Division had attacked the Forest of Romagne and gotten nowhere. Savage German counterattacks had thrown the other two V Corps divisions back half a mile. Shaken division commanders were reporting companies and battalions down to half strength. Even Wiley Parker was sounding discouraged.

Without any announcement of his arrival, Pershing stalked into Bliss's office. He looked slightly better than last night. He walked up and down the room, glancing at a map on the wall, the books on Bliss's desk, whipping a short malacca cane against his leg.

"I'm forming two armies," he said. "The Second Army will operate east of the Meuse. I'm putting Bullard in command of it."

Bliss said nothing. Robert Lee Bullard was a good choice. He had performed well as commander of III Corps.

"I'm putting Liggett in command of the First Army. But we're not going on the defensive. We're going to keep attacking."

Bliss still said nothing. Liggett was another good choice. The fat man with no fat above the neck was big enough and smart enough to stand up to Pershing if necessary.

"I'm relieving you as Five Corps commander. I don't think a corps suits your style. I'm putting you back in command of the Lafayette Division. I'm moving Wiley Parker to the Third Division. They need some shaping up."

He walked up and down, whipping the cane against his leg. "How does all that strike you, General? Can you live with it? Can you fight that division of prima donnas you've created?"

"I can live with it. They'll fight," Bliss said.

"I want you to summarize, on a single page, possible changes in tactics for the First and Second armies."

Bliss promised to get something on paper within the hour. "What about these negotiations between Wilson and the Germans, Jack?"

"I don't know a thing about them. I haven't heard one word from our commander in chief. As far as I'm concerned, we're still fighting a war."

Pershing strode to the door. Bliss decided to go on living dangerously. "Jack," he said. "Are you going to see Michie?"

Pershing flung the answer over his shoulder. "I'm on my way to tell Foch about the new arrangement. I may stop in Paris on the way back. But it's none of your goddamn business."

He was gone. Bliss was still a general—a diminished one. He did not give a damn. Let the world think he was relieved as corps commander for incompetence, drunkenness, or whatever. He had rescued his division. He might even have rescued the American Expeditionary Force. That was more than enough to satisfy a man who had graduated from West Point at the bottom of his class. Especially when, despite some appearances to the contrary, John J. Pershing was still his friend.

56. ROUNDHEADS AND CAVALIERS

MAJOR GENERAL CHARLES P. SUMMERALL, THE new commander of V Corps, brushed aside the gas curtain at the dugout entrance and slouched into the command post of the first brigade of the Lafayette Division, a former German bunker in the Forest of Romagne. Rats skittered in the dim tiers of bunks against the rear wall. Brigadier General Douglas Fairchild and his staff leaped to their feet and saluted.

Major General Malvern Hill Bliss said, "Hello, Summerall." All he got was a glare. He was not supposed to be here. The new commander of V Corps had called Fairchild directly, ignoring Bliss, who found out about it from Brigadier Jorgenson, still the corps chief of staff. For some odd reason, Grimjaw had decided he liked Bliss. Maybe it had something to do with working for Summerall.

One of Bliss's professors at West Point used to say American soldiers were either cavaliers or roundheads. Cadaverous Charles Summerall was a quintessential Cromwellian. His training as an artilleryman gave him a mathematical approach to battle. It was all as impersonal as the trajectory of a howitzer shell. Individuals simply did not matter. For the past two days, he had been lashing the exhausted divisions of V Corps to break the Germans' grip on the heights of Romagne, the key to the Kriemhilde Stellung. He had spent the previous week driving them through the murderous Forest of Romagne.

Summerall had reportedly announced he did not want Bliss and his Lafayette Division in V Corps. Hunter Liggett, the new commander of the First Army, had told him he would decide where divisions belonged. Nobody pushed Liggett around.

"Fairchild," Summerall said, "I want the Côte Dame Marie tomorrow or a casualty report of five thousand men."

Had Pershing told Summerall this was the way to drive Bliss crazy? Was this a carefully calculated form of torture? No, it was just Pershing's way of telling Bliss he was still the boss. He did not worship long casualty lists but he expected results, and Summerall had gained more ground with the First Division than any other general in the army. That was why he was commanding V Corps.

With a mighty effort, Bliss remained silent and let Douglas Fairchild reply. "General Summerall," he said, "you'll have the Côte Dame Marie tomorrow or that casualty report—with my name at the head of the list."

Who was it Summerall resembled? Bliss groped for the name that was teasing his memory and found it: Thomas J. Jackson, better known as Stonewall. The artilleryman had the same humorless intensity and tenacity and ruthlessness as that lemon-sucking genius who regularly marched his infantry beyond human endurance and gunned down deserters and pressed home every attack until the last reserves were dead or victory was in his grasp. Maybe every army needed this dose of Cromwell in its veins. Robert E. Lee thought so. He had called Jackson his right arm.

But we know what you think of Robert E. Lee, whispered the mournful voice of the thinking soldier. Bliss stifled it one last time. He had gone as far as a man could go. He had been forced to choose between love and knowledge and had chosen love. Maybe that was an extravagant word for what existed between him and Jack Pershing. But for several reasons—one of them a certain red-haired ambulance driver—it was the most satisfactory.

Summerall departed without even suggesting a battle plan. Bliss jammed his finger into Fairchild's chest. "We'll take that goddamn hill. But if the casualty report is five thousand I'll hang your ass if it's the last thing I do in this army."

Fairchild looked as if he might spring at Bliss's throat. "You heard what I said!" he cried. "If it's five thousand my name will be at its head."

Another glory seeker was in danger of finding death a friend. Bliss softened his voice. "It won't be. We're going to figure out how to do it the smart way."

As dawn turned the sky slate gray above the Argonne, whizbangs crashed in a continuous stream on Company A's position at the northern edge of the Forest of Romagne. Generals Bliss and Fairchild strolled to the door of Captain George Eagleton's dugout and did an Alphonse and Gaston about who should enter first and escape sudden death. Bliss finally shoved the Brigadier inside. Captain Eagleton was dozing on some sandbags in the corner. The company clerk was too tired to yell attention. He shook Eagleton and said, "Coupla generals here, Captain."

Sergeant O'Connor burst through the gas curtain on the dugout door. "We just lost Korda!" he said. "The little bastard kicked me out of my foxhole. Ten seconds after I left, a whizbang made a direct hit. There's nothin' left of the scumbag but a piece of his raincoat."

Fairchild waited for Bliss to reprimand O'Connor for calling the late lieutenant a scumbag. Instead, Bliss suggested the Sergeant join the meeting. "We're trying to figure out the best way to attack the Côte Dame Marie," he said.

"Good luck, General," O'Connor said.

The fourth major to command the first battalion joined them in the tiny dugout. The company clerk grudgingly lit an extra candle. Bliss passed around a bottle of brandy. "We've got orders to take this lousy hill by tomorrow night," he said. "Anyone got any ideas?"

Eagleton pulled out a sketch of the Côte Dame Marie and spread it on the dirt floor of the dugout. "The Krauts have an opening in their wire here," he said, pointing to the southeast slope of the ridge. "It's zeroed in by ten or twelve machine guns. If we did something clever to distract them, maybe a small party with plenty of grenades could get through it and up the slope to clean out those guns. The rest of the battalion could come through the opening as soon as we finish the job."

"You're going to do it yourself?" Bliss said.

"All my lieutenants are dead or wounded, sir," George said.

"Who's going to lead the rest of your company up the slope after you?"

"Sergeant O'Connor, here."

"We better make him Lieutenant O'Connor. You're going to need an executive officer, and there's not a chance of getting any replacements for the next three months."

"You couldn't find a better man," Eagleton said.

"How about it, O'Connor? Do you want to become one of us bastards?" Bliss said.

Brigadier General Fairchild was appalled by Bliss's description of the officer corps. O'Connor did not disagree with it. "If the old gang was still around, I couldn't do it, General. But the replacements ain't been here long enough to know the difference. It's a deal."

"If we pull this thing off, tell them the coq au vin's on me for the whole company—even if Solange is charging Paris prices."

Bliss went to work on taking the Germans' mind off that opening in the barbed wire. Around noon, two 75-millimeter artillery pieces appeared among the foxholes of Company A, hauled there by the sweating, cursing gunners. The artillerymen fell down every ten feet as whizbangs burst around them. But they wrestled the guns into position and began pumping shells into the slopes of the Côte Dame Marie. The artillery captain asked Bliss how long they had to stay in this exposed position. "Until Christmas Eve," he said.

A few feet away, Lieutenant O'Connor was organizing his company for the attack, briskly distributing hand grenades, talking confidently to sergeants and corporals. A quarter of a mile away, Bliss could see Captain Eagleton and seven men running in an infantryman's crouch toward the opening in the barbed wire. They all carried sacks of grenades.

Bliss got on the field telephone to Harry Quickmeyer. His regiment was supposed to attack the other side of the Côte Dame Marie. There was no break in the wire there. Quick and his rebels were going to have a tough time. "A blue rocket will be the signal for the attack."

"Tell him I'm leading the attack on this side," Fairchild said. "I'll see him on top of the ridge."

Bliss heard the edge of competition in the remark and did not transmit it. "He doesn't need any encouragement to kill himself," he said.

A cascade of whizbangs bracketed the two artillery pieces near Bliss. The gunners, including the captain, broke for the rear. Machine-Gun Joe Perry appeared out of the swirling black smoke. "I knew the white-livered sons of bitches were going to do that," Perry said. "I've got the machine-gun battalion standing by to cover you with indirect fire."

"Red rockets will let you know we need more men. Send them in at battalion strength, will you please, General?" Fairchild said.

The blue rocket rose into the gray sky. "Here we go, men," Fairchild shouted. "For God and country—and democracy!"

The battalion swarmed up the slope of the Côte Dame Marie, Fairchild striding erect in front of the line, without a helmet or a gun as usual. At any moment in the tangled thickets Bliss expected to see a machine gun spit death. The Brigadier was practically begging the Germans to extinguish his luck. He had spent a good part of last night damning Wiley Parker, Summerall, and the other casualty-list collectors in the American army.

The crash of guns and shells on the southwestern slope of the ridge was tremendous. Through the clatter rose the *yi-yi-yi* of the rebels' Confederate yell, the same war cry that had carried their South Carolina grandfathers into the muzzles of Union artillery at Malvern Hill and Gettysburg. Bliss had taught these boys to stay close to Mother Earth. He hoped they were remembering their lessons.

No one fired a shot at Fairchild and the men of Ireland's Own. They found Captain Eagleton halfway up the slope, presiding over fifteen prisoners and at least as many machine guns. The Germans had fled into their dugouts in the face of the point-blank artillery fire. Eagleton had rushed the guns and taken them without losing a man.

The Celts had some dirty fighting to clear the half-mile summit, but by nightfall there were no living Germans on top of the Côte Dame Marie. The resistance on the southwestern slope quickly melted away and the two regiments soon linked up. Bliss watched the rebels and the Irish Americans slapping each other on the back, exchanging war stories. He started telling Joe Perry about their slugfests back at Camp Mills on Long Island.

"Where's Colonel Quickmeyer?" Fairchild asked one of the rebels.

"He's hit bad," a captain said. "Some machine guns messed us up for a while. He was tryin' to get B Company reorganized when—"

Near the bottom of the southwestern slope of the Côte Dame Marie, Fairchild and Bliss found Quickmeyer on a stretcher, the front of his blouse soaked with blood. Fairchild knelt beside him. "I'm sorry," he said.

"The same goes for me, Quick," Bliss said.

Quickmeyer ignored Bliss. He was glaring at Fairchild. With a terrific effort, he summoned the strength to speak. "Dougie—take the only honest advice—I've ever given you. Don't marry her."

Bliss ordered four men to take Quickmeyer to the nearest aid station on the double. "Is he talking about Louise Wolcott?" he asked.

Fairchild nodded. "Without her I don't think I could have survived this—this slaughter pen."

What did the French say? The more things change, the more they remain the same. Against machine guns and artillery and poison gas, two cavaliers had been fighting for *la belle dame sans merci*.

57. LOST LOVE

Outside Field Hospital 23, another sea of canvas with huge red crosses on the sides and tops of the tents, Polly Warden watched dozens of soldiers swarm to greet the young woman who ran the local Red Cross canteen as she arrived with the latest newspapers in the back of her Ford. The car was pockmarked with shrapnel. Its back windows were long gone. But she made the run every morning because she knew how badly the men wanted to keep up with the news these days.

Her canteen was a crude wooden shed surrounded by sand-bags—far from the cute, stylish affairs the Red Cross had featured in fund-raising exhibits in America last year. Life in the mud and shell fire of the Argonne did not encourage cuteness. Three Vassar graduates ran this canteen, keeping it open twenty-four hours a day, serving coffee and doughnuts and good cheer to all comers. There was one like it in every division's sector. General Pershing had abandoned his opposition to women participating in the war.

Today's headlines boomed stories of spectacular British and French advances in the north. Of course, they also trumpeted American successes in the Argonne, which made Polly a bit suspicious. But there was not much doubt that the Germans were talking peace. The word "armistice" was floating back and forth in exchanges between Berlin and Washington.

Meanwhile, Americans and Germans were dying. The casualties in the last three days, as the First Army battered its way up the slopes of the main German defense line, the Kriemhilde Stellung, were awful. The 42nd Division, fighting to the west of the Lafayettes, had sent out an emergency call for extra ambulances.

The Lafayettes' losses were almost as heavy, according to her gloomy friend, Sergeant Walsh, still in charge of evacuating the wounded.

Martha Herzog and several other members of the ambulance group thought the generals were acting like maniacs. If peace was a real possibility—and they must know whether it was real or a fiction—they ought to stop attacking and save lives. Polly had no real answer to this earnest mixture of hope and sorrow. She wished she could talk to General Bliss. She had not heard a word from him since their chance meeting a week ago. She only knew he had gone back to commanding the Lafayette Division—an apparent demotion.

Polly had told Bliss she still loved him. But the words had been torn from her lips by seeing him sacrificing his career, his reputation, and his life for his ideals. Now he was back in command, ordering men to attack-attack-attack in Pershing's name. She was assailed by the same confusion and anger that had overwhelmed her at Saint-Mihiel.

"Miss Warden?" a medic said. "Colonel Quickmeyer wants to see you. He's in Tent Five."

He did not have to say anything else. Tent Five was where they put the wounded who were beyond help. Polly ran through the usual chaos of writhing men and exhausted doctors and nurses. She glimpsed Isaac Pinkus leaning over a sobbing soldier with a smashed leg, a dozen other doctors working on body and head wounds. She seldom went into the operating tents these days. The scenes aroused too many memories of the Château Givry.

Quickmeyer lay on a stretcher in a far corner of Tent 5, four haggard infantrymen hunkered beside him. "They ain't doin' nothin' for him, ma'am," one of them said in a thick southern accent. "Can't you get some attention? He's hurt real bad."

"Beat it," Quickmeyer said. "I want to talk to Miss Warden."

The soldiers retreated to the other side of the tent. Polly knelt beside Quickmeyer.

"I've got something—I want you to tell Louise Wolcott," he said.

He struggled for breath. "I know you don't like her. But— promise—to tell her."

"Of course I will," Polly said.

"Tell her not to blame herself—for what's happened. I would have gotten into this end of the show one way or another. Tell her I loved—every minute of it. I was doing—what I was born to do."

He gathered his strength for the last time. "Tell her I loved her—from the first minute I saw her—that night in Fort Myer. Before she said a word to me. ..."

Polly stumbled out of the tent, her eyes glazed with tears. Martha Herzog seized her arm. "What's wrong?"

"Harry Quickmeyer," Polly said.

Rushing into Tent 5 before Polly could stop her, Martha knelt beside Quickmeyer and pressed his hand to her breasts. As far as Polly could see, they did not speak. In about five minutes Martha stood up and walked away, her head bowed. Quickmeyer's eyes were closed.

Dr. Pinkus rushed up to them. "I'm sorry," he said. "You know how the system works. We couldn't do anything for him."

"I loved him," Martha said, tears streaming down her cheeks.

Pain distorted Pinkus's cherubic face. The guns thudded in the distance. "Let's go," Polly said. "The ambulances are loaded."

"Loaded and loaded and loaded until doomsday!" Martha said. "Why are we still fighting? Can't you find out from your friend the General? They're treating their men and us like children—or cattle!"

The road was the usual tangle of traffic. Polly's sitter was a German American, a shell-shock case. They had put him in a straitjacket and tied his feet together. He had been unable to bear the agony of fighting his own people. He recited long passages from imaginary newspapers about a German victory. At the end of each story he would shout, "*Deutschland über alles!* Germany over the whole world!"

Beyond the Argonne they picked up speed. All the way to the evacuation hospital, Polly's ambulance wheels seemed to say *the-war-is-not-over the-war-is-not-over the-war-is-not-over.* Why hadn't she heard from Malvern Hill Bliss? Did he know something he was afraid to tell her? Something that might make her agree with Martha Herzog and Anita Sinclair about the callousness of generals?

58. ROOTING FOR WOODROW

AFTER THE CAPTURE OF THE CÔTE DAME MARIE, Bliss demanded the Lafayette Division's relief. They had been in the front lines two weeks, attacking almost every day. No one had changed clothes or eaten a decent meal or gotten even half a night's sleep in that time. In many companies casualties were over 50 percent. The survivors were turning into zombies. Hunter Liggett, the new commander of the First Army, told Bliss virtually every division in the Argonne was in the same condition. They were going on the defensive while he brought order out of the chaos on the roads and moved fresh divisions into the line.

The commander of V Corps, glowering Charles Summerall, thought this decision was a colossal mistake. He refused to let the Lafayettes escape his Cromwellian grasp. They were assigned to a reserve area only ten miles behind the lines. "You'll be getting five thousand replacements," he told Bliss. "They'll probably be worse than the last batch. Get them ready to fight. Don't let them read those newspapers full of peace rumors. I don't think they mean a damn thing."

Inclined to disagree with Summerall on principle, Bliss did his own research on the prospects for peace. While the Lafayettes recovered from their ordeal and his staff bemoaned the replacements, whose training appeared to be nil, Bliss sat in his headquarters reading letters and diaries taken from the bodies of German soldiers. All of them reverberated with growing desperation and despair. The failure of the Friedensturm peace offensive in July had been a terrific blow to the army's morale. The realization that thousands of fresh American troops were arriving in France every day only added to the pervasive gloom.

The division intelligence officer stuck his long Yankee face through Bliss's doorway. "General, we just finished interrogating a pretty big fish, a staff colonel from the army group opposite us. He was visiting the front and got caught in our assault on the Côte Dame Marie. I thought you'd like to talk to him. He's got some interesting things to say about the dawn of peace."

Colonel Hans von Falkenhayn was a tall austere man in his thirties whose suave emotionless face reminded Bliss of several Jesuits he had known in his Baltimore schooldays. "Sit down, Colonel," he said. "I understand you're ready to talk quite freely about Germany's situation."

"I wish to clear up some misunderstandings about these armistice negotiations," he said in unaccented English. "They are the product of civilians around the Kaiser who have succumbed to pessimism and unfortunately influenced him."

"You don't consider your army beaten?"

"By no means. We are retreating slowly before superior numbers. We intend to make a stand at a point of our choosing that will make even you Americans consider a peace treaty on our terms an excellent proposition."

"What sort of terms?"

"We'll agree to evacuate Belgium and France. But we'll insist on control of Poland, Russia, Rumania, and our other eastern territories, all fairly won."

Bliss offered him a cigarette. "How do you see Germany's future?"

"Quite promising, in spite of our present frustrations. We have the greatest arms industry in the world. There is no doubt that you Americans will become embroiled with another foe, who is eager to challenge you for control of the Pacific."

"Japan?"

The Colonel smiled superciliously, as if Bliss was a kindergartner who had managed to recognize the first letter of the alphabet. "We'll supply weapons for both sides, and at an opportune moment join one of them—probably Japan. An unpalatable thought to those of us who wish to see the white race remain supreme."

Bliss asked him if he was related to General Erich von Falkenhayn, who commanded the German armies at Verdun in 1916. "My father's first cousin. I call him Uncle."

"I think you should call him a few other things. Such as mass murderer."

Colonel von Falkenhayn's smile grew somewhat less supercilious. "Perhaps the Japanese will be easier to deal with in the long run," he said.

An hour after the Colonel departed to a prisoner-of-war camp, Pershing stamped into Bliss's office. He was not the exhausted beaten man Bliss had seen six nights ago. There was a spring in his step, the glint was back in his eyes. "I never thought your prima donnas could take the Côte Dame Marie," he said.

Bliss grinned. He could live with these left-handed compliments. "We fooled the Germans too. We even fooled Summerall. He wanted five thousand casualties."

"How many did you have?"

"A thousand."

Pershing's nod was noncommittal. He was not defending Summerall; he was not apologizing for him either. Bliss could not resist slipping in another needle. "It took us a little longer to bust the Kriemhilde Stellung than your Leavenworth geniuses predicted."

While the Lafayette Division was seizing the Côte Dame Marie, the 42nd Division, fighting on their right flank, had captured another key height, the Côte de Châtillon. The twin conquests meant the First Army had finally reached the objective the planners had given the infantry for September 26, the day they attacked. It had taken three weeks and 175,000 casualties to advance those ten bitter miles. "They had to learn the hard way, like the rest of us," Pershing said.

"How's Liggett doing on the defensive? Are the Germans going along with the idea?"

Pershing stared at a map on the wall. "I guess so. They don't want me around First Army headquarters any more. Liggett practically told me to go away and stop bothering them. Isn't that a hell of a thing? That fat old bastard is almost as bad as Tasker."

"Liggett knows what he's doing, Jack."

"I hope so," Pershing said. "He's leaving me full time on Foch's griddle. You know what that little twerp said when I told him we were creating two armies and I was going to be group commander?"

Pershing wiggled his mustache in a good imitation of Foch. "I 'ope thees does nut me-an you will retrate to Chaumont and hide from zee lack of results."

"Did you hit him this time?"

"I damn near did. Then we got into something even messier: this armistice stuff. Wilson's made an incredible botch of it. He's got the British and the French in a fury by negotiating on his goddamn Fourteen Points without even consulting them. What do you think of an armistice?"

They had reached the purpose of the visit. Pershing was picking brains, one of his favorite habits. "It's a lousy idea," Bliss said. "It practically guarantees this won't be the war to end wars."

Bliss told him about his conversation with the German staff officer who was already planning the next war. Pershing said he had seen similar stuff from other parts of the front. "So what's the answer?" he asked.

"The one Teddy Roosevelt is recommending. Unconditional surrender. An armistice means the German army can march home with their guns on their shoulders and flags flying. They can tell themselves they haven't really lost, they've just stopped fighting because the civilians panicked. Only unconditional surrender in the field will change that. If we march them home as prisoners, it will make all the difference."

Pershing seemed surprised to hear Roosevelt had made unconditional surrender the Republican Party's main issue in the midterm election campaign currently raging in the United States. The First Army had absorbed all Jack's waking thoughts for the past three months. He paced the room again, thinking hard in his direct cutting way. Other men thought their way to opinions. Pershing reached decisions.

"I agree with Teddy," he said.

"What does that mean for us in the Argonne?"

"It means we attack again as soon as the First Army is ready. Maybe we can break them before Woodrow and his Fourteen Stupid Points let them strut home like winners."

Pershing departed. Bliss sat there, staring into the darkness for a long time. He had said exactly what he thought. Wasn't that what a general and a friend was supposed to do? Duty—honor—country, those ideals hammered into his soul at West Point. Hadn't he told Pershing what honor and duty to the United States of America required him to say?

Unquestionably. But it meant the corpses would continue to multiply for the burial parties. The shrapnel-gouged, bullet-torn wounded would continue to flood the field hospitals.

More headlights flickered outside his window. Footsteps. Arthur Hunthouse appeared in the doorway, disapproval on his sycophant's face. "Miss Warden would like to see you."

Bliss sensed trouble the moment she walked in. She was exhausted. The vivacity, even the intelligence, had drained from her eyes, her face. "I know I shouldn't be here. It could lead to ugly gossip. But I can't understand why you haven't written to me," she said in a leaden voice.

"When you're only five miles away a letter seemed silly. I hoped we might meet at the field hospital. I was there once or twice, but we were on different schedules."

Her feminine antennae picked up the evasion in his voice. "You were more or less pleased by that, weren't you."

Bliss took a deep breath. He had told Pershing the truth and survived. Why not keep pushing his luck? "In a way."

"You don't think it's a good idea to tell a mere woman the whole truth about this mess?"

"I'm afraid I toyed with that thought. Not because you're a woman, but because of the job you're doing. It would turn me into a drunk in a week."

"Is there anything to these armistice negotiations?"

"There's a lot to them, but we're disregarding them. We're going to keep attacking."

"Why?"

He tried to sum up what he had helped Pershing decide. He told her about Falkenhayn and Teddy Roosevelt's campaign for unconditional surrender. It did not impress her. "How can you ask men to keep dying for a theory?" she said.

"It's part of what they pay us for," Bliss said. "Generals are in the history game. Like presidents and premiers"

"It's—it's abominable."

"It'll take twenty years to find out which of us is right. How about a stay of execution?"

She shook her head. They were down to fundamentals. Grim-eyed men against tearful women, the judging head against the pitying heart, Jehovah's justice against the Virgin's mercy. General Bliss talked desperately, urgently, and got absolutely nowhere. He doubted if Pershing would have done any better.

Polly Warden vanished into the night. Bliss lay awake until dawn, almost rooting for Woodrow Wilson.

59. *THE VIRGIN SPEAKS*

IN PARIS, ON THE RUE DU BAC, LOUISE WOLCOTT walked up and down her blue and gold bedroom, Polly Warden's letter clutched in her hand. The bosom of her pink nightdress was soaked with tears. For the hundredth time she read the words of forgiveness Harry Quickmeyer sent her with his last breath.

That piece of porcine pomposity, General Tasker Bliss, had telephoned her last night, inviting her to dinner with General Henry Wilson, the British Chief of Staff, and other luminaries of the inner world of power and push. She had declined without even offering an excuse. She was through denigrating General Pershing, through applauding sneers at his failure in the Argonne. She was through with all the mean and petty games men played with one another, using women as convenient pawns.

Still the tears flowed. She had wandered the streets of Paris, wondering where and how she could expiate her sin. A drunken American officer had picked her up, thinking she was a prostitute. She had taken him home to the Rue du Bac and let him have her. He was a big brawny Westerner with all the finesse of a moose. It was over in five minutes and he spent the next hour thanking her.

Still the tears flowed. She thought of the loaded gun in the drawer of her dressing table. Was that the answer? It would be simple and quick. She would regain the initiative, finally and forever. For a moment or two she would share his pain.

At dawn, while her impromptu lover snored in her bed, Louise dressed and took a taxi to the Church of the Dome of the Invalides. A ten-franc note gained her admittance. She gazed down at

Napoleon's red porphyry tomb and wandered off into the dark recesses of the nave. She had not come to worship the bundle of rags and bone inside that marble sarcophagus. She was here to consult darker, larger powers.

She found herself in a dim side chapel gazing up at a shadowy statue of the Virgin, her arms outstretched. She thought of the thousands of women in black kneeling before similar statues at Notre-Dame and a hundred other churches in Paris. She was one with them now, one with their grief, their agony. They were a kind of force, drawing her into the arms of the Divine Mother, Mater Dolorosa, the Woman of Sorrows.

She needed someone with special powers of intercession, someone who could ask God to forgive her failure to acknowledge love, its harsh hawk-eyed reality, when it entered her life. Only a woman could forgive another woman for such an enormous sin. Louise did not know how long she knelt there, rapt and pleading, asking the Virgin Mother for help.

Clump clump clump. Male footsteps were marching toward her. A hand touched her shoulder. She turned to gaze into the somber face of Brigadier General Douglas Fairchild. "Your maid said you'd left the house at dawn. I knew you'd be here."

He lifted Louise to her feet. Her legs, her whole body, felt numb. "Were you praying for me?" he asked.

Yes, whispered the statue of the Virgin.

"Yes," Louise said.

"The Argonne's changed my mind about war. I felt stripped, naked—except for you. Only you gave my life meaning."

I'm glad, whispered the statue of the Virgin.

"I'm glad," Louise said.

"Quickmeyer was killed. I felt terrible. I've told you how much I disliked him. But I still felt terrible. He was a good soldier. He was just—unlucky."

Too bad, whispered the statue of the Virgin.

"Too bad," Louise said.

"Did you love him? He said something that made me think you did—before you met me."

No, whispered the statue of the Virgin.

"No," Louise said.

He put his arm around her waist, and they walked slowly back to the tomb of Napoleon. Louise felt the Virgin's eyes on her every step of the way. "I'm still a soldier. I'll never be anything else," Fairchild said.

I don't want you to be anything else, the Virgin said.

Her voice was no longer a whisper. It was a dark moan that filled the entire church. It swirled up into the dome above the tomb. Louise trembled. "I don't want you to be anything else," she said.

Louise saw what the Virgin wanted her to do. She would marry this haunted soldier and spend the rest of her life pretending to love his pomposity, his ambition, his egotism. He was the total opposite of Harry Quickmeyer in every way. Night after night she would place her lips on his self-satisfied mouth; she would open her body to his fumbling thrusts; and ultimately, in some distant moment of private glory, she would know she had expiated her sin.

I love you, the Virgin moaned.

"I love you," Louise said.

"Oh, my darling, my precious one," he said.

He swept her into his arms. Her lips were as cold as the red porphyry of Napoleon's tomb. He did not notice, of course. He would never notice. That was part of the Virgin's plan.

60. DOING THEIR DAMNEDEST

HORNS BLARING, CARS ROARED THROUGH THE darkened streets of the villages where the Lafayette Division was billeted. Officers fired off guns. Rough hands shook heavy sleepers awake. Bliss stood on the steps of his head-quarters listening to the uproar.

"What the hell's goin' on?" someone shouted.

"The goddamn niggers in the Ninety-second Division broke and ran. They left a hole about three miles wide. We gotta plug it."

"Who ever thought those black sons of bitches could fight any-way?"

"Black Jack Pershing. Get in those goddamn trucks!"

"I'm gonna get killed this time, I know it."

"We're all gonna get killed eventually!"

A call from Hunter Liggett had awakened Bliss at midnight. "You asked me to give the Ninety-second another chance. I did it against my better judgment," the fat man roared. "Get the hell up there and clean up the mess."

The convoys rumbled down the main streets of a dozen villages, scooping up soldiers and thundering north into the Argonne. Bliss and Captain Hunthouse and Mile-a-Minute Murphy were in the middle of the first dozen trucks. To everyone's amazement, the roads were smooth, solid—and practically empty. Military policemen waved them through every crossroad. It was like riding a good rail-road. "It looks like the First Army has finally gotten things orga-nized," Bliss said.

At dawn the Lafayettes reached the three miles of front where the 92nd Division had collapsed, to be greeted by a ferocious German artillery barrage. There were dead black men everywhere, literally hundreds of them in front of a woods called the Bois des Loges. The Germans were dug into La Ferme Rouge, a red-roofed farmhouse with machine guns all along the perimeter. Indirect fire poured over the tops of the trees of the Bois des Loges. The 92nd had taken over the wood and the farm from the 78th Division. Within six hours the Germans had counterattacked with precision and fury.

The Lafayettes dug in while battalion and regiment and division tried to get a handle on the situation. Sergeants and lieutenants screamed curses at the new replacements. They had been in the army less than two months and barely knew which was the business end of their rifles. There had been no time to train them. Bliss could only hope the veterans would teach them by example.

American artillery, a lot of it, suddenly began answering the German artillery. It was another welcome change. The veterans watched the big shells hiss overhead in the gray half-light and cheered when huge explosions erupted a mile or two behind the German lines. The whizbangs dwindled, though the machine guns continued to be lively.

Bliss went up to the front with Company A. They were more than his sentimental favorites now, they were his luck. He watched Lieutenant O'Connor check the platoons and report to Captain Eagleton they were in good shape. "We'll attack at noon," Eagleton said. He showed O'Connor the orders from the regiment. "Our objective is those blockhouses on the west side of the Red Farm. We'll have a couple of French flamethrowers for support."

Bliss decided he had nothing to worry about at the Red Farm. At noon the division advanced behind a rolling barrage. The moment the barrage lifted, flamethrowers unleashed their tongues of fire at the blockhouses on the Red Farm. About thirty Germans came running out with their hands up, screaming *kamerad*.

Elsewhere on the farm, the Germans surrendered in droves or headed for the Bois des Loges. They got no rest there. The rest of the division was attacking this half-mile-square chunk of trees, backed by plenty of artillery. Bliss feared a replay of Belleau Wood. Again, the Germans simply declined to put up a fight in their old style; they either surrendered or ran. By 2 P.M. Joe Perry sent Bliss a mordant message: ENTIRE WOOD NOW PROPERTY OF U.S. ARMY.

Later that afternoon, Bliss stumbled through the tangled terrain of the Bois des Loges. The stench of death was thick in the air. In his ears rang the sulfurous words of the commander of the 78th Division, who had lost three thousand men taking this patch of woods. "If my boys weren't so spent, I'd send them back with you. What the hell does Liggett think he's doing, trying to get niggers to fight like white men?"

Bliss had not tried to answer him. The General had not been at San Juan Hill. Or in the west, where the Ninth and Tenth Cavalry had held their own against Sioux and Apache warriors, the best horse soldiers in the world. He had no hope of changing his mind about black Americans.

Bliss was looking for proof that not everyone in the 92nd Division had run away—and dreading to find it. One of their white staff officers had their order of battle in one hand and a compass in his other hand. "I think it's a little to the west, General," he said.

They broke through a thicket and looked down on a ravine full of dead black men. There were at least a hundred and fifty of them, most of them badly mangled by hand grenades. At the northern lip of the ravine, just beyond the company line, Sergeant John Henry Turner lay on his back, a bloody trench shovel in his stiff hands. In front of him lay a dead German with a hole in his chest. More dead Germans lay in a veritable carpet in the woods beyond the perimeter.

Sergeant Turner's company had not run away. The white officers had run. Bliss had already talked to them at his headquarters. His military police had spent the morning rounding up the fragments of the 92nd Division. Bliss knelt beside Turner. His long lean face was utterly peaceful. Like Joe Doakes in Tucson, he had died doing his damnedest against a ferocious enemy.

Four and a half days later, at 3 A.M. on November 1, Bliss sat in his headquarters, reading the latest news of Woodrow Wilson's danse macabre with the Kaiser and his government. The Germans kept trying to pin the President to a peace of nonsurrender, while Wilson desperately tried to convert his Fourteen Points into an agreement with some teeth in it. So far no one seemed to be winning.

That was why, in half an hour, the First Army was going to attack again. Hunter Liggett had taken two full weeks to straighten out the mess in the Argonne. He had also issued open warfare instructions that had an interesting resemblance to the Mother Earth squirm-ahead-in-squads tactics the Lafayette Division had been using since July. Henceforth Americans were to avoid frontal assaults on machine guns ("reserves should not be piled against difficult obstacles" was the way the Leavenworth geniuses put it). They were to attack from the flanks whenever possible and call in artillery more often before they went forward. There were even a few words for Joe Perry's faith in the machine gun as a support weapon, using indirect fire.

"Hunthouse!" Bliss bellowed. A bleary-eyed Arthur Asskisser tottered to the door. He had been up all night, rushing final orders to brigade and regimental headquarters.

"Get up to the front and make sure that order to move the first wave five hundred yards into the open beyond the woods is obeyed to the letter. You might as well stay there and go forward with them. Use company runners to report back to me on the situation as it develops."

Hunthouse wavered into the night, leaving Bliss with no other entertainment. He paced and waited for the barrage, cursing the inching minute hand on his watch. He had not heard a word from Polly Warden. If this offensive became another bloodbath, he would be persona non grata for life.

At 3:30 A.M. the guns crashed, the earth shook. The flashes illuminated Bliss's windows as if the whole world were on fire. He could have read a newspaper by them, they were so bright and continuous. At 5:30 A.M. the infantry went forward, seven divisions, almost two hundred thousand men. Bliss waited tensely to see if his ruse of advancing the first wave of the Lafayette Division worked. At 6:30 A.M. a runner arrived from Joe Perry's headquarters. NO CASUALTIES FROM ENEMY ARTILLERY. FIRST WAVE HAS GAINED ONE MILE AGAINST SPASMODIC RESISTANCE.

"Murphy!" Bliss whooped. "Let's get going."

Mile-a-Minute hauled himself off a nearby couch. "Where to, General?"

"The front! This may be our last chance to get killed."

"General," Murphy said, "you're breakin' my heart."

Four days later, a groggy Bliss told Mile-a-Minute to stop as they approached a company sprawled by the side of the road. They looked as tired as Bliss felt. Arthur Hunthouse had collapsed with the flu two days ago. Half the division staff had followed him to the hospital. Instead of a bloodbath, the First Army was in a footrace. The Germans were retreating so fast, there was no time for anything but minimal sleeping and eating. Bliss was practically living in his car.

The soldiers were his old pals, Company A of the first battalion of Ireland's Own. Captain Eagleton and Lieutenant O'Connor squatted side by side pondering a map. Around them the men lay in various postures of exhaustion. "It's all over," Eagleton said. "They're not even trying to stop us. It's like a football game. Once you get the momentum, the other side is finished."

"These guys never played for Yale, Captain. They still got a lot of guns," O'Connor said.

They noticed Bliss standing in the road, his hands on his hips. "Hello, General," Eagleton said, giving him a casual salute. O'Connor did likewise.

The men remained on their backs, which was perfectly all right with Bliss. "What's your schedule?" he asked.

"We're supposed to pick up some trucks in Chaudron. That looks to be another two miles down the road," Eagleton said.

"I'll drive ahead and tell them to meet you halfway," Bliss said. "It'll save a few blisters."

He had been leapfrogging the division after the retreating Germans, half in trucks, half on foot. Bliss got back in his car and pulled ahead of them as Eagleton ordered the company out on the road for the slog to Chaudron. In two minutes, at Mile-a-Minute Murphy's usual pace, Chaudron appeared as they topped a ridge line. It sat at the bottom of a small valley, a typical French country town with one narrow winding main street. There was no sign of any trucks.

As they rolled up the main street a hatchet-faced man in a U.S. captain's uniform came out of a house and waved them down. "Do you know where the hell my trucks are?" Bliss said.

He found himself staring down the wrong end of a Luger. "Why don't you step inside, General, and we'll discuss it," Hatchet Face said in perfect English.

In the parlor of the house, Bliss was introduced to smiling six-feet-three Major Carl von Alter. "Your headlong pursuit begs for a bloody nose, General," he said.

At the window, two men in faded battlefield gray crouched beside a machine gun. The Major pointed out other guns in a half dozen ground floor windows along the street. Riflemen filled at least forty upper-floor windows. "How many men do you have in the vicinity, General?" von Alter asked.

"Five thousand," Bliss lied. "All coming down this road."

Alter was much too experienced to swallow this story. "Our scouts have seen only a single company. We should have no difficulty demolishing it," he said.

In the next half hour, Bliss grew to detest Major Alter. He had spent the war on the Russian front. When he took over Chaudron he had shot all the men in the village to make sure they did not try to warn the Americans. That was how they did things on the Russian front. This operation was to be the first of a series of bloody noses his division planned to give the Americans.

The thud of marching feet reached the room. Hatchet Face stepped into the street in his American uniform. "Are you looking for the trucks?" he called.

Bliss was standing about ten feet from the window. He watched Company A come up the street, marching casually, carelessly, their rifles at various angles. Eagleton was out front. O'Connor was back with the second platoon. The Germans were waiting for them to reach point-blank range.

"Mother Earth!" Bliss roared and leaped on top of the machine-gunner in the window. The gun tilted on its tripod and went off as Bliss clawed the German's hand on the trigger. The bullets blew out the top of the window and smashed a second-floor window across the street. The other machine guns and rifles opened up an instant later. Eagleton was hit by the first blast but a lot of the men behind him had gone flat at the warning.

With a curse Alter dragged Bliss off the squawking gunner and slammed him against the wall. He shouted something about shooting him, but Bliss knew that was unlikely. Generals did not get captured very often. They were full of interesting information. He kept his eyes on the situation in the street.

The veterans rolled underneath the stream of bullets and got to the walls of houses on both sides. Lieutenant O'Connor pulled a grenade off his belt and flipped it through the nearest window, waited ten seconds for the blast, and dove in after it. Seconds later he was at the door of the house, waving men to safety. He had survived Sergy and Fismette and Romagne. He knew how to run a street fight.

A big corporal they called Killer had done the same thing in the house opposite O'Connor. He shouted for people to join him. At least half the first two platoons got into houses that way. Soon Chauchat gunners sprayed bullets from upper windows, eliminating many of Major Alter's riflemen. The third and fourth platoons, saved by Bliss's warning, retreated to the edge of the town and their sergeants sent men swarming through the gardens behind the houses on both sides of the street. The crash of rifles and the boom of grenades from the rear sent Alter and Hatchet Face scurrying to direct a defense. They gave the assistant machine-gunner a pistol and told him to keep it trained on Bliss and Murphy.

O'Connor dove out and dragged six wounded men from the second platoon into his house. A sergeant and several privates did the same thing on the other side of the street. A hundred feet away, in the middle of the street, Captain Eagleton rolled over and tried to crawl toward the nearest house. He was too badly hurt to move more than an inch.

The curve of the street gave Bliss a clear view of O'Connor crouched in the doorway of his house. Bliss realized he was going to try to rescue Eagleton. It was much more suicidal than Eagleton's swim across the Vesle. Maxims were still firing from windows on both sides of the street, less than twenty feet away from the fallen company commander. "I'm gonna get the Captain!" O'Connor yelled to Killer, who was firing a Chauchat in the doorway across the street.

"You're out of your goddamn mind!" Killer roared.

O'Connor threw a smoke grenade down the street. It exploded into a white haze. Killer threw another one, and O'Connor charged out the door into the fog. In blurred outline Bliss saw Killer crouched in the doorway, Chauchat blasting at the Maxim on the right. Another man was firing his Chauchat at the German gun on the left. O'Connor lunged through the smoke, slipping once on a puddle of blood, almost tripping over bodies.

As he reached Eagleton, O'Connor flung a grenade at the Maxim on the left, a second grenade at the one on the right. Bullets struck sparks from the houses on both sides of him as the dazed Germans fired wild. O'Connor staggered away with Eagleton on his back, the bullets hissing around them. He made it to the house and dove headfirst through the doorway. Someone slammed the door just as a hundred bullets thudded against the wood. The Lieutenant's mother must have lined his crib with shamrocks.

Five minutes later, the windows of the house across the street exploded as grenades and rifles demolished the machine-gun squad on the ground floor. Seconds later, the same thing happened in two other houses. The Maxims were promptly turned on the Germans in the houses on Bliss's side of the street. Bullets poured into Bliss's parlor, all but decapitating the resident machine-gunner and his assistant.

From the hall Bliss heard Major Alter and his friend in the American uniform talking excitedly in German. Something about "Schleppwagens." A moment later the rumble of several dozen motors filled the air. It was the rest of the first battalion—in the trucks that Company A was supposed to meet in Chaudron. Alter appeared in the doorway, gun in hand. "Come, General, we must leave," he said.

Bliss declined to move, hoping O'Connor or one of his friends would start shooting that machine gun across the street again. A second later the *pop-pop-pop* sent a stream of bullets through the shattered window into Alter's chest, flinging him ten feet into the hall.

The other Germans did not stop to take Bliss prisoner. A grenade killed Hatchet Face as he tried to get out the back door of the house. Most of the surviving Germans met similar fates. As the gunfire died away, Killer appeared with his smoking Chauchat on his arm. "Your car's parked out back, General," he said.

Bliss ordered the wounded loaded into the trucks and had Eagleton put in the backseat of his car. The Captain was barely conscious, his chest and belly swathed in bloody bandages O'Connor had wound around him from their first-aid kits. A lot of the men were crying, some mourning Eagleton, others friends who had died in Chaudron's blood-soaked street. Company A was in bad shape.

"Can I come with you, General?" O'Connor said.

"You're the only officer left. You better stay with the men," Bliss said.

"General, I know what those field hospitals are like. I want to make sure the Captain gets taken care of. You got a division to run."

"O'Connor," Eagleton whispered, "stay with the men."

O'Connor held out his hand. There were tears on the tough guy's face. "You're one in a barrel, Captain," he said.

Bliss told Murphy to change his name to Mile-a-Second. They roared down the muddy road, Eagleton propped in a corner of the back seat, Bliss beside him to make sure he did not roll onto the floor. "What went wrong, General?" he said. "Was it my fault?"

"No. It was my fault, son."

"Thought we had them licked."

"We do," Bliss said.

The Captain coughed up blood. Bliss wiped it away with his handkerchief. "Wasn't that great, General? The way O'Connor got me out of there?"

"I'll make sure he gets a medal for it."

"Didn't—do it for a medal, General. People do things—in the infantry—for friends."

"I know that. Generals like to give medals. It makes them feel a little less useless."

Captain Eagleton was silent for a long time. He seemed to be slipping away. Then he was back, smiling in a rueful nostalgic way. "Women, General. Women drive you crazy?"

"From birth."

"Why is that? Why can't they—listen? You know what I mean, General. They only hear half of what you say to them. Why is that?"

He was silent again. The speedometer hovered around 100. Mile-a-Minute hurtled around trucks and tanks and artillery pieces. But the blood soaking the back seat made Bliss wonder if it mattered.

"Yet you can't—do without them, can you, General?"

"Women? No. I've tried. It doesn't work."

"I tried too. It didn't work. I kept seeing her—sitting beside me in that hansom cab—going up Fifth Avenue. That red hair. So damn—beautiful."

The car rocketed over a hill. At the bottom were the tents of the Lafayette Division's field hospital. Eight or nine ambulances were parked in the field just beyond it. Captain Eagleton was very still; his eyes were closed. Bliss hoped he was seeing that red-haired modern woman who refused to listen to him. He feared the Captain was not seeing anything but the blank cool darkness of death. He dreaded what the woman they both loved would say to General Bliss.

61. EMERGENCY SURGERY

THE-WAR-IS-NOT-OVER THE-WAR-IS-NOT-OVER THE-*war-is-not-over* drummed the wheels of Polly's ambulance as she ascended a steep hill in the bare rolling farmlands of the valley of the Meuse, miles north of the Argonne. For the previous twelve hours—the entire night of November 5–6—she had led eight ambulances along a road so mushy they were up to their hubs in mud most of the time, in constant danger of skidding into the ditch. The American army was advancing so fast, it was almost impossible to keep up with them. This put unbearable pressure on the whole medical service, with special strain on the ambulance drivers. The evacuation hospitals were now fifty miles in the rear.

The sleepless night left Polly dazed, almost trancelike. Occasionally she heard Dr. Giroux-Langin's voice, warning her that ambulance drivers too break down. She ignored it; she ignored all the order givers, the arrogant domineering proponents of war-to-the-death. She was vaguely ashamed of her outburst at Bliss's headquarters, but also proud of it. Someone had to speak out against this murderous determination to kill and wound as many men as possible.

She knew that judgment was unjust. She saw the pain, the doubt, the regret on Bliss's face as he told her what Pershing had decided. A part of her mind warned her history might well prove the generals were right. She remembered the Germans at Château Givry roaring "*Gott mitt uns!*," the long-range shells killing schoolgirls on the boulevards of Paris.

Polly was beyond arguments. She only knew she wanted the killing and maiming to end. She did not want to see another morphine-numbed soldier without an arm or a leg or an eye or a jaw;

she did not want to run her finger down another casualty list. She did not want to hear another scream or sob from the back of her ambulance.

But the world, the generals, even the wheels of her ambulance declined to listen to her. *The-war-is-not-over the-war-is-not-over the-war-is-not-over* the wheels mocked. The pistons in her engine beat the same ironic refrain. The war, Anita Sinclair's vortex, continued to whirl her toward some unnamed and unnamable consummation.

A mile ahead on the road, Polly saw about two hundred American engineers trying to fill a huge hole, probably from a mine. A shell came whining out of the sky. There was a tremendous explosion, a swirl of black smoke, and cries of agony. Polly and Martha and Alice Hedberg and the other drivers waded into the water-filled bottom of the hole, helping to drag out wounded men before they drowned. It was mucky, sickening work. Nothing makes an uglier wound than shrapnel.

Polly knelt beside a sergeant with a gash in his chest, through which blood was spurting and air was being sucked in. She whipped out his first-aid packet and plugged the opening with gauze, then pulled a needle and some silk gut from an oilskin pouch in her pocket and sewed the wound shut. The man was in such shock, he barely noticed the minor pain.

Isaac Pinkus had taught her that if these perforating wounds were closed promptly, the danger of hemorrhage was reduced and the soldier had a far better chance to survive. They bandaged other wounds, applied tourniquets, injected morphine. The survivors loaded the sergeant and the other wounded into the ambulances, and the column headed for the field hospital, about ten miles up the road.

At the hospital, Polly asked Isaac Pinkus to look at her sergeant with the chest wound. "I couldn't have done a better job myself," he said. "I think he'll make it."

Polly felt a glow of pride out of all proportion to the accomplishment. Maybe the desperation engulfing her was a wish to do something more positive than drive an ambulance. "Any news of an armistice?" Pinkus asked. He was hollow-cheeked. His eyes, his voice, were gray with fatigue.

"Still a fog of diplomacy," Polly said.

"Don't they know men are dying?" Pinkus said.

"Generals and politicians don't worry about such things."

Careening into the evacuation parking area was a car that belonged unmistakably to a general. Two stars fluttered on small flags from the front fenders. Malvern Hill Bliss leaped out of the back seat and roared, "Get a stretcher and a doctor! I've got a badly wounded officer here!"

Pinkus and half a dozen orderlies and nurses forgot how exhausted they were and rushed to obey. Polly followed the crowd, wondering what officer had rated a ride in the rear of the General's car. A colonel, at the very least.

They lifted George Eagleton onto a stretcher and Dr. Pinkus knelt beside him. He looked up apologetically. "I'm afraid he's dead, General."

"Goddamn it," Bliss said.

He turned away with an angry frustrated swerve of his body and saw Polly. He walked toward her, arms spread wide. All she could see was George's blood on the sleeves of his uniform, on his hands. "I'm sorry. His company was ambushed in Chaudron," Bliss said.

There was more. Something about advancing as fast as possible to trap the Germans on this side of the Meuse. Polly stared down at George's riddled chest, swathed in crude bandages. What a pathetic mockery it made of her primitive skill with perforating wounds. What a mockery it made of everything. Polly Warden, heroic ambulance driver; Malvern Hill Bliss, victorious general.

She was glad the war was not over. She was glad she still had time to find Anita Sinclair's solution. Somewhere north of this tented circus of suffering, where German machine guns were still chattering, she would find death. That was what she wanted and deserved. It was absolutely intolerable that an egotist like Polly Warden with her absurd ideas about women's destiny should go on living while so many others—women like Anita; men like Paul Lebrun and Harry Quickmeyer and George Eagleton—died.

She stumbled away from George's body, away from the hospital tents. Bliss followed her. "Polly," he said.

She whirled. "You have his blood on your hands, General. Are you aware of that?"

"Yes," he said. "Can you forgive me?"

"No," she said. "Never."

She meant it. She could never forgive him. She could also never forgive herself. That was the really immovable transcendent never. Nothing mattered now but death. Did Bliss see it in her eyes? Not surprising, he was an expert on the subject, like all murderers.

"Get in the car," Bliss said.

"I have an ambulance to drive."

"They'll find someone else to drive it."

He led her to the open door of the car and half lifted, half shoved her onto the backseat. The car lurched out of the evacuation area and headed south. "You're kidnapping me!" Polly raged.

"I'm not going to let you kill yourself."

"I have no intention of killing myself."

"You're going to let the Germans do it for you."

"Why did I ever think I loved you? I let you kill the man I really loved!"

"You didn't love him. You wished you'd loved him. I had exactly the same experience with my wife. When the person you wished you'd loved dies, it's agony."

"He deserved someone better than me, someone less selfish, someone—"

"Dumber. He needed a woman with less brains. I needed a wife with more brains."

"How can you be so arrogant?"

"I'm not being arrogant. I'm being *blunt!*" He shouted the word in her face.

He fell back on the cushions of the hurtling car and said nothing for a mile or two. The only sound was the roar of the motor and Polly's sobs. Then he began to talk in a different voice.

"If you refuse to forgive me, I'm fairly certain I'll never forgive myself. I know exactly how responsible I am for Captain Eagleton's death and all the other deaths of the last two weeks. I have no defense except the one I offered you the other night. History. The judgments a man makes in its name. I know it's absolutely useless before a woman's scorn."

"I hate it! I hate it and I hate you and John J. Pershing and

Wiley Parker and Charles Summerall. You're all the same! You're all killers!" she raged.

"You're about fifty percent right," he said. He waited for another silent mile, perhaps hoping she would retract some of her condemnation. Then he spoke again in that low intense voice.

"History can break your heart. You've seen it break mine once. Now I've seen it break yours. But I don't think people have to die of heartbreak. I used to think so. It was an essential part of my southern heritage. I thought it was the only honorable way to die. You helped me change my mind. Now I want to change your mind. Will you let me try?"

He did not touch her; he did not even look at her as these words poured out. Polly realized this man was telling her the truth. No matter what she felt about him or that truth now, she could not deny it without risking an oblivion far worse than the one she was planning to seek from the Germans—an obliteration of her self, her woman's soul, the identity she had been struggling to understand since the war's vortex swallowed her. She could not deny those days in Paris, that authentic surrender to love. That was as much a part of her woman's self now as her determination to be an independent person.

What else did she see on this man's tired face? Sadness, regret, and pain. She had dismissed those feelings the other night when she berated him about unconditional surrender. Now they were part of this truth, this self he was asking her to accept. She had the power to lessen that pain, console that regret, banish that sadness.

She saw something even more important. He would somehow bear it if she imposed her imperious *never* on their lives. There was strength on that face, resolution, and courage—above all, courage— that she needed now as never before.

With a cry, Polly groped her way into his arms. "A part of me loved him," she said. "A part of me will always love him."

"I know that," Bliss said, kissing her gently on the throat.

It was the lost part of her, the Polly Warden who had ridden up Fifth Avenue with George Eagleton on that last day of March nineteen months ago, the naïve conflicted feminist who had been obliterated by the war. Perhaps in this man's arms she could finally look back on that woman without rancor or regret as a being from another time.

"I'll let you try to love me," she said. "But it won't be easy."

"I know that," Bliss said.

"Now take me back to the field hospital. I don't want anyone else running my ambulance."

"I thought you were going to say that. Murphy's been driving in circles for the last half hour."

In five minutes they were back at the hospital. Martha was standing beside Polly's ambulance, talking to Pinkus. They looked relieved as she walked toward them. "That didn't take too long," Pinkus said, beaming.

Martha gave him a glare and studied Polly anxiously. "Are you all right?" she said.

Polly nodded. "Let's go," she said.

She slipped behind the wheel. A long-range German shell came whining in to explode near the road the engineers kept trying to repair. She reached out her hand to Bliss. "Thank you," she said.

She saw George's blood on his khaki sleeve. For a moment she wondered all over again if she could bear it. A soldier cranked her motor. It coughed and sputtered into life, and Polly led her ambulances onto the dangerous road.

62. ON HIS OWN

THE CALENDAR ON MALVERN HILL BLISS'S DESK read November 8. He had set up a semblance of a headquarters in a wrecked château overlooking the Meuse River. The turgid stream took a left turn north of the Argonne and meandered west, roughly parallel to the German border. They would be ready to attack tomorrow morning. The Germans, with the river swollen by two months of rain at their backs, might put up a nasty fight. Sedan, key to the vital north–south rail line, was only a dozen miles away.

Sedan was a city of great historic symbolism. In 1870, the French had surrendered to the Germans there, ingloriously ending the Franco-Prussian war. The French had already announced that the Fourth Army would take Sedan to erase that blot on France's honor.

For the twentieth time, Polly Warden's tearful eyes accused General Bliss of wasting lives. But in John J. Pershing's army, a man disobeyed an order at his peril, especially with a corps commander like Charles Summerall breathing down his neck. Everything Bliss heard and read made him think an armistice was imminent. Should he ask Pershing for permission to cancel the attack? He shuddered at the beating he was certain to take and reached for the telephone, half hoping the line was cut.

As his hand grasped the receiver, Alexander Graham Bell's damnable invention rang. He picked it up and heard Pershing's growl: "Get me Bliss."

"I'm on the line, Jack."

"I just got the word from an AP reporter. The Republicans have won control of both houses of Congress. Teddy beat Wilson's socks off, calling for unconditional surrender."

"Does that mean the end of the armistice stuff?"

"No. Wilson stopped talking to the Germans when he realized he was blowing the election. He told them to negotiate the terms of an armistice with Foch. The Field Marshal's been dickering with them for the last two days."

"Have you told Wilson you recommend unconditional surrender?"

"Yeah. I almost got my head taken off. I was told it was a political question and none of my stupid business. Woodrow's still the commander in chief for another two years. He doesn't have to listen to me—or to the voters."

Pershing said Foch, working both sides of the street as usual, claimed he too was against an armistice, but he had to obey orders and negotiate. Haig was backing him because the British army had used up their last reserves. The British and French politicians were panting for peace terms. They were afraid if the Germans turned around and gave their troops a pasting, bolshevism might break out.

"But we've got two million Americans in France!"

"That's another reason why the French and British politicians want an armistice now," Pershing said. "They don't want to let us say we've won the goddamn war for them."

"What do we do?"

"We keep attacking. We don't know when—or if—Foch can make the Germans swallow his terms. Among other things, he wants them to hand over their fleet, their airplanes, most of their locomotives, and thirty thousand machine guns. It's damn near an unconditional surrender—but not near enough to make it the real thing."

"What's our objective?"

"Sedan."

"That's in the zone of the French Fourth Army."

"Not any more. I just told them we're going to take it. At the very least I want the satisfaction of making Foch and company eat the sight of the American First Army in Sedan."

If he were Jack Pershing and had been forced to swallow six

months of Foch's insults, maybe he too would want to stuff Sedan down the Field Marshal's craw. Come to think of it, he had ingested a few insults from Foch himself. But there were American soldiers involved in this nasty feud.

"Jack, is Sedan worth ten or fifteen thousand casualties? We've got the railroad under fire from our artillery now. Nothing's running on it."

The silence on the other end of the phone was thunderous. "I thought we settled this," Pershing said.

"We did. I'm thinking of my men."

The silence grew even more thunderous. "Give me an order," Bliss said.

"I just gave you one," Pershing said, slamming down the phone.

Five hours later, Bliss still had not issued the order to attack. He paced the floor and stared out at another icy drizzle, thinking of his infantrymen freezing in their watery foxholes. He summoned Mile-a-Minute Murphy and told him to head for Evacuation Hospital Six, sixty miles away. They got there around nine o'clock. He waded through the puddles to the barracks that housed the Kingswood Ambulance Group. A light burned in the office at the rear. Field Director Warden was still at work.

She looked as melancholy as he felt. It made him glad he had made the trip, even if she thought he was crazy. He sat on a lopsided couch and told her about the attack on Sedan. As he hoped, it stirred her affection for France—and her wrath at the prospect of more casualties—to an instant boiling point. "You can't do it," she said.

"Do you have the nerve to say that to General Pershing?"

Bliss was warning her she was not going to see the genial man with whom she had danced and chatted on the S.S. *Baltic*. This Pershing was the grim-eyed commander-in-chief of the American Expeditionary Force. "Yes!" she said.

Bliss smiled bleakly. "Now I've got to find the nerve to take you to him."

They roared down the dark muddy roads at Mile-a-Minute Murphy's usual speed while Bliss accumulated second thoughts on what he was doing. If his red-haired accomplice started lecturing Pershing about casualty lists, his career in the U.S. Army might yet end ingloriously. But it was too late to back out without looking like a coward. They reached the railroad car on the siding in Souilly around 10 P.M. Pretending they had an appointment, Bliss saluted the dripping sentry and escorted Polly up the steps into Pershing's suite. He was at his desk, reading reports.

"Jack," Bliss said. "You know this young woman. I happen to love her. But that has nothing to do with why she's here. She served in the French medical corps. She majored in French at Wellesley. She knows more about French history and the French people than you, me, Liggett, and that whole crew of Leavenworth geniuses at First Army headquarters. She's here to tell you why we shouldn't take Sedan."

"It's nice to see you again, Miss Warden," Pershing said. "I've heard about the fine job you've been doing with your ambulances."

"Thank you, General," Polly said.

"I can understand why this screwball is in love with you. I hope you're not in love with him."

"I'm afraid I am, General."

"Deplorable. Tell me why I shouldn't take Sedan."

Bliss braced himself for annihilation. Something about the set of Polly's jaw made him certain the lecture on casualties was on its way. But as she looked into Pershing's tired eyes, something wonderful happened. Polly's face softened, saddened. She was remembering what Bliss had told her about the two Pershings. She saw the suffering man behind the iron mask, the man who had wept for Frankie aboard the *Baltic*. She answered Jack with one word. "*Cafard*."

In a low voice, Polly talked about France's pain: the million dead, the two million wounded and maimed and disfigured, the twenty million mourning parents, sisters, mothers, wives. She told Jack where and how she had seen that pain and learned to feel it in her months at the Château Givry. She talked about what *cafard* did to a man's soul.

Watching, Bliss saw something even more wonderful begin to happen. Pershing understood exactly what she meant. He seemed to grasp it from the moment she spoke the word. Was it because *cafard* named his own pain for the first time and naming gave the human

Pershing a chance, a hope, of dealing with his anguish?

"Can a screwball suggest another reason for second thoughts, Jack?" Bliss said.

"He can try."

"As you know, I was born in Maryland, right across the water from Yorktown. I grew up studying that battle. I've always been struck by the fact that there were thirty-two thousand Frenchmen there—and about nine thousand Americans."

Pershing glowered at some papers on his desk. "I just got a call from Pétain begging me not to do it. Foch and Clemenceau are having kittens." A dour smile flickered across the iron general's face. "Maybe that's enough satisfaction."

Bliss asked if there was any news about the armistice. "It goes into effect the day after tomorrow at eleven o'clock," Pershing said. "The eleventh hour of the eleventh day of the eleventh month. Maybe it'll be a lucky number. But I doubt it."

"It will be lucky for some people, General," Polly said.

"But will it be lucky for their children?" Pershing said. "Pétain and I see it another way, from the point of view of the men who died. Pétain thinks his million poilus died to win a genuine victory over Germany. I think our American boys died for the same reason!"

Polly made no attempt to answer this final ferocity. She knew what she had accomplished with her invocation of *cafard*. Women were absolutely uncanny creatures, Bliss thought. It was the thousandth time he had reached that conclusion. He would naturally forget it as fast as possible.

Pershing walked them to the door of the railway car. As the sentry helped Polly descend into the rainy night, Pershing seized Bliss's arm in an iron grip. His eyes had narrowed to those familiar slits. "I want the attacks to continue tomorrow. The Germans can still back out. That's an order, General."

As they drove back to the evacuation hospital, Bliss told Polly what he had just been told. She said nothing. She did not have to speak. He knew how she felt. They sloshed through the rain while Bliss wrestled with the unthinkable, the unimaginable. When he finally spoke he heard his own voice echoing inside him, like a man talking in an empty barrel. "I'm not going to obey that order."

Again, the uncanny instinctive creature beside him said nothing. "Pershing may court-martial me. I'd do it if I were in his shoes."

Still the uncanny creature declined to say a word. Why should she? He was as trapped as the 77th Division's lost battalion in the Argonne forest.

What the hell do I do now, Turner? Do I really have the nerve to ignore a direct order from John J. Pershing? How do I get out of this mess?

You're on your own, General.

63. BLESS ME, FATHER

AT DAWN ON NOVEMBER 11, MALVERN HILL BLISS found the 116 surviving members of Company A in their foxholes overlooking the Meuse River. Above the infantrymen's heads the division's artillery poured shells into German positions along the winding stream. The guns had been firing steadily for thirty-six hours. In spite of the drizzle and the numbing cold, the infantrymen were looking almost cheerful. It was always nice to see the other guys taking a pasting.

"How do you like those fireworks?" Bliss yelled in the doorway of the company command post.

"We can't figure it out, General," Lieutenant O'Connor said. "Are you tryin' to scare the Krauts to death?"

The Lieutenant was eating a breakfast of sardines and hardtack. Beside him, two men were oiling Chauchats. The guns lay on a raincoat on the dirt floor like large dismembered insects. "We've been hopin' you'd send us after them so we could even some more of the score for Captain Eagleton," O'Connor said.

"I think you've evened the score pretty well."

"Some of our wild men didn't think so. They went out on a sort of free-lance patrol last night and got in a hell of a brawl with some Krauts in the woods. We lost the big guy, Kilpatrick, the one everybody called Killer."

"He was a friend of yours?"

O'Connor nodded. "The last of my Jersey guys. I brought a dozen with me."

"What are you going to do when you get home? Put together another gang?"

O'Connor shook his head. "I liked the excitement, General. You know what I mean? But this war's given me enough excitement to last the next fifty years. I'm gonna settle down." He nudged the stock of one of the Chauchats with his foot. "The Captain said we're all gonna be livin' on borrowed time—borrowed from the guys who didn't make it. I sort of like that idea. What do you think, General?"

"I like it a lot."

"He said we oughta try to do somethin' for them—for the country. A sort of memorial. He was goin' into politics. He wanted to try to change a few things. Give everybody a better break. I was gonna work for him."

"You're on your own now," Bliss said. "You've borrowed his time too."

O'Connor nodded. "I'm gonna give it a try. I got a letter from my brother. He tells me some Hearst reporter wrote me up. Commissioned in the field for heroism. It's mostly bullshit, but the Democrats want to run me for the state assembly."

Was this the way the world worked? Bliss wondered. He had no idea what this Irishman could accomplish in New Jersey, where politics was at least as corrupt as New York or Maryland. But O'Connor had borrowed more than time from the war. He had a sense of purpose, a glimpse of idealism. Who knew where or when the seed might flower?

He asked him if he was going to take Solange home with him. The Lieutenant shook his head glumly. "She found out her husband ain't dead. He's a prisoner of war." He brooded for a moment. "I think she knew all along."

"The French are different, Lieutenant."

The Germans started returning the American shell fire. Shrapnel slammed against the dirt walls of the command post. "How much longer do you think the Krauts'll last, General?" O'Connor said.

"I wouldn't be surprised if they folded up any day," Bliss said.

A soaking-wet runner from regimental headquarters slithered into the command post. "It's over!" he gasped. "It's over at eleven o'clock."

"You mean the war?" O'Connor said.

"I don't mean the goddamn World Series!"

O'Connor ordered the company clerk to spread the word. "Tell everybody to keep their heads down."

He grinned at Bliss. "I guess maybe you had some idea this was comin', General."

"Let's say I was hoping," Bliss said.

That was an understatement. Their Cromwellian corps commander, Charles Summerall, had issued orders for everyone to attack relentlessly, to the very hour and minute of the armistice. Bliss had ignored him too. If the armistice failed to materialize and the war continued, he had no doubt that Summerall would try to hang his insubordinate scalp out to dry and Pershing would grimly approve the procedure.

A half mile to the right, over the crash of exploding shells in the Lafayette line, came the clatter and bang of machine guns and rifles. The First Division, true to Summerall's merciless code, was attacking. The Germans shifted their big guns to that sector. For another two hours the Lafayette artillery continued to conceal Bliss's premature armistice as he walked along the line of foxholes, slapping men on the back. His cold-weather friend, neuritis, sent slivers of pain up his legs.

Suddenly it was very quiet in the drizzle. Bliss's watch read eleven o'clock. Men stood up in their foxholes and looked around, grinning at each other as if they had all gone crazy. In a way they had. They had lived through the war. Two days ago that had been only a crazy hope for an infantryman.

O'Connor led a well-armed patrol into the woods. About a mile from their lines, they found Kilpatrick and a dozen dead Germans around a wrecked machine gun. Killer had gotten them all with his Chauchat and his trench shovel. He had died with his hands around a German's throat.

Through the trees came half a dozen men in gray. They looked at the bodies and shook their heads. "Crazy Americans," one of them said. For a moment O'Connor considered killing the six Germans. Bliss saw the murder in his blue eyes. It would be easy. A single burst of the Chauchat on his hip. A glance asked Bliss's permission. He shook his head. He was telling O'Connor he was no longer a mug from a New Jersey slum. He was an officer in the United States Army.

Back in the American lines, Bliss shook hands with O'Connor and walked through a patch of woods toward his car. Down the winding path came Chaplain Kelly. His uniform was still a mud-smeared wreck. His face wore the same devastated look Bliss had seen when they met in the German barrage. "I want to pay you the five dollars," Kelly said.

At first Bliss did not know what he was talking about. Then he remembered their bet at Camp Mills on whether the war would prove the army did a better job of teaching brotherly love than the churches. It seemed remote, irrelevant now. "Keep it, Father," he said.

"Take it," Kelly said, holding out a grimy bill.

The Chaplain's haunted eyes revived the anguish of the deaths on the Marne, the Ourcq, the Vesle, Jonathan Alden's wasted heroism, the slaughter in the Argonne. Bliss heard Lieutenant O'Connor—or was it Captain Eagleton?—saying *borrowed time*. "I've got a better idea, Father," he said. "Give me your blessing."

"Don't mock me!" Kelly cried, tears streaking his muddy face. "You know what my blessing is worth."

"Father, remember the man who stood in the back of the synagogue and told God his prayers were worth nothing? He was the one Jesus praised."

Kelly shook his head. He was more than unworthy, he was lost. Bliss took the five-dollar bill and tore it to shreds. He seized Kelly's arms and reached back to words they both shared, the opening line every penitent speaks in the confessional. "Bless me, Father, for I have sinned."

A flicker of hope and understanding passed over Kelly's face. "Kneel down," he said.

Bliss dropped to his knees in the mud. The Chaplain raised a shaking hand to draw an invisible cross in the silent November air.

64. PEACE THAT SURPASSETH UNDERSTANDING II

OVER OVER OVER WHISPERED THE WHEELS OF POLLY'S ambulance as she drove up to the unloading platforms of Evacuation Hospital 6. The war was over! These men on stretchers, mostly flu cases and a few shrapnel wounds, were the last soldiers the Kingswood Ambulance Group would carry from the Lafayette Division. Polly's mind could not grasp the fact, much less its meaning. She had lived through the war. She had a future to contemplate. For the moment it was an utter blank.

Outside the Kingswood barracks, Malvern Hill Bliss was striding up and down beside his car, looking impatient. "Get in," he said, flinging open the rear door.

"Where are we going?"

"Where else? Paris!"

"What about the rest of the group? I feel I should say something, do something."

"They're free, white, and twenty-one," he said. "Let them celebrate any way they please."

He summoned Martha Herzog and wrote out an official-looking order requiring Gwendolyn Warden to accompany him to Paris and appointing Martha the new director of the Kingswood Ambulance Group. "This is a very good idea, General," Martha said. "She owes herself at least a dozen forty-eight-hour passes."

"This one is good for forty-eight years," Bliss said.

Martha obtained another order, empowering Dr. Isaac Pinkus to commandeer a staff car and drive the new director of the Kingswood

Ambulance Service anywhere she wanted to go. Obviously it paid to flatter victorious generals.

Paris was wild. There were a million people in the streets singing the "Marseillaise." Polly listened to the magnificent words thunder above the rooftops: *The day of glory has arrived!*" She remembered the first time she heard them, when John J. Pershing and his staff rode down these same streets. That had been a day of false glory. She remembered Paul Lebrun's words, *un ancien démence*, and Pershing's doubts about the armistice and wondered if this glory was also false. Had France—and the rest of the world—really escaped the looming menace of Germany?

History. It was too vast, too remote to worry about for the time being. The only thing to do was join the rampaging joy around them. Soldiers were mobbed and in some cases in serious danger of being kissed to death by legions of women. Military bands marched haphazardly in all directions, their musicians mostly drunk. Champagne was being given away by the gallon at the sidewalk cafés. Even the gendarmes were smiling.

At Polly's suggestion, they drove to Premier Clemenceau's residence, hoping to catch a glimpse of him. Within ten minutes he emerged and saw them in the crowd. He plowed through a line of policemen and two ranks of bystanders to give Polly a ferocious embrace. "I've been kissed by five hundred women so far today. Now it's my turn!" he said.

He kissed her violently and hugged her again, tears in his eyes. "I wish I could give you a medal for what you did for France. Instead I can only wish you happiness."

He regarded Bliss with less enthusiasm. "Your friend Pershing turned out to be a better general than I thought," he said.

"He's not a bad politician, either," Bliss said.

Clemenceau conceded that with a curt nod. "I wish I could keep him around to get the kind of peace we need to tame the Germans for a century. Your president is coming over here to turn us all into choirboys. Is he in for a surprise!"

Polly shuddered at the livid hatred on the old man's face. The Tiger did not know how or when to sheathe his claws.

Back in the car, Bliss anticipated their next destination. "I bet you want to see Madame Doctor."

The hospital on the Rue Desnouettes was celebrating the armistice with the "Marseillaise" and champagne in every ward. On the third floor, they found a different atmosphere. Dr. Giroux-Langin was in her office, chatting quietly with Charles Louis Lebrun. She leaped up and embraced Polly and even gave Bliss a kiss on both cheeks. "You look exhausted," she said in her accented English. "But what does it matter now?"

Lebrun poured them champagne. They drank to France and peace. Polly asked for Charles and Louis Lebrun. Had they survived their service at the front? Lebrun nodded. "Charles won the croix de guerre. I had nothing to do with it. He actually deserved it."

They drank to Charles and Louis. Polly decided she had to find out the reason for Lebrun père's presence. "He's a patient," Dr. Giroux-Langin said. "He's been suffering from a rather severe depression. So far I've declined to give him the treatment he swears would cure him."

She glanced mockingly at Lebrun, who meekly acquiesced in her scorn.

"But who knows what tomorrow will bring? Now that we've saved France, anything is possible," the Doctor said.

It was Giroux-Langin's turn to ask questions. "What will you do with the rest of your life?" she asked Polly in French.

The answer came to Polly's lips as though she had been thinking about it for months. In fact she could not recall giving it a moment's conscious thought. "I'm going to become a doctor," she said.

Giroux-Langin's dark eyes glowed. "I've been praying you would make that decision. I knew if I suggested it, you would have resisted me as the tyrant I undoubtedly am. Where will you study?"

"I don't know. I didn't realize I was going to do it until you asked me."

That produced a frown. "Yet you're serious?"

"Totally."

Still speaking French, Giroux-Langin said, "What about this general? Will he approve?"

"I think so," Polly said, smiling at Bliss. "He's a rather unusual general."

"Get your degree first. Then marry him. He may be unusual, but he's still a man."

"Don't worry. I'll get my degree," Polly said. "Then I'm going to give him a son."

Bliss could not follow this exchange in rapid French. "I know you're talking about me, but I don't know what you're saying," he complained.

"It doesn't matter, General," Lebrun said. "Even if you spoke French like a Sorbonne professor you wouldn't really understand them. They communicate in secret codes."

They drank to the mystery of womanhood and exchanged another round of kisses and good wishes. For a moment, as Charles Louis Lebrun embraced her, Polly heard Paul whisper, *When you hear my name, does you heart always glow?*

Yes, she was able to answer without pain. Forever yes.

Dismissing Mile-a-Minute Murphy, Bliss and Polly wandered the chaotic streets, savoring the joy. Outside the British embassy, a singer wearing a dress cut from a Union Jack stood on a taxi's roof and sang "Hail, Brittania." At the Café de la Paix, captains and majors from all the quarreling armies raised glasses and bellowed drunken compliments. At one of the outer tables, a pretty French girl on his lap, sat Major Rodney Blake, General Gough's former aide. "I thought you died on that ridge behind the Chemin des Dames," Polly said.

He shook his head cheerfully. "We ran away to fight another day."

At twilight, the Place de l'Opéra blazed with light for the first time since 1914. Ignoring a chilly wind, the greatest singers in France came to the balcony of the opera house and sang the "Marseillaise," "God Save the King," and the "Star-Spangled Banner." Then a French bugler blew the *barloque*, the all-clear signal after an air raid. Everyone laughed, gave a final cheer, and went home.

Polly and Bliss dined alone at the Hôtel du Quai Voltaire. As they finished dinner, the headwaiter rushed to the table and practically saluted. "A message from General Pershing!" he said, handing Bliss the note.

Around nine o'clock they taxied to Micheline Resco's apartment. Pershing was already there, a glass of champagne in his hand. *Lohengrin* boomed triumphantly on the phonograph. Micheline welcomed Polly gratefully as a fellow French-speaker. Polly liked her instantly, although at first she was too full of compliments for her service at the front. When she realized she was embarrassing Polly, Micheline turned to the generals. "Aren't they wonderful? These conquerors!"

"Now you know how to win a woman's approval," Pershing said to Bliss. "Beat the German army now and then."

"We've done more than that," Bliss said. "We've won two wars: one against the Germans, the other against our allies."

"What shall we drink to, besides these magnificent generals?" Micheline Resco said.

Pershing's face grew grave. He raised his glass. "The men. They were willing to pay the price."

The words hung there in the quiet parlor. Polly wondered if it was as close as a victorious general could come to admitting he had made some mistakes. Was her presence—and Bliss's—another way Pershing was facing that truth in his laconic style? Perhaps. They drank to the men.

Bliss gazed at Polly for a moment and shook his head. "I'll never understand it, Jack. Why have a couple of killers like us been allowed to live and love again?"

Micheline Resco was visibly distressed to hear her adored general described as a killer. Knowing Pershing's temper, Polly was almost as dismayed. She could not imagine a more undiplomatic remark.

Pershing's eyes narrowed to those ominous slits. But there was no explosion. On this night of all nights he was not going to let Imperfect Bliss irritate him. "Why can't you just be grateful—and not ask dumb questions?" he said.

65. CODA

On her last day in Paris, Polly Warden strolled through the sunshine to the Café de la Paix, where she found Martha Herzog and Isaac Pinkus, hands entwined. They were going to be married as soon as the Lafayette Division was demobilized. Martha was planning to get a graduate degree in political science from Baltimore's Johns Hopkins and devote herself to preventing another war.

In the distance, bands began playing. They paid their bill and strolled to the Champs-Élysées to see the victory parade. The generals came first, on horseback. At the head of the French detachment rode Field Marshals Foch and Pétain, exuding mutual disdain. Field Marshal Haig was alone at the head of the British contingent. Finally came the Americans. Never had Polly seen a man sit a horse more splendidly than John J. Pershing. Behind him trotted no less than thirty-two generals, riding eight abreast. Polly waved to Malvern Hill Bliss in the second rank, but he was too busy looking martial to see her.

Behind the generals came fifteen-hundred-man detachments of poilus and Tommies and Yanks. As the cheers thundered down on them, Polly could not restrain her tears. She had seen them at their worst and at their best, shaken by a terrible enemy, yet somehow determined to prevail.

They retreated to the Café de la Paix, where Bliss joined them. He kissed Polly and ordered a round of drinks. "Have you ever seen so many generals in one parade?" he said. "You'd think they won the damn war."

He waved to a young woman selling flowers and bought a rose

for each of them. They joined the people of Paris in an immense procession down the Champs-Élysées to the Arch of Triumph. It was dark by the time they reached the massive marble monument to *la gloire*, with its sculptures and friezes of the victories of Napoleon's armies. Beneath the lofty curve of the arch lay an unknown soldier in a bronze coffin. Beside him each person placed a single flower in memory of a brother, a son, a father, a husband, a lover, or a friend who had died in the war.

Bliss looked back at the throng still jamming the length and breadth of the Champs-Élysées. "In Lorraine I met a French Jesuit who was serving as a stretcher-bearer. He told me the war would prove there was a God by revealing how much love was in the human soul. I told him he was crazy. I wish I could apologize to him."

"You don't have to apologize to anyone for anything," Polly said.

Arm-in-arm, the lovers walked into the darkness. By morning, when they left Paris to begin their life together, a million men and women had created a mountain of flowers beside the silent soldier.

SOURCES

THE EXPERIENCES OF THE THOUSANDS OF AMERI-
can women who went to France in World War I
are described in many memoirs and biographies. Among the most
vivid are recollections by two women who served in the French
army's medical corps, *The Forbidden Zone* by Mary Borden and *I Saw
Them Die* by Shirley Millard. Published anonymously, *The Uncen-
sored Letters of a Canteen Girl* is rich in anecdotes and incidents.
David Mitchell's *Monstrous Regiment: The Story of the Women of the
First World War*, is a good overview. Also enlightening is *Behind the
Lines: Gender and the Two World Wars*, edited by Margaret Randolph
Higgonet and several other historians, and *Into the Breach* by
Dorothy and Carl J. Schneider.

Bobbed hair, liberated sexual morality, and demands for equality
are usually associated with the women of the 1920s. In fact, as
Henry F. May demonstrated in his book *The End of American Innocence*, large numbers of women vocally impatient with male assump-
tions of superiority began appearing around 1910. An even more
graphic and factual account of this transformation can be found in
James R. McGovern's essay "The American Woman's Pre–World
War I Freedom in Manners and Morals," in the September 1968
issue of *The Journal of American History*. B. H. Friedman's biography
Gertrude Vanderbilt Whitney recounts the early revolt and liberation
of a woman at the summit of American society.

Sexual experimentation in Paris, dramatized by Natalie Barney,
is discussed and analyzed in many books, such as *Women for Hire* by
Alain Corbin, *France: Fin de Siecle* by Eugen Weber, and *Wine,
Women, and Song: A Diary of Disillusionment* by an anonymous

American who fought *la guerre de luxe*. Barney's flamboyance is well described in *The Amazon of Letters* by George Wickes and *Portrait of a Seductress* by Jean Chalon.

Joseph Caillaux's plot to negotiate a white peace with Germany in 1917 is the subject of several books, notably *Dare Call It Treason* by Richard M. Watt and *The Enemy Within* by Severance Johnson. There are many biographies of Georges Clemenceau, the man who smashed this plot. Perhaps the most vivid glimpse of him in word and deed is *The Tiger of France* by Wythe Williams, a *New York Times* correspondent who knew him intimately. Winston Churchill, who was present in the Chamber of Deputies when the Tiger roared *"Je fais la guerre!"* also provides a trenchant sketch of him in his *Great Contemporaries*.

General Pershing's sharp disagreement with Wilson about the armistice is spelled out in the second volume of his memoirs, *My Experiences in the World War*. Clemenceau's *Grandeur and Misery of Victory* and David Lloyd George's *War Memoirs* document French and British dismay with Wilson's naïve diplomacy. The President's clashes with Theodore Roosevelt over the conduct of the war, Roosevelt's call for unconditional surrender, and his rout of Wilson in the 1918 elections are recounted in *The Warrior and the Priest* by John Milton Cooper.

Through Malvern Hill Bliss's eyes we see a very different version of America's military experience in World War I. This too is supported by recent scholarship—as well as by some of the memoirs and diaries of the men who fought in France. The diaries of James G. Harbord, Pershing's chief of staff, and Robert Lee Bullard, III Corps and Second Army commander, are especially revealing about the British-French attempt to amalgamate the American army and the pessimism that engulfed the American high command during the long wait for troops to arrive from the United States. Another invaluable source is George C. Marshall's *Memoirs of My Services in the World War*, which was discovered in manuscript after the General's death. Marshall was chief of staff of the First Division and later worked for Pershing at Chaumont and on the staff of the First Army.

In his book *The Great Crusade*, General Joseph T. Dickman, the commander of the Third Division, was among the first to point out the fiasco in Belleau Wood was a meaningless battle that should never have been fought. For the misuse of the American infantry by French generals in the counteroffensive against the Marne salient, a primary source is Hervey Allen's memoir *Toward the Flame*. He was a lieutenant in the 28th Division. His company was wiped out in Fismette in a debacle not unlike the fate of Company A in this novel. For a broader view of this campaign, Barrie Pitt's *1918: The Last Act* tells the story with cool irony. General Robert B. Alexander's *Memories of the World War 1917–1918*, details the bitter truth as it was experienced by the 77th Division. Also valuable is the history of the 42nd (Rainbow) Division, *Americans All,* by Henry J. Reilly. The Rainbow fought from the Marne to the Ourcq to the Vesle.

The shortcomings of Pershing's ideas on open warfare are discussed in Paul Braim's book *The Test of Battle*. Edward M. Coffman has graphic details on the chaos in the Argonne in *The War to End All Wars*. Donald Smythe's fine biography, *Pershing: General of the Armies,* is another rich source for this crisis, as well as for many other aspects of Pershing's experience in France. For an individual view of battle in the Argonne, it would be hard to better *Fighting Soldier* by Joseph Douglas Lawrence. The author also had the benefit of many discussions with his father, the late Thomas J. Fleming, Sr., who was a lieutenant in the 312th Infantry of the 78th Division.

The new tactics the Germans devised for their 1918 offensives have been analyzed in two recent books, *Stormtroop Tactics: Innovation in the German Army, 1914–1918* by Bruce I. Gudmundsson and *The Defeat of Imperial Germany* by Rod Paschall. For the impact of the German offensives on the French and British armies, *Crisis 1918* by Joseph Gies analyzes the leading actors and strategies. *See How They Ran* by William Moore chronicles in painful detail the rout of the British Fifth Army in March 1918, the near rout in Flanders in April 1918, and the smashing of the British section of the front in the attack on the Chemin des Dames in May 1918. The Fifth Army's tragic story is well told from another perspective in *Goughie* by Anthony Farrar-Hockley, a biography of the unfortunate general.

For personal relationships between the generals, the diaries of

Harbord and Bullard are revealing. Bullard had a particularly low opinion of Tasker H. Bliss. In their memoirs Harbord and Pershing can barely disguise their loathing for Field Marshal Ferdinand Foch. Pershing's clashes with Haig and Foch are described by Smythe and other biographers, notably Frank E. Vandiver in *Black Jack: The Life and Times of John J. Pershing*.

Pershing's love affair with Micheline Resco, carefully concealed during his lifetime, is amply documented by his biographers. Although they never married, Pershing spent part of every year in Europe with her until the outbreak of World War II. On the day after Pershing died in 1948, his son, Warren, handed her a letter, written some years before the General became ill, in which he told her he hoped they would meet again "in some brighter clime ... where you will hold me in your dear arms and I shall be your own."